INDA

SHERWOOD SMITH

DAW BOOKS, INC.

DONALD A. WOLLHEIM, FOUNDER

375 Hudson Street, New York, NY 10014

ELIZABETH R. WOLLHEIM

SHEILA E. GILBERT

PUBLISHERS

http://www.dawbooks.com

First Hardcover Printing, August 2006
1   2   3   4   5   6   7   8   9

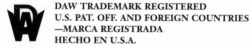

Acknowledgments

I would like to thank my editors; Betsy Wollheim for her insightful advice, and Debra Euler for her cheerful and prompt returns whenever I had questions.

I'd like to thank all the people who read Inda in various drafts, especially my writing group, The Horse Latitudes. They patiently listened to me maunder and agonize, and gave me not just one but several reads. Finally and most gratefully, Beth Bernobich, who generously gave of her limited time to go through this story again and again for me.

Last, music is always problematical—a writer says *Such-and-such was my inspiration*, and the reader thinks, *I hate that band!* Still, I will pass on for anyone interested in such things, the first time I heard the soundtrack for *Amistad*, and did not know what it was, I was stunned—for the second and last tracks sounded just like the scrubs on the open plains, and the end of the sixth like the "Hymn to the Fallen."

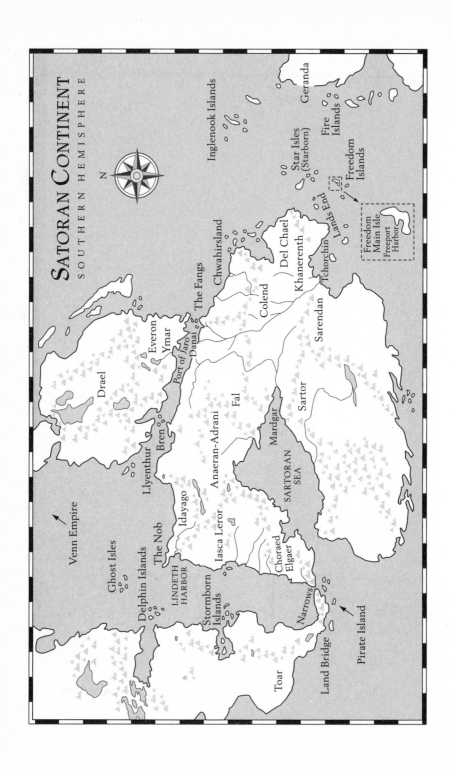

SATORAN CONTINENT
SOUTHERN HEMISPHERE

N

Venn Empire

Ghost Isles

Delphin Islands

The Nob

LINDETH HARBOR

Stormborn Islands

Llyenthur

Bren

Idayago

Iasca Leror

Anaeran-Adrani

Choraed Elgaer

Narrows

Land Bridge

Pirate Island

Toar

Drael

Everon

Ymar

Danai

Port of Jaro

The Fangs

Fal

Mardgar

SARTORAN SEA

Sartor

Chwahirsland

Colend

Del Chael

Khanerenth

Sarendan

Tchorchin

Lands End

Star Isles (Starborn)

Freedom Islands

Fire Islands

Geranda

Inglenook Islands

Freedom Main Isle

Freeport Harbor

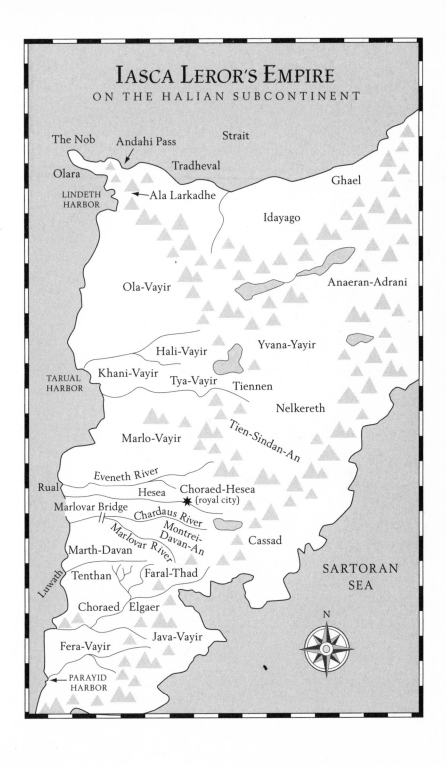

IASCA LEROR'S EMPIRE
ON THE HALIAN SUBCONTINENT

The Nob   Andahi Pass   Strait

Olara

Tradheval

Ghael

LINDETH
HARBOR

Ala Larkadhe

Idayago

Ola-Vayir

Anaeran-Adrani

Hali-Vayir

Yvana-Yayir

Khani-Vayir

TARUAL
HARBOR

Tya-Vayir   Tiennen

Nelkereth

Marlo-Vayir

Tien-Sindan-An

Eveneth River

Rual

Hesea   Choraed-Hesea
            (royal city)

Marlovar Bridge

Chardaus River

Montrei-
Davan-An

Marlovar River

Marth-Davan

Luwath

Tenthan   Faral-Thad

Cassad

SARTORAN
SEA

Choraed / Elgaer

Fera-Vayir

Java-Vayir

N

PARAYID
HARBOR

PART ONE

Chapter One

"LET'S go fight the girls!"

Inda Algara-Vayir's shout signaled the end of morning chores. Broom handles clattered against the stable walls and buckets thumped down as the boys of Castle Tenthen whooped with joy. Dawn had brought the first clear day of a late spring. After winter's bleakness, the sunlight shafting from the still low northern sun cheered the castle's people going about their work.

For the young, it meant the first war game of the year.

"What's your plan, Inda?"

"What're we gonna do, Inda?"

Some of the older stable hands laughed as the boys romped like pups, exchanging shoves and yapping questions that no one listened to. Might as well be barks.

A hard thump across Inda's back came from cousin Branid, the tallest and oldest of the boys. "Be a short war if the girls aren't ready for us." Some of the other boys paused, and Branid added, smirking, "Unless you want us to attack 'em while they're up studying scrolls with your mother, or restringing the bows."

Inda shook his head. "They'll be ready. Worked it out with Tdor at breakfast. Both to finish by midmorning bells."

The boys yelled again, then Inda said, "We'll have a short one today.

On account of the mud. Later in the week, if the ground dries, we'll have our first overnight game."

This time the cheer the boys sent up was very close—as close as they dared—to the notorious academy fox yip.

The girls waiting at the lakeside heard the cheer and grinned at one another in readiness.

And up on the castle walls, some of the Riders on sentry duty and the women of the Princess' Guard who were on watch smiled, remembering the first war games of spring in their own youth, for these were the days in Marlovan history when both men and women guarded the castle walls, men outward, women inward.

One of those Riders' sons sent a sour look at Branid, then muttered to Inda, "Liet says we'll never get anywhere. She told me they got new ideas."

Branid sneered. "Everyone knows Liet's full of bran gas." He jerked his thumb toward the forge, from which smoke rose into a still sky. To Branid, everyone's value or truthfulness related strictly to their rank. Liet's family were distant cousins to the Algara-Vayirs, and Liet's brother did not train for the Riders, but worked in the forge. "Now if *Joret* said anything . . ."

"Liet?" Inda ignored Branid from habit. Yes, Tdor had grinned in a strange way while they'd talked. He'd thought it caused by spring's arrival. So, the girls had a ruse.

Someone punched Inda. "Where'll we find 'em?"

Inda jabbed his thumb back over his shoulder. "Down lakeside." He sighed inwardly, wishing he'd thought up a good plan, but he hadn't believed it wouldn't rain yet again by the time morning chores were finished. "Let's go," he said aloud in Marlovan, unaware of his shift from Iascan to the language of his ancestors, the language of war. *No,* he thought, *make the plan when I see the girls. More like a real fight anyway.*

The echo of the midmorning bells bounced off stone walls as the boys raced out of the stable yard, through the massive side gates that were now standing open, and down a trail toward the finger of the lake that was one of their favorite battlegrounds, well away from the thick growth of cattails and the sharp, waxy leddas. As soon as they passed the budding hemlock and the great ferns all covered with shiny, pale green leaves, they saw the girls at the lake edge ranged behind a waist-high fort. From this distance, the girls' voices sounded like gulls as they jumped up and down screeching taunts and threats in a mixture of Ias-can and Marlovan. A couple of generations ago only Marlovans had spo-ken in the language of war, but time, peace, and intermarriage with the Iascans they'd conquered and now lived with made it more practical for everyone to understand one another. Nobody thought about it: Marlovan was for war drill, and Iascan for regular life.

That is, simple for the castle folk. When dealing with outsiders, the language used could change the intent of words, if not the meaning. This was why the princess—Fareas-Iofre—had decreed they always use Ias-can with outsiders.

"Let's get 'em!" Cousin Branid yelled, looking back for followers.

"Parley first," Inda countered, and the boys slowed.

Branid snorted. "You didn't lay down the rules this morning? *I* would have. M' grandmother says, you *always* lay down the rules first to your men, or—"

"Didn't have time," Inda said, once again cutting into Branid's half-boast, half-whine, familiar since early childhood. "Set 'em now. See what they reveal."

The boys slowed to a stop, eying the girls, who continued to yell in-sults, waving their arms and capering about, some slapping their butts, others holding up the backs of their hands and wiggling the fingers. In-sults meant to entice the boys to attack now. Inda scanned them until he found Tdor, his betrothed, right in the middle, brown braids flapping against her skinny back as she hopped.

"They've got to have a whole mess o' mudballs behind there," a Rider captain's son observed. "All ready to throw."

"And they want us to charge now," Inda agreed. "So let's go easy. Spread out, start picking up your weapons."

The boys studied the enemy's stronghold as they sauntered forward, bare toes digging down in the pungent mud. The girls' fort was built in a semicircle, stones in front, then mud and brush, the edges curving back to the lake shallows. Water was as effective a barrier as rock, as they'd learned from generations of plains-riding forebears.

There were a lot more girls down there than boys, now that the older boys had gone either riding on spring border patrol with Inda's father, or to the royal city as part of Tanrid's Honor Guard. A lot more girls, but Inda wasn't sure they were all there. It was hard to count, the way they jumped around.

The boys picked up clumps of turf and mud and piled their weaponry into their smocks. They stopped within hailing distance.

"Take the fort or capture commanders?" Inda called.

"Commander only," Tdor yelled back, as Inda had expected.

Whoever captured the other's commander won. Shorter game.

"Prisoners?"

"No," Tdor yelled. "Honor system: death blow you're dead, otherwise you can fight."

Good. Taking prisoners meant having to guard them, and Inda needed every one of his boys.

The rules of war having been established, the stable master's son asked, "Charge in a line?"

"No. Three prong," Inda said, putting his evolving strategy into the form of an order. "You lead left, Vrad. You right, Cousin Branid. I got the middle." Tanrid, Inda's older brother, had told him over the winter to try to break superior numbers into smaller groups, and Inda had used much of his free time scouring through old records, trying to find accounts of battles wherein the strategies Tanrid mentioned had worked—or hadn't. "Divide 'em. On my whistle, all swoop on Tdor."

Inda looked about, saw comprehension, jerked his chin up and the boys charged, yelling wildly, pausing only to throw mudballs. Branid, trying both to run fastest and throw the hardest, was the first to slip on the slimy mud and fall, the girls' mudballs pelting him with pitiless accuracy. He looked around in despair and was relieved when he saw two of the other boys go down face forward, each under his own slurpy brown hailstorm.

Inda watched them all, sensing that something was not quite right. His offensive charge progressed steadily despite the formidable barrage of defensive mudballs. He ducked as a big, squishy one whizzed overhead and straightened up—just in time to catch one square on his temple. He scrubbed his sleeve over his eyes, squinted against the sting, and glimpsed Vrad and another boy reaching the fort. They began climbing over, Vrad glancing back toward Inda.

"In! In!" he yelled, motioning them to close on Tdor.

He expected the girls to form around her, but she leaned up on the fort and whistled once.

New shrieks caused all the boys to turn their heads toward a clump of trees. At that moment what had looked like scrubby brush broke apart. Dead branches and old grass arced into the air as a flying wedge of girls raced round to flank them.

"Awww," Inda moaned, and the boys lost what little order they'd had. All that screeching and jumping had been a decoy!

Tdor grinned in triumph at Inda from the fort wall. He grinned back. A good ruse, but he hadn't lost yet.

He kept throwing his mudballs, looking around to assess his forces as best he could through smeared vision until a tackle from behind splatted him face-first into the mud.

"Pin his joints," came a brisk female voice.

Feet thumped onto each elbow, sending pangs up his arms. He pulled his knees under and stuck his butt in the air in a desperate attempt to fight free and the feet lifted away. He scrambled up, ready to defend himself, but no one attacked.

Tdor saw him rubbing mud from his eyes. "Runner!" she said in a low voice; they were no longer enemy commanders.

Boys and girls all stopped fighting, watching the tall, sturdy young woman in Runner blue who trotted down the path. It was Chelis, Fareas-Iofre's youngest personal Runner.

Chelis scanned the group, now fairly equally coated in mud. In the center of the boys she spotted a short figure with light brown curls escaping from a mud-draggled braid, his brown eyes just visible in an equally mud-smeared face.

"Indevan-Dal." Chelis brushed her fingers over her heart.

Indevan-Dal. Inda's name with the courtesy title, and Chelis' salute, caused silence. Just like that rank had been reestablished; Inda was no longer another mud-covered boy, he was now second son of the Prince and Princess of Choraed Elgaer.

"You're wanted by Fareas-Iofre right away," Chelis said, using the Marlovan word for the princess' rank, Iofre, though the rest of her words were in peacetime Iascan.

Inda frowned. Summoned before his mother? Midmorning? He began a hasty mental appraisal. Had someone found out about the spiders in Liet's bed? But she wouldn't blab, and anyway she'd gotten her revenge. Then was it the mudshoes? But the older boys (who'd been strutting far too much, in the younger boys' view, about the prospect of their ride to the royal city) were gone, and anyway his brother Tanrid had already thrashed him for that.

Chelis recognized both the consternation and the blank eyes of rapid internal review. "Messenger from the royal city," she murmured, exactly as ordered. She added in a low voice, "I suggest, if I might, you stop by the baths."

Inda nodded once, then loped up the trail toward the castle. The massive high walls, built of honey-colored stone, reflected warmly in the bright morning sun. Above the walls, long rows of windows set into deep arches in the main building—the glass casements framed by thick iron-reinforced shutters for defense—reflected gleams of light from the lake. Each corner tower also reflected shards of morning light, rendering the castle as mellow in appearance as a castle ever can be; it was home, as familiar and as comfortable as the brackish-smelling breeze coming off the marshy expanse north of the lake, where a line of servants, dressed in brown-dyed cotton-wool, walked a stone-flagged trail, carrying baskets that would at day's end be full of leddas to be boiled and dried and woven into shoes and belts, singing as they went.

Their world intersected with the children's only rarely, despite proximity; the leddas harvest song, weirdly minor key and ancient—from long before Norsunder had nearly swept humankind from the world three millennia ago—went unremarked as birdsong as the children began talking.

Almost all. Tdor waited patiently, for she'd seen Chelis glance her way, her brows lifted just a little.

The boys followed Inda toward the castle. Over their talk rose Branid's whine, "*I* knew those girls were there, but I thought Inda knew, too. Now, if you'd just followed *my* command—"

Three or four of the girls rolled their eyes.

"Tdor-Edli?" Chelis held her hand out, and when Tdor stepped near, dropped onto Tdor's muddy palm a heavy metal object. A ring! "Messenger brought this from Hadand-Hlinlaef to you as an early Name Day gift," Chelis said in Iascan, using Marlovan titles.

Hadand-Hlinlaef: not just Hadand's name, but her rank as future wife of the king's heir. Tdor knew a warning when she heard one. Her fingers closed round the ring. "Thanks."

Chelis left, her long yellow braids swinging as she ran back up to the castle. The girls crowded around Tdor.

"A ring!"

"Is it pretty?"

"Why did she send it here? Why not to your family?"

"She promised before she went back to the royal city to send me something I could wear home for my Name Day visit," Tdor lied automatically, holding the ring out, and knowing that the beaten gold object would not garner any admiration.

Sure enough. "It's ugly," Noren stated, wrinkling her nose.

"I've seen prettier stones in the pickovers on Lastday market." Liet flung back mud-streaked braids the color of flax.

Speculative glances all around. How quick some were to hope for gossip! "It's an old heirloom," Tdor stated, quashing the idea that Hadand had sent the ring as an insult. In her experience, even false gossip sometimes took on life, just because people wanted to believe it. "The Iofre gave it to Hadand-Edli when she turned twelve."

The Iofre had worn it? And her daughter Hadand, one day to be queen? Oh, well then, that was different.

"I'll put it in my heirloom box," Tdor finished. "Against my visit to Marth-Davan." As she spoke, she brushed her fingers down her grubby tunic, a gesture that only Noren understood.

Noren's frown cleared. "Huh! I itch," she declared. "Who's for a bath? Liet, did you *see* the surprise in Inda's face when you swooped down?"

The girls followed Noren, talking about their win—and what they would do next time—as they trudged up to the castle.

Tdor fingered the ring, longing for a moment of privacy. However two Algara-Vayir cousins were still watching her. You couldn't be third in rank behind the princess and then Joret, Tanrid's betrothed, and not be watched. Tdor had lived nine years here in Tenthen Castle, betrothed to Inda. She had learned how to wait.

While she walked, Inda ran. Sentries in their ceaseless patrols atop the battlements saluted, fingers brushing over hearts, as he passed below. He waved back without slowing.

Fiam, Inda's young personal servant, met him at the lower door. "Clothes laid out at the baths."

Inda smiled. "Thanks."

No more was said as the two boys skimmed downstairs to the baths. Inda breathed the scent of hot water in deeply. He undressed as he ran, flinging off his smock. At the edge of the bath he kicked free of his riding breeches and drawers, then dove in. The water, diverted from an underground stream, was kept warm and clean by the mysterious magic spells renewed by warrior-escorted mages every few years. It felt so good, the cleaning magic flicking over his skin and hair and teeth, and always reminded him of the snap of a fresh ginger root just under his nose. Fiam silently picked up the mud-encrusted clothes. Naked boys splashed into the water all around, and of course they began a water fight. For once Inda did not join them.

Laughter and chatter echoed from the women's side as the girls began arriving. Branid was last through the men's side.

"What d'ya think the summons is for?"

"Probably something or other from my father," Inda called.

Branid shrugged, losing interest. Though great-uncle Jarend was a prince, he was also old and boring. Branid held his nose and dove into the bath.

Inda scrubbed his fingers vigorously through his hair, then stretched out to float on his back. He watched the reflections of the water on the stone wall opposite the high windows, wondering idly if Tanrid had reached the royal city yet. Then he began mentally reviewing the map, trying to figure out where his brother and the Honor Guard might be.

"Inda?" Fiam said in a low voice, glancing upward.

The messenger! Inda popped up, slinging his hair back. It smacked his shoulders with a splat. He grabbed a handful and inspected it: no mud in sight. "How do I look?"

"Clean enough," Fiam pronounced, after scanning him with a critical eye. Fiam looked at the ugly splotches of bruises in various states of healing that marked Inda, and was glad once again that he was part of the household. Everyone knew that Randaels—Shield Arms—had to be tough, they were to hold the castle when their brothers traveled. But he wondered privately if anyone alive could ever be tough enough to please Tanrid-Laef, Inda's brother, who would one day rule Choraed Elgaer as prince.

Fiam did his best to towel Inda's hair as the boy tugged on new clothes: drawers, his best riding breeches, his one good long tunic, green with the silver hunting owl stitched on the breast, new riding boots, and his knife-sash.

Inda contained his impatience as Fiam's swift fingers braided his thick, curling hair, and then whipped a ribbon round the end, letting it drop between Inda's shoulder blades.

Inda looked down at himself. The boots were new, good black-weave, well shined. They were stiff and uncomfortable, but Inda was proud of them, and of his new knife. Ten years old and he could hit a wooden post with either hand. Tanrid had seen to that all winter, every day, even during the worst weather. *You think attackers will wait for a nice day?* he'd snarled, shoving Inda out into sleet and even snow, but by the time Tanrid left for the academy, Inda was the best of all the boys at knife throwing, and so Tanrid had given him his first academy knife for Inda's very own.

He was still grinning about that when he reached the floor where his mother and father resided.

His mother was thinking about Tanrid and Inda as well.

Inda entered the formal audience chamber and politely laid his hand over his heart. His tall, straight-backed mother was not wearing her usual undyed woolen robe over linen shirt and breeches, but her green velvet gown, her usually bare head hidden under the silver-stiffened lace cap that she only wore for holidays or special occasions.

Fareas-Iofre studied her lastborn. A purple and yellow bruise framed one of the questioning brown eyes, mottling the brown skin that otherwise glowed with good health. The Iofre wondered with familiar anguish if she would become accustomed to what everyone else accepted, that the heir must thrash his brother into toughness and obedience. To her, raised in a family without a younger brother, the custom was cruel and Tanrid seemed kinder to the stable dogs than to his brother. Yet of the entire household only Tdor appeared to mind.

Fareas-Iofre said in a low voice, "I called you in first, though there's a risk. I exhort you to bear change with honor."

"Risk?" Inda asked looking around for weapons. "Change?"

The Iofre's heart ached from visions of possible futures whose only shared characteristic was danger, visions she could not will away. But her son's surprise caused a tiny blossom of humor to bloom behind her ribs, just for a heartbeat or two. "Nothing is 'always,' my dear. Except the greater truths, one of which is that power begets politics, and politics are more dangerous than war because there are fewer rules."

When his mother talked like that Inda watched as well as listened. He saw her worried eyes, the same light brown as his. She always sat straight and tall, just like his father, but she leaned forward a little now, her hands clasped tightly.

"Circumspection is honorable," the Iofre murmured.

Questions crowded Inda's thoughts. Nothing his mother said made sense yet, but he knew she was never frivolous. And Tdor would help him figure it out later, if he could just tell it to her correctly.

A little silver bell tinkled somewhere.

"Go straighten your tunic," the Iofre murmured, waving to the far door. "It is crooked, and you must not appear before the King's Voice in that manner."

He crossed the room and carefully opened the door with its gilded inner edges. It was the only room in the castle that had been decorated, and to Inda, his mother's audience chamber was pretty enough for a queen.

He walked through into his mother's dressing room, where two of her women waited. Though his tunic looked fine to him, their calloused fingers twitched and smoothed and patted, retying his sash, adjusting his knife to the correct angle.

At the same moment, up in the tower where they stored old furnishings, Tdor crouched down behind an enormous iron-reinforced wooden chest that had been blackened by fire twenty-five years ago. She had practiced the unsealing spell over and over, since she was six. But this was her first message, and when she whispered the key-words, made the sign, then touched the ring's stone, the brief flicker of light, the faint sting on her fingers of a magic spell broken, made her gasp with joy and wonder. The stone lifted, and there was a tiny coil of paper.

She unrolled it, saw the vertical script of Old Sartoran, no longer spoken even in faraway Sartor, oldest kingdom in the world. But it was the language of archives, and of magic.

The words said only *Make certain he comes to me.* And Hadand's sigil, which she'd shared with Tdor two visits ago.

Tdor read it again, turned the paper over, saw nothing else. The princess had once said, *Anything you commit to paper you must consider your enemy will read.* Hadand, now fourteen, had reinforced that lesson during this winter's visit, with all the earnestness of someone who knew danger. Who had enemies, even.

Enemies. Tdor had always thought the context of enemies was strangers in wartime, but in recent months—since Hadand's last visit home—she was no longer so sure. She already knew that certain of the girls she could entrust some things to, but not everything. Others were always unreliable. Yet she had to live with them, and work with them every day. So she learned to hide her secrets.

In the distance Tdor heard the faint, sweet chime of bells. She ate the rice paper, then drifted out to wait for Inda.

Chapter Two

INDA returned to his mother's audience chamber. Joret, Tanrid's betrothed, had joined the Iofre, and a young man wearing the expected
war coat of Runner blue. Over his heart was stitched a crown. Inda
stared. Of course he'd seen the King's Runners before, but always from
a distance. They'd only had business with his father, when he was here,
or with his mother, or once a year with Tanrid.

His mother beckoned as if she hadn't seen him all day, and Inda reacted instinctively: he saluted her again, palm to heart, saw faint approval in her nod, and so he saluted Joret as well. Not even a smile from
Joret. Just a tiny nod.

Then a glance at the young man, who gazed with bemusement at
Joret. A laugh bubbled in Inda's gut, but he breathed hard to squash it.
Every one of the few strangers he'd ever met goggled at Joret as if their
brains had been boiled away.

Joret's eyes, bluer than a rain-scrubbed midsummer sky, were lowered so that her long, thick lashes hid them. Her gaze stayed on her fingers as if something of import was written there. Her smooth black hair,
so unusual in this part of the world, which mostly bred yellow and light
brown heads, gleamed with subdued blue highlights. The only sign of
emotion was the faint rose along the smooth honey-colored skin of her
cheeks.

The princess said, "My son, here is the Herskalt with a message for you." She spoke of course in Iascan, the language of peace, but she used the Marlovan word for King's Voice, underscoring the importance of this audience.

Recalled thus to duty, the young man looked startled, then he blushed. The Herskalt said formally—in Marlovan—"Indevan-Dal, a message was sent to your father, Jarend-Adaluin Algara-Vayir of Choraed Elgaer, with this same royal communication: you are required to present yourself by the turn of the month to the king's academy for training in field command."

Inda gaped. For a moment he was too stunned to question this yank of the shuttle from the steady warp and weft of his life. The Runner, watching as he had been commanded to watch, saw no anger betrayed in hands or eyes or mouth, nor false surprise. He couldn't figure out why the Royal Shield Arm thought that another messenger might have brought the news first, or why that would be a problem. But then everyone in the royal city knew that the Royal Shield Arm did not, for some reason, favor the Algara-Vayirs.

The King's Voice glanced toward the Iofre, who sat, her face unreadable, as expected. He couldn't prevent a hasty glance toward the heir's betrothed, but that was a mistake, for he caught her interested gaze straight on, and its impact, so unexpected, made his nerves fire, scattering his wits.

The Iofre's voice recalled him. "Are questions permitted?"

"Yes." Relief. Duty was so steadying!

The Iofre turned to Inda. "My son?"

Inda struggled for words, veering between the strangeness of his mother's earlier warning and his own feeling that he'd stepped out on what he'd thought a sturdy trail and found too late that his feet had overreached an unseen cliff.

"Why?" Inda said, framing the first word he could catch in his freefall. "I always wanted to go to the royal city and learn what my brother learns. But I'm to be his Randael, am I not?"

"Yes." The King's Voice smiled. "That has not changed."

"Well, so, isn't Tanrid supposed to train me? It's always been that way for the younger brother, except of the king. The heir trains the next Randael so he'll execute his brother's commands the way he wants when he's away riding the borders."

The King's Voice said, quite kindly, "You know that your father is oath-sworn to Tlennen-Sieraec." He used the Marlovan title for ruling monarch in peacetime instead of the Iascan word for king, just as he'd called Inda's father by his Marlovan title, Adaluin, and not the Iascan prince.

Inda's brow puckered as he considered. "Of course."

"That means not only does Tlennen-Sieraec come to the aid of his protectorates, as happened here twenty-five years ago . . ."

Inda ducked his head. That horrible story was familiar from earliest childhood.

". . . but you—meaning your father and his kin—must come to his aid with the oath-stipulated defense force if war threatens and the king must ride out as Tlennen-Harvaldar."

Harvaldar: Marlovan for *war king.*

"So there's a war coming?" Inda grinned with anticipation.

The Herskalt smiled back. He liked this boy. His report on his mission would be favorable, so the Iofre and Joret saw.

"Perhaps. Now, you know the purpose of the academy, yes?"

Inda recited Tanrid's oft-said words: "An army's strength in the field depends on all the king's captains being trained together, so they know the commands, and the chain of command."

The King's Voice added, "That last part means being familiar with the commands of the Royal Shield Arm, Anderle-Sierandael." And watched closely, as he'd been ordered to.

Inda did not bridle, pout, frown, look away. He said with a revealing lack of self-consciousness, "That's why he oversees the academy. My brother told us that."

If there is any conspiracy here, I will eat my boots, the Herskalt thought. Not that his report would contain those words. "Well, the Sierandael believes that if we must raise another army for defense, it will have to be captained by the shield arms, so they too must be able to follow his commands."

Inda's brow cleared. This reasoning made sense, and his conviction showed in his expression. He nodded. "What about Tdor, my Randviar?" Inda used Tdor's future rank in Marlovan, for the wife of a Shield Arm was also a defender, and Iascan had no equivalent words. "Will she go to the queen's training early?" Inda jabbed a finger Joret's way, and then added, "Joret goes next year, when she's fifteen. Is Tdor going with me

before Joret goes? That would be strange," he added, though inwardly
he very much liked the idea of Tdor being with him in the faraway
royal city.

The King's Voice managed not to glance at Joret, and kept his composure. "No. The queen's training has not changed, so your Randviar will
go at fifteen, as usual. Have you any more questions, Indevan-Dal?"

"No." At a gesture from his mother, Inda saluted the Herskalt and
added, "Thank you."

The Herskalt then saluted them all, palm over heart, and said, "With
your permission I will withdraw and give your steward the orders for
your dispositions." Two steps back, eyes scrupulously averted from Joret,
and he was gone.

"Dispositions?" Inda turned to his mother.

"That means your personal weapons, clothing, bedding, riding boots,
and money for your subsequent needs."

"Oh." Inda fidgeted with his sash. "May I withdraw?"

The Iofre inclined her head, and Inda saluted again, still on his very
best behavior, for the change in his life seemed to require no less. He
closed the door carefully behind him, and ran his fastest upstairs to the
school wing, where he and his siblings, their intended spouses, and the
family wards all had their rooms.

When he reached the upper landing there was Tdor, still muddy,
lying in wait. Before he could speak she thrust him into the heir's suite,
which was behind the door nearest the landing.

Inda glanced around, distracted. He had never entered Tanrid's rooms
without permission. Habit was strong, and so was imagined presence,
for the heir's gilt furniture and fabulous rugs sat here, furnishings inherited from his forefathers, heavy, beautifully carved raptor chairs and
tables, that no one was allowed to touch. Even Tanrid was careful here,
so careful he was seldom in these rooms, and almost lived in the stable.

"It's cold in here," he said, trying for the right words to express his
unease. "No, it's not that. We shouldn't be here."

"Never mind," Tdor said, plopping down cross-legged in the middle
of Tanrid's ancient rug, all blue and green and silver with owls in flight
worked in a pattern. "What Tanrid doesn't know he can't thrash you for.
Tell me what happened. And keep your voice low. We don't need half
the castle with their ears pressed against the door."

"No one saw me come upstairs," Inda protested.

Tdor sat back, eying him with tolerant scorn. There was only a year and a half between them, but sometimes she felt years older. Only sometimes. Inda was the best commander on the field, quicker even than the fourteen-year-olds. But he was too honest to spy at stairwells, for instance, as Branid did.

Right now she wanted his attention, so she said, "Everyone sees everything. Except you, right now. Talk."

So Inda told her about his interview, as clearly as he could. When he came to the end, she said, "And Joret was there from the start?" At his nod, she chuckled. "No wonder he was so nice to you. I wonder if she planned it that way?"

"Who? Mama?"

"Of course!"

A brief silence ensued, during which Inda thought about how much Joret hated being stared at. She hated it so much she often hid when strangers came, unless her position as princess-to-be required her presence. Nor was it always strangers who were guilty of bad manners. Tdor had pointed out once how some of Jarend-Adaluin's Riders stared at her, even though she still wore the shapeless children's smocks and lived with the children, and Inda had realized it was true. Not that Joret complained. She just went silent—unlike her usual self when it was just the children alone. Then she talked and laughed like his sister Hadand, who on her visits home was as merry as she was loved.

Tdor considered the news, for now she understood why the earlier messenger had come and gone so secretly. She also realized what Hadand's note meant. Inda going to the royal city! She wondered why, what the real reason was. If there was a single reason. That, too, was a new lesson about politics, that there was seldom a single reason for anything. You were told reasons, but there could be hidden ones as well.

This was the first year that Fareas-Iofre and Joret and Hadand had begun to tell her anything secret, and they didn't yet tell her everything. What she was certain of was that sending Inda would increase the House expenses, already strained by the need to feed all those extra men and horses for the watchful guarding against another surprise attack by pirates so far inland. On top of that was Tanrid's academy expenses. And now Inda would require the same. Somehow they would have to find the money. *You don't feed this many mouths, horse and human, and lie about in luxury,* Fareas-Iofre had said, when the household was finding yet another way to make old cloth last through another season and to repair worn furniture.

"Well, I wish I did get to go early, but that's that. Now, look," she said, grabbing Inda by the shoulders. "This is very important. No matter how busy you get in the royal city, you have to go see your sister."

Inda stared back in surprise. "Of course I'll go see her."

Tdor shook her head, wondering how much to say. "Don't forget, no matter how busy you are. She never sees Tanrid, for example. She says the academy boys are almost never inside the city. But sometimes they do go, and Hadand thinks it important enough for you to see her to send a message to me, in secret. She needs to tell you things. *Dangers.* Do you see?"

Inda touched his sore eye with careful fingers. After a rough morning in the mud, and all this running about the castle, his head ached a little. Not that he'd whine, because that was weak. And, he knew, his anticipation faltering a little in its headlong gallop, if what Tanrid had said was true—he frequently began his thrashings with *You think this hurts? You will never have to see real beatings, like we get in the king's training*—then aches, bruises and pains were about to become both more frequent and more nasty.

"Dangers," he repeated. "Do you mean in the academy?"

Tdor's thin face puckered. She leaned forward. He could hear her breathing, and knew from her eyes that she was upset. He leaned forward too, and their foreheads thumped together, the way they'd exchanged secrets since they were small.

"There's talk about the Royal Shield Arm, the Sierandael. How he doesn't like this family," she whispered. Her breath was warm and moist on his face, smelling of rye bread and of cinnamon-baked apple.

"Why?" Inda thought of cousin Branid, whose grandmother thought Branid should have been the heir, and all the trouble that caused. "Is it because Father's a prince? Someone wants his place? Or thinks he's making claims to something higher?"

"No," Tdor said, twitching in impatience. "Everybody knows Adaluin is just an old territory title. Your family would never be kings. And Hadand says they all know your father is loyal to the king. They were good friends when they were in the academy. It's something else, but if your mother knows, she hasn't told me yet. Hadand either."

Inda thought of his father: old, patient, usually weary, riding the borders through all seasons in protection of Choraed Elgaer. Inda could not imagine how he could possibly make enemies, except of pirates, and sighed, grinding his brow gently against hers. Somehow it felt soothing. "I hope it's something interesting."

Tdor put up her hands on either side of his face. "I always wanted to know secrets," she whispered, low and soft. "But then I started hearing them. And they aren't fun, most of them. Not ones about the grownups. They are sad, or terrible, or I don't understand them."

"I promise to visit Hadand as soon as I can," Inda said in a long-suffering voice. "And ask her then. Is that good enough?"

Tdor nodded. "Yes." She got to her feet, tipping her head consideringly. "If all the Randaels your age are going, you'll meet Mouse."

Inda groped in memory, then remembered Mouse was Tdor's cousin. Because Tdor had no brothers, Mouse would be Randael to the older cousin she'd never met, as he'd gone off to the academy each year just before her birthday visit and who was now doing his first year in the Guard.

Inda also remembered that except for her mother, everyone in Marth-Davan was nasty to Tdor, except this cousin Mouse.

Their thoughts had paralleled. Tdor said with her usual sturdy practicality, "My home visit will be worse than usual. At least I know ahead." She shrugged, then smiled. "But you know about Mouse."

Inda tried to remember Tdor's tales from home, but the truth was, he'd scarcely listened to stories about people he'd never meet. Now he recalled that Mouse was small, but he'd gotten his nickname from the fact that all the castle cats had been his friends and slept in his room all winter. Until he discovered horses. Now he was horse mad. "Mouse likes animals more than he does people," Inda said.

"He trusts them more. Because he's small, people aren't always kind."

"You want me to look out for him. If I can."

Tdor opened her hands. "He's always been kind to me. Be kind to him."

Inda flicked his fingers over his heart, his mind galloping ahead from Mouse to the academy. "I won't know anybody," Inda said, realizing for the first time he'd be among strangers. Strange Runners came and went, sometimes old friends of his father's riding through, but he'd never met any strange boys. "They'll all be on the strut," he said gloomily.

Tdor laughed at him. "You're the son of a prince, and they'll be just sons of Jarls. They'll think *you're* on the strut."

Inda tossed up his head, indignant, then he realized she was probably right. Boys here accused one another of strut all the time, but that didn't make it true.

Inda got to his feet. "I'm going to tell the others the news about the academy." He grinned. "Think Branid will be mad that I'm going, or glad to get rid of me?"

"Both," Tdor predicted.

Downstairs, the Iofre called for refreshment as she considered her next words. Joret had not needed to be present for that interview. Of course it did the Herskalt honor, but the Iofre's own presence would have been sufficient since the business did not concern Tanrid. By requiring Joret's presence and exposing her thus to the almost inevitable hot-eyed stare, she had transgressed her own private code, the one that guided her relations with castle inhabitants. But greater need had prompted her. The young man almost certainly was hand-picked by the king's brother. Distracting him had been a tactical success—he had expressed himself more freely, and she was convinced that she now had a better chance of hearing the truth. She also knew that to refer directly to the matter in any way would be intolerable to Joret.

Refreshment came. Not child's fare, but the precious, expensive golden-green Sartoran steeped leaf that smelled like midsummer after a rain, served not in their flat Marlovan wooden bowls but in pale, gilt-edged porcelain imported all the way from Colend at the other end of the continent. It was a silent gesture, one that Joret immediately understood: the conversation now would be princess to future princess.

Joret held her dish in both hands, emulating the Iofre, who never spilled, or slurped, or splashed. Sip, sip.

The Iofre said, "I desire you to take my place and command tomorrow's defense. Practice cannot begin too soon."

Joret turned her palm up in agreement. Everyone in the castle knew the horrible story of Tenthen's attack by pirates twenty-five years ago, when the Adaluin's first wife—Joret's aunt, for whom she'd been named—and the Adaluin's brother Indevan-Randael had not been able to hold the castle. The fire marks were still to be seen here and there, and the story had shaped everyone's lives.

"Very well," Joret said, both apprehensive and grateful, for she suspected that the Iofre was being kind, in her way, to make up for the
rudeness of that fellow from the royal city.

And so they talked about Joret's study progress, switching between
Old Sartoran and Iascan, then to Marlovan, when they came at last to
the first House war game of spring.

Joret finished her steeped leaf, saluted, and withdrew, her mind already dashing away into plans for that war game. How many were to attack the castle? Perhaps it would be one of the two flights of the Riders
on home detachment, or a riding or two of the household, being given
secret word right now by the former Riders' captain who served as Randael, so they could get ready.

As Joret considered plans for her defense, Fareas stood at her window, gazing out at the misting rain.

She tucked her hands inside her sleeves, her mind flitting between
images: Joret's happiness at her first defensive command outside of children's games; the tiny drops of rain forming along the edge of the rail of
her balcony, underlit by the reflected sunlight from beyond the passing
clouds; Inda's happiness at the prospect of the king's training, how his
expression had matched Tanrid's, seven years ago, on the eve of his first
departure to the royal city; how those drops there looked like pearls,
and that would that be a handsome effect on a gown, tiny pearls edging
sleeves, a neckline.

She permitted the images to skip and tumble through her mind, like
the children below in the courtyard, and then she forced herself to examine the hard truth, the almost unbearable truth, that all three of her
children would now be in the royal city, within reach of the power factions there.

Custom took the oldest boy away to mold him into a Marlovan commander, and the oldest girl, to be fostered into the family where she
would one day marry. She had known Tanrid would be trained at the
academy and that his personal alliances would form there. She did not
know if that academy had shaped Tanrid into the hard young man he
was now, or if his nature had found its true expression in that training.

What she did know, with profound conviction, were three things.

First: that she, and everyone in Tenthen Castle, was bound to the
memory of the Adaluin's first family, killed in their failed defense. Not
only did the story of that horror inform the decisions, and actions, of

every single day, but she also endured the whispered comparisons to the dead Iofre. The stories of Joret-Iofre's beauty had shaped the outlook of the younger servants, so that Young Cook knew as well as Old Cook what the first Iofre had liked to eat, and when, and why. The stable master knew what kind of mount Joret-Iofre had preferred. The grizzled old Riding Captain from the Adaluin's generation who, until Inda came of age served as Shield Arm, knew Joret-Iofre's skills at castle defense; the equally old and tough arms mistress her abilities at personal defense; and always, always, the comparisons, whispered, betrayed by speculative glances, driven by the question: if the next attack came while Jarend-Adaluin was riding the borders, would Fareas be able to hold Tenthen?

Second: perhaps because of the memory of her husband's first wife lingering in almost every person in the castle, or perhaps because Fareas had not been sent here at age two, but at sixteen, forced by royal policy to marry the widowed Adaluin instead of the Montredavan-An son she had grown up with in beautiful Darchelde, this place was not, and never would be, her true home.

Therefore, the third thing, the unspoken one, which gave meaning to her life: she was devoted not to this castle, though her duty lay here. She was not devoted to the Montredavan-An family, though her heart lay there. All her devotion belonged to her children, most particularly her cherished third, he of the loving heart, of the brilliant mind. The first two children, if a boy and a girl, belonged to other people. The third was supposed to be kept at home, and so she had given him the education of a royal, looking to a future of enlightened leadership while his older brother rode the borders.

He, too, was now to be taken to the royal city as a hostage.

Chapter Three

EACH spring since Inda was three his brother Tanrid had ridden off at the head of an Honor Guard, banners snapping, while the guard galloped like raptors in flight toward the royal city and the glories of the academy. Inda had watched, longing to go but never speaking of his desire. He knew his place was to remain at home all his life, first training and then defending the castle while his brother ranged the principality during the spring and summer seasons.

He didn't believe it would actually happen until he walked down to the courtyard and found his very own Honor Guard waiting, a Guard led not just by any Rider, but by Captain Vranid, his mother's cousin, all of them wearing their green and silver House riding coats, tight through the body, long skirted, knives through the silver sashes. How splendid they looked! And all for *him!* Inda endured his mother's embrace and whispered exhortations with a polite attempt at hiding his impatience.

It was harder to say good-bye to Tdor, but his parting pangs eased once he rode through the gates into the cold wind.

There was no galloping toward adventure for Inda. They had to camp in the lee of a hill while a bitter, sleeting storm from the coast battered them, their glorious coats hidden by thick gray cloaks and hoods. And when they resumed their ride, the road was filled with puddles the size of ponds.

Their slow pace became a full stop when they reached the river that marked the northeast border of Choraed Elgaer, a river that looked to Inda's eyes impossibly wide with rushing brown water surging over logs and swirling up onto the banks to shake the trees that grew there. The road leading up to the bridge had two logs laid across it, reinforced by stones.

"You'll have to halt," came a voice from the hillock next to the bridge, where they saw a small round house with a pointy conical roof of sandy-colored tiles.

As rain pelted down a short, squat man emerged, holding a rain-canopy over his head.

"We ride with Jarend-Adaluin's son to the royal city," responded Captain Vranid. He indicated the rain-sodden green banner with its owl in flight. "We must not be stopped."

The man shook his head. "The bridge isn't safe, not with the water runnin' past the mage-mark."

"Mage-mark?" Fiam muttered.

Captain Vranid said, "We will retire to the guardhouse. Send a Runner when we may pass."

They rode back to the walled fort on a hill, and as the Guard saw to the horses, Fiam said to Inda, "I thought spells protected bridges for at least ten years. Or is the spell gone?"

"No, or we'd have heard about Mages being brought in to renew all the water and mine spells," Inda answered, watching as an aide spoke familiar words over a waiting Fire Stick. That was everyday, boring magic. The kind one grew up with, not great spells of the sort only read about in the history scrolls.

Flames shot up obediently in the fireplace, over which was set some water to boil. Inda slung off his wet cloak and plopped down next to Fiam on the hearth.

Fiam was still looking perplexed, so Inda added, "A 'mage-mark' is a safe-measure mark. I guess on that bridge even magic won't hold the water if it goes too high. Back in the old days your ancestors might have brought a Mage from the royal city to do it, Mages being common enough, but now it would take months to contact one and bring him here, always under guard."

Fiam nodded, more interested in warming his hands than in considering the old days, before his ancestors were ruled by Marlovans. "Glad we don't have that big river near us," he said. "If it bursts its banks."

"If that stupid rain doesn't stop all of Choraed Elgaer will turn into a river," Inda grumped, sitting back in disgust as the tapping overhead solidified to a roar.

But they crossed the bridge at last, and two days later adventure seemed to beckon, in the form of the brigands that were seen riding parallel to them, like shadows, on the eastern side of the even larger river that formed the border of Faral-Thad. The shadows paced them as they rode up the river valley that bisected the mountains.

Inda assumed that his seeing them meant they were fools, until Captain Vranid said, without once taking his sideways gaze from those distant green, clover-covered hills dotted with swarms of roaming, peaceful sheep, and the occasional glint of steel helms behind, "They're letting us see them to gauge our reaction."

Inda asked, "Can't we attack 'em anyway?"

"If you were not along, we might," was the smiling reply.

Inda flushed. He knew that, even despite his brother's rough training, he would not be useful as a fighter, not until he got some size and muscle—and far more drill.

"No one doubts your courage," the captain said, knowing at a glance what Inda was thinking. "But we don't know how many there are. They don't know if we have anything worth attacking us for. And if they do attack, and we lose, and they find out who you are, at best it means death for us and a terrible ransom for your parents, Indevan-Dal." He hesitated, wondering how much of the truth to tell young Inda, whom he liked. He reflected on where the boy was going—and who might call him to question—then said only, "They know the King's Guard patrol the border of Montredavan-An land, directly north and west. I have sent a Runner ahead, by covert route. We should have aid soon."

So they did not gallop, but looked expectantly northwestward. That night the inner perimeter was paced ceaselessly and the outer ridden by armed guards, though the brigands seemed to have vanished.

By the next morning there was the expected relief party—not one but two sets of armed Riders, half in crimson and gold, the royal colors, and half in old gray coats much like those the Algara-Vayir Riders usually wore, but their banner was a golden eagle, wings outspread, against black.

Inda realized what he was seeing: the Montredavan-An Riders, who were permitted to patrol just inside their border, but they could not ride beyond, and the King's Guard, who rode just outside the same borders, making sure no one else entered or exited the forbidden land.

Inda watched as the Montredavan-An Riders lined up at one side of the road, the only sound the clopping of horse hooves and the snapping of their black and gold banner in the wind as they deferred to the King's Guard.

The captain of the King's Guard indicated the silver and green banner as he said, "Algara-Vayir?"

Captain Vranid saluted. "I am Riders' Captain Nollan Vranid, charged with the safety of Indevan-Dal Algara-Vayir, who is summoned to the king's training."

The Guard captain said, "Your road lies east."

"So it would. We rode westward to avoid brigands. I sent my Runner to report to you." A wave of the hand toward the Runner who'd rejoined them that morning. On the nod of acknowledgment from the Guard captain, he continued. "We counted a dozen, all well-mounted, just over the Faral-Thad frontier. If they ride true to form there are at least treble that number hidden in the hills."

The Guard captain said, "Yesterday I dispatched half a wing to investigate. They have not yet returned to report."

Vranid saluted again.

"Captains," the Montredavan-An leader said. "We will patrol and watch for these brigands. But first I feel obliged to offer this truth: the Jarlan, herself granddaughter to Tdanar-Gunvaer, would take it amiss if a party from Algara-Vayir, from her kin-sister, in finding itself so near our border, did not pass through Montredavan-An lands for a single night."

The Guard captain considered. Treaty forbade any war parties entering Montredavan-An land. But this was no war party, it was an escort to a boy summoned by the king's brother.

He looked at the leaders. The Montredavan-An captain studied the horizon, the other frowned between his horse's ears as though something of import lay there. They awaited his decision, without plea, argument, or persuasion. There was no suggestion of conspiracy here. More to the point, there seemed little to conspire about in a second son being conveyed on order from the royal city. And there was that reminder that the Montredavan-An Jarlan was related to the king and the Shield Arm through old Queen Tdanar. Occasionally parties were allowed in—and of course the border was crossed all the time by women's Runners as they wrote letters back and forth, like women everywhere. The captain himself had to spend many weary evenings dutifully reading long letters about home affairs that the women always seemed to be writing: letters about children, horses, dogs, crops, even gardens, punctuated with all kinds of historical references, as the girls always seemed to get more training that way. Never about kingdom affairs, at least. He wondered what he'd do—that is, how he'd feel—if he ever did have to confiscate a letter then arrest one of the tired, patient female Runners—

—And shook his head. That was irrelevant right now.

So. His decision? In his experience, men would hide their true thoughts, but boys did not. Therefore the Algara-Vayir boy's reaction would decide the matter.

He turned his attention to Inda, looking for either a smirk or anxiety, and saw only faint question and mostly boredom.

Inda stared back, idly wondering what the granddaughter of so fierce a Marlovan queen would be like to meet. He knew that his mother had been intended to marry the Jarl of Montredavan-An, but was sent instead to his father through a complicated treaty, and the king's cousin brought here to marry the Jarl. He was curious to see where his mother had grown up.

The Guard captain finally sat back, and his mount shifted beneath him. Even she was bored. "Bad weather on the west. It would seem ill, I believe, to deny the Jarlan's hospitality for a soggy camp bed." He smiled faintly, saw no response in either the Montredavan-An or Algara-Vayir parties beyond polite acquiescence, and so he raised his fist and his men trotted past, around a green hillock, and out of sight.

The Montredavan-An captain handed off the patrol to his next in command, taking three men with him as the Algara-Vayirs reassembled into columns. At their head, the captains rode side by side north toward Darchelde. Vranid said, "It was far too easy to lure those brigands after us."

The other nodded. "There will be trouble. But it will happen in your lands, not here. You must have been sent so far west by the Iofre to a purpose, then?"

"Yes. She wanted to make certain the Jarlan found out about this new arrangement with the second sons." They paused, both reflecting on

how difficult it was to get communication across the Montredavan-An
borderland. Vranid glanced back at the road where the King's Guard
had vanished, their dust still hanging in the air. "Your watchdog does not
seem a bad sort."

"Could be far worse," the captain replied as he motioned his own
Runner ahead to report to the castle. "We nearly had one sent by the
Sierandael." They both paused, thinking of the king's brother. "And so
we take care that his reports will never betray the slightest sign of
friendship on our part."

Vranid laughed.

No one spoke to Inda during the winding ride up into increasingly
forested hills. After the road descended into a cool, dark green-lit valley
they rode upward again, and when the forest cleared they saw before
them a magnificent castle, built of the familiar sand-colored stone in a
very old style, with columned archways. Built across the broadest hill, it
conveyed the impression of widespread wings, overlooking the river valley below. Inda, gazing up at that vast edifice, remembered that it had
once been the royal castle. Black-and-gold banners at all eight towers
lifted in the wind; bow women stood on each tower, composite bows
strung but held, no arrows nocked. There were women at the sentry stations where Inda would have expected to see men with their long bows.
These women—big, strong women all—held long bows. There were few
men in sight.

The gates opened. The Riders entered the court.

What drew the eye first were the two massive iron-studded doors at
the top of two stairways sweeping in impressive curves to either side—
curves, Inda realized, impossible to get a battering ram up.

One of those doors opened and a short woman bustled through.

She ran lightly down one of those broad curves, and Inda saw a wide,
youthful smile and prominent eyes the color of spring grass. She was followed by several women, bows at the ready, their robes and riding
trousers probably hiding several knives. Skimming down the staircase
last of all was a short girl with a merry face and golden curls escaping
her braids.

"Welcome to Darchelde," the woman sang out in Iascan.

"Jarlan-Edli." Vranid struck his palm over his heart. "Fareas-Iofre would wish her greetings to be given you."

"When you return," the Jarlan said in her clear voice for the two spies that the king's brother had placed among her servants, "you are to convey my best greetings to her. Do come within. Accept our hospitality before you resume your journey."

Inda wasn't listening. He saw the girl studying him from behind her mother. She laughed soundlessly when her eyes met Inda's. Then she stuck out her tongue.

Inda would have stuck his out right back, but he was aware of everyone turned his way. At a sign from Captain Vranid, Inda dismounted, and stable hands led his horse away.

The Jarlan gestured to the girl. "My dear, take Indevan-Dal in charge. When time permits, introduce him to your brother."

"When time permits." Inda heard the faint emphasis the Jarlan put on those words, an emphasis that reminded him of his mother when she spoke to Joret or Hadand or sometimes Tdor, and he knew instinctively the words carried extra meaning.

He kept silent as the girl stepped forward, and saluted with palm to heart. She looked more or less like the children at Castle Tenthen: bare feet, smock, baggy riding trousers—but her smock was embroidered, and clean. "Come along, Indevan-Dal," she said, and when they were away from the slow-moving adults, who were still exchanging stiff and formal politenesses, "I'm Shendan Montredavan-An, but you can call me Shen. Everyone here does, and we aren't allowed to see anyone else."

Once again she laughed soundlessly, eyes crinkled.

"I'm Inda," said he, following her up the stairs.

At the top Shen paused before the huge carved door that stood open, and gave him a mocking smile. "Know you the 'Hymn to the Beginning'?"

Inda shrugged, instantly wary. Was this Shendan about to test him on *history?* "Since we've been singing it at New Year's Firstday, oh, since I was able to talk, I guess I do."

Shendan just crossed her arms as she led the way into an enormous hall built between the huge fireplaces from before there were the magical Fire Sticks. "So let's hear it."

Inda glanced around, hiding his surprise. This castle was obviously far older than his own home, yet all the joins in the stone had been smoothed with plaster, and the paintings of stylized eagles, of riders and old legends on the walls, were fresh. It really did look like a castle for kings—but then it was really the first Savarend Montredavan-An who had conquered Iasca Leror, despite all the songs about Bederian Montrei-Hauc and his prowess. He had made the peace, formed the kingdom, and then lost the throne by a knife in the night, right in this very castle.

This family had produced the first real Marlovan king, and now were exiles on their own lands. Old history seemed suddenly immediate, and he wondered what Shendan was going to say next. He suspected he would not find out until he answered as she wanted, so he chanted in Marlovan, the words sounding to him, as always, like the galloping of a horse:

> *Maralo Venn of ancient day, riding Hesea Plain*
> *Wide as the wind's home, free as the eagle.*
> *Led by three warlords wielding the sun:*
> *Montrei-Hauc the mountain-gift,*
> *Montrei-Vayir plains masters,*
> *Montredavan-An, lords of the forests.*
> *Allies and equals, before they were kings*

Shendan echoed in a derisive singsong, " 'Allies and equals, before they were kings.' How many lies in that line?"

Inda knew plenty of girls, but not one was anything like this Shendan. "Not lies," he stated. "Poetic embellishments. That's what my mother calls 'em."

Shendan cast him a sideways look, full of inward laughter. "I should have known you'd be familiar with such things. Your mother grew up here, after all, and I'm glad she taught you. I'll bet a horse you even know the dates in Sartoran time."

Marlovan history was sung, and time was measured by great deeds, not years. But Inda said, "Your ancestor made a treaty by marriage with the Cassadas family in 3682, when he took over Iasca Leror." *After which they changed their name to Cassad, and became as Marlovan as the rest of us.*

"And do you know when Anderle Montrei-Vayir had my ancestor, as you call him, assassinated?"

"3718," Inda said, feeling uncomfortable—as if it had happened last week, and not almost two hundred years ago.

"Well, lies or poetry, it sounds good, doesn't it? All right, then. Skip away to 'riding the ranges'—"

Inda chanted,

Riding the ranges, valiant and venturous,
Marlovan war kings defended the holdings
Great Vayir strongholds, from the high throne.
Yet treaties beholden, deeds of famed prowess
Bound Jarls and King at year's Convocation.
War drums and danger through all four seasons
Brought fire and feud by—

The old words, sung over and over since Inda was small, suddenly took on different meaning now that he was standing in the stronghold of the Montredavan-Ans so vilified in the song.

Shendan's mouth curved in her soundless laugh, then she continued:

—gold-greed and fame-fire
Burned a hunger never to assuage.
Bones broken like spear-shafts,
Shields piled in towers,
Such was the vision of the Montredavan-An king.

Fame-fire—the craving for never-ending renown—that was the way the words translated, but until now Inda had never thought about what they really meant. His face heated under Shendan's trenchant gaze. What came next were the triumphant verses about how the new Jarls swore allegiance to the new Montrei-Vayir king who pledged peace and plenty. He said, "So the old songs lie, is that it?"

Shen snorted. "Didn't it ever seem silly to you that all the dogs yapping at Anderle Montrei-Vayir's heels added 'Vayir' which means 'plains,' onto their family names, just when they left riding the plains and moved into the castles they'd stolen from the Iascans? 'Great Vayir strongholds' indeed!"

Inda had always liked those verses. He grimaced. "Dogs including my own ancestors." He pointed at her. "But it wasn't strut when the

Haucs and the Davan-Ans and the Vayirs put 'Montrei' *before* their names?"

Shen's lips tightened. "It was always part of our name. It had all slurred together by the time the Haucs and the Vayirs thought to put 'Montrei' to theirs. Montrei means leader."

"It means 'fist' in ancient Venn," Inda retorted. For the first time he was glad of all those afternoons studying with his mother when the rest of the boys were out running around, free as air. "Marlovans changed that to mean the strongest leader. Montrei-Hauc, leaders of the mountain families, Montredavan-An, leaders of farmers and forest, and Montrei-Vayir, leaders of the plains. It was supposed to unite them. But it didn't."

Shendan lifted her shoulders, then gave him a reluctant grin. "You're the first boy I've ever talked to who knew that. Besides my brother."

"My ancestors pretty much had to add Vayir onto their names, I was told," Inda said. He was ready to make peace if she was.

Shen nodded, and indeed returned a kind of peace offering. "I learned that too, and why: because they got their title by marriage even before my great-father rode into Darchelde. I think old Anderle, so good at backstabbing, probably expected your Algaras to turn Iascan, and maybe expand Choraed Elgaer's borders at the expense of the incoming Marlovans, and so your ancestors had to add Vayir or find his army at your castle gates."

Inda's mother had told him that some families spoke of unity when tacking "Vayir" onto their names, but most of them had done it to avoid Anderle's wrath—and his retribution. Only the very strongest landholding families, like the Tlens and the Sindan-Ans, could really choose whether to add it or just keep their names as they were.

But he didn't say any of that now.

Shendan was used to being the smartest of any boy or girl she met, not that she met many, exiled here on her own land. A daughter of a king without a crown. And here was one who would ride out free and easy, and she just had to test him one more time.

So she laughed softly, hugging her arms to her, and stepped closer, staring straight into his eyes. "Did you know," she asked in that goading voice, "that that very next generation stopped speaking Marlovan? Except for all their silly titles they were acting more Iascan than the Iascans, because the real Iascans thought us a lot of barbarians."

Inda retorted, "Iascans had writing. Marlovans did not. They used Iascan for records, and Marlovan for war. It's a matter of what's easier, not
if they were barbarians."

" 'Marlovan for war.' Not until recently. No one spoke it at all, except
at your academy, did you know that? Until the last generation or so,
Marlovan was for ignorant boys in a stupid war school!"

At home Inda would have taken that as a challenge to be settled out
in the fields, the other boys and girls yelling encouragement, but he remembered he was a guest, and so he had to behave like one. No matter
how much frost this daughter of kings flung at him.

Shendan snorted again, then she noticed Inda's red face and his
tightly pressed lips, and all the anger drained out of her. She'd expected
arrogance, maybe even pity, and all she'd found was more civility than
she'd offered—that and equal knowledge.

So she finally spoke the truth. "Anyway Mother says we live with the
result, which is the treaty that binds us here to our land for ten generations, on pain of death if anyone enters or leaves without due escort.
We can only defend our land, we can't go beyond it. So while I can go
to the queen's training in a few years, my brother has never been to your
academy, can never go, is supposedly forbidden to learn to use a sword
here, though he can learn while at sea. But he can never bear one here.
Understand now?"

Inda drew in a breath. So it wasn't just a test, it was a way—maybe
the only bearable way—for this strange girl to warn him. "You don't
want me strutting about getting to go to the academy when I meet your
brother." He might have added that he hated strut, but he didn't. Such
statements, usually in Branid's mouth, just sounded like more strut, and
anyway it was a fair warning since Shendan didn't know him at all.

Shendan nodded once. "Just don't mention it. And when you leave,
don't talk about us. To anyone." She cast back a serious look from her
wide-set eyes, then added, "This way. We have most of the castle shut
up, since we are the only ones here." She waved. "But you can have your
choice of beds. There's a great old thing, all carved over with horses, that
my great-great-grandfather died in when he was assassinated. Want that
room?"

"Only if there's a ghost."

Shendan laughed. "Do you see ghosts, then?"

"No. There's supposed to be one at home. Jo . . . one person has seen it, and Tdor wishes she could see it. Maybe if I saw one here, she'd be satisfied."

Shen pointed to a door beautifully carved with horse heads, kingscrown blossoms intertwined in their manes, and Inda felt strange when he thought of his mother at home here when she was Shendan's age. For the first time he wondered what it had been like to grow up in this castle, and then, at around the age Tanrid was now, to suddenly be sent south to Tenthen, to marry a man she'd never met. He shook his head.

Shendan waved a hand at one of the hallways. "That leads to our rooms. I'll put you right across here. It'll make it easier for everyone, as the old king's room is a day's ride away." She flapped her hand behind her at silent corridors leading off to other portions of the castle, measured off by steadily decreasing shafts of light from the high slit windows. "So, what is Tdor like?" Shendan gave him that funny smile again. "We will probably be bunkmates when I go to the royal city, as I understand she and I are the same age."

"She's . . . she's . . ." Inda frowned. No one else had ever asked him such a question before. Tdor's face rose vividly before his inward vision, her serious eyes, her sudden grin that made her bony chin even bonier, her quick soft laugh. Her kindness to everyone, including the animals.

"You like her," Shendan observed.

"I . . . she's my Randviar," Inda said, as if that explained everything. "We'll be married one day."

"Good enough. I'll wait for . . . ah, here he comes."

Inda had already heard the familiar sound of riding boots on flagged stones. A tall, thin boy midway between Inda's and Tanrid's age appeared at the top of the steps.

"My brother Savarend," Shendan said. "This is Indevan."

"Indevan-Dal," said this newcomer by way of greeting. He had a strange sort of smile, one side curving up higher than the other, a sardonic smile suited to someone much older than he appeared to be. His eyes were the same color as his mother's, not the muddy hazel usually called green, but a bright shade the color of spring grass. His hair was red, as unruly as his sister's. It was wet, as if he'd come straight from the baths.

"Inda," said Inda, feeling awkward.

Savarend raised a long, thin hand. "No, no. Formality only. They'll be most chagrined if we display any hint of friendship."

Brother and sister exchanged glances, quick as the flick of a firefly, but not too quick for Inda. He remembered Tdor's last shaky-voiced warning: *Don't talk. Listen. That's how you learn fastest where danger is, without drawing its attention.*

So he said nothing, not even to ask who "they" might be, and when Savarend asked if Inda would like to see the treasures garnished from his duties at sea, Inda agreed.

On the ride away two days later, Inda reflected on how kind the Montredavan-Ans were, once Shendan had decided not to make him an enemy. Both of them were older than he, and therefore could have been expected to ignore a ten-year-old thrust on them. But they had made him laugh. Savarend had not only showed him curiosities gained from his travels as a ship's boy (duly sanctioned by the treaty, obviously), but he'd told him stories about pirate attacks and terrible storms, about sea legends concerning Ghost Island, where all the dead killed by pirates were said to walk. Shen had shown him around that great castle herself, pointing once to the highest tower where her father apparently had a room. "We will not go there and you will not see him. It's better that way," she'd whispered under her breath.

Marend Jaya-Vayir, Savarend's betrothed—who was also Inda's second cousin—had kindly asked what foods he liked best to eat. The Jarlan, granddaughter of a queen, had brought him fresh bedding herself, and seen that he was comfortable.

But he had not met the Jarl, who stayed up in his tower, and so he told the Guard who was waiting at the border two days later, after the storm that struck soon after their arrival had blown past. Even though they were going to be very late to the royal city, they still had to stop at an inn there to be questioned. By then Inda understood how very rare it was for anyone to be permitted inside of Montredavan-An lands, and so he hid his impatience at the long, detailed interrogation. The captain of the King's Guard and his two Royal Runners listened closely when he told about Savarend's sea stories, and Marend's baking, and Shendan's pretty singing voice.

He had become convinced that Shen's fit of anger, certain wry words Savarend said before laughing off the subject, were because they were the son and daughter of kings through both sides of the family. But for an assassin's knife in the night he would be at the academy, and Shen would get to marry, have children. Not that she wanted any of that. Inda heard in the songs she picked that what she wanted was a life outside of Darchelde, in a new place, where she wouldn't just grow up to be a Randviar with no Randael.

Inda, already missing his home, couldn't understand that part. Though he looked forward to the academy, he wanted also to be home at Tenthan, with Tdor and his parents and cousins and friends and everything just right. He didn't understand the desire to leave home forever, but he could sympathize with the wish for justice that would never come.

So he kept to himself the things he knew he was not supposed to have seen. Such as the looks of secrecy between mother and children, between brother and sister, and the expert way that Savarend had handled a knife when he thought no one was looking.

Chapter Four

"FROM this moment on, you have no rank."

Twenty busy minds braced against the harsh voice while trying not to stare at the great stone walls or to listen to the ferocious rhythm of clashing steel from beyond the tallest wall as the echoing bells of noon died away.

"The 'Dal' added to some of your names, the deferential 'son of Jarl of Whatever-Vayir,' is mere courtesy. Signs of rank you haven't earned, that you were merely born to."

Of those twenty, some were distracted by the snapping of pennants in the wind, the wink of sunlight on the steel helms of the King's Guard and the steel tips of the bows of the Queen's Guard. One, the king's second son, looked beyond at a sky as unnoticed by the rest as the distant cry of birds.

"Courtesy. There is no courtesy in war."

Inda's gaze snapped from those steel helms to the speaker.

Around him, two lines of weary, excited, easily distracted ten-, eleven-, and twelve-year-olds gave all their attention to their new leader, whose sun-lined face revealed none of his thoughts. Master Gand, veteran dragoon captain and now their principal tutor, easily read the expected delight, apprehension, excitement, and exhaustion in the young faces, and in several a poor attempt to hide a knowing smirk.

Not from Evred-Varlaef, though. The king's younger son—small for twelve, with auburn hair, just like his father's at the same age—looked down at the ground, his countenance shuttered.

Still watching them, Master Gand finished his speech. "From now on, you have only your family name. If I could take the 'Vayir' off of some of those names, I would. You're here because your family, Vayir or not, has earned honor for its service. Your family. Not you. Your rank here must be earned, just as you'll earn the right to wear your hair in horse-tails. If you live." Another pause. "You will call me Master Gand."

Most now looked thoroughly intimidated, except for two of the smirkers whose expressions had altered to speculation. The third's ex-pression had gone wooden.

"Most of you have older brothers here, the rest cousins who are heirs. This is the first year we've brought Shield Arms outside of the royal family for training, so there is no tradition. We've determined that you will be referred to by your family names, as I said, with the addition of *Tvei* when necessary to differentiate you from your *Ains*."

Ain, tvei. One and *two* in Marlovan. So far, those were the only Marlovan words Master Gand had spoken outside of the titles he scorned. *I will be Algara-Vayir Tvei*, Inda thought, trying to accustom himself to the sound.

"You have liberty for the rest of the day. At the dawn bells, you will line up here, ready to begin work. Questions?"

One of the smirkers said, "What if it's raining?"

"You will be here. In this line. Ready to begin work." The threat—quite chilling—was back. "Further questions?"

The smirk vanished. As for the others, nobody wanted to ask ques-tions, at least not here, though their minds burgeoned with nothing else.

"Firstnight bell for you younger boys is your supper mess, and you'd better be done eating when the older boys come in at second bell. Dis-missed."

Inda waited until others started moving; by showing up so late he had missed the tour, and had no idea where anything was. His arrival at this huge parade ground was still a blur of quick murmurs and pushing hands.

The others milled about, friends or relations banding together as they walked away. A big boy with long pale hair gave a whoop and ran off. Another one said in a loud voice to the boy on Inda's other side, "Come on, let's get to Daggers before all the good tables are gone." Neither boy glanced Inda's way.

Daggers Drawn. He'd heard Tanrid talk about the academy's own tavern so many times. But they only went after their father introduced them.

From the way these boys strutted the rule was clear, you still couldn't just go. Someone—father, perhaps brother—still took you first.

Well, that was easy, then: no Daggers. *Maybe never,* Inda thought sourly, for his father almost never came to the royal city except when he was required to. That left Tanrid, who hadn't been anywhere in sight, unlike some of the other curious older brothers, and that brought another question probably no one would answer: why didn't the order come before Tanrid left, so the brothers could travel together? Not that Inda really wanted to be under Tanrid's orders on the road, but when he thought about it, it was strange.

"Lost?" A boy with reddish hair approached.

Inda nodded, tired thoughts instantly scattered.

"Where did you want to go?"

"Bunk." Inda added, "Learn my way around before tomorrow."

"Good idea," put in a small, skinny boy with lemon-colored hair. He jabbed a thumb Inda's way. "Like him, I just got here before noon."

"Me too," said another boy, and two more nodded. A fourth, a long-faced boy, just stood, looking resigned.

"Well, I can help with that," said the one with reddish hair. "This here is the academy parade ground, where we'll meet mornings the first week or so, I'm told, and then afterward when the entire academy assembles. We'll have our own court at our barracks. Come along, if you like."

All the boys in that uncertain little group were sensitive to tones of command; the redhead had invited, not demanded.

Satisfied, no one spoke. At home Inda would have asked questions, but he still remembered Tdor's last words: *Listen. That's how you learn fastest where danger is.*

Danger. He hadn't really believed any danger would find him, not at the famous academy he'd never gotten tired of hearing about, but he'd agreed because their hearts hurt at parting.

Now that he was here in the royal city, and there were all these questions, he thought the advice good.

"Here's what you ought to remember." The redhead pointed upward. "That is the royal castle bell tower. Highest of all the castle towers. Everywhere you go, if you stop and find it, and fix its direction in your mind, you'll learn your way about."

Inda squinted. The noonday sun sat just above that tower.

"As for the city, its bell tower is at the south end. If you can see it or hear it, you can orient yourself in the city."

Nods all around. The small boy with the lemon-colored hair said, "I take it you live here."

The redhead glanced at Inda. His gaze went cloudy. "Yes."

"Oh," Lemon-hair observed. No one else spoke.

"So, turning this way from the tower, the scrub pit lies that way. Remember: three archways . . ."

The boys moved out of the parade court, watched, unseen and unknown, by Inda's sister, Hadand-Hlinlaef, future queen. She sighed in relief when she saw the redhead near her brother's dear, familiar form, as the last of them vanished under the mossy archway. How strange, how unaccountable to see her little brother here, he who should never have left home. She knew the order about this change in tradition must have come from *him*—the Sierandael—and that meant it was for no good reason.

She stepped back inside the secret passage.

Inda kept his back to the tower, aware of it behind him as he followed along the worn flagstones between the plain stone-and-wood barracks buildings. Scouting unfamiliar terrain using landmarks could be applied to cities, Inda realized. In the time it took to cross another court his bewilderment, that sick sense of being lost, shifted to internal mapping, using the tower as principal landmark. Thus steadied inwardly, his eyes and brain continued the task almost without interfering with the stream of his conscious thoughts.

Most of that stream was concerned with the memory of his arrival, and speculation about the inevitable first meeting with his brother. Tanrid had not been among the seniors who galloped forth so suddenly from the academy gates just before noon, when Inda and his guard were arriving, so desperate, so anxious not to be late. Inda did not notice the age-smoothed stones under his new boots, nor the archways they passed through. Instead he saw the beautiful dashers in exact formation, tails high—as if they knew they looked good—and on their backs young men in new gray academy war coats, tight to the sashed waist, long and full-skirted for riding, their hair tied up in the horsetails of their plains-riding ancestors, the bugler calling a fall of three notes that caused citizens in the street to immediately give way so fast that the horses' headlong pace was not checked, and by they thundered, smelling of horse and human sweat and oil and steel, a smell that filled Inda with yearning.

Inda had felt pride in his name, in his land, in his family. That pride had lingered until Captain Vranid and the Riders silently gave way to the horsetail-wearing seniors thundering by.

That's what the arms master meant by earning, Inda decided, as the redhead said, "And the third archway. There's our pit." He dashed through the archway, the boys following as they scanned the clean-swept stones of their little court and the low stone-framed building beyond, with its plain wooden walls and row of glassless windows. All the shutters were open.

Pit. Inda and the boys at home had quickly nipped any bits of academy slang that Tanrid had let out, though all of them, especially Inda, had been beaten severely for presuming to use it.

"Our tack ought to be stashed by now," the boy added, and Inda translated mentally: *Someone got our gear in storage*. Still in Iascan.

They clattered inside, their boots loud on the plank floor, and stopped in a clump, taking in the long room that smelled of old wood, dust, and wool, a particular blend of scents that worked its way down into the memories of every boy who came through here, evoking a welter of emotions.

Inda just stood, thinking *I'm really here*, and gazed at the two neat rows of empty wooden beds—only twenty, instead of thirty-six, the traditional maximum number of boys taken for training each year. Then he turned to the redhead to find he was being studied. Both boys glanced away before they could see one another flush.

Lemon-hair sighed. "Looks to me like a good half of these bunks are already claimed. But lotsa choices are left."

Inda cleared his throat and mumbled, "My brother said you don't want to be near the door, where inspections are always worst."

"Same with t'other end," another boy said in the exact same tone—that of the younger brother with a deadly fear of being accused of frost, which was worse than mere strut. Anyone could strut, but frost was scorned as a kind of arrogant superiority, an assumption of rank. Strut might get you a clout, but frost could get you beaten, and everybody would say it was earned.

"Windows are best," Inda ventured.

"Taken," Lemon-hair noted gloomily, and all saw that each bed under a window was already made up, or had gear on it.

"Well, I see some free ones on that side in range of a window. When there's a west wind there might be some air," Redhead said, so carefully neutral he sounded half-strangled.

Nods, shuffles, furtive looks, and the boys decided they might claim them. Much better than being alone, and so far at least, none of these others seemed a pug, a frost, or a lick.

Conversation was easier by the time they'd each located their strictly regulation storage chest, lugged it in, and stashed it (properly squared) at the foot of their bunk. In their chests they each had sheets and coverlets, undyed and nearly indistinguishable, which they brought out. Inexpert hands did their best to smooth the bedding over the thin mattresses stuffed with old mail-quilting.

They all wore riding trousers, stockings, and riding boots, and the plain gray tunics, not much different than the smocks they wore at home, carried no device over the heart, which was also regulation; two of the tunics were obviously worn hand-me-downs from brothers or cousins, but no one said anything. Those who had everything new had, however they'd felt the day before about family and home, a desperate wish for the security of anonymity now, and were glad of the gray, protecting them from an accusation of strut or frost. For the first time in lives that were supposed to be spent within sight of the castle walls of home, no one knew who anyone *was*.

The distant tower rang the midafternoon (*Daylast*, Inda thought, in Marlovan) bells. Inda's stomach lurched. He hadn't eaten since a very hasty slice of bread at lastnight bells, three hours before dawn.

The king's second son, he of the red hair, looked at the other boys, and saw varying degrees of uncertainty. His own dread of discovery and treatment (bad as well as good) that people gave to a prince as opposed to a person, the certainty of some cruel gesture on the part of his brother, became concern. He realized these others would not speak, and they did not know what to do. He glanced at Hadand's brother, looking so much like Hadand he'd recognized him right away. Hadand had said, *Please watch out for my brother.* He would do anything she asked.

He said, "I know a good bakery."

"Don't got a flim," Lemon-hair admitted, grinning as he pointed to the pockets of his worn breeches.

"I happen to have lots left over from the journey south," said another boy, the one with the long hound-dog face and short dark hair. "May as well get rid of 'em now."

Nods. The boys moved off in a group. The king's son—still enjoying his anonymity—took them by a back route (away from the stables and weapons courts) to the gate to the city, and suddenly they passed from the austere military atmosphere to one of comparative light and color. The walls were still the same honey-colored stone, but the buildings were a jumble of sizes, some with signs, windows with painted shutters, and window boxes growing early flowers. People moved about, some on horseback, others driving carts and wagons, many more walking. Everywhere the new boys observed guild colors, and what seemed to their eyes, accustomed to the sameness of provincial castle life, a wild variety in civilian clothing. The air smelled of horse, of blooms, of roasting chicken and cabbage and bread.

Then came the moment the king's second son dreaded. Lemon-hair grinned. "So what shall I call you?"

"Inda."

"Flash," another said, laughing. He was a wiry boy with sun-streaked brown hair. "M' brother started calling me that when I was little. On account of how slow I was."

"Lan," mumbled another blond boy shyly. "Lan Askan."

"My family name is Toraca, but you may as well call me Noddy," said the dark-eyed, dark-haired boy with the hound-dog face. "Everyone at home does. Noddy Turtle."

"Why?" someone asked.

"Turtle on a fence post."

The boys snickered, even though it didn't make sense.

"Turtle?" Lan murmured. "Fencepost?"

Noddy didn't smile. They were to learn that he almost never smiled. "What I looked like when I was little." He shrugged his shoulders up under his ears, his arms dangling, and they saw it: he did look rather like a turtle. "You never get away from these things." He shrugged again, a normal shrug. "So why try?"

Lemon-hair grimaced. "I thought about that all the ride down," he said. "Picking a new name. Something heroic, maybe. I mean my first name's Kendred, but I never heard it, that I recollect. If someone called 'Kendred!' I'd think it meant for one of the other Kendreds. Has to be a handful of 'em here."

Everyone agreed with that. Marlovan names were always repeated back and forth across generations, families, allies, and clans. Of course there would be others with all their names.

"So," Lemon-head went on, waving a grubby hand. "So I thought, a new nickname, see? Then I saw me the arms master that's been to our house for sup at least once a year since I was born, and of course there's my brother in the pigtails."

"So?" Inda prompted.

"So you're gonna hear my dad's name, sure as fire, and then it's all up," the boy went on. And, as it chanced, the very moment he said, "On account of my dad being Horsepiss Noth, everyone calls me Dogpiss," a local hound lifted his leg against the corner of a shop.

The name, spoken just as the blithely unconscious dog let go the yellow stream, strengthened by the taboo nature of urine in a world where the Waste Spell had been almost the only magic to endure from the terrible war that had nearly wiped magic—and humans—from the world centuries before, it made them all laugh, even Noddy, though his laugh was a kind of snort, his long face still blank.

The stream was only there for moments. A member of the Wanders Guild popped round the shop corner (probably following the dog, who'd been sniffing about) and waved his wand over the dark puddle. Glitter, flash, the puddle was gone, the Wander walked past, and the boys continued on, still gasping and shaking with laughter, some of them considering the news: here was the son of the famous Horsepiss Noth, who captained the King's Dragoons. The Dragoons were tough (many said the toughest) and their captain had to be even tougher. Those boys with brothers in the pigtails had already heard of Whipstick Noth, Dogpiss' older brother, and knew he was going to be the same.

"Oh, oh, oh, it hurts," Dogpiss said, holding his sides. "Oh. Someone say something quick! Something sour—"

"We'll be sour enough come morning," Noddy predicted.

"True," Dogpiss agreed, but he still laughed, his thin body shaking, wisps of short yellow hair hanging in his eyes.

"How'd your Ain escape being a 'piss'?" Noddy asked, his long face blank, which got the others laughing all over again.

When Dogpiss could breathe, he wheezed, "B-brown hair . . . like Ma's . . . I got the piss-yellow . . . like Dad . . ."

When his snickers subsided they turned expectantly to the red-haired boy, whose voice and manner so subtly set him apart.

Evred-Varlaef, the king's second son, felt and instantly repressed the familiar sense of sick certainty at what was to come. His brother would see to that, he knew it, he just knew it. But he would postpone the inevitable as long as possible. "Well, you may as well call me Sponge." At their surprise, he added, "Got it from my cousin, who was sent to sea."

The others nodded, thinking of the reddish-brown sponges pulled up from the ocean floor and used in cleaning.

They turned to the last of the group, a tall, powerfully built boy with unruly black hair. He'd not spoken once, though he'd been quite helpful in shifting heavy chests without any apparent effort. Even his laughter was silent. Now his face creased in misery. In a tiny voice like a kitten's squeak, he, well, he *mewed*, "Camarend Tya-Vayir. Cama."

Inda had to bite hard on his tongue to keep from hooting. Though he could not have described to Tdor how he knew, he recognized instantly that while Dogpiss didn't mind being laughed at, this boy would feel terrible.

Half the others identified him as younger brother to the horrible bully hated by most brothers: Horsebutt Tya-Vayir.

Sponge studied Cama's square face under his shock of black waving hair, and thought, *he doesn't look at all like Horsebutt*. But he didn't speak, for he was still elated over his anonymity, the easy acceptance of the others. He'd enjoy it while he could.

They turned down an alley that dead-ended against the city wall, and ducked through a narrow door below a weathered bakery sign. Those with money crowded up to the counter. Inda sat on the edge of a bench, breathed in the smell of baking rye bread, a scent that reminded him so forcibly of home he felt a squeezing in his throat, and his tired eyes burned. He propped his elbow onto a barrel; on his other side sat a boy whose name he'd already forgotten. A moment later he heard footsteps, and a big plate of berry cakes appeared, with hot jam to pour over them.

He took one, but scarcely tasted it. The other boys crowded onto the bench and passed the plate back and forth, chattering about home. Inda leaned his head on his hand, hearing only boys' voices, no words.

His mind slid away, back, back to being woken at lastnight bell, the third hour of the morning, for that cold, long ride across the plains of Choraed Hesea. He had not even had time to say farewell to Captain Vranid or Fiam . . .

"Supper!" someone exclaimed, and Inda jerked awake, his hand numb, drool on his cheek. He wiped his mouth on his shoulder, got to his feet, and followed, legs heavy, mind stupid, longing for bed.

The musical clang of the sunset bells—*sundown*—announced the end of the day, as did the lengthened shadows. Inda followed the others into the mess hall, a long room with a wooden roof, bright with glowglobes and loud with skull-smiting noise.

Sponge watched Inda covertly, but said nothing. At twelve—older than most of these boys—he was very experienced in the silent, deadly riptide of power politics, and had learned the still patience of prey.

Inda carried his tray, received the doled out fishcakes into the worn, shallow wooden bowl that looked exactly like the bowls at home. Boiled cabbage. Rice. At the end of the serving table sat a dish of round wooden spoons, also like those at home. He picked one up and followed Sponge, glad to have the decisions made by someone else.

The others sat at the end of a long wooden table, apparently for the scrubs, at the far end of the room. Images, unconnected, caught Inda's attention: Sponge, sitting down, looking somber. Dogpiss, at the end of Inda's bench, taking a bite.

The riding boot that caught Dogpiss in the ribs and shoved. A boot belonging to a brawny boy with long butter-colored hair.

The world narrowed to dreamlike slowness as Dogpiss' blue eyes teared from surprise and pain, his food went flying and he landed backward, his head knocking the edge of the bench behind theirs. Bright blood spotted his yellow hair.

Inda was too stunned to feel anything. He was only aware of his hands moving as if someone else moved them, and his mind was somewhere else, watching. That someone used his hands to thump his food

on the table and smash the wooden tray across the laughing face of the
brawny boy, who squawked in pain.

Reality jolted Inda back into his body when another hand gripped his
braid hard and yanked.

Inda squirmed and managed to strike something meaty. The world
narrowed to heat and yells and the struggle of arms and legs, until strong
hands seized the scruff of his neck, ripped him free, and thrust him with
a skull-rocking smack onto the bench.

"Sit down and eat," an older boy snapped in an urgent whisper. "You
want to bring King Willow down on us all?"

Inda tried to protest, but he saw another older boy fling the yellow-
haired bully onto a bench. And there was Sponge lifting Dogpiss, who
winced and touched his head, and Noddy picking up their cups and settling their trays. So Inda sank back onto the bench, his head and heart
drumming, his breathing shaky.

"Eat."

Inda didn't even look up to see who spoke. He sat without moving,
aware of everyone staring. Except Noddy, who glared at the yellow-
haired boy and said loudly, "Already laying claim to tables and we
haven't even been sheared yet? What frost."

Frost. Frost. The eyes turned away pair by pair, and talk resumed, leaving only a last glare from that yellow-haired bully. Dogpiss and Inda
picked up their spoons in trembling fingers.

Chapter Five

UP in the royal wing Hadand sat with Queen Wisthia, who insisted on the Sartoran word for queen, *Sarias*, which was put before her name, the way it was done in civilized kingdoms. Twice a year she endured the Marlovan word for queen, *Gunvaer*, the bloodthirsty connotations of which she detested. Her rooms were arranged in the Sartoran style of her youth, and she kept Sartoran customs. Music played during evening study. No war drums were ever permitted. Some of her women were trained in wind and string instruments, and these four sat with steel-stringed lutes and lap harps, plinking soft melodies that chased like butterflies up and down the scales.

Hadand saw her own Runner, Tesar, drift across the open doorway. She forced her attention back to the scroll she was translating. *The shearing songs calm the animals, and in turn the children are calm, and glad to see the lambs dash off into the fields, free, light, and dancing in the sun . . .*

Shearing. How odd, these coincidences. Tomorrow would be the infamous scrub shearing. *Inda.* Tesar's being here meant something had happened, to either Inda or Sponge or both. Hadand could have groaned with impatience, but like Sponge she had long ago schooled herself to stay still. So her mother had taught her, a lesson reinforced by Ndara-Harandviar, wife of the king's brother, the Sierandael.

The music pattered on, syncopated as the last drops of rain from a passing storm, until the distant bells rang.

"My dears, we will retire," the queen said, rising.

Hadand also rose. At last! But here was poor little Kialen Cassad, designated by treaty before she was even born to marry the king's second son and be his Harandviar. Kialen's frail fingers crumpled like spider legs close to her thin chest, her dark-ringed eyes wide and fearful. She'd seen Tesar as well.

Hadand made the finger sign that represented lilies, the sign for danger, the signal for a smooth face. Kialen obediently did her best, trotting close behind Hadand as they moved to Hadand's rooms down the hall. Hadand had been given her rooms at age ten, after eight years in the royal nursery with Sponge and the other royal children, though they still sometimes used the big nursery room for study. By the time she was twelve she did not require Ndara's warnings—real lilies, drawn ones, or finger signals—to know which rooms were safe to speak in and which were not.

Tesar, Hadand's trusted personal Runner, fifteen and equally old in deception, said, "Kialen-Hlin, Hadand-Hlinlaef, the stable master bade me inform you that Evred-Varlaef has made his riding horses over to you for the summer. He awaits your orders."

"Very well," Hadand said, carefully bland. She turned to Kialen. "There is just time enough to bathe, and then we might work on your Old Sartoran vocabulary before we attempt that scroll on the seasons. Tesar, please bring clothes to us in the baths."

They passed by the Runner, who saluted while her other hand, so deft, so practiced, slid a tiny roll of rice paper into Hadand's fingers. Then Tesar vanished on her errand.

On a landing down the narrow back stairwell, Hadand paused and read the tiny Old Sartoran script: *He struck at supper, through Marlo-v. 2. I. fought back. Noth boy target.*

That was all. Hadand translated. "I" meant Inda. "Marlo-v. 2." was Marlo-Vayir Tvei, the second son of the Jarl of Marlo-Vayir, who had done something to the son of the famed Captain Noth of the Dragoons. All of it designed to get at Sponge in some way—just as they had predicted. "He," of course, meant Aldren-Sierlaef, king's heir, the enemy, Sponge's brother.

Hadand's future husband.

Poor Kialen's face was blanched with fear. "It's all right," Hadand whispered. "It's about my brother, not Sponge."

The girls passed down the last stairway to the warm stream-fed baths under the castle, Hadand having swallowed the note. Voices of off duty female Guards echoed off the old stone walls, and nearby two of the queen's women talked quietly about the new fashion in the queen's old country: chimes braided into women's hair for dancing. They would never do that here.

When Inda woke, just before dawn, he couldn't remember where he was. He was aware of that wool and wood and puppy dog smell again, the sounds of many boys breathing, then "Up! Up!" someone yelled. "You know we'll have an inspection after the shearing. Let's clean now, and save our backs."

Inda had no idea how to make a bed look smooth or how to sweep a floor. Fiam had always taken care of that. But Fiam was on the long ride home, probably looking forward to wargaming all the summery days . . .

Trying to fight away homesickness, Inda thrashed into his clothes. Habit caused him to fling his nightshirt down, but he picked it up again. Those hooks on the wall beside the headboards, yes they were for night-shirts. He watched the rest of the boys, did what they did, and at last stood back and in the blue predawn light compared his efforts with everyone else's. He didn't see any difference.

"Straighten your breeches. You've got ankle rumps," Noddy whispered to him, pointing down to where he'd stuffed his breeches into his riding boots, and saw that they were flat in front and pouched out behind. He pulled at the loose material until it draped more or less evenly around each boot, then he reached for his braid—and dropped his hands. No use in struggling with two-day-old knots when it would soon be gone.

Besides, the others were already running out to the parade court, to be in line before the sunup bells. Torches still lit the court, for the sun at this time of year still rose after the sixth-hour bell. A fine mist had moved in, making it darker, but at least it wasn't miserably cold.

On the first clang of the bell Master Gand marched out of the big building opposite the castle wall, where the masters lived. If he was pleased to see this year's scrub class neatly lined up and ready, he showed no sign of it. His mouth soured. "So how many of you are going to waste my time telling me you've been riding from the time you could walk?"

By now they'd learned not to volunteer any commentary.

"Good. Because those would be the ones needing a month or two of wanding the stable floors, to unlearn all the rotten habits they'd picked up since they started walking."

Pace, pace, high-heeled cavalry boots crunching bits of gravel on the old, worn flagstones.

"You are eventually going to learn command of cavalry. All three branches: light, heavy, dragoon. But if you think that means you are ready to ride horses, think again, my little lambs. You are ignorant. And as such you are more danger to the horses than you are to any enemy. You little Vayir-dals left the real horse care to your armies of stable hands at home. Well, here's news for you: in the field, there are no servants, and farriers don't follow you about in case your horse throws a shoe. You're going to learn how to take care of your horses, including their feet. And you're going to do it fast. And right. In the dark. Before you ever sit on a horse's back."

Silence, except for the wind rushing through the pennants overhead.

"The first month or so, you ignorant lambs are going to learn everything there is to know about horses' habits and needs, and that means you are going to work. Hard."

Pause. Pace, pace, no answer.

The tutor lifted his hand toward the gate to the training areas. For the very first time he spoke Marlovan, the language of war. "And now, my little lambs, it is time to be sheared."

A great shout went up from behind the gate, and Inda and the boys all drew together instinctively. Inda, remembering his brother's lavishly described horror stories about the traditional shearing of the scrubs, saw the tall blond boy who'd kicked Dogpiss in the mess hall—his name still unknown—looking pale and scared. Inda turned away, pleased, but not two breaths later a painful jab in his back brought his head around to see that same boy, a big, brawny boy, staring straight ahead, a telltale smirk twisting his lips.

The scrubs shuffled through the gate, to find the expected, seemingly endless two rows of older boys waiting. Not the seniors, the ones who had earned the right to bind their hair up into horsetails. These were the eleven- to sixteen-year-olds, the older ones with hair in clubs, the younger with their shorter hair pulled into squirts in back: the pigtails.

"Go! Go! Go!" The Marlovan chant sent birds squawking.

The first boys began running down the middle of the lines, and of course got slapped and shoved from side to side, some of them falling, to be kicked until they rose again and ran on.

Three. Four. Inda felt a spurt of anger almost as hot as the one he'd felt at the senseless attack on skinny little Dogpiss who hadn't given that big turd the least trouble.

It was his turn, and he began to run, shoulders hunched, jaw tight, until he realized that the slaps were mere stings, and he'd received much worse from his brother. He did stumble and fall once, but the kicks thudded with more sound than sensation against his sturdy tunic. He scrambled up to the sound of laughter, felt the hands propelling him onward. Run, run, and there was the end, and the *Go! Go! Go!* was laughing, not cruel, and then one of the orderlies reached for him, whipped out his hair tie with expert fingers, and snip, snip, there went his braid. His head felt light, his neck cold, and he couldn't help fingering his hair as he joined the small group of shorn boys. His hair, never neat, had sprung up in curls all over his head, but at least he wasn't the only one with that problem.

They all looked strange. No, they all looked the same, with their squared off hair in back, and Inda, staring at the boys, realized that the shearing run wasn't just a way to humiliate them with this silly short hair. He realized it had made them into a group, even that big blond horseapple. Well, they were academy boys now, and city people would know them as academy, commanders-in-training, set apart from civilians. They *belonged*.

He rejoiced in his heart, grinning foolishly like most of the others. *Why, that wasn't nearly as bad as I'd heard.*

Some of the boys had already vanished, and the arms master howled at the rest of them to get ready for inspection and their very first callover, and if they weren't ready, they'd be scrubbing floors for a month . . .

Inda laughed as he ran back to the barracks, noticing that he had no problem finding it. Breathless laughter, joking insults about looks, easy chatter—until they reached the pit. The blond boy and a couple others were still missing.

But that was not what made them all stop, staring in shock.

There was his bunk next to Dogpiss', but their carefully smoothed sheets were trampled all over with dirty, horse dung-clumped hay, their mattresses ripped and scattered, their gear chests open and full of *something* that reeked enough to make their eyes water.

Inda looked up, dazed, sick. Several boys backed slowly away, their gazes averted. He remembered Tanrid's stories, and knew what it meant.

He and Dogpiss had been bunk-scragged.

Chapter Six

TWO days later, Inda finished up his punishment chores in the stable and trudged back toward the scrub barracks. He tucked his cold hands inside his armpits—

Pain! Elbow! The world spun. A familiar grip on his arm, familiar breathing, and Inda resigned himself to a thrashing. He just hoped Tanrid would tell him why.

Tanrid pulled Inda around the side of the stable, next to one of the huge feed sheds, held him against the wall, and frowned down into his face. There were his hard brown eyes, his unsmiling mouth, his sun-streaked brown hair now pulled proudly up into a tail high on the back of his head.

Tanrid's frown was not angry, it was urgent. Inda could see that clearly enough in the reflected light from the torches on the castle wall just behind the sheds. "I heard you got shit-scragged. First morning! *And* a fight in the mess hall?"

"Not shit-scragged—" Inda gasped.

"What were you thinking?" Tanrid shook him, thumb pressed agonizingly into that awful place just beside his elbow joint.

Inda blinked away tears and managed to get out two words: "Attacked . . . Dogpiss . . ."

Tanrid abruptly eased the pressure, but kept hold. Inda drew in a shuddering breath and spoke faster. "The fight in the mess hall was instinct. Marlo-Vayir Tvei kicked Dogpiss Noth off the bench, his head cracked, and, well, I just acted."

"Did the beaks come in? Wave the willow?"

Inda shook his head. "No beaks, no caning. Pigtails landed on us, pulled us apart. But I—"

"No buts. Do. *Not*. Fight in the mess hall." Another jab in the elbow joint, and Inda gasped. "Any fight, they don't like the reasons—and they never do—we all eat outside. All. Rain or not. There's always rain this time of year. No justice, no negotiation. Happened twice to me so far, both times from scrubs scouting the rules. If your fart-faced litter of scrubs lands us outside, we'll scrag you all. Got it?" Another poke.

"Yes." *You never told me that*, Inda thought with resentment. *You never told me anything that didn't make you look good.*

"So you weren't shit-scragged?"

"Not dog turds, or shit." Inda looked down in embarrassment. He'd only actually seen human excrement once—the inevitable experiment of the small child. But he'd heard about how not using the Waste Spell, and putting your own shit in someone else's shoes, or room, or bed, had not only sparked feuds between entire clans, but even wars. "In our bunks."

"Horse?" Tanrid spoke in relief.

"Yes."

Tanrid nodded once. "That's what I thought. Just a bunk-scrag, but there are three different rumors going around, and like usual people only tell the story they think is the funniest. I had to check, because if it wasn't horse Father would want to know. It becomes a family matter. Details?"

"After the shearing, we got back for inspection and our first callover, and there were our beds, torn up, horse plops in hay all over. Our tack, full of horse piss. We got wands, of course, but we couldn't fix the beds in time—"

"You *didn't* blab."

Inda couldn't hide his scorn. "Course not. We got a jawing for being slobs. Stuck with a month's stable cleaning, only it's swap-off. One, then t'other. Entire pit got mess hall gag."

"Ah." Tanrid's expression altered. "The swap means they knew you weren't to blame."

"That's what a couple of boys said."

"But the mess gag, well, it could mean anything. Go on. You know who did it, right?"

"Not sure. They must've done it right after they were sheared, because they weren't with the rest of us. But they kept laughing when we tried to clean up before inspection."

"Who're 'they'?"

"Marlo-Vayir Tvei and someone called Basna Tvei. I learned their names at callover. Who are the Basna family?"

"Northerners. They owe fealty to Sindan-An from way back, before they allied with Tlen."

Sindan-An and Tlen, two powerful landholding clans, so famed for their prowess their names appeared in most of the ballads. They were the crown's supporters in the north.

Tanrid added, "Basna Ain is one of the senior horsetails, going into the King's Dragoons next year."

"Oh." The king. Inda had also learned that Sponge was the king's second son—something Sponge had tried to hide and which Inda was still trying to comprehend. "But I don't know who else bunk-scragged us. Or why."

Tanrid glanced about again, then muttered, "I don't know—yet—if there's any connection, but you better know this. The Sierlaef hates his brother."

Inda gaped. "Why? Sponge is the future Sierandael!"

"The rumor is, he wants Buck Marlo-Vayir as Sierandael. I don't know how true it is. I don't run with the Sier-Danas."

Sier-Danas. The Marlovan term for "high rank Honor Guard." So the royal heir had a gang of privileged followers, then. Huh.

Tanrid said in a rapid whisper, "As for the bunk-scrag, there are other ways to find things out. You can't bribe the stable hands to get wands and not have someone pay more to find out who bribed 'em. But you listen." He shook Inda once, hard. "If you disgrace the family, I'll scrag you myself."

Tanrid let him go and strode away. Moments later the sunup bells began to ring, and Inda dashed through narrow causeways between stone buildings, falling in with the scrubs who tumbled out of the barracks, still warm and sleepy-eyed.

Dogpiss was first, his wispy yellow hair drifting into his watchful blue eyes. He mouthed, *Where were you?* and Inda mouthed back, *Brother ambushed me.*

Dogpiss grimaced in sympathy, but they did not speak as they followed the others to the parade court, some still tugging and tucking at clothing.

Master Gand waited, his sun-bleached horsetail flagging in the wind, his old gray military coat straining at powerful arms crossed before him, booted feet planted apart. A single glance at him was enough to straighten up the lines of boys.

Master Gand looked down their neat rows, expression blank, and began the callover. A visceral awe, a kind of thrill-pang, suffused Inda when he heard "Montrei-Vayir," the name of the royal family, and Sponge sang out, "Here."

In Marlovan. Now they spoke the language of the old plains warriors from whom most of them had descended. The bunk-scrag had taken some of the joy out of that. But it was still so strange to be standing right next to a member of the royal family, about which he'd heard so many stories—good ones as well as bad—bringing a brief image of Shendan Montredavan-An to mind.

Gand said, "After inspection report to the stable. First-bell after noon, report to the east practice court. We'll find out if you know which end of a sword to grip."

Intake of breath. Everyone wanted to get at weapons—whether bow, lance, or sword, it didn't matter.

"In a day or so we'll form up ridings. Questions?"

"Captain Gand."

Inda kept his eyes forward and suppressed a wry look at the voice of the annoying lick everyone was calling Smartlip.

The arms master looked around with exaggerated surprise, and someone muffled a snicker. "Is there one of my dragoons about?" Gand asked, and of course no one answered. He then faced Smartlip, and studied the scrawny boy for a long, long pause. A very long pause, during which not just Smartlip but his friends began to feel the prickle of fear, as did others who were afraid of more mass punishments than they'd already gotten. Smartlip's sharp face lost its smirk, his expression going from blank to lip-biting fear, and sure enough, out came his tongue licking round and round his chapped lips.

Gand finally spoke. "You are not a dragoon, last I heard, Lassad. Am I misinformed?"

"No, Master Gand," Smartlip quavered.

Only the cold breeze moved, bringing the smell of rain.

"You are a scrub, and I am your tutor. I am not your captain. If you ever manage to gain the age, the experience, and the wit to be put into a dragoon riding, then, and only then, will you address me as Captain Gand. Until then, you will not presume, or you and I and 'Captain' Willow will have a little discourse on assumptions. And Captain Willow has a lot more to say than Master Willow. Understood?"

"Yes, Master Gand."

"Now, ask your question."

Smartlip swallowed, his sweaty hands stiff.

"Are we going to wait all morning?" Gand asked in a low voice that struck fear into every single boy.

Smartlip glanced in fear his crony's way, getting a glare in return, and Smartlip realized he was in trouble no matter what he said or did. So he stated in a wooden voice utterly devoid of the enjoyment he'd so looked forward to, "Master Gand. We . . . I . . . it's been two days. You haven't permitted us to speak. At mess. Master Gand. I just wanted to say that some of us . . . I . . . feel that we ought not to be punished for the sloppiness of two people."

Master Gand stopped right in front of Smartlip, but his eyes—pale they were, and merciless—appraised the entire row. The breeze fingered the pennants overhead, and scoured the bare necks of the still, silent, frightened boys.

At last Gand said in that terrible low voice, "You will stay silent at mess for a month, Lassad. A month. Do you comprehend *month*, Lassad?"

"Master Gand." A nod.

"Thirty-six days. Perhaps, in that time, you will come to realize that I am not stupid." A smile. "I suspect that the reverse probably won't happen." He looked up. "As for the rest of you, I think silence is to the benefit of all. You will continue to remain silent at mess until I see . . . shall we say . . ." His gaze drifted along the row. ". . . a better attitude toward learning." His gaze did not stop on Inda, or Dogpiss, whose beds had been scragged and who had gotten stable duty as a result. His gaze lingered on the husky boy now called Tuft who at Landred Marlo-Vayir's insistence had put Smartlip up to the questions, a boy from a powerful family made up of two great clans. The boy swallowed, feeling very small just now, and hoped that Smartlip wouldn't break and squeal.

Meanwhile Master Gand's gaze moved to Marlo-Vayir, who kept his sneer hidden, though it made his teeth ache.

"Dismissed."

The scrubs filed out in silence, most of them so relieved their knees shook, a couple of them angry, one or two thoughtful, and Dogpiss—as usual—barely restraining laughter.

During breakfast Dogpiss kept making horrible grimaces and insulting gestures toward the miserable Smartlip, encouraged by the strangled snickers of his own friends.

Most of the boys ate fast and bustled out. There was no reason to stay, enduring the inventively derisive comments of the pigtails and being unable to respond. Inda ate a little more slowly, grateful for the chance to sit, think, and watch.

Beginning with freckle-faced Kepa, who was sitting next to Sponge. Inda had seen him snickering with Marlo-Vayir Tvei, but he was always making jokes with everyone, mostly stupid jokes, about which masters looked like which horse butts, and the like. His laugh, his grin, brought to mind Cousin Branid at home in Tenthen. Branid grinned just like that during the winters when he bootlicked Tanrid by spying on everyone and reporting it back—and then joked around with his victims, insulting Tanrid behind his back, all as if he really thought no one noticed.

Dogpiss grinned all the time too, but after two days it was clear that he thought everything was funny, even getting muzzled at mess and having to talk with hands and grimaces.

Dogpiss made jokes just to make jokes, Kepa made jokes to bootlick, that was the difference.

Not that any of it mattered. Inda dug his wooden spoon into the thick oatmeal that was considered good for both boys and horses who were facing a heavy day of training.

The important thing first. Sponge's royal brother evidently didn't like Sponge, but Inda couldn't imagine why not. He bent lower over his food, eating slowly as he thought over the past two days. Sponge had not done anything wrong by Inda's standards.

The urge to ask Tdor, so habitual, had to be dismissed. But in remembering that she was far to the southwest, Inda also remembered his promise. He was supposed to talk to Hadand, but he had no idea how to find her—if he even got the time away. So far they had not one free moment, and how was he supposed to get into the royal castle without getting himself in more trouble than he was already in?

Inda sighed, shifted on the bench, then brought his mind back to Sponge. He remembered Tanrid's words about the Sierlaef. Hadand was to marry him! Did she hate Sponge too?

The questions bred more questions, multiplying so rapidly he groaned and got up, his food half-eaten, to try to distance himself from his thoughts. A mistake. They stayed right in his head.

He remembered the long labors lying ahead until midday meal, and as he walked he forced himself to swallow down the last few bites, shoveling them in so fast his nose stung. He stashed bowl and spoon in the barrel of magic-cleaned water, surreptitiously brushing his fingers over the rim to feel the tingle of magic. He liked the weird sensation of magic, rare as it was.

Inda then ran back to the scrub barracks, apprehensive of what he might find—especially when he spied Marlo-Vayir Tvei and Smartlip over by their own beds. But then he saw Noddy and Sponge busy tidying things, then Noddy took up the broom from the corner and slowly started sweeping it over the already clean floorboards, which were scuffed by several generations of boys' boot heels. Inda, old hand at practical jokes, knew instantly that they were on guard. But they weren't guarding Dogpiss's or his own bed. Oh, of course! Oldest trick there is.

A single bell rang, echoing against the stone walls.

Sponge just stood, arms folded.

"Come on, we'll be late," Smartlip muttered.

Marlo-Vayir cast a glance back, then vanished out the door.

Inda said, "They were going to do their beds and blame us."

Sponge whistled softly. "I wasn't sure if they'd have the frost, after that warning today."

"We stayed around to make sure they didn't try," Noddy said over his shoulder as he restored the broom to its place.

Dogpiss appeared, breathing hard. "They scrag their own bunks?"

Inda shook his head. "But we can't watch every day. What if we're late?"

"I'll watch," Sponge said. "You go from mess to work."

Noddy's dark gaze was sober. "You'll get gated for delay." His voice was tentative—more question than statement.

"Oh, yes, I'll get gated." Sponge shrugged. "But I don't care. Then it's just me."

Noddy's face was blank as usual, except for a faint pucker between his straight dark brows. He said slowly, "You know Marlo-Vayir Tvei's brother is—"

"—Buck Marlo-Vayir, one of my brother's Sier-Danas." Sponge lifted one shoulder. "If you mean, was the Sierlaef probably behind that?" He waved at Inda's bed, and none of the listening boys missed the fact that Sponge did not use his brother's name, but only his title, just like everyone else. "I say yes. That boot, the bunk-scrag, were aimed at me, but Marlo-Vayir didn't know who I was. Thought Dogpiss was me, probably because my brother has the same color hair as Dogpiss. My brother'll be mad at Marlo-Vayir Tvei for being too obvious, as well as the mistakes. I think . . ." He paused, staring down at the old, kick-scarred doorway.

"Go on," Inda urged.

Sponge's mouth was tight, reminding Inda of Joret when people talked about her looks as though she weren't there. Then he faced them. "Here's what I believe—what I guess, anyway. My brother won't let them touch me now. What he'll do instead is make the rest of you the targets, just because you're seen to be . . ." He paused, looking away, as if unable to get the word out.

So Inda said it, wondering why it was so difficult. "You mean they'll go after your friends, right?"

Sponge looked down.

"Well, that's easy," Inda said, relieved. He knew how to plan for that. So did Dogpiss, for whom barracks life, with all its rough games, was home.

Noddy gave his turtle-on-the-fencepost shrug and led the way out. They found Cama hovering just outside the pit. He asked in his kitten squeak, "They scrag their own bunks?"

"No. We stayed there the whole time." Noddy sighed.

Inda contemplated that as they loped toward the long rows of stable buildings. It was a nasty ruse: wreck their own beds and then get the blame shifted to Inda and Dogpiss, who would then get the blame among the boys for not passing first week inspection. That meant daily callover in the parade court, and daily inspections, for a whole month. And that meant getting up earlier. Everyone else got callover in their own courts after meals, and only weekly inspections. A sure way to get them hated by all the boys.

All because the Sierlaef hated his brother and because Marlo-Vayir had mistaken Dogpiss for Sponge. *Not just the yellow hair but because Dogpiss was the center of attention,* Inda thought. *Like the Sierlaef is, among the horsetails.*

What did make sense was this: "So Marlo-Vayir and his clan-cousins are the enemy," Inda said aloud.

"Mine," Sponge said. "Not yours if you sheer off from me."

Inda didn't bother trying to figure out why. This problem seemed way beyond his reach, like the towers of the royal residence that they all could see but never would enter. *I need Hadand to explain it,* he thought.

Reminded again of his promise to find his sister, he shifted his pace so he ran next to Sponge, who looked over in mute question. Inda hesitated.

Sponge, son of a king, felt the hesitation, and held his breath, his heart thumping as he jogged. Was Inda about to say, as politely as he could, that they'd be better off not talking to one another? And if he did, what was Sponge to say in return?

Plays, songs, poems make much of those moments that affect, unalterably, the remainder of people's lives. Most decisions don't have irrevocable consequences; lost ground is recovered, sometimes rapidly, sometimes slowly. Sometimes there is an awareness of those moments that seem to change the world. Inda was aware of no such thing. He hesitated because of his brother's words, because so much of what was going on he didn't understand, but instinct had been his surest guide so far, and instinct prompted him to look over and say, "I need to get to Hadand. In secret, I guess. Know a way?"

Sponge nodded once, his face pale, hazel eyes wide and, right now, very green. He could not bear to speak, right then, and anyway they could smell the proximity of the stable, a familiar smell they'd known all their lives.

So Sponge said nothing more. He knew Hadand wanted to see her brother. He knew it would take thought, and care, to arrange the meeting, but all that could wait. What he cherished now was the realization that Hadand's brother had not rejected him. In fact Inda trusted him, in the same unthinking way—as if it was as natural as breathing—as his sister Hadand did. People in Sponge's life so far despised him, watched him, scorned him, judged him, flattered him, ignored him, lied to him, told him what they thought he wanted to hear, beat him, tried to influence him, but no one, except Hadand and his cousin Barend (the rare times he was home) trusted him. Until now.

Chapter Seven

DOGPISS was the first inside the practice court. He slunk inside warily, stopping with his back to one of the high stone walls, where he could watch the rest enter and not be taken by surprise. The single clang of first-bell had long since faded into the breeze, but no master was here. Curious.

Dogpiss watched the boys shuffle uncertainly. Three days ago they would have scrambled for the practice weapons in the racks. Now they stood in two rough rows, waiting for a master to arrive and issue orders—or for someone to go first, and take the blame. Dogpiss whistled softly under his breath.

Horsepiss Noth had said, *I won't tell you the tricks of the training trade, my boy. You won't learn anything, then. Just remember these two things: first, that most of those boys will forget within a day that they're there to learn command . . .*

Wrong. At least, that Marlo-Vayir horse plop had certainly acted fast enough, their very first day, there in the mess hall.

Except now Dogpiss wondered if Landred Marlo-Vayir was just a follower after all, doing what his brother ordered; who did what the Sierlaef ordered. For whatever reason.

Look at him, Dogpiss thought, repressing a grin. Marlo-Vayir wanted to get at those weapons so bad he was almost drooling. *But look at the way he's nudging Smartlip and his cousins and muttering. He's trying to get them to go first! That's not command.*

Meanwhile, no sign of a master.

Dogpiss saw he wasn't the only one scanning the bare stone walls for clues, and the blank windows of the masters' building above, but no one else seemed to want to move either. Why not get them started? Marlo-Vayir wouldn't listen, of course. Dogpiss wondered if any of the others would. Supposedly they were all equal, but what had his father said about that? *There isn't any "equal." Not with human beings. First will probably be the king's son and his friends, the ones with "Vayir" hanging on their names, if he's anything like his older brother. Then come the smart ones, and the ones with skill.*

These boys're like dogs, Dogpiss thought, watching the two rows slowly break into tight knots. Scout dogs, he thought, trying to be fair. Not pugs, which were lapdogs, usually spoiled. Scout dogs, but still dogs. Those quick looks at everyone else, the mutters, even the snickers, were ear-twitching and butt-sniffing and prowling around and around, maybe showing teeth, hackles not quite up, tail tips waving warily.

What was the rest of Dad's advice about command? *Second thing: that natural command arises less out of being strongest than out of knowing what to do and doing it.*

Dogpiss decided to test it. He knew what would happen if he stepped out and began organizing people: loud hoots about frost. Marlo-Vayir would surely see it as an excuse to start pounding him.

But if he just acted? He walked to the stack of practice padding on a long table, and picked up the first jacket.

"Sure that's a good idea?" There was Inda, looking uneasy.

"We weren't ordered to wait," Dogpiss said. "We were just ordered to be here at first-bell."

Inda's light brown eyes narrowed, then he gave a short nod. "True. But could it be a trick of some sort? Are our shoulder blades gonna kiss the willow for frost, or something?"

Dogpiss shrugged. "Aren't we here to learn to command?"

"That's right." The soft voice was from Sponge, coming up on Dog-piss' other side. "But we haven't the authority to order the others, and wouldn't they love to see us try."

"So we 'order' us." Inda grabbed a jacket. "I'm for it."

The three got into practice gear, followed a few moments later by small, quiet Mouse Marth-Davan, who usually lost himself inside the biggest group or else somehow managed to vanish altogether. Inda had not exchanged more than a dozen words with him so far, but for Tdor's sake, he'd made those words friendly. And now Mouse, with a determined air, silently joined them.

Behind him came several of the others, some with furtive glances both at the open entrance to the court and at Marlo-Vayir.

Dogpiss kept his gaze on his companions, but his attention on the bullies behind him. For a time there was silence, then furtive whispering from the perimeter. *Now watch. As soon as we touch a weapon and no master appears and lands on us, Marlo-Vayir will grab a practice blade, and he won't put on gear. He'll say something about how only pugs use gear.*

Inda and Sponge hefted some practice swords—then moved to a corner, and squared off into a familiar warm-up pattern, Dogpiss following along, but keeping Marlo-Vayir in view. Cama and Noddy, hastily fastening their gear, joined them, and for a moment they regarded one another, wondering who would signal the beginning. Sponge felt eyes turning his way, and he studied the ground.

"Hep!" Inda grunted, and weapons came up. As he counted in Marlovan under his breath, they began the double-circle swing that every boy learns first, then the blocks and thrusts.

When they began on the square form—and no master was yet in sight—Marlo-Vayir, who had been muttering insulting comments to his snickering cronies, lifted his voice. "Just follow me. Unless you're afraid."

He started toward the weapons. With a look of scorn the big blond boy eyed the rack, yanked out the biggest practice blade, and sent it round in so fast a circle it whooshed in the air.

Dogpiss sighed. He'd figured the Marlo-Vayirs would be well trained, though it would have been fun if the bully had turned out to be clumsy and slow. Marlo-Vayir's thick, bony wrists showed the ease of long drill, and he handled the blade deftly.

"All right, square off," Marlo-Vayir ordered Smartlip, who had gotten his own blade.

"But what about gear?" Smartlip asked, picking nervously at his lips.

Marlo-Vayir sneered Sponge's way. "That's for rabbits and pugs."

An intense thrill burned through Dogpiss. He knew bullies. Most of 'em were predictable. The ones you feared were the smart ones, the ones who seemed to think ahead of you. Marlo-Vayir Tvei was not a smart bully.

Within moments the other boys followed, and you could divide their partisanship by how many first put on practice padding and how many didn't.

They'd paired off and begun old routines when Master Gand and two other tutors walked through the archway, put horny old hands on their hips, and looked around with a pensive air. All three masters then strode to the padding bench and pulled out the bigger jackets and helms. They alone used real swords.

Then, without wasted words they called names, and began to put the boys through basic drill, and then a bout. Nobody made the unpadded ones get padded, but when Dogpiss turned away from his bout, sweaty and his arms feeling like spindled wool, he stared at Marlo-Vayir, crimson with tiny cuts all over his face and arms. Smartlip had them too, though he had fewer. And each of the other unpadded boys had at least three or four cuts, tiny ones, the sort of cut that the practiced duelist inflicts as a humiliation, or a goad.

One by one the scrubs went silent in shock, uneasiness.

We're training for war, you brickheads, Dogpiss thought.

Sponge thought, *There's blood in all the old stories, but no pain. All you hear about is honor and courage.*

Inda thought, *Master Gand is warning them.*

Dogpiss had grown up in barracks under a father who taught him to be observant, so his assessment of his fellows' abilities did not vary much from the masters'. But few are universally vigilant, and so it was with Dogpiss. His attention was on the other scrubs, and the masters watching the scrubs. He never once looked up, and so he did not see five horsetails slip along the new walls adjoining the nearby barracks and vault lightly up to run along the rooftop. Of course the sentries could easily see them from the higher walls of the royal castle along the eastern perimeter of the academy, but they immediately recognized the Sierlaef and four of his five Sier-Danas. They'd no sooner report them than they would a passing flight of birds or the prowling cats.

The rules were that they'd be caned if they were caught, but by their second year the Sierlaef's chosen band knew the difference between what the masters had to officially notice and act on, and what they could ignore. As long as the five lay quietly and didn't talk loud, much less hoot or throw things, the masters wouldn't notice them. Not officially, anyway.

With dispassionate expertise the royal heir's four friends observed and commented on the scrubs at their swordwork. The Sierlaef stayed silent, watching.

"Hoo. Your Tvei's wilder than Peddler Antivad the Drunk when he met the wind funnel, Cassad."

Cassad Ain snickered. "Weird. Seeing Rattooth down there." He hid how anxious he was as he watched his buck-toothed, yellow-headed brother Rattooth busily hacking away at a hound-faced boy. The thing about brothers being here was that your own training was right there, being seen by everyone. Your own brother you never thought anyone outside of home would see—

Brother.

Pause. Glances the Sierlaef's way. All four saw the king's second son fumbling through a practice bout with another boy. He was by far the worst. Clumsy, slow, tentative. *Untrained.*

The Sierlaef felt those gazes, but kept his focus on the court below, and the others returned to their comments, keeping them general, and by unspoken agreement avoiding the subject of the red-haired boy known as Sponge.

The Sierlaef scanned the academy, both the older buildings and the new ones his father had ordered built last year, now occupied by the seniors. The academy was his own domain, for he and his companions were the leaders among the leaders. But the royal heir was impatient of this pretend command. He wore a horsetail now. He was no longer a boy, but was not yet regarded as a man, and he hated it!

He squinted against the hazy sunlight, gazing beyond the academy compound to the real world: the guard barracks commanded by his uncle. Here, it was just boys and play war, and though he was a horsetail, he was only a first-year horsetail, with two long years before he could go over to the guard side and live with men, and war would be real.

Real, and one day mine, he thought, glancing up at the great walls surrounding the castle, and the sentries in their steady, vigilant tread. *All of it mine to command.*

To command! I will not be Aldren-Sieraec, I will be Aldren-Harvaldar, the war king, and afterward they will proclaim me Aldren-Harvaldar Sigun. The Victorious.

His gaze returned to the court, and the hated red-haired figure down there, flailing away inexpertly with the practice blade, and anger boiled in his guts.

Memory images, unwanted, of four years ago: *Your brother has already mastered the Sartoran script; why can't you trace your name right in simple Iascan?*

And just last week:

Your brother can already read this entire record. Can't you get through a single phrase?

Anger forged into hatred, but of course the Sierlaef did not speak of it. His father thought him stupid when he couldn't read a damned line of that damned Sartoran squiggle, but Uncle Anderle-Sierandael knew he wasn't stupid.

The Sierlaef sensed the others waiting for a cue from him before they said anything about his own brother. He had no interest in their appraisal. He knew Sponge was bad because he got little training. Was it his fault if the brat was always sneaking off to the library, or hiding with cousin Barend whenever they knew he was looking for them?

It was not, and his uncle knew it. That's what mattered, that his uncle knew. His uncle even agreed: Sponge was only good for heraldry, for grubbing in an archive, not for war.

His uncle would be the real leader, if the Venn made war.

Down in the court Sponge flailed grimly away, taking hit after hit without flinching. The Sierlaef, watching, felt beneath the anger a pool of cold fear, but he refused to accept it. Sponge was *not* smarter, that was all. And he'd prove it.

He took a deep breath, watching Sponge's partner, a small brown-haired boy who looked a lot like Tanrid Algara-Vayir. The voices around him resolved into words again.

"Tlen, your Tvei's not bad on defense," Cassad said. "Gand seems to like him."

Hawkeye Yvana-Vayir sat back, powerful arms crossed. He spoke for the first time. "All of 'em look solid."

Tlen, whose chunky little brother was already being called Biscuit, flicked a look at Hawkeye. The latter alone didn't have a brother in the scrubs, as his twin brothers were nine. Tlen got a wild grin in return.

The Sierlaef watched that exchange, quick as it was. His uncle had warned him when he was a pigtail that the Tlens and the Sindan-Ans were as tight as they were ancient clans, along with the Tlennens that his father was named for. And the Marlo-Vayir family was allying with them through a complicated series of intermarriages.

Hawkeye Yvana-Vayir alone of all his companions didn't care about power alliances, though his mother had been the Sierlaef's aunt. *My uncle picked the clan heirs for my friends,* the Sierlaef thought, his mood shifting from anger to approval. *And he was right, and I like them well enough, and I know they will back me in my future wars, but Hawkeye I chose myself.*

Not because he was a royal cousin, but because he was wild. His nickname was the result of his getting drunk his first week at the academy and walking straight into a door. All he cared about was fast horses, good drink, and being the best in a fight.

"Montrei-Vayir!"

Hearing his name snapped the heir out of his reverie. It was Sponge's turn to be tried by Master Gand. He got an idea.

The others saw his shift in focus, and watched as the Sierlaef pointed down at the scrub court and said, "Coward."

The surprised companions snapped their attention down onto that red-haired boy. A coward? That was the worst thing you could accuse anyone of—even worse than being thief! Sponge was a *coward!* Was that why he was so slow?

But he stood right up to the master, not flinching, nor crying, or cringing. He took the blows—and he earned a lot—with no change of face at all.

The seeming contradiction struck all the Sier-Danas, one by one. They turned assessing gazes from the boy on the court to his royal brother, and with practice the Sierlaef's companions gauged his thin, bony face. Most of the time the royal heir listened to their opinions, but rare was the mood that permitted contradiction. The jut of his jaw, the narrowed hazel eyes, those were the signal flags for Agreement Only.

The Sierlaef's Sier-Danas read the signals with the ease of long habit. Sponge was to be considered a coward, then. They shrugged, then returned their attention to the court.

"Who's the tall butterhead with all the cuts?" The quietest Sier-Danas, Manther Jaya-Vayir, spoke up. His brother, too, was nine and would be in the next Tvei group.

"That butterhead's Buck's brother," Tlen said.

"Best start calling him Cherry-Stripe," Cassad said, looking at all those tiny sword cuts.

"He shows promise," Manther said agreeably.

A grunt of agreement came from the Sierlaef, who never spoke if he could help it; single words and sometimes phrases he could manage without stuttering, but rarely a whole sentence, unless he practiced it over and over.

"Three lefties altogether," Tlen observed. "No. Four. That last one there switched to left."

Approval. Lefthanders were usually faster with a sword, because they had to be, and they were unexpected; also, the Sierlaef was left-handed.

"Algara-Vayir Tvei's solid," Cassad said, eying Inda with judicious interest.

"Slow," the Sierlaef said. "Like his Ain."

Tanrid Algara-Vayir of Choraed Elgaer might be considered slow by some, but he was fearless, strong, tenacious, and could be vicious when crossed. He was also the son of a prince, the highest rank after the king's own family. The Algara-Vayirs had, by marriage and treaty, acquired their title even before the Montrei-Vayirs had taken the throne from the Montredavan-An family. Everyone knew that old history, but they didn't know why the Sierandael hated the Algara-Vayirs.

The Sier-Danas figured the Sierandael's hatred had something to do with why the Sierlaef had not invited Tanrid Algara-Vayir into their circle, but that was one of the questions you didn't put to the royal heir.

So no one said anything as the five watched Inda stand up to an onslaught from a master bent on finding out every weakness.

Just about then the last of the Sier-Danas, Buck Marlo-Vayir (so named when he was just a scrub and climbed up on a war horse to strut his riding skills, just to be launched butt over head), slid up onto the roof, and at a gesture from the prince the other four obligingly wriggled over to make space.

"I have to do a signal run with the ponies," Buck reported. "Just got my orders. I leave after supper."

Shrugs and acknowledgments. Part of the horsetails' duties was commanding the rides of the upper-level pigtails—the level they'd all been last year—called ponies.

"Gand tickled up your Tvei," Cassad said, waving a long, muscular arm. "We're gonna call him Cherry-Stripe."

Buck Marlo-Vayir, now an Ain, looked down at his brother Landred, who was waiting against the wall. "Coo," he said, thinking about how Landred would feel when he hit the baths that night—and how much worse it would hurt in the morning when he woke up. He snorted, with no vestige of sympathy. "Cherry-Stripe, yah. Look at him strut."

"Won't," the royal heir said. "If."

From long practice Buck decoded the threat. "He won't drop the reins again," he promised, remembering his swift, brutal confrontation with his younger brother the night before. "He just got overeager, and he mistook his target. He also didn't understand the rules of the mess hall. He does now."

The royal heir said, "Good."

Down below, Gand said, "All right, put your equipment away, and we'll move on to archery, and then knives."

The king's heir and his five companions watched the scrubs file into the far court, now empty of older boys. Two of them remembered their scrub days; Buck wondered if he was going to get more orders concerning Sponge. Probably.

They watched as Dogpiss Noth and two other boys picked up bows, strung them, took aim, hit fast, three times in a row. Noth's arrows smacked straight into the center ring three times, with a force surprising from one so little and stringy. Cassad thought of entertaining ways to run 'em; Tlen scorned them for a litter of pups, as clumsy and unaware as the young dogs in the scout kennel. The royal heir grunted.

Hearing it, the other horsetails waited for him to speak.

"Good," the Sierlaef said. But his tone promised more.

So they watched in silence as another three boys shot, and then a third group.

"Good group. Mine. One day."

For the Sierlaef, that was a very long speech.

The Sier-Danas bent their minds to decoding it, as below, another three scrubs came up to shoot: Inda, Sponge, and Noddy.

"So you don't want us to ride 'em, then?" Cassad Ain finally asked, seeing that the others were reluctant.

"Only ones w-with *him.*"

The pronunciation of "him" singled out Sponge as effectively as if he stood alone.

The five big boys, strong, well trained, leaders, and favorites, all considered the Sierlaef's words. An exchange of glances. First at the thin face of future royal command, the humorless eyes, and then by semaphore at Buck, their speaker.

"Want us to scrag him?"

Thump! The last arrows slammed into the targets: Inda's shot first ring, Sponge's on the outside ring, Noddy's center.

"No."

The five reacted with the philosophical disappointment of the seventeen-year-old for whom life has been one continuous wargame that he always wins. And at a sign from the Sierlaef they slipped back down the roof, dropped to the wall, and ran easily along the two hand widths' span of stone twice the height of a man from the ground.

Back in the archery court Sponge turned his face upward at last. He'd known they were there. From his earliest days he had grown sensitive to inimical eyes. Now that they were gone, he could look up. What he— and he alone—observed now was the brilliant beauty of the rain-washed sky above them all, the flights of spring birds arrowing toward distant fields, the shape and color of the stone walls and towers, peachy in the morning light, their lines an intersecting work of art.

Along one of those walls he saw the six horsetails move away, and then stop, their focus elsewhere.

The Sierlaef paused where the new wall intersected the old and stared down into the vast parade ground where the Guard gathered only for formal occasions: Convocation, command promotions, formal punishment.

The Sierlaef turned his head and gave his Sier-Danas a faint smile. "Barend."

The Sier-Danas identified the single name with Barend-Dal, the only son of the Sierandael, and absent for at least a year, sent to sea to train as a ship commander.

The Sierlaef pointed at the clean sweep of the parade ground. "Chwahir."

Barend-Dal visited the land of the Chwahir on his sea journeys, they translated, still staring uncomprehendingly at the parade ground.

Chwahir, military kingdom far to the east. Chwahir, seldom seen this far west. Chwahir, constantly at war with their neighbors.

"Post," the Sierlaef said, pointing.

The court below was bare, but they had all seen the flogging post set up from time to time.

"Chwahir. Have 'em. Permanent."

Yecch, Tlen thought, and Cassad repressed a wince. What was the heir on about now?

Good question, but for someone else, Buck thought, for they were the Sier-Danas, and the Sierlaef's weird mood was no threat to them. Their lives were laid out before them: the future king's Companions, first in honor, first in war, first in power. So long as they never showed cowardice or treachery they would never be tied to that post down there, to be flogged before the assembled Guard—and maybe even the academy, if the crime was heinous enough.

Main thing was, the heir didn't want his brother scragged. Fine.

The Sierlaef said, "S-scrag. His f-friends. Hard."

He looked up, saw muted surprise in his followers but didn't care, nor would he explain that he wanted his brother alone, friendless, so he would beg their father to let him quit. To let him spend his life in the archives, scribbling his worthless Sartoran messes. He would never go to war, he would never interfere with Aldren Harvaldar-Sigun, war king triumphant.

Sponge would be the stupid one, the one without fame or honor.

And if he tried to refuse the future his brother planned out for him— which was treason—he'd end up down at that post.

At that thought, the Sierlaef smiled, and he said it again, as back in the practice court the masters waved the scrubs over to the throwing knives. "Scrag 'em hard."

Chapter Eight

HEADMASTER Brath faced Master Gand across the old desk. "There's no proof. No accusations. We cannot act on hearsay."

Gand shook his head. "We both know how to sift rumor from truth. There's no use wasting time debating what we can notice and what we cannot. Look, I have to get down to the stable. Olin just told me Clover's begun foaling. She'll want me there."

Headmaster Brath scrubbed a hand through his thinning sun bleached hair, his gray eyes anxious. "Have you a suggestion?"

"Yes." *And you will dislike it for all the wrong reasons.* "Fix up some excuse, take the Sierlaef and his followers out, and thrash them till they can't stand. Tonight. Or you are in for a summer of trouble."

The headmaster blanched. Then fury suffused his face, even his neck, but Gand sensed fear behind the headmaster's diffuse gaze. Brath began in a strained voice, "I could be wrong . . ." That only to satisfy convention, so that Gand couldn't call him out for a duel. ". . . but I fail to see how a dishonorable misuse of my position of authority will solve today's trouble, much less that of a season."

Silence. They stood there in the bare, quiet office, dust from the riding rings drifting in the open windows, and regarded one another: Gand, placed by the king in charge of the new boys; Brath, commander of the academy, appointed by the king's brother. Brath never would have sent

Gand down to run scrubs. No one understood why the king had. As for Gand, he had become accustomed, since giving up the field, to the idea of spending the rest of his life training the senior horsetails without family position who were destined for dragoon command. This order had puzzled him as much as it had Brath.

Gand gently rapped his knuckles on the desk. "How much truth do you want to hear?"

Brath's mouth tightened, then he took Gand by surprise. "Whose truth?" he said, so softly Gand had to bend forward to hear it. "At what cost?"

Gand shook his head. Brath sank back into his chair, his forehead beaded with sweat. His gaze dropped to the neat stacks of paper lying in a row across the top of the ancient desk. Gand touched palm over his heart in salute, for the forms had to be maintained. They had to live in this place, and see one another every day. Brath nodded in return, and Gand departed.

Spring. Time for young animals to enter the world.

Olin, stable hand for the past forty years, squinted at the hazy green treetops, just visible over the walls. Trees only interested him as gauges of season. He shifted his attention to Gand, approaching now, correctly assessing that walk. Gand's face was about as wooden as expected from a dragoon, but his walk was as good as talk.

Gand stalked in and overhead the small brown sparrows and finches fluttered, chirping, then resettled in the rafters.

Olin grimaced at his crony Yennad. They both knew Brath. But no one spoke; Olin bent down to massage Clover's shivering skin, her spasming belly.

The mare looked up at him, her great brown eyes patient, still, apprehensive. The bond between horse and human was as old as the Marlovan language. The plains people loved all their animals, but especially those few that descended in a pure line from the wild horses on the blessed plain of Nelkereth, like Clover: proud of neck, with a small graceful head, beautiful line of chest and leg, made for running before the wind, color the silvery cream of snow in the sunset, faces and feet pale brown.

Olin murmured soothingly to the mare, his voice more tender than any lover had ever heard it.

"Here she comes," Yennad said, from over Olin's shoulder. He was certain that the foal was a filly. He was usually right.

Yennad was even older than Olin, both of them wounded too many times, decades ago, to ride easily anymore. Yennad said to Gand, his brown, seamed face sour, "Me granddad always told us, no good'd come o' this training 'em on one ground. Walls all around. Marlovans don't live natural within walls."

Olin inwardly dismissed Yennad's prognostications. He too had inherited a distrust of castles and the owning of land. But in Olin's view, the problems lay not with Marlovans adopting the Iascans' castles and pottery and the exquisite folded steel they made in their mountain forges out beyond the royal city. The true problems lay between fathers and sons, between brothers and uncles, and those problems were not new. It's just that their ancestors, when they squabbled, could ride off to fight somewhere else instead of being forced to hold their ground.

Yennad muttered under his breath as Clover shivered and rolled her eyes. Gand stroked Clover's nose, murmuring in a low, steady voice.

He pretended not to hear the condemnation of change, the dire predictions of what happened when tradition was set aside. Gand's own grandfather had said once, wheezing with laughter before the winter fire, *No one likes change unless he makes it himself. Then it's innovation.*

The foal made her entry into the world to the sound of human voices, the gentle touch of human hands, the smell of human and horse combined. A filly—most welcome—soon stood shivering near her mother, lipping the air.

And in good time. Gand heard the noon bells, and remembered his twenty charges. He left Clover to expert hands, veering between buildings with swift steps. His own skill, it appeared to the distant royal eye, was with human young, though he himself would never have defined himself that way.

Gand sometimes contemplated why the king did.

At what cost?

The question unsettled him because he couldn't define it, unlike a problem on the field. The king could have, but he had not. To his brother he'd said only, *We must put someone in charge of the Tveis who can identify the varieties of training the young Randaels inevitably will show, and form them all to your standards.* To which the Sierandael had agreed. The king had not spoken his real reason to anyone, lest it seem a criticism of his brother, or show favoritism to his second son, in whose training he must not interfere any more than he had in his heir's. But for some reason the Sierlaef had neglected his brother and the Sierandael, usually so observant, had missed it. Gand, the king believed, would fix it.

Gand sidestepped down the alleyway, with a quick and silent tread. His pace eased when he recognized his nephew, who was pushing a cart full of clean practice jackets between the storage buildings. Neither looked at the other while a string of first-year pigtails erupted from the practice court archway, shouting, laughing, thumping against each other as they ran up the stone alley toward their pit and vanished into its court; when the alley was clear, Emad did not stop, but he shifted his grip, waiting until his Uncle Gand was next to him.

Emad said under his breath, "On way to mess, Marlo-Vayir, Cassad, Basna shying gravel at the boys around *him*." The pronoun meant Evred-Varlaef; neither actually spoke his name.

Gand looked each way along the narrow space between the weatherworn buildings made of unadorned stone and wood, and up, then sniffed the air. No witnesses. Still, the less said the better. "And at mess?"

"Joal reports nothing. *He* sat with Cassad. No trouble."

"Stable?"

"No trouble. All separate tasks."

They parted, Gand continuing on to the scrub court. There stood his charges in their two rows of ten, barely containing their anticipation at the prospect of their first war game.

He let the moment draw out, knowing how effective silence was. Amusement rooted deep in his belly, but no sign of it was permitted to shoot past his chest. There must be no laughter in his voice, though they so strongly reminded him of all the young animals in the stable and kennel. They really were young animals, barely able to see past themselves. But holding their invisible longe lines were men who for their own purposes appeared to be training some of these boys for disaster.

He would avert it if he could.

"*Kek-kek-kek!*" A blue-tail hawk cried, stooping some smaller bird, just behind the bell tower. Two or three of the many flaxen heads lifted, and then faced forward again.

"You will have noted," Gand said, "that this group is not the traditional thirty-six. We'll still divide into four ridings, but each with only five. You select your leader. You'll each have a flag to defend. The goal is to protect your own flag, and capture as many of your enemies' flags as you can. Questions?"

Pause. The boys exchanged looks.

Dogpiss Noth said, "Master Gand. Do we take prisoners?"

"You decide that."

Emboldened by the fact that Noth hadn't been annihilated, the other boys started in with questions.

"Weapons?"

"What you see is what you get."

"What bells do we have to stop at, if nobody's won?"

"Sundown."

"What if—"

"I think that's enough. Wait until you see your terrain, and figure it out from there. Now. The ridings."

They stilled, some betraying partisanships by little signs. Gand did no more than purse his lips, but Sponge, Inda, and Dogpiss, watching narrowly, knew what was coming next before Gand even spoke. Dogpiss grimaced. Inda repressed a sigh.

Sponge, as always, hid his reaction.

Gand noted it all, though he gave no sign. He called out, "Sindan-An. Noth. Ndarga. Askan. Tya-Vayir."

Of course they'd split up friends, Dogpiss' wry glance, his slight shrug, signaled to Inda.

Inda's roll of the eyes, his sideways glance, returned awareness of the fact that at least the followers of Marlo-Vayir Tvei (now known through the academy as Cherry-Stripe, a nickname he would have resented had he gotten it from his fellow scrubs, but because it had come from the horsetails, he used it with pride) would be split as well.

Whispers burned through the others, quick as grassfire, and Gand paused. The whispers ceased. "Marlo-Vayir. Algara-Vayir. Kepri-Davan. Lith. Fijirad."

A groan from Smartlip, quickly stifled.

"Basna. Montrei-Vayir. Fera-Vayir. Lassad. Arveas. And obviously, the rest of you are in the final group."

Cherry-Stripe looked stunned, as if he'd really thought he'd have his own followers.

Inda watched Noddy sigh, his long face resigned, as he studied Mouse Marth-Davan. Tdor's cousin was the youngest, smallest, and most timid of all the boys. He still didn't talk unless forced to.

Tdor. It still hurt to think of home. At least he was getting used to that ache just above his gut, just like his feet were getting used to the unfamiliar ache of wearing boots every day. Only when would he see Hadand?

Forget that right now. See who else was in Marth-Davan and Noddy's group. Ennath, Biscuit Tlen—separated from his kin, when they usually moved as a mob—and Rattooth Cassad. He surveyed the two sturdy, pale-haired boys, and wondered what would they be like when not following Cherry-Stripe's orders.

Impressions streamed through Inda's mind, most wordless, made up of images, tones of voice, bits of conversation half-heard over the past few days.

"Your flags will be waiting," Gand said. "As for the masters: your Ains may have told you that we are effectively invisible on the field, unless we talk to one of you. If we do, you will not like it, I promise you that. We are testing your brains here, not your strength. Save that for the targets, not for one another. Let's go." Gand gestured toward the north.

The boys loped off through the stone archway and along the newly flagged path. Some ran faster, anxious to get to the site first, others matched pace with friends seemingly to commiserate, but actually to test old alliances against the new. Gand vanished somewhere behind them; Inda watched the Tlen cousins hang back and wait for Cherry-Stripe, presumably for orders. Oh, great. And Cherry-Stripe was in Inda's own riding.

Sponge's eyes turned his way. He altered his stride. Dogpiss loped up on the other side.

"No expectations," Sponge said. "Right?"

"Play to win," Dogpiss said, grinning.

Inda saw his relief, but pain across the back of his head banished further thought. Then Dogpiss gasped, stumbled, felt the back of his head, still healing from the bruise he'd gotten the first night.

They both spun around to see Cherry-Stripe staring straight ahead, but Smartlip's smirk betrayed them. Dogpiss flashed up the back of his hand, and Inda snickered. Smartlip flushed, then deliberately bent and picked up a bigger rock.

Cama jogged sideways and whapped him so hard Smartlip stumbled and measured his length on the ground. Laughter from all the boys, Rat-tooth and Biscuit included, caused Smartlip to bounce up and take a wild swing at Cama.

A willow wand snapped across his shoulder blades. Smartlip yelped with pain. Cama was next. He gasped.

Gand loomed over them, having appeared seemingly from nowhere. "Report for five apiece at evening callover."

"But I didn't do anything," Smartlip whined in outrage.

"You are," Gand said in a soft voice, without breaking stride, "imply-ing that I am blind? Or that I lie?"

Smartlip cringed. "No, Master Gand."

"Good. Then you only need add on three, for stupidity always re-quires its own reward." Gand glared at them all. "Run," he commanded, and they ran.

As the boys streamed up the road toward their war game site, a fire arrow arced over Castle Tenthen far to the southwest.

Spring was the season for war games all over Iasca Leror. The defense of the land around each castle was the Shield Arm's concern, but the in-side the walls defense belonged to the women.

Joret, who would one day be Iofre, commanded the day's defense of Castle Tenthen.

The signal arrow sputtered against the gray, cloudy sky, and moments later a band of attackers led by Branid obeyed the signal and stormed the back gate, where they found defenders ready for them.

Pans of lake water poured down into the boys' faces and screams choked off into gasps. Younger boys wailed in disgust; the water was brackish and nasty-tasting. Despite Branid's assurance (emphasized by his fists on the smaller boys) that if they were fast the girls would be taken by surprise, the girls had obviously figured out their feint so long ago they'd had time to fetch and drag mucky lake water up to the walls. They could see Liet up there, laughing.

Elsewhere great poles were tapped symbolically against the invaders' ladders, which meant everyone on the ladder was either dead or hurt—had they been real attackers the ladders would have been poled away from the wall with the invaders midway up, and the swamp water would have been hot cooking oil with rolled balls of rice paper set afire, floating on top.

Lightning crackle-hummed overhead, bright, sudden, and lethal. Thunder roared, drowning out voices and the creaking of the wind-tossed trees. Joret, high on the tower, waved the blue flag that signaled a cease. The gates in the north and south opened, and the castle denizens—family, ward, servant, stable hand, and guard alike—abandoned the semblance of battle and retreated inside the great gates to seek warmth and a change of clothes.

Tdor, who had commanded the south gate defense against the boys, watched from behind a hay shed as attackers streamed in, mixing with defenders running down the guard stair. As she expected, as soon as Liet's back was turned, Branid attacked her, flinging her into the mud edging the horse pond. Caught by surprise, facedown in the slippery mud, Liet could not flip over or use wrist or ankle to hook one of Branid's limbs.

Branid rubbed her face in the liquid mud, then yanked her head up by the hair. "You're a pug," he yelped. "Say it!" Back into the mud. "Pug! Pug! Pug!"

Liet gargled for breath, writhing weakly.

Two, three loping steps and Tdor closed her fingers on Branid's collar. He was solid, and slippery with splashed mud, but Tdor had been training all her life in the fighting form the women called the Odni, which used men's size and strength against them. Now she used his own surprise, his instinctive turn, to pull him off balance. A hard palm-strike under the chin, a foot hooked into his armpit, and he squelched into the mud with a satisfying splat while Liet rose, sobbing with fury.

Branid began to yell, saw who had attacked him, and fell back in surprise. Tdor caught up a clump of muddy grass and stuffed it into his mouth, then dropped onto him.

Branid gagged, his hands trying to claw the mud from his mouth, but she had his elbows pinned securely under her knees.

Words formed—"You will leave Liet alone"—but she heard Fareas-Iofre's calm voice from a year ago, *Never issue a command you cannot enforce*, and so she crowed, "See how you like it!"

And she forced herself to roll off and get to her feet. "Allies means allies," Tdor said, slinging mud off her hands. "Liet's my ally. When we have a real attack, she'll be yours."

Branid's muddy face contorted with his convulsive spitting and gagging. When he could speak he shrieked, "Allies! Shit! You should hear what she says about you behind your head."

Tdor raised her palm, pushing away his words. "Who cares? When we fight, she does her job. Same when you're on my side."

Branid mumbled in Marlovan, just loud enough for her to hear, *Marth-Davan coward.*

Tdor wiggled her hands at her ears. *I don't hear you!*

Branid ran off without a backward glance. Lightning flashed again, and rain came suddenly, cold needles that turned into warm drops by the time Tdor reached the door to the baths.

The scrubs reached the fields beyond the academy.

A few boys, Inda and Sponge among them, watched who was talking and who scouting as they ran. Dogpiss shut out the other boys' chatter and scouted the terrain: rectangular, big enough for running, but not for riding. Walled at the closest short side—a low, ancient stone wall, the rocks fallen from it at some points—trees at the far end, the left long border a stream, and the road the right. In his experience, ground was picked first, then a strategy is developed.

"I see the best digs," he said, cutting through his riding's chatter. And he took off, the others running after him.

"Now, first thing, we have to pick a captain," Cherry-Stripe declared, eying his riding. Only two listened—Kepa was trying to get rid of that sniveling Smartlip, Inda watched the field. Why?

Noddy and Rattooth, who ordinarily had little to say to one another, saw what Dogpiss had done, exchanged a couple of brief remarks on what was the second best ground to claim. They began to run, the remaining three of their riding following.

Arveas, Fera-Vayir, and Basna grouped together, glaring at Smartlip, who lurked behind Kepa. They could see from his sullen expression, his angry gestures, that he was whining. "Does Gand want us to lose?" Flash asked, arms crossed. "A snitch and a royal rabbit."

Glances Sponge's way. Coward or not, he was still a king's son. He was standing apart, watching the ridings.

Basna rubbed his chin. "Have you seen him rabbiting yet?"

Fera-Vayir Tvei shrugged. "Cherry-Stripe's brother in the Sier-Danas says he's a rabbit, so he must be a rabbit."

"We can test," Flash offered. He grinned. "It'd be fun."

Basna snickered. "Why not? We lost anyway."

Abandoned by Kepa, Smartlip caught up. He glared with his characteristic challenge and anxiety. "So who's captain?"

Basna pointed at Sponge. "He's captain. Of course."

Sponge looked at them one at a time, then said, "No."

Meanwhile, Cherry-Stripe kept glaring at Inda, waiting for his attention. He had to be the leader. Buck would thrash him if he weren't. "I'm riding captain," he stated in a louder voice. Kepa, Lith, and Fijirad obediently twisted their thumbs skyward in agreement, but Inda still kept looking around. What a pug! Cherry-Stripe spoke right at him. "I say we don't bother with thumbs-up vote, but fight for it."

He stepped right up to Inda, who stood on tiptoe, looking over Cherry-Stripe's shoulder at the other boys across the field.

Cherry-Stripe said louder, "Strongest wins. We're supposed to be leaders, and—"

Inda turned his way at last. "All right," he said, waving his hands. "Be the leader, Cherry-Stripe. We all know you and Cama and Tuft are the strongest, and blah blah blah. But do it fast, because look! I just knew Dogpiss would find the best defense digs straight off. See, he's got that bend in the stream, all those rocks. No one's going to flank him now, and a straight on attack will break all of us up. And there go Rattooth and Noddy, heading for those trees over there. If we jaw all day, we're going to end up with the worst spot."

Lith looked back, then at Cherry-Stripe. He said to Inda, "We're closer. If we run, we can take the trees first."

Inda promptly started running, Lith and Fijirad on either side. Kepa hesitated, and Cherry-Stripe irritably waved him on. Stupid bootlick. "I'll run Rattooth off," he shouted, and forced himself to sprint his fastest, until his side hurt and his heart thumped in his ears. He caught a glimpse of Rattooth's face, and felt satisfaction burn through him when the smaller boy swerved.

Now Cherry-Stripe needed to know if the others had seen that. He loped toward his riding despite the stitch in his side.

". . . and Cherry-Stripe is our captain," Inda was saying, waving his way. "Make it fast! I see Dogpiss scouting all the leaders. You *know* he's going to think the same thing."

"What?" Cherry-Stripe gasped.

"Alliance," Biscuit said. "We go after the other ridings one at a time, share the flags square, two apiece."

"But I—" Cherry-Stripe saw the other boys all thumbing or speaking agreement, and knew he'd lost his chance of issuing a counter command. Anyway Inda'd told them *he* was captain of the riding. Since everyone was watching him, he said, "So now we have ten. We rush them. I can take any two or three." His confidence was back. *This is how war games ought to be fought, just like home. The strongest always wins—*

But they were *looking* at him again. He frowned, realizing someone else had spoken, and he'd missed it.

"And what then?" That was Inda, repeating himself.

"Thrash 'em, of course—" Then he remembered that stupid ruling he'd scorned back in the courtyard.

"Can't," Kepa said, looking disgusted. "Beaks'll land on us if we have any real fun."

"Pin 'em," Noddy suggested. "Join us or be our prisoners."

Nods of agreement.

"Who do you want guarding prisoners?" Inda asked.

"You guard your own." No, wait, that wouldn't work. Cherry-Stripe didn't want to be stuck watching some stupid boy when he could be capturing flags and glory. "No. No."

Inda glanced Kepa's way, and Cherry-Stripe did too, just to meet that eternal bootlicking grin. *He* was no help. So—ah! Cherry-Stripe laughed in relief. "Kepa, you'll be jailer."

Kepa's grin stretched even wider. He loved the idea of being jailer. He could kick and punch anyone who tried to escape and get away with it.

Noddy sighed, stone-faced. "Dogpiss kipped the best digs."

"Yeah." Inda snorted a laugh. "We got to roust 'em out."

Cherry-Stripe opened his mouth to say they should rush Dogpiss' riding, except he looked across at the boulders, the water behind the riding, the driftwood the boys were busy piling up, and knew that the suggestion was stupid. Desperate for a command he could hand out, a good one, he looked around. "Let's get our own fort," he said, then hated how his voice didn't sound commanding, it sounded more like a question.

But the others agreed, and Cherry-Stripe felt easier, that he was properly in command. They secured their trees, took up guard positions, and looked out to assess the other groups.

Cherry-Stripe now needed to score a flag on his own.

Dogpiss, watching them from across the field, muttered, "Inda's riding's going to go after Sponge's first. You watch. Get the weak riding off their flank, then come in strength against us, 'cause we got the best digs. Let's strike first." He jerked his thumb at Cama and Ndarga, one big boy, one small. "I'll go too—maybe we can get Flash and Basna to join in with us."

Tuft and Cama both agreed. Tveis of big brothers who would one day command vast plains, they both recognized in Dogpiss a future dragoon captain, just like his father. Sindan-An Tvei (now known as Tuft from the day of the shearing) rounded on Lan and said loftily, "You and I guard the flags."

Lan rolled his eyes at Tuft's Vayir frost.

Inda watched them all, intent, loving the prospect of battle, relieved that the way he used to let Branid lead, or think he led, worked with Cherry-Stripe. Dogpiss' pale yellow head turned—he was planning a fast attack, probably on Sponge's group, maybe try to get them to ally.

Inda said to Cherry-Stripe, "Are you going to take command against Dogpiss' advance?"

Cherry-Stripe looked wildly around the field. He saw Dogpiss, who just seemed to be running around like the other boys. Advance? Yes, he was heading straight for Sponge's riding. He shouted, "After me!" and launched at his fastest run, well ahead of the others, and pounded straight for Cama, the biggest of Dogpiss' three-man advance charge. Fijirad flung himself on Dogpiss, and the two tumbled wildly over the grass, legs and arms scrambling for holds; Tuft forgot he was to guard the flag and launched over the rocks to Cama and Dogpiss' rescue.

Lan hesitated, took the square of old canvas that served as their flag and shoved it under a flat stone. Then he too ran after them, yelling wildly.

As Dogpiss' riding gathered around the fight, all shouting insults or orders that no one listened to, Inda muttered to Noddy, "You and your riding go take Sponge. You just know they made him their riding captain."

Noddy shrugged, his long face not changing. He motioned for his group and repeated the order, adding, "Take Flash first. And Basna. Then Sponge." The others agreed—they knew by now that Flash and Basna were among the best scrappers in the entire scrub class.

Noddy watched them aim straight for Sponge's riding, but he lingered, observing Inda, who beckoned to little, skinny Mouse Marth-Davan, and when the boy trotted over, Inda bent his head and whispered to Mouse.

Mouse smiled, then scudded lightly away from the battle through the trees, heading up to the far end of the field and back down—unnoticed by anyone. Noddy felt his armpits go cold when he realized that Mouse was going to make the pinch on at least one flag—maybe even two. And no one outside of Inda and Mouse realized it.

Except Noddy. And . . . Noddy saw Sponge watching, too. Just before the attackers reached Sponge and Flash and Basna, taking the three boys down onto the grass. Flash and Sponge wrestled with their attackers, Flash with skill and Sponge with clench-jawed determination; the others watched for a moment, seeing the prince fighting desperately, then they all dove into a mad scramble of arms and legs, grass and dust flying in all directions, as everyone tried to take everyone else prisoner.

Meanwhile Mouse skirted the entire field, collecting the flags, observed only by Noddy, Sponge, and Inda.

And the masters.

Chapter Nine

TDOR was summoned to Fareas-Iofre in her private chamber.

It was too early for study; as she straightened out her clothes she reviewed the war game. Her tangle with Branid was not a problem. Even if the Iofre had heard about that, there would be no objections. Except maybe from Branid's old granddam Marend-Edli, and no one listened to her if they could help it.

She ran to the Iofre's room. When she saw Noren's familiar small, round body, her hair neatly braided and her tunic fresh, she realized what the summons had to be, and her heart seemed to fill with light. The two girls exchanged grins before they entered the Iofre's chamber.

Fareas looked at the two faces before her, one thin and serious, the other merry and freckled and round, though right now Noren's expression was strictly schooled.

"Noren," the Iofre said, hiding her own amusement, for this was a serious matter, "Tdor tells me that you have expressed an interest in becoming her personal Runner."

Noren slapped palm to chest, not daring to speak.

"You are eleven, old enough to make the decision to begin the training. It means long days, and you will no longer live with your family, but upstairs. The training is hard. You must learn to defend your Edli, and care for her things. You will study, not just to write in Iascan but in Old

Sartoran as well, and you will above all learn to keep your own counsel. Do you think you can do these things?"

Noren nodded once, her little chin almost knocking her collarbones, then once again she smacked her hand over her heart. They all heard the thump.

The Iofre smiled briefly. "Now, you know this, yet you do not really know it: though one day you might have lovers, Runners never marry. If they choose to marry and have children, they must give up Runner blue and the accompanying privileges. There can be only one loyalty for a personal Runner to an Edli, something I do not expect you to understand until you are older. But you must keep it in mind. Is this acceptable?"

For the third time Noren struck her hand over her heart. This time she could not repress her grin.

"Very well. Then you must go to your home and see to the transfer of your gear. Chelis will help you settle in." Noren saluted, and was gone in two heartbeats.

"I think she is a good choice," the Iofre said to Tdor. "But you must remember her honor is in your hands. If it turns out you cannot trust one another, if you grow apart, then you must speak at once. She could always be one of the House Runners. Your Runner is someone who will, we hope, be at your side for life. Remember that as time goes on."

Tdor saluted, and the Iofre rose and without further words led the way to the archive, a long corner room with double sets of windows that stood wide open. The cherished shelves of carefully dusted books and scrolls were set against the inside walls.

There they found Joret waiting. As the Iofre moved to the far table Joret semaphored a question with her brows raised, and Tdor murmured, "Noren. My Runner."

Joret smiled. Noren was a good match, just as she had found a good match in her own silent, tough Gdand.

The Iofre approached with a scroll. She sat down at the worktable and gestured for Tdor to open it.

Tdor bent over the rolled end of the ancient manuscript, recognizing it as the one that had just arrived the day before. The paper crackled as she unrolled it, and she smoothed it with careful fingers, setting weights along its length.

"I think it's a bad copy," Joret said, frowning.

The Iofre looked up with quick concern. "Oh, I trust not," she murmured. "My sister sent it. The seal bears her sigil."

Tdor scanned the Old Sartoran lettering. Until she started parsing it, the flowing script, going top to bottom instead of side to side, looked like vines and strange, stylized flowers.

"Here," Joret said, pointing to the first row. "And here. Look!" She whispered the words to herself, feeling the world reform around her in a way she could scarcely define. "*Shaping root-buds of light*—isn't it? Does that mean something?"

"No . . ." The Iofre's high forehead puckered in perplexity.

"Shaping root-buds of light?" Joret and Tdor both felt, and hid, their mirth. The Iofre usually did not mind, but today she seemed tense. No, *intense*, Joret thought.

"It is 'cloud,' " the Iofre said in her soft voice.

"But the word for 'cloud' ought to be written with the 'ei', not 'eh'. 'Clouds' has the double vowel, does it not?" Joret asked.

"Yes. Tdor? The ascription?"

Tdor bent over the writing at the very end, mouthing the words, then translating out loud. " 'This taeran was copied from one captured from a Venn warship in Geranda.' " She looked up. "Dated three hundred years ago."

"That explains it, then," the Iofre said. "Some mage in the Land of the Venn must have written it down as spoken out loud."

Tdor and Joret knew that Marlovan had altered its vowel sounds over the generations since they had been exiled from the Venn. Some words—such as Jarl—had changed a consonant instead, from "hya" to "jha."

The Iofre said, "Yet my sister writes that its title matches with one on an ancient list, a taeran purported to be one of the few that address magic as understood in Old Sartor."

Unsaid was how much of a price the sisters had paid.

Joret looked up, her eyes wide, the color of rain-washed sky. "I see that phrase we have discussed before—'dena Yeresbeth'—but it is spelled in the Venn pronunciation, 'deneh Ieresbedh.' "

Tdor rubbed her thumb over her lip. *Dena Yeresbeth*. Everyone knew that "beth" in Old Sartoran was "three," and "dena" was a verb that usually meant "made of." "Yeres" was the word that mages all over the world debated.

" 'Shaping clouds of light.' Now *that* sounds Sartoran," Joret whispered to Tdor as the Iofre checked a glossary.

"You mean makes no sense, right?" Tdor whispered back.

Jarend-Adaluin, standing in the open doorway and looking in at the three of them, saw the secret mirth in the girls' faces. Tdor was a dear child, but his gaze did not linger on her uncomplicated features and untidy brown braids. It tarried, painful as an unhealed wound, on the color under Joret's smooth brown skin, the long eyelashes, the light that seemed to gather in her remarkable eyes. The shape of bone in socket and jaw and skull, the waving fall of her glossy black hair, all of it a fresh reminder of his own beloved Joret.

He shifted his gaze away, used to the pain of that too, and met his wife's eyes across the width of the room. Fareas' patient brown gaze never changed as the girls belatedly noticed the presence of the tall, straight, gray-haired man there in the doorway and rose hastily to their feet, slapping their hands to their hearts in childish politeness. The Iofre saluted and he returned it. They never relaxed the courtesies before any other person. They had far too much respect for one another.

"Your pardon, Fareas-Edli," he said, "for my interruption of your studies."

"You are welcome," she responded, pulling from inside her robes his heavy seal-ring on its fine chain. She unhooked it and held it out on her palm. "Welcome home, Jarend-Dal. I can lay aside the work if you have need to consult with me at once."

"No, no, do continue," the Adaluin said. "And you had better keep the seal," he added. "I am not home long."

The girls looked from one to the other, then Joret sat down and returned to the manuscript. She knew that the Adaluin would never notice her unless there was a need, and then he would be formal, kind, impossible to understand. She no longer bothered trying to gain his attention. She saw him too seldom for that.

Tdor sat down too, and bent over the manuscript, but she listened to the adults. Living people were more interesting to her than those in old records.

"Just before I reached our home gates I received a Runner," the Adaluin said. "From Standas on the coast watch. There is word of a pirate ship having been seen. I must depart again tomorrow. But my route will take me close to Marth-Davan, so if you wish, I will escort Tdor there for her Name Day visit."

Tdor's mouth rounded in surprise. Pride mixed with dismay.

The Iofre turned her way, and smiled. "Should you like a royal Honor Guard, my dear?"

Tdor rose and saluted. "Thank you, Adaluin-Dal." There could be no other answer.

"That means you must be prepared to travel tomorrow," the Iofre said. "We had better see to your arrangements."

The Adaluin said, "I will leave you to it. I must rotate the ridings for our journey." There would be no leave for the Adaluin, of course, but it would never occur to him to complain. The purpose of his life was to ride his lands all year long, defending, inspecting, judging. His household ready in case the pirates ever returned.

Tdor, still watching, saw the Iofre look distracted, but not at all upset. Tdor wondered if she someday would feel just distracted, and not upset, if Tanrid were to send Inda away to inspect the coast. She couldn't imagine not being upset, nor could she imagine Inda not being upset. Though he was excited to go to the academy, she remembered the quiver of his mouth as they said their farewells.

She wondered what was missing in adults that was there for children. Maybe she had it backward, that something was missing in children which made adults so difficult to understand.

"Come child," the Iofre said softly. "This is not the time to stand over our studies."

Tdor realized she'd been staring at the scroll that now she would not get to read for an entire month, until her return. She followed the Iofre out, while the Adaluin crossed the castle to his own private rooms, unchanged for twenty-five years.

He passed through his workroom and the small room he used for a bedroom, then opened the door to the grand and princely bedroom that everyone thought permanently closed, the chamber untouched by his command. Unlike his own rooms, which were as clean as they were austere, this room lay under a twenty-five-year film of dust, the bedding rumpled, his dead wife's night robe crumpled on the brown-stained rug; the room smelled of dust and faintly of mildew, for even the mold-spells had not been renewed. No one had been permitted in the room at all except himself.

The windows let in long, golden shafts of light. Jarend-Adaluin's single step to the threshold was enough to stir the dust motes upward in lazy swirls. They floated, tiny points of fire in the light; out of the light they extinguished to the softness of ash.

But the light, the dust, were not what held his attention. They only enabled him to see the form limned in gold luminosity, the young shoulders, the exqisite line of brow and jaw and neck, the soft fall of black hair a shadow-contrast to the shimmering ghostly form of Joret, his beloved first wife, as she stood near the spot where she had bled to death, gazing through the windows into eternity.

Chapter Ten

THE scrubs' first Restday finally arrived.

"Beginning with Firstday tomorrow, you will revert to academy schedule: callover once a day, weekly inspections."

Master Gand ignored the whoop for one breath, then he tapped against his boot the willow wand that all the masters either carried or wore at their belts. The voices stilled.

Master Gand said, "After breakfast you still have your stable duties. There is no Restday for those under our care."

Meaning animals, a few thought, those few who had listened past the word "duties." Sponge was the only one who heard the underlying message, though as usual he gave no discernable sign.

"You will also," Gand said, "beginning with the midday meal, be permitted to speak in the mess hall. All that is, except Lassad." Pause, several smirking looks sent Smartlip's way.

"See that you do not lose the privilege again. Next time will be at least a month. You have liberty from noon to sundown bells, when you'll report back for drums. Dismissed."

The boys stampeded from the parade ground.

One good thing about morning stable work was seeing all the new foals. The scrubs all managed to find business at that end of the stable, and Master Olin smiled at tender strokes from small, grubby hands, the covert kisses on the velvety-soft newborn muzzles. The sooner humans and horses accustomed themselves to one another, the better for each.

Midday meal, their first with the gag lifted, added their treble voices to the adolescent uproar in the mess hall, amid the clatter of wooden spoons against wooden bowls used by three hundred ravenous boys.

Now that the scrubs could talk, the pigtails lost interest in teasing them by sign and grin, and the scrubs, left to themselves at last, squeezed onto one table instead of their usual two, ten to a side, in a rival-free merriment that they had never before experienced. The mess hall was the same: the hard butt-worn benches, the ubiquitous smell of baked rice balls and cabbage, slow-roasted garlic-and-onion rubbed chicken, and rye bread, but now that they could talk everything seemed new.

But after all only nineteen added to the general noise. Smartlip still had to sit in silence. And no one paid him the least attention. He attacked his food in a rage, sploshing his water and clacking his spoon against his bowl until he saw the glances of ill-concealed mirth sent his way.

Oh, he expected frost from Cama (he was going to start calling him Meow) and Noddy the Slacker (another nickname Smartlip was trying to generate), but Kepa and Rattooth and Cherry-Stripe were supposed to be on *his* side.

Cherry-Stripe never noticed Smartlip's inward agonies. He was too busy fuming over his own problems.

At least you were captain of your riding, his brother Buck had said, catching him on the way to the baths last night, and slapping him two or three times to emphasize his words. *But that Mouse Marth-Davan getting the enemy flags? You should have gotten at least one! Don't disgrace me again.*

And then he'd vanished into the night, without even letting Cherry-Stripe have a chance to explain that Mouse had been a decoy, sneaking around to grab the flags while he, Cherry-Stripe, fought valiantly against Cama. Of course then his brother might ask who made that plan, because it wasn't like any plan they'd ever made at home. He'd have to admit it had been Inda's.

Cherry-Stripe rubbed his arm where his brother had gripped him, staring at the others. Cama's face was puffy on one side and showed a new bruise under his unruly black hair. New bruises, from last night:

Horsebutt had obviously thrashed him as well, probably for the same reason.

Cherry-Stripe sighed. He didn't want to sympathize with anyone who had to be related to Horsebutt, not when Cama stubbornly stayed friends with Sponge. Cherry-Stripe had his orders. Once Cama decided Sponge was no good to be around, Cherry-Stripe could take him into his own group.

Sponge. Where was he? Sitting with Rattooth, talking quietly at the other end. That was another thing. Sponge was, everyone said, a rabbit, but Cherry-Stripe hadn't seen any sign of it. Bad training, yes. He was the worst of the scrubs. Not that it mattered. He had his orders.

What did matter was when people acted, well, like you didn't expect them to act. How could you plan against that?

Like that Inda. Truth was, he'd really been the leader yesterday but he wasn't strutting. In Cherry-Stripe's experience, if you won, you strutted. Most likely it was all accident. Yes, that was it. Accident.

Assigning motivations that he understood eased Cherry-Stripe's inner debate, until noise broke into his brooding. He looked up, saw them all laughing—all except Noddy, who never changed expression, and Cama, who laughed soundlessly.

". . . and so we put an egg in each of their boots, see, and then—" Dogpiss' face was crimson as he wheezed for breath.

"C'mon." Tuft smacked the table. "What happened?"

Dogpiss shook his head, still wheezing with laughter.

Inda reached over and pounded him on the back.

"M-me . . . mmmm . . ." Dogpiss gasped, tears squeezing between his eyes, and he waved a helpless hand at Inda.

"Here's what he told me in the baths the other night," Inda said, grinning down the table. "Whipstick slipped into the bell tower and rang the alarm. So the guards ran out of the barracks." He paused to snicker.

"Th . . ." Dogpiss whimpered. "The . . . b-boots . . . oh!"

Inda said, "Patrol jumped straight into their boots. Ran out. Or started. Some of 'em got four, five steps. Slowed down. Then they started dancing like their feet were on fire—"

"Wailing!" Dogpiss forced the word out. "Howling!"

"By the time they all got out to the parade court, they were all hopping around—" Inda said, then he caught sight of Dogpiss' sweaty, snotty face, and he too succumbed to paroxysms.

"What? What? What?" Ndarga demanded.

Noddy sighed. "His Ain laughed so hard he fell off the bell tower. Broke his arm."

The listeners whooped. Noddy, of course, looked resigned.

When the laughter had died down, Kepa asked, "So they found you out, huh?" And at Dogpiss' nod, he bent forward, his freckled face eager. "Did you catch the willow?"

"Oh, something fearful." Dogpiss snickered. "M' father whupped us himself."

Kepa giggled, wide-eyed and avid. "Didya get welters?"

"We couldn't lie on our backs for a month, and Whipstick with a broken arm." Dogpiss wriggled his shoulder blades, and two or three boys twitched shoulders in unconscious empathy. " 'twas worth it. We started calling the captain Dancing Tderga."

"To his face?" Basna asked, looking skeptical, impatiently tossing a drift of pale hair out of his eyes.

Dogpiss looked at him like he'd grown another ear. "Of course not! You think we're stupid?" He poked Inda. "Tell 'em the one about the paint soup."

Inda shrugged, grinning. "Not as good as the Egg Dance."

Kepa sniggered. "Just don't try that here. Or *you* can, Inda. But not Dogpiss, unless you want to get flogged before the entire school."

"It's not a real flogging," Tuft said, waving a hand. "Just a dusting with a willow wand."

Kepa leaned forward. "Hundred dusters'll raise weepers."

Most of the boys grimaced. Cherry-Stripe scoffed, "Oh, nobody gets a century unless it's theft, or cowardice. Something big. Not stings."

"You Vayirs wouldn't get it anyway," Kepa said, still with that avid grin. "At least, you have to agree. Or your father does. So, Dogpiss, if you want to run a sting, better let Inda do it. Or Cassad. Or Sponge."

All the fun had gone from the talk, despite Kepa's big grin.

Sponge looked away; Inda said, "It's a matter of honor. Not a matter of refusing to stand up to a punishment you earned just because of your rank. Read the histories. That rule came in the early days of the academy, when it was just Vayirs here, and there were accusations against boys for political reasons—"

"No history! No history," Dogpiss said, waving a hand. "If I think of a sting, I run it myself, Vayir or no Vayir."

Inda looked around the table, saw disgust, unease, even anger. "Look, everyone's done! And now we got our first real liberty. Who wants to waste it blabbing?"

They all remembered that it was really Restday, and yelling with joy—with relief—they grabbed up their dishes and fled.

Inda followed more slowly. He didn't like the way Cherry-Stripe had been watching him, before Kepa started that hare about flogging and the rules governing Vayirs. It had to either mean another scrag or else something worse.

He dropped his dish into the barrel and ran out, looking for Sponge so he could find out how to get to Hadand.

A rough hand on Inda's shoulder made him jump. He whirled around and stared up into his brother's face. Tanrid looked taller than ever, and old, and hard, with his hair pulled up in back, and his gray war coat outlining the shape of his arms.

"Took you long enough to eat," Tanrid snapped. "What did you do, go back for fifths?"

Inda knew better than to answer, of course—and Tanrid didn't wait for an answer anyway. "Come on, we're going to Daggers," he snarled, as if Inda had somehow resisted.

Once Tanrid hadn't shown up in the first three days, when everyone else had gotten sponsored—everyone, that is, except Sponge—Inda had accustomed himself to the idea that Tanrid would not come. He was now amazed, and it showed.

Tanrid glowered around, chin jutting and eyes narrowed. Not angry, even if he looked it. Inda knew to a nicety all the gradations of his brother's temper, but this mood was a new one.

Tanrid let Inda go and struck off through byways Inda was just beginning to master, his pace so fast Inda had to skip-walk in order to keep up.

As they emerged from the stable-scented austerity of the academy, Inda wondered if, like Cherry-Stripe and Cama, he too was going to catch it for not having personally snatched flags.

They passed through the high gates and into the city itself. To one side was the outer boundary of the king's castle, the honey-stone walls smooth, the windows so lofty nothing of the inside could be seen. To the right, little streets opened off here and there, narrow gaps between ivy-covered stone buildings.

The weather was fine, so windows were open; Inda, rounding a corner, passed a low one at his own height and he glanced inside to see a snug room with bunk beds, a worktable, and steps leading down into some room on a lower level. The houses, though made of stone, were far more adaptable than castles, with walls pulled down or built up, rooms added onto rooms not just adjacent to them, but below or above.

Then they were past, and he turned his attention to the Restday revelers in their best clothing, all except for the sentries. After a week of Marlovan it was strange to hear Iascan again.

"Here we go," Tanrid said abruptly, as they rounded a corner and now they heard Marlovan once more, the loud chatter and laughter of boys.

Daggers Drawn was a long, low building, indistinguishable from the others around it except for the weather-beaten sign outside, the golden fox of the academy on a black background.

That fox was so familiar to Tanrid he no longer noticed its strange beaklike muzzle or the raptorish slanted eyes. It was old, Inda thought, lingering on the threshold. Really old—

"Move!" Tanrid thrust Inda through the low door.

Inda kept his retort in his head, and looked around.

Tanrid, unlike Inda, did not notice the long-familiar odor comprised of horse and boy-sweat and spiced cider and the thick, dark, mildly fermented brew that was called rootbrew though its main constituent was barley. He didn't notice the tattered banners on three walls, donated years before by graduating horsetails after wins in the traditional banner games of summer, or the battered, knife-furrowed tables and benches. As Inda looked around, eyes wide, mouth open, Tanrid watched his brother and realized that Inda, far from being annoyed at how long it had taken Tanrid to get over to the scrub den to do his duty, had not expected him at all.

Tanrid, so self-conscious his manner was surly, thrust Inda toward the proprietor, a gimp-legged old lancer who paused in the act of dipping ceramic mugs into the barrel with the magic cleaning spell on it, and set them down.

"My brother, Indevan-Dal Algara-Vayir," Tanrid muttered, hot-eared and self-conscious. And to Inda, "That's Mun. Keeps score."

Ketha Mundavan, Lancer captain to the old king, eyed the Algara-Vayir pup with concealed interest. His sun- and scar-seamed face never gave the least sign of this interest, but he listened to all the boys' gossip, freely canvassed in this retreat from the rules and regulation of the academy, and he'd heard a surprising amount about this newly arrived scrub.

But he didn't speak, just gave a nod, and that was that.

Tanrid recalled vaguely that on his own introduction here, his father had spoken with Mun about old times, and felt that he ought to be doing something like it, or something, anyway. He wondered what he was supposed to say. "See that you never overrun your score," he snarled.

But that just sounded like a beak. Acutely embarrassed now, he thrust Inda so hard toward a bench he stumbled.

Mun recognized that embarrassment with practiced ease, and so he resumed washing glasses, knowing that it would be a little while before Tanrid recovered.

Inda sat where he was told and scowled down at his hands. On one side of them a party of pigtails laughed about some private wager; beyond them, in the stuffy corner farthest from either window or fire, were five scrubs, and Inda sensed five speculative gazes on his back. On the fire side of the room, the preferred area, several seniors in their gray academy war coats held court. Inda could hear their rumbly voices, but he didn't look their way because that would be perceived as frost.

Not that it mattered who they were, or what they talked about. They were all having a good time, and he wished he was anywhere but here, with Tanrid of all people, and wondered when he'd ever get the chance to talk about interesting old battles with Sponge, who, it turned out, loved reading old records as much as he did. Or if he'd ever get to see Hadand.

He repressed a sigh, and Tanrid glared at him and said, "I had reasons for not coming sooner. All-day field runs, then got sent out on a two-day scouting run. Lasted till yesterday."

Inda once again looked surprised.

Tanrid was so surprised to see his brother's surprise that he forgot his own unease. "You thought I wouldn't?"

Inda mumbled a few words at the floor.

"Speak up," Tanrid commanded, exasperated.

". . . or something," Inda muttered, and a burst of loud laughter from behind them drowned out the rest of his words.

Tanrid looked at those moving lips, the averted gaze, and suppressed a desire to slap some sense into the brat.

"What's with you?" He leaned forward so they wouldn't be overheard. He, too, was aware of those staring scrubs, and if the rules about fighting hadn't been even more stringent here than at mess, he'd go knock some heads together. "Who are those pugs, anyway?"

"Oh, it's just Ennath and Fijirad and them," Inda said. Then he frowned at Tanrid. "If you're going to thrash me, go ahead. I hate waiting."

"Thrash you?" Tanrid repeated. "Why?" Then a brief, somewhat bleak crease of humor deepened the corners of his mouth. "Even if I wanted to, Mun'd be on me fast. And then it would take a week to crawl back to the barracks."

"Oh." That hadn't occurred to Inda.

"So don't you fight here either," Tanrid admonished, belatedly—and unnecessarily. He knew it as soon as he spoke, and saw the grimace of impatience that tightened his brother's face. The unease closed in again. "It's too strange," he muttered to the opposite window. "This having brothers here. Where everyone can watch, and talk about how you're training."

Inda's lips moved, but there was no sound.

Tanrid scowled. "Say it, don't just sit there like a dog turd waiting for a wand."

"I already got enough people who want to thrash me."

"When do I ever thrash you except if you're lazy, or give me lip?"

"Lip being an opinion that's not yours," Inda retorted. "There's also when I don't—" Inda stopped, then shook his head. To his own ears, he sounded too much like Branid, whining about what couldn't be helped. "Doesn't matter."

Tanrid scowled even more ferociously. He didn't even notice when Mun came near, set down the foam-topped dark brown rootbrew that Tanrid invariably drank, signed to Inda *The same?*, and got a nod in return.

Tanrid didn't notice because he didn't like change, didn't like thinking, really. He liked things orderly, the way they were supposed to be. He was Tanrid-Laef Algara-Vayir, future Adaluin of Choraed Elgaer. He would marry Joret, who along with his brother would defend his home when he was away, and about that his father had said once, *Train your brother well, my son. I was too merciful to my own brother, your Uncle Indevan, who loved his ease. And you know what happened.*

That was clear enough: it meant thrash the silliness out of Inda, thrash out any sign of disrespect or of avoiding orders, of cowardice or sloth. Inda was no coward, and he was seldom lazy and almost invariably the times he was idle were not spent lolling in the kitchen or his bed, but frowsting in the archive among their mother's books. But he did get mouthy, and he'd started questioning Tanrid's orders almost as soon as he could walk.

So Tanrid thrashed him. Did it as hard as they got it here—that seemed a fair standard—but he never used a stick. How he hated being thrashed with a stick! Always his hands. Fair. Honorable.

But he had no idea how to explain that and not lose his brother's respect. Especially when everything was so . . . so different, so restless, so *uneasy.* "Talk," he said.

Inda shrugged as if to say, Here goes, then. Indeed he was no coward, but he saw no reason to invite pain.

"It stinks, having Ains around all the time. Spying us out, landing on us when they don't like what we did." He recalled Cama's bruises, and seeing Cherry-Stripe Marlo-Vayir jerked by his Ain into an alleyway the night before, on the way to the baths. Not that he cared what happened to Cherry-Stripe, but all the boys had seen, and some looked around anxiously for their own Ains. It didn't take any insight to know they were wondering if they were next. "Grabbing us and yelling orders at us and slapping us around, if they don't like what we do. As if we weren't already catching it from the beaks."

"Scrubs always catch it from everyone," Tanrid pointed out. "Then when you make your way to the top it means something."

Inda shrugged, and slurped at his rootbrew. "Hoo." His eyes widened. "That's good. Much better than ours at home."

"I told you that."

"I thought that was just strut," Inda said, testing.

Tanrid knew it, and confronted thus with a semblance of normality, he sat back, giving a derisive snort.

Inda could see that perplexity, even discomfort, underlaid that scowl, though anger was there too. He waited.

Tanrid said finally, "So you thought you'd catch a knuckle-dusting from me because Mouse Marth-Davan got the enemy flags t'other day?" A slight, sour grin, then he added, "I wasn't spying—I was a day's ride away—but I heard about it when I got back."

"It was a ruse, that's why Mouse got 'em. But it was my ruse. And my riding didn't lose their flag." At a gesture from Tanrid to continue, Inda said, "It was also my idea to let Cherry-Stripe lead the main feint because otherwise we would have lost our flag, and the game, by the time Cherry-Stripe had to fight his way through us to be riding captain."

Tanrid gave a single nod, staring at Inda with narrowed eyes. "So you did scan the field, then."

Inda said, "I always do that. It's easy enough. You made me start doing that before I could even read maps. It's scanning the men that's harder."

"Scanning the field at the start of an attack is not easy," Tanrid said. "No matter. The flags. Why didn't you get one?"

"My plan won. Don't care about flags."

"You should. That brings us honor . . ." Tanrid hesitated again, then shook his head. Then his jaw jutted. "Remember what I keep telling you about Uncle Indevan. You can't go soft."

"There's soft," Inda said, "and there's stupid."

"I'm stupid?" Tanrid was too taken aback for anger—yet.

Inda had him actually listening for once, and hastened to speak. "No! Look. You'll one day command warriors. If the Riders are away with you, as they were with our father, whom do Joret and I command? Mostly cooks and stable hands and weavers along with the few Riders left behind on home rotation."

Tanrid's expression eased a little. "Go on."

Inda opened his hands. "Mama keeps saying to Joret and Tdor, *You have to live with these people all your life. Your first reaction should be mercy.* Well, I have to live with 'em too, don't I? I mean, though I'm commanding the outer defense and Joret the inner defense, we pretty much share the same people. That means making everyone . . ." Inda twiddled his fingers together, seeking words to define a strategy for which instinct had hitherto sufficed.

"You unite your command," Tanrid said.

Inda's expression cleared. "That's it! It's how I get cousin Branid going one way, and Vrad the other, the ways they go best, so they don't just attack each other trying to be first. Forgetting the real plan."

Tanrid didn't say anything about how the horsetails were just learning about uniting their command and that a lot of them still couldn't see it, they just saw command as being fastest, toughest, most skilled in weapon and riding, competing against your men instead of deploying them where they would serve best. It had certainly never occurred to him before, and he frowned into his brew. Was that why Inda mouthed off so much when Tanrid told him what to remember, how to run a tactic? Tanrid struggled inwardly in the grip of a new idea: that Inda might not be arguing just to give him lip when he disagreed with Tanrid's understanding of the rules of war.

Maybe. Maybe. One thing for sure, he was glad now that he'd said nothing to Inda about the Sierlaef's warning—delivered through Buck—*When you see your Tvei, tell him to sheer off mine, and he'll do better.* Tanrid couldn't see anything wrong with the younger prince, other than bad training, and that could be fixed fast enough, especially under Master Gand, who was by far the toughest of all the tutors. But it fit with so many other strange things: the years of ugly looks Tanrid's way, missed honors, and stricter punishments whenever the Sierandael commanded field runs; the Sierlaef's hostility when they were small, his distance now. It all seemed to have something to do with bad blood between the royal family and their own.

He drank off his rootbrew. " 'Mercy.' I just hope if you defend Tenthen without me you won't show pirates any mercy."

"No chance," Inda promised, swallowing his own drink.

They left then, and walked back in silence, but it was a different sort of silence than before, for neither was apprehensive or embarrassed, only busy with his own thoughts. When they reached scrub territory Tanrid left after a flick of the hand and a grim sort of smile; Inda ran off in search of Sponge, and found him in their pit, which was warm, stuffy, and still smelled a bit like dog fur, even though all the windows were, as usual, open. Sponge was playing Cards'n'Shards with Noddy and Cama. Noddy had a new bruise forming on his forehead, his clothes looked rumpled as if from a struggle, and there was a white look to Cama's jaw.

All the scrub problems galloped back to Inda. "Deal me in?" Inda asked, and stepped behind Sponge, mouthing the word *Cherry-Stripe?*

And Smartlip, Noddy mouthed back, his expression unchanging.

"Markers," Cama said in his kitten voice, pushing some over.

The boys butt-sidled, making space, and Inda sat down. He dismissed the scuffle from his mind. That was business as usual. What occupied his mind now was Noddy and Cama being here, wasting time with cards. No brother was going to take Sponge to Daggers and the idea of the king doing it seemed somehow unthinkable. Kings were . . . kings were . . .

Inda picked up the grubby, paint-chipped cards and looked at them unseeingly for a moment. Though the king obviously lived right behind them, somehow he seemed just as distant as he had from Tenthen Castle.

No, it was right to give up Daggers until Sponge could go.

And so they played until evening mess. Then they went together to eat, and after that it was Restday wine at the fireside. They did not have bread because there were no women to pass it out, so it was just drums and wine, like their ancestors had had in the old days, when riding the plains. They sang and played the old, familiar drum songs and chants, and learned new ones. And after that baths, then bed, and as Inda lay down, half-aware of the rustles and breathings of nineteen boys around him, he wondered again just when and how he would see his sister.

He still did not know what dangers threatened; so far he had never even seen the Sierandael. What he did know was that life here was far different than he expected, and that Sponge, though a prince, seemed to have fewer privileges and more worries than the lowest-ranking stable hand.

Chapter Eleven

F AR to the southwest, the villagers along the coastal hills above Pah Luwath watched the Adaluin's entourage ride up in double columns, bridles jingling and pennants flaring.

Tdor watched them watching, studying the people and their homes with intense interest. Pah Luwath: ancient estuary renamed Luwath Harbor by the Iascans, then Port Fera-Vayir by the Marlovans, names steadfastly ignored by the locals. *You will see our shared ancestry in their homes,* the Iofre had said to Tdor the night before Tdor's departure. *We abandoned our yurts when we moved into Iascan castles. The coastal folk rooted their yurts to the ground, replacing reed mats with stone, but keeping the old round shape.*

And there they were, round houses of stone with conical roofs still made with poles, but laid over with baked mud and grass tiles, neatly overlapped in patterns, doors all facing the east—houses built to ward off the frigid sea winds of winter.

Tdor noted the houses, but it was the people she studied. They were like statues, except for the way the breeze ruffled clothes and light-colored hair.

Tdor saw their faces turn her way. She rode next to the Adaluin and was the only child, though not the only female. The Iofre had sent Che-lis, her youngest Runner, to look after Tdor, as Noren was not yet ready for this responsibility.

Tdor met the interested gaze of a girl her own age who was holding a flat basket of round breads. Restday breads. Instead of summer tunic and riding breeches and boots, the girl wore a single long garment that reached to the tops of her bare feet, kept snug against her body by a colorful bodice that laced up the front. Tdor wondered if the girl had embroidered the poppies along the narrow sleeves and the hem; the girl, meanwhile, wondered who wove those fine boots the Marlovan girl wore so proudly, and if she did really learn to fight with a knife, like everyone said those women did.

Tdor watched the girl vanish behind, as words from "Hymn to the Beginning" sang in her mind:

> . . . . *led by three warlords wielding the sun:*
> *Montrei-Hauc the mountain-gift,*
> *Montrei-Vayir plains masters,*
> *Montredavan-An, lords of the forests.*

Three clans successively claiming kingship, the symbol of which was the display of gold in their banners. Supposedly the people of Pah Luwath were the descendents of the Montrei-Haucs, who left no art or written records after they swept down out of the northeastern mountains to the plains of Hesea, joining with the clans there that subsequently called themselves Marlovans. After the conquering of the entire kingdom of Iasca Leror by the first Savarend Montredavan-An, the Montrei-Haucs had vanished among the coastal peoples here.

They hated us, the Iofre said. *Though we are all related, them to ancient Venn explorers, us to more recent Venn outcasts.*

The Marlovans had ridden for generations looking for war—if not with outsiders, then with one another. Now, it seemed, since they had settled into castles and taken up reading and writing, war sought them. Marlovans protected the local people against roaming brigands and corsairs and the ancient threat of the Venn, the tall warriors from the part of the world so far away their winter came in summer and summer in winter: their common ancestors, now their enemies.

Tdor felt an urge to slide off her horse and go running back to that girl with the poppies on her dress, and talk to her.

But the girl was out of sight now, behind an old line of budding trees planted to mark a border. And so the Adaluin's party rode sedately along the shale-paved road with planted fields stretching to either side, and then wound down a hill toward the shoreline cliffs. The breeze was suddenly cooler, smelling not just of soil and plants, but of brine.

When he saw the sea, the Adaluin raised his hand. The cavalcade halted.

Tdor studied the town below. It formed a semicircle on the last shelf of land before the estuary marshes, bisected by the river. Beyond the estuary was the sea itself, silvery blue, the afternoon sun stippling it with a path of sparkling light that seemed to stretch from the breakers to the horizon. Etched against the horizon drifted a flock of fishing smacks and way, way out beyond, Tdor made out the silhouette of a real ship, with two masts and a lot of beautiful triangular sails, gracefully curved in the wind, their shape reminding her suddenly of the tear-shaped shields of the Riders.

Her mare shifted her weight. Tdor swung a leg up, crooking it over the saddlepad to ease her leg muscles. Her aching butt couldn't be helped. Only twice a year did she ride all day—traveling to and from Marth-Davan for her Name Day visit.

The Adaluin had ridden ahead alone to meet a waiting man who had to be Standas, his coastal eyes. Tdor could just hear Inda's voice, *If you want to take someone by surprise, you don't use the roads.* Inda. What was he doing right now? Was he happy? Tdor sighed, and then heard the clop of horse hooves.

Chelis eased her mare alongside Tdor's. Behind them, the Riders talked in low voices. Chelis said, "Sore, Tdor-Edli?"

"A little," Tdor said. It wasn't anything new. She'd been saddle sore since the end of the first day's ride. But Chelis seemed to want to chat, or maybe she was asking questions that the Iofre had told her to ask, to make sure she was comfortable.

Tdor thought back to the village and the girl and Hadand and Inda, and then said, "What do you know about love?"

Chelis' heavy brows went up, and she laughed. To Tdor's surprise, and interest, spots of color ridged Chelis' hard cheekbones. Chelis was tall, and tough, with two thick shining golden braids—tough enough to ride alone to the royal city despite having just turned eighteen. She'd left off children's smocks two years ago, that Tdor remembered.

"What sort of love were you thinking on, Tdor-Edli?"

"Love love. Grownup love," Tdor said.

Chelis grimaced, leaning forward to run a thumb along her mare's neck just below the mane. "What do you know?"

"I don't *know* anything, or I wouldn't ask."

Chelis gave a nod. "Fair enough. You know about mating."

Tdor shrugged. "I've seen the dogs and horses at it, and I'm told that people are much the same." She did not say that last summer she and Inda had talked about this very thing, knowing that they'd be expected to do it some day. So they'd retreated up to his room and taken off their clothes and stood looking at one another in their skin, and laughed at the idea of boys having nipples just like girls; they both *knew* it, but no one actually ever *thought* about it. Even funnier was how their butts looked exactly alike from the back. They snickered, and looked at the parts that were different, but nothing happened. So then they'd lain on the bed together, and still nothing happened, except that Inda fell asleep, for he was tired from early rising. Tdor, thinking back, remembered how pleasant it had been to lie there with their arms and legs touching, how nice he had smelled, sort of like a puppy. But that hadn't meant anything, any more than it meant to cuddle pups or kittens and sniff their fur. She said, "But that's not *love*. Is it?"

"Not really, though it can be." Chelis grimaced. "You ought by rights to be talking to the Iofre, Tdor-Edli. You're still in smocks. This doesn't feel right, somehow."

Tdor waved a hand. "I want to know how it is that—some adults—can ride off for long times, and it doesn't matter to the other one. Some are all kissy and such." She thought of Hadand, how one day just before she had to leave Tenthen and return to the royal city, she'd said, *I only get one more visit home,* and she wiped her eyes, and then it seemed she'd forgotten that Tdor was there, for she'd said to Joret in a fervent, shaky voice, one Tdor had never before heard from her: *This will probably be the Sierlaef's year to cross from boy to man. Oh, how I hope it's other men he'll want, for it runs in the royal family, doesn't it? How unfair, how horrible, if—* Then she'd seen Tdor, and shut her mouth so fast her teeth clicked.

Tdor said in a low voice, "Can hate turn into love?"

Chelis grimaced again, then said, "I can tell you about fun in the pleasure houses, but I haven't found love love, like you mean, and to tell you the truth, I don't really want to. I like being a Runner. I don't want to have to choose between the freedom of my life and life in a home with one person. Children."

"Oh," said Tdor, puzzled now. How would someone *know* how to pick? She couldn't imagine growing up and not knowing that Inda would some day marry her. Weird.

Would I choose him, if I were to choose? she thought. She believed so, but she knew he was what she was used to. *Would I pick him as a favorite?* But the idea of lovers—people you liked to have sex with, but didn't have families with—seemed another strange idea, like clothes that didn't fit, and she turned her head to ask Chelis.

The Runner, eyeing her with trepidation, saw the question coming but to her relief, the sound of hoofbeats caused everyone to quiet and form up again.

Chelis eased her horse back into place, and the Adaluin rejoined Tdor, giving her a courteous nod.

He looked back at his captain, now riding next to Chelis, and said, "All's well enough here. The alarm was a false one."

They turned their horses and rode northeast until sunset. They found a pleasant glade on the side of a hill and set up camp, for the day was Restday, and unless there was war or similar emergency, no Marlovan rode past sundown on Restday. Tdor walked around, delighting in the new flowers, the scents of the trees, the ribbon of ocean still visible in the west.

Swiftly the great fire was set up, and the guards who'd ridden round the perimeter to scout returned, the first watch sentries standing right behind the Adaluin to take a piece of the nut cake that the Iofre had sent with Tdor.

It fell to her, as ranking female, to break the pieces off and to say, over and over to each male, from the Adaluin to the horseboys, "As strength to the body, so strength to the spirit."

Then the Adaluin was handed the wine flagon, and he squirted a red arc into the air, glowing ruby against the last limb of the sun, saying, "Wine in place of our blood."

First squirt to Tdor, sweet and stinging, then to Chelis. And then to the sentries of the first watch, who would only get to hear the drums from a distance, and not drink or sing or dance. One by one they swallowed their sip and then retreated to prowl through the deepening twilight as others brought out drums and reeds and began the old chants: "Hymn to the Beginning," for the Adaluin liked tradition, and then other songs.

As the wine passed round, laughter replaced solemnity, and some of the younger men got up to do the men's dances round the fire, the beautiful water-marked steel of their swords flashing and gleaming. More than one speculative glance was cast Chelis' way. This being Rest-day, when camp discipline was relaxed, and she the only female of adult age, she had her pick of the men if she wanted one.

Not long after she vanished into the darkness with a tall fellow with bark-colored hair, her laugh drifting on the soft air behind, the Adaluin sat down next to Tdor, a tall, gaunt figure in his sun-faded green House coast, his furrowed long face pensive. He smiled at her, and then looked away, not at the fire, but into the purple smear on the western horizon.

"Are you enjoying your studies?" he asked, quite kindly.

Tdor said, "Yes, Adaluin-Dal."

"Do you read upon interesting subjects?" he asked. "Or are you confined still to learning the meanings of words?"

"Oh, no, the Iofre wants us to find subjects we like, once we've done our part in parsing Old Sartoran texts. She says we make better leaders if we read what people did in the past. What they did right, and what they did wrong."

"Ah." The Adaluin inclined his head, the firelight making his brown skin ruddy, smoothing the lines years of sun and wind had carved into his lean cheeks, and gilding his silver horsetail with golden highlights. "She is a fine scholar."

"Yes, Adaluin-Dal."

He shifted position. "The reports, I discovered, were confusing. Some insisted they saw a fleet of pirate vessels. Others a single one, a ghost ship. Though it had a Venn shape, there are too many witnesses that swear it flew black sails, impossibly black, and that it vanished into a–a tear in the world. Have you read about such curious things?"

Tdor swallowed. "Do they think it went to Norsunder?"

"I do not know," the Adaluin said. "Such things are rare enough, except in stories, that at times I believe people see what is not there. I have never heard of anyone who has seen the damned taken beyond the world into Norsunder."

"Yet we read about it, time and again. Especially in the Old Records. But then Norsunder was supposed to have been made and shifted beyond time and place by Old Sartorans. Who still wait there, so the records say."

The Adaluin agreed. He'd heard enough about those great and mysterious powers in his own youth—powers impossible to even the greatest mages now. He had, in truth, no interest in Norsunder, or in magical powers. His interest lay with his own experience. "Have you read about . . ." A slight hesitation, too slight for Tdor to really notice. "Ghosts?"

Tdor began, "Joret made them a study a year or so ago . . ." And then she stopped, for she did not want to trespass on another of the secrets she had learned so recently.

Hadand and Joret both had been quite earnest: *Do not tell the Adaluin or Iofre about how Joret once saw her Aunt Joret's ghost, on New Year's night, coming out of the fire.* How Joret had thought she was dreaming, for she'd been half asleep, and she'd been so small, but she could not have dreamed of her aunt saying "Treachery" in Marlovan when Joret hadn't even known the word in Iascan, much less Marlovan. *Treachery, treachery.* She'd said it three times, and then walked into the cold, dark night.

Tdor had only told Inda, who instead of being excited and deliciously scared had just shrugged. He had no interest in ghosts.

Now Tdor swallowed, and said, "I don't know much, except what Joret told me. About her project. She has a lot of projects, you see, Adaluin-Dal. Ghosts were one. She said that there are only a few people who can see what most humans cannot. If someone sees a ghost at all, it's because the ghost is tied to a place by violent death and violent emotion both. And those who see them share something with them. Like the experience, or a shared emotion, or sometimes shared blood. Then, some say that white kinthus will make some see ghosts where there are none, but of course we don't know if those are dream-images or actual ghosts."

"Yet kinthus makes one tell the truth," the Adaluin murmured, the shadows now hiding his eyes. "But it can kill."

"So I am told. At least, the Iofre said that people drinking white kinthus tell truth as they believe it. But you ought to ask Joret. Or Fareas-Iofre. They know more than I."

"Thank you, Tdor. So I shall. The Iofre says good things of you," he added. "You will be missed at Tenthen during your Name Day visit."

I only get three more after this one, Tdor thought, and didn't feel anything. She tried the idea that she was just tired, but she really knew, though it hurt a little to put it into words, that Tenthen was her real home. That except for her mother and Mouse, no one in Marth-Davan wanted her there. And now Mouse was gone.

The Adaluin moved away to talk to the captain, who waited respectfully on the other side of the fire.

Tdor sat yawning, and finally decided to climb into her bedroll, where she lay watching the fire and thinking. Presently Chelis returned, and rolled up into her blanket next to Tdor just as Tdor's thoughts were beginning to weave into dreams.

Tdor looked up, blinking tiredly. "About pleasure houses."

Chelis gave a muffled laugh, and then said with some asperity, "Did I not say you ought to ask the Iofre, Tdor-Edli?"

"Just tell me about the first time. They tell you what to do?"

"Yes. They tell you, and even show you if you want."

"Oh, well, then," Tdor murmured, relieved. Of course mating required lessons, just as did riding and writing and reading and anything else. So she needn't worry about it until the time came, and if she and Inda couldn't figure it out, they'd just go to the pleasure house and hire some lessons.

On that comforting thought she dropped into sleep, as across the low fires, the Adaluin paced back and forth along the edge of the campfire, staring out to sea.

Chapter Twelve

THE slow days gradually accumulated into a week, and then weeks, until the end of the month dawned on Tdor. By afternoon she was riding southward toward Tenthen under the green and silver banner of Choraed Elgaer.

Tdor was glad to leave Marth-Davan. Her father had never troubled to hide his disappointment that she had not been born a son. He blamed her that his lands would go to a nephew. Her mother, kind but distracted, had little time for her. Her big cousin's intended Jarlan ignored her as if she didn't exist, and Mouse's intended Randviar, jealous of her own rights, watched Tdor with an unfriendly eye, always anticipating presumption. She made it clear that Tdor's last visit to Marth-Davan couldn't be too soon.

Inda moved down the line at evening mess, getting his food and listening to the high-voiced chatter around him. This was the eve of the first all-academy war game of the season. Tomorrow morning they'd all ride out and camp in the field for days.

Everyone was excited. Inda hoped it would be fun, but he remembered some of Tanrid's stories about how the older boys captured scrubs of the opposing army right off so they had to do all the camp scut work. Whatever the commanding horsetails' grand strategy was, he and Dog-piss had decided over morning stable chores that their private strategy was to Not Get Caught.

Inda carried his tray to the scrub table and chose a new place to sit. He didn't care whose group sat where. He wanted to sound out some of the others on his Not Get Caught strategy.

Cherry-Stripe watched Inda sit between Lan and Mouse, of all people. Who would ever *want* to sit next to Mouse? The only thing he was good at was horses.

Cherry-Stripe felt dissatisfaction boil in his gut as he got his last item, a cup of hot honey-milk, and headed over to the end of the first scrub table, where his crowd always sat. Why couldn't he just go sit next to Inda? He reviewed the usual reasons: he was a leader, he had to set an example, his brother's orders. He had tried it once, accidentally on purpose. Mistake. Inda joked and talked with just about everyone, but that time he didn't laugh or talk. His face just looked distant. Wary. Like a scout in enemy territory. *That's right*, Cherry-Stripe thought, *he's the enemy*.

The enemy who always had the good ideas. Not just once or twice, but always. That was the only thing you could predict about him. He never showed any strut or frost, he never insisted on being riding captain when they were put in ridings. In fact, the two times Inda and Cherry-Stripe had been teamed, Inda had said, right away, "Of course you'll lead, Cherry-Stripe, but I hope you saw . . ." And he'd point out something Cherry-Stripe *hadn't* seen. It was all very well for Kepa and Smartlip and Biscuit to scoff, but they always lost. Then Smartlip would whine and lay blame, and Kepa would want to gang up and scrag some-one, but Cherry-Stripe knew the truth. They were pugs. Licks. Follow-ers. Inda was a leader.

While he brooded, the rest of his group thumped their trays down next to and across from him.

Behind them came big Cama Tya-Vayir, ignoring the older pigtails heading for their tables. Scrubs were supposed to be last and least, but pigtails got out of Cama's way.

Cherry-Stripe fought another hot surge of anger. He so wanted Cama as an ally. *No one* was stronger or fought as well, not Tuft, not even Flash, whose temper, changeable as a summer storm, made him the scrubs' hastiest scrapper.

Cama gave him a surly glare, then banged down his tray across from Mouse, who jumped, his thin shoulders hitching close to his ears. His small face flushed when he dropped his bread onto the table. Everyone saw his wince and compressed lips when he bent forward slightly to retrieve it.

Kepa chortled, a smug, mean sound.

Cherry-Stripe realized what must have happened but the urge to laugh vanished when Flash and Fij gave him sour looks and sat with their backs to him. Cherry-Stripe grimaced. He couldn't really say Flash was part of his gang. He sometimes joined the scrapping—he liked any excuse for a dust-up. But unlike Kepa, who seemed to really like everyone scragging a single victim, Flash hated scrags. He liked scraps and scraps only, loud with scorn if the numbers weren't fair.

Cherry-Stripe sidled a glance at Inda, who was busy talking to Lan, hands gesturing, while Sponge, across from him, listened.

Cherry-Stripe said to Kepa, "You and Smartlip scragged Mouse?"

Kepa smirked, and Smartlip sniggered.

Cama sent an angry look their way and leaned forward to say something to Inda. His voice was far too low to hear.

Tuft frowned. "Not the rules, scragging Mouse. Two on one. He wasn't even with Sponge."

"He was with him just after chores," Kepa protested, as if that explained everything.

"Teach 'em something," Smartlip said. He sniggered again, an irritating sound. "You shoulda heard him squeak. Eek! Eek!"

Biscuit Tlen smeared jam on his fifth bun. "But the rules—"

" 'Rules,' " Kepa sneered. "Are there rules in war? Don't we want to *win?*"

Win what? Cherry-Stripe thought, for the first time. Then he stared down into his tomato soup, appalled.

Noddy sent a quick glance down the table. Those in the middle, Dogpiss included, were mostly involved in a foot-shoving contest under the table, judging from their unnaturally still bodies, their sudden jerks, and their smothered laughter. At the other end, Cherry-Stripe glowered at his dishes, Tuft glowered at Kepa, and Biscuit looked at the pigtails as if he was sitting out on a field somewhere.

Cama said to Inda and Noddy, "Kepa needs a rein. Guard me?"

The "guarding" being to watch for beaks.

Inda stirred his soup around, then said, "Bad idea." Noddy and Sponge both noticed how people wanted Inda's approval of schemes.

"Good idea," Cama started, and as usual so hated the high squeak of his own voice—higher than Mouse's!—he shut up.

Noddy sighed. "Kepa broke the rules in jumping Mouse."

"Rules," Inda breathed, thinking how strange it was that even in covert warfare the beaks would punish them if they got caught breaking the rules. There were spoken and unspoken rules that were understood by everyone. Almost everyone.

He leaned back and glanced down at the end of the table. Cherry-Stripe's face was flushed as he said something to Kepa, who just laughed.

Cherry-Stripe understood rules. Kepa didn't. Smartlip didn't either, but he seemed uneasy at times, was always watching the others, and then reacting the way they reacted. Kepa would show a friendly face, his words were usually friendly, but they all could see the only time he showed his real feelings was when he scragged someone. Or watched a scrag. Or a beating. Cherry-Stripe loathed the way he licked his lips over and over.

Cama leaned forward, breaking Inda's thoughts. "Kepa wants his own war. Let him have it. Start with him." He crossed his arms, waiting for agreement.

Noddy, Lan, Mouse, Inda, and even Cama looked Sponge's way, but as usual Sponge looked down, mouth tight.

Inda said, "I know. I saw it comin'. When Kepa got Biscuit and Flash and the others to chase Noddy, after the shooting practice." He twiddled three fingers, meaning three days before. Sponge and Noddy had been dismissed early. "Look. We get worse, you know what will happen? They get worse. Where's it stop?"

At his end, Cherry-Stripe repeated, "Don't do it again."

Kepa just grinned. When Biscuit and Flash finished, Kepa followed them, whispering. All three looked back.

Cherry-Stripe sat there hating Smartlip's snicker, hating Kepa's grin, hating the fact that he was losing his command.

He did not see Cama get up and follow Kepa.

When Secondnight bells rang, Cherry-Stripe lurked under the archway to the horsetail pit. He peered across the new stones of their court, past the slanted wide bars of golden light from the long row of windows to those windows themselves.

Cherry-Stripe knew what would happen if any of the horsetails caught him even here, on the extreme edge of their turf, but he had to talk to Buck. He hoped the darkness, and the general liberty—customary the night before an overnight field game—would protect him until his brother emerged.

They had to come out. Surely they'd be going off to Daggers, or more likely (being horsetails, with more freedom) one of the town pleasure pits that the older boys called Heat Street. But all he heard was horsetail laughter and talk, their voices lower than boys' but not yet men's, and from one of the windows drifted the soft, sinister thump of a war drum.

The echo of Secondnight bells faded. A heavy hand clapped onto his shoulder and spun him around, leaving him gasping.

"Well, what have we here?" drawled one of the horsetails.

Not one of the Sier-Danas, either.

Cherry-Stripe backed up against the wall and gaped in dismay at not one but three assailants, teeth and eyes fire-lit by the torchlight from the castle walls, stable gear needing repair slung over their shoulders, hands still strapped in the steel-studded wrist-and-palm guards that were given as horsetail training began. Apprehension gripped his gut when he recognized the heavy face, the almost white hair of Horsebutt Tya-Vayir. Cama's Ain! He hoped they didn't bother learning who the individual scrubs were.

They knew who he was. But they were not going to let Cherry-Stripe know that. These three were second-year horsetails, and they remembered quite well last year when the Sierlaef and his gang had been mere ponies. And Horsebutt resented how the Sier-Danas strutted as if they ruled everyone, and how they had gotten their Tveis to bully the rest of the scrub pit.

Not that anything was said directly to the king's heir, who would one day rule. His strutting friends, that was different. So here was a tasty opportunity to get in an oblique strike at the Sier-Danas, maybe melt a little of their frost.

"Came to wash our floors?" A hand thumped into Cherry-Stripe's chest.

"Naw. He wants our stable chores." A shove, and Cherry-Stripe stumbled into the court. Now he was in their territory, and therefore their legal prey.

"What are you doing here, scrub?" Shove.

"Spying?"

"No, he wants a duel." *Smack!*

"A thrashing."

Back and forth they slapped him, their easy strength bringing tears of pain to Cherry-Stripe's eyes. They were still laughing when a voice from the doorway stopped them. "Scrub."

The Sierlaef.

The horsetails backed away from Cherry-Stripe, picked up their gear, and flowed around the Sierlaef, who stood unmoving in the doorway. They vanished inside, leaving the two alone.

Cherry-Stripe blinked, the light revealing his terrified face. He could not see the Sierlaef's expression, for he stood backlit in the door.

But the Sierlaef did not address him. He turned his head, motioned at someone. "Tvei," he said.

Buck appeared a moment later, dressed in his war coat, sashed, his boots polished. He stood there arms crossed, surveying Cherry-Stripe with no welcome in his countenance. The Sierlaef and the other four Sier-Danas filed past, the royal heir waving a hand around in a circle, meaning *Get rid of him and come along.* Their high-heeled cavalry-booted stride drummed down the stone alley toward the city gates: horsetails were silent as cats only when it suited them.

Buck cursed under his breath, grabbed his Tvei's tunic front, and hauled him back out of horsetail territory and into one of the adjacent passageways.

He thrust Cherry-Stripe against the wall so his head thocked against the mossy stone. "What?" His tone—*it had better be good*—promised trouble.

Cherry-Stripe swallowed and knuckled his eyes. "Kepa got jumped. Just now."

"And?"

"Bunked. Can't move."

Buck frowned. "Go on."

Cherry-Stripe went on rapidly. "It was Cama Tya-Vayir. Made him say he was a lick three times, then thrashed him. Bad."

Buck pursed his lips.

"Look, Buck, it's not working," Cherry-Stripe whispered in agony. "We done everything you said. We hit 'em when they're with Sponge, or try. But it's hard because when they're with him, it's in a group. A group that gets bigger, not smaller."

Buck waved that off. "That Kepa Kepri-Davan *is* a lick." Yet Kepa's Ain, a horsetail, was popular. Strange, that.

Cherry-Stripe almost retorted, *He's near all I have left to command— him and Smartlip.* "He does what I say. Likes to scrag."

"Does he like getting scragged?" Buck laughed. "What's Cama's work worth?"

"Bruised ribs, black eye, wrenched arm."

"Beaks?"

"We made sure Kepa told 'em he fell down the steps." Cherry-Stripe shrugged, his voice scornful. "He won't dare snitch. They know nothing. But he can't go on the game with us tomorrow; he's bunked three days."

His Tvei's easy dismissal of the masters was the ease of ignorance; Buck suspected the masters knew what was going on. As usual. That might explain some of the sudden, savage punishments, the arduous assignments that seemed to come out of nowhere, the gatings when one expected free time.

It had been a difficult month. In the past no one paid any attention to squabbles among scrubs. Buck had counted on that when he'd given his orders to his brother. It was different now because there were brothers here. That had to be it. At first it had been fun watching the brats busy scragging one another, on his orders, but since then there'd been trouble not just with the beaks but other horsetails.

Not just horsetails. Even pigtails, like Whipstick Noth. Sidelong glances *his* way, and even the Sierlaef's way.

Buck sighed. The truth was that it was all on account of the Sierlaef and his insistence his brother was a rabbit—when no one had reported any signs whatsoever of cowardice from Sponge. Nothing but his bad training, and who was responsible for that? No, no, no it was crazy to even *think* that.

While he brooded, with a lifetime of practice Cherry-Stripe successfully assessed his brother's mood; not violent, not yet.

So when his brother looked up, he went on. "They won't stop running with Sponge."

"Why not? Don't they see he's poison?"

"Somehow . . ." Cherry-Stripe's shoulders tightened, and he looked away. "Somehow it's become a matter of honor to stick it out."

"Honor," Buck repeated, frowning. "How did that happen? Has Sponge come on the strut? Giving orders?"

"No. He won't. He won't even captain a riding."

"So he is a rabbit, then?" That would make everything so much easier.

"No," Cherry-Stripe muttered. He, too, felt life would be easier if Sponge showed the least hint of cowardice or frost. "Everyone knows he tries the hardest, and he's learning."

"Landred, if *you've* done anything cowardly—"

"No, no, no," Cherry-Stripe said, hopping from one foot to the other in his desperation to make his brother understand before he struck. "We did everything you said and we're not *winning.* We're looking *stupid.*"

Buck's lip curled.

Cherry-Stripe went on quickly, "I think even Rattooth would be one of them if his Ain wasn't a Sier-Danas, for he's always sneaking off to talk to Sponge when he thinks I don't see. And he always has an excuse not to scrag."

"Talk to Sponge about what?"

"About *history*. Great battles. Rattooth knows the ballads best of any-one in the pit. He sings for Restday drums. He talks about the stories in the songs. Sponge reads all that stuff up there in the king's books."

"Hunh."

"And others are joining 'em, like I said. I hate it, Buck."

Buck shook his head. "Stop whining. Look, here's what matters. You know the Sierlaef wants me as Sierandael when he's king. If I get that, you'll be Jarl of Marlo-Vayir. You want to be Jarl?"

One nod.

"Then you have to fight for it. I'm tough, so I get to be Royal Shield Arm. You get to be tough, and you'll be Jarl. I'll sound the Sierlaef, but I told you what he wants right now."

Cherry-Stripe grimaced, searching for words. His brother poked him in the chest. "You said it's a matter of honor. If you haven't rabbited, then someone made it that way. Who leads 'em?"

"Inda," Cherry-Stripe said with conviction, and then looked puzzled. "That's another thing. He doesn't give any orders, they always just *listen* to him, want to know what he thinks—"

"Never mind. You know what the Sierlaef wants. Scrag Inda, then. And Cama. And Noddy as well, as he's Cama's riding mate. Don't just scrag 'em, bunk 'em."

Cherry-Stripe grimaced. Buck looked down into his brother's face, and saw reluctance and dismay, and wondered just what was going on in that scrub pit. Before this strange order that brought brothers to the academy, he'd been fighting mean, trained to thrash anyone who showed any hint of competition. The perfect future Randael to uphold the family honor.

Buck poked him again. "Clear strategy. They bunk one of you, bunk three of them. Cama, Inda, Noddy. All tonight. Make sure all are bunked before the game tomorrow. Got it?"

Cherry-Stripe gulped. "Yes." Talk was over, then and it was amazing that he'd gotten that much.

"I want to hear scrub squeaking and squealing about it at morning mess. I'll expect to hear it. Right?"

"Right." Cherry-Stripe wondered miserably who he'd get to carry out these orders.

"Then get out of here, and don't come back. Everyone knows you were here, and if there's trouble from it, you're the one who's going to feel it." Buck shoved his brother back toward the other side of the compound and strode rapidly off.

Chapter Thirteen

"**B**UT . . . I can't . . . breathe," Inda whispered.

Gentle fingers brushed hair away from Inda's closed eyelids, a furtive caress that brought his mother to mind so vividly and so suddenly that Inda sighed on his outgoing breath, "Mama."

Sponge winced. Inda seemed to be out of his mind. He tried again. "Inda. You must get to the east postern of the throne room. The archive is adjacent, and Hadand will be there. Do you hear? Hadand will be waiting for you, at Secondday bells."

A soft moan escaped Inda.

Sponge put his mouth close to Inda's ear. "Hadand. She will be there—I just saw her, for it was I the master sent to find the healer. It's the only way you can see her. We'll be on the road, no one here except Kepa, and you can sneak out."

Inda gave a single, brief nod.

"As for getting up—if they offer you kinthus, take it. It kills pain." He watched Inda for comprehension and reaction.

Inda, roused to awareness by the urgency in Sponge's whispering voice, felt his dreams dissipate in the running stream of pain, the effort that breathing took, in, out, in—not too much, not too deep, or he'd get that sharp stab of lightning.

"Did you hear me, Inda? Kinthus. Take it."

Another nod. Inda did not seem to know what kinthus was. Or he knew but did not care. After a month of precious moments of wide-ranging conversations, of shared laughter and effort, Sponge was certain that Inda did not care—if he even knew about white kinthus, which was the strongest painkiller, far stronger than green. So strong it was dangerous, for it killed pain by sundering the ties of body and mind instead of just masking them. Some minds, unmoored, did not find their way back.

Sponge, looking down at Inda, realized that Inda would not care that the herb removed not just pain but inhibition, that under its influence one talked, that secrets were impossible to keep. Inda did not appear to have secrets, at least not the dreary little secrets of betrayal, of ugly ambitions, of covert cruelties and weaknesses that could occasionally be glimpsed behind the bland masks of those in power or those who tried to gain power.

Sponge looked at Inda's profile against the weak predawn light and anguish stung his eyelids, for he knew that his own friendship was the direct cause of Inda's pain, yet he could not bear to give it up.

He touched Inda's forehead again, just the smallest touch, a wordless gesture of friendship, of sympathy, of kindness, apprehensive that he might be perceived to have crossed a personal boundary.

Inda said nothing, and so Sponge moved away and slipped back into his own bunk, to wait, eyes wide open as he listened to Inda's painful breathing until the wake-up bell.

Dust motes hung suspended in the air far above Inda, who stood, panting softly, just within the door to the vast throne room. The light slanted down from the tall windows on the east wall, splashed with startling vividness along some of the banners hanging below the windows, and painted squares of light on the smooth stone floor. The silence was profound, the moment so still that he seemed to drift in light-stippled eternity.

Those banners, motionless above him, he could just about name them all, and the battles at which they'd been borne. He could hear the war ballads in Marlovan, sung each New Year's Week to the beat of the war drums, and on Restdays that fell closest to each battle during the year. Beyond the rumble of drums and soaring voices he could hear other sounds in the distance: the thunder of hooves, the shouting of voices, the clashing of weapons, the wind moaning across the plains—

"Inda."

The gentle whisper sundered the vision and reformed the ties between spirit and flesh.

Inda looked up, mildly pleased to see his sister at last. She seemed taller. Brown eyes much like his own, the same square-cut chin he saw reflected in steel or glass, waving brown hair, though lighter in color, pulled back in the child's tail. Her eyes brimming, he saw in vague surprise, with tears that glittered with refracted light.

She took his hand, her own as rough as his, or nearly.

"Inda." Her voice trembled. "You're hurt."

He smiled. "The orderly wrapped me tight. So I can't turn sideways. The Healer said they can't reknit bone. Only bind it together with magic. And then bandages, to keep it in place." He winced slightly, paused to draw a slow breath. "Did you know the Old Sartorans used. To be able. To reknit broken bones?"

Hadand gazed down into her brother's face. His pupils were huge, his expression bemused. She considered what effect kinthus would have on him, other than bringing out the truth as he perceived it. He might remember this conversation all his life, or it might vanish like a dream. He couldn't be one of those rare visionaries that occasionally turned up in records, ones who hear others' thoughts, much less the one who sees beyond the veil of time. Not Inda, who Tdor said had shrugged off Joret's ghost with total disinterest. Straightforward Inda, truthful Inda. She could not endanger him further.

"Yes. Now, tell me what happened." Hadand dug her nails into her palms. *Be precise with those full of kinthus, or you will get their entire life history.* "Last night. To your ribs."

Inda whispered, "Cherry-Stripe's cousins and Smartlip. Cut out Cama and Noddy and me. Scragged us. All at once."

"Why?"

"I—I don't know. Cherry-Stripe didn't talk. I just stepped outside, and there he was. Punched me in the face. I couldn't see. Fell on the stones. Torches, all alight. People yelling. Tuft and Noddy wrestling. Then Smartlip—that's Lassad Tvei—kicked in my ribs. Laughing, like Branid at home . . ."

"What did they say? Anything?"

"I . . . it was all at once. *Think you're gonna run a riding, Prince Strut?* That was Smartlip. *That's enough, that's enough.* Cherry-Stripe said that, very loud. Smartlip left me alone. Then I heard Cama crying out *My eye, my eye!* And Cherry-Stripe yelling at Smartlip to stop."

"Damnation," Hadand whispered, sickened. She'd heard that a boy had been carried over to the Guard lazaretto, but not why.

"The rest all fades together," Inda murmured, his voice hoarsening. "Why couldn't I see you before? I mean. I know why I couldn't come. Why didn't you come. To see me?"

"We are all watched, not just you boys. I'd hoped I could sneak down to see you, or Sponge could bring you, but it just wasn't possible. I'm sorry, Inda," Hadand said, and kissed her brother. His brow was warm and clammy; when the kinthus wore off, he'd be in considerable pain. She must get him back before it did.

"Inda. *Listen.* Will you stay away from Sponge? You're a target only when you are with Sponge. It—it's his brother behind all this scragging. There's reasons why, but I will tell you later." *When you are not full of kinthus, and blabbing everything you hear and think.* "It is for you to choose to stay away from Sponge, because he won't send you away."

"No," Inda said. "And. Tell me now. Tdor said. Ask you. I'm asking. Why does the Sierlaef . . . hate Sponge?"

Hadand repressed a groan. What could she say? No, what *dare* she say?

She took his face gently in her hands, and pressed her forehead against his the way she'd seen Tdor and Inda do when they were upset and talking just to each other. "Listen. But never speak about it. It's because the Sierlaef cannot read. It's the same with Barend, too, though not quite as bad."

"What?" Inda tried to pull away, but she kept him in her grip.

"He cannot read. The healer once thought something might be wrong with his vision, but he can see a hawk on the wing as well, or better, than most of the men. But when he tries to parse the simplest writing he bleats like a sheep, much worse than he speaks."

"But Sponge?"

"Well, that part is my fault. I was learning my letters at four, like we all do, but it seemed natural to me to practice by teaching him even though he was only two. He got it so quick, and he was so interested. It never occurred to me not to teach him. We were always together, see, when the Sierlaef was training, so we shared my lessons. So when it came time for the tutor to teach him, he was already reading."

Reading and thinking, Ndara-Harandviar had said just the year before. *Reading and asking questions, and then beginning to check ancient history texts against the answers. My husband does not want a Sierandael who thinks, he wants one of brawn and no brain, one who will further tie powerful families to him in loyalty.*

Hadand did not dare voice that aloud, not now, when Inda was still full of kinthus. Maybe never, it was so very dangerous.

Inda, meanwhile, struggled for clear thought, though it felt like trying to see underwater. Everything was distorted, except for the dancing, lancing shafts of light. He had been about to say that tradition required the second royal son to be Sierandael, but throughout history it had not always been true. The exceptions had always been trouble between grown brothers. In this situation, the Sierlaef, still a boy, was getting his way because the adults let him. Why?

"Not enough," he murmured.

"Oh, yes it is," Hadand retorted. "You were not there, but I was, when Sponge was just barely five. And the Sierlaef was trying to parse a line, and Sponge offered to help him." She tried to force away the shocking memory: the little boy's generous nature, the guileless kindness behind his offer, the Sierlaef turning on him with a snarl and knocking him down, and kicking Sponge as the tutor, a herald, watched, horrified, not sure if he dared to interfere.

Hadand sighed. The Sierlaef had been ten then—huge and old and strong to the others so much younger, but now she could see how galling it had been to a ten-year-old boy who couldn't read to have his brother, just out of babyhood, already at ease with entire scrolls. She said shortly, "The beatings began then."

"But the . . ." Inda hesitated before saying "Sierandael."

Hadand recognized that calm, unshakable expression. Inda was kind, even biddable, except when he was convinced of what was right. Or he had questions about what was morally right. Then he was worse than Tanrid for rocklike endurance. "Listen," she said. "And obey."

He nodded, instantly obedient.

"Mama has told me, if—if you got into danger, you are to train in the Odni."

"The women's combat?" Inda said, looking bewildered.

"Yes. But you will not tell anyone, anyone at all. You are off your stable gating, right?"

"Yes. Two days, now."

"Good. So you have liberty before dawn, then."

"We can go . . . early to the baths."

"Then you'll be the cleanest boy in the scrubs. You are to come here to the throne room, Firstday, Thirdday, Sixday, before dawn. Never fail. My own arms mistress will train you."

"But the throne room. Is forbidden . . . except on royal orders."

"That's why it's so perfect a place," she responded, smiling with irony. She glanced over at the dais, empty now, except for the gold and crimson hawk banner of the Montrei-Vayirs, hanging above it. One day she would have to stand there with the Sierlaef by her side, and pledge him her loyalty . . .

"But how can it help?" came the dreamy whisper, with slow, careful breaths between phrases. "Tdor told me. The Odni trains you . . . to disarm."

Hadand said, "You learned that women traditionally defended the camp when the men were away. Or stepped between feuding men on their own side. But you don't really know what it *means*. Few do nowadays," she added, thinking of the Sierandael, commanding the Guard, the army, the academy.

But not the women.

She drew a deep breath. "In our history women killed wounded prisoners with mercy. Fast. You see? And when men did get within home borders, we used their strength against them. To strike once. Fast, and final. You're going to learn it, just to protect yourself. Promise me you will keep it secret."

"I promise."

"Then go back, and you are to sleep. And heal."

Inda smiled, and she shepherded him out into the fresh air and sunlight. She knew something of kinthus and its effects; she did not know if that strange focus in her brother's eyes as he looked up at those thrice-damned blood-smeared old flags was the borderland of vision or merely sleep, but she did not trust him in this vast room imbued as it was with centuries of passion.

Chapter Fourteen

WHEN the sun touched the western edge of the great plains, the academy halted to set up camp. Soon a signal arrow, followed by the rumble of horse hooves, sent birds flying skyward. The scrubs paused in their labors and peered eastward, descrying two outriders with streaming pennants of gold and crimson: the king!

Dogpiss whistled. Noddy turned to Sponge, who shrugged. Then their camp captain, Cassad Ain, strode over, smacking heads left and right. "Get busy! Those tents need to be taut, and the hay unloaded. Get moving!"

"He thinks we'll make him look bad," Rattooth remarked sourly to Basna as he glared back at his brother.

Basna snickered. "Like the king cares about camp setup." He rubbed the back of his head with resentful vigor; Cassad Ain had showed a lofty impartiality with his palm.

They were wrong, of course. The king, if he came at all, had a distressing habit of seeing exactly what he was looking for, and remembering it, though it might be weeks, or even months, before he said anything. And the masters knew it.

Awareness of the king's approach was signaled through the camp. While the pigtails and scrubs chattered and wondered, the masters noted that the king did not wear his splendid crimson and red House battle tunic, but wore gray just as they all did. That meant the king was officially not to be noticed, so at least they could continue setting up.

The relief at not having to drop everything and form up in ridings for parade was short in duration.

"Why is he here?" Rattooth whispered to Sponge as soon as his brother was busy yelling at boys dragging hay off wagons.

"To see how Tvei scrubs measure up to Ain scrubs, of course," Tuft muttered.

"You butt-brains sure took care of that," Dogpiss stated, his usual humor gone. "Inda and Cama bunked, as well as Kepa. We'll look soooooo good."

"Shitheads," Noddy snarled, glaring with cold hatred at Smartlip. His expression was far more shocking than the insult, for it was the first time he'd ever been anything but expressionless.

"Right."

"Soul-sucking shitheads."

Several thought of Cama's bleeding eye, and Inda with those kicked-in ribs, and scowled at Smartlip and Cherry-Stripe.

Sponge murmured, "Do our best. All of us. Can't let them think we're weak just because we're Tveis."

It was the first semblance of an order he'd ever given.

"Right." "All right." The agreement was different in tone, it drew them together into a superficial truce, all except for Smartlip, whose syco-phantic "Right, Sponge!" went ignored by all.

Cherry-Stripe didn't speak and avoided everyone's eyes.

They heard the approach of horse hooves, and felt the scrutiny of the royal gaze. They kept working, intensely aware that the king was sup-posed to be invisible unless he spoke to you.

No one could be less invisible. He rode slowly by, not pausing even when he saw his son, short red hair ruffling in the wind, slicing up the blocks of steamed rice wrapped in cabbage leaves. The king watched, for a moment, the small hands wielding the carving knife.

Then the royal attention moved on, and tension released its grip on the scrubs' necks, leaving them inclined to clown and snicker in an ef-fort to shed their surges of giddy relief.

The king rode by the pigtails and their horsetail commanders, some of whom paused and then at covert nudges and kicks self-consciously returned to checking saddles and gear. They were ready to ride the field and mark the perimeters with flags on lances, waiting only on the signal from the headmaster.

Brath observed the royal progress in between questioning glances at his peers. They just stared back, awaiting his order to disperse the boys. Gand alone seemed oblivious to the king and his outriders with their snapping flags.

"Go," Brath said to the boy serving as signal captain, who thrust a crimson flag into the air. The drummers rumbled the *ride out!* tattoo, and horns blasted quick rising notes of three.

The king wheeled his mare, who, nearly in heat, watched the young stallions. They kicked high, tails up, as they thundered by. The king bent, an absent hand smoothing the mare's neck.

Off they raced, boys and long narrow-flanked scout hounds and horses dashing through waving grasses, young animals all, strong and fast in their precise formations, hair flying, wind streaming over muscled bodies.

The Sierlaef flashed a hand up in salute, mocking the invisibility rule. You could do that if you were royal heir, of course, but maybe the king would shame him by not responding.

Up came the king's hand in salute, and the Sierlaef turned away, gratified—and then angry that he had cared at all.

As the boys galloped away to the designated battle perimeters, the king trotted back to the command post. He dismounted, the signal that he was now visible. Everyone in sight put right fist to heart.

"Master Brath," said the king.

"Sieraec-Dal." Brath's hairline was beaded with sweat.

"I count fewer first-year boys than I expected to see."

"Yes, Sieraec-Dal."

"Why is that?"

The royal eyes looked green in this light, the royal hair mostly gray but with enough red remaining to echo the crimson of the royal banner just behind him. Brath felt the urge to turn his gaze away, to seek support from his masters, but he knew that they would just peer back at him, trying to hide their dismay. Except for Gand, damn him, who was at the horse picket.

"Accidents," Brath said after a protracted pause.

Wind toyed with clothing, flags, hair, long plains grasses. They all smelled rain on the wind; camp would be wet by morning.

The king smiled. It was that same terrible smile his elder son some-times had, only colder, more deliberate. "My brother," he said, "will not like hearing about so much clumsiness."

Pause. Everyone reflected on the Sierandael, War Commander and head of the academy, and what he would and would not like.

The king went on, then, to other subjects—horses, mostly. His questions were specific. Gand, listening just within earshot as he continued his inspection, reflected on how revealing those questions were. The king was far more conversant with the details of the academy stable than Brath had realized.

Finally the king remounted, everyone saluted. He rode away.

Brath, blinded with relief, waved at the others to carry on.

Presently the delicious smell of rice-and-cabbage cakes sizzling in olive oil drifted eastward on the soft twilight breeze. Under the hazy night sky rose the noise of speculation, laughter, bragging. In shadowy corners were softer, angry mutters; Brath saw Horsebutt Tya-Vayir gazing with hatred at the Sierlaef and his Sier-Danas, there at the first fire. Brath shook his head and wandered along the edges of the golden circles cast by the row of campfires, listening to unguarded young voices, and exchanging glances with various masters.

He found Gand at the weapons tent, overseeing the cleaning and stowing of the gear that had been used on the scouting run.

Gand looked up, appraised the headmaster's face, and gestured to the darkness. "Carry on," he said to the watching pigtails, who bent sedulously over their work.

The two masters, veterans of years of barracks and camp life, knew exactly how far to walk to carry them out of earshot.

They had not spoken of personal matters since the day Gand had warned Brath to thrash the Sierlaef.

Brath winced, thinking over his own words: *I fail to see how a dishonorable misuse of my position of authority will solve today's trouble, much less that of a year.* Stupid, stupid. "Honor" was one of those words that ended communication. Gand had not spoken of anything but academy matters since, and they both knew it was Brath's duty to breach the barrier.

And so, "No doubt you heard what *he* said."

Gand turned his thumb up.

Brath resisted the urge to wipe his clammy palms on his tunic. Even out here, alone except for night birds and the chirring insects among the grasses, it was unsafe to say, "The Sierandael hates Evred-Varlaef worse than he hates the king's mate, Captain Sindan." They didn't know why, they just knew it was true. He said, by way of reconciliation, "I've had Kandoth and Nem land hard on the first-year horsetails during the past couple weeks."

But Gand just shook his grizzled head. "And they'll blame someone else, or else scout out ways to get around you. The damage is done. The boy now thinks he's above the rules."

Until this year *the boy* had only meant one boy: the Sierlaef. Now there was *the boy* and *the younger boy*.

"He's the heir," Brath whispered, bewildered. "He *is* above the rules."

Gand hesitated, knowing whatever he said would have repercussions that could cause more harm than good. There was so much they did not know about the relations between the royal family. But Gand had some guesses, which apparently were invisible to Brath. Brath had been picked by the Sierandael because he was obedient, because he was reliable with logistics, with all the outward details of the academy, not because he thought about the unseen.

Gand restrained himself. "I suggest a lot of field exercises, the farther away the better, and pick good storms to send 'em out in. Might steady the reins a little."

It wouldn't, but at least the Sier-Danas' absence would give the masters some breathing space.

Chapter Fifteen

THE healer came once an evening to check on Inda. During the day orderlies brought him food. Otherwise he was left alone to sleep. And since Cama was kept in the lazaretto on the Guard side, there was only Kepa, who either napped during the day or pretended to, if he thought Inda might be awake.

Kepa was asleep when Inda passed noiselessly by.

The last bell before dawn found Inda just outside the throne room, terrified that the Guard would discover him, that trespassing here was some sort of treason. He was alert to every sound, nevertheless he was startled by a flicker of movement that resolved into a stout woman with long gray robes over loose trousers and scouting moccasins. He jumped. His ribs twinged.

Hadand's arms mistress, a tall, strong older woman, put a hand under his elbow. "Come along within, young dal," she murmured in a gruff voice. "The pain will pass. And I will teach you how to breathe. Do this now: In through the nose, out through the lips. In-whish, out-whoosh."

Inda obeyed. This breathing just felt strange, didn't seem to help, though the nausea did fade, then vanished, leaving only the familiar twangs of pain across his chest whenever he moved.

"I don't think I can lift a knife," he admitted.

"You won't," was the reply, as they moved across the vast flagged ex-

panse of flooring. "Not for weeks. Longer. Until you learn to move." The
air smelled old in here, somehow. Old and cold, the flags overhead
ghostly in faint angles of fluttering orange light from torches outside the
high windows.

"Today you're just going to learn to fall," she whispered. "All week. You
learn to fall first. Then you learn how to move. Then how to block. All
before you ever hold a knife. And you have to learn how to hold a knife
before you fight with one. You men hold them like swords. Idiocy! Ignore
the ribs," she added. "In war, no one cares if you are ready and fit."

Falls. Inda thought about being knocked to the stone floor, and wondered if he'd live until dawn.

The arms mistress said wryly, "They have their own ways, in your
academy." A snort, then, in a different, brisk tone, "You men, you fall
hard. You expect to fall hard, except when you ride. With us, falling in
a fight uses the same principle. You want to make the motion work for
you, and against your opponent. Why help him by jarring your own
bones? So you will use your leg muscles, not your middle. We make the
little girls practice falling for an entire month . . ."

Using her strong hands, she showed Inda where to bend, how to
throw himself if attacked from the front or from the back, to use the
speed of the fall to propel himself up again. She first eased him down
slowly, and then had him do it himself, always keeping his middle
straight, using his legs and arms. Down, roll, up. Over and over, until his
middle was glowing with constant pain, and his legs felt like string.

Finally she said, "That is all for today. You must return. Rest. But
every time you rise, practice these falls. Again and again, until you fall
like water and rise like the grasses after the wind has gone."

His second lesson was much like the first. By then Kepa was pronounced
fit, and he was sent to the stables to tend foals. While Kepa was gone
Inda forced himself to practice, using the entire length of the scrub pit
between the rows of beds, falling and rolling until he was dizzy with
pain, but it did come easier by the third day. And his ribs were healing,
just enough for him to perceive a difference.

His third lesson, on the day the academy students returned, involved
more falling, this time sideways as well as forward and backward, plus

learning the arcs of blocks. Women blocked differently than men, Inda discovered. Men beat the opponent's sword back, women used the opponent's own speed to change the direction of the weapon while they applied their own blows elsewhere to change the opponent's balance. It was a new way of thinking about attacks, and he realized he was going to have to unlearn a lot of what he'd learned before he could use it. While still drilling in the old, familiar way.

He practiced the new movements every time he was alone.

Midway through the second week, he woke as usual, slipping out into heavy rain. The arms mistress ignored his sodden state and put him through the drills until he warmed from the inside.

On his way back lightning flared almost directly overhead and thunder caused the stone to reverberate. Rain hissed down in stinging needles, blinding him, and so he ran into Smartlip Lassad, who had been lying in wait just outside the barracks.

Smartlip was afraid of thunder and lightning, something he would never admit. It was this fear that woke him earlier and that now kept him close to the barracks, until at last he saw Inda stumbling through puddles back toward the pit.

Triumph, fear, and curiosity roiled inside him when Inda recoiled, his hands going to the ribs Smartlip had kicked that horrible day, after which everyone suddenly turned against him.

"Where were you?" Smartlip demanded.

Inda looked around wildly, then his eyes narrowed into suspicion, his face slick with rain, lit by the torch on the other side of the archway. "I'm not gated."

"We are only permitted the baths before dawn," Smartlip stated the obvious as an accusation. "And don't try to tell me you went to the baths." He jerked his thumb over his shoulder, in the opposite direction from which Inda had come. Excitement seeped past Smartlip's fear. Inda had a secret. Inda of all people.

"Who else knows we're up?" Inda asked.

" 'We.' Uh-uh, you don't drag me in," Smartlip retorted. "I only got up because I saw you leave, half the night ago."

"It wasn't half the night ago, it was only last-bell . . ." Inda realized he'd been trapped. He sighed.

Smartlip yearned to use Inda's secret to force him to run under his command. *Inda Algara-Vayir. That* would give him a weapon against those other turds! No one would even speak to him now unless they had to. Anger boiled in Smartlip's gut.

And while he was thinking, Inda watched. Smartlip spoke with all that bluster, but the way he was standing, it was like he expected someone to hit him. Inda was so surprised he felt his hatred ease a little.

"Can you keep a secret?" Inda asked.

Smartlip almost missed it, so busy was he with his own brooding. You think you are doing the right thing to be a leader, and what happens? Someone wisecracks, you make a better one, someone makes a fart joke, yours is funnier, they scrag, you scrag harder, but then they all suddenly just turn on you, like you're a turd lying there in the sun waiting for a wand. No one had spoken to him for days. Even Cherry-Stripe. *Especially* Cherry-Stripe, when *everything* was all his fault.

"Secret?" he repeated, hazily, his eyes first widening with hope, then narrowing in distrust. "What's your threat?"

He *was* afraid, Inda realized as he recognized at last what caused that furtive way of looking at people, that weird snigger that wasn't a real laugh. Smartlip Lassad, who had kicked in his ribs, who had kicked in Cama's eye, was afraid of them all!

Inda pressed the heels of his hands against his eyes, then looked up. "No threat. Look. The secret is yours to tell or not. I've been going to visit my sister, Hadand, who is going to marry the Sierlaef."

Smartlip gazed at Inda in disbelief. "So what's the threat?" he repeated for the third time.

Inda opened his hands. "Either you keep the secret, or you don't." He walked on by.

Smartlip stood where he was, feeling cheated, until a shock of blue-white lightning over the castle tower sent him inside.

Inda was changing slowly into his second smock and trousers, the sight of the bandages round his body a reminder that made Smartlip falter in his step. Neither of them spoke, not even when the bells rang, and tousled heads popped up from blankets up and down the room.

During morning chores, Smartlip watched Inda from afar. Inda, he realized, paid no attention to the scrub gag. If he had to talk, he did, including to Smartlip. He just did not talk much, not even to Sponge, probably because of those ribs.

At midday meal, Inda was sitting next to Cherry-Stripe, who gave Smartlip a sour face when he approached.

Angrily Smartlip marched past his accustomed corner, and thumped his tray down on Inda's other side, glaring around at the others. It was the bravest act of his life so far; fear mixed with the heat of anger, his heartbeat loud in his ears.

They all glared back. None of them knew what to do.

He didn't miss how most of them looked at Inda for clues, but Inda just went on eating like nothing had happened. So Smartlip picked up his spoon and pretended that nothing *had* happened, digging into the soup thick with onions, rice, carrots, and chicken, with a better appetite than he had had in days.

On Restday, the king summoned his heir to the midday meal.

The Sierlaef dressed in his crimson and gold House tunic, put on his embroidered sash and tucked his polished knife in at the correct angle, combed up his hair into its tail, and walked through the academy into the castle, where the sentries saluted him. He clattered past, ignoring them. Two more *years* of mucking about in the rain with little boys.

But he also knew how much his father liked tradition, and the tradition was to join the Guard at age twenty.

He was still brooding about that when he entered the residence wing. He stopped to pay his respects to his mother, hiding as usual in her rooms with all the strange furniture and frilly stuff. He knew his father would ask.

She put aside her letter writing. "How are you, my son?"

"I'm. Well. Mother," he said slowly; Iascan made his stammer worse. His gaze roamed over the girls the queen had chosen this year as attendants. Were there any pretty ones? Of late that question, so uninteresting in the past, had become increasingly pertinent, ever since he'd discovered stubble on his chin, and had to go to the healer for the beard spell. "Field run. Rain." He shaped his words to add that they'd begun taking the three-year-old horses out, but he could feel the flutter in his lips and at the back of his mouth that presaged the breaking up of his words into that hated sheep's bleat, and so he gritted his teeth and just stood there.

"Ah, good," she said, and patted his hand. "Carry my best to your brother, will you? I have not seen him since he was taken to your academy. I wish you would bring him to see me."

"Can't. Scrubs stay. In their pit." He forced the words out.

"Yes, so I am told. But my greeting? You will remember?"

"Yes, Mother." He touched his heart and withdrew down the hall to his father's private rooms.

They were in the study, before the fine tiled hearth extending out from the massive fireplace, each seated in one of the carved raptor-chairs at either end of the crimson and gold rug, his uncle dressed in war coat, riding trousers, and boots, his father in the long robe of the scholar, his feet in expensive soft leddas and silk indoor moccasins.

His uncle grinned, his father smiled. "Enter, son."

The Sierlaef struck his fist against his chest and grinned back at his uncle, so glad to have an ally.

Then he saw the third occupant of the room. Captain Sindan, who always wore plain Runner blue, gave him a grave salute.

The Sierlaef returned Captain Sindan's salute with a careless flick of his hand. No words were exchanged, the Sierlaef quiet from habit. The tall man with the gray-streaked black hair was too familiar a sight to evoke even a moment's brief interest. He'd been present in the Sierlaef's life since babyhood, a kind if somewhat remote figure whom all the royal children called Uncle Sindan. So too had the Sierlaef until the day his uncle considered him old enough to take him aside and say, *The Sindans are poor cousins to the Sindan-Ans, so he has little clan interest. But worse, far worse, he gave up a good command—a well-earned command—in the Guard just to be near your father. I can't respect anyone who gives up rank to be a mere Runner Captain, just for love.* That summed up Captain Sindan in the heir's eyes: no power, no rank, so worth only politeness.

"Welcome back, my boy," said the king in Iascan. Damnation! "Did you salute your mother?"

"Yes. S-said to greet Sponge."

"I trust you will carry out her wishes, then."

"How was your first field run as a horsetail?" Uncle Anderle-Sirandael asked. "Which side were you on?"

"Won," the Sierlaef said.

The Sierandael laughed. "Of course you did. Come, boy, I want details. Whom did you ride? How many prisoners did you bag?"

While the Sierandael coaxed answers from the stammering heir, he watched his own brother sitting next to the fire. As yet Tlennen hadn't mentioned having ridden out to view the exercise, a most surprising change of habit.

Anderle-Sierandael hated change of habit. To him, it meant nothing but danger. *Why* would anyone change habit, unless dissatisfied? His brother was in many ways a great king, managing councils and guilds and money matters, foreigners and their demands. It was the Sierandael's job to oversee the defense of the kingdom, and to his eye all was running as smoothly as trained four-year-olds on a straight road: the academy; the making of the heir into a future war king against the inevitable coming of the Venn; the Guard and the Jarls ordered to drill in preparation for that very same war; the focus quite properly with land and not with the sea, which no one but a madman could think a suitable field for war. How could anyone control anything on the sea?

The king had interrupted the academy portion of that smooth run with his presence, and without discussing it beforehand. That meant something was on his mind.

The Sierandael repressed a frown as the heir stuttered on in his account of the war game. All the while the Sierandael watched his brother, who listened without any change of expression. When the Sierandael got to the question he'd designated as his tactical shift, he turned to the king, saw Captain Sindan's watchful eyes, and forced himself to say in the same tone of jocularity that he'd used with the heir, "And so you rode out to watch 'em, eh, Red?"

The king spread his hands. "The Adrani envoy was ill and the Novid harbormaster canceled our meeting, as he had no news."

The Sierandael forced a laugh. "So the ships have not returned? And some think they can be relied on for defense!"

"So I have come to believe," the king murmured. "But I await the report of our captains. After all, this is the first cruise of our first fleet. And if all is well, it is your own son I wish to sail on the next cruise, a more venturesome cruise, to learn seaward command."

The Sierandael struck his fist against his heart. He knew Tlennen meant it well, so well that the Sierandael struggled to hide his distrust of ships and his contempt for his own son. Ships, dangerous and creaky, were not to be trusted—and Barend was better on them than on land, the noisome little rat, a magic-born rat of a Cassad without any vestige of Montrei-Vayir in his face or form.

"And so," the king continued, "as there was no ship captain or harbormaster to interview, and as it was a fine day, I betook myself to horse."

In other words, he was saying his visit to the war game was impulse. But in Anderle-Sierandael's experience, his royal brother never did anything on impulse.

The king discussed what he'd heard about the academy stables. When he was home the Sierandael had reports twice daily on every aspect of academy affairs (and when he was on maneuvers they were run to him once a week) but one did not interrupt a king, even when he was your brother.

At last the king finished, adding, "I also thought I might see for myself how Evred is fitting himself to barracks life."

"What did you find?" the Sierandael asked.

The Sierlaef grinned, thinking of Sponge's clumsiness.

"That he is obedient, willing, but badly trained, and apparently generally believed to be without much talent."

Exchange of looks between heir and uncle.

The king turned to his heir, who was so difficult to comprehend. "Is it not your duty, my son, to see that your brother will one day be fit to command the home defense?"

The Sierlaef looked his uncle's way, to be met with a faint shrug. Swallow, swallow, force the lips to shape words, the throat not to spasm: "Reads. Hates drill. Always in arch-ar-ar-*books.*" He snarled the last word.

"Perhaps, when the season is over, you might persuade him to attend to drill a little more, and history a little less?" the king responded, smiling at his son. When he turned back to his brother, his face smoothed to seriousness. "More surprising, far more, was the number of serious accidents among the other first-year boys. Very serious. During the recent month it seems few of them could even emerge from an ordinary building without falling down."

The Sierlaef scowled at the fire. The king knew! Who snitched?

The king said, "I am most concerned. Most concerned." He looked up. "I must write a letter to Jarend-Adaluin Algara-Vayir, but I do not know what to say."

The Sierlaef, indifferent to the Adaluin of Choraed Elgaer, sensed his uncle's wariness. His uncle had always spoken bitterly of the Algara-Vayirs, but he never knew why.

"You all will remember," the king continued, speaking in Marlovan now. The language of their ancestors, of war. "That twenty-five years ago we came to the rescue of Tenthen Castle—too late to save his family, but in time to kill the pirates who had lingered. It's a credit to our House that half the wing riding the borders of Darchelde made their famed all-night run south in little more than a day, for we honor our oaths."

Old history. The Sierlaef stirred impatiently, then saw his uncle's frown, his tight lips.

The king went on. "Less known, and for a reason, is why Jarend-Adaluin was away. It is assumed he was riding his lands, and he has never revealed his real mission. A loyal man." He paused to adjust one of the Fire Sticks, but on the periphery saw the quick glances, a third exchange, between his brother and his son. "A loyal man," he repeated, sitting back in his chair. "He was scouting a traitor under my direct orders, when the pirates attacked his home. So though the official histories hold that he is obliged to me, in fact the obligation goes the other way. He was doing my work, visiting Uncle Eveneth on my behalf, because my forces were spread too thin. Because of this decision of mine his family was killed."

Silence, except the crackling of the fire.

The Sierandael sensed danger—a lightning bolt out of a clear sky. "You never told me about Uncle Eveneth." *All I knew was that you'd sent a secret message to Jarend-Adaluin.*

"I was a new king then, as you will remember. I have not spoken about the difficulties of assuming the throne, the compromises between what I perceived as duty and as necessity; at the time I had to pretend there weren't any difficulties, and since then . . ." A shrug. "It became ancient history, suitable only for boring children in the archives." Now a smile. "You were away in the east, giving Stalgoreth a salutary show of power, do you remember? You had the rest of the Guard, outside of those we had designated to patrol Darchelde."

"Yes." The Sierandael's worry eased. He was not being blamed, then. He had been on the king's business, of course. He repressed a sigh. His brother, smart, loyal, an excellent heir and then an excellent king, was just so soul-rotting secretive! The only way to contend with that was to spy on your own, and make your own plans to avert ever being taken by surprise.

"Because you were away I did not tell you that Great-uncle Eveneth had been . . . courting the Montredavan-Ans."

Montredavan-Ans! Another danger, but an inherited one. The Sierandael acknowledged, and then dismissed them. Their sons stayed home, or went to sea, or to foreign lands, and his own hand-picked men, under the command of one of the king's most loyal captains, rode their borders year round. They could have no influence, no power, now.

Jened Sindan, watching all three, king, brother, and son, saw the indifference in the Sierlaef's flat gaze, relief in the Sierandael's change of color, and the nearly hidden regret narrowing the eyes of the king.

"But that is the past. To the present. I do not want to write to Jarend-Adaluin, to whom I have owed obligation for twenty-five years, that his boy has broken ribs from falling down stairs, any more than I like the prospect of sending a messenger to the Tya-Vayirs with the news that their prospective Shield Arm is now one-eyed. We will try to mitigate that, at royal expense."

"As is right," the Sierandael said, nodding several times.

"You have great authority among the boys, my son," the king said to the Sierlaef. "You have done exceedingly well. All your masters attest to it. The boys all look up to you."

The Sierlaef grinned. Well, finally! A little praise. For once. Tonight would be the night to ask to be transferred.

"Therefore I know that this request—no, I really must make it an order, but nothing you cannot easily compass, situated as you are. I want you to oversee those boys yourself. From a distance, of course—do not interfere with Master Gand or the others. Just . . . make certain they are safe. Your brother, and all the Tveis," the king said, rising. "I do not want to have to write any more letters about their lack of safety in my city, in my service. Especially when we have so recently broken with tradition, and brought these future Randaels here, something I do not wish the Jarls to have cause to regret. Are we agreed?"

"Yes, Father."

"Ah, good. Then let us go in to the midday meal. I know you will wish to enjoy some of your free time before the Restday drum."

As the sound of Lastday bells echoed through the stone streets, the Sierlaef passed back through the gate into the boys' world again, his strides long and angry. After a long, tedious meal, the Sierlaef made his request, just to hear his father deny him the right for early entrance to the Guards. Behind his back his uncle had spread his hands in sympathy, indicating *What else did you expect?* But the Sierlaef had thought that his father's strange, reminiscent mood might indicate a new mellowness, a willingness to listen, for once. Wrong.

The Sierlaef stalked his way to the scrub pit, heels thudding the stones like execution drums as he practiced words under his breath. He ducked through the doorway, the same beat-up, kicked doorway he'd run through seven years ago. The dark smudge was still on the wall above the door, from generations of boys leaping up to smack the top of the doorway, just to be doing it. Now he had only to stretch up his hand to touch it, not that he would. He was far too angry to be amused.

The inside was as stuffy as all the barracks were, but did not smell like sweat and gear oil as did those of the older boys. It smelled like dusty pups. They were busy doing typically stupid scrub things: cards, of course, and a bunch of them were trying to train three kittens to do tricks. Another group was racing beetles, and in high, excited voices they bet things like chores and extra foods. Stupid puppies!

When they saw him they all stilled. In another mood the Sierlaef would have laughed at those goggling faces.

But even that faint urge to smile burned to cinders when he saw his brother, who did not goggle or gape. He sat there on the floor with four others, his round face composed, looking startlingly like their father. He couldn't read that face any more than he could read that damned squiggly dogshit in the archive rooms. Sponge even had their father's red hair.

The Sierlaef marched up to him, looking magnificent to the startled scrubs in his scarlet and gold, his boots loud on the much-swept wooden floor. The other three boys playing cards scrambled away, some of them dropping their cards and markers, leaving Sponge alone on the floor.

The Sierlaef said the words he'd been practicing, and managed to get them out without a tremor. "Queen's greetings. Any more accidents. You tell me. King's orders."

Out he marched, boots scattering the debris of the boys' game. He had better things to do, like figuring out how to make the masters sweat, and sweat hard, and beg the king to send him to the Guard by summer.

Inda and Sponge did not catch a moment alone until two days later, when they were both moving hay from a wagon into a barn. "What's it mean, your brother coming in?" Inda asked. "Are we safe?"

"Only from Cherry-Stripe," Sponge whispered back, pointing with his chin in the direction of their pit.

"But he already mutinied against Buck. We all heard that."

They'd all heard Cherry-Stripe getting thrashed behind the barracks, when his brother had confronted him. They'd also heard Cherry-Stripe yelling, "I don't care! *You* do it. I won't! Go away, this is *our* pit!"

Sponge looked up. "I should say, you're now safe from any more scraggings on my brother's orders."

"Are we safe from your brother?"

"I think so. I think my father must have interfered. That should buy us the rest of this year without any more trouble than we'd normally get."

Inda pitched more hay. The familiar clean, good smells, the sounds, were barely discernible to him. He only felt the pull of unexpected muscles, residue of the new training. He also felt his healing ribs twinge.

He had promised Hadand he would keep his training secret, as well as the other secret, the one about why the Sierlaef hated his brother. As he looked at Sponge now, he wondered why Hadand wasn't training him, but then he remembered that this breach of the women's rules was on his mother's orders.

Before he'd come he would not have believed terrible things could happen, but since the night Smartlip had laughed as he booted in his ribs and then kicked in Cama's eye when he was already down, he'd begun to realize that the academy was no place of safety. Not for those who were close to those who angered those in power.

Inda thought back to that sudden appearance of the Sierlaef, his un-smiling face, the way he addressed Sponge as if he were a servant, the way he'd kicked apart their games. He remembered what Hadand had told him about the Sierlaef and his reading.

Sponge caused anger in those close to power.

So . . . he wouldn't tell Hadand.

Inda considered the matter from all angles, and found it good. Hadand would be protected by ignorance; Sponge, a prince, needed to learn to protect himself if his brother, for whatever reason, ordered any-one to attack him.

And so, for the very first time in his life, he broke a promise. "I think I know something that will help," he said. "We'll start with how to fall."

Chapter Sixteen

ONCE Inda started getting up extra early, it was easy enough to continue, especially when a quietly determined prince would waken him if he slept in.

Life settled into a routine. The older boys were kept on grueling field runs and extended drills—in preparation, the masters said, for the war with the Venn that everyone knew was coming. The scrubs, left alone, started enjoying life at the academy.

Except for Smartlip, who was still mostly an outcast, even after Cama (who'd begged and pleaded) was allowed back, wearing a black patch over his eye that looked so tough, so interesting, that half the boys would almost have surrendered an eye of their own to get to wear one as well. Inda sometimes addressed Smartlip, and so did Sponge, but no one besides Kepa spent any time with him—and that always in secret, when the others weren't watching. Smartlip, hating that, watched with resentment the way Kepa grinned and flattered everyone, especially Inda and Sponge and Cherry-Stripe, and only gossiped about scraggings and who got flogged with Smartlip when no one was around to see or hear.

Smartlip despised Kepa for that—and despised himself for listening to it—but it was better than no company at all.

And so the sun, unnoticed, tipped past its highest arc and slowly started dropping northward each day. Now the topic of conversation was the academy banner game, which was a week-long wargame in the field, the entire academy divided into two armies, competing to capture one another's flag, which could then be displayed outside a chosen barracks until the next spring.

After the banner game came the academy games at the end of the season, which was the chance for the academy boys and the girls in the Queen's Guard training to compete before the city and their families. The culmination of the games was a battle in the great parade ground between the older boys and girls over a construct erected solely for that purpose. The winners set it aflame and danced and sang and celebrated around the bonfire half the night.

The older boys redoubled their efforts in drill, thinking they could bully their little brothers into doing their chores to give them more time for practice. But the scrubs were nowhere to be found during free time—they had some secret or other.

Down in the pigtails' barracks, Whipstick Noth smiled to himself, but as usual he said nothing.

Far to the west, all along the coastal border existed a different sort of watchfulness. Not against the Venn, but against pirates. Everyone was afraid of pirates. Word of a bad attack somewhere in the southern seas whispered from harbor to harbor, and the rumors Standas had reported to Jarend-Adaluin months ago of a mysterious pirate ship with sails black as a starless night had spread.

The night before the games were to begin, at Tarual Harbor on the west coast of Iasca Leror, Barend-Dal Montrei-Vayir stepped onto his home soil after two long years at sea. The first thing he did was sniff the brisk autumnal air. During his four years as a ship's rat he'd discovered that ports, and the land immediately around them, looked more or less the same. It was the smell that differentiated them.

Mardgar's southern port smelled like olives. The Sartoran port at Yldes smelled of steeped leaf, though Barend was assured the plants were many days' ride away, on the mountainsides. He didn't care. The offshore winds there carried the aroma of green, summery steep-leaf, like nowhere else in the world.

Home smelled of sedge, grass, and spiced cabbage, a plains smell also unlike anything in the world. Barend sniffed as he walked up the quay, stumping at each step because land always threw a sailor's balance off until his body realized it didn't have to adjust to the heel and roll of a deck.

Then he looked around, seeing but not seeing the crowds of porters trundling goods to and from the various ships, the fishing fleet at the south end unloading the day's catch, sailors of various lands lounging along Port Street, the row of inns and pleasure pits of various sorts and prices.

He lifted his eyes to the sunlit hills behind Port Street and scanned the roads for the disturbance in traffic he dreaded. But instead of a crimson and gold banner-waving Honor Guard that would force its precedence over everyone, what emerged from the jumble of traffic were four riders with no banners, two of them in Runner blue, the other two in the gray-dyed woolen coats that Marlovan plainsmen had worn for uncounted generations.

His first impression—not a new one—was how short Marlovans were in comparison with most other people. It wasn't obvious when living among them. Or when the warriors rode. Or when they looked at you.

The realization, mixed with the relief of recognition, made Barend grin. None of his father's men came but Uncle Sindan had!

Barend did not yell or run. His first ten years of rough treatment by his father, and in the royal schoolroom by the Sierlaef, followed by four rough years at sea, had made him learn patience. Uncle Sindan would see him in a moment. For now Barend could watch as his two worlds mixed and separated, like the intersecting ripples of two rocks thrown into a stream.

People flowed around the four riders on their exquisite horses, animals so well trained that only flicks of their ears betrayed their awareness of the banging, bellowing noise of the harbor.

On shipboard, each time he was reposted, Barend earned his rating, low as it was, until he was finally accepted on his own merit. Now he felt himself drawn back into the invisible circles of power that propagated out from his father, the Sierandael, and from the king—those rocks in the stream again.

"Barend." Uncle Sindan greeted him, his rare smile making his long, lined face look a little younger.

"Hullo," Barend caroled. He recognized Ranet, his mother's favorite Runner, like Uncle Sindan wearing her blue tunic blank, without the crown over the heart. As for the two in gray, he thought he recognized his mother's armswoman, but the man he did not know. This man held down his hand for Barend's seabag, and pulled it up behind him.

"Come," Ranet said, reaching.

Barend took her hand and scrambled up awkwardly behind her, mostly tugged by the woman's strong arm. He always had to relearn riding when he came home.

Home. Barend felt his gut knot. When he was in far waters, he used to like to think of the cozy warm nursery rooms, drinking hot cider or chocolate and drawing endless pictures while farther down the table Sponge and Hadand sat reading, talking over what they read, and little Kialen listened, silent as always. Just the four of them, for he'd grown up knowing there would be no wife for the son of a Shield Arm, that he was basically a spare heir, and if something happened to Sponge, he'd have to marry Kialen and take his place.

Four of them together, long pleasant afternoons, warm afternoons. Even the Sierlaef didn't seem so bad when Barend was far away, shivering on watch during dark, bitter winter nights, because his memories would dwell on the days when they successfully hid from him, holing up somewhere—preferably with food snitched from the Sierlaef's own rooms—in warmth and comfort, as the bullying heir stamped by, bleating Sponge's name.

But now that he was on home ground, his desire to see his mother again, and Spongie and Hadand and even quiet little Kialen, was outstripped by dread of his father.

He wished suddenly that they were in Lindeth Harbor, at the northernmost limits of the kingdom. That would mean a long, quiet ride home. But Tarual Harbor was much farther south; home was only a week or so of hard riding to the southeast. *So think of the good things, then.*

No one spoke as the horses threaded through the crowds. It did not take long. Harbor mobs were like a long rope following the shape of the harbor, unlike a walled city, where they formed a circle or rectangle, becoming more knotted toward the middle.

Quite suddenly the businesses gave way to warehouses, their weatherworn wood sidelit by the westering sun. Those gave way to houses, most of them round, and the open road pointing up over the palisades toward the plains of Khani-Vayir, one of the westernmost, and largest, of the Jarl-holdings.

It wasn't until they had passed a long row of wagons rumbling harborward that Uncle Sindan looked over and said, "And how was your journey, young Dormouse? Two years!"

Barend wriggled on the saddle pad behind Ranet, delighted to hear his nickname again. Soon enough they'd cross some invisible line and Uncle Sindan would assume his wood face once again, addressing him as Barend-Dal. That meant the bad side of home: spies and Father's sudden, unearned beatings.

"Oh, it was mostly all right," Barend said.

He'd learned that nobody wanted to hear about splintered masts, or horrible storms and beating miserably westward against east-moving currents when no progress was made for one long month, or passing too near to a terrible sea battle between the powerful Chwahir and the even more powerful Venn. No one at home knew a thing about winds, or sails, or other lands, nor did they care. "Convoy duty is always the same, if there are no pirates. At the end of winter the winds were wrong in the straits, and we were months too late to make the big convoy out of the Sartor Sea, so we had to wait to come west. We were stuck at Ymar until the Venn and Chwahir finished their fighting."

"Ymar!" Ranet whistled. "Did you see any morvende? Are they really pale as bleached cotton? And bird-clawed?"

Barend said, "White hair, yes. Whiter than winter snow. Pale skin too. You can see their veins, which is kind of disgusting, but they don't let you see much skin, for they wear these robes of real thin material with lots of folds. But their fingers are like ours, just with long talons at the ends, kind of. They don't wear shoes, either."

"Did they sing?"

"Yes. It was a death wake for some ruler." Barend looked back in memory to Ymar's great harbor, gazing awestruck at the slow-walking figures with their drifting hair like bird down, the wide light eyes, and he heard again the beautiful antiphonal singing in running triplets, all plangent minor key, so beautiful it hurt his throat and made his chest ache. "The music was a little like the real old songs, the New Year songs, that some of the people in the south sing. Only better."

Ranet whistled again, this time appreciatively, then said, "It was the Queen of Ymar who died, was it not?"

Barend smothered a yawn. "I dunno. I don't know their lingo, and none of 'em use Dock Talk. But it touched off a war."

Sindan and Ranet exchanged glances. It was Ranet who—first wetting her dry lips—asked, "Did anyone say why the death wake was in the harbor, and not the royal city?"

"Nobody tells us rats anything." Barend gave a one-shoulder shrug. "And it's not as if it was someone we knew. I confess I was more worried about the inns being closed and that we wouldn't get a hot meal before it was back to rocks and gruff."

"I heard somewhere that they call ship's biscuit rocks. But gruff?" Ranet asked, smiling.

Barend's mind suddenly shifted, making him feel he was on deck again and the ship giving a sudden lee lurch. "The Guards call it slurry. Same sort o' thing, you know. Only potato, instead of rice. Cabbage, cheese, the same."

Uncle Sindan said, "The Venn did not give you trouble?"

Was there something funny about Uncle Sindan's voice? No, he was only looking at those people planting winter rye.

"Not us. Once they saw us sailing west, they cleared the straits—the sea battle part of the war was east of us. The Venn don't do anything if you obey, and don't carry forbidden cargos, and if you pay up," Barend said carelessly, watching some birds high overhead. The sea birds had given way to land birds now, but they still acted the same: the flights indicated a wind change nigh, and maybe rain out of the west. Ugh. If it was out of the west this time of year, that meant cold.

"So, hear any news when you landed?" Ranet asked.

Barend shrugged. "Lots of talk, of course. Too busy complaining about trade cuts. Any late convoys going east had to turn back—" A yawn caught him by surprise, a huge, gaping yawn that made his eyes water. "Sorry." He smiled. "My watch this week began before dawn, y'see, and we had to prep the ship against coming in. Captain said I was good overall, says that I ought to be posted as a mid into the *Talas*. Or maybe even the *Cassad*, since . . . you know." A whirl of the hand, indicating family influence. Another yawn took him. "It's all in the letter to m' father, he said," Barend added, pointing to his battered seabag behind the armsman.

"Full of praise?" Uncle Sindan asked. "May I read it?"

"I would say yes, except it's sealed." Barend saw Ranet and Uncle Sindan look at one another, one of those annoying adult sort of looks that
mean they could hardly wait until he was gone to talk—and he might
as well forget asking, because they'll just lie like rugs.

"Did you see the *Cassad* at all, then? Or our other two ships?" Uncle
Sindan asked, and Ranet looked sharply at him.

Barend shook his head. "Heard they were supposed to make landfall
at Novid or Lindeth, but you know what the winds are like. Well, you
don't know, I guess, but—" Another yawn.

Uncle Sindan laughed. "Sorry, Dormouse. I suspect you need food
and sleep, and no questions. We'll see to just that."

Barend sighed with gratitude. "Oh, good."

Uncle Sindan clucked softly and the horses increased their gait.
Barend daydreamed and dozed, noting with vague interest that they did
not take the road turnoff inland but kept to the south, along the coast,
though that was the longer way back home.

He didn't care. It was fine to ride like this, no watch bells, no rope's
end if he was caught napping . . .

Not long afterward they settled into a crossways inn, just before the rain
began tapping at the windows. The inn was old and plain and never used
by aristocrats. Jened Sindan knew it well, netting them a small but snug
pair of rooms up under the roof. While the armsman went down to the
common room to eat and listen, and the armswoman to the stable to see
to their animals and listen, Sindan and Ranet got a good, hot meal into
Barend.

For a time both stood there, looking fondly at the small, scrawny boy
who, despite his fourteen years seemed not to have grown much since
he was about eight. But then that was the way of Cassad descendants,
to be small, thin, with those distinctive broad foreheads and wide-set
eyes, the narrow, pointed chins, the short upper lip and prominent front
teeth. Barend did not look in the least like a Montrei-Vayir, but like his
mother, Ndara-Harandviar, wife to the Royal Shield Arm.

No one spoke while Barend ate with the concentration of a totally
exhausted boy—a familiar enough sight—and then they offered him a
bed, but he insisted on pulling his summer hammock from his seabag

and slinging it from clothes hooks in adjacent corners of the room. "I'll have to sleep in a bed soon enough," he said, rubbing his eyes. "Truth is, I sleep better aswing."

And it seemed he did. Within a few breaths he surprised them by going boneless, his breathing deep, his cheek pressed into the hammock in a way that looked uncomfortable, but apparently wasn't.

Sindan and Ranet turned to one another.

Sindan's loyalty was to the king, Ranet's to Ndara-Harandviar; they were allied in their concern for Barend.

He said, tentatively, "Shall you do it or shall I?"

The question betokened not just alliance, but a measure of trust. It admitted that Sindan tampered with messages—and also implied that he knew she was also as skilled.

She said with a slight grimace, "It ought to be me."

If there was reason to destroy the letter, he would not be lying if he said he had not touched it.

Ranet pulled the letter from the seabag and expertly slit the seal. She read swiftly through, and then held it up. "Just what the boy says. He will take no harm of it." She hesitated, then added, "And nothing about the missing ships."

Sindan scanned the neatly written letter, saw measured praise of the boy's industry and courage, a formal letter, just what was expected from a captain whose parents were Iascan shepherds to write to the powerful brother of a king. And, indeed, no word of the tiny Marlovan fleet.

Ranet skillfully remelted the underside of the seal and pressed it with delicate care back onto the refolded letter. When it had been replaced in the seabag, she turned to face Sindan, who frowned down at the floor, his gaze abstract.

"Jened?" There were probably four people in the world who used his first name. He looked up, and she continued, "Shall we turn inland on the morrow?"

Sindan said, "Why don't we ride south a day, and listen? Give Barend an easy journey, to rest. And then, after a pair of days, if there's no news, you return with him. The king ordered me to ride south to Algara-Vayir after Barend was safely met."

A delicate issue. Ships were kings' business, home defense women's. But Jened could understand Ndara-Harandviar's concern, since her son was supposed to join the fleet next time he was sent out.

Even more delicate: the method of conveying news back home. Ranet said nothing more, touched her heart, and withdrew to the room she was sharing with the armswoman. Once there she eased the bolt across the door, took from her pack a feather quill, a twist of darkberry ink, and a tiny roll of paper, which she smoothed out one-handed. A tricky business, but she was practiced. She dipped the quill, and wrote very swiftly in Old Sartoran: *B safe. No word of 3.*

Ranet rolled the paper into a tight little wick, and then pulled from her shirt a golden locket on a thin chain. She opened the locket, put the paper wick in it, closed the locket, and held it pressed between her palms.

She sat cross-legged, breathing deeply three times before she fixed the image of an identical locket, with the same three starliss flowers carved on its face, in her mind. Voicelessly she enunciated the words of transfer, felt her nose buzz and her bones tingle, held the image, held it, finished the last word—and sensed the inner snap of a successful transfer spell.

Drained and dizzy, she threw the feather into her pack, eased the bolt back, and then rolled gratefully into bed.

Chapter Seventeen

IN the royal city of Iasca Leror, Ndara-Harandviar felt the tap of magic transfer against her breastbone.

Queen Wisthia noticed the little buck-toothed Harandviar stiffen. The queen's slack-lidded gaze shifted to the muscular, dark-browed man standing next to the Harandviar. The Sierandael had noticed nothing. Though custom required them to be next to one another, he seldom looked his wife's way. Instead he spoke in a low murmur to the Guard and academy commanders on his other side, who stood stiffly in their House tunics, their gazes straying toward the king at the window, hands clasped behind him.

Wisthia hated the king's brother, who never talked about anything but war, or training for war, never feigning any other interest even for politeness' sake. Nor did he hide his scorn for her own tastes in music and art, but at least he kept his thoughts locked behind his sardonic expression, and never actually said anything. She had found over the years that if she pretended he was not in the room, she could bear his presence.

In contrast Wisthia liked his little wife, who obligingly oversaw the dreary details of castle defense training, the education of Runners, and all the similar repellent martial arts expected of a queen in this benighted land, but who seemed to enjoy the arts Wisthia had brought along with her—or she had the grace to pretend she did. Because of her indefatigable hard work all Wisthia had to do was preside at the summer academy games and the New Year Convocation of Clans, and yawn through the interminable ballads about glorious wars of the past—and sometimes she even managed to evade that.

The queen lifted her head and signed to her musicians to strike up a livelier melody. The flourish of sweet-sounding stringed instruments drew attention their way for a brief moment.

Ndara saw her husband's back turn, and her hand strayed to her bodice. The queen understood immediately: magic message, though she did not know from whom. It was she who had given the pair of lockets to Ndara, long ago when she'd first come as a bride. The lockets had been a fad at home, where magic was far easier to come by, meant for lovers who were parted and wished to send little tokens. Wisthia had not known then that Ndara had no lovers, would never have any lovers.

What she did have was some sort of communication web with quiet, impassive women, some in the castle, some in the great Houses, some who served. Wisthia did not react. It was Ndara's business, and she never troubled Wisthia with any of it.

The Sierandael frowned, his head turning—

"The children are late, it seems," Wisthia said to him.

Everyone, including the Sierandael, faced her way.

She beckoned to her lady in waiting. "Go find them, my dear."

The Sierandael's back was now to his wife.

Ndara-Harandviar felt a spurt of gratitude for the queen's action. Surely Wisthia had done it on purpose. The queen might refuse to learn anything about Marlovan customs, but she was an acute observer of human beings, Ndara had learned over the years.

She turned her shoulder and tried to slide a hand into her bodice. It was an act of madness. She knew she should wait. But, oh, two years, two long years she had not seen her son. Word had come that his ship had appeared at last; she had to know if he was safe—especially with the troubling dearth of news about the three Marlovan warships.

Her fingers trembled. The queen said something to the Sierandael, he was engaged in a polite reply, and so, using their conversation as protection she twitched out the locket, retrieved the paper, replaced the locket. Her fingers unrolled the wick. Then, holding her breath, she glanced down. Safe. Safe! She swallowed the rice paper, fighting against tears.

Wisthia watched covertly, thinking: Ah. Message indeed. Politics, no doubt. Her mother had said, before Wisthia made the long journey to royal exile in Iasca Leror, *Politics is another term for war with the mind.* She had added, *With us, political defeat means disgrace, for a time. With them—as with war—it means death.* Her father had said, *We made the marriage treaty to keep their warriors from crossing the border. They will treat you well enough if you do not meddle in their affairs.* He'd then added with wry-voiced meaning, *They will also leave us alone.*

Headmaster Brath cleared his throat. "Sierandael-Dal, what say you then to shifting the winter storage to the old stable? We haven't used it these three years . . ."

The Sierandael resumed his low-voiced conversation. Ndara looked bemused, her thin cheeks flushed.

"Rain comes," the king said, moving away from the dark window. "I trust it will not ruin the games."

Games. How odd, his tone. But Wisthia had long since given up comprehending her soft-spoken, distant spouse. It was enough that he was kind, that he had not required her to learn that barbaric tongue they spoke when they talked of war, or to ride for days in dirt and weather, smashing and clashing willow weapons, as poor Hadand would be forced to do on Fourthday, and then again on the day of the youths' great siege.

The maid returned with Hadand and Kialen, who saluted.

"Enter, girls," the king murmured. "Kialen, are you looking forward to this week's prospects?"

Kialen trembled when she saw so many eyes on her. But the king's voice was kind, and low, and she could talk to him without getting sick with fear. "Yes, Sieraec-Dal. This year we have permission to watch the new boys. I shall see Spo—Evred in the games, shall I not?"

Wisthia shifted her attention away from the little lisping voice in time to see Ndara brush three fingers downward against her skirt, and flick her thumb toward the window. Hadand's eyelids flickered to the side and back. Otherwise she did not move, or change her expression. What control the child had!

The king—what did he see?—went on, "Indeed you shall. But you must remember he is just finishing his first season, and I'm afraid he will not yet be participating in the gymkhana, or the sword or knife exercises. What you will see is the horseshoe competition, the relay race, and some target shooting. Perhaps you will enjoy that."

Wisthia turned her attention to Hadand's intelligent brown gaze in that still childish round face, then to frightened little Kialen at Hadand's shoulder, and felt her heart squeeze. These two she had helped Ndara to raise as daughters, and they had become dear to her.

The only demand she'd made in the marriage treaty had been that any daughter of hers would not be fostered out among these barbarian Marlovans at the age of two, but would remain with her. There had been no daughter. Instead she had two sons, first her beautiful Aldren—called in their barbaric tongue Sierlaef—who had by degrees been transformed from a sweet babe in her arms to a steel-muscled boy, almost a man, who looked at her with killing indifference. Then there was Evred, he of the beautiful soul, who at first she had not dared to love lest the same happen to him. Now it was too late.

She pushed aside the familiar ache, grown fainter with time.

Kialen's thin fingers fiddled with the ends of her flaxen braid as she looked up at the king. "Yes, Sieraec-Dal."

Wisthia saw her chief steward at the door to the dining chamber, and so she said, "Let us go in, then, shall we?"

And the king came to her, grave, courteous, holding out his arm. She placed her hand on his sleeve and led the way into the dining room. She loved that room. The king had permitted her to strip out those ugly war tapestries and cover the walls with silken hangings of pale yellow, the floors with fine woven rugs in yellow and deep blue, and banish those hideous Marlovan chairs, so heavy and martial with their strangely styled wings and raptor legs ending in claws. What she had were graceful goldenwood furnishings that looked like chairs and tables, not like hunting birds. A civilized room, which now smelled enticingly of chicken pie and mulled wine; in her own chambers, the manners obtaining in her own home prevailed. The wine was served in crystal flutes, not those ugly flat dishes with the square handles, and people ate with fine silver spoons, not those flat round ones, and they cut their food with thin dull knives. Those nasty curve-tipped Marlovan knives they cut and served and ate with were kept in their sashes, where she could ignore them. Once she had hoped to teach this nation of barbarians proper manners; now she suspected that, though those around her were polite enough to heed her wishes, as soon as she was gone, her eastern manners would be forgotten.

Wisthia sighed inwardly. Tomorrow would be far worse, being Restday, the day that most of the leaders of the great Houses who had sons and daughters here would arrive, and there would be the tedious banquet filled with Marlovan war chatter, and those interminable ballads in harrowing minor keys, accompanied by the ever present, sinister drums.

Then six days of supposedly friendly combat, but she had seen those boys breaking arms, she'd seen bleeding mouths and slashed flesh, and the hot-eyed smiles of challenge between the older boys and girls before the Sixthday siege. Her insides tightened, and she leaned over and said to Ndara, "My dear, with this sudden change in the weather I fear I am unwell. Will you preside in my place on the morrow?"

Ndara bowed her assent.

The king murmured concern, for which she thanked him. The Sierandael attempted to hide his disgust. Hadand, Kialen, and Ndara continued with their meal. No one was surprised. It had been the same for the past ten years.

Wisthia permitted herself to smile only when she was alone at last in her rooms, with her own ladies, with whom she could speak and write letters in her own tongue, and listen to the music of home, and thus spin away another year in the hope that some day, she might at last return.

The Royal Shield Arm accompanied his wife back to their wing, a rarity that she would gladly have forgone.

So would he. Pacing beside her, he looked down on her untidy hair, always slipping out of its comb, the flat front of her gown, the freckles and buck teeth, and he felt a surge of rage that had not diminished in fifteen years, ever since she finally consented to emerge from the nursery at age twenty, put off smocks for her first gown, and the night before their wedding, she faced him and said, *You will never come to my bed, or ask me to come to yours.*

For *her* to make such a demand! Her! Ugly, small, repulsive. How close he'd come to reaching for a knife, but he dare not touch her, not the daughter of the powerful Jarl of Cassad.

I want an heir, he'd said, blunt for blunt. There had not yet been a second child to the king and queen, and if there were, one could always hope it would be the girl the queen so desired.

I will take your hand, and we shall see if the Birth Spell works for us, she'd retorted. *If not, I will adopt any child you have by another woman. But there will be no one in my bed.*

Betrayal clawed at his vitals. The memory, fifteen years old, was still as fresh as a salted wound. Blow after blow, all pointless, undeserved: the mysterious Birth Magic had finally worked to give them a son, but instead of a big strong Montrei-Vayir boy, he was a rat-faced scrap of a Cassad. That blow was followed scarcely two years later by the queen's bearing of a second boy.

A boy who might as well have been born to heralds, who haunted the archives instead of the stables, who spoke his secrets to his father in Old Sartoran. How could anyone defend a kingdom with *that* as leader?

The Sierandael shook his head, hating it when memory jabbed him. He couldn't fix memory. And thinking about Tlennen and those scrolls and books was disloyal. Tlennen was a good king, and a good brother. But his second son should never have been born. Or should have been sent away to sea. Or something.

Well, he could not fix the past, but he could make plans for the future, and all for the good of the kingdom—that was the meaning of Sierandael.

His goal—his true meaning—always reassured him. He turned to face his wife. The only way he'd found to control her had been to force her to watch him beat senseless the puling, buck-toothed boy that they'd made by the mysterious magic that no one really understood, that came, or didn't come, as it willed. Or someone willed. No one could explain how the Birth Spell worked.

His mind, as always, shied away from the threat of the unknown, the unknowable. When they stopped outside the doors to their opposing rooms, he snapped, "The king and I will preside tomorrow. There is too much of import to discuss with the Jarls. Hadand can preside at the Sixthday banquet. The Jarls will like that. When Barend returns, he stays in the schoolroom. I don't want his sea habits embarrassing us before the Jarls."

They parted without any further words.

Chapter Eighteen

RAIN swept through the plains of Hesea all the next day, bringing mud-splashed cavalcades with sodden banners. The entire city was torch-lit that night, the streets full of armsmen and liveried servants amid the city folk, the castle full of clan leaders.

Missing from those leaders was the Adaluin of Choraed Elgaer.

Tanrid, prepping in the horsetail barracks, had received his father's Runner and the message of delay with philosophic stolidity. Seven years, he'd been competing at these games. It had come to matter little who watched and who did not.

But this year Inda was here.

The next morning, the games' first day, Tanrid was there when the scrubs marched out to the great parade ground adjacent to the Guard barracks. And so he was there to witness his brother's mirthful, chortling grin, that, in Tanrid's view, meant trouble.

The scrubs gamboled, smothering snickers, until they reached the gateway. Then they straightened up. As they marched out onto the beautifully swept stones, most of them scanned the stands that the guard had set up. Heh. Sparse, just as their brothers and cousins had warned them so loftily and derisively they would be.

Inda scanned the long picket line, set up the night before all along one wall, with tables of supplies, fodder, and tubs of water for the horses, who had been brought out at dawn, and now stood munching, shaking heads, or snoozing in the early sun, which was already warm.

Inda had said a month ago to the other scrubs in a night conference on the middle bunks, *No one will come to watch us anyway, and the few who do will come to laugh at the scrubs running about sabotaging one another. Who cares which riding wins? So let's spit in the eye of those strutting pugs who happen to be older than us, and beat the sand-glass instead of one another!*

Cherry-Stripe snickered under his breath as a smirking pigtail pointed out the waiting shoes and equipment, as if they'd never seen horses or gear before. Cherry-Stripe restrained the urge to give the offending pigtail the back of his hand. For a whole month they had practiced in secret—only old Olin knew, and he'd promised, cackling and slapping his thigh, not to tell.

The young Guardsman in charge of signals gave a blast on his polished brass horn, and the scrubs formed up in their line, growing mops of hair lifting in the wind, many of them with their shapeless gray tunics noticeably short at wrist and knee.

Inda watched the other boys bump up shoulder to shoulder. The surreptitious nudges and whispered mutters were those of shared conspiracy, and not of threat or anger. Joy made him giddy—it was going to work, he knew it was going to work.

Ra-ta-ta! Ra-ta-ta!

Master Brath motioned them into ridings. From behind the wall came muffled laughs of anticipation.

The scrub shoeing always provided vast amusement for the older boys who had once been down there, busily disrupting one another and fumbling in their anxious—and usually ineffective—efforts to get to the supplies first, fight off the other ridings, and get their horses shod, all before the sands poured through the glass. Horsetails drifted alongside the picket-fence and weapon racks. The scrubs heard their coarse guffaws.

In the stands were a few Guards with the same expectation, and some city people who liked the free entertainment, and some of the scrubs' family members who watched, out of either partisanship or appraisal.

Blat! the last trumpet rang off the castle walls above.

"Ready?" Inda breathed.

Twenty pairs of eyes stared straight ahead.

He whispered, "Begin."

And each boy leaped to his assigned post. The great bubble of laughter in Inda's chest expanded as his plan unfolded with startling effect. All those watching stared in amazement. And then the comments started.

"What's that?" Manther thumped Hawkeye in the arm and pointed. The two stood at the end of the picket line. Hawkeye had been looking inward, appraising the moods of the horses.

Hawkeye gave an impatient glance over his shoulder that swiftly altered to puzzlement. "What?"

"They're like bees," Cassad Ain murmured, rubbing his jaw as he watched his brother handing shoes off to Mouse Marth-Davan, who assessed each horse, spoke briefly, and sent feisty Flash Arveas running down the row, to be replaced by big, strong Tuft. Tuft! Waiting for orders from Mouse! "Bees," he said again. That was the closest he could come to that peculiar, utterly unexpected humming efficiency.

Behind them Olin and the older stable hands watched in delight, promising one another tankards of ale later. The competitions meant nothing to them. What did was the rapid, drilled skill with which the boys worked.

"They're taking direction from *Mouse?*" Buck asked, sounding outraged. The smallest, spindliest scrub. And the other boys obeyed! *All* of them—including his brother!

"Mouse knows horses. Gotta give him that," Tlen murmured, watching the little boy's rare assurance. "But he's not in command."

"No," Buck said, and he thought, *And neither is my rockhead of a brother.* He turned away with a sour face. Winter was going to be full of thrashings before he dared bring Cherry-Stripe back again. "Why?" he asked, feeling quite injured.

The Sierlaef's shadow fell over them, and the five looked up quickly. In answer he flicked up his hand, and showed them the back of it, the supreme insult. "To us."

The others made signs of agreement. Oh, that made sense. They'd been in the field for weeks, working on archery, and lances, and training the horses in maneuvers. But on each return, when they could even find the scrubs, those with brothers had sustained exhibitions of lingering mutinous resentment.

"Command?" the Sierlaef asked, narrowing his eyes.

No one spoke, but they saw at roughly the same time that Sponge was not directing this remarkable exercise, never before seen, as far as any of them knew, in the history of the academy. The second prince was busy with one horse, and never looked up, except to watch for hand signals from—

"It's Jarend's boy," the Sierandael exclaimed suddenly, up in the stands, next to the king, as he watched the sturdy brown-haired Algara-Vayir boy waggle a hand, whereupon the tall, weedy Ennath scrub at the other end of the line of horses ran to the Marth-Davan boy. He leaned forward, surprised and angry. That was not how the competition was to be run. He looked over, saw his brother nodding in approval.

"It's a remarkable feat," the king said.

The Sierandael knew he did not mean the fact that the horses were shoed, and neatly, at least three sand-glasses sooner than the best record. He meant command. That damn brat down there had somehow managed to turn all those boys' loyalties to him, even if the main motivation was typical boyish rebellion.

Tanrid was still silently laughing to himself later in the week. He, like the rest of the academy, had no trouble interpreting the scrubs' remarkable performance in the shoeing as a defiant back of the hand to the Sier-Danas. It didn't matter that Firstday's afternoon competitions had proceeded regularly, that the Tvei scrubs had performed well at archery and relay races, but those were so basic few had stayed to watch them, finding basics boring, whether skillfully performed or not. Nor had it mattered how well the fifteen year-old first-year girls had done, to their own disgust. The talk was all of the Tveis' shoeing.

The sky was bright as a polished steel bowl beyond the army of marching lambkin clouds, the air hot and still. Yet the stands were crammed with spectators. Tanrid rode to the parade ground with the rest of the horsetails his face impassive. His fingers checked the sweat-soaked wrist guards on each hand.

He'd ceased to care about the competitions years ago, ever since he'd realized the Sierandael always called against him. But today he couldn't let Inda's gesture, however silly, go unsaluted. Today, he would win, no matter what the calls.

Sitting in the stands, Hadand leaned forward, watching her older brother. Tanrid was uncommunicative at all times, but she, like Inda, had come to gauge his moods by how he carried himself.

He looked different today. She ignored the sun baking her scalp and her back in its sturdy riding tunic—she would go directly down to the court to join the girls for their competitions—and watched Tanrid. Instead of his usual hard-faced carelessness, there was a lift to his chin, a stillness in the way he rode his mount that reminded her of the fox poised to run, just before the dogs stream over the hill.

The horns blared, not just the two simple falls that called for the younger boys' competitions, but the interwoven triplets in four chords that tightened muscles, sent blood rushing, causing the older boys to sit tall on their saddlepads, bootheels jammed down in their stirrups. Many flashed casual glances over their shoulders at the girls who stood, or sat, equally still, watching.

When the last note died away, the Sierandael dropped the red pennant. Everyone paused now, watching for the red flutter to strike the ground—

"Hi-YAH! Yip! Yip! Yip!" They were off, ridings thundering from both ends of the court over sun-reflecting stones worn by nearly two hundred years of Marlovan riders in rigid competition. Dashing around the spiked obstacles toward the central straw-stuffed men, horses nearly nose to tail in a precise line, the spears thrown in precision.

They did not appear to perceive the danger of those obstacles over which horses had to leap or veer around, almost on their haunches, the targets were so narrow. A single miss from one of those spears would bury the steel point in the boy riding so close on the other side. Queen Wisthia, seeing the races for the first time as a young bride, had been sick with apprehension, her breath held, her guts cramping until the ridings had galloped past, the target buckling under the weight of the spears pincushioned all over it. She'd realized that this was not even the real competition, just the gymkhana. The howling audience regarded what happened as fun, as mere horse tricks! It was *expected* that they hit the target each time, with spear, bow and arrow, and knife as they rode past. Not to hit it culled a boy out of the riding, to hooting derision from people in the stands, children, townfolk, gray-haired oldsters.

Back and forth, back and forth they galloped, the horses' pretty tapered heads held high, their gait smooth, their glossy manes and tails streaming as the boys' hair streamed. The boys somersaulted on the horses' backs, and dropped down and up again, and then leaped from horse to horse, laughing at one another, or harshly shrilling the fox yip, the ancient war cry.

Hadand, watching, felt the trickle of sweat down her armpits, and not just from the heat. Horses picked up on moods, everyone knew that. Good the boys were, yet the eye was drawn to the loud thud of Tanrid's spear, always right in the heart, and the speed of his mare, so fast she flew like a hawk on the hunt.

The boys finished the last round, carrying streaming torches in each hand as the crowd howled and stamped their delight. Unnoticed, the noon sun blazed down on them all. Hadand began to surmise what the next phase would be like, and wavered between dread and anticipation.

But she was still outside the mood that gripped them all, still an observer, as the trumpets called the end of the gymkhana and the girls began to flow onto the field to the roar of the off duty females of the Guard and the women of the city. She was still an observer as the horsetails vanished to hand off their foaming, sweat-streaked mounts to the younger boys and dash water onto their heads and down their parched mouths as they readied themselves for the next phase, everyone's favorite phase, girls against boys.

In the beginning, it was just a weapons competition.

Hadand was the youngest of the girls. This was her first year as participant, watched by everyone because one day she would be queen. Despite the years of personal training, her attitude with the big girls had always been circumspection, cooperation, deference. *Listen*, her mother taught her. *You learn more being last than first*, Ndara had told her. *First will come soon enough, with all its responsibilities.*

But those inward voices stilled, replaced by pride and triumph as Tanrid, last off the court, looked back straight into his sister's eyes, mouth twisted in a faint smile of challenge.

I dare you to win, the thought came, through the shimmer of heat and the fine white dust the horses had kicked up, through the roar of approval from the watchers.

Done, she cried in her mind, even though he was now getting water poured on him by shouting boys, even though she knew such thoughts never got past the thin bone wall of her skull.

But there is a kind of call that echoes from spirit to spirit at such times, transmitted not in words, but in smiles and posture and in the meeting of eyes; she felt the impact of her answer in her brother, a rare moment of communication—of kinship—that surprised her. Maybe the only one they would ever share. *Make it good,* she called, and he called back, *Oh, we'll make it good.*

And so all caution fell away, all the distance of the trained observer who tries to plan ahead to avoid disaster, who defers to diplomatic necessity, even in games—skills her mother had taught her since she was very small. She was young, and strong, and the single thing she shared with Tanrid was the intensity of focus that could be terrifying to those who did not know them, yet thought they did.

The boys watched at first in careless amusement, then a shared wild joy as Tanrid won game after game in the boys' eliminations, and the girls watched with surprise (and some of the older ones, who were superb, gracefully deferred) as Hadand won game after game, beating girls older than she with her strong arm and steady eye and remorseless aim, until the rest of the boys and girls seemed to recede into the distance, leaving the two Algara-Vayir siblings in a smiling, challenging, duel of skill.

At the end of the afternoon the two Algara-Vayirs, each champion for their sex, faced one another alone for the last game. The sun had set, a smoldering ball of fire, on the distant walls, and torchlight cast its uneasy, ruddy glow over the parade court when the last target appeared, the painted man, the weapon the thin-bladed double-edged dagger that both men and women wore in bristling multiplicity during times of war.

The rhythmic stamping in the stands, the hands drumming war tattoos on fence and bench, the sight of the scrubs screaming themselves hoarse—Sponge and Inda among them—intoxicated Hadand with triumph, with the same recklessness that had goaded her brother to break his wall of indifference and strive to win.

And so she jammed the knives in her sash crosswise, turned her back, held her hands out, empty, palms up. Some of the girls gasped. They knew what was coming. The older girls only performed this sort of sport for themselves. But Hadand whirled around, both hands pulling the knives in a blur of speed and hurling them to thud in the heart of the target.

A shout of joy exploded skyward. In the stands, the king sent a mildly questioning look at his sister-in-law, but she did not see it. She stared down in horror.

The Sierandael saw her pop-eyed dismay, and thought, *She has no control over those girls.* Out loud he said, "A mockery."

Ndara heard, and clasped her hands, bone squeezing bone.

She could not answer, but the king could. "No," he said. "A display of skill. And the exuberance of youth."

Ndara looked up quickly, to meet his encouraging smile.

The Sierandael grunted. He was used to the boys' capers, and the masters had orders when the boys got out of hand. So girls cut capers as well! He'd never seen them, but then he only went over to witness their training twice a year. They were always strictly behaved, displaying drills in rigid formation.

From the shock in his wife's face, it was clear she had no idea what the girls were doing when she wasn't there supervising them.

He sat back, arms crossed, as down on the court Tanrid Algara-Vayir, now glistening with sweat, slammed two blades into his belt. He turned round, hands out, just like his sister, then his fingers nipped the blades from his waist and he threw them high, whirling over and over, glittering red-gold in the firelight, until he caught them by the sharp steel tips and sent them speeding to slam to the hilts in the target's head.

Again, the crowd shouted, a vast upwelling voice of might.

The Sierandael thought, *He must have taught his sister those tricks. Only why haven't I seen this from him before?*

Antics, for during war no one would do handsprings and then fling knives in a row down a target, nor would they toss them over their shoulders, but the audience indeed adored it. Even when the darkness, the flickering torchlight, the heat-scorched dizziness of which Tanrid and Hadand were as yet only subliminally aware, caused Hadand— younger, not as well practiced or as strong as her brother—to fling the knives more wildly, the audience no longer cared.

The king said, apparently in answer to Ndara's face of dismay, "It seems the people approve."

Tlennen would never trespass on his prerogatives. It was for his brother, the Royal Shield Arm, to choose to award the accolade or not. Anderle-Sierandael knew that despite the bravado, the flagrant disregard of strict rules the two had earned it, but he hesitated, not because of the flouted rules, but because he hated being taken by surprise. A Shield Arm could not afford to ever be taken by surprise. Ever.

The Sierandael looked down at the row of horsetails along the fence.

There, outlined in torchlight, sat the Sierlaef and his five friends, all of them cheering madly, even Hawkeye Yvana-Vayir, whose father, full of overweening ambition, would thrash Hawkeye bloody for not winning. The Sierlaef had never won, though the Sierandael had overseen his training himself. The boy was just as strong as the Algara-Vayir boy, just as fast, but after he'd passed his sixteenth year he seemed to have stopped caring about winning. Yet he was cheering now.

Then the Sierandael understood at last. The horsetails all cheered because Tanrid was one of them, and Hadand was the royal heir's intended, so it was a horsetail win and a royal win.

No, it was a *Marlovan* win.

He breathed slowly, his puzzlement, his distrust, the ever-present anger, all leached away, leaving him with a conviction of the rightness of his training, of his far-seeing policy.

It is a Marlovan win. If the Venn come to war, we will be the stronger. But it has to be on fields, not out on the sea.

He thrust his fist into the air, and even the Guard on watch added their deep voices to the great shout that sent birds scolding to the far end of the city. Weapons brandished, torches waved, and boys and girls ran out onto the court, swarming around the two in the center, who stood, their mouths sticky, laughter and joy and exhaustion turning their bones to water.

The Sierandael smiled, and the king smiled to see his brother's smile; Ndara watched Hadand through a mist of tears, and inside she wailed in fear, *Oh, daughter of my heart, what have you done?*

Chapter Nineteen

THE night of the scrub exhibition with the shoeing, Sindan sat alone at a tiny table overlooking the great harbor at Ala Voar, listening to a pair of newly returned sailors talking to some other mariners about a sea battle.

He felt the locket hanging against his chest thump as though an invisible finger had tapped it. He knew what caused it: a little puff of air through the tiny holes on top, the sudden shift in weight from the appearance of paper.

". . . so next thing we knew the Strait was full o' Chwahir roundhulls, and them light-lined Everoneth war-trysails, all headin' north-northeast, while the winds're followin' . . ."

Magic was a strange thing, Sindan thought, his attention divided between the sailor's words and the golden locket. A shame they couldn't find a way to transport people instead of little paper messages. He sipped at his fresh autumn brew and looked around the inn room. Mages in other places could transfer people. He'd learned that after the king had seen Ndara's gift from his bride, and had in secret had sent Sindan seeking more of them; the military advantage had been instantly clear.

He had also discovered on that trip the Marlovan reputation outside their own land. For a time it worsened the farther east he traveled.

Mages there might have been, but they vanished like mist until he crossed the Sartoran Sea and ventured to ancient Eidervaen itself, capital city of great Sartor, where the lockets were for sale to anyone who had enough gold, and where the words "Marlovan" and "Iascan" were nearly unknown. He'd had just enough gold for three of the lockets.

". . . one of those neat little Delfin cutters come racing down the strait, sky-sails flying, and reported enough smoke clouds drifting over the water to look like a storm coming."

The sailor's audience leaned forward. No one paid Sindan the least attention. Practiced after all these years, he hauled out the locket one-handed, removed the paper, and dropped the locket back inside his shirt.

It was not from the king, who held the first locket, but from Pavlan, Sindan's armsman, whom he had sent farther on so they could cover twice the territory in the given time.

Sindan felt his heart slam against his ribs as he read the cryptic message: *News of three.* The rest told him where to go.

He looked up, his gaze resting on the worn casement of the window, its frame carved with stylized wheat tips, an old Iascan decoration. His ears heard the sailor still going on with his account of the surprising sea-alliance between the Chwahir and the Everoneth, old enemies, bound together against the greater threat of the mighty Venn fleet; his mind considered logistics.

By midnight he was on the road.

Five horses a day run to lather, three meals total eaten on the road, and very little sleep brought Sindan to sunset Fourthday, while the royal city talked about the remarkable exhibition made by the future queen and her brother at the games.

The sun had just vanished into a mist moving slowly over the ocean toward the coast as Sindan rode down toward the third village above Rual Harbor, at the extreme western edge of Marlo-Vayir territory.

Exhaustion caused the light from emerging stars and gold lights in distant windows to blur ever so slightly as Sindan rode along an old trail. There, hanging from a tree, visible only from that trail, was a lantern in blue glass.

He clucked softly to the horse, which grunted up the hill to the copse. A pale blob of a face emerged and murmured, "Sindan."

"Pavlan. More news?"

"Come now. We might even have lost him already." Pavlan threw a wad of cloth to land across Sindan's saddlepad. "You will have to be an herb healer, or they will not let you in."

Pavlan, tall, thin, dark of hair and eyes, had grown up in this area, part of the reason why Sindan had sent him here.

Pavlan extinguished the lantern, relieved that Captain Sindan had been so fast, but sick with sorrow over what he would find. While they waited for their eyes to readjust to the darkness, Pavlan said, "This village is small, all Old Iascan, most folk in the sea trades. Fishers found a skiff drifting on the tides, and brought it in. Hesti is—was—on board the *Cassad*." Pavlan looked away, then continued in a quick, dispassionate voice, "Ship's boy. Thrown overboard with the fishing skiff before the ship sank, as far as we can make out. Been floating for days. Internal wounds. He is alive, but barely. He probably won't last the night." A faint ching of metal, and the third locket landed on Sindan's leg. "There's that."

Sindan dropped it round his neck to join his, then wrestled into the unfamiliar clothing made mostly of cotton instead of wool, loose instead of fitted, long and narrow. It would be uncomfortable for riding. The pale color was that of unbleached cotton, except for the spring-green dye edging the front lacings of the robe.

Just as he looked up, lightning flared out over the sea.

"That storm has held off for days," Pavlan said. "But it's coming now. We'd better hurry."

"I'll need a healer's satchel, will I not? Spell book?"

"I have all that waiting."

Sindan thrust his rolled-up tunic into a loop on his saddlepad and mounted up. The horses' ears flicked back and forth, and they sniffed the wind. They, too, smelled a storm about to break. But the ride was not long, and Pavlan was familiar with the old paths winding about the hills.

They dismounted at the top of a rise and led the mounts down a narrow trail between terraced gardens, the neat rows of vegetables briefly revealed in the flare of lightning out over the water. They could hear the surf booming and hissing below.

A small girl took the horses around the side of a cliff, toward what smelled like a byre for cows and chickens. Pavlan started down a narrow footpath to a round cottage, golden light glowing from its windows. Sindan followed in silence.

Pavlan sent a curious look over his shoulder before opening the door, which was, like all the doors in these old round sea cliff hugging houses, located on the east. Doors on the east. Just like their Venn ancestors, those who were now their enemies.

Pavlan's glance was easy enough to parse. Sindan's Runners, carefully chosen, were never asked for family details; in entering this house, he was crossing from the king's affairs into a private life. Hesti was obviously kin. Sindan, feeling a surge of compassion, hoped the child was not close kin.

Inside the single room a young woman waited, standing next to the clay fireplace in the center. Sindan cast a swift glance around, noting and dismissing the worn wooden furnishings, the brightly colored rugs on the stone floor, the ladder to the sleeping areas above. The woman wore an unbleached healer's robe with the spring-green stripe down the front lacings.

Her face was pale, drawn with repressed emotion. She said directly to Sindan, "I have been giving him the green kinthus. Now I will give him the white. Everyone is there: if he talks, they want to hear, for half the village youth had hired onto one or another of those ships."

Sindan said, "I understand."

"You are to be a master healer, summoned to help, though nothing will really help," she said, her voice trembling. "Hesti wants to die. Whenever I ask you a question, answer with yes."

She thrust a bag at him, and pushed past, opening the door. Sindan took the unfamiliar weight and shape of a healer's satchel, from which rose a faint whiff of some sweet herb, and followed the woman. Pavlan, silent, tight-lipped, fell in behind.

The first big spatters of rain stung the three as they wound down the steep pathway to a double cottage below.

The entire village appeared to be inside, all of them silent, gathered around a pallet laid next to the fireplace. Sindan repressed an inward wince when he saw the battered youth lying there, eyes sunken, mouth bleeding.

The villagers made way. With gentle fingers, the healer took the kettle from the slate atop the fireplace and poured steaming water into a red clay cup.

She looked up at the supposed master. "Is this the proper dose?" Sindan did not look away from the boy's face. "Yes."

In went a pinch of fresh-smelling herbs, with the faint, uncanny not-quite-smell that seemed to brush the back of the eyes from inside.

It was Sindan who supported Hesti in his strong, steady arms as the boy sipped, and his breathing eased, and he even smiled. Sindan wiped gently at the obscene crimson bubbles that leaked from the side of the boy's blue lips, but he did not speak. The healer spoke in a soft voice, asking questions, to which the boy responded in a restless, almost voiceless whisper.

"We sailed in a line, yes. We were to make fall at Novid. Some of us were to go on leave, before we sailed for Lindeth . . . but the lookout at dawn saw them just south of us, six sails all told, and they held the wind . . . captain said we could try to run, and if . . .they were larger, see. Fighting crew, sailing crew . . . we have to have both, captain said, but we could fight . . . no breakfast, the galley fires were doused . . ."

The account rambled as the boy's mind wandered from memory to memory, not just of the attack, but farther back, through good memories, mostly centering around his twin brother, who had been on one of the other ships. He tried to smile as he muttered about old pranks, secrets, plans for the future they shared.

The mother wept, trying to be soundless, but her harsh breathing formed a counterpoint to the inexpertly guided rambles. Still, Sindan, who knew the intricacies of interrogation, did not speak, not even when it became clear that the binding between spirit and flesh was on the verge of becoming severed—not even the magic spells in the healer's book lying useless at Sindan's side could reknit it. The boy smiled, for in his sightless eyes his brother beckoned, unseen by those still dwelling on this side of the boundless divide.

Custom is quite clear on the subject of healers and kinthus: what is said by the sufferer must never be repeated. There was no conflict here. The boy's memories were those of a youth, and would remain locked in the hearts of the silent family.

What Sindan could take away, and did, he wrote to the king by the light of a candle in the cow byre, and closed into his locket, as rain drummed on the roof:

All three warships were sunk, the crews taken or killed outright.

Chapter Twenty

THE last bell before dawn rang, muffled by the roar of rain. Inda found his sister in the throne room instead of the arms mistress. He exclaimed in delight, "Hadand! But—my lesson?"

"She can't come," Hadand whispered, her breath frosting in the air. The bite of winter was near. "Other duty. Too many people in the castle. Oh, Inda, I am going to command the defense today. Me!"

He said in surprise, "I thought the older girls did that."

"They all gave me the thumbs-up last night. Everyone. It wasn't me who suggested it, I wouldn't dare, because I'm too young. I never even had a drill command. Not until next year."

Inda rubbed his hands up and down his arms. "I wish we could find Tanrid. Get some hints on the boys' old tactics."

"We." Impulsively Hadand hugged her brother. "We." As always, anyone's problem was his problem. "It's all right," she said. And, added proudly, "I never went to bed last night. I was in the archive all night, looking through the records for tactics on defense against enemies storming walls, because the boys always seem to storm, from what I've seen in the last few games. So I drew out a map, and planned where every girl will stand, and what she will do. When we go down to get in place, I won't dither, don't you worry."

Inda, thinking of his own games at home, grinned. "It's after that you have to worry about. If the horsetails are half as smart as Joret and Tdor."

She heard distant footsteps. "Look, Inda, sweet, I have to go, and you too. The castle is too full. If I don't see you before you leave, promise me you'll continue your lessons at home. And here again in the spring."

The urgency in her voice made him nod fervently, feeling a wash of homesickness and excitement both. He would miss Hadand, and even more he'd miss Sponge, and Dogpiss, and Noddy, and the others. But he'd see Tdor, he'd be home!

A swift, warm kiss pressed against his forehead, and he reached for his sister, felt her solid body against his, then she was gone, flitting along the hall. He made out her smock in the weak light from the high eastern windows, then he ran back to the barracks.

Hadand continued on upstairs, hesitating outside of Ndara-Harandviar's rooms. She knew her aunt was awake, and busy.

Hadand pressed against the wall, fingers running back and forth along the painted head of a stooping hawk, dark gray against lighter gray, as she wrestled with the rare conflict between pride and doubt. It seemed a pretense, to be commander, when she stood here in the cold, empty hall of Sponge's ancestors and thought about it. But she did know what to do, she did, she *did*. That careful map upstairs was proof.

Yet she knew Ndara would be concerned about what the Sierandael would think, about a hundred ways for possible disaster. Just once, Hadand decided, just once she would not worry about disaster.

Therefore the best use of her time would be to eat a good breakfast, and then visit the girls, and make sure each one knew her place for the coming attack. A strong Gunvaer must sound assured and be ready to lead with self-assurance and conviction.

Rain slashed indiscriminately at faces, bodies, and drummed on the wooden ramparts dismantled from the Guard practice fields and brought to the great parade court by an army of sweating servants the day before. Lightning flashed. Thunder rumbled, almost drowning the trumpet call that released the waiting horsetails.

While the horsetails splashed across the flagged court, Hadand took a moment to draw in a slow breath of anticipation, and look around her.

The wall, built roughly in a U shape, bristled with girls standing at the ready, willow knives in their sashes and hidden up their sleeves. A few of the older ones exchanged speculative comments about the senior boys.

Then the boys arrived. Out came the makeshift ladders, as expected. Rickety ladders, barely able to hold them. The boys gave cadenced shouts and raised the ladders, one to the middle of each wall, just as Hadand had predicted, and she repressed a grin of expectation.

The mass of boys pressed together, their faces upturned, as a few boys began laboriously crawling up those ladders. Hadand waited, jittery, feeling the weight of the girls' expectant gazes. *Don't push the ladders down until the boys almost reach the top. Wait for my signal*, she'd said.

When the first group nearly reached the third rung from the top, she whistled sharply, and the girls sprang into action. The ladders began to fall back, the boys on them jumping to safety. Hadand glanced at the girls hiding behind trapdoors and false windows where she'd predicted the ladders would be set up.

She whistled again. The girls streamed out below to attack the boys dealing with the falling ladders.

But as soon as her girls emerged, yelling shrill insults, someone among the boys kekked like a hawk about to stoop, and the crowd of boys who had been waiting in front of the wooden wall produced two hidden ladders! Big, sturdy ladders!

The ladders were hustled one to each outer wall, while the main portion of the girls were concentrated in the center!

The boys streaming upward, Hadand screaming "Wait! Wait!"

Some of the girls looked her way, but all she was doing was waving her hands and yelling "Wait!" so they threw themselves at the boys already topping those two big ladders onto the rampart wall, yelling, laughing, exchanging mock blows and insults.

Hadand saw her defense splinter with those feint ladders, and listened in despair to the yips and crows of triumph as two wings of boys swarmed up, unimpeded. In two heartbeats her well-organized defense disintegrated into a brawling, laughing melee.

At least, Hadand thought as rain beat down on her face, *no one can see me weep.*

Then she had no time to think as scrambling boys began chasing the girls in order to get prisoner points. They chased all except her. The big boys dodged around her as if she were invisible. She turned around and around, dismay and humiliation thick in her throat as she helplessly watched the chases and scuffles, heard curses, grunts, and sometimes laughter.

Without warning a hand seized her shoulder and she began to protest, but found herself flung facedown and her arms wrenched behind her. A knee thumped across the back of her legs. Her chin ground into the wood, lightning-bolts of pain shot up her arms into her eyeballs, and all she could hear was breathing above her, and despite the rain she sniffed the wet-dog scent of sodden wool, the sharp odor of boy sweat.

Boots appeared near her face. Knees appeared next as the boots' owner crouched down. Two big hands clapped onto the knees. She craned her neck to peer up sideways. There was Manther Jaya-Vayir, her own cousin. His long horsetail, hanging over his shoulder, dripped rain onto her face. "Yield?" He was grinning!

She grunted, and the hands holding her wrists let go. Someone grabbed the scruff of her tunic, catching some of her hair, and hauled her one-handed to her feet. She looked up into a rain-slick face: the Sierlaef. No one else would touch her.

"Bad job," he said, as around them the boys called, with hoots of derision, "She yielded!"

And the girls made noises of resignation, disappointment, and even a few mutters; to one of them she heard Cassad Ain say, in no low voice, "Well, what do you expect? She's just a baby. You were idiots to put her in command."

And the senior girl's indifferent answer, "Wasn't my idea."

Hadand's eyes stung. It wasn't? But just last night, the older girls had all smiled at her, praised her, and it was they, not she, who had brought up the idea of her commanding the siege. They'd all seemed to want her.

Then she remembered Honeytongue Ola-Vayir's extra-sweet voice, "Oh, Hadand, you are *so* clever, *you* should be in command tomorrow!"

Hadand winced. Of course Honeytongue had been making fun of her. But Hadand hadn't seen it then. She gripped her elbows, facing the truth: She hadn't wanted to see it, even though she knew Honeytongue hated her, even though she knew Honeytongue's compliments were always false, though there had been nothing false about the genuine cheer from the younger girls.

Maybe that was why Honeytongue had fawned over her so. *She knew*

I'd fail. I should have seen it, I should have stopped it, Hadand realized, wincing.

Yes, she had seen what she wanted to see, despite all Ndara's and Mother's warnings about flatterers and how easy it was to believe them.

She stifled a sob, crossing her arms tightly to hide the shuddering of her chest. The tears kept coming as the boys all separated off to the academy side and the girls to the Guard side of the castle, past the stands that had begun emptying as soon as she lost control of the exercise. The rain wouldn't have stopped them from watching if it had been a good siege. She'd sat up there with them, year after year, ever since she was little, in all kinds of weather, and had watched the crowds packed on the benches, yelling.

She wanted to be alone, but that wasn't possible. She had to endure the well-meant reassurances of the oldest girls as she passed through the barracks on her way to the baths. There she had to endure the gazes of the younger girls she'd been jumped over in this disastrous command, the glances of contempt, compassion and sympathy just as awful as derision, and, worst of all, the false, sweet, gloating words of pity from Honeytongue Ola-Vayir, and pretend she did not care, that it was just another game.

Pride steadied her just enough to enable her to dress in her House tunic of green and silver.

Her personal Runner Tesar appeared just before she was ready, saying nothing, but holding out a ceramic cup that steamed faintly. Hadand took it, smelling the grass-bitter scent of a willow decoction. She drank it all down, ignoring the sting on throat and tongue.

"Kialen?" she whispered, through aching throat.

"In her room," Tesar said.

They both knew Hadand would talk it all out with Tesar later, when the pain eased. Now Tesar knew, without sign or speech, that Hadand would want her to sit with Kialen until Hadand could come and coax her out. Kialen, so easily terrified, could not bear seeing Hadand upset.

Tesar took the cup and vanished noiselessly.

The worst aches had begun to fade by the time Hadand reached the great dining hall. She stood straight-backed, head high, to salute each father, uncle, son, or daughter who entered, the young people all seniors of the great Houses who had completed their last year of training.

They walked in rank order down both sides of the table, each dressed in the splendid old-fashioned battle tunics adopted from the Iascans for use in formal ceremonies, the devices raptors and running beasts for old Marlovan Houses, some with the addition of stylized plants that they had taken from the Iascans along with their castles. Ndara stood at her right, wearing Montrei-Vayir crimson and gold, smiling in welcome.

Shame also sharpens the ears. As the line passed by Hadand heard the Sierandael mutter to Ndara, "Why did you let her command the siege defense? You are made to look like a fool."

"The girls won year before last," was the tranquil reply, as if it didn't matter, as if this were just another game.

Hadand watched the Sierandael grunt a nonanswer and proceed to his place at the right of the king.

Hadand's eyes burned again. She had to raise them to the banners hanging overhead to remind herself that time passes, and so does pain, and she must not disgrace herself with weakness. What hurt now was the faint pleasure in her aunt's face, as though she were actually pleased at the Sierandael's scorn.

Ndara was indeed pleased. She looked with compassion on Hadand's barely concealed misery, but refrained from speech—she would give the child time to regain her composure. What was far more important to Ndara was that the Royal Shield Arm had seen what he wanted to see, what he expected to see. He would assume Hadand's knife exhibition was mere trickery, and forget it.

The Sierandael smiled as the king entered at last, with the newly arrived Jarend-Adaluin at his side. The long habit of resentment pricked at the Sierandael as he surveyed the tall, gray-haired prince who looked so old and tired. He was sixty at least, for he'd had several years on the king, back in their academy days. Old, and could fall in battle against the brigands and pirates he rode restlessly in search of most of the year's fighting season. The new Adaluin would be Tanrid, who was now under Anderle-Sierandael's hands and who had surprised them all the other day during the games.

I pride myself on being far-sighted, the Sierandael thought. *But I have not been far-sighted enough.*

The king and Jarend-Adaluin both came to Hadand, for with the queen absent the table was hers. She laid her hand to her chest, doing her best to smile. Even if her father hadn't arrived in time to see her disgrace, he'd hear about it.

Ndara winced inwardly at the forlorn smile the child tried to summon, but noted that Hadand's chin was high, and her lower eyelids, though rimmed with the gleam of unshed tears, did not puddle. She nearly had herself under control.

Jarend-Adaluin stooped to kiss his daughter's brow. He smelled of wet wool and grass and horse—newly arrived indeed. He took his place behind the chair at the king's left as the king passed behind Hadand. He cupped his palm and gave her cheek a brief caress, and her eyes stung again, but just for a moment. The wordless gesture of sympathy buoyed her. He was not angry, or disgusted, by her failure today.

The king sat. Everyone sat. Servants came forward to pour wine. Since Queen Wisthia was not there they used the shallow Marlovan dishes, and their knives for cutting food, although they no longer sat on pillows, but at tables, on big chairs with high enough backs to make attack from behind difficult. Sweet wine gurgled into the wide, flat cups with handles at either end: they were made out of gold, instead of wood, as suited a royal household. But they were still cups that required two hands to lift, two hands that could be watched.

Hadand lifted hers first, and everyone followed. The king nodded to her, they drank, everyone drank, then conversation began, an agreeable buzz of voices, as servants brought around the wine-braised chicken, and the rice balls. Hadand looked down at hers, knowing she ought to eat. She plucked from her waist her dagger with its handsome golden handle etched with raptor wing markings, fit for a queen, and toyed with it.

Ndara murmured in Old Sartoran, "What did you learn today?"

Her voice was soft, and none of the guests looked their way; the focus was all at the king's end of the table.

Hadand sent a quick, hurt look at Ndara, who did not look back, only smiled a little, and lifted her cup to her lips. From behind the broad, shallow vessel she added, again in archival Sartoran—except for one word—"Would a Gunvaer have the leisure to cultivate her sorrows?"

Hadand felt a sting of pain as if she'd been slapped. She sat very still, and then stole another sideways peek to see Ndara smiling at someone farther down the table.

Hadand looked up to catch a curious look from Tdon Eveneth, a senior horsetail. She remembered him laughing as the boys slipped and slid down the wooden rampart after her defeat. Pride forced her chin up. He gave her a quick grin and saluted her with his cup, but before she could respond the Tlen sister—his betrothed—on his other side dug him in the ribs and he turned away, chattering in a low voice. They got along as merrily as Inda and Tdor. They laughed, easy laughter, and along the table Hadand saw sons who would be Jarls and girls who would be Jarlans or Randviars chattering about the games, about the year, and asking for news from home. She fought against loneliness and desolation at the thought of her own marriage. That way led to self-pity. *So what can I learn?* she thought.

First observation: most of them think the siege was funny. Funny! It doesn't matter to them. It matters only to me.

Gunvaer, Hadand thought. *Ndara said gunvaer. Not queen in Sartoran, or Iascan, but in Marlovan. I will be a Marlovan queen, not an outlander. I can't be weak.*

Ndara, watching, saw the wide, blank look of pain in Hadand's brown eyes narrow to resolution.

"What two errors did you make?" she asked.

Hadand thought: *This talk, right here, right now, it's practice for the real thing. A Marlovan queen will never be able to go to her room and cry, no matter what happens.*

And so she forced herself to eat a bite of rice. Then, "I let myself show off on Fourthday. I should not have."

Ndara drew a slow breath. "Good. Why?"

"Because." Hadand's gaze strayed down to the Sierandael, who was talking to the Jarls. Laughing. "If there is war at home, we must be able to take them by surprise."

Ndara thought, *She's been saying it all her life because I taught her to say it, but maybe now she believes it.* "Second thing. What did you do wrong today?"

"I am too young. I should not have let the bigger girls praise me into command. I'm not ready for a real command."

Ndara sipped wine, looking down the table at her husband, the Sierandael. "But you might be forced to assume it anyway. You have read history. Do you think defense, ruling, violence—the bloody change of rule—only happens when one is ready?"

Hadand drew a deep breath. Her perspective reeled again, and she murmured, "No."

"So what did you do wrong today?"

Watched covertly by her father, Hadand reviewed the siege. Jarend-Adaluin saw his daughter's expression alter from mute misery to concentration, and his own unease vanished. The king watched as well, and listened to the talk around him.

". . . when my warship gets back," the Jarl of Cassad said.

The king, shifting his attention to the Jarls, quickly reviewed the situation. No one here had had sons on board those ships, thereby requiring a private interview. Two of the Jarls had paid for the building and outfitting of a ship each, true, but they had the wherewithal to do so, and to do it again. But they must be convinced of the necessity.

He said, "The ships were destroyed by pirates."

"What?"

"Pirates! Damnation! Where?"

"When did this happen? How many?"

The reactions were surprise, indifference, anger. Only Hasta Marlo-Vayir sent a covert glance the Sierandael's way, but that was to be expected. They'd been old friends since their academy days, and Hasta—as loyal a man as the king's own brother—disliked and distrusted ships and the sea for what appeared to be exactly the same reasons as the Sierandael's.

It was time for a new point of view.

"We will not be able to carry out our prospective treaty with the northern kingdoms unless we can build a fleet," the king went on. "We cannot offer protection from pirates in return for bases if we cannot actually protect."

"We can *take* the north if they sneer at us," Mad Gallop Yvana-Vayir, who was married to the king's sister, proclaimed, striking his fist on the table, then looking to see who was with him.

The king watched who agreed, who abstained. The Sierandael nodded slowly, his furtive, anxious expression meaning he flatly disagreed. But he stayed silent, which meant he would listen.

So the king said, "Most of you were here when we announced ten years ago that we would commit time, and much gold, to building three warships. Beginning with those, I had intended to build a fleet not just to protect our own coast, but also to extend our protection north, all the way to the west end of the strait. We all know the Idayagans up north could never withstand an attack from the Venn. The Venn must know it too. So it makes sense that they won't attack us along our well-watched west coast, but along the northern coast, beginning with Idayago and its neighbors. And once they've taken both sides of the straight, they will use the northerners' supplies to ride southward in strength against us."

He paused, saw nods, shrugs, pursed lips.

"Where we have disagreed is in our response. I believe if we had bases along the peninsula and in Idayago, we could prepare for the Venn, no matter from which direction they come. If we knew they were about to launch an invasion, had we those bases we could even launch a preemptive strike against them. I would prefer to meet them in battle in the north, keep them from destroying our land. Let them spend years recovering, instead of us."

Mutters of vexation, warlike exhortations, cursing at the damned pirates. But among the mutterers, there was old Tya-Vayir's low voice: "Not if we make it our land." He put down his ale—too much of it, damnation—and looked around, startled and uneasy, to see who had heard him.

But the king's eyes were on his brother.

At the other end of the table, in a low voice, Hadand said, "I lost control almost at the outset." She sighed. "I memorized those words, but they didn't really have any meaning: 'Don't lose control or you will not get order back.' "

"Yes." Ndara's eyes flicked up at the sound of a thud.

Marlo-Vayir thumped his fist onto the table. "So we can't carry war to them across the strait. If they come, then at least we are on familiar ground. We are strong here, on home soil."

Mutters of agreement.

Hadand felt her nascent self-pity vanishing like mist in the sun. "So then the girls' defense teams lost integrity. They stopped looking to me and looked to each other."

"Give me specifics."

"Once I saw the new ladders, I should have had a back up plan. And I should have been ready to implement it. As it was, I forgot our hand signals," Hadand said, after some thought.

"Good. Go on."

"I didn't see—no. I saw things, but I couldn't make sense of them. It was just a big crowd of boys all swarming around, and climbing, and yelling, and not at all like drill. The girls turned into a swarm as soon as the boys breached the ramparts. Everything was moving too fast. When they all moved like during drill, I could see and comprehend everything. Feel I was in command. But that wasn't command, not really. My only real command was before the siege, when I placed them and told them the plan. I lost command as soon as it stopped being like drill."

"The Venn," the king said, and the men's voices ceased, "want complete control of the strait, not just our end—they have that—but the eastern end as well. They tried for it, and reports are they lost recently, against an alliance of Chwahir and Everoneth. It was, from what I gather from my foreign contacts, a tremendous loss. Perhaps there will be no war in our generation, which gives us more time to prepare the next."

At that, the young raised their glasses and cheered.

Under the sound, Ndara murmured, "And so shall battle be, quick and chaotic, according to true records. What else?"

Hadand wriggled her aching shoulders, and could not repress a wince. "I forgot all my training. Just stood there and let the Sierlaef fling me down like an old doll."

"So?"

"A commander can only command if she's free. I should have at least tried the evasion blocks."

Ndara offered Hadand more rice balls. "The knife defense is worthless if you do not stay out of your enemy's grip."

Hadand winced again. After years of drill and practice with her armswomen, she finally understood what she'd been told so many times: no matter how fast she could spin a knife into the air, or how good she was with a stationary target, no enemy was going to stand politely by and wait for her to take aim.

It was time—past time—to start making her lessons real.

Chapter Twenty-one

TWO mornings later, a hand smacked Tanrid's shoulder, spinning him free of dreams. He sat up, blinking at the weak light coming through the row of barracks windows.

"Come." The familiar silhouette was the Sierlaef.

"For what?"

The Sierlaef jerked his thumb over his shoulder toward the castle, then walked quietly past the still-sleeping bodies of the other horsetails, most with their gear all packed and ready to go, neatly stashed by each bed. He was already dressed.

Tanrid pulled his clothes on, shoved his feet into stockings and boots, then fingered his hair up into its tail, pulling it into his grandfather's silver owl-in-flight hair clasp as he sorted through possible reasons for this strange, unexpected summons. Then he stopped at the door, lifted the dipper from the bucket and drank a few mouthfuls, feeling the snap of cleaning magic over teeth and tongue. He dropped the dipper with a plunk and left.

Outside he found the Sier-Danas conversing in low voices, their breath puffs of vapor. His cousin Manther gave him a covert salute. The others nodded without a break in their talk.

Tanrid turned his face up toward the sky. He shook his head, blinking away the residue of interrupted dreams: jumbled images of riding mingled with the voices of the pigtails from their barracks, who had stayed up far too late, thumping the hand drums and singing the old Away songs. In their grandsires' time, those songs had preceded raiding forays. Tanrid remembered his mother saying they were songs of nostalgia now, not intent, and she hoped they would stay that way. He thought it odd, but she often said odd things.

The Sierlaef gestured for them to follow him to the stables.

Though it was against regulations, everyone knew that the Sierlaef and his friends sometimes went over to ride morning evolutions with the Guard. No one resented this on the part of a future king, however they felt about the Sier-Danas being a part of it. Tanrid wondered why he was now to be included.

The Sier-Danas accepted Tanrid's presence with no particular emotion; most of them liked Tanrid, or at least respected his skill. His cousin Manther had thought all along that Tanrid ought to have been a Companion, though of course he'd never said anything aloud.

The boys flung the light saddle pads over their favorite mounts, fixed halters and reins, all with practiced speed. Soon they were riding in the cold wind round the perimeter of the academy, over to the Guard garrison on the other side of the great parade ground, a place of much fascination and speculation.

Early as it was, the Sierandael was waiting at the huge iron-topped gates, dressed also for riding, and holding the signal flag affixed to a lance. A trumpet call brought a wing of the Guard out, riding toward well-trampled fields.

The morning's evolution was lance practice. The Sierandael and the six horsetails watched from the roadside as the young men whirled the lances in unison up, round, side, round, forward, round, in maneuvers that would never be used in war, that were meant to build strength and versatility in arm and wrist. The horsetails, having experienced the rudiments of lance circles for the first time this year, appreciated just how tough it was to make it look so easy.

The sun slowly mounted in the sky, and the wind rose, bending the brown grasses and rippling over the tops of puddles left by the recent storm, smelling pungently of mud.

"Ride with me," the Sierandael said abruptly to Tanrid. He handed his flag off to the Sierlaef. "Signal the change."

The Sierlaef watched his uncle ride off with Tanrid at his side with a surge of jealousy.

"You depart today, do you not?" the Sierandael asked.

Tanrid struck his chest. "Yes, Sirandael-Dal."

The Sierandael said, "Just as you woke up, too." His tone did not mean that morning, causing Tanrid to look up in question.

The Sierandael smiled. "It took seven years. And now that you've finally woken up, it's time to go home. I want you to return awake in the spring. Then I'll not regard the time as lost."

Tanrid rubbed his knuckles across his chin. Were there really hairs there? He'd had body hair for nearly two years, but he knew the beard usually came later.

The Sierandael watched the Sierlaef wave the flag. The Guard obediently couched their lances and separated into ridings for the next stage of the evolution. As horses rumbled by, kicking up clots of mud, he said, "Nothing exceeded my pride the other day, when you finally exhibited some of the skill I have always seen as potential in you."

Tanrid looked over in surprise.

The Sierandael's mouth tightened in irony. "Why do you think I rode you as hard as I did all these years? Why I called against you when I could? I wanted you to wake up years ago. You have the potential to be a great captain. Not just of your own flight, or maybe a wing, but of an army. We will have need of such, if the Venn come."

Tanrid felt strange, as if still caught in his dream.

The Sierandael stretched out a hand, rubbing his mare's bony head between her ears. "They will come, someday," he said. "They have established strongholds all along the north side of the strait. They need our plains, I'm told. Their lands in the far north are cold and soggy, and they need more food to feed their great army and their mighty fleets."

Tanrid turned his hand up. He'd heard that all his life.

"My brother the king thinks we ought to carry the war to them. I think we are strongest here. Whichever way it happens, we must be strong. Strong leaders make for strong warriors."

Tanrid considered. Yes. That made sense.

"Do you agree?"

The Sierandael was asking his opinion. Tanrid heard again the measured words of praise, and years worth of puzzlement and resentment vanished, just like that. It made so much sense now. His own father had said much the same, over the years. War was hard, so you were hard on those who would command warriors.

"Yes, Sierandael-Dal," he said, and the Royal Shield Arm, who knew boys, heard the conviction in this boy's voice.

"Good. The king will need a strong arm in the south, whenever war does come. So work hard this winter," he said. "Work hard not just on your own skills, but on your leadership."

The Sierandael watched Tanrid, saw a nod of conviction, and laughed. He had the boy, as simple as that. Why didn't he do it years ago? Well, late was better than never. But there remained one very important matter. "Your brother. He resists leadership, which makes him a poor leader."

Tanrid seemed about to speak, but remained silent.

The Sierandael said quickly, "You disagree?"

Tanrid flushed. He knew better than to disagree with a commander. So he turned his head, watching but not registering the perfect lines of Lancers forming, galloping, wheeling, galloping, reforming. Resists leadership? From what Tanrid had seen—admittedly from afar—Inda was a hard-working scrub under Gand's strict training. In fact, Tanrid privately thought the Tveis were far ahead of where the Ains had been at Inda's age. Obviously Gand had given them more than a taste of dragoon training, but that was good, wasn't it? It certainly had improved the one they called Sponge.

He glanced up, and realized the Sierandael was still waiting for him to answer.

Embarrassed, he said haltingly, "I think—he doesn't mean to be disobedient. He thinks, see, his ideas . . ." Tanrid groped in the air, then shut up.

The same flare of danger the Sierandael had felt on the games' first day burned in him again. "If you are in the midst war and you depend on one wing to take a hill, but the captain of that wing decides he has a better idea, what will happen?"

Tanrid frowned. "If it works, well . . ."

"Tanrid. If the *entire army* depends on you to take that hill, but you decide to follow a scouting party instead, however good your idea is, what happens to the army if they follow up, expecting the hill to be secured?"

Tanrid's eyes narrowed.

The Sierandael said, "Use your strength to command your own brother. See that he learns obedience. That skill will help you to command men one day."

Tanrid nodded slowly, but not in resentment or disbelief. He thought back to the scrubs' shoeing exhibition, silly as it was. What had seemed like an innovative idea now took on a new, more dangerous meaning: he realized what had really motivated his brother was insubordination. "I will," he promised.

The king found Sponge in the archive room. He smiled, having wondered when Sponge would find his way back to reading. In his own academy days, it had happened within two bell-changes. Sooner, if it was possible. "Did you miss books, then, son?"

Sponge looked up from one of his favorites, an exquisitely illustrated Iascan translation of an old Sartoran ballad, complete with inked and gold-leafed illustrations. Now that he was old enough, Sponge could see in the handsome faces the careful resemblance to the few Marlovan portraits in the queen's audience chamber (the old Marlovans themselves had no portraits—they passed down only flags and emblems of war), and the detailed shields all bore the raptors and wild canines of the Marlovans, though the battle in the ballad had taken place over a thousand years before, in Sartor.

The king saw Sponge's finger resting on one of the shields and guessed Sponge's thoughts. "Diplomatic flattery from the Cassad queen, who was the supreme commander of the diplomatic arts."

Sponge sighed, unsurprised. He knew that history, how the Cassads— then known as Cassadas—had been the former royal family, how the queen had married the first Marlovan king instead of fighting a war the Cassadas knew they'd lose. And so, by changing their name and adopting Marlovan customs, this family had managed to keep their personal holdings and position in a way that never would have been possible if they had been conquered.

"Diplomatic flattery, I might add, of the sort my great-father Anderle swallowed down like old wine. You know it was he who declared that every second or third generation we must marry outside the clans, and perhaps his view was long-sighted, but I suspect he just liked the presents."

Sponge laughed.

"Are all your friends gone, then?"

Sponge lifted a shoulder. "Don't know. I didn't want to say good-bye, so I didn't go to breakfast mess, but came straight here." With anyone but Hadand he would not say that much.

"I never did either," the king said. "So I always just left my things there and walked home. Your uncle used to stay until the last one was gone, seeing them off."

The king did not miss the flicker in his son's eyelids at the mention of his uncle, the lengthened upper lip. And as always the king felt a pang of helpless regret that his first son should have so resembled Anderle and his second himself.

He shook away the regret stemming from a situation about which he could do nothing. Sponge watched his father pace slowly along the shelves, one finger moving over the silk-covered spines with their graceful gold lettering. Sponge was still too unpracticed with the vertical Old Sartoran script to see it in groups of words. It looked like interwoven leaves to him, until he concentrated on each form and sounded out the letters.

"Ah." The king pulled down a book. "I think you might be old enough to discern the importance of this record."

Sponge studied his father's expression. *He looks sad because he tried to get my brother to read it,* Sponge thought. From his earliest memories there was the Sierlaef's halting voice in the nursery, cursing with passionate intensity about the stupid books and the fools that had nothing better to do than write them. How Marlovan kings of the past had never had to read, and they had conquered an empire.

"It is a real description of a battle," the king said. "By a prince. Not written years afterward, by a scribe with one eye looking to please a king, but for his own private journal. It was Fareas-Iofre of Choraed Elgaer—though she was still living in Darchelde then—who sent it to me as a gift, on the eve of my wedding," he added. "She copied it out herself. That is her hand you will see there. It's very clear. My Sartoran is not as good as it ought to be, but I can read it."

Sponge took the book with both hands, understanding that there was much of importance underlying his father's words.

"If you finish it, come to me," the king said. "We shall discuss it." He left; duties were always waiting.

Sponge sat in his cushioned chair, so comfortable after all those weeks of hard benches, and looked out the windows, thinking. The light reflecting off the warm stone of the walls muted from golden to pale sand to a grayish blue: rain was nigh.

In the distance the noon bells clanged, and he thought of Inda riding through the gates, bracing against the oncoming weather. Inda, riding south, not to be seen for the months of winter.

Sponge crouched over the book.

The Sierlaef leaned against a stone battlement and scowled into the distance, where bands of rain obscured the hills with gray shadows. The last entourage was just barely visible, a dark snake winding along those hills. He could no longer see the sky-blue Marlo-Vayir banners, but he could imagine Buck with the armsmen right behind the pennants, joking back and forth, Cherry-Stripe snuffling at the back, after the thrashing his brother had given him that morning out behind the stables for giving Buck frost about the scrub shoeing.

Not that the Sierlaef cared. What he did care about was his uncle's private talk with Tanrid Algara-Vayir. Why?

The sound of boot heels recalled him. A Runner said, "Sierlaef-Dal. The Royal Shield Arm requests your company."

The Sierlaef dismissed the Runner with another wave, and followed more slowly behind, taking the long way down through the sentry walks to the garrison. The aides, Runners, and stable hands all took one look at the arrogant tilt to the chin, the taut, hard-boned cheeks browned from weeks of sun, and stepped far out of the way as he stalked to the mess hall.

Despite the ceaseless labor involved in the closing of the academy for the winter, and in addition to his ongoing chores, the Sierandael was on watch. His first glimpse of his nephew made him repress a sigh. "Later," the Sierandael said to three aides, all waiting patiently. They bowed and withdrew.

Royal Shield Arm and royal heir walked to the front of the line and got a plate of fishcakes and spiced slurry.

The uncle said presently, "Why the sour mouth?"

The Sierlaef thought, *He will say he favors the best, so why does he truly favor me?*

The troubled brow, the wariness in the Sierlaef's gaze, warned his uncle that the fit of sullenness he'd expected had somehow smoldered into something very close to rebellion.

"If you're missing your friends, the remedy is to keep busy. If it's because Tanrid Algara-Vayir was part of our review this morning, it's because you yourself ought to have invited him."

The Sierlaef's eyes widened in surprise.

His uncle waved his knife. "He's good. Better than I'd ever thought he would be. He might even be the best."

The Sierlaef flushed.

The king's brother said, in a low, measured voice, "Here's the truth of kingship. You don't have to be the best, you have to command the best." He sat back, watching the impact of that.

The boy's mouth lost the grim tightness. Anderle-Sierandael laughed inwardly, but out loud only said, "Eat up." And, after a time, "I told Tanrid that command begins at home. He needs to get that scrub brother of his in order." The Royal Shield Arm smiled. "The shoeing was an amusing prank, but one we can't afford, not with the threat of war within our lifetimes."

The Sierlaef frowned. "You. S-s-said s-soon."

"I thought it would be soon. That is, within the next ten years. Your father did as well," his uncle said. "The Venn have established those outposts across the strait, and one day they will bring down transports full of warriors."

The Sierlaef put his knife down. "No ships."

His uncle sat back, smiling a little. "It's true, we have had no success building a fleet. Just as I predicted. I regret the loss of good men, and the money that went into the building. It does seem to mean, though, that when war does come, we will do the best if we meet it with our strengths. Also, one of those lost was the Montredavan-An boy, who your father sent aboard the *Cassad*—a generous gesture, but frankly, I am relieved a pirate's knife or sword or boat hook took care of potential trouble that one day might've threatened your reign right here."

Savarend Montredavan-An dead? They had never met, of course. The Montredavan-Ans were forbidden to step on any road but those that led directly to the sea, and even that only under guard, but still the Sierlaef had heard things about the red-haired Savarend, only a couple years younger than he was himself: how brilliant he was with the bow, how superlative his skills at riding. How they thought he might have even had sword training, though no one had seen him at it, forbidden as it was. Just as well he was dead—the Sierandael had said the Montredavan-Ans were nothing but trouble, and the rumors about Savarend had proved it.

The Sierlaef grinned.

His uncle opened his hands. "Your father says that all the reports from the east are that the Venn fleet has taken a smashing from the Chwahir and Everoneth. As much as anything can be decided with ships," he added, shrugging dismissively. "On the water, battle can't be decisive, for who can possibly hold command over water? But a fleet can be diminished, and if the reports are true, then the Venn will need time to rebuild. That might take two years, depending on what has happened—or it might take ten. More. If so it will be you who defends the homeland."

"Me." The royal heir licked his lips.

The Sierandael saw the anticipation. Now it was time to redirect the Sierlaef's anger. Part of command, of course, is to know who is to be cherished for the greater good, and who is expendable. He drummed his fingers on the table. "If you are one day to ride north as Aldren-Harvaldar, as our royal great-fathers did in the old days, then you need to think about the matter of command. Who are you going to leave behind to defend your kingdom? We do have plans, but if those do not come to pass, are you going to leave a fumbling archivist in command, someone who hides from his duty in order to waste his time translating worthless old papers into worthless new papers?"

The Sierlaef's face hardened again, but this time the anger was not directed at his uncle.

The Sierandael watched as the boy picked up his plate, jammed it into the barrel with a liquid *splorch*, and strode off in the direction of the palace.

Sponge had puzzled over a page or so of the Sartoran record before he realized that he had not yet eaten that day. He recalled the noon bells ringing. So he tucked the book under his arm—glad that it was a book, and not a scroll, as those were so unwieldy—and trod up to the school-room in the residence wing.

He smelled hot cream soup with baby carrots in it, and his mouth watered. He ran inside the central chamber that all the royal children shared, with its plain, battered wooden furnishings and the sturdy woolen rugs on the floor, woven with bright birds and flowers, sent by his mother's brother.

Sponge looked around, sensing a difference. Nothing had changed. Except—"Dormouse!"

The small, scrawny boy at the far table looked up, grinning. Though he'd been gone two years, Barend did not look the least bit different. His triangular head and prominent front teeth still made him resemble a rodent. "Spongie!"

"When did you get back?"

Barend's bony shoulder jerked up to his ear. "Yesterday, early. You all were busy with the end of the games. Mama and I spent the day together in her rooms."

Sponge sorted through what was unsaid, and opened his hand.

"You're a little taller," Sponge observed.

Barend looked wry. "A finger's breadth. Not as tall as you, and I never will be, despite the two years I got on you." He shrugged. One's size couldn't be helped. And the years away from his father's scorn had done a lot for his self-respect. "I'm glad you're the first one back," Barend said, his smile fading.

Sponge shook his head. "Don't spoil it. What's to eat?"

Sponge helped himself to the food, which was still warm in the crockery dishes, and saw that Barend had paper and chalk next to him. He was busy drawing, as he always was, whenever he could get the chance. So Sponge opened his book, and the two boys ate and worked in companionable silence.

. . . the screams of those on the field rendered it impossible to hear the horn calls. I never considered before how alike are the two sounds, horns and screams of agony. I will not forget . . .

Sponge shuddered. The beginning of this one was far different from the ballads.

He bent over, and his lips moved as he shaped the words.

. . . I saw my cousin shouting as he hacked at the tor-helm . . .

Tor-helm. Tor. People, us. That would be a term for the leader of the other side, without knowing his title or rank.

. . . who had already thrown down his sword. At this sign the rest of his war-party swarmed the opposite side and began killing . . .

Sponge winced, and skipped to the next page.

. . . had forgotten our own family, lying on the ground, and so, despite my own wound, I felt I ought to commandeer those who could pick up a pole and tear cloth to fashion stretchers and bear our wounded from the field . . .

Sponge sighed. He'd only read five pages of the thirty in the book, but so far, there had been no hint of glory. Yet it was a famous battle, one seen in tapestry and heard of in old songs.

Sponge looked up at the tall row of windows. The rain had begun, soft and steady, for this was no short summer storm.

Barend snorted, rubbing his nose on his sleeve, then went back to his sketching; it wasn't just horses anymore. Barend drew ships, in amazing detail. Sponge admired his ability, but secretly wished Barend would return to drawing horses. Horses were alive, beautiful. Ships were boring.

Sponge sat back to think about what he was reading. The room was quiet, except for the snap of the mage-fire in the fireplace, and the hiss of rain outside the windows.

So when the door slammed open both he and Barend jumped.

The Sierlaef strode in, and the sight of Sponge sitting there in his gray academy tunic, with a book open before him, sent a lightning strike of hot fury right between his eyes

Both boys stilled. The Sierlaef closed on them in three hard strides, and glanced down. Not even Iascan! It was one of those soul-eating Sartoran things that they'd tried to force him to learn. So Sponge was already bootlicking the king, was he?

He grabbed the front of his brother's tunic and hauled him away from the table. "Train." And he flung him against the wall.

"Papa asked me to read that," Sponge answered, trying dizzily to get to his feet.

The Sierlaef backhanded him into the wall. Sponge couldn't think past the lightning searing through his head, but his body had learned this lesson. He twisted, just enough to fall heavily, distributing the force of the fall along his length.

"No lip," the Sierlaef said. "Listen. Obey." His voice started bleating on the consonants in the last word, and in frustration he lashed out, slapping Sponge again.

Now Sponge was conscious of falling right, of how it really did work. It was a tiny triumph, but it was still a triumph.

It didn't keep him from biting the inside of his mouth when he was struck there. The sight of blood spurting from between his lips caused the Sierlaef to step back.

"Obey," he said again, to justify the sight of that blood. "No disgrace. In spring. Hear?"

"Yes, Aldren-Sierlaef," Sponge said, and coughed on the horrible taste in his mouth.

The Sierlaef slammed out.

Barend went for a wet cloth, holding it against Sponge's aching head until the blood stopped flowing. No need to speak. Sponge would do the same for him when Barend's father came for him.

When Sponge pulled away, Barend got shakily to his feet. He was home, all right. And he could sketch all he wanted, pretending his mind was out there on the water, skimming before the wind, but he knew he was here, and winter would be long and full of pain and fear.

Sponge wiped his mouth. "I'll teach you something," he said, stumbling toward the casement that opened onto the sentry walk, his old retreat. "Maybe it'll help you if pirates attack. It'll definitely help you here."

Barend grinned. "Well, we have until spring." He ventured a joke. "By then, pirates might be welcome."

When Hadand and Kialen came in at last, having finished their duties with the queen, it was in expectation of a cozy nursery party, a welcome for the two who had been gone. But they both felt the tension in the air before they saw the blood on the floor, being cleaned up by Barend. Kialen Cassad, never far from fear, began to tremble and feel faint. Hadand kindly sent her to her room to lie down, and Kialen was glad to leave, closing the door soundlessly behind her.

Hadand looked at Barend, saw no bruises. "Sponge?"

Barend jerked a shoulder at the window.

Hadand knew where to find him. He'd always gone out into the rain. He'd said once that it felt good, that it numbed pain.

She opened the casement and walked out onto the sentry walk. There he was, at the far end, a small bony figure crouched down. She went to him and put her arms around him, not caring about rain, or about the clamminess of his skin, or how he shuddered.

He leaned against her, and they were both silent. When the shuddering eased a little, she said, "Was there a reason?"

"He said that I won't disgrace him in the spring, that I have to train. In obedience."

So that was why Sponge was so upset! They both knew what that meant: a long winter of dreary chores, of no books or talk, except in stolen moments. The Sierlaef would have him wanding horse droppings, and pitching hay, and doing the chores of servants. And there would inevitably be more beatings.

Sponge waited, blinking rain from his eyes. He could hear from Hadand's compressed breathing how upset she was, and yet, and yet, there was nothing more. No word, no offering of that valuable lesson in the evasions, that Sponge wouldn't have even known about had it not been for Inda.

He could not believe her concern was false. He must not look for falsity, or he might find it where it did not exist. It was terrible enough to doubt. Hadand loved him. He knew that. She had shown it in uncounted other ways, all his life. But it seemed she didn't trust him enough for this one thing.

"It's cold," Hadand said at last, when she realized that Sponge had withdrawn by degrees, that he sat quiescent in her arms, without leaning against her.

Perhaps he thought himself too old for comfort. Only two years lay between them, after all; he was not really a little boy any more. She sat back, and looked into his face, but it was cold, his lips blue, one cheek swollen, tangled hair in his eyes. She had no clue to what he was thinking.

They both walked inside, and Hadand ordered hot cocoa with cream, rare and expensive, and she made it herself, the way Sponge liked it. But Sponge's pensive mouth stayed pensive, and after a time she went to her own rooms, feeling that she had somehow lost something important.

She cried herself to sleep.

Chapter Twenty-two

SPRING arrived at last.

Inda had just slipped inside his room after another secret Odni training session when Tanrid strode into his room, causing him to jump guiltily.

But Tanrid didn't smack him, or order him to stop lazing about, or order him down to stable duty. He just said, "There you are. Listen. We're leaving for the royal city."

"The royal city?" Inda repeated, disbelief warring with joy. "When?"

"Father's orders, we're to ride by noon. We're meeting a war party on the road. Going after those brigands that killed mother's Runner."

"War party?" Inda asked. "Then it wasn't a few skulkers?"

"Father says some spy discovered a whole wing's worth of 'em, maybe more, massing at the river fork in the south of Hesea, to attack all spring travel—south, north, west." Tanrid grinned. "Instead of farmers and tradesmen, they're gonna find us." He strode rapidly down the hall.

Inda laughed with an elation he hadn't felt for months. "Fiam!" he yelled, dashing out the door. "Fiam!"

Long before noon he stood in the sleety rain by the horses the Riders had gathered in the courtyard. A war party! And after that? The academy! With Sponge, Noddy, Dogpiss, and Cama!

He was full of joy until Tdor appeared at his side, rain making her thin nose glow dull red and turning her lips blue. She gazed into Inda's face, wincing away from the new black eye and the cuff-mark on the opposite cheekbone, upset to see the joy he did not try to hide. "Just remember this plan is not a war game, you haywit," she scolded.

Inda stared at her in surprise. Of course he knew that. And he could have explained that he was just so happy to be getting away from the long cold winter of drudgery, beatings, of enforced silence, of hard stable work and even harder work down in the women's court, unseen by his brother, who had assumed he was lazing around in bed, and punished him for his own good.

But she should know all that, he thought hazily, feeling angry, betrayed even, so he snapped, "Of course it's not a game." His voice came out sounding hard, with as much derision as Tanrid used on a good day. She stepped back a pace, her eyes rounding in hurt surprise as he added, "What d'you think we've been training for, anyway?" which was another of the things Tanrid had said, usually before one of those beatings.

Tdor's lower lip trembled. Remorse snuffed his anger but she was already headed back to the castle.

His father appeared then, like all of them wearing his winter riding coat, bespelled against cold and wet weather. He was escorting Joret and her personal Runner, who were riding with them, as Joret was to begin the queen's training this spring.

The noise of everyone mounting up was louder than the rain.

They formed up swiftly into two columns. The bannermen moved to the front, their horses shaking their heads. The Adaluin raised his arm then flattened his hand in the signal to wait as the Iofre appeared, rain speckling her robes darkly.

She came to Inda and reached up to caress his face. "Be well, my son," she murmured, then she turned to Tanrid and spoke her farewell, touching the hand that loosely held his reins.

She moved to Joret and stood on tiptoe to whisper to her. Joret leaned down to clasp her hands, her blue eyes serious as she spoke her soft farewell. Inda looked past them for Tdor, who did not appear. But they were about to ride.

He gestured to his mother, "Tdor—" He realized he didn't know what else to say without sounding whiny.

The Iofre read his unhappy, half-ashamed, half-stubborn expression, and recognized the underlying regret. She said, "I will carry your farewell to her."

Inda winced, swallowing in a tight throat. It was better than nothing; it would have to do. He'd make it up to her when he returned in the autumn, he promised himself.

The Iofre last exchanged a few low-voiced words with the Adaluin, who bent from his saddle pad to hear her, then she stepped back, now thoroughly wet, but she did not heed it.

Her worried gaze lingered on Inda as the Adaluin raised his fist. The cavalcade rode out through the gates, turning westward instead of to the east.

Two weeks later they met the Jaya-Vayir war party on the coast road at a small village a day's ride north of Marth-Davan. By then Inda was familiar with his father's plan, as amended by the king and agreed to by the Jarls of Cassad and Jaya-Vayir.

Inda's excitement bounced between the plan and the prospect of seeing some of his scrub friends again: not just Rattooth Cassad, but Cama Tya-Vayir, who had been sent south out of Iasca Leror in search of a healer trained in arts unknown in Marlovan-held territory. The Cassads still had connections in that part of the world, and so the Jarl of Cassad had sent his sons to keep Cama company as well as to see a bit of the world.

The Algara-Vayir war party halted when they saw dust hanging high in the air. Inda peered down the sunny road past the last round-walled house, spotted the yellow-and-white banners of the Cassads, the green and purple of the Jaya-Vayirs. Past them . . . He gave a yip of joy when he saw the pale yellow head riding between Cama's dark one and Rattooth's straw-colored, messy locks: Dogpiss!

Inda fidgeted until the outriders met, followed by the Adaluin and the Jarl of Jaya-Vayir. As soon as the leaders signaled consent to break formation, he yelled, "Dogpiss!" The younger boys all rode to one side, the horsetails to the other. "What brings you here?" Inda exclaimed.

Dogpiss grinned. "M' father was sent down by the king himself as a reinforcement to your dad. Since we were leaving for the royal city anyway, he brought Whipstick and me along. We rode down the coast road,

missed you, met these pugs," his thumb jerked between Cama and Rattooth, "so we turned back."

"Pugs!" Rattooth snorted. "I loved how Whipstick pugged you good
last night, when you kept farting and wouldn't let us sleep."

On Dogpiss' crack of laughter the boys glanced at Dogpiss' brother,
who had not been invited into the horsetail group. Whipstick, thin,
brown as a seasoned dragoon and almost as tough, knew better than to
join the horsetails uninvited so he stayed with his father's men. When
the scrubs all turned his way he lifted a hand in salute. Inda saluted
back.

The three scrubs did not have the frost to summon him over, not
Whipstick Noth, captain of the pigtail scrappers. And Dogpiss, who
could have beckoned his brother over, did not because he wanted his
friends to himself.

Dogpiss said, "Cama was sent south with the Cassad boys for his eye."

"I know. How was it?" Inda asked, turning to Cama, who was silent as
usual. "Did you see any—"

"Later. Blab about sightseeing later. You got a hoof-kiss," Dogpiss observed, examining Inda's almost-healed black eye. "Fall down the stairs?"

Hearing scrub slang again was weird after a long winter only seeing
family. Inda snorted. "Most every day."

Dogpiss snorted as well. It was easy enough to see that Inda had had
a nasty winter. Well, it was time for some fun now. They weren't scrubs
anymore, not strictly, though there wouldn't be a regular Ain-scrub
group until next year. Oh, they'd still be at the bottom rank, but at least
it wasn't all new. More important, Dogpiss had prepared for some prime
practical jokes.

"Have any fun this winter?" he asked.

Inda just shrugged. "Naw. You?"

"Oh, I have some good stings," Dogpiss whispered. "But I won't tell
you. I'll show you. Too good to risk spoiling. I don't trust the Ains not
to nose 'em out." He turned his head, his pale hair lifting on the breeze.
"Hey, Squint! You know they're gonna call him Squint, now." Dogpiss
snickered. "I'm trying to get him used to it."

Cama, standing out amid all these fair heads with his dark curls and
his black eye patch, shrugged and tried to look sour. It was evident he'd
already resigned himself to a new nickname—they didn't know he privately preferred anything to Meow.

The Adaluin, as ranking commander, gestured to his bannermen to signal *fall in*. Scout dogs scrambled in and around the horses' legs, sniffing, tails waving warily, but returning to heel at the snapping of the handlers. Tanrid whistled to the Algara-Vayir dogs, who raced to him, muzzles lifted, tails wagging as they pranced around his horse. He leaned down to pat every head before turning back to his friends, who, having been accustomed for eight years to parting before winter and meeting again in spring, had exchanged brief greetings. All faced the northern hills on the other side of the Chardaus River, where through the interlaced trunks and branches of budding trees they glimpsed the great east-west road.

Inda, riding across the bridge behind the horsetails, saw them exchange fierce grins of pleasure at the prospect of battle.

"What happened?" Dogpiss asked Inda from behind his hand.

"One of my mother's Runners was attacked and killed by brigands. Just before New Year's, on the edge of Cassad lands. Shepherds found her, recognized the Runner blue and the owl badge. They reported it to the Cassads, who sent a Runner to tell us. Their attacks across the plains all the way to the mountains have worsened. And now they burn what they can't take. Father asked the king if he could raise a force and clear them out."

Dogpiss rubbed his hands. "Won't Cherry-Stripe howl when he hears we were in a battle!"

"And Tuft," Rattooth added.

While the scrubs were exchanging their news, the horsetails had been doing the same.

"Have you had a Galloper recently?" Cassad Ain asked, his prominent front teeth gleaming in the soft gray light.

"At dawn," Tanrid said. "Not long before we met you. Came up from the southeast under cover of dark. He said your father's hiding out at the attack site, along with handpicked warriors from Tlen and Tlennen. I guess they were doing some training runs together in the hills over winter."

"Hoo! M' cousin'll be with them," Cassad pronounced with conviction. "They'd have to tie him up else."

The four Tveis, now all listening to the horsetail conversation, exchanged grimaces. That meant three of the Sier-Danas along with Inda's Ain. At the very least they'd be doing the horsetails' field chores. Still, chores were inevitable, and meanwhile, the prospect of action was delightful.

All was happening according to plan, Inda thought, glimpsing his father's profile at the head of the column. Jarend-Adaluin's lined face was watchful, but the set of his mouth, the ease of his shoulders, indicated that he was pleased with the unexpected augmentation of their war party.

"So where's the attack going to be, then?" Cassad asked.

"Your father and his people are camped up behind the hills above the big bridge where the Chardaus River meets the Marlovar River . . ." Tanrid began. He outlined the plan, and who was to be there, and how they would trap the brigands against the river, force them to surrender, and sweep most of them off to the eastern hills to dig for ore in the mines, accomplishing two things at once: giving the local farms and villages relief from the constant raids, and gaining more miners. "It should be prime fun, at least for us to watch. We don't get to be in it. King's orders."

Groans at that, but the word "king" kept them from expressing themselves more fluently.

"We should be able to watch, at least," Tanrid finished.

Inda didn't listen. He knew the plan. He had also studied the great field map in his father's tent the first night of their journey, while rain drummed around them: he knew that no one would be south of the Chardaus, which was the northern border of Montredavan-An territory, forbidden to them, and patrolled by the King's Guard. What he'd learned was that no one patrolled north of the river—the king's forces were stretched too thin—so that brigands had been preying on travelers across the southernmost reaches of the plains of Hesea, despite its being the heartland of Marlovan territory.

Inda remembered the Galloper arriving in the bleak, bitter darkness just before dawn, his horse steaming, his blue tunic obscured by mud. Inda had watched the man gulp down hot brew with shaking fingers. He couldn't even talk at first. He'd sat there with bowed head, hands around the mug as Jarend-Adaluin waited until he could croak out, "They are there."

Yes, everything was according to plan. Excitement and anticipatory triumph made Inda grin, but along with it came, well, worry, though he wouldn't actually say it out loud, not before the others—especially the horsetails.

But he had to figure out why he was worried. It had begun when he first saw that grown man shaking with cold, the near-dead horse. You didn't ride horses like that in war games; you'd get yourself thrashed. As well you should.

Inda could almost hear Tdor's voice: *Just remember this is not a war game, you haywit.*

But now, watching how some of the men checked and rechecked weapons, the way the horses' ears twitched northward, he realized what she'd meant: that the attack was real, that someone might die. Someone besides brigands.

Inda's stomach swooped. *That's just cowardice,* he told himself angrily. *Especially since* we *don't even get to ride to the attack.* Jarend-Adaluin had made that clear. The boys, Joret and her Runner, and the horsetails had to remain on the outside. He'd promised the king.

No one argued with *that*.

A shifting in the lines snapped everyone's attention forward. They'd been riding up a ridge, shaded by early leafing nut trees. The flag dipped twice, meaning it was time to break column and set up camp.

As always, the young people were assigned to the middle of camp, directly under some leafing birch. Dogpiss and Rattooth happily squabbled over the grassiest spot for their bedrolls.

Tanrid chirruped between his teeth and the roaming scout dogs bounded instantly to his side, lolling about, muzzles grinning, tails beating the air. Tanrid bent, examining paws, rubbing backs as the animals stretched, noses high in bliss. Inda wondered how it was that the dogs merely obeyed him, but loved his brother. Meanwhile the boys were on watch, expecting the horsetails to land on them in some form or other, but to their surprise they paid the scrubs no attention.

It was Inda who spotted why: Joret. Even Tanrid watched her with a kind of brooding expression that Inda could not define; he was too young to recognize it as a kind of baffled mix of embarrassment and desire. Maybe it had to do with that sex stuff. Inda still didn't understand it, nor did he care, except for enjoying the little respites over the winter when Tanrid went off to the pleasure houses with some of the younger Riders.

Inda saw with a rush of sympathy that Joret had withdrawn into that closed, tight-shouldered manner she drew on like a cloak when she was aware of being stared at. The color in her cheeks, the extravagant curve of her lowered lashes, did nothing whatever to hide her startling beauty. Being still in smocks—and the future wife of the Adaluin's heir—gave her the choice of speaking or not, but she hated those restless gazes.

And so she performed her part in the Restday bread-giving with a graceless, unsmiling brevity, relaxing only when she handed bread to the restless Tveis who cared not whose hand they received it from. They only wanted to be singing, dancing, and talking. She was especially kind to one-eyed Cama Tya-Vayir, at first out of pity, but when she looked into his face, a strange coldness tightened along the insides of her arms. *One day he will be beautiful,* she thought, *and he doesn't even know it.*

"As strength to the body, so strength to the spirit." Her hand pressed his, and Cama gave her a shy, absent smile, for he was wondering what Dogpiss was hiding in his kit.

Then the first watch departed to their posts. Inda, Cama, Rattooth, and Dogpiss perched themselves along a row of rocks that jutted up like green dragon's teeth, remnants of an ancient fence, now moss covered, as the men began the songs. No drumming for the boys; the horsetails claimed the shallow drums used by youth. Joret was handed the drum with clashing brass cymblets. She performed her rhythms with competence, if not inspiration, her gaze on the fire, and not on the boys who waited, in vain, for her to look up so they could show off before her.

As the songs soared and thrummed, Inda said, "So, Cama, Rattooth, I want to know what it was like down south. Any interesting sights?"

Dogpiss put in, "Any good jokes, Squint?"

Cama shrugged, hating to talk, of course, but at least these were friends, and used to his squeaky voice. "Different," he said. "Real different. More than Iascan and Marlovan differences." He waved a hand, struggling for the words. "Their songs are different. They don't have drums at all, way south, near the Sartor Sea. There were some palaces, but no castles. Big cities. Very big, and the clothes are all different."

"Iascans didn't have drums, not until the Marlovans came," Dogpiss said, shrugging. "Mother told me that."

"What did they have, then, on Restday?" Cama, Dogpiss, and Inda turned to Rattooth, whose family was Iascan in origin.

Rattooth Cassad wiggled his fingers, looking like a blond rodent with his prominent front teeth. "Reed-pipes. Though we now use 'em for Marlovan songs, of course." A careless, confident statement resulting from that far-seeing great-mother who had said to her family on the eve of her wedding to the king of the Marlovan conquerors, *We will wear their style of clothes, and speak their tongue, and learn their songs and stories, but they will learn ours. And they will use our fine swords, our pottery, our castles and farms. And one day they will forget to see us as "them." If so, then in a sense we win the war, for we will keep what is ours, and lose no more lives.*

"I want to hear about your eye," Dogpiss said, waving away the blather about musical customs. "Did they do anything disgusting?"

"What was the magic like?" Inda asked, leaning close, the better to see Cama in the flickering golden light of the fire, around which young men danced, swords whirling in unison as the war drums rumbled.

"Slow," Cama said. "If I want to see out of this eye again, they said I have to go back. You remember, it kept opening, the cut, I mean, and I'd wake up and this gunk came out, and it hurt. It wouldn't heal. They had to take care of that first, and then wait. First heal this bit of skin, and then that muscle. And afterward, always waiting, and the mage gets sick as if he'd fought ten duels. During the spell-casting you feel as if a thousand bees stung you. No, it doesn't hurt. As if a thousand bees walked over you, their wings humming."

"Ecch," Dogpiss exclaimed with delighted revulsion.

"They do one little thing at a time, like I said. And so it will cost a lot. They says our ancestors knew such magic as common."

"Aw, that," Dogpiss said, waving a hand. "We always hear that, how they knew it all in the old days, and we lost it all."

"But they did," Inda said. "Tdor and Joret are always reading me things. Everything was different then, even time."

"Time," Dogpiss scoffed, "is time. It can't be that different. Not *here*."

There was no need to speak of what they all knew: that time did not progress at all in Norsunder, where the soul-eaters lurked, waiting for another chance to try to take the world again. If one wanted to escape from the effects of time he found his way to Norsunder. The price was that his soul belonged to the masters of that terrible place.

"I didn't believe time could vary in the world either. At first." Inda thought back to that dreamlike memory from the year before, when he'd been given kinthus. But he couldn't explain what had happened. So he said, "What Joret told me was that time here isn't always going forward, the way we assume."

Dogpiss snorted. "If you try to tell me it goes backward, then I'm going to rub your face in that mud."

The boys laughed, Inda included. He thought, but did not say, that he had once stared up at a banner in the throne room and heard the sounds of battle, as if two times met.

"Boys."

Four scrubs leaped to their feet. Four faces turned upward.

Jarend-Adaluin stood silhouetted against the fire, the mail under his war coat jingling faintly as he gestured toward their bedrolls. "Sleep," he said. "We shall ride hard on the morrow."

Chapter Twenty-three

JUST before dawn, the younger boys were kicked awake by the horse-tails. Over the gratifying yelps and howls of younger brothers Tan-rid, the ranking horsetail, issued orders for the breakdown and packing of their gear. The horsetails fixed their hair and smoothed their clothes so they could happen to stroll over for morning mess when Joret did.

Tanrid had just tightened his hair in the silver owl clasp when he realized the scrubs had gone quiet. Instantly suspicious, he whirled around to see Horsepiss Noth standing nearby, arms crossed. *Captain of Dragoons* Horsepiss Noth. Nobody knew what his real name was—if he even had one. Twenty of his forty-five years a captain, sun-seamed and hard as old wood. So hard the horsetails, who'd just been thinking themselves so very tough, looked like a row of guilty youngsters, all failing to see the faint narrowing of the eyes, the slight shadow at the corners of the thin lips, that hinted at strictly controlled mirth.

"Time," he said, "for you boys to run a little drill, eh, while the scrubs finish your packing?"

His tone promised that the scrubs were not getting the worst of morning's work. As the horsetails picked up their weapons and trooped off to the trampled ground where the guard had already finished warm-ups, Dogpiss chortled, and Inda, who had seen the humor in Noth's face, joined him.

"Make it quick," Dogpiss said to the other scrubs, and ran off to where his brother stood near the horse lines. Whipstick Noth, rejected as a mere pigtail by the lofty horsetails, had stayed with his father's men, all of them known to him by name.

As Inda packed Tanrid's bedroll with efficient, absent-minded speed, he watched the Noth brothers. The grins on their faces were startlingly alike: they were up to something.

"Come on," Rattooth grumped. "Just because his dad's here, Dogpiss seems to think he can buck drudge."

Inda whispered, "I think they've got a sting in mind."

Rattooth's face cleared into an expectant grin, strictly schooled by the time Captain Noth released the crimson-faced, sweat-soaked, slow-moving horsetails.

The scrubs sat in a row eating their breakfast, watching as Whipstick put just enough saunter in his stroll toward the cook pot to catch the attention of the wary Ains. Was he gloating?

Dogpiss drifted alongside the cook pot as the horsetails lined up, last of all, to get their food. They all watched, with ominous intensity, Whipstick's swagger as he returned from getting seconds. Was that the back of his hand, or was he just scratching his head? They were paying scant attention to the food doled out into their bowls, and no attention whatever to Dogpiss standing helpfully right by the Rider on cook duty.

The Ains got their oatmeal, topped with honey. Inda, observant of detail as always, frowned when he glanced in the wide, shallow wooden bowls. There were dark bits in the oatmeal, as if it had burned. But his had been perfectly cooked.

Still eying Whipstick, who was definitely on the strut as he moved toward the horses, the horsetails began to eat.

"Get the saddle pads on the mounts," came the command, and Inda and Dogpiss turned their hands to that work, Dogpiss' face crimson with repressed emotion.

Cama was the first to realize what Dogpiss had done. The horsetails' mouths were green—startling, bright green—as were the fronts of their tunics where they slopped in their haste to eat fast before the horses were ready.

Laughter from the men busy gathering their gear brought the horsetails' attention onto one another. They exchanged swift, shocked glances then realized what had happened, which of course caused universal merriment: added to their food had been tiny pellets of an herb so rich in color it bled off at the slightest touch of moisture.

"Right," Tanrid Algara-Vayir said, and the men laughed the more heartily, and his father smiled, as he and the other horsetails dropped their bowls onto the grass and efficiently surrounded the wheezing, weakly running Dogpiss.

He fought mightily, but without success, as the bigger boys held him down and scrubbed the remainder of their food over his face and clothing, then carried him down to the stream and tossed him in.

Dogpiss emerged, streaming, shivering, green-splotched, whooping with laughter. The horsetails' green mouths were evidence of their having been royally stung. They realized too late that Dogpiss' green skin was a banner of triumph.

The horsetails nursed their grievance in silence during the wearying days following.

The last jog was accomplished single file at night, under cover of rain, after they had set up a false camp and waited until the sun went down. All they got was cold food and a long walk, stopping frequently so the scouts and scout dogs ahead could find and be certain of their trail, everything metal muffled against jingling, and no talk whatever allowed.

That cold, soggy walk seemed eternal to the youths, but it did finally end. Midway through the night they were separated, all according to plan. In silence the young people were taken up the trail to a ridge lying east of the battle site, accompanied by a young Jaya-Vayir Rider captain popular with the boys, and two each of Algara-Vayir and Jaya-Vayir armsmen. Shelter meant a sort of warmth, and their first thought on reaching that camp had been to burrow down and sleep.

The Adaluin and the Jarls then turned north and eased up through a silent forest of beech and pine toward the northern end of the bridge, where they took cover and waited out the night.

Dawn found the young people camped amid trees and rocks on the far side of a little gully, with strict orders to lie low. Captain Samred and his four Riders had spent the night on a ceaseless patrol bounded by the gully, the road lower down, and the river. Weak light showed to the west, thick trees forming a dark, tangled line between the road and the great Marlovar River that flowed toward the bridge where their fathers lay in wait.

The next thought of the horsetails was vengeance on Dogpiss, and that no adults were present to interfere with their creativity.

Tanrid muttered in surprise, "Hey. Dogpiss isn't here."

Inda kept his face averted so no one saw his grin.

"Shall I fetch water?" asked Joret's Runner, Gdand.

Sudden silence behind him brought Inda's attention around. All the older boys were staring, or trying not to stare, at Joret, who sat beside a tree, her face turned resolutely toward the forest as she swiftly braided her glossy blue-black hair.

"I can wait," Joret replied softly.

Unconcerned with Joret, Gdand, and the riveted horsetails, Cama picked at his eye, which made Inda's stomach turn, all purple and pink with healing flesh. The imprint of Smartlip's heel was still clear. Rattooth watched as well, his lips curled in fascinated revulsion.

No one spoke. The horsetails made hasty, self-conscious groomings of clothing and hair, and everyone packed up their bedrolls. Tanrid had been given charge of the cheese and biscuits. He passed out shares with quick efficiency. Inda took Dogpiss' and laid it aside.

"Where did your brother go?" Cassad murmured to Whipstick Noth, who shrugged. Whipstick was in a rotten mood because, until last night, he'd thought it was only these Vayir boys who'd be stashed away, that he'd be able to ride with his father. But Jarend-Adaluin had insisted the king meant all the youths. Even those accompanying unexpected reinforcements.

Was that a scream?

No, it was probably some bird. Much as he wanted to, Whipstick knew he couldn't hear the battle. They were not far, but definitely out of earshot.

"Soon as he sticks his nose up we'll find out where he's been," was the grim answer from Tanrid. He added, "And we don't have to be nice about it, either, since he's broken bounds."

With this prospect before them, the horsetails' moods improved, and they fell into quiet conversation, with no more than occasional glances Joret's way to see if she was listening.

Joret piled her gear neatly, her unstrung bow in its weather wrap, sat against a tree, and unrolled a scroll to study.

Inda scanned the area. The Chardaus flowed behind them; right below them was the great east-west road leading to the bridge. Elsewhere the land was a lot steeper, more forested, than it had seemed on the map. Their little valley was protected, especially in this low-cloud, drizzly weather—

He frowned, listening. Riders on the road! They didn't look like danger, they were just ambling along. Brigands didn't ride out in the open like that. These fellows were talking like it was Restday in the city.

"Should we warn 'em, d'ya think?" Cama asked, adjusting his eyepatch. "They won't want to ride into a battle."

"Silence," Tanrid ordered. "We're to lie low, remember?"

Inda frowned. Something was wrong. Six riders, no weapons in sight, dressed like farm folk, except for—

"Horses," he breathed. "Down."

He hadn't meant to issue a command. The horsetails looked surprised, and Tanrid raised a hand to smack him for frost, but Cassad Ain caught his wrist. "Inda. What do you see?"

"No farmers have horses like that," Inda whispered back.

They peered through bushes at the riders, who chatted and laughed, but yes, they all glanced furtively about them as they gestured, and the horses were pretty, not purebred Nelkereths, but definitely high-bred, and what was more important, definitely trained. Nervous, too, they could tell by looking at their ears.

Inda's mind was fast adding up the details. "They keep scanning west," he murmured, thoughts racing faster now, like a plunging stream, no, a waterfall, but sharp and clear: the details all converged somehow from endless possibility into a continuous stream of probability.

"Do you think they're searching for the main battle?" Whipstick elbowed up next to him. "It couldn't be for us." His tone made it a question. "Could it?"

Inda was more sure by the moment. "If they know about the battle, why aren't they over there? And if they don't, why are they scouting? I think they *are* looking for us."

Silence. Joret, the horsetails, and the scrubs all peered down through leaves and tall grasses. Now that the riders were nearer, that the idea had been put into their minds, they could see how the men were scanning methodically, despite laughter and a lounging posture that looked more and more false. Scanning—watching—with expectation.

"We should call the perimeter guard," Cassad whispered.

Whipstick jerked his thumb up. "I'll go."

A noise behind them brought their heads around, and the bigger boys scrambled for knives—

A green-splotched face, perfectly camouflaged, emerged from a shrub. Dogpiss!

He belly-crawled into the camp, eyes wide with terror. "They're dead. I saw two of 'em. Throats slit. One b–b–bleeding to death, killed just now. They killed a couple of *them* first."

"Who's dead?" Whipstick clutched the front of Dogpiss' tunic. His brother trembled in his grip. "Samred? Our guard?"

Dogpiss' muddy hand pointed shakily down toward the river.

"Then we fight," Tanrid said, mouth thinning.

"No, no," Inda said, agonized. "Look!"

Again his brother raised a hand, for he was the ranking boy here, but again Cassad halted him. "He's right. If they're searching, and others attacked our guards, then we had better double or even triple the number we see." He indicated the six riders, passing westward along the road. "A trap. They're closing in."

"A trap . . . for *us*," Tanrid murmured, and the impact hit them all at once: they'd been betrayed.

And if they had been betrayed, so had their fathers.

"Say twelve to eighteen of them, maybe more. Even with the ones Captain Samred and the riders killed, there have to be a *lot* of them to kill our men. We only have our knives and bows," Inda said, not even aware of talking. His mind ran too fast.

"We fight," Tanrid stated. "We won't be rounded up like sheep for shearing."

"We run," Cassad countered, grim. "We're no use dead."

"Run where?" Tanrid snapped, looking around at the unfamiliar territory, and the others looked around too—except for Inda, who had already scanned the terrain.

He considered them: Tanrid, Cassad Ain, Manther, Whipstick, Cama, Dogpiss, Rattooth, Joret, Gdand, himself. Ten against maybe close to twenty grown men, armed men, used to fighting.

His thoughts ran faster, falling into a pattern of order. Turned his head. "Dogpiss. Where were you? River?"

Dogpiss turned his thumb up. "Wanted to see if I could spot the bridge where the battle is. Big turning—"

"Never mind that. You lead the way. And Joret. You're good with a bow, so you cover us as we come after." Joret thumbed up—she was already strapping on her palm guard with its steel thumb ring. "You both," Inda added, looking at Gdand. "Then we make it to the river. Swim to the bridge."

Gdand was short and sturdy, and she would be as good with a bow as she was with knife fighting, or she wouldn't be an Algara-Vayir Runner. "I'll scout the trail," she murmured, and backed away through the shrubs that Dogpiss had emerged from.

Joret had already strung her bow, the only signs of emotion a glow along her cheekbones, and a slight tremble in her fingers. She crushed her scroll into the front of her smock, and shook free all her arrows, so carefully made all winter, feathers beautifully fletched in the tight Marlovan spiral. She looked down, and then hesitated, glancing up at Inda.

It was Inda, not the older boys, who knew each person's strength, whose mind shaped action and order out of the shock that gripped them all. "Leave some for Tanrid and Cassad Ain," he said, and Joret complied.

The older boys had only a few arrows along; theirs awaited them at the academy. Joret and Gdand had each designed and made her own, something that the arms mistress at Tenthen House required for the honor of the House.

Cassad saw the plan. "You and I cover the rear, Tanrid."

Yes. Like in wargames. They knew that drill.

Drill. If life fell into the patterns of drill, they could act, even though the adults set to guard them were dead, the plan betrayed.

"Now," Tanrid said, and they could move: they not only had a plan, but orders.

They abandoned the camp, leaving their bedrolls and gear, everything except for weapons, and withdrew swiftly, Dogpiss, Joret, then Whipstick, who would not let his brother out of his sight. Inda followed Rattooth, and as soon as he moved that ephemeral clarity disintegrated into impressions, worries, sensory details that formed no more order than the dancing motes of sun on running water.

He'd been in command only long enough to set them into motion. Then he was merely a terrified boy, especially when they were spotted by a dark form in a tree who shouted, "They're here! To me, to me—"

Twang! Tanrid shot. They all heard the smack of the arrow's impact and the dark form fell, now making hoarse, gurgling noises, until he landed with a sickening, meaty thud.

The younger boys followed Dogpiss' trail of slippery mud and broken weeds, as insects chirruped angrily around them. Horse riders emerged from the brush to the north, two abreast, in a frighteningly short time.

The two *twangs!* from Tanrid and Cassad were almost simultaneous; a fletched arrow sprouted in one's throat and in the other's gut, and both fell.

"Fan out! Fan out!" the boys heard a man yell.

"That one's got whistlers," Tanrid cried, but Cassad was already belly-crawling through the long grasses to grab the dying man's warning arrows, while Tanrid took aim at the bobbing heads retreating through the trees.

Faster. Crawl faster! Impressions splintered then, and afterward none of them clearly remembered that retreat, or how they got the various scrapes and bruises that marked them. The horsemen, hampered by the uneven terrain and by the deadly aim of the skilled bows, followed at a discreet distance, forming a ring that advanced at a thundering yell when at last the children tumbled onto the rocky riverbank.

But even as they charged, *Wheng! Zang!* Again and again, with trained speed, Joret, who was now poised behind a rock on the river's edge, emerged just long enough to shoot arrows, each hitting its mark, and the five horsemen behind their dead leaders veered off. From the other side of a tumbling stream Gdand sent two arrows, one thunking squarely into a rider's back. He tumbled into the brush.

Cassad and Tanrid had already run out of arrows. Yelling wildly, the boys splashed into the river and began swimming directly out into the middle of the current.

Joret, still perched on her rock, shot until she saw no enemies, then she slung her bow over her shoulder and dove in, Gdand following. The remaining brigands appeared cautiously, and ranged along the riverside. One or two splashed into the water, but were called back by those who realized they would never catch up, not in that icy water, and so they stood and watched as their quarry swirled away down the river.

Inda, looking back once, realized the brigands were not shooting, though two of them had bows. That had to mean they'd had orders to take him and his companions as hostages.

That's proof, Inda thought hazily, as he gasped and kicked hard through the bitterly cold current sweeping him along. *If they had orders, then they definitely knew we were coming.*

Chapter Twenty-four

BLEAK gray light leaked between the eastern cloud bands when ten or twelve of the brigands appeared, riding slowly toward the bridge.

Enticingly slow.

They were watched by the three commanders, who were crouched down behind a jumble of rocks and shrubbery on a hillock from which they could see the converging roads.

"Another decoy," the Jarl of Jaya-Vayir said, drawing out his knife and running a thumb along it.

The Jarl of Cassad eased his position, wincing against the lightning radiating from his hip. Up all night, waiting, watching. *War is a young man's game.* "Decoy from what?" he forced his tired mind to think. "We know where they are."

"The question is if they know where we are," the Adaluin murmured, thinking of their own forces lying on the other side of the bridge, waiting; Noth's men scouting in two perimeters, and their reinforcements down the road waiting for a signal arrow that had yet to be shot. The brigands, instead of following their customary pattern of attacking in force, had been sending out these little scouting parties all night, as if—

"Impossible," the Jarl of Jaya-Vayir muttered, thinking of those long, wearying treks through the night forest in the rain, doubling around and then back again, splitting the parties and doubling yet again, as they crept into position.

The Adaluin's hand tightened on his sword, but from uneasiness, frustration. He glanced eastward, now seeing instead of blackness the forested ridges, and farther out, the hills. Nothing there, of course. No one could attack through that terrain. Which was why they sent the boys there—

No. It was impossible. Was it? All the sorties had come from the west, north, south, never from the east. He faced the other Jarls. "The only thing in the east is the boys." And in saying it, realized he had it at last.

Cassad's face changed from disbelief to anger.

Jaya-Vayir's jaw slackened. "But that would mean—"

"They not only knew we were coming, they know our plan."

The Jarl of Cassad glared at the Adaluin, both their minds grappling with the stunning realization: betrayal. Jaya-Vayir got to his feet, feeling old and stiff as he turned his eyes from one to the other. Both of them looking as creaky as he felt, and he wished he hadn't been so generous through the long night with sips from his flask of distilled rye. *Never again,* he thought tiredly. *Unless it's the Venn themselves.*

"But it's the king's plan," Cassad murmured.

And all three faced east. The boys—sent to the east, to be safely out of the way, by order of the king.

No one wanted to speak. They looked at one another, and then all three of them thought of Captain Noth, sent at the last moment as re-inforcement, directly by the king.

The king hadn't betrayed them. But someone close to him—

Sick terror gripped the Adaluin, followed by hot, killing rage. *I will not lose a second family.*

He motioned to his waiting Runner. "Get Noth." The man struck fist to heart, then vanished noiselessly into the underbrush. The Adaluin turned to Cassad. "If they don't know about Noth, we can bring the dragoons around the back way to close the trap on their own trap."

Cassad bared his long teeth. "And hammer them." He gripped his weapons, the cold, sour wind off the marshes whipping his long graying horsetail.

Jaya-Vayir said, "First we need to secure those children—"

Faint over the roar of the river warbled a triple owl hoot. The commanders paused, as poised for action as their highly bred scout hounds, until a message was relayed from the far perimeter: "Someone in the river!"

A young Jaya-Vayir Runner dashed up. "River patrol's pulling the boys and girls out of the water." He panted, smacking his fist to his chest.

Cassad said to the Adaluin, his hands flexing, "They must have figured it out."

"Or the attack went awry," the Adaluin replied. "Either way, we no longer stand between the enemy trap and our heirs."

Captain Noth arrived, moving silently and swiftly.

The Adaluin said, "It's a trap. But we're going to close it." Noth's grim expression hardened. The Adaluin said, "I am afraid it is you yourself who must take the boys and Joret to the royal city. I don't trust anyone else. Take a single riding of your most trusted men, and leave me all the rest."

Noth saluted and backed away, speaking in a rapid whisper to his second in command.

All three leaders motioned to their runners and started giving orders, in quick, cryptic words—as speedy as they were in their young days in the academy so long ago. All three were furiously angry, the cold anger that comes from a narrow escape from the unthinkable. They would not halt until they spent all their rage in exacting retribution.

But the boys and girls would not see it.

They emerged from the river, shivering violently, to find themselves surrounded and bundled up in heavy, severely cut dragoon winter coats, woven wool hats pulled over their wet heads, a fiery swallow of double-distilled rye shot into mouths, after which each was placed on a horse.

Then they were riding hard to the north. They knew better than to demand halts, or reports, of Horsepiss Noth, no matter who their fathers were. There was no talk until they camped that night in a narrow grotto with two rings of guards in ceaseless patrol. Over the fire, as they stone-grilled newly caught trout and stale oatcakes, Noth questioned them. His hard face, its furrows harshened by the flickering shadows of the firelight, gave nothing away as he listened to their reports.

Tanrid protested, "I still think we should have held and fought. I was ready to fight." But his eyes were anxious with the implied question, were we cowards to run?

He was still thinking like a boy who plays wargames, it was clear, as was Manther Jaya-Vayir. Cassad Ain had a better sense of reality; he grimaced, then added in a low voice, "The only one who used his head was Inda. Um, Algara-Vayir Tvei."

Joret added, "Inda knows what everyone is capable of. It was a perfect defensive retreat. I think his mother would be proud." Gdand opened her hand in silent corroboration.

Dogpiss, his green-splotched face serious, ended on a sober note. "Captain Samred and the other Riders were killed. They cut their throats." His voice was strained. "Dead."

Inda gave the briefest account, wonderfully succinct. "Dogpiss said the guards had been killed. We had to retreat. So we did."

"Who ordered the retreat?"

"My brother Tanrid."

"Who made the decision to retreat?"

Inda looked perplexed. "I don't know. We all did, I guess." And when Noth waited, he added, frowning into the fire, "Dogpiss had seen the territory. Tanrid and I had seen the map before we left home. It made sense to retreat, using the bows as cover." He looked up and added soberly, "They didn't try to kill us. I think they had orders to take us hostage. Doesn't that mean they knew all about the plan beforehand?"

Captain Noth said, "It's possible."

Cama and Rattooth asked more questions than they answered.

Whipstick, last, chewed his lip, poked at the fire, then murmured, "We woulda been dead. Inda took command without even knowing he took command, first by seeing what was there, not what he expected to see. We all just saw what the enemy wanted us to see. Me too, at first. Cassad Ain made the horsetails listen to him. Tanrid claimed rank, and after Inda laid out the strategy his brother said to move, then we moved." Whipstick added, "We were betrayed."

His father pursed his lips, and that was that. He said little more, writing an official report for the Royal Shield Arm, who was the top of his chain of command, but his verbal report was saved for the king.

Chapter Twenty-five

WHEN the sun rose over the royal city a week after the battle at Marlovar Bridge, the Sierlaef woke up. He looked out his window. Plenty of time before he would have to order his gear shifted down to the academy for another long, wearying season with the little boys.

Dawn. Old habit—dawn sword drill—prodded at him, to be dismissed. He no longer went down to the practice courts every day. His uncle had said, *You don't have to be the best, you have to command the best.* What was the use of sweating sword work and archery drill when he would command his men to do that? No, he had far better things to do!

He whirled out of bed, took a fast bath, dressed hastily and pulled his wet hair up into its clasp. As he did he thought scornfully of himself at this time last year, so proud of that horsetail at last. But he'd still been a little boy in the ways that mattered. The entire world had changed, ever since New Year's Week, when his cousin Hawkeye took him upstairs for the first time at their old pleasure house, and he found out what the big boys had been doing while he and his Sier-Danas had been sitting below, drinking, playing Cards'n'Shards for real money and thinking themselves so old.

He yanked on his coat, sashing it in place as he kicked his door open. Outside he heard Hadand's familiar voice—"So how did it feel to really shoot someone?"—followed by a different voice, a clear female voice, "I don't know, everything happened too fast. I thought of them as targets like the arms mistress always said, and just when the after shakes she told us about caught up with me, we had to dive into that ice melt—"

That voice. It was so . . . *compelling*. He lunged through the door, and the voice stopped.

The Sierlaef stumbled to a halt, staring.

"Have you sent for Sponge?" Hadand asked, dragging the Sierlaef's attention away from the girl accompanying her. "He should be seeing to his gear transfer to the academy, don't you think?"

The Sierlaef frowned, trying to remember where Sponge was, and why he should send for him, but his wits fled again when his gaze whipsawed back to the girl standing next to Hadand.

The shock of Joret-Dei's startling blue stare made his entire body flame and then just as suddenly turn to snow.

Hadand, looking into her betrothed's face for clues to his thoughts, interpreted them closely enough. She said, "This is Joret, my brother's intended, here for the queen's training."

The Sierlaef struck his fist against his chest. Joret touched her palm over her heart, but did not speak.

The Sierlaef liked how this girl with those amazing eyes, that beautiful mouth, that smooth black hair, didn't giggle or bridle or ask him coy questions.

"Shall I summon Sponge, then?" Hadand persisted. "If you're busy, I can send Tesar."

The Sierlaef opened his mouth, but already he could feel the sides of his tongue quivering when he even thought of speaking, and so he just shrugged.

"We'll do that right away then." Hadand set off briskly, and the other followed without any backward glance.

The Sierlaef leaned against his door, watching them go: Hadand short, Joret medium tall, straight as an arrow, her body hidden by her smock and loose riding trousers. Long glossy black braids swung free down her back.

Joret felt that gaze all the way down the length of the hall, breathing easily only when they turned a corner at last. "I take it he discovered sex," she said in Old Sartoran.

Hadand smiled. "Here I dreaded what it would be like if he decided he liked girls, but it has worked out so, so very well. He's been on Heat Street nearly every day, almost never at the practice courts or stable. The Sierandael took a trip for treaty purposes—the king has been far too busy with his own troubles—so no one issued orders about Sponge at all."

Joret's brows puckered faintly. "Has Sponge been left to work in the stable all winter?"

"Yes. It's been boring but at least no one had to beat him, because he obeyed the Sierlaef's orders. He never trespassed in the archive, not once, after those first two or three horrible weeks. Then the Sierlaef was too busy on Heat Street to remember to issue any more orders." She looked around when they reached an intersection, but except for one of the Queen's Guard pacing a floor below on her rounds, no one was in sight and anyone listening at one or another of the hidey-holes that Hadand knew about would not understand Sartoran.

Hadand breathed a soft laugh. "The Sierlaef is unlike his father and grandmother in not choosing his own sex, but he's like them in that he's already found a favorite. Kies is also very nice, and I've paid her a good deal extra to keep him very busy for a long time, and never ask him to speak."

Joret laughed. "So if he's happy—"

"Everyone around him is happy," Hadand said. "I may be only fifteen, and sex is still a mystery to me, but I already know what my future strategy as queen will be: if Aldren is happy, everyone will be happy. And if he's picked Kies as his favorite for the rest of his life, like his father picked dear Uncle Sindan at about the same age, well, he could have picked far worse. She's kind, easygoing, has no interest whatever in war politics, she just likes her comfort and pretty things." Hadand gave a short nod of satisfaction. "Life ought to be much, *much* easier now."

Joret looked back over her shoulder and murmured, "You haven't had to use the Waste Spell for your woman's cycle yet?"

Hadand shook her head. "But probably this year," she said, making a face. "Look at me." She pulled her smock tight. "Last year Inda and I were pretty much of a size and build—but all of a sudden I got these and this." With one hand she tapped her chest and with her other she smacked her hips, which had indeed widened considerably, though she was not any taller than Joret remembered. Hadand's eyes narrowed. "You?"

Joret took a step nearer, until Hadand could smell the horse scent on her clothes, and the herb she stored them in. "Four months now," Joret whispered, color heating her face and fading again. "But I won't leave off smocks, as long as I possibly can. I don't want sex, not with anyone I know. It's unbearable enough, to feel *eyes* on you, like invisible crawling things. The thought of someone's hands . . ." She shuddered.

Hadand chuckled. "Well, you're here. And Mama will expect you to work in the archives with us, hunting old mentions of magic. You won't have time for sex, if you don't want it. Ndara-Harandviar will see to that!"

"Good."

They ran downstairs, down another long hall, through slanting rays of light from the western windows, then through shadow again, light and shadow, as Hadand smiled and said, "Even Sponge is happy. It was I who brought him reading from the archive, something new every night or two, especially after Barend was sent off to sea again. He's been so good, everyone in the stable has come to love him as I do. He's actually a little like his uncle in that when he has to do something, he does it all the time, hard, and doesn't do anything else. He set himself to master shoeing and saddle repair and he did. The stable master reported to the Shield Arm that no one, at all, is faster or neater at trimming horses' hooves." They started down the last flight of stone stairs. "So, though he did not get any of the weapons training he was supposed to have, he is now so thoroughly accomplished in the stable that no scrub will be better this year. Here's the stable, and the queen's barracks is through that way. We may as well stop together."

They found Sponge out in the back, mending halters. He looked up at the girls' arrival, his face unreadable, his attitude as courteous as if he stood in his father's study.

"This is Joret," Hadand said.

"Welcome," Sponge said politely.

"And Joret being here means Inda is here," Hadand said. "He ought to be down at the academy now, unloading his gear."

Sponge's face changed. Joret, watching with interest, realized he'd looked old, in a way, but now he looked like a boy again, a merry one. "I . . ." He sat down again, the joy fading from his expression. "My brother . . ."

"Gave his permission. Go. I saw him on the way."

Sponge set the halter down, replaced the mending gear, and was gone before anyone could take more than five breaths.

He stopped at his rooms only long enough to summon Runners to transfer the gear he'd already packed himself, then he raced down through castle halls, skipping round armsmen, bursting into the street and running through the mossy archway to the academy.

He arrived, breathless, face glowing with delight, at their new barracks—officially in cub territory—to find Dogpiss, Cama, Rattooth, and Inda sitting on the worn wooden floor between rows of battered wooden bunks exactly like the ones in the scrub pit, playing Cards'n'Shards. As his entrance, they all sprang up.

Inda was not much taller but a little broader, muffled in what was obviously one of Tanrid's castoff gray academy tunics. His brown eyes were the same brown eyes, wide with honest emotion he never thought of hiding: surprise, and a delight to mirror Sponge's own.

"Sponge!" He pointed. "Good thing about getting here early is, we nipped the best bunks. There's yours."

Sponge glanced at the narrow, plain bunk under one of the coveted windows; his joy belonged entirely to Inda's arrival.

But it did not do to fuss, of course. He said, "Good thing? As in there are bad things?"

"Chores started right away," Dogpiss said, sighing.

Sponge bent closer. "Your face is green. Is it?"

Dogpiss looked dismayed. "It's not *fading*, is it? Think I could smear some more on?"

Cama shook his head, and Rattooth said, "Strut."

Dogpiss sighed.

Inda, eying Sponge, said cautiously, "Winter interesting?"

Sponge shrugged again. "I did get lots of reading done, after my cousin was sent back to sea," he said. "Mostly firsthand records. They differ from chronicles—"

"No, you don't," Dogpiss said, waving a hand. "You two are not going to start blabbing about history first day we're here. Save it for the beaks."

Cama looked relieved, Rattooth disappointed, but no one was surprised. Inda gave a one-shoulder shrug that promised private talk later, and Sponge sat down to watch the game.

Before the current round was finished and he could be dealt in, they heard the quick tap of boot heels on the wooden floor outside the door, and looked up in time to see Tanrid Algara-Vayir stride in, resplendent in House coat, fringed formal sash, his best dagger, and highly polished boots.

"Get to the baths," he said briefly. "Clean up. Meet at the great court at the bell-change."

"What?" the boys cried, but Tanrid whirled and stalked out, his long brown ponytail flapping on his shoulder blades.

Inda turned to Sponge, who said somewhat diffidently, for he hated displaying inside knowledge, "I think it might be that we're all to attend Master Gand's wedding. Since we're here."

"Wedding!"

"Master Gand?"

"Masters can't be married!"

Sponge shook his head. "I'll explain as we get ready."

They raced off to the baths. As it happened, only Rattooth Cassad and Inda were interested enough to listen as Sponge said, "It has to do with those ships that sank. Treaties. Master Gand and his wife will be Shield Arm and Randviar in the north."

Cassad looked amazed. "Gand? Married?"

Inda splashed them. "Seems strange. Something's missing."

Sponge thought of the things he could say, and what he ought not to say, and kept silent as he splashed back.

Weddings were pretty much the same all over the kingdom, Inda thought later, after stuffing himself with lemon cakes. Even when held in the vast Guard Hall instead of a castle, the long tables exactly like the boys' mess tables in the academy pushed against the walls, the stone floor swept clean, wreaths of fir fashioned round sconces for decoration, filling the air with a sharp scent of pine. Standing around clean and neat while the two people getting married, equally clean and neat in their wedding clothes, gabble the vows about fealty you've heard all your life, but afterward they share out the wine and the cakes, and then comes the drumming and dancing.

Men's dances, women's dances, men's, women's, the children weaving in and around them, either dancing in silly competitions or else playing tag games, or cramming more sweetcakes into their mouths. The youths watched one another dance, and the older adults watched the youths watching one another, and on the perimeter, the ranking guests sat at the plain wooden plank tables and held up wine cups to one another, talking in quiet voices, testing or redefining alliances.

It seemed strange to Inda to see the academy masters in a wedding setting, especially strange to see hard-faced Captain Gand in a wedding shirt with a silken sash round his waist, all made by his new wife. But he smiled, and seemed pleased, and the boys were pleased for him—at a respectful distance.

The king even came, but he didn't stay, at least. Not that the boys minded the king being there, except for the fact that they all had to behave like they were on parade.

Afterward it was fun, trying to sneak wine and cracking a continual stream of jokes. Dogpiss' face was crimson with laughter when at last the signal went round for the boys to retreat to the academy.

The walk wasn't long, of course. No one left in any kind of order. Inda looked around for Sponge, but not finding him, he started off, pausing in the doorway when he saw a tall man standing just outside, talking to two masters and blocking the way. The light from behind Inda shone on a familiar face: the Sierandael, Royal Shield Arm and overseer of the academy.

Inda was not about to shoulder past the masters, much less the Royal Shield Arm, so he waited. The two masters presently saluted, fists to chest, and walked off speaking a last cheery wish for a good evening, and Inda, expecting the Sierandael to follow them, lifted a foot, ready to sprint for the academy.

But then the Sierandael glanced over his shoulder, and his brows lifted when he saw Inda. Not just saw, but recognized.

They had never spoken. Inda would hardly expect so exalted a figure to take notice of a scrub. In fact, he wouldn't want that to happen, because far too often "taking notice" was just another definition of trouble. He mentally reviewed his behavior that evening. But that assessing look, that wasn't puzzlement, that was definitely recognition.

"You're the young Algara-Vayir, are you not?"

He *was* in trouble! Dismay made Inda stiff and solemn. Should he salute? His right fist balled, ready to strike his heart. "Sierandael-Dal."

The Sierandael, looking down into that face from which all the humor and intelligence had been studiously smoothed out, put his hands behind his back and assumed a more jovial tone. "I hear from Captain Noth you had a near miss with brigands."

Inda worked to repress his relief. "We were disappointed, Sierandael-Dal."

"Come along. Tell me about your end of things."

Somewhat bewildered, Inda followed the Royal Shield Arm out into the cool night air. "Nothing really to tell. We weren't part of the real plan—wasn't it the king's order?"

The Sierandael smiled, nodding. "Yes. Though you boys have the courage, you do not yet have the experience for warfare."

"Well, we were separated off, as ordered. At dawn, we saw some riders. They looked suspicious. Dogpiss came back—he'd, ah, gone down to the river to scout—and found our guards dead, and so we had to retreat, and we did. Then Captain Noth was detailed to whisk us off here to the royal city, and we didn't get so much as a sniff of the battle."

The boy was unprepossessing to look at, but the Sierandael remembered the games last summer, and said with a laugh, "I would have been put out when I was your age. A swindle!"

Inda murmured agreement, thinking, *Why does he laugh?*

Then the Sierandael said in the same joking tone, "So what do you think your father did, after you boys were whisked away?"

"Well. We talked about it . . ." He began doubtfully, afraid of what Tanrid called Blabbing Too Much.

"I don't want to hear what the others thought. I want to hear what you thought," the Sierandael said, which took Inda utterly by surprise.

A flame of gratification burned through him. No adult in his experience showed the least interest in what he thought! *So make it clear, dolt,* he told himself.

The Sierandael had fallen into step beside Inda, who gazed up at the torches on the castle walls, no longer oil-dipped as of ancient days, but kept alight by magic, painting with reddish glow the familiar wood-and-stone buildings of the academy that would comprise his world for the months ahead.

What he really saw was the map lying there on his father's table, overlaid by the glimpse of the bridge, of the terrain as seen from the river, that the boys got before Captain Noth took them away. And again he felt that strange sensation as all the details, past experience, what he'd heard, thousand of bright pinpoints of possibility coalesced into probability. His mind floated down that fast stream of conviction and he said, "My father would be angry, and he'd use that, I think, to reverse the plan. Since we were betrayed. So . . . instead of waiting for them he'd charge right over the bridge, straight toward where he knew they were lurking. They'd think their trap closing. But if Father sent Captain Noth's dragoons to veer round to the headland that way, down along the riverside . . ." His hands dipped like moths in the ruddy light, over the map he saw so clearly in his head. "They think they're closing a trap, but one closes on them." He smacked his hands together. "The dragoons dropping off to fight on foot through the marshy area, the others forcing the brigands down to the water, which is the barrier. They'd have nowhere else to go, and so the dragoons could . . ." Inda talked on.

The Sierandael felt his own palms prickle. The boy's words were an eerie echo of the report he had received just two bells ago, from an exhausted Cassad Galloper who had ridden straight from the thorough rout at the bridge, so complete, so merciless it would probably gain a name, and the king might even demand a banner for the Great Hall.

The boy could be lying for effect. He could have heard some part of Jarend-Adaluin's orders before leaving. Maybe he'd heard them without quite realizing. But Noth had been quite definite about plucking those children out of snowmelt waters, and about the fact that the boys had been nowhere near the commanders. Jarend-Adaluin's anxiousness for his sons, an anxiousness intensified by his having survived the murder of one family a quarter century ago, would have driven him to get them away from impending danger just as fast as possible.

Inda, realizing he was rambling, stopped, his face flushing. "Um, that's how it works in my mind, but of course I haven't actually seen a real battle," he said contritely.

The Sierandael forced another laugh, a forgiving one, an indulgent one. "Quite all right, boy. We all like to imagine what we might one day be called upon to command. No doubt you look forward to that, do you not?"

The Sierandael smiled down into that face, thinking rapidly ahead. Of course he would set the same problem for the older boys, but he already knew what he'd hear: a lot of bravado, making maybe tactical sense, as he'd expect from seven years of good grounding. But none of them, not even Tanrid Algara-Vayir, would see the solution. No one except an eleven-year-old boy.

Inda, meanwhile, was troubled by his reaction to the Sierandael, his commander while here, the king's own brother and Shield Arm. He could not define why he felt so ill at ease.

Prodded by a stab of guilt, of perplexity, he realized that he had been asked a question, and he said more than he ordinarily would. "Oh, I do, Sierandael-Dal. Well, not at home, not really. I've heard enough about the burning, and how long it took for the land to recover." Adding in a burst of feeling, "If the Venn come, like Tanrid keeps saying, well, then, if it's when the Sierlaef becomes king, then I shall be able to fight under Sp-uh, under Evred-Varlaef's command. I'd like that."

The Sierandael laughed as they passed through the last stone archway between guard territory and the academy proper. Inda realized why he felt uneasy with this man, academy commander and king's brother though he was: his was a laugh without humor, without cause. It was Kepa's laugh, and Branid's at home.

The Sierandael, looking down at that reserved expression, forced himself to smile, and to wave a casual hand in dismissal as he said, "And so perhaps you shall. But there's much to be learned between now and then. Go get your sleep, then learn it."

"Yes, Sierandael-Dal." Now Inda knew he should salute.

The Sierandael watched him run down the narrow stone corridor between the walled-off barracks courts, saw the relief in that springing step, and pursed his lips. He had had command of men and boys for enough years to recognize in Indevan Algara-Vayir the most dangerous type of all: the born commander who is utterly loyal, and as utterly without ambition.

And that loyalty had already gone to the wrong prince.

Chapter Twenty-six

S PRING slid into summer, Inda's days resembling one another in their sameness: drill, work, never enough sleep, and occasional moments of conversation with Sponge, all the more cherished because they were so few. Their new tutor, handpicked by the Sierandael himself, saw to it that these boys were not "coddled" as they had been last year. Coddled? The boys' surprise was immense at their first callover before Master Starthend, when with his very first words he declared just that. Coddled!

But Starthend kept his promise. Because he'd been instructed to ride them hard, and because he had his own private grudge against Captain Gand—who'd been promoted over Starthend back when they were both dragoons—he decided he'd show these boys what *real* dragoon training was.

At this year's games, these boys would outshine everyone in the lower academy, and thus outshine Gand.

The boys, used to rough handling at home, and Gand's exacting standards the year before, adapted. Inda still forced himself to waken early three times a week in the cold, often rainy hours before dawn, in order to make it to the Great Hall for his practice in the Odni with Hadand's arms mistress. Lessons he continued to teach Sponge every chance they got.

It was far from being a bad year. The boys loved getting training ahead of their year—they expertly judged the pigtails' annoyance by the variety and heat of their insults about strut, frost, and stupid scrub clumsiness at mimicking dragoons, and thus the lessons Starthend had meant to be so grueling (and they were) were also secretly gratifying, though the boys knew better than to let Starthend see that.

Smartlip was tireless in his efforts to please everyone. Kepa was subdued. Mouse Marth-Davan not only spoke of his own accord, but had become riding mates with Lan Askan, who was as horse mad as he. Cherry-Stripe was relieved when Inda, the unacknowledged leader of the barracks, made certain he was always chosen commander of ridings in scrub wargames—when the boys could chose. It was an unspoken alliance that thwarted nosy brothers, and Cherry-Stripe was the more grateful that Inda never seemed to expect gratitude.

All Inda wanted was for the scrubs to win.

The masters always picked the sons of the Jarls as leaders, except for Inda, son of a prince. No one wasted time questioning why. Cherry-Stripe and the others depended on Inda for plans; Inda's plans didn't always work but they were by far the best, and he always figured out why they didn't work, explaining it to the others afterward. Not that everyone listened—indeed, along with Cherry-Stripe, only Sponge, Noddy, Cama, Cassad, and sometimes Flash (if he and Dogpiss weren't busy with more important matters, like stinging off the older boys and getting away with it) listened.

Inda, delighted when his tactical experiments worked, was content to keep his leadership strictly within the confines of their pit. He'd already learned the difference between being appointed leader by someone outside and leading because others chose to follow.

But, unknown to most of the boys, political tensions rapidly worsened, tightened by the sinking of the three great ships that had been intended to form the core of the king's envisioned fleet, and tightened again by the repercussions of the Battle at Marlovar Bridge.

Men sent Runners back and forth with messages questioning the truth of the rumor that someone had betrayed the king's plan—which meant that someone had put a price on the heads of the Jarls. And a prince.

Of the young people only Sponge and Hadand saw some of what was happening, Sponge by watching the tension and whispered conferences among masters, and Hadand by observing Ndara-Harandviar's tension, her worries about her Runners until they arrived safely back, but neither was able to see the other long enough to safely talk.

Inda was oblivious to the political realm outside the academy. But he was not unobservant within his own world.

"Dogpiss, I don't think a sting is a good idea."

Dogpiss paused in the middle of pitching hay, his blue eyes wide and surprised. "What? Why?"

Inda glanced at the hay sifting down through the tines of the pitch fork onto the hard-packed ground that they had just swept, and snickered.

Dogpiss, glancing down, sighed. "Aw, horseshit." He jabbed his pitchfork into the pile of hay on the cart, and flung it over into the horse's stall. "I think we need a sting."

Inda shook his head. "Haven't you see how the beaks are always watching, whispering? I think if we do *anything* on the banner game, Starthend is going to use it as an excuse to gate us all. If not worse."

"I'm not afraid of Starthend." Dogpiss frowned over his shoulder. "Why are you?"

Inda sighed, knowing he'd expressed it wrong. "It's not fear, it's keeping your head low when there's lightning all around. There's something wrong somewhere. Haven't you heard about some of the duels fought over in the Guard? Duels! If they get caught, it's a flogging!"

"That's just Kepa drooling," Dogpiss scoffed. "He wants to see a flogging, so he's listening to every rumor he can find—"

"Dogpiss, do you really think I give Kepa's rumors the worth of half a horse fart?"

Dogpiss sighed again, this time because he knew Inda was right. In fact, Whipstick had recently taken him aside and muttered, "Father says lie low. There's trouble up in command. Don't draw attention."

Dogpiss said, "But, see, when it's like this is when we need a laugh most. A good sting would get everyone laughing."

Inda paused to wipe his forehead against his sleeve, hating the hot still weather. He couldn't remember so rotten a summer. Miserable heat trading with fast, violent storms. Maybe that was the reason for all the vile tempers.

Vile temper. "If your great sting tosses a shoe, Master Starthend is going to land on us all with willow aswing. And you know he doesn't think anything funny. Ever."

Dogpiss grimaced, and for answer threw another load of hay so violently it scattered clear over the horse's back like spindly snow. His last attempt at a practical joke, aimed at the pigtails just above them, who had been (in the scrubs' opinion) far too assiduous in staff practice, had failed—they were spotted by a pair of pigtails illegally perched on a wall, gambling, who promptly snitched on them.

Though only Dogpiss, Basna, Flash, and Fij had been involved, Starthend had punished them all, making the scrubs sweep down the great parade ground on Restday, since they obviously had too little to do. And he promised the punishment for their next infraction would be far more painful.

Dogpiss thought about that, looked over at Inda, and said, "Maybe, but I tell you, that's exactly why we need a hoot." He grinned wryly, and then his smile faded. "And the horsetails need a lesson."

Inda grimaced. The way the horsetails—no, the Sier-Danas—had been riding the younger boys of late might be just a result of the weather, or it might be anger at the fact that they had been closed out of the great city-game. And Master Starthend had seen to it that the Tveis hadn't enough free time to hide out like last year: in fact, he sent them over to the horsetail pit to work. "Training," he called it. "In obedience."

Dogpiss leaned on his pitchfork and wiped his forehead. "Once we're out on the banner game we might be able to hide."

"True." Inda heard Starthend's hard heels on the warped wooden flooring leading to the tack rooms, and hastily turned back to work.

And while the boys did their best to look diligent, on the other side of the castle, Chelis the Runner self-consciously smoothed a plain tunic over her own Runner blue, and joined the other girls. No one gave her a second look. They were too self-conscious themselves, and too awed by their surroundings.

Ndara-Harandviar appeared moments later, dressed as plainly as they were. "Come, we have plenty to accomplish."

She led the way to the first of the long barracks rooms used by the girls in the queen's training, which looked like barracks rooms the kingdom over: bunks, trunks, windows. Dust circling lazily in the hot, still summer air caught the eye, drawing attention to slanting golden shafts that fell on worn linen quilting neatly smoothed over each bunk.

"I have found that it is much swifter to do my yearly check on the bedding when the girls are out. They all have such different ideas on what constitutes wear and tear . . ."

Ndara-Harandviar continued in a calm voice, describing exactly what to look for, and what to do, and the city girls hired for the occasion forgot they were in the very rooms the Queen's Guard and future Jarlans and Randviars used, breathing their air, touching their things. There was practical work to be done, and they knew well enough how to do that.

And so it began. One by one the girls were divided between the rooms, Chelis held back for last. "You will work here." Ndara-Harandviar led the way down a dark, worn-stone hall.

But no barracks waited. They turned through a narrow door, and climbed narrow stairs. Up, and up, to another door that opened onto bales and bales of undyed wool. The smell of it was strong in the windowless little chamber.

With shaking hands Ndara clapped alight a glowglobe, shut the door, and kept her back to it. She observed Fareas' chosen emissary, a tall, strong, quiet, capable girl, and drew a deep breath. "Fareas-Iofre has a message?"

Chelis said, "My message is: What have you discovered about the betrayal of the plan for the attack at Marlovar Bridge?"

Ndara said, "Brigands are not born from rocks. They come from families, and even have families of their own. Many are former Riders, dismissed for breaking rules or stealing or fighting. One of my Runners has a daughter who works for a tavern keeper in town who hears and passes on careless castle talk to his brother, who is an ex-Rider."

Chelis gripped her hands. "And so the treachery they all speak of. The betrayal of the plan. It was a gabby servant in the king's employ, or a drunken guard who hinted at the plan?"

Ndara whispered, "I believe it was my husband."

Chelis felt her heartbeat in her temples. Pandet, the Runner killed, had been her guide when she first began training. She worked her lips, then said, "The Sierandael plots against the king, then, is that it?"

Ndara gave an impatient, dismissive shake of the head, a gesture too desperate to be perceived as arrogant. "If only it were that simple! If the Sierandael sought to murder his brother and take the crown, I could shout *Treason!* before the throne, and might even be heard. The Sierandael loves his brother. He adores his brother. He loves and adores him so much he would do anything to be first in Tlennen's heart, first in his respect. And being first in his respect means proving that he is always right about matters military—even if it means careless talk of the sort that leads to pirates finding where our ships are and careless talk about Jarls and an Adaluin who he considers troublesome, therefore bad for his plans, therefore bad for the kingdom. Do you see? He is in his own mind's eye the rescuer of the kingdom."

Chelis turned her thumb up, her mouth still dry.

"Further, you must remember that the king adores the Sierandael. Honor and love bind them both, and the Adaluin is also bound to the king by the same bonds. Therefore the message I have for you is for his wife, and not for him."

Chelis passed a hand across her forehead, then said, "I don't understand. I mean, I see why we cannot tell Jarend-Adaluin without proof. But I do not understand how the Shield Arm is not betraying the king by talking carelessly, as you say, about the king's own plan for the Marlovar Bridge attack, so someone heard and passed it on."

"Because he always has to be right. Up there with his brother the Sierandael loves glory. If he can win glory and his brother's regard, he would do anything. Anything," she repeated, her voice a mere whisper. "Including bring war to us."

Chelis looked confused. "War. But we are prepared for that, are we not? We always hear about the Venn coming—"

Ndara sighed. "Never mind the Venn. For now, you must realize that you are now involved in high politics. Everything I tell you, everything the Iofre tells you, must stay secret. Who the person was who overheard him, and brought word to the tavern keeper to pass on to his brother, we may never know. My Runner's daughter only accidentally heard the brothers talking out at the stable. What we do know is that the repercussions are severe. Angry Jarls who feel that betrayal of some could lead to betrayal of all. Others making demands for the price of alliance."

Chelis could understand that. So the Sierandael was feeling the effects of the betrayal, then, even if he wasn't *consciously* aware of betraying anyone.

Ndara said, "We must return, and you must leave with the girls, and wear that servant gown right out of the city. One of the Iofre's Runners has already died this year, and three of mine. Brigands still exist, and for them torture for information is campside entertainment. Do you know how to go to ground?"

Chelis's mouth was now very dry. "We trained."

"Do it. Always. A different route every single time. No matter how bad the weather is. Pandet's mistake was reusing the same route, thinking winter protected her."

Ndara saw comprehension in Chelis' face, and said, "Last. A spy—and I am one, make no mistake; I spy on my own husband—a spy seldom hears everything she must hear. Usually it's a caught word, a night of searching papers for a single line, days of sitting and listening to the chatter of the unwary for the possible mention of a name, a place."

Chelis' insides tightened. Here was something new.

"So we have to listen to everybody my husband talks to when we can. One is the royal heir, the Sierlaef. One of my ears, shall I say, overheard last month a scrap of, oh, not protest, but surprise from him. The exact words were *Inda Algara-Vayir? Why a disgrace? He's just a scrub.* Repeat that."

Chelis easily repeated not just the words, but also the careful tone. That had been one of her earliest lessons.

"Fareas-Iofre must hear it exactly that way, so she can help us interpret what it might mean. We listen, we spy, but as yet we cannot fathom what it means."

Chelis rubbed her sweaty hands down the gray tunic. "The Iofre has been afraid for him ever since he came here. She fears he's a hostage."

"He is." Ndara sighed. "No one understands why the Sierandael does not like the Algara-Vayirs, it's just accepted that he doesn't. And it's also accepted that having both his sons here would insure that Jarend-Adaluin does nothing in the south without the king's sanction. We assumed that would be the end of it, and so it was last year, but not now. What inspired the Sierandael not just to notice Indevan, but to order the heir to disgrace him—if that's what it meant—I don't know for sure. I wish I did. There is something, as near as I can tell, about the Marlovar Bridge Rout that started this new plan. And I have been waiting a month for Fareas to send you to me, because three of my trusted personal Runners have died mysteriously since last summer, and I have only one left. I dare not send her south."

Lockets. Magic. War. Ndara pressed her thin fingers against her temples, and then sighed. She had a headache, a bad one, getting worse. Not the imminent storm, but the sense that clues, important clues, were escaping her, and the kingdom was sliding toward disaster. The mind wills unceasing vigilance, but the body is not, cannot be, unceasingly vigilant.

Ndara said, "You must go. Whatever Fareas can do must be done soon. Of that I am certain."

Chapter Twenty-seven

THE Sierlaef and Buck Marlo-Vayir perched on the north tower battlements, watching the Guards' wargame in the city below.

The boys were sour. All summer they'd expected the horsetails to be running in this game as attackers. The Guard was in it, the girls were in it, but only the senior year horsetails from the academy were in it.

The Sierlaef had been watching Tanrid's betrothed perched on a low roof, her profile highlighted against the honey-colored stone of the high building beyond her. The girls were snipers, all armed with jelly-bag tipped arrows, as the Guard and seniors chased one another through the streets below.

The Sierandael had arranged for the two to watch on the excuse that they would one day be commanding such exercises, but it did not gratify them. They wanted to be down there now, running, fighting, shooting, being watched from behind windows by the civilians who had been forbidden to leave their homes this day.

Instead, later tonight they had to take the brats out for a stupid, worthless banner game. Oh, once those had been fun enough, but that was when they were boys. Now they were too old for those games.

Buck watched a riding of senior horsetails come charging around a corner, swords out, fanning efficiently. Up on the roof one of the Queen's Guards gave a hand signal and nine girls shot, all hitting their targets, the blunt-edged arrows with their little jelly bags making an odd thumping sound.

The horsetails faltered, looking down in dismay to see where they were wounded; those whose trunks had been hit had to fall, but the others who showed smears of red on limbs got to stagger off, scrupulously not using the "wounded" limb.

Buck groaned, longing with the intensity of one who has rarely been thwarted to be down there with them. "Oh, what fun."

The Sierlaef's gaze scoured down Joret's body: hands, legs, shoulders taut, form perfect as she took aim, her profile cool, severe, unchildlike. Her shapeless tunic pressed against her by hot, fitful breezes, revealing the swell of her breasts, the enticing curve from waist to hip. *Two years,* he thought. *She'll be here two years. Surely she'll leave off smocks.*

Frustration of a personal sort made his mood vile. "Go."

A stupid banner game. Fun for boys, but for men, it just meant a whole week out in the field, away from Heat Street—away from *real* fun. *It's all stupid,* the Sierlaef thought.

Well, if he had to do a banner game at least he was in command of one army. And the only master who would be along would be that stupid bootlick Starthend. Maybe he could get some fun out of his uncle's stupid commands.

Buck Marlo-Vayir glanced at that smile, and sighed inwardly. Trouble ahead.

Chapter Twenty-eight

BANNER games were the oldest form of Marlovan wargaming, dating from before there ever was an academy.

Banner games during Inda's day were played by all the academy boys, who were divided into two armies. The regulations over the years had evolved into a bewildering complexity for the outsider, with rules both overt and implied, that it was nearly impossible to explain beyond the obvious goal of capturing one another's war flags.

Tradition dictated that the games be six days, the first three days on foot, weapons confined to willow swords, the second three days on horseback, weapons increased to blunted spears and imaginary knives. Most of the rules governing interaction in banner games were on the honor system, with a fierce emphasis on honor, stressed by residual memories handed down as stories of ancestors' banner games suddenly turning into vicious brawls that did far more damage to one another than to any prospective enemy.

The boys thoroughly understood that the banner game was a metaphor for war, that each boy represented a riding, and that if you captained a riding, you were in actually in charge of a flight—three ridings—or even a wing—three flights.

Points were awarded by the master or masters accompanying the boys, otherwise the boys were completely in charge of themselves. The winning ridings got to hang the banner for their level outside their barracks for the rest of the season and the beginning of the next. To win over the group just ahead of you was considered a score off; to lose to a younger group was a deadly insult.

As soon as his neat double column of boys was out of sight of the city, the Sierlaef's interest in the city defense game faded. Out of sight, out of mind. As he rode at the front of the column, the academy fox banner just behind his right shoulder, and the second-year horsetail banner behind his left, he had to acknowledge that yes, his uncle was right, command was sweet. Especially when you had not just one goal, but several, at least one of them being secret.

He was the one who picked the terrain, though Master Starthend had the final say. He picked the campsites, as usual with a stream that ran down the middle, marking an easy boundary.

And though he really didn't care one way or another about Inda Algara-Vayir (what was his uncle on about, anyway?) the Sierlaef's emotions were stirred in the boy's disfavor the first morning when he toured the camp for inspection and heard three scrubs—his own brother, Inda, and Rattooth Cassad—blathering away in Sartoran while setting up the campfire. Not just Sartoran. From the weird pronunciation, it had to be that archival stuff that Hadand sometimes used when she gossiped with Ndara-Harandviar.

That made him angry, and he decided that his uncle was right, the scrubs were full of frost. Were they becoming a lot of damned heralds? Obviously they didn't have enough to do.

With a few stammered words to Buck, he fixed that.

Five long, wretched days later, the scrubs rose well before dawn to set up campfires at both camps. That was quite within the rules. It was also within the rules to deny them horses and confine them to foot maneuvers. Five long days, three of them rendered superlatively hideous not only by the long hours of labor and horsetail willow-swats but by fast-moving thunderstorms, had left them exhausted, wet, and miserable.

So it was with considerable surprise that Inda saw Dogpiss smirking in the bleak light of a cheerless, cloud-streaked dawn as he returned from the other campsite across the creek. Summer, Inda was thinking grouchily as he watched his breath steam. Hah.

"What are *you* so happy about," he muttered. It wasn't a question, but a statement of affront.

To his surprise Dogpiss sidled looks in every direction. Inda's glum mood eased a little, replaced by faint interest. Usually Dogpiss did not care who heard him talk—unless he had some sort of great sting forming in his mind.

Dogpiss stuck his hands in his armpits. "Campfire done?"

Inda waved a hand. "Fire's started. Wash time." He pointed at the cookware resting on a rock, then knelt at the edge of the stream, grabbed up some sand, and started cleaning. On banner games, there were no buckets with the cleaning spell. All very well to do things like the old days, except when it was you who had to do the grunt labor.

Dogpiss dropped down next to him and snickered softly, his breath puffing. "*He* talked to me."

"He?" But as soon as Inda said it, he knew that Dogpiss meant the Sierlaef. Probably out along the inner perimeter, inspecting the other camp. "Talked to you?"

The Sierlaef didn't talk, everyone knew that. He stared at you with his pale eyes, never smiled, just tipped his chin, or snapped his fingers and pointed, and you'd better know just what to do, or one of the Sier-Danas would reinforce the order with slaps and kicks.

Dogpiss sat back on his heels, his hands still in his armpits. He'd already had to wash the other camp's gear, and his fingers were still numb; they were the only clean part of him, just like the other scrubs. "He said, 'Good run?' And of course I started blabbing the proper things—I don't want to be wanding horse shit for the next three days, all by myself—but he cut me off and said 'Good run?' again in a real impatient voice, like he wanted a real answer. I said, 'No.' Know what he said?"

Inda set aside one of the big pans and reached for the next, holding his breath against the smell of burned olive oil and old cabbage. He sighed. "What?"

Dogpiss leaned forward, his blue eyes reflecting the distant sun, grimy yellow hair hanging across his brow, unnoticed except when it itched. "He said, 'Need a laugh.' That's what he said. Just the same thing I was saying before we left." He sat back, grinning in triumph. "And who better to come to for a laugh? When the future king comes to you, well, you've got a rep, right?"

Inda frowned down at the pan he was washing. He knew if he tried to get Dogpiss to hold off on whatever it was he'd planned, the response would just be a scoff unless he had specific reasons. So what were his reasons? He couldn't think of anything specific, just . . . feelings. Tension. *Looks.*

His mental review ended suddenly when Dogpiss smacked his arm. "Don't mug like that," he said, impatient. Inda was going to come out like a beak. He could just see it in his face.

To prevent himself from hearing it, he took off across the camp. He'd brought his itchweed along, hoarded all year. A sting, on a banner game, and all but ordered, practically, by none other than the heir to the kingdom. What a score! What could make it better?

To sting the horsetails. It'd be a laugh, all right, but they'd be the butts of it. And they couldn't say a thing. Or at least they could, but the Sierlaef couldn't. After all he hadn't said "Horsetails out of bounds." No, he'd said, "Need a laugh."

Dogpiss' gut fluttered with hilarity, half-repressed. As the scrubs drudged through cooking breakfast, watching the others gobble their food and eating last, before they faced the cleanup, he told three boys, ones as wild as he, as instantly ready to move, but quiet and quick as well. Just three, beside himself, for this sting of all stings. If, say, four of them moved in a group, they could nail every horsetail bed in a heartbeat.

He was so excited he didn't feel tired, though they'd had four days of no sleep until midnight and rising before dawn.

After breakfast the trumpet assembled the two camps.

"We're still even," Buck said, which of course they all knew. What he didn't need to say was that if they didn't capture the other band's flag by sunset, then the rules changed: the last night you didn't stop at sunset, you could carry on maneuvers all night.

They all knew that meant they'd be up all night.

The scrubs were just exchanging grimaces—no surprise who'd be guarding camp all night while the older boys were on the fun night sneaks—when the Sierlaef stepped forward to select the day's riding leaders for their army.

Older pigtails first. Inda watched with little interest as the Sierlaef snapped his fingers and pointed at various people. He had never been picked once this year, so he was taken completely aback when the long calloused hand shifted his way, the snap, the finger, and then picked out Basna Tvei for the second riding. Inda just stood there as the finger rapidly divided the scrubs into the two ridings.

Riding captain! Joy, tiredness, apprehension, all made Inda's gut unsettled. He was glad he did not have to speak.

"We'll hide the flag twice," Buck announced, his voice low, though the other camp on the other side of the stream was probably in the middle of plans, too. "That means we have to be covered when we make the switch."

He handed out the orders: one riding of pigtails on watch for where their opponents searched first. Another decoying them, so the older boys could shift the flag to where they'd already searched. Inda's riding of scrubs to guard the old site, as if the flag were still there, Basna's tending horses. If they came, retreat, call for the bigger boys, and they and the pigtails could make a pincer sweep and capture them.

Easy enough, Inda thought, trying to rouse his foggy mind.

So when can we get near the camp? Dogpiss thought, trying not to betray himself with laughter.

The ground was too soggy for good riding, so nearly everyone was on foot. When Master Starthend appeared on the makeshift log bridge, the Sierlaef gave him a single nod, and the master signed to the trumpet boy, who blew the three triplets of the forward.

So began another long day, a very long day, with no midday meal, just a lot of running, yelling, shivering when crouching too long, then more running, which at least created warmth.

Sponge endured the day, miserable with apprehension. Long-honed instinct warned that his brother was planning something. There had been too many grim smiles the scrubs' way. If only he could talk to Inda!

Inda tried to comprehend the plan, but he was too tired, he just couldn't see everything before things changed, and why was Sponge over in the other riding? If only they could talk!

Dogpiss writhed with barely concealed impatience. The older boys never let them get anywhere near the bedrolls.

Inda, who gave up trying to command about noon, was not the only one in his riding seeing light rings and double shadows when the sun began to set. He reacted when the pigtails or horsetails yelled at them, ran when the other boys did, dropped when they did. Too many days without enough sleep caught them gaping with yawn after yawn when they stopped, and so most of them never quite knew what had happened until it was too late: suddenly a riding of ponies surrounded them, yipping in triumph, and though they tried to run, and then to fight, then were all flung facedown in the mud and arm-bent until they flat-handed the mud, signifying surrender.

They trooped miserably past the horse pickets toward the stream to cross to enemy territory. Dogpiss made loud comments about the smell of their captors, but the ponies just smirked, a couple of them gloating equally loudly over not having to do any cooking chores.

Lan, Mouse, Fij, and Sponge appeared, horse tack in hand, to make sympathetic noises. Sponge's eyes summoned Inda, and in a low voice he said, "They knew where you were."

Inda sighed. "We'll lose points, but then we hadn't a hope anyway. Why'd we get landed on so hard this week?"

"You don't have to ask," Sponge said moodily. "I think—"

"You prisoners fraternizing?" a gloating pony sneered.

The two separated before they could get smacked.

His brother, Inda thought. Again. But why did the Sierandael let the Sierlaef make a target of his brother? Did they think it good training? Except why wasn't his real training any good? You could say he expected more of Sponge, except Sponge had been so poorly trained until he entered the academy. And he'd been learning steadily since, especially with all the extra secret practice in the Odni, but no one knew about that. Sponge worked hard, he never strutted, and he took smacks and cuffs just like everyone else.

It just made no sense, why the Sierandael let the Sierlaef treat his brother this way. Inda felt frustrated at the lack of opportunity to see Hadand and ask her. He couldn't ask Sponge, who loved talking about everything else, but he never talked about himself, or his family.

Inda shook his head, and then there was no time to think, because the sun had set, and it was time for supper. As prisoners of war they still had to work, but at least only for this camp. They could not cross the stream. Prisoners cooked, ate, then retreated to sit on their bedrolls and watch the rest of the game. They couldn't even sing or dance at the campfire. They could only drum for the dancing. But at least they couldn't be forced on any night maneuvers. They were honor-bound to sit tight until sunup, at which time they could try to escape. That thought swiftly resigned most of them to having lost house points by an entire double-riding of ten being captured.

After a week of outdoor cooking the scrubs were quick and efficient, and so the enemy campfire started early, the first-year horsetails and the youngest pigtails doing war dances and fox-yipping because they were sure they were going to win.

Yet from the look of the growing leaps of flame on the other side of the stream, it seemed the Sierlaef thought his group would win.

"Look at that strut," one of the pony captains exclaimed, hands on hips.

"Yeah," said two or three pigtails.

"Not just strut," muttered a fourth, glaring at the Sier-Danas. "Midwinter frost."

The others glowered in that direction as the other army finished feeding the big campfire on the top of a knoll, then began dancing round it, drums thrumming, like they'd already gotten the banner!

"Frost," muttered an older Tlen cousin. "On a banner game."

"Royal frost," said Ennath Ain sourly.

"Shut up, shut up, shut up," came several agonized whispers. Whipstick Noth just stared, arms crossed, his lips curled in the same way his father's did when he saw a sloppy drill.

"Get to work, you dog turds," the pony captain snarled with a glance across the stream at the Sierlaef, silhouetted against the golden flames, and the crowd hastily dispersed.

Banished, sitting under the stars with blankets round their shoulders, the scrubs stared across at the other camp.

"What ice," Dogpiss whispered, his eyes so wide and excited the firelight reflected in them, two dancing flames. "And won't we just burn their butts. Come on. We can be over and back in three songs, just four of us."

Tuft was, of course, instantly ready to go. So was Flash.

Inda, half asleep in his warm blanket, roused enough to realize that Dogpiss wasn't just talking generally, he actually intended to do something.

Dogpiss had his sting *here*, whatever it was.

Alarm flared in Inda. Working his reluctant tongue in his stiff jaw, he whispered, "No."

Dogpiss and Tuft turned his way. Tuft sat back. Cama—half the time now called Squint, due to Dogpiss' indefatigable efforts—grimaced in disgust, but he was resigned to waiting. After all, they were really honor-bound to stay. Flash flopped back in his blanket.

But Dogpiss scooted near, lowering his voice to a whisper. "Just a few moments. You could count to ten and we'll be back."

Noddy said tiredly, "Not on a banner game, chicken-wit."

"We're not *doing* the game, turd-face," Dogpiss murmured, leaning closer, so as not to rouse the other boys, most of whom had fallen asleep already.

Only Kepa lay awake, but he said nothing. He was furious that Dogpiss hadn't picked him to help with the sting. Well, he still had a chance.

He sat up and muttered, "Whatever it is you're doing, I'll go. Even if Algara-Vayir is a rabbit's foot, some of us aren't scared."

Dogpiss flipped up the back of his hand in scorn and dismissal, then scooted closer to Inda, so close Inda could feel his breath on his cheek.

He whispered, "Why, if the flag was right out, I mean, if it was the other side, I'd leave it right there, a-lyin'. This is better than a sting, it's a score, the fastest, the best yet. A royal score, you might call it." He snickered.

Before he could blab again about his conversation with the Sierlaef, Inda shook his head. "No."

Kepa saw that shaking head. *They're talking about me. Inda's in charge—he's always in charge—and he's a coward!* Fury burned him. He'd never done anything to Inda!

Noddy, disgusted with Dogpiss, flung himself over in his blanket, face turned away.

Inda returned to watching those fires. How strange, that the Sierlaef would stage a triumph campfire, especially so far from where the bedrolls lay. *Especially* when he was pretty sure they were hiding the flag right there, in the—

How long had his thoughts drifted? Not long, but long enough. Something bothered him besides the Sierlaef's strange ruse; it had to be a ruse. And Dogpiss—

Dogpiss was mighty quiet. Tiredly Inda counted the shapes, and then, his heart thumping, he counted again.

And yes, there was Dogpiss's blanket, draped over a rock.

He edged close to Noddy and whispered in his ear, "Dogpiss bunked out. I've got to get him back. Keep everyone silent." He sat up, and saw the gleam of firelight in Kepa's watching eyes, but he paid no attention. Noddy would keep them still.

(Chapter Twenty-nine)

THE Sierlaef sat near the campfire, not hearing the wild drumming, the songs, horsetails singing with two of the Companions yipping counterpoint, not seeing the old war dances around crossed swords, brought out just for the campfire. He smiled, laughing inside because he knew they'd think his smile was at the songs, the dancing, but it was actually because he'd set up his plan so perfectly.

Dogpiss Noth was an idiot. If he wasn't over there doing something nasty at the campsite right now, well, then the Sierlaef could call himself an idiot too. But he wasn't. No, that boy had been so easy to set up. The Sierlaef didn't care what it was that Dogpiss had smuggled into the game. It was enough to know that he'd put him in the right place.

Too bad that idiot Sponge, strutting Sartoran all the way, couldn't have been in that riding too, but his uncle had said to keep Algara-Vayir Tvei and Sponge separate.

All was going according to plan.

And to fix it all in place he'd put Hawkeye on guard, his wildest, hardest-riding and fighting Sier-Danas, with a few sips of strictly forbidden double-distilled rye in him to make his temper worse for being detailed guard duty. Liquor always made Hawkeye wilder. And meaner.

Any moment now the yells would crack the sky, Dogpiss getting thumped and Hawkeye doing the thumping. And so there would be no chance of Dogpiss getting collared quietly by some sympathetic Ain and hustled back to the other side. The whole camp would hear, and that meant the whole camp would see those scrubs nicked honor points while under Inda Algara-Vayir's command.

Those points would lose the game for his own side, not that the Sierlaef cared. He was too old for banner games anyway.

Well, tomorrow he'd go back in private instead of public triumph. His uncle would be proud of his cleverness, and maybe the rules governing royal heirs could change for next year.

He chuckled softly, his ear turned toward the quiet camp.

But when the yells came, the sound too quickly turned wrong. "Hey, you!" And then a scream.

A *scream?*

The drums stopped.

Honor, the game, rules covert and overt were forgotten. The Sierlaef ran with everyone else, stumbling toward the stream from both campfires, to find Inda standing there, his face bleached pale in the starlight, and Hawkeye Yvana-Vayir wringing his hand as though he could shake free from his fingers the impact of Dogpiss' face.

"I thought he was a pigtail spy," Hawkeye cried. "Just gave him a smack! He, he was wet, I guess, and so he slipped—"

No one listened. The boys stood around staring down at Dogpiss' dark form lying half in and half out of the stream, until Cassad snapped, "A light!"

Several boys ran to fetch torches.

"Master Starthend," Buck declared.

"He's still riding the far perimeter," Manther said.

"Shoot off a whistler, dolt!" Tanrid yelled, his voice cracking, and Buck ran off himself to fetch a bow and one of the eerie whistling arrows that they knew were only for dire emergency, and which they'd never before had to use.

Whipstick said nothing, only bent down and gently tried to lift his brother, backing away when the first torch came bobbing down, and in its uneven light they saw the killing gash from the rock point that had bashed in his temple.

"He's still breathing!" someone sobbed.

But he was wrong, it was just the flickering torchlight.

Inda could see it, and would, over and over again, that night, and all during the long, terrible ride the next day, how he'd caught up with Dogpiss, grasping his wrist, his living wrist, all bony like his own, and then Dogpiss launching himself away over a rock, and both boys being taken by surprise by Hawkeye, who had been skulking behind a huge stone, so unmoving they hadn't seen him in the darkness, and how Hawkeye had risen, and moving fast—like all horsetails moved fast—cracked Dogpiss across the face.

Wet, shivering, his boot heels sliding on stone, Dogpiss hadn't had a hope of catching himself, and at the first contact of the side of his head with that jagged stone, his spirit had fled, still laughing, maybe a little surprised.

Inda could still see, as he would all his life, Dogpiss' face as Whipstick turned him over, his eyes still wide open, reflecting the cold, distant stars overhead.

When the Sierlaef finished his report, Anderle-Sierandael threw his head back and laughed.

The Sierlaef stood before his uncle in the Royal Shield Arm's private room, the big doors closed, his personal Runners on double guard outside. That laughter, so amused, so calm, made the royal heir ashamed of the tears he had wept all during the night. Shame brought anger, defensive anger.

The Sierandael stood there silhouetted in front of the window, against which rain drummed. "Summer!" he exclaimed. "This must be the wettest summer I've seen in my life."

No answer from the boy.

His uncle turned around, his dark eyes narrowed, the smile still creasing the sides of his mouth. "Think, boy. Did you really believe that command, that training for command, for war, would see you all safely to old age?"

The Sierlaef gripped his hands tightly behind his back.

The Royal Shield Arm regretted the laugh, but really, it was so perfect, so much better than he ever could have hoped for. When he thought of the time he'd wasted concocting the next stumbling block for that damned Algara-Vayir brat, he could crow with laughter. Oh, the boy could still grit his teeth like a hero through the punishment, but he would never in the future command anything more than his House guard. Not after he couldn't keep a boy in his riding from dying while dishonoring his barracks! And the Sierandael would see to it the blame stayed right there on Inda's shoulders. The Sierlaef—still so very much a boy—didn't need to know his uncle had received a report at dawn, nor did he need to know just how far he'd thought ahead in order to make certain the incident avoided disastrous results.

The immediate issue here was that his nephew's trust had faltered over an imagined moral question, and that had to be resolved fast.

He could already see doubt in the familiar pucker between the Sierlaef's brows, and quickly sought the words to alter that into conviction. "The fact that an accident occurred, and the boy slipped on the rocks and cracked his own head open does not rob you of your success. You managed it all with skill. And you will continue to manage with skill."

The Sierlaef frowned, ramming his knuckles against the back of a chair. "Why *him?* Inda."

"Why Indevan Algara-Vayir? You did not see him stand there before me and gloat about how much he looked forward to fighting by the side of Sponge as Royal Shield Arm."

The Sierlaef grimaced.

His uncle said, "The Algara-Vayirs are trouble. Their father courted your father back when we were young, and now this Indevan, who of course won't inherit, wants to use Sponge to gain influence. You've just put a halt to that. You must think in the long term, my boy. Never lose sight of the long term, because you want a long reign, am I correct?"

The Sierlaef waved a hand in agreement, his lips working, until at last he uttered the word, "Noth. D–dog–p–piss."

His uncle felt a spurt of alarm. "What about him?"

"Talk. I s–set him—"

The Sierandael raised a hand. "Let me get this clear. Did you *order* him to try anything outside of the rules?"

"No." The Sierlaef gripped his hands behind his back. "Hint. S–st–sting—"

"Did you give him clear direction? In other words, could he have taken your words as permission? No. An *order* to run a ruse outside the rules?"

The Sierlaef thought back, frowning. His head ached, he knew what Dogpiss had understood and what he hadn't but how could he explain it without revealing his uncle's command about Inda Algara-Vayir? He couldn't.

Relief and regret warred inside him. He looked into his uncle's face, and realized what his uncle wanted him to say. It would make things so much easier. And it wasn't as if anything they did or said could bring the Noth boy back to life.

"No," he said.

The Sierandael smiled. "Then that matter is cleared up."

The royal heir nodded once, then turned around and stalked out, because he knew his uncle was right. He was always right. But all he could see was that dead boy, and tough Whipstick Noth sobbing his guts out, and so he plunged down through the private wing and out to the street, straight to his favorite pleasure house to bury himself in Kies' ready arms, where he didn't have to hear the boys playing the memory drum songs, where he could drink himself insensible. So what if he didn't have leave. No one would throw him out of the academy.

And so the Sierlaef was thoroughly, numbingly drunk that night, when the academy stood at attention in the great parade ground, the older boys tapping the big drums with a slow, steady beat, as everyone, young and old, hummed the "Hymn to the Fallen," the melody so deep-rooted no one could trace it, they just grew up knowing it, as they grew up knowing that it was never sung for those who died peacefully in bed, but for those who fell honorably on the field.

Inda stood in line, physically present but morally ostracized. The rules required him to be outcast, surrounded in silence, until judgment had been passed. But the isolation of the rules could never match the isolation of his own anguish, intensified by physical misery. The torches held high by Whipstick's barracks-mates streamed like fire-ribbons toward the sky, the colors smeared not just by the tears he could not prevent, but by mounting fever, as yet unnoticed, unacknowledged.

Whipstick stood straight and alone before the small bier that held his brother's still body, a black sash of mourning tied round his middle. At the right stood the Sierandael, at the left the king and his heir. Whipstick waved his torch once over his brother, and then began the Words of Disappearance, but Inda never heard them.

The ache in his body, clamoring now as insistently as the ache gripping his mind and heart, overwhelmed him, and Whipstick's falter, his pause to choke on one valiantly strangled sob, sent a pang so fierce through Inda that mind and body could no longer cope. The torches snuffed, one by one, and then the world died.

He crumpled up without a sound, and didn't wake even when two of the bigger boys, at a gesture from Master Brath, carried him down to the lazaretto.

When he woke, the headache tightened round his skull, and for a time he could not think, did not know where he was.

But then he saw a face. Familiar. Long, hound-jowled, or would be one day.

"Noddy." His voice was gone.

"Don't talk yet. You've been asleep two days. We've swapped off checking, when we can." Noddy smothered a cough, then sneaked a look over his shoulder, a gesture so uncharacteristic the first faint stirrings of alarm tingled through Inda.

"Sick?" Inda asked.

Noddy shrugged slightly, his turtle shrug. "Near all of us. You're the only one who went toes up." He coughed, sniffed, then said, "I'm not supposed to be here, but Sponge somehow got the healer's assistant decoyed. First this." He held out a cup.

Inda tried to raise his head, and winced against the hammer of headache. Noddy helped, and Inda drank down an infusion of expensive steeped Sartoran leaf laced with willow bark.

Almost at once he felt some of the fever-ache ease.

Noddy sat there, waiting, his dark eyes so serious that Inda gradually realized something was very wrong.

Dogpiss.

Fresh grief ripped into Inda's heart, and the silence stretched.

At last Noddy said, with another sideways look, "I daren't stay long. Since I don't have any fever I'm supposed to be in the stable, but Cama is doing my chores." He smothered a cough.

"Why shouldn't anyone visit me?" Inda whispered. "Oh. Judgment. But they know it was just D . . ." He couldn't say the name. His eyes prickled. "His sting."

Noddy sighed. "No. It's not that easy. Somehow the beaks have got the idea that you and Dogpiss were running a ruse."

"What?"

"Yes. And you were in command."

Inda thought that through, and gasped, which set off a fit of coughing.

When he lay back, exhausted and pale, Noddy grimaced. "Maybe coming was a bad idea, but we thought you had better know. Judgment was postponed for a week or so—that's how long the healer said you would likely be sick—but then you're going to have to face Master Brath."

For a long, horrifying moment Inda tormented himself with thinking about what that meant: not only would he lose honor points, but as a riding commander, he'd lose double riding points for the scrub barracks. And wouldn't that be worse now that something horrible had happened? Oh, much worse, much worse. Didn't that kind of thing require punishment before the entire academy?

But wait! He frowned. "A ruse for what?"

"To get both flags, and score off everyone else—a double win for the Tveis. Our army's flag was in our camp. That's why Hawkeye Yvana-Vayir was there on guard."

"But we didn't know that. Did we? Maybe we did—I can't remember. We didn't know where the other side's flag was."

"How can you prove Dogpiss didn't know?"

"Of course he didn't. He'd tell us. Dogpiss was hot on a sting." Inda struggled to sit, and forced words past his fiery throat. "Everyone knows what he's like. All I have to do is tell them that it wasn't a ruse. Of course he knew we were honor-bound to stay. He wouldn't have touched the flags, not if they were lying in plain sight. He just wanted to sneak over. Plant his sting. Whatever it was." A sudden hope. "They must have found it!"

Noddy shook his head once. "He might have had it in hand when he fell, but if so it was long gone downstream by morning. And we did search. Rattooth, Cama, and I. Nothing."

Inda winced. "But Cama, and Tuft and Flash. They all heard me tell him not to run."

Noddy shook his head slowly. "Yes and no. They heard you say not to run, but Cama and Tuft admitted they didn't hear what Dogpiss said next. Flash said he rolled up to go to sleep and didn't hear a thing. But he was farthest away. Kepa said that the two of you were whispering plans—you being in command—and then took off together." Noddy grimaced. "And Smartlip said he saw and heard it too."

"He did not! He was asleep! Wasn't he?"

"He says he wasn't."

"But he lies. Kepa, too. We know that from last year."

"Everyone knows Kepa's a sneaking, lying, bootlicking snitch, and that Smartlip can talk himself into believing whatever gets him attention. But we still have to prove they're wrong. How? And listen to this, Inda. Brath has had Smartlip and Kepa in two or three times, and Cama, Tuft, and me just once."

Inda groaned, his hands roaming restlessly over the blankets. "I have to talk to them. Have to tell them it was a sting. Dogpiss was hot because the Sierlaef put him up to it."

"What?"

"Yes. Didn't Dogpiss tell the rest of you?"

Noddy sighed. "I don't think so. No, I'm pretty sure he didn't, or I'd have heard. And he wouldn't, would he? Most would think it strut, but he'd tell you." The faint emphasis on "you" slid right past Inda, who was sick, distressed, and confused.

Noddy got to his feet, coughing slightly, looking as distressed and confused as he felt. Maybe it was a bad idea to come. He and Sponge had thought it best to prepare Inda, except he looked so terrible, with those red patches in his cheeks and his eyes looking so wild.

He couldn't think of any way to take it all back, or to make it better, and so he retreated, as noiselessly as he could.

Ten days later Inda stood before Master Brath in the office off the academy parade court, his fever too recently gone, leaving a heavy lassitude and a very soggy cough. Master Brath, with Master Starthend standing behind him, wooden of countenance, asked Inda for a report. Inda had had days to consider what he would say, and so out it came in logical order, sparing nothing. He watched those blank faces—blank until he recounted Dogpiss's conversation with the Sierlaef, after which Starthend pursed his lips and Brath said only, "You overheard it? You didn't? Ah. Continue." Inda got the feeling they weren't listening so much as waiting for him to finish.

As soon as realized that, he tangled his words, then he thought he sounded desperate, and his face burned, and his sentences tangled farther, and it was almost a relief when Master Brath said, "That's enough, Algara-Vayir. You stopped making sense on your second, or was it third, iteration of your version of what happened in the prisoner-of-war camp before you and Kendred Noth broke boundaries."

Kendred. Hearing Dogpiss' real name brought back, so vividly it was like a knife inside, those sightless eyes, the defenseless hands that would never move again.

Inda fought hard to regain equilibrium, and almost missed Brath's quick, low voice. "You know the rules. The offense would have been serious enough for you both, but compounds because you were captain, and thus responsible for everyone's honor. That a death occurred because of your actions requires public expiation. Ordinarily that is a hundred strokes before the gathered academy, for their honor, too, has been compromised. The king has seen fit to reduce the sentence to fifty, since this was so obviously an accident, and it was not your hand that struck him down. The sentence will be carried out before the gathered academy in three days. Do you understand?"

"Yes. *No.*"

Both masters reacted, one surprised, the other bemused.

Inda went on, fighting desperately to keep his voice still. "I refuse. I have that right. I can't be caned in front of everybody against my will, unless my father orders it, and so I won't. Because I didn't do anything wrong." The Masters did not speak, and to fill that terrible silence, Inda gripped his hands hard behind his back and said, "I demand the right to tell my father what happened, and abide by what he says."

Master Brath said, "If you refuse my judgment, you must be remanded to the Sierandael for his judgment. He will decide whether or not you have the right to send a Runner all the way to Choraed Elgaer— which would take about a month, there and back, and we're two weeks from the end-of-season games."

Starthend snapped, "Do you really want the entire academy kept here longer just so you can stand on privilege of rank?"

Inda saw it then, that he had been trapped. He did not know why, or

how, but instinct—no, conviction—sang along his nerves. He gritted his
teeth and said, "I won't do it."

Master Brath gave him an angry, cold look. "You could have that sentence increased for cowardice."

"I won't agree to a punishment I don't deserve."

"I have no choice but to place you in a holding cell pending the judgment of my superiors." He sent a look at Master Starthend—what do I
do now?—and then glared at Inda. "Wait here. And I mean do not
move."

Inda's knees felt like water, his head ached again, and tears threatened
behind his eyes, but he gripped himself hard, determined to stand there
all day and night if need be.

Such resolution turned out to be unnecessary. Very shortly thereafter
two big guards appeared, both with stiff demeanors that didn't quite
hide their embarrassment, and he had to walk between them over to the
Guard side, and to the prison there.

His last sight of his academy mates was brief glimpses of pale faces
peering from archways, and barracks windows, some of them looking as
stricken as he felt, but some cold, forcing him to realize that there were
those who believed the false story just because the beaks did.

Chapter Thirty

INDA sustained three interviews while he was in that stone cell. The first was by no means the worst. The Royal Shield Arm came that night, but the interview went exactly as Inda had come to expect. The Sierandael held to the story that Smartlip and Kepa told; he refused to believe that the Sierlaef had had any such conversation with Kendred Noth.

"But it's true," Inda said almost voicelessly. "Dog—Noth Tvei told me himself. The Sierlaef said everyone 'needed a laugh.' D—Noth Tvei said the Sierlaef wanted a sting, to make everyone laugh—"

The Sierandael's eyes narrowed. "Are you asking me to believe that the royal heir, commanding the banner game, talked a boy secretly into scoring against his own side—against the rules? Into sneaking out of a prisoner-of-war camp, when you are honor bound to remain?"

Inda winced. Did it sound like he was trying to put the blame on the Sierlaef? Was that some sort of treason? "Oh, please, Sierandael-Dal. Ask Noddy—um, Toraca. He'll tell you. I mean, he didn't hear it or anything, but—"

"I have spoken with Nadran Toraca, but it is well known that he is your own personal friend, and as such, his testimony might be, shall we say, suspect. As it is, I do not see why I should ask his opinion on conversations he never heard. Nor did you, by your own admission."

In other words, they believed that not only was Inda lying, but that Noddy was, too, which effectively shut Inda up.

The Sierandael then said, in his most friendly, most persuasive voice, "Come on, now, boy. I don't believe you're a coward. You can face fifty smacks. It's not even a whip, for you're still in smocks. Just a willow wand, and if you like, we'll stuff you full of liquor before and kinthus after. You won't even feel the welts until they heal. You surely do not want to dishonor your father's House. Why, what do you think he will say if we have to turn this into a kingdom-wide affair? Your father has a formidable reputation for honor."

"So much so that I know he will listen to me," Inda said, lips trembling. "He knows I tell the truth. And I will abide by whatever he decides."

The Sierandael's anger was more a relief to Inda than not. His persuasive voice contrasted with all the signs of hostility—the steady, searching gaze, the taut shoulders, the angry angle of jaw and elbow— signs Inda was scarcely aware of except that he was made uneasy in this man's presence.

"You might have forgotten," said Anderle-Sierandael Montrei-Vayir, brother and Shield Arm to the king, "that refusal of justice on the grounds of cowardice, or untruth, is a dishonor that never can be amended. You could be stricken from the House lists, stripped of name and inheritance, and your father has the right to hang you as a thief, a thief of honor." A narrow, white-mouthed look. "And so does the king."

"I won't do it," Inda whispered. "I did nothing wrong."

The door slammed shut.

The next two interviews were harder, because he had no defenses.

In the morning Tanrid showed up, in full dress, knife in his wrinkle-free sash—and not just an everyday knife, but his grandfather's gold-handled knife, with the fine wing-markings along the haft—his boots polished. All he was missing were wrist guards and mail coat and shield, which were never worn unless one was riding to battle. Even so he looked too large for the cell to Inda's aching eyes; Inda's fever had returned, because he could not eat and was too angry and frightened and grief-wrung by turns, to sleep well.

"Talk," Tanrid said, his arms crossed, his strong right hand resting lightly over the left elbow in a way Inda knew well.

Inda's voice was going hoarse again, but he managed to get it all out. This time, when he recounted Dogpiss' talk with the Sierlaef, his brother narrowed his eyes and looked quite angry. "I thought so," he said. "The whole thing stinks. It was a damned setup, but I can't figure out why. I will," he promised, jabbing a finger toward Inda. "For my own honor, and yours. In the meantime, you have to uphold our honor and stick it out before the academy."

"But I didn't do anything. You don't believe me?"

"Of course I do," Tanrid retorted. "You are not, as some are saying, a liar. Never were. And no one has dared to say it to my face, either. I caught Kepri-Davan Tvei out, and he wouldn't tell me to my face that you were a liar and coward—he tried to worm out of it. Is he a rabbit? His brother isn't. Anyway, I gave him a prime thrashing out behind your barracks, and not one of your scrubs snitched, though half were watching on the sneak."

Inda said, "Does Whipstick believe me?"

"He will. He's waiting to find out what you tell me."

Inda opened a listless hand, swallowing with difficulty. His throat was raw again. Not that he cared. He couldn't eat anyway. What he longed for was sleep, and no dreams with Dogpiss falling, falling. "So if you believe me, then you see why I won't go out there and take that beating."

"No," Tanrid said brutally, "I don't. You have to stick it out, just like I said. Look, I know you told the truth and that Smartlip lied as well, and won't I thump him when I do catch him out. Right now he's sticking as close to the masters as a turd in straw. But see, Inda. You can't stand out against the Sierandael, or even worse, force our father to do so on your behalf, which is really against the king. It's riding too close to treason. Far too close. It's not fair, and it's not the truth, but they hold the power, not you. We find our own ways of getting justice, so long as the House retains honor. You have to go through with it, just like others have before, and no doubt someone else will next month, next year."

Inda shook his head. "I won't."

Tanrid took a step toward him, mouth thin, eyes dangerous. "It's our honor at stake."

"Honor," Inda croaked, "requires me to stand to the truth. Dogpiss *died.*" He gulped on a sob. "And it was not. My. Fault. I. Will. Not. Take. The. Blame."

Tanrid raised his hand to strike Inda, but he looked down at Inda trembling there, his upper lip long, his eyes bruised, not from violence but by fever and grief and sleeplessness. He was a pitiful object, scrawny, dirty, obviously sick, but there was no sign of cowardice in that face, or of guile, just conviction, as total as it was hopeless.

And so Tanrid lowered his hand, and even wiped it on his tunic, and then, because he didn't know what to say, he did something he hadn't done since Inda was two, before his brother had been given to him to train: he ruffled his head, scratching a little behind his ear, like you do to a favorite puppy, an awkward, wordless caress that made Inda's lips quiver. Tanrid felt his own throat constrict, and so he left.

The last interview was when the fever had worsened, and for a long time Inda thought he'd dreamed it. The night before he was either to give in and take a punishment he did not deserve, or to have his life ruined, maybe his father's as well, he woke up to find a hand touching his brow, and Sponge was there.

"Hadand found a way to get me in," Sponge breathed. "She thought— we thought—it might be better if you weren't alone."

Inda rolled over, his head pounding. Sponge touched his hot brow and drew his breath in. "Your brother said you might be sick, and asked the Sierlaef to get a message to Hadand—"

"The Sierlaef?"

"Yes. Mark you, he has not said anything to me. He wouldn't. But he let Hadand know, even asked her to do something for you if she could. She thinks, just because he's hiding out—he won't talk about what happened to anyone—that he feels terrible about Dogpiss. That he never meant anything of the sort to happen. So anyway she arranged for me to be here. With this. Here, drink. You'll sleep."

Inda didn't care what it was. He sipped something pungent that smelled like flowers, that wiped cotton-softness through the pain behind his eyes. He whispered, "I told the truth."

"I know. We all know. But no one dares to speak. Yet. I promise you, Inda, on my honor, on my soul, you will get justice." The voice was so soft Inda almost thought he dreamed it, except there was a deep tone, almost an adult note, a note of truth, that caught Inda's fleeting attention and held it, just for a moment. And then he sank back, and

Sponge's arms closed round him, and held him, in compassionate, loving silence while he slept.

Just before dawn the Sierandael was considerably surprised to hear the clatter of galloping horses echoing up the walls. He was, though he would never admit it, tense enough about the Algara-Vayir affair (really, why was that boy so stubborn? So stupid? What did he possibly think he could win?) that he was already dressed by the time his personal Runner arrived.

He admitted the man, who smacked his fist against his chest in absent salute, his eyes wide as he said, "It's Jarend-Adaluin of Choraed Elgaer."

"Impossible."

The man opened his hands. "He's here, with an Honor Guard."

The Sierandael frowned. "The fastest messenger would have taken two weeks, and then a two weeks' hard ride back." He did not say that he had had Runners on watch along all the southern roads to find out just who would have seen fit to apprise Algara-Vayir, outside of the official royal Runner who had not even been sent yet. Shoving aside that knowledge—and the memory of his Runners coming back empty-handed—he said, "Where is he? Seeking audience with me?"

"No, he's closeted with the king."

And so he was.

Tlennen-Sieraec had been on watch, as much as a king can be on watch during his days of ceaseless activity, ever since he had sent a message to Jened Sindan about what had happened via the magic locket.

Captain Sindan had been only a couple days' ride from Tenthen Castle, for he was, on the king's orders, painstakingly investigating the spectacular near failure at Marlovar Bridge.

Sindan had ridden straight to Tenthen to bring back Jarend-Adaluin himself, using not the regular roads that bounded provincial lands, but the narrow unmarked Runner trails that ran through them.

Now the three men faced one another in the king's study, two weary from almost ceaselessly riding day and night, one from stress. The king bade them both sit, and for once Jened Sindan relaxed his own rigid rule when in anyone's presence but the king's. He was too tired to stand, but he avoided the two great wingback chairs and chose the hassock farthest from the fire.

In a very few words, the king told the Adaluin what had happened.

The Adaluin's mouth tightened at the end. Not anger, so much as pain. "No, Inda won't back down. He'd go up against the wall first."

"No one doubts his courage," the king said, moving to the window overlooking the parade ground, and the academy beyond.

The Adaluin held out his hands. "Then what do I do? My choice appears to lie between ordering him to be flogged before the academy for something he swears on the honor of our House he did not do, or riding up to your throne and throwing down a war-pennant in Indevan's name."

In other words, either he betrays the trust of his son or his oath to the king.

The Adaluin sat back in one of the great winged chairs, facing the king, who remained at the window, the side of his face highlighted with the blue colors of impending sunrise. Inda's father pressed his lips together. First the betrayal of the plan at Marlovar Bridge, and now this business with Indevan. It was perhaps too easy, too convenient, to assume some mysterious form of treachery on the part of the Sierandael, whom he'd loathed ever since their academy days. The Adaluin's memory of the king's brother was of a shifty-eyed rat of a scrub, but that scrub had grown into a competent leader, an excellent trainer, and his loyalty to his brother was undoubted, a loyalty returned by the king.

The possibility of treachery against House Algara-Vayir was not treason. Accusing the Royal Shield Arm without proof was.

The king paced to the fire and back to the window again. "In a sense, the warded threat of war with the Venn has done us ill. We are not a people accustomed to peace. There are signs of internal strife, of frustrated expectations, that must be investigated, and shall be. For now, we must consider what is to be done with your boy."

The Adaluin realized that the political repercussions he'd foreseen on the long ride were, somehow, already echoing through the kingdom.

"Young Indevan will not compromise," the king said. "And I cannot see my way clear toward using my authority to force him. And without proof either way I cannot act." The king paused, still staring out the window.

The other two paused as well, seeing in the unforgiving morning light the pain deepening the lines in the king's face. The Sierlaef obviously knew more than he was telling, but three times the king had tried to get him to talk, to no avail. The implied lack of trust hurt worse than any of the other troubling news of late.

The Adaluin sighed, and sat back. "From what you say there is no clear trail of events, not unless someone can prove that those two boys lie."

"But we cannot. Headmaster Brath and my brother both have interviewed everyone concerned. There are two conflicting stories. Whichever way I decide, the political strife realigns, perhaps worsens." The king turned away from the window. "During the past week I've had far too many Runners demanding justice be done, or I had better give my reasons why I did not believe the two boys standing against Indevan, for then they can claim their Houses have been dishonored."

The Adaluin remembered their academy days, how Kethadrend Kepri-Davan had veered between bootlicking the royal sons and complaining bitterly behind their heads about Vayir privileges. Of course Kepri-Davan would use this incident as an excuse to try to gain political advantage.

"I see." The Adaluin sighed, his hands flexing. "Either I act, and worsen your strife, or I accept dishonor."

Tlennen turned to the dark-haired man sitting on the hassock opposite the fire, rain dripping off his clothes and pooling on the floor. "Jened?"

Captain Sindan said, "I believe there is a third way. But it will be difficult for you both."

Both men turned toward him.

"Tlennen," he said to the king. "Your part is easiest. You will say nothing at all."

The king's brows rose faintly. "There are enough anomalies in the various stories to cause questions among those who are not sided with the Kepri-Davans and their ambitions for a rise in rank by whatever means. Perhaps a complete silence could be quite effective. If . . . ?"

Sindan turned to the Adaluin. "If your son vanishes, without trail or trace, if you do not see him, or know where he has gone."

"I will agree," said the king, "only if you will contrive that he be put in a place of safety. The boy is not at fault."

Sindan struck his fist against his chest. "That I promise."

They both turned to Jarend-Adaluin, who showed nothing of the pain those words gave him. In his long life he had learned to accept pain. He looked down at his hands, and then up. "Very well," he said. "When must it be done?"

"Today." And, "Now."

PART TWO

Chapter One

A S the merchant brig *Pim Ryala* drifted down the long Lindeth Harbor toward Lookout Point, the girl the ship was named for hitched up her skirts and thumped her skinny butt onto the taffrail. Two middies joined her, knowing the beck of command from the owner's daughter when they saw it.

Ryala Pim nodded at the taller mid, a swarthy Idayagan. "Heyo, Fass. Whatcha got there?" She examined the second mid, a compact boy with a thatch of rust-tinged light hair and the slanty blue eyes found all over the southern hemisphere on either continent.

Fassun said, "Heyo. Testhy's new, just come off snooze-watch. Captain hired him down south. Testhy, Ryala Pim."

Testhy made a creditable bow.

Ryala snorted. "So you southerners think you know something about sailing the strait?"

Testhy sucked his lip. That kind of challenge from another mid, or a ship's brat, he knew instantly how to answer—and where—but this was the owner's daughter.

So he shrugged. "We'll see."

Ryala and Fassun exchanged looks of qualified approval. A hotheaded answer might mean a hothead on watch. Mama Pim was fluent about keeping contented ships, which was why the Pim family usually got the best pick at harbor hiring.

"So what'd ya sling at us this time?" Fass asked, leaning on the taffrail next to her.

"Just three for you, and one for *Pim Olla*. You get two rats and a likely-seeming carpenter's mate." Ryala felt her guts lurch—which was why she never actually sailed in any of her mother's little fleet. "We also saw us a prime Delf topman, but he turned out to be related to the Gams." Another look exchanged.

Testhy, goaded, said, "I suppose that means something. I mean, I've heard of the Delfin Islands, but what's a Gam?"

Fassun's answering grin was both amused and superior. "You obviously haven't spent much time around those Delfin Islanders."

Ryala laughed. "The Gams are a clan."

Fassun added, "The Delfs' clan feuds are worse than . . . worse than . . ." He groped in a circle.

Ryala said, "Worse than a Bren at the bargaining table."

"Or worse than a Chwahir and an Everoneth in the same sluicehouse," Fassun offered.

Testhy lifted sun-bleached, almost invisible brows. "You mean worse than the Brotherhood of Blood and everybody else?"

This reminder of the pirate fleet that had become maritime traders' biggest fear in the entire southern half of the world sobered the other two. "We don't have many Delfs down south," Testhy added.

"They seem to mostly sail big waters, north and east." Fassun shrugged. "Some say they even understand the Venn sails, though if they do, we haven't met any."

"Maybe the Venn get 'em all," Testhy said. "Square-rigging has to require more top hands, especially the way they flash."

Ryala wrinkled her nose at the notion of flashing sails. It was unnecessary to change sail all at once, a sort of showing off. If not worse. Merchant ships did not have all those skyscraping towers of square sail whose sheets and braces just had to get tangled, nor did they squander money on hiring too much crew. That was the sort of behavior you expected from warships. Or pirates.

"Anyway," Ryala lectured Testhy in a tone meant to be kindly. "Pricklish or not, every captain wants Delfs on board. Mama says it's because their babies learn to net, reeve, and steer before they can walk."

Fassun waved a hand. "What I know is that they also drink too much, fight too much, get insulted over nothing, but they gang right up at the first sniff at their precious islands—and go after everyone else."

Testhy rolled his eyes. "So we only have the one, then?"

"One is all you can ever get, unless they come with kin, or kin-allies. Niz is captain of the tops," Ryala added.

Testhy nodded. That explained everything. This was his first cruise on a merchant ship, but even on the little coastal brigs, your upperyard hands were the ones you valued most.

He also decided he'd had about enough of Ryala Pim's and Fassun's condescension, but four long years as a shiprat had taught him not to react to anyone who ranked above him—which was everyone, as he was a newly hired rat. So he said only, "Who are the new hires?"

Fassun sighed. "You said just two? I saw eight or ten brats over at the bench. The owner is pickier than . . ." He groped, but before the other two could offer comparisons, he said in haste, ". . . anyone I know."

Ryala lifted a shoulder. "One was barely eight years old. No sved on that one—they said she was ten, but she still had front teeth comin' in. Ma says eight is too young, they cry for their own ma, nights. Biggest one smelled like drink, another almost as big talked snappish. Rough knuckles. Probably a scrapper."

Now it was Fassun and Testhy who exchanged a covert look.

"This and that wrong w' the rest. Mama says you'll have to fill the other two berths round the Nob. Our two are the right age, though one's an obvious landrat. But he looks young enough to learn." She didn't add that she thought she might have heard him speaking that nasty Marlovan to his guardian—it couldn't have been family because there was no hugging at the farewell like happened with new rats just signing on and leaving families for the first time. Was it really Marlovan? She wasn't sure. It wasn't like she knew any—she heard it so seldom— and there were so many tongues around a harbor.

She also remembered the misery in the boy's face when he trod all alone up the ramp. No, much better not to bias the others against him. She knew that Norsh and his mates could be rough on new rats.

She moved on to other, mostly technical subjects, while below, with a minimum of words and a maximum of shoves the mid of the watch, Norsh, directed the two new rats where to stow their bags and hammocks.

"Yes, that's it. Now you report to the purser. Turn in your sved. Get signed in, or you won't get your pay."

Without waiting for them to respond, he batted aside the canvas doorway that divided the rat cabins from the other tiny cabins along the forepeak. They clambered down one of the ladders into the hold. Glow-globes swung overhead, their light blue-white and steady, though the shadows around the edges of the hold rippled with each swing.

There, a neat, small balding man sat at a desk directly under one of the glowglobes. He set aside his work, his mouth downturned, as the two newcomers were pushed in.

"Here's Indutsan. Purser." Norsh paused in the doorway, a big strong young man of twenty, dark of hair. The two silent newcomers had immediately seen from the tight sides of his mouth that he had a temper, and they hadn't spoken once.

"Thank you, Norsh," the purser said.

Norsh vanished down the companionway.

"Now," the purser stated, pulling a huge, somewhat battered bound book toward him. He opened to the right page, ruled neatly, and then peered up at the two before him. The girl was bouncing slightly on her toes, short brown hair, round body, an air of experience. She thrust herself in front of the other one, who just stood, face blank, hands stiff and slightly held away from his body.

"Give me the sveds."

Each child handed over a hiring paper, given them by the ship's owner on the dock. Indutsan scarcely glanced at them, except to verify they had the magical seal; in his experience people would lie to the scribes, but if Mistress Pim actually hired them, lies became her responsibility, not his.

"Name?" Indutsan asked. "And previous experience."

"Jeje sa Jeje," the girl stated, her voice unexpectedly low for someone of her size. "I been—"

"Just a moment." The purser neatly lettered the name in. "Now."

"One season on the *Mrana*. Before that, fishing smacks."

"What training?"

"Sail-maker. I finished the cruise fourth mate to Sails on the *Mrana*."

"Age?"

"Twelve," Jeje said, gloating inside as Indutsan wrote it down. She was really fourteen, but some merchants did not hire new rats older than twelve. This was her family's ploy to get her out of fishing smacks and onto the big merchants, where pay was good and steady, and life was much easier.

"You're a rat now. If Sails wants you, she'll speak up."

Jeje crossed her arms. "I know the ropes."

The purser turned to the other. The boy stood there, brown eyes utterly incurious. He looked sturdy enough, though underfed. Underfed, and stupid. "Name?" Indutsan asked.

The boy's eyes blanked even more, as if he searched inwardly for something missing, then he said, "Inda."

"Have you a family name? A village name, even?" Indutsan asked with exaggerated patience, and Jeje snickered.

But Inda didn't hear, because his mind snapped him back to the dock near the hiring bench where a woman was asking people incomprehensible questions in the slurring Iascan characteristic of northerners.

How long must I be here? he had asked in Marlovan, looking up into Captain Sindan's face.

Light reflections from the water beside the dock flickered over the man's face, showing deep lines that could be anger, or grief, but all Inda saw was the remoteness of his dark gaze. *You are now a sailor, and this is your ship. You must find another name, another life.*

A lurch of the ship snapped him back to the present. The other two watched, the girl in disbelief, the man frowning.

"Elgaer," the boy said slowly, as if trying it out. Ducked his head. "Elgaer."

"Very well, Elgar," Indutsan said in his northern slur, and the boy did not correct him. "Age?"

Again the inward look. Jeje knuckled her lips, unsure whether to laugh or feel badly for someone who seemed to have to reach far, far inside his head for the simplest thoughts.

"Be twelve in the fall," the boy finally said.

Indutsan wrote it down. "You are a rat, which means you berth forward. This is a privilege, one you will probably only appreciate if you are deemed, after a year, unable to be promoted to mid and so you join the crew, and thus have to share your hammock space with the other watches." He paused, saw no reaction, thought that this dolt would probably join the crew in far less than a year, young as he was. "You are in Vorzscin's watch for the nonce," to the girl. "And you in Fassun's," to the boy. "But any mid, any mate, any warrant—and of course the captain—wants something, you hop. You hear the word 'rat,' you run."

Jeje snickered, sidling a glance Elgar's way. Obviously a rockhead. His stolidly blank face, and her own apprehension of what it meant to start at the very bottom rank on a new ship, made her decide in favor of humor over sympathy. At least she wouldn't get the grief that new rats usually did, not with such a good victim right at hand.

"We're a four watch ship. That means you work two, third for learning and leave if you earn it, and one for sleep. Did you understand pay at your sign in? Each stop a portion, balance after we complete the cruise?"

Jeje nodded, and after a moment the other did as well, though with no change of expression. Indutsan rather thought the boy hadn't understood a word, and he was right, but he decided it wasn't the time to go over it all again, not with a long cruise before them. He could always make the attempt before they paid off at their first liberty.

"All right, then. Mess dawn, noon, sundown bells." And to Elgar, "That's when you eat, if you do, no matter what watch you draw. And the watches change each week. Your middie will explain it to you."

Jeje ducked her head, and when the other hesitated, Indutsan flicked his quill in dismissal. Then he sat back and watched the girl dash out toward the ladder to the tween deck, and the boy lurch with the stiff-limbed care of a landsman or a drunk. He shook his head and returned to his work, the new rats already gone from his notice.

To be fair, the pursuer was also gone from the rats' notice. Jeje ran up to the deck to scout the other rats. She knew how important first impressions were in the small, confined wooden world of a ship at the start of a trade run that wouldn't be under eighteen months, and could stretch two years or longer if wind and tide and human events conspired against them.

Inda, still below, saw the ladder, tried to put a foot on, but the ship flung him against a bulkhead.

A man's face emerged into his swimming vision. A blond man, ordinary features characterized by good humor, who somehow reminded Inda of men from home.

But the man said in one of those slurry northern accents, "Hands first, rat." His voice was low, abrupt, but kind. "One for you, one for the ship, and you'll stay on your feet."

Inda shifted his weight, grabbing onto the ladder with his hands, and then reaching with his feet. It worked. When he emerged in the next deck he looked around. Now he was lost again. The ship creaked, the wood sounding like something tormented, and his guts lurched. He tried to take a step, and fell into a bulkhead.

"Way there," came a voice, and he flattened himself against the damp-smelling wood of the hull as a row of brawny young men stamped by, carrying long folded lengths of canvas.

Now he had to find out who Fassun was, not to mention what a "mid" was.

Inda poked his way down the narrow corridor. It looked vaguely familiar. It curved around, and there was a canvas flap—yes! He lifted it, and there were the four people in hammocks he'd seen before. Three of them were breathing long and slow, but Inda saw the fourth awake, eyes barely open. His face was a mess, puffy and bruised; Inda's first reaction was the pity of the scrub for another scrub caught out behind the barracks by a horsetail, but of course that life was over. It had no more meaning. He just hoped the pain would end.

Taumad, hanging there in the hammock, saw the new boy staring, but the stare was nothing he'd ever seen before. It looked like the new rat had gotten the thumping instead of him. So he swallowed back the insult he'd been forming, and let his breath out in a snort.

The new boy seemed to see him then, and before Tau could speak, whispered, "Fassun? I am supposed to find this Fassun." He spoke with care, in a flat voice. Was there an accent? Or was he just slow?

Tau said, "On deck."

The boy looked around, and then his frown eased. "Oh. Up on the ceiling? The—the outside floor?" He pointed upward.

Not slow. A landrat.

"Up." Tau spoke without moving. It hurt too much otherwise. And the landrat had better not stand around gabbling, or Tau would spit out the insult after all.

But the rat gave a quick duck of the head and left.

Inda found a ladder, climbed carefully up, and emerged into brightness and wind and the salty smell of brine. The lurching movement was just as nasty here, but at least he had air in his face, which helped his guts settle, if not his sense of balance.

He looked around. People were busy everywhere, doing things with ropes and canvas and buckets, and other kinds of tools. Overhead was a confusion of wood and more ropes, and at the front end, up high, a single sail. At either end of the ship stairs led up to what seemed to be balconies, where yet more people worked at incomprehensible tasks.

A fresh wave of misery seized him, as he thought, *Why must I be here?*

It was a question he could not ask during the entire ride west, at first because he'd been too sick, and then because the king's Runner had been so silent, and Inda could not shake the horror of memory. Straight to the harbor, the buying of new clothes, the loss of his academy clothes and boots, all interspersed with whispered talks with unnamed Runners in blue, and long looks that were not angry. But no one had spoken to him, and then this morning early Captain Sindan said, *They are hiring on the dock now. Come.*

A fresh jab to his innards. Inda tried to ignore it and searched the deck. There was that girl Jeje. She was talking to a group of boys and girls near the stairway to the front balcony, and when Inda turned their way, she pointed at him, laughing. Some of the others laughed as well.

They were laughing at him, Inda realized, as the ship gave another of those senseless lurches and he staggered. He shrugged inwardly. Didn't matter. Nothing mattered anymore.

He reached the group, four boys and two girls. They all stared at him. "Fassun," he said.

"I hoped you might find the time to join us," retorted the tallest of the boys, swaying easily with the motion. His hair, eyes, and skin were dark, and he looked strong and competent. Horsetail age.

Horsetail. Academy. Another jab of memory, this time Hadand running into the cell, the healer behind her. Hadand's face pale, her eyes red-rimmed. She put her arms around Inda, and held him, whispering, *Captain Sindan will take you away so you can disappear. They cannot find out who you are.*

Not finding out who he was, well, he'd taken care of that with the . . . the purser. So now he said, unaware how long he'd stood there looking inward at the pain of memory, "I couldn't find you."

"Yes," Fassun said, even more slowly. "I . . . see . . ."

The others grinned, some of them laughing.

"Well, let's get you started." The shortest one spoke with exaggerated care. "This . . . is . . . a . . . ship."

"These are *masts*," Jeje said, pointing upward.

"And *sails* are on the masts," another girl enunciated.

"*Three* masts," the short boy with the invisible brows said, and when he held up his fingers and counted off each one the others all convulsed with laughter.

"Foremast in the front, *main* mast in the middle, and *mizzen* last," the girl said, pointing and waving her arms, her voice insultingly slow.

"These are *sails* on the *masts*," a boy said. "See these *big* sails right *here* above the deck, that you're going to be raising? These are the *mainsails*, called *courses*!"

"Courses . . . courses . . . courses . . ." Everyone repeated the word over and over, nodding their heads violently up and down as they made antic gestures.

"So the captain has declared general leave, then?" a not-quite-genial voice interrupted, from a tall tough-looking young man with pale hair sun-bleached almost white.

Seven faces looked up, six displaying variations on guilt and apprehension, one empty.

First Mate Kodl swung a rope-end suggestively, and everyone except Fassun and Inda scattered.

Fassun said to Inda, "You'll be expected to know the standing rigging before we show you running rigging, and how to bend and reef."

Kodl strolled on, his weather-browned face showing the faintest hint of humor. It was that slight narrowing of the eyes, the deepened quirks at the mouth corners, that brought Captain Noth to Inda's mind, and again the invisible knife stabbed him deep inside.

"Here's the—are you going to puke?"

Inda blinked, and saw dark eyes peering into his with wary impatience.

"No."

"Better not. You do, and can't manage the Waste Spell, you'll scrub down the entire deck, and swab it dry."

"I said I won't," Inda replied.

His voice was flat, and Fassun wondered if they might be wrong about his being slow, then shrugged. He didn't care one way or another, as long as the rat did what he was told.

"The very first thing we teach land rats is *starboard* is to the right, and *larboard* is to the left, when you're facing forward. Now, you will see that the shrouds and stays are made of wire-strung weave," he said, pointing to the complicated webwork extending down from each mast to the sides of the ship, and then to the lines slanting down between the nearest two masts, and out to the bowsprit. "These hold up the masts. The shrouds to either side, and the stays fore and aft. Or as you landrats say, forward and backward."

Fassun, watching, saw the landrat mouth the words "Starboard, larboard, right, left," and "Shrouds and stays, fore and aft." The boy's brown eyes moved from one to the other, not in bewilderment, but with intent.

Relieved that he might not have to repeat the simplest, most boring basics over and over, Fassun bestirred himself enough to show Inda each item, sometimes giving a brief reference to its purpose.

Inda concentrated his attention, repeating the new words, a running stream. *Gangway*, the wooden path along the sides, *waist* the sunken space in middle of the ship filled with boats and spars and barrels, *forecastle* the flat-topped balcony in front, *aft castle*, or aft, the balcony at the back, which was where the higher-ups had their cabins, the *captain's deck* the one highest up aft with the wheel on it. It helped, he discovered, to give all his attention to these unfamiliar things. Memory could then not devour his thoughts, nor could the endless questions he could not answer, that had no answer.

The lessons broke off just about the time he was beginning to feel overwhelmed, and gaffs, booms, and beckets began to chase one another around the names of the various ropes and not-ropes-but-looked-like-ropes; there came a call of "All hands!" and Inda discovered that he was expected to run back, no, aft, to listen to pale-haired Kodl reel off a set of incomprehensible commands.

He was pushed and jostled into place along the gangway, took hold of a heavy rope, and soon found himself helping to lower a small boat into which a well-dressed, scrawny girl who looked vaguely familiar from his hiring ("That's the owner's daughter!") had climbed.

"Yo, heave! Ho, heave!
Stamp and go, stamp and go!"

A fellow with a fine singing voice chanted out,

"The water's a-risin', the sails ain't set.
The wind is a-howlin', the watch's all wet! And a . . ."
"Yo, heave! Ho, heave!" the rest sang out, tromping forward and
yanking in unison.

Down, down the boat went, everyone handling the rope in time to
the song, which mostly seemed to be about various types of disaster. As
Inda wondered what a wrung mast was, the boat lowered in jerks,
swinging, but staying level, until it smacked onto the waves. The girl did
something and a triangular sail similar to most of those above flashed
out and the wind caught it, the girl grabbed a tiller with her free hand,
and away the little boat sailed, leaving a flat path of a wake for a brief
time. Inda watched her tack toward Lookout Point, which was where
the Pims had their house, wondering how she knew how to judge wind
and sail—

Thump! Fassun rapped Inda's skull smartly. "Did the captain give you
liberty?"

Inda did not answer, just turned to the next task.

Fresh air, plenty of plain but good food, the roar of noise tween decks,
more lessons, and then a climb up the mainmast, a trip that left him
trembling and drenched with sweat, tired Inda so much that when at
last he was sent down to sleep he had just enough presence of mind left
to watch how Dasta, the other rat he'd been pulling ropes with, climbed
into his hammock.

Once he was in it, he disliked the motion, the way he was bent, but
he was too tired to do anything except lie there. Accented Iascan voices
blended with the weird creakings and thrummings. He realized incuri-
ously that the boy in the next hammock over was not a boy but a girl—
a sturdy girl with long black braids—then he sank down into sleep.

He woke when a rough hand pitched him out of the hammock. Even
in sleep his body remembered how to fall, and so he was more angry
than hurt, but when he looked around he saw the other new boy, Dasta,
lying on the deck rubbing the back of his head.

"Bells," Fassun said, and as Inda watched, his hands readying for self-
defense, the bigger boy turned to the one in the hammock. "Healer says
you got one more day, Taumad. You better be out sharp at dawn."

Tau said, "Watch me."

Fassun gave a crack of laughter. To Inda he said, "You got a good berthing, and don't mistake it. Plenty of ships start the new ones on dead-watch circle, but your first week you get to sleep at midnight bells, nice and polite."

Inda said nothing.

Fassun eyed him. "So what are you standing around for?"

The girl, who had been changing, said in a slow voice, "It's time to roust out your duds and get ready for mess."

Inda looked her way. A girl, right there, in the barracks!

"What are you staring at?"

Inda's thoughts splintered. "You're a girl."

Faura whooped. "You mean you noticed?"

Fassun snorted a laugh and gestured with his hand in a circle. Inda knew that one: get busy. Trying not to think of Tanrid, who'd gestured just the same way, he dressed, hesitating when it was time to put back on the new flat soled, fleece-lined green-weave shoes Captain Sindan had bought for him, and that he'd worn for the first time the day before. The shopkeeper had insisted these were sailors' shoes, but Inda saw that the other rats were all barefoot.

Dasta paused with the canvas flap up. "Sooner you get used to no shoes the better. Shoes are slippery aloft. We only wear 'em in winter."

Inda ducked his head and took them off again, sliding them into his bag, which was ranged along with the others against the sweeping curve of the cabin. It was almost a relief to feel his bare feet on the deck boards, somehow steadier. His feet were tough from all those years of going barefoot before he was sent to the academy.

Inda straightened up. The light filtering in from a square hatch in the hull shone on hammock hooks overhead, and painted a square on the stained canvas that served as a door. He gazed around without really taking anything in, trying to sort out his jumbled thoughts. *Mess.* He had to go to mess, though his stomach felt unsettled.

A voice startled him. "They'll run ya."

He swung around. The speaker was the one with the puffy face. Eyes a distinctive light brown, really more gold than brown, gazed at him—or one eye, anyway. The other was too swollen. Inda glanced from the face to the hand resting on the hammock edge, and he saw red, swollen knuckles. Not a beating, but fighting.

He paused at the canvas door. "What exactly is a sved?"

"Seal with magic on it. Guarantees cargo is as stated, and signed off to captains. The sved you got at hire promises you are not a deserter or criminal."

"But they say 'sved' to one another."

Tau sighed. "Slang for telling the truth." And when Inda hesitated, wondering if it meant honor, the other said, "G'wan. You'll not get any grub else."

Inda ducked through and followed the noise down the narrow, bending corridor to the huge tween decks area, where tables and benches had been let down from overhead, and square wooden dishes slammed down. The food was a lot like academy food, and like the academy, everyone ate fast, shoved their dish into the magic bucket, and ran out. The sight of that magic bucket reminded Inda of the academy, and he wondered if reminders would ever cease to hurt.

Chapter Two

THAT second day, Inda realized that his difficulty in understanding the others was not just a matter of accent or unexplained ship terms. The sailors spoke in something called Dock Talk.

Not that anyone told him until he asked the fellow rat named Dasta. The other rats and middies seemed to think it funny to use it around Inda, switching back and forth from Dock Talk to Iascan. But Inda figured it out when he recognized familiar Sartoran verbs—often simplified to the singular and one or two simple tenses—tying together bits of other tongues. Dasta had been hired the month before Inda. He told him the name of the sailors' trade tongue, and they shared what they learned as they scrubbed, hauled, practiced reeving, frapping, worming, and pulling ropes.

Dasta realized that Inda was not stupid. In fact, he was the quicker with parsing Dock Talk, but like most small, skinny boys without any sort of influence, Dasta'd learned to keep his mouth shut.

The third morning Taumad left his bunk, and Inda saw that those spectacular bruises masked another Joret. Tau was slim, his hair was not just the usual straw-color seen all over the Iascan plains but gold, a gold with faint silver highlights, falling in waves, matching the gold of his eyes. He was so handsome that people stared or smirked; that girl Jeje watched him like a wolf watched a rabbit, and Faura giggled, fussed with her hair, or tried to poke or tickle him to get his attention.

Taumad's reaction was not to draw inward, like Joret's. He was sullen, goading, and rude. Inda was not surprised to see that the older boys goaded right back, the worst of them being the ranking mid, that senior-horsetail-aged one called Norsh, who also slapped, grabbed, shoved, and head-buffeted Tau more than anyone. Norsh's knuckles were as red and swollen as Taumad's.

Inda watched, but he too kept his mouth shut. He had enough to endure with the running game about his stupidity and the corresponding stings: he was sent aloft to fetch horses' feed bags—a search that caused derisive laughter until Dasta whispered to him that the "horse" was the rope one climbed along under the yard to work the single square sail on the fore-mast—he was sent to the hold to find ropes or sails that didn't exist, he was sent to various officers to ask for insults cloaked in technical gibberish.

The mates watched, enjoying it. They'd all endured much the same thing, and in their opinion rats learned their craft, and learned their place, all the quicker for good-natured ribbing.

But is such behavior ever really good-natured? It never is to the victim, and can very rapidly turn poisonous. So Inda barely spoke. He never smiled, laughed, or frowned. He had been trained to endure, and so he endured, so thoroughly it seemed he had no reaction at all. And so the ribbing escalated by degrees, as the others sought a response, for effect.

Jeje came by the same degrees to regret her laughter. Everyone ganging up on one victim was not fair. She comforted herself with the thought that Inda was too stupid to notice.

The fourth morning her comfort ripped away when her watch and his worked together to load new stores. Inda paused, and she heard his sharp intake of breath at the sight of a barrel of red sponges freshly dug up. She could not imagine what in the sight of a sponge bucket could cause such a reaction, but the look of pain in his compressed mouth and tight-closed eyes dealt a slap to her own psyche. His stolid face was not stupidity, but endurance. Solitary endurance.

She, like Dasta, knew better than to speak up to Norsh and the other mids, not when she was at the bottom of all the ranks. It wouldn't fix anything, and would only make her an added target. Instead, on the fifth evening Inda found a little gift of food in his hammock after he was too late to mess, and his hopeless tangle of a mended net—an assignment by Norsh that Jeje knew was to entertain his particular friends—neatly finished when he woke up on the sixth day.

Restday morning Inda woke up just before the others, after a heavy sleep and wild, disturbing dreams. For a few moments, hearing the breathing of others, smelling the familiar dusty-dog smell of many children in a small space, he thought he was in the scrub pit at the academy.

It was the movement of his hammock that broke the grip of dream, and doused him with a cold, indifferent splash of reality. There was no callover, no Sponge. No fresh, crispy crusted rye-buns baking for early mess. Sponge and Tdor were gone. Gone. And Dogpiss was dead.

Inda slid his hands over his face, dug the heels of his palms into his eyes, and held his breath. He thought he'd stopped crying on that long ride with Captain Sindan across the western plains of Hesea, where no one could see. Damnation. He must be the one damned. Norsunder could never be worse than this life.

The ship's bells rang, *ting-ting, ting-ting.* Dawn watch. Restday, and then another week in this place, and another. He could never go home again.

No. Don't think like that. Tanrid had believed him. And what was it Evred said about justice—

Thump! A hard hand whirled him out of his hammock.

And he landed, rolled, launched himself up, used the power of his own momentum to strike twice and fling his tormentor onto the deck, and for a moment he crouched there, knees immobilizing the enemy's arms, knuckles pressed against his neck, until his mind caught up and he realized this was no academy scrap. He had Fassun pinned down. Fassun, a mid. On a ship. Who could have him beaten with the rope's end for insubordination.

Fassun stared up in shock at brown eyes narrowed with murderous intent, but before he could form the simplest thought that killing stare widened into realization, and the boy's face bloomed from pale to scarlet.

Inda lifted his hands and got to his feet, his mouth now set, his eyes averted. Fassun's anger cooled into questions. He too got to his feet and stood for a breath or two, trying to control his aching gut as he gazed down at the smaller boy. "Where did you come from?"

Another scarlet flush, and a low mumble. "Elgaer."

Silence from the others as they contemplated Choraed Elgaer, which to them just meant a stretch of extremely rocky coast that had no decent harbors. Faura grimaced, astonished that that stupid rat could deck cousin Fass. Maybe she would drop the rock-brain comments. Taumad rubbed his knuckles, watching.

"No," Fassun said. "What's your family, what do they do?"

"Where did you learn that fighting?" Testhy asked.

Inda shook his head.

"What's all the thumping up here?"

Everyone turned. First Mate Kodl stood at the canvas flap that served as their door. Then they looked Fassun's way. It was within his rights to report what had happened.

"I knocked over a gear bag," Fassun said.

Kodl pursed his lips. "Shall I tell the captain that the larboard mids are too busy yapping with the rats to hold inspection?"

They all got moving, the atmosphere thoughtful, the looks sent Inda's way covert.

The lower ranks rolled and stowed their hammocks on deck between the shields hung along the railings as they would if they were attacked, scrubbed their cabins and then themselves, dressing in the plain, sturdy shirts and canvas trousers of sailors, and then lined up on deck for the captain and first mate to come by for ship inspection.

For a time the ship was the only speaker, the timbers creaking with musical (to the trained ears of those whose lives were lived on water) contentment, the ropes humming to the percussion of the sails as the ship plunged through a gray sea under a low gray sky.

Inda and the captain saw one another for the first time. The new rat, to the captain, was unprepossessing but clean. To Inda, Captain Peadal Beagar looked alert and commanding in his green captain's coat with its round brass buttons, and he exuded a benign sense of authority, settling to a boy whose world had been blown into scattered leaves by the winds of ambition.

The captain studied the sails, the neatly coiled-down ropes, the swept deck, and then inspected cabins, galley, hold. All was clean, orderly. And so he gestured, and the bosun sent his mate to ring the bell for Restday mess. The upper ranks scrambled down tween decks: first served.

Taumad, standing next to Inda, studied the shorter boy. Inda glanced up briefly, and then away. Tau liked that. This boy didn't stare or leer like so many others did, didn't grab, touch, caress. Tau remembered the first day, when Inda looked like someone had given him sixty with a rope-end before the entire ship's company.

"You're going to have to sved the others," Taumad said.

"No." It wasn't a snappish response. Just unyielding.

Inda was stubborn, but so far he had never been sullen or mean. He was interesting. Tau had grown up hearing his mother expose, in a mocking voice, far too many secrets of human weakness. Most of them were predictable. The other rats were very predictable. Inda was impossible to figure out.

Nothing more was said between them as the rats were dismissed to stampede tween decks to fetch dishes and stand in line for grub. But there were those who observed the troublesome Taumad sitting by choice next to the new landrat, and later offering to help him learn to use a needle and thread.

One of those who noticed was Captain Beagar. Later on in his cabin, while the Restday singing floated down through the skylight, he said to his first mate, "Did you note your hot-blooded Prince Dawnsinger seems to have found manners, at least with that young landrat?"

Kodl nodded, grinning. "Being as we're landmates, I collared Testhy and got the sved. If he isn't farting down the wind, the rat decked Fassun in about a heartbeat, at dawn bells. Small as he is."

"Fassun?" the captain repeated. "Decked by that small boy? Hm."

The two dined alone. The second mate had the watch, the third was asleep, and the skylight was closed. That meant they could talk, if their voices were low enough, with what semblance of privacy existed aboard a cramped wooden world.

Kodl passed the Restday wine back, adding, "I hoped Taumad would find himself a mate. If he stops fighting everyone who looks his way, we might not have to put him off at the next port, promising as he is."

The captain dismissed Tau and his problems. What concerned him was the cruise, more specifically the return spring season after next, when they might be kept by weather from meeting the yearly convoy, and when they would emerge from the Narrows dividing the land bridge into waters that were dangerous, and becoming more so, for the last leg of their journey home.

"Give the landrat a month to learn his ropes and sails, and then put him with the forecastlemen," the captain said.

Kodl hesitated; the captain, seeing his hesitation, indicated he had permission to speak his mind. "The forecastlemen will take assignment of a small boy, and a landrat at that, as an insult."

"I don't care what they think," Captain Beagar stated, and Kodl knew he would have to repeat the captain's words. "Not when it comes to defending my ship." He sat back. "If the boy is as good as you say, he will adapt." He smiled a little. "In fact, if he is as good as you say, and he survives the forecastle's welcome, Scalis will probably make him a pet. If so, whatever he knows had better show up in the repel-boarder drills. And if that comes to pass, he'll move up to mid by next cruise."

Kodl opened his hand. That was an order, and they were captain and first mate again; it was not for Kodl to say that he had doubts a boy would be permitted to teach that irascible old Scalis anything.

Chapter Three

NEARLY two years passed before the Pim ships again reached the coast of Iasca Leror.

The convoy that emerged from the Narrows that second spring was a magnificent display, stretching to the horizon, the complicated geometries of fore-and-aft rigged ships with square topsails interstitched by the long, elegant triangles of single-masted cutters racing up and down the line, signal flags snapping in the strong, cold spring winds.

The trade convoys always gathered in masses just south of Sartor as self-protection against the pirates infesting the unpatrolled southern waters. This year's convoy, held a full extra month beyond the usual time due to contrary winds, had benefited by the strengthening of another forty vessels, discounting the odd little smacks that stuck close lest they be snapped up by the pirates lurking to the west in the inlets of the land bridge.

Next cruise's worry about getting safely through the Narrows was a year or two off. They'd made it safely through the Narrows in a long string, framed by cloud-touching cliffs, and now the Pim ships were sailing to the north, almost home, after nearly two years' trading. Those who had family, friends, or lovers along the Iascan coast watched every plunge of the bow, how each sail drew.

Inda watched as well, standing with ease on the foretopsail yard with

Tau and Jeje. The rise and fall of the ship had become a part of life, as unthinking as breathing. The wind, a stiff breeze sweeping up from the southwest, stayed steady. No one had had to touch brace or sheet since morning, so the three were watching the other ships, how they handled their sails, and half-listening to the sailors on the mainsail masthead behind them, their words carried forward on the wind.

"Well, I wonder if m' wife'll still be there. Night before I left she chucked a cook-pot at m' head."

"My boy oughta be talkin' by now."

"My ma'll be surprised I made it a whole year and a half without being hanged," Tau observed.

Jeje snickered. They knew her home was up in Lindeth, the next harbor north, but she had relatives in the Parayid Harbor, and she'd heard of Tau's mother's pleasure house.

What Inda thought about was the land east of the harbor—his Fera-Vayir cousins' land. Part of Choraed Elgaer, just a few days' ride south of Tenthen. His homeland.

He had tried to forget. But oh, sometimes at night, especially during the long winter they spent tacking grimly through the dangerous waters south of Sartor, he had shivered on deck picturing Tdor there on the dock as the *Pim Ryala* spilled wind and glided in on the tide. She would be waving and shouting, "Come home, Inda! Come home! It's all made right." His imagination never quite decided what "it" was. Sometimes the false accusations were denied by the Sirandael himself before the entire academy, and then he was surrounded by Sponge and his bunkmates, ready for him to join the games again. In other daydreams Tanrid spoke up on the parade ground denouncing Kepa and Smartlip. The worst dream was his father coming to explain why he had sent him away without seeing him, but Inda could never hear the words, because no reason he could think of made any sense.

No, it didn't make sense. It was just inescapably real.

He turned away, a sudden physical movement. Tau and Jeje exchanged looks. They'd gotten used to that strange face of Inda's, the way he'd go blind and deaf to whatever was around him, and then he'd shrug, or jerk, or move restlessly from one location to another, his mouth white and thin.

Tau said, "Now, where're you staying, Jeje?"

She opened her mouth to say "With my cousins, of course," but his tone, the meaningful glance Inda's way, caused her to amend with an unconvincing, "Not sure I rightly know."

False as it was, Inda didn't seem to hear it, or at least to react, so after a pause too long to be natural, Tau said, "Well, then, you can always swing a bunk at my ma's. I'm sure she won't charge—not much, anyway," he added, thinking of the lightning and thunder at home before she'd sent him off to sea. "If business has been slow. But room, there always is." He turned Inda's way, adding in a casual voice, "You too, Elgar, if you've a mind."

To their relief, he said, "Oh, thanks. If there's room."

"And I'm going with you," came a loud, determined voice.

They turned to see Faura hanging in the shrouds, listening, her dark gaze steady on Tau. For a time no one spoke, the only sounds the wind singing in the rigging and drumming the sails. Tau just stood, his face blank.

Faura finally tried for politeness. "If there is room."

"There usually is, in a pleasure house," Tau said evenly. "But doesn't Fassun have digs for your family?"

Faura tossed her head. "I can do what I want."

Jeje rolled her eyes. No one spoke as they all slid down to the deck.

The landing of the *Pim Ryala* involved the entire crew. The Pim captains took pride in anchoring creditably. Inda, as the smallest forecastle hand, was in charge of foremast signal flags, which meant readying and hauling up the white flag on Kodl's gesture of command.

Then, when the lookout up high had bawled out that the harbor master had dipped their white, it was time to put the helm down, and bring in the topsails, jib, and last the mainsails while the ship rounded into the wind.

The larboard watch had to tighten everything down and lower the boats, while the starboard watch lined up for pay.

The larboard rats groaned and cursed. Inda said nothing, but as soon as his job with the signal flag was over, he swept a spyglass over the crowd lining the nearest dock.

No one there for him. Of course no one was there. For a short, fierce time he loathed himself for being stupid enough to have expected anything else, but the anger gradually faded into the old numbness, and he made himself busy until the bosun tweeted the signal for the larboard watch to line up at the capstan for their pay. As he held out his hand for his share of coins, Inda thought, *If she knew, Tdor would be here.*

It was true. Little else made sense, but that was true enough to ease some of the constriction in his heart. And more true, he thought as he dropped down into the long launch, and took up his oar at the third mate's hoarse shout, life was easier with friends. Even if it didn't make sense.

He glanced across at sturdy dark-haired Jeje, and behind her Tau, who had taught him how to navigate in strange harbors. There was Dasta, his hawk nose lifted as he surveyed the town for family, and Yan, the quiet Chwahir boy.

"Pull, ho, heave, ho!
The ship's on fire, the first's a liar,
but we're done and gone for ho-ome!"

So I will stay with Tau, he thought. Searching inside, he found that the prospect did not hurt; he knew that he, Tau, Dasta, Jeje—if her relatives let her loose—and the others would find things to do. They'd laugh. Odd, how many jokes they already had, jokes that had nothing to do with academy jokes and slang. Though he was very close to his ancestral home, no one would know, and his secrets would stay secrets.

As the boat slowed to weave in and out of harbor traffic, some of the hands sat upright, one or two waving to people on the dock. Right before Inda, at mid-oar, sat yellow-haired Dun, the carpenter's mate hired the same day as he. A strong man of medium height and build, seen most often in defense drill—for he shot a good bow—Dun had been kind to Inda in an absent sort of way over the long cruise.

They had to pull in their oars to permit a fast little trysail to pass. Dun turned his head to scan the harbor, and caught Inda's gaze. "Find a place to stay, young Elgar?"

From his accent in Dock Talk, he was Iascan—southern Iascan—though he spoke Iascan with the slurry northern intonations. *I'll have to get used to hearing the sounds of home again,* Inda thought. Out loud he said, "Sure."

Dun gave a nod, and squinted out over the harbor. His yellow hair was tied off in a stiff four-strand queue like a sailor's, and he wore sailor's gear, but he still sometimes reminded Inda of a plainsman. He said, "So what did you think of your first voyage, eh?"

Inda lifted a shoulder. He said what he thought he was expected to say. "I liked it right enough."

"Get drunk?" Dun smiled. "They always get the rats drunk at least once. A tradition, though every captain hates it."

"Just one time, during the first winter." Inda grimaced and looked down, his upper lip lengthening for a moment. That day still knifed him in the heart: walking round a corner in a strange city, and seeing a scruffy brown dog pee against the side of the building. He'd heard Dog-piss' laugh so clear, so sharp! To get away from that pain he'd let Scalis and the other forecastlemen talk him into drinking whisky-laced punch until he found that though he couldn't see, and he had to puke, drink didn't numb memory. If anything it made it worse.

But he'd never tell anyone that. "What I liked best was that I saw Sartor. Oh, just the coast, but still."

Dun grunted, wondering what had caused that long pause, the desolate gaze a thousand years beyond the horizon. He knew the boy wouldn't talk, so he just said, "I think everyone ought to see Sartor once. Whatever your family name or place, we all connect there somewhere, if you go far enough back."

The third mate bawled, "All right, mates, if you don't want to sleep in the boat, let's put a little back into it."

The way was clear. Dun picked up his oar. Within a short time they pulled up dockside and clambered out, some of the crew making flourishing bows to Tau, who flushed but did not retaliate; even Tau knew, after all this long voyage, that the teasing—except from Norsh—had dwindled to mere habit.

Dun was lost almost immediately in the crowd. Inda, Tau, Yan, and Dasta watched, grinning, as a group of short, barrel-shaped, deep-voiced people who looked just like Jeje trundled up in rolling sailors' gaits, all talking at the same time.

She threw a roll-eyed glance over the shoulder of a brawny-armed aunt who was squeezing the breath out of her, and the boys knew they wouldn't see much of her for a time. Faura smiled in satisfaction.

They started down the dock to the street, all of them feeling the ground heave beneath their feet. Inda and Dasta stamped, only Tau walked with no less grace than usual. Faura hung back, watching Tau and thinking, *I'll have him all to myself with that frog of a Jeje out of the way, and why does he talk to her so much anyway?*

Tau led the way down a back alley that smelled strongly of fish to the main street of the harbor. Up on the hills behind the harbor one could make out the round shapes of Iascan houses, but here they were square, built on a grand plan that the young travelers now recognized as modeled on Sartoran and Colendi buildings.

Tau paused to peer through the tall ground floor windows of a prosperous pleasure house. His laughing grin of triumph back at the other two caused a passing woman to falter in her step, and then blush and hasten on when she saw by the nature of his clothing that he was underage.

Tau ignored her. "Plenty of company within," he told his two companions. "That means Ma will be in a welcome mood."

And indeed he was right. The golden-haired, beautiful Saris Eland scudded lightly across the shining floor, her draperies fluttering like the butterfly whose name she had adopted, and embraced Tau with tender emotion. She gave no sign that she had seen them through the window. Or that she had seen the woman's reaction to Tau, and his studied lack of response; that she observed Faura's hungry gaze on her son.

Tau mumbled something and she turned her glorious golden eyes onto Inda and Dasta, saying, "Of course, my darling. Your—your mates are welcome here! Take them back to your room, and I'll order you a supper. You must be hungry!" She walked away, her skirts whispering over the shining floor.

"Food," Dasta murmured, his eyes wide and glistening. "Real food? No gruff? No rocks?"

Tau grinned. "No gruff, no rocks. Sleeping as late as we want. No night watches, no rope's end. No prison, either. We can run all over the harbor, and nobody can make us pick up a rope."

Dasta rubbed his hands. "That," he said, "is what I call liberty."

Chapter Four

DUN the carpenter's mate entered a small, weather-beaten inn behind the grand main avenue. The inside was dark, and the few customers all seemed to be landsmen.

In the far corner near the kitchen partition, facing the room with his back to a wall, sat a tall, long-faced man with gray-streaked dark hair, wearing anonymous Runner blue: Captain Jened Sindan.

Dun slid into the seat opposite.

"Welcome, cousin," Sindan said.

"How is the family?" Dun replied in the pure central-plains Marlovan of their ancestors, his posture altered, though he still wore the loose clothing of a sailor. Now he was Hened Dunrend, King's Runner.

The short, buxom woman who trod heavily to their table did not betray the slightest interest in them or their conversation; if she understood Marlovan, she gave no sign. She stated—in flat southern Iascan—"The supper is either fish cakes with cabbage balls or chicken pie. We have summer ale, brown porter, and white wine from the north."

The men ordered, the woman trod heavily back toward the kitchen, boards creaking beneath her feet.

"Is he alive, Dunrend?" Captain Sindan asked, leaning forward, his voice low.

"Yes. Do you want me to show you where?"

Sindan shook his head. "I must not risk being seen. Tell me every-thing."

"That compasses much," Dun said. He paused.

Creak, creak, the floorboards groaned, announcing the advent of their porter. *Thunk, thunk.* The mugs clunked down, and *creak, creak,* the woman retreated.

Dun smiled a little. "He was desperately unhappy in the beginning. But broke his isolation by befriending the wildest of all the rats, one named Tau, the one I'd least expected."

"Misery," Sindan repeated, taking no interest whatsoever in Tau. "He said nothing?"

"Not a word. Not one single word about his family, friends, or what brought him there."

"So they don't know, then," Sindan said, relieved.

"Oh, they suspect he's a Marlovan, but he doesn't know that. The name he chose, I should mention, is Inda Elgar."

"Elgar." Sindan frowned. "Too easy to put that together with the miss-ing son of the Adaluin of Choraed Elgaer."

"But you have to remember how profoundly uninterested they are in Marlovans as individuals. To north coasters, in particular mariners, we are a mass of ravening villains, bent on nothing but conquering—what is it? Did I say something?"

"My news," Sindan murmured, "can wait."

Tromp, tromp. Two plates slammed down. *Tromp, tromp.*

"How did they find out he's a Marlovan? Language?"

Dun's fingers scrabbled emptily at his waist, where of course there was no sash and no knife and hadn't been for two years. But speaking Marlovan again, smelling home food, brought back the habit he had so carefully suppressed. "No," he said, using the fork to spear a cabbage ball. "It was his fighting. Which in turn got him promoted into the fore-castle watches."

"That means nothing."

"Forecastle sailors are usually men, and big, for they are accustomed to handling the anchors and the head sails. In heavy weather . . . well, think of fighting to control, say, four runaway horses, all that wild strength connected by one rope, while balanced on a tree branch in a high wind."

Sindan nodded once. "Understood. So, to the fighting."

"He got angry and duffed a bigger boy. So the captain wanted him with the forecastle. Those men are largely responsible for repelling boarders on merchant ships."

"Go on."

"Well, the forecastlemen ran Inda, as you'd expect. Here's this small boy, knows nothing about the sea, and the captain insults them with him instead of the sturdier shiprats. Inda said nothing. He never does. Just watched the repel-boarder drills, bad as they were. Did his part if told to move. But I'm not telling it a-right. He has this hothead friend Tau that I mentioned, run a lot by the biggest of the mids, who command the rats and oversee watches. Think of them as senior horsetails, training for command."

"Ah."

"The biggest is this one called Norsh, who had been riding Tau, Inda's friend. Riding hard. There'd been two fights before we were hired on. So anyway, there'd been another tussle, and Norsh used his rank to get Tau roped. Inda didn't say anything, but on the next real shooting drill, when Norsh was jawing at him he turned away and shot fast, hitting the barrel—they float a barrel in the water with a target painted on—time after time, his form perfect, straight line fingertip to fingertip, just as we're taught, and I was so careful not to show though they have me on that crew. It was a sting, and the forecastle howled."

Sindan frowned. "So he was betrayed by his training?"

"Only in a sense. Merchant sailors are untrained. Some captains won't even give them arrows, because they can't be retrieved from the water, so they go up onto the mastheads—few of them even have longbows— pull the strings a few times, and that's drill! Ours shoot, but they send poorly made arrows out without any sense of aim, figuring they have to hit something. To them Marlovan means skill with weapons. They don't recognize anything like styles of fighting."

"Good."

"So to resume, Norsh couldn't thrash Inda for frost, because he'd followed the orders of the drill captain, and the forecastlemen were all shouting their approval. So Norsh says he will show Inda how to fight hand to hand."

Sindan toyed with his knife. "And?"

"Well, at first Inda just stood there taking it, because he thought he had to. Rank's privilege of punishment, that much he understood. It'd been impressed on him that you can be rope-flogged for insubordination. And he's used to it from his brother, no doubt."

"You are right."

"It's a bad way to train," Dun said, his tone serious. "I didn't see it until I got away. This tradition of boys beating boys in the families of rank, one day it's going to cause big problems."

"Already has. Go on."

"So the boy said nothing, just stood there silent, taking it, until Scalis, uh, he's the captain of the forecastle watches, well, he said, 'This here's drill! Go to it, boy!' And Inda was like an arrow to the mark. They'd never seen anything like it. He was wild, his style reminding me more of the women's Odni. That is, he did not have the knives, but it was the way he used his hands. Flowing like water, hands and kicks." He demonstrated with the heel of his hand to his own chin and breastbone. "He had a broken wrist by then, not that he noticed. But he blackened one of Norsh's eyes, knocked the wind out of him, and Norsh went down hard twice. The second time Inda flung himself onto his neck. The men all stood around with their mouths gaping. But before Inda could do Norsh serious damage—before I could find some way to intervene without betraying my origins or orders—that hand gave way and he dropped like a rock on top of Norsh."

Sindan looked grim again.

"As soon as he woke up he apologized to Norsh for losing his temper, the first mate and captain approved, and so Norsh was forced to let it end there. The forecastlemen did not. They started teasing the training out of him, a block here, a strike there. Their fighting drill is not much beyond 'Wade in and swing whatever weapon you've got, roaring like a bull.' Inda sees that, and it seems a part of his nature to organize, to teach, perhaps to command. One day, finally, he showed one of the men staff work. Once his wrist had healed he was leading the drills, and they were like colts in clover." Dun gave a rueful smile. "They have no idea what it is, of course, or only enough to permit themselves to think it, like his shooting, some sort of general 'Marlovan' defense. Their mouths are full of curses like 'drunk as a Marlovan' or 'stinking as a Marlovan horse turd' but they're doing academy scrub drills, only without drums, calls all in Iascan, if you can imagine such a thing."

"You should not have permitted that to happen."

Dun said, "I thought about it, but two things stayed me. One, not one of those men will ever set foot a hundred paces inland. They'll never know what they learned. And second, the rumors of pirates are growing worse. You did say to keep him alive."

"And that is still my mandate."

"Well, then, the ship's crew had better know how to fight," Dun stated with grim conviction. "Things are going from bad to worse in the east, and there's troubling news closer at hand."

Sindan was silent for a time. Neither had really touched their food. Dun began to eat in an absent way.

"Then leave be," Sindan said finally, and Dun realized he was not going to find out what had happened to cause the son of a prince to have to vanish. Especially since the boy was obviously not a thief or a coward, the usual suspicions.

Dun again regretted that his Runner duties had kept him so long on the coast, that his family background in ship carpentry had made it easy to assume this disguised self. But he'd been patient for a year and a half, and now that duty was done.

Or? *It's still my mandate,* and *Leave be.* Those suggested he was not free after all.

Sindan broke into his thoughts. "You said he has the way of command. Is it just the drill, then?"

"No. The reading classes."

Sindan raised his brows, and for the first time smiled a little. "Tell me, frivolous as it may seem."

"Little to tell. I didn't know the academy taught them reading and writing, even Sartoran."

"They don't. Classes are spoken. The education in letters was the doing of Fareas-Iofre."

"Ah. Well, few hands can even write their names, and of course it's not needed. Now, mids can't become mates until they pass a test, because there's writing involved. Well, it's the purser's mate's job to teach the mids, there being little clerical work while the ship is at sea, but this fellow either is an extraordinarily bad teacher, or else he doesn't want competition. Inda didn't know any of that. He saw a couple of the mids struggling over some text, glanced down, corrected them. Imagine their surprise that he could read! Soon he conducted classes in the rat-hole— uh, their cabin."

"But that's teaching, not command."

"And I don't perceive it?" Dun retorted, but without heat. "The cruise was largely uneventful, as I said. Until we got caught in the middle of a civil war in Khanerenth. The ship was impounded, all the sailors were seized and imprisoned in an old barracks. Nothing much happened while we waited for them to sort it out; this was beginning of spring last year, you see. We were penned in adjacent warehouses. Captain and mates controlled the sailors in the big one, but the boys, next door, started dividing into factions, fighting, that kind of thing. Kodl, the first mate, who was permitted to check on the boys, reported that Inda got several of them learning to read and write, and then drilling. Gradually they absorbed the rest of the young ones. The only ones who stood out were the older mids who despise the rats. That, my friend, is the instinct for command."

Sindan sighed. "Now I see. You're right."

The regret in his voice silenced Dun. But only for a moment. Obliquely approaching the subject that meant most to him, he said, "You mentioned trouble."

Sindan leaned forward. "As soon as the ground dries out from the last snow, Tlennen-Harvaldar raises his war banner and sends Anderle-Harskialdna to march on the north."

Dunrend betrayed his shock only in the widening of his eyes. Tlennen Harvaldar, *war king*, not Tlennen-Siraec, *ruling monarch*. For though the Shield Arm could command defense, it was only the king who could declare war; his brother defending at home would remain Sirandael, but if he rode to war, he took the coveted title of Harskialdna.

Sindan saw the question in Dun's face, and murmured, "He was forced into it, of course. The Venn sea war in the east just postponed that trouble, and those who counted on glory and land have been poised to turn on one another. And so our excuse is the Idayagans' refusal to accept the treaty sent north last summer."

"But I thought that the treaty offered our warships in sea defense, and had to be dropped when our ships were sunk."

"Another treaty was sent—the Sirandael went himself. The new treaty would shift the defense from sea to land, requiring them to quarter warriors there for defense against the Venn when they do come. The Idayagans have not answered, and the year they were given is up."

Dun compressed his lips. *The Sirandael went himself.*

Putting that together with the remarks about brothers, and Dun knew what Sindan could not say, and something of what he himself had come very slowly to realize, ever since he'd traveled to other lands, and could compare what he saw to what he had always taken for granted at home.

He had never been sent to the academy, of course, for his family had no influence. Runners were trained differently, but one of the ways they were trained was to comprehend those they might one day have to represent, to protect, and as they traveled ceaselessly around the kingdom, they listened.

He had heard enough to imagine what the Sirandael's life had been like: raised not just to train for defense at home, but for war. Everything in his life an arrow to that one target. It wasn't just duty, it was his life's meaning.

Far away, while sitting and thinking in a Khanerenth jail, Dun came to realize that a man whose entire purpose for living is to command a war will not want to spend his life waiting for its possibility. He was going to have one, and he was going to see to it—after all, it made military sense—that he would have it on his own terms, the ones with which he expected to win.

Dun leaned forward. "You'll need Runners. Send me north."

"I need your skill as personal guard more. There is no one better than you, even among most of the Guard. You must protect Indevan-Dal."

Dun protested softly, "He will survive. When he discovers how capable he is, he will even prosper."

But Sindan shook his head, and said, reluctantly, "You have to understand that I speak with the King's Voice in this matter. Though I do not wear the crown sigil," he touched his breast, "and carry no written orders you see me as Herskalt, and these are the king's own words: *You are to stay with the boy as his shield.*"

Dunrend closed his eyes, drawing in a slow breath. He needed that time to recover from the nearly overwhelming bitterness the command caused. Then he saluted, fist to heart

"That's it, then," the server thought to herself, standing soundlessly behind the wooden divider, and she retreated through the kitchen, where the cook and her mates were busy, heedless of anything going on in the outer room. Step, step, out the door and up the back way to the barren attic room she'd held since she'd taken this job two and a half weeks ago, two days after the arrival of Jened Sindan, captain of the King's Runners. Who had come here to sit every day, obviously waiting for . . . something.

Back in the eating room, both men sat in silence for a time, Dun wondering if the war would come while he was gone, if his beloved Hibern knew he was still alive, above all if he would ever be able to return; Sindan watching his young relative struggle to master disappointment, and considering the reach of the Sierandael's decisions, consequences the king's brother would never know of. Some he exerted himself to make certain the king's brother never knew of.

Finally Dun said, "At least I can now tell Inda who I am."

Sindan frowned at the window, which looked onto the busy street and the cloudy sky above the rooftops. At last he said, "Do you think Indevan-Dal wishes one day to return home?"

Dun said immediately, "I know he does."

"Yet you say he has not spoken."

"Not about his family, or homelands, or anything Marlovan. But you cannot spend close to two years watching someone, even a small boy, without coming to understand a little of what goes inside his head. I would say he longs for home. It's there in his silences, the way the others tease him about bad dreams that he will never explain."

"Then he cannot know who you are," Sindan murmured, his hands open. "Do you not see? If Indevan-Dal wishes to return home, he will return home with stories of his experiences while exiled, and those stories cannot include a guard ordered by the king himself."

Dun realized that the order extended to himself as well, and he sustained, in silence, the sharp pang of disappointment. *If I do not know the reasons for the exile, then I too can return home one day.* And he thought of Hibern, also a Runner. She knew about long missions, and silence. One learned to accept that in the royal service.

But she would not wait forever, and he could not blame her.

So the exiles must continue together, without the comfort of communication.

A Sartoran would have negotiated, a Colendi might have smiled, agreed, and done what he wished, a Delf would have argued, and a pair from Old Faleth would inevitably have ended up outside fighting a duel of honor, but Dun was a Marlovan. "So shall it be," he said, and saluted again.

"Then let us part," Sindan said, rising from his chair.

Meanwhile, the former server crossed the alley to another small inn, where Ranet, Ndara-Harandviar's Runner, waited. Ranet sat alone at a table, toying with bread and cheese, as she'd done every day since she followed Jened Sindan south. The server sat, murmuring, "I have found the Iofre's son." And leaned forward to describe everything she'd overheard.

While out in the alley, Sindan arrived, and with his own silent step approached the door, waiting until someone came out. When at last a stable boy banged the door open, he glimpsed the two women in the crack between door and frame, smiled, and noiselessly withdrew.

Chapter Five

HADAND raced down to the throne room, her breath clouding in the cold air. Outside the last snows were still melting, but she was warm with inward joy.

Sponge was there, standing just below the three steps to the throne on its dais, where the shadows seemed to pool the deepest, the air was coldest. Weak morning light just reached him; his silhouetted profile turned sharply at the soft sound of her footfalls on the stone floor.

She grabbed Sponge by the arms. "Inda's alive!"

Tiny lights flickered across his vision, resolving into tiny golden gleams in Hadand's tears, reflections of the torchlight outside the high clerestory windows.

"He's alive," she whispered again, just for the joy of saying it.

Sponge's throat had gone tight, his mouth dry. When he could speak, he said, "Where?"

"They sent him to sea! On a ship, of all things! I just found out last night. A message sent to Ndara by Ranet."

"A ship," Sponge repeated, because at first the words made no sense. Then meaning came, a superb protective strategy. "Like Barend. My uncle would never guess that." *Sindan told the truth. He is safe.*

Hadand's thoughts paralleled his in an unsettling way. She sat down cross-legged, face in her hands. "Captain Sindan didn't lie to me, then," she whispered, and her shoulders shook as she silently wept.

Sponge stood by awkwardly. Hadand almost never cried. He could probably count the times he'd seen her do it.

And as always, it was brief. She drew in a shuddering breath, pulled down her hands, pressed them together, then looked up at him with those wide-set brown eyes so much like Inda's, and said, "Do you forgive me?"

Sponge stared at her in amazement.

Hadand swung to her feet and faced him, chin turned up. He was fully a head taller than she. "Have you forgotten, then? The day after Inda disappeared."

It was Sponge's turn to feel warm inside, the painful warmth of embarrassment, of regret. He remembered it well, the wild anger, the urge to strike out at someone. But he couldn't strike at his father, or his uncle, or his brother, or his bunkmates who couldn't be told anything at all, and so when Hadand had sent him a message saying *Come when you wish to, we can comfort one another,* he had written in white-hot anger, not even troubling to convert it all to Old Sartoran, *Comfort yourself with your secrets.*

Sponge winced. "I thought we talked that out. Before we started in here." He flicked his fingers at the throne room.

Hadand opened her hands. "Oh, you said you understood when I explained my promise to my mother to just teach Inda. My promise to Ndara. But I have never felt you . . . forgave me." She still could not bring herself to say the real word: *trust.*

Sponge sighed. "I did understand that it was not your secret to give out. That training Inda was your mother's decision, and I agreed. How could I be enough of a pug to hold onto a grudge when you've trusted me enough with your training ever since?"

There was the word, and he'd used it. But Hadand, sensitive to every subtle modulation of his voice, still felt his hesitation, the care with which he chose words. Real trust, the old trust, did not require one to choose words.

He sensed her doubt, and said with even more care, "I just don't want to compromise you any more than I already have, forcing you to choose between me and the secrets you share with your mother and my aunt."

Sponge watched Hadand press the heels of her hands into her eyes—

Inda's gesture. The real truth was, they were here because Inda had broken his promise. Hadand knew Sponge believed he'd done it because he had valued Sponge above the necessity for secrecy.

The logical corollary was that Hadand did not value him as much, though she had grown up with him. He could not know how determined, how desperate the women were that their secrets not be discovered—for the good of the kingdom. If they had to make men stand down from violence, they needed to know skills that the men did not know.

Hadand's mother and aunt were not aware of these throne room training sessions. She lived ever since with the sickening knowledge of just how dangerous it was to betray a single secret—that it could lead to more betrayals so very, very easily, even for the best of reasons. She understood why Inda had broken his promise; to try to mend Sponge's broken trust Hadand trained Sponge herself, and did not tell him about the nights of worry about what it might mean in the future.

Her only reward was this precious time with Sponge all alone, where they could talk, however briefly, and exchange news, however much must be left unsaid.

So she had better not waste any more of their time, then!

She flexed her cold fingers. "All right. Now I'm being the pug. I'm unsettled because until last night I never dared to believe that Uncle Sindan hadn't lied to comfort us."

Sponge felt his gut tighten. "You feared that as well?"

"Yes, but I thought it was my burden," Hadand stated. "At the time I was just glad to have Inda safe, away from *him*, but then I thought what if it was to a quiet death? That they sent me knowing that Inda would come without question if it was I who brought him?" Then her jaw came out. "My single comfort was that Uncle Sindan never lied to us before, not like—Never mind. Right now you must have your lesson, before we have to get ready for the war council with your father."

The war council was the reason Sponge could come so late in the day, instead of before dawn, as usual.

Hadand watched Sponge straighten up. He was getting his height at last, the bony jawline and big knuckles, elbows, knees, and feet of the fifteen-year-old. But almost two years of intensive lessons from Hadand, every day they could, had trained him out of the coltish clumsiness that was characteristic of most boys his age.

Hadand swung a practice knife at his neck. His forearm snapped at an angle across her wrist, binding round and using her own momentum to deflect her blow; she whisked her other hand in, flicked her knife from its position along her forearm to a stabbing angle and before he could recover from the block, she slashed the wood across his gut.

"Oof. What was that?"

" 'Change of the Wind.' You learned that sequence with your hands. Now learn with the blades."

They practiced the same move over and over, their breath smoking in the frigid air. Then they shifted from drill to sparring, the only sounds in the vast room their harsh breathing, and the hiss of their shoes on the floor. Finally he managed to use his size to throw her off balance. She fell. He extended a hand and pulled her up. "All right," she murmured. "You take the knives now."

She hadn't begun teaching him the knife moves until New Year's Week, and it was still new, how the girls held the knives angled up their forearm, blade out, not point out like a sword. It was lethally effective, he could see that, even though they only used a wooden simulacrum of a knife. Even the bruises were nasty when he was slow in blocking.

They fought on until the bell clanged in the tower outside, echoing down the cold stone; the house stewards clapped out the torches. Morning light was no longer blue in the windows, but pale gray. They stopped at once, trying to compress their breathing. They had the same meeting to attend.

The practice knives vanished inside Hadand's robes—for she wore robes now, having put off smocks just before New Year's—and they paced side by side toward the King's Residence. Hadand's profile was somber, her expression closed, and so Sponge turned his thoughts to Inda—alive, and living somewhere on the vast ocean. Did he ever think back on the academy?

Of course he did. *And he probably thinks about my damned vow of justice, and how I have not kept it.*

It was twin expressions of bleakness that the king saw in their faces when they arrived in his chamber. The king's brother and heir were already there, looking at the big map on the table and talking about their force, the Sierlaef confining himself to single word responses, as usual.

The king stood with his back to the fire and stared down at the map, wishing he could tell his younger son and his daughter-to-be that Indevan Algara-Vayir was well, was safe, was watched over, but silence was best. He could not risk one unwary whisper. The kingdom was too close to the conflagration of inner strife, and he had to exert himself to direct that outward, if he could.

Anderle-Sirandael—or now Anderle-Harskialdna as he privately named himself, though he had yet to be officially named so by the king—watched his brother for signs, and saw no hint of why those two brats had been summoned. At least Sindan wasn't here. He hadn't been seen for weeks, not since he was sent to inspect harbor defenses along the coast. That meant he had his brother to himself, and that meant he would listen to no one else but the Harskialdna.

So he should think out what he must say. He frowned at the carefully inked territorial borders, all in gold. Those would change soon enough, at least. His promises would be kept to those who were loyal.

As for the others . . . oh, he couldn't really say that Cassad was disloyal. Nor Jaya-Vayir. Or even Algara-Vayir, damn him. Not when the king, his own brother, insisted the Noths were in Choraed Elgaer on his own orders. And so strange, for them to go there when Algara-Vayir's damned boy had killed their own Tvei.

Jarend-Adaluin now needs a Shield Arm for his heir, Tlennen had stated, using his King's Voice. *Captain Noth shall go to Choraed Elgaer, his boy training with them winters. When he is of age, his son shall be their Randael.* Unanswerable.

"Sit down," Tlennen invited. "I want you two young ones to hear not just the plans, but the reasons for them."

A pause. The Sierlaef made little effort to conceal his impatience. Sponge and Hadand sat quietly.

"The Venn," the king said, feeling for words, "will come. We all know that. Over the past generation or so they have expanded their old watch-posts to garrison size on the north side of the strait." He touched the map above the blue line that marked the strait. "We are taught by history that their plans are long. It would explain not just the garrisons, but their sea strategy."

To whom did he speak? The right words would come if he could identify that. To them all, that was the problem; he had a different message for each, but they heard in different ways.

He turned his attention to the map. "We are isolated from land invasion by the Mountains of Ghaeldraeth to the north and east, the weak point being the Andahi Pass."

Here he swept his fingers across the west, north, and east of the subcontinent.

"The terrain of the north, mostly hills and mountains, has held little lure for us. We can take the Andahi Pass, but we are not accustomed to mountain warfare. Neither are the Idayagans. Life has been too easy for them, too peaceful. They had only to wait for winter to come to their hills and freeze enemies out. This strategy, if it can be called that, will not suffice against the Venn, whose lands are reported to be far colder than ours. Meanwhile, none of these northerners can agree on what must be done to defend against imminent attack. Some of them think that treating with the Venn will prevent the attack, and the people of Olara on the peninsula do not really care who claims to rule them. All their walls of defense are aimed toward the sea. They fear pirates, not war from the land side."

A pause. No one spoke. The only sound was the snap of the fire, and the Shield Arm's breathing.

"If the Venn come, they will establish bases on the coast, then take the Andahi Pass. They can then attack us on land through the pass, as well as from the sea. If we march north, secure the pass, and establish our own bases first, we change a weak defense to a strong one."

A glance. The king watched his brother nod in agreement. It was his plan, after all. The heir looked out the window, his profile bored. He'd already heard the plan described, of course, as he must. Sponge studied the map. Hadand sat with hands hidden, in the manner of the women. She would make a good queen, if she and Evred together became strong enough to rein in the heir by the time he became king.

A surge of pain forced Tlennen's thoughts away from that. He said, "But I do not want a bloody rout. Those only touch off badly organized defenses of desperation, and long slow wars of attrition. We will mass in Ola-Vayir's lands and ride north fast, each to specific targets. No violence offered until they attack. No looting. We carry our own supplies, establish supply lines, and eventually trade. These orders are mine."

And so to violate them was not just a military matter, but treason. That message was not for the Royal Shield Arm, who had known it from the outset, but for the king's heir, who still stared out the window.

The next message was for the king's brother. "Do not make the mistake of thinking that my strategy lessens our honor."

A flicker of a look. Until now Tlennen had not discussed the north

other than to state his wishes. Now was the time for seeming pre-
science, a subtle reminder of who was king. Tlennen had never been to
the north, but he had eyes in Sindan, wise eyes, observant eyes; he also
had the benefit of instant transfer of messages, even if sparingly used.
And so he said, using Sindan's words, though the Royal Shield Arm
would never know that, "They hate us in the north, with the deep hatred that fear inspires. This fear, this hatred, will do our fighting for us,
if we let it. If we are fast, and avoid senseless slaughter, they will surrender faster."

The Shield Arm sneered, of course; he expected, no, he wanted desperate, glorious battles, but he would remember Tlennen's words.

The king knew that his strategy was a gamble. If he was right, his
foreknowledge would propagate through his people. If it turned out he
was wrong . . . well, disaster, already threatening in those mighty outposts being built along the north shoreline of the strait, would probably
just hasten.

The king smiled at his brother. "You shall raise my banner and ride
tomorrow, Anderle Harskialdna, you and my heir."

There, now it is done, the king has spoken, thought the Royal Shield
Arm, with that expansive inward sense that at last hard work brought
its reward, and the world was right. Tlennen had used the King's Voice.
Anderle was no longer a mere Sirandael. He was now Harskialdna, war
leader. And Tlennen was no longer Siraec, but Harvaldar, war king.

Anderle-Harskialdna, Anderle-Harskialdna Sigun.

The king inclined his head, and they all rose; Hadand was the first out
the door, Evred right behind her. The message for them was far more
diffuse, because in a sense everything for them had been. The truth was,
Tlennen thought bleakly as he watched his bored heir saunter out, the
kingdom would one day rest in their hands—inner defense in hers, outer
defense in his. Aldren would wear the crown, but those two would do
all the work.

The Sierlaef strode away, his sash dancing, his boots clattering. Why had
his father insisted on having the brat there? He shrugged impatiently,
knowing that his uncle would be rattling on about the very same question. The Sierlaef realized he really didn't care. Sponge had been doing

a competent job in the pigtails of late, but he wasn't any Tanrid Algara-Vayir. No leader. That was Cherry-Stripe Marlo-Vayir. That meant Sponge was no trouble.

And he wouldn't ride to war, either. The Sier-Danas would, and the Sierlaef meant to see to it that they returned with drum songs already sung about them. Tanrid Algara-Vayir was fast, strong, and no one could stop him, but Hawkeye and Buck came close, and the latter was the Sierlaef's right hand and would one day be his Harskialdna.

How didn't matter. It would happen. What his uncle wanted he eventually got, the Sierlaef had learned that much in life. So the heir was beginning to make sure his uncle knew what *he* wanted.

And what he wanted right now . . . he paused before his mother's doors, and smoothed his clothes with suddenly damp palms.

Then he thrust the door open, surprising one of the queen's women, who bowed and stepped out of his way.

They were still in the parlor. He could hear those string things sawing away, and a voice reading. Was that Her voice? He licked his lips, and felt sweat prickle in his armpits.

Two steps, his heels unnaturally loud on the wooden parquet; in the parlor the voice silenced. He walked in and saluted his mother before he let his gaze seek Her out, and there *She* was, with a scroll open before her, a finger poised on a word. He repressed the intense desire to take that scroll and kiss the writing she touched. Blue eyes looked up, blank, polite, blue as the twilight sky over the plains.

"My son?" Wisthia repressed a sigh. Poor boy, he still was enamored of young Joret, embarrassingly so. She'd thought he would have gotten over it by now, which was the only reason she'd acceded to his surprising request last summer, to invite the girl to stay an extra year as one of her ladies.

The Sierlaef swallowed again. Now he'd have to speak. Before Her. Damnation! "We leave," he said. "Dawn."

The queen gazed into his face. So this terrible talk of war was real. And her boy would be a part of it.

She considered and discarded words. Her years among these frightening Marlovans had taught her that conventional wishes, such as one gave at home—that there be peace, that one come back safely—were unwelcome, were considered cowardly here. So what could she say? *Kill lots of other people's sons?*

Revulsion made her angry, a helpless sort of anger that was gone as soon as it came when she stared up at her firstborn. Instead she took his rough, strong hand, and kissed it. At least he did not resist.

"Be well," she said. That, surely, was acceptable.

He nodded awkwardly. And because he had not resisted, because his hand was warm, recalling for a precious instant the baby she had held against her breast, she said, "My dears, let us go in to breakfast. Joret, please return the scroll to the archive, then join us as you will. My son, will you carry it for her?"

The Sierlaef flushed to the roots of his hair. Let him say good-bye, then, in his own way. Signs of tenderness in him were so rare, they probably ought to be encouraged, even if desperately inappropriate. Why did he have to yearn for the future wife of a prince? Because she was beautiful, of course. And they were young; silliness of this sort was expected in the young.

The women began to withdraw, some with covert looks over their shoulders as they passed through the door.

Joret paid them no notice as she rolled the scroll with quick, competent movements. The Sierlaef stood where he was as the women flowed around him, and watched Joret's hands, so neat, so strong. His hot gaze traveled up her arms to the swell of her breasts just hinted at beneath her robe, up to her long neck, to her face, which looked down, oh, that face, framed in the smooth hair that fell like silk down her back, the soft, austere lips. Her lashes brushed her cheeks, so long they cast shadows, hiding her eyes.

"Joret." He croaked her name. At least he didn't bleat.

She looked up, lips parted. Those lips, how he longed to taste them, to press his own in those shadowy corners.

"A kiss. War," he managed.

She kissed her own fingers, and then touched his hand, the briefest touch. "Give this," she said, "to Tanrid."

He couldn't flush any hotter, he was already as red as fire. Her touch flamed through him. "For me?"

She looked up then, those blue, blue eyes, not angry, not passionate, just calm, as calm as when she stood down in the parade ground shooting fire arrows with the rest of the girls, straight to the center of the target. "I told you, Sierlaef-Dal, I don't dally. It is not in my nature."

It was true. The others her age, even Hadand very recently, had all been to the pleasure houses. He had made sure he found out who and where, because he had the power to do so. Joret's name was never among them.

He took up the scroll, his arm brushing against her shoulder, and he leaned down and sniffed the scent of her hair. Desire made him tremble.

They walked in silence, which was a relief in a way, because though he longed for her to talk to him, at least he didn't have to talk back. When they reached the archive, she indicated the place where the scroll should go. When he turned around she was gone, leaving him reflecting on her beauty, her perfection, her qualities, one of which was loyalty. He just had to win that loyalty for himself.

Chapter Six

IN her aunt's round house on the north shore of Parayid Harbor, Jeje sa Jeje rose to sunlight brightening the latticework of clay-colored tile roofs climbing eastward up the hill. Jeje didn't need to stick her head out the window to know that the wind had shifted at last, and at most she and the crew of the *Pim Ryala* had a day to finish their liberty.

Jeje clambered down the ladder from the loft, finding the family at breakfast. "Wind shifted," she said as a greeting. The others made various gestures of assent. They knew it, and also what it meant.

She picked up a hunk of rye bread from the table, dug her finger into the soft center and pressed some crumbly cheese into it, then sank her teeth into it as she ran outside.

Everyone else was aware of the wind change. People seemed to be moving faster, with intent. She bent her head, toiling uphill to Hilltop Row where the rich lived. In the midst of them was the Golden Butterfly, the pleasure house owned by Tau's mother.

Already the world seemed a little brighter, the light and air cleaner and prettier. How did they *do* that? Jeje did not define "they," just snuffled in the scent of fresh-baked butter rolls as she eased in the back way, where the deliveries were made. She never thought much about her appearance (in fact, it would be safe to say she never had thought about it at all) until the first day she arrived here to meet the others, and caught sight of herself in one of the many gold-framed, candle-lit mirrors, a small black-browed barrel with short legs and arms, standing between the most beautiful woman she'd ever seen, more beautiful than stories and songs, and that beautiful woman's beautiful son.

Though the Butterfly, as the locals called her, had been kind and welcoming, Jeje felt too shy to go inside. She preferred to wait until the others emerged, so they could wander over the harbor, counting incoming ships, and listening to gossip about pirates and rumors of war in the north.

Even here in back everything was charming, with ivy vines and flowering trees in pots around the edges of the warm brick court. Several workers stood near the door to the kitchen, laughing at something, mugs of sweet coffee in their hands.

Jeje sidled toward the main door, listening for the voices of her shipmates. The rooms right off this door were where Inda and the rest stayed, she knew. Not upstairs, where the adults all paid to go.

The first rat she found was pale, black-haired, flat-footed Yan, the displaced Chwahir. He perched on a branch of the flowering tree that blocked the unsightly view of the alley, eating fresh-baked spiced peach tarts. Jeje's mouth watered, though she'd just finished the bread and cheese.

Silently he held out his last tart, and she took it.

"I'll get some more. They're packing up their dunnage," Yan said in Dock Talk, his Chwahir accent flat. "First we'll go see if Kodl or Fassun left any messages for us at the harbor master's." He jumped down and loped inside.

Overhead, one of the casements opened, the diamond-shaped little panes of glass acting like prisms in the bright morning light, throwing sparkling reflections across the courtyard and up the climbing roses against the far wall, swifter than a flock of starlings.

"But my dear," said Saris Eland, gazing skyward. "My darling Taumad *is* a romantic." Her voice was so sweet, so lovely, reminding Jeje of one of those silver flutes they had in the east. But her eyes, Jeje remembered those dark-fringed golden eyes that seemed to see all the way through your skull to the back of your head. "Or he'd not speak so cynically."

Another woman's voice, fainter—from farther inside—said, "That is convoluted even for you, Saris." Saris. So close to Sarias. Wasn't that the word for queen in Sartoran?

"Oh, no! Don't you see, my love? A true cynic expects all that is base in human motivation. Thus the cynic stays calm and unperturbed. My dear boy has always sought heroes, even when he was quite, quite small."

Sarias, queen. *Elend,* grace. It was Tau who'd taught Jeje that, though until they arrived here she never knew why. Those were the original words behind the Iascan sarasaland, the golden butterfly sometimes called queenwings up north.

"How very fragrant the morning is, is it not?" The pretty voice was right overhead. Jeje hunched up her shoulders, knowing she shouldn't be listening, feeling embarrassed but fascinated. No one else heard; the workers were laughing over something in one of the carts, and across the little court someone else, humming softly, was cutting climbing rose blooms to take inside. "It was why he left, though he has had my training since he could walk and talk. Oh, my dear, my spirits would be quite low were I to reflect on how much we should have prospered had he stayed! Alas, it is not to be. He loves the sea. He will take all my expertise to his ships, and everywhere he goes he will meet with desire, and his face and his skills will grant him any bed he wishes."

The other voice came faintly over the sound of Inda and Tau and Dasta inside, approaching rapidly. "You speak, dear Saris, as if that were a tragedy."

"Ah, but it is, do you not see? For a romantic, it is a tragedy. A romantic strives to win what is worth winning. To surround a romantic with greed, passion, the very desire to possess him, is to close his heart and lock it against you."

"There's Jeje," Inda said cheerily, bounding through the door. "Come on, let's go find out how much liberty is left."

Overhead the casement shut again.

Yan, comfortably unaware, handed Jeje three fresh tarts, still warm. She looked down at them, and realized that her stomach had closed.

Faura snatched them from her hand. "If her majesty doesn't like them, *I* am not so picky." As usual she turned her long-lashed eyes upward to see if Tau was listening, then her hand pounced, mouselike, and caressed his arm. These furtive, possessive touches, every one of which Jeje noticed, never failed to make Tau go stiff.

But he said nothing. He never said anything, as long as she didn't grab him or punch him, like Norsh did, and Jeje thought, *Can't you see how much he hates being touched?*

"Let's go." Faura turned the caress into a coy poke.

Inda peered into Jeje's face, and though he didn't say anything nosy—he never did—he looked so concerned she forced herself to smile.

Past the ironwork gates, vine shapes with dancing butterflies along the top, and out into the alley they moved as a group.

The upper casement opened again, and Saris Eland leaned there on her elbows, smiling at the fall of the lace of her bedgown away from her wrists, then lifting her gaze to catch a last sight of those bobbing heads before they disappeared down the next turning.

"I am a good woman," she said, turning her eyes westward, toward where she could just see the ocean above the rooftops of the houses built along the street below hers. There it was, placid and blue with winking splashes of reflected sunlight.

"A very good woman," she repeated, whirling away to face the amusement of her chief confidante, the short, red-haired Rainbird, who specialized in first timers.

Rainbird dropped into a chair, layers of lace mostly hiding her charmingly rounded form. "To not charge your own son for coming to me all these nights?"

"To pretend I did not see it," Saris Elend said. "My dear Tau is so very unaccountable! But then seventeen, no, eighteen, is so very unaccountable an age. I remember." A brief, secret smile. Rainbird knew it was one of the rare references to the Butterfly's unknown life under another name, somewhere else. Somewhere with money and influence—her education had been too good for her to be the child of stonecutters or shepherds—but no one knew who, or where. The Butterfly could talk for days, but never say a thing about her true beginnings; she made up stories that changed as did her taste in clothing. "I trust Taumad has not importuned you with his moods."

Rainbird poured out fresh steeped leaf, brought in straight from Sartor just the week before. Spring scents filled the slowly stirring air, banishing the residue of perfume and heat and physical endeavor. "Not at all. Nothing private, no confidences, no passionate vows of love. Sex is a game for him, one he plays very well."

"Of course. I lectured him very carefully for years on what to expect, and what others would expect," Saris Eland said, and at the friendly quirk of the eyebrow Rainbird gave her, she added less loftily, "It is a relief to discover that he does listen. As did that poor dear child in the courtyard just now, what is her name? Jolly? Jasa?"

Rainbird shook her head and spread her hands. "I can't tell those children one from another. They were here too seldom when I was awake. You don't mean the pretty dark-haired one? She's trouble brewing."

"Oh, Faura's just spoiled, having always had her way. She'll learn or she'll refuse to learn. No, the one who wrings my heart is the little toad-shaped one with the bull-calf voice that will be rough and ravishing one day, though she doesn't know it. Jeyna? Jeje! She already wants my dear boy, though she's at least a year or two off from discovering why, or what she'd wish to do with him. Oh dear, I did try to warn her, but she probably will not remember my words past midday. I do not pretend to omniscience."

"Yes, you do," Rainbird contradicted, pushing a fine blue-and-gold porcelain cup toward her.

"True, but I don't expect them to remember it. Ah, How difficult it is to be a mother. Taumad and I must have one last talk, I think, before he leaves. I must impress upon him that to wear the clothing of the young is absurd. It's been at least a year since he could make that claim. Longer. One's true defense when everyone wants one is to take them first. Go to sleep, my dear. You have earned it."

Rainbird saluted her with a wry gesture.

Saris Eland studied her expression and laughed suddenly. "He's that good? Or is it merely his lovely face?"

Rainbird just shook her head, still smiling wryly.

The next morning the Butterfly kissed Taumad and his companions, wishing them a pleasant journey and handing each an expensive basket packed with delicacies. Inda spoke polite words of thanks, though in his heart he faced the northeast, where Tenthen Castle lay, and bade them an inward farewell.

He could not know that his father was scarcely half a day's ride inland, overseeing a dispute about road repair; that his brother was not on his way to the academy at all, but riding northward at the head of a mighty force in company with the Sierlaef, his Sier-Danas, and the king's brother, who was no longer a mere Sirandael but Harskialdna at last.

He could not know that while he and Tau and Dasta and the rest shouldered their gear and started the long march down to the jolly boat,. their baskets of good things bumping against their legs, at that same moment, Ranet, personal Runner to Ndara-Harandviar, was riding a tired horse into the courtyard of Tenthen Castle.

Tdor was down in the courtyard, organizing the girls for bow drill. She saw the mud-spattered woman in blue ride in. By the time she'd turned the girls over to the arms mistress and run upstairs, the news had already been spoken.

"Inda is alive," the Iofre whispered, tears in her eyes.

Tdor gasped. Joy was so sudden, so intense, it hurt.

Fareas-Iofre, ever mindful of others, rose and with her own hands pulled Ranet to one of the great wingback chairs. "Sit. I will summon food, and you must rest." She dashed her sleeve across her eyes.

Ranet smiled tiredly; she had hurried the faster, knowing how welcome her news would be.

Fareas said to Tdor, "Captain Sindan put him on a ship."

"A ship?" That was Chelis, standing with her back to the door so it could not be accidentally opened.

Tdor rejoiced. *Oh, Inda, you are still in the world.*

Fareas turned to Ranet. "It does seem strange that he is put to sea, yet no one knows. My husband was there, he agreed to his being taken away, yet he did not know to where." *And he cannot know now*, she thought, and saw concurrence in the other's countenance.

Aloud, Ranet murmured, "No one did, only Captain Sindan."

Fareas understood. It was the only way the king could circumvent his brother's seemingly unaccountable behavior, whatever the king thought of the Harskialdna's reasons. He sent a boy into exile; he started a war.

The Harskialdna saw my Inda's potential for greatness, and was afraid, Fareas thought.

Tdor stood silently, blind, deaf to the others in the room. *Inda is still alive.*

The world was right again. And she needed it to be right, because in two weeks she would depart for Marth-Davan, for her last visit, and after that she would go to the royal city to begin her two years of training with the Queen's Guard. For she was now fifteen.

Chapter Seven

SPRING warmed into summer as the *Pim Ryala* and its two consorts sailed down the strait toward the east. One day, when the
winds were particularly timid, most of the merchant traffic (and
there was plenty of it) lightened sail, to the relief of crews. Strings of
signal flags were hauled up, various captains inviting other captains
for ship visiting.

High on the mainmast, Inda watched Niz the Delf sling his arm
around a brace without pausing once in his speech about the intricacies
of square sails.

Niz liked this new mid, who seemed to want to learn his trade, instead of shirk duty like some young sparks he could name. "No. With
them topgallants, you sheets home to weather-side first."

Inda, standing on a boom nearby, nodded respectfully. "That's better
than running the lee sheet almost all the way out before homing the
weather sheet, and then the lee sheet?"

"Three moves," Niz said, raising three gnarled fingers as he bobbed his
head, his high bridged, sharp nose poking forward just like a bird peck-
ing seeds. "That's three, and three takes longer as two. Sure as fire, boy,
sure as fire. With them topgallants, which is tricksy sails, you know—"

"Sail hai," came the call from the mizzen lookout. "Brig. Comin' up
fast on the weather quarter."

Inda groaned, hoping it was no one the captain knew. But moments later, sure enough, "Pass the word for flags!"

Inda heard the words relayed from aft forward by various voices, in a variety of accents. He sighed. Lesson obviously over. "Thanks, Niz."

He slid down the backstay. Tau handed him the glass.

Tau studied Inda, who looked so ordinary—brown of skin, hair, and eyes, sturdy, his unruly hair escaping a sloppy sailor's braid. "Why d'you set that old fart on about sails we'll never fly?"

"You don't want to know how Venn ships rig?" Inda asked.

Tau snorted. "No. I won't ever hire out on anything but merches, and comfortable merches at that. Nothing ever to do with those damn square-sailed Venn. The only thing I think about, and I admit it's a comforting thought, is those Venn aloft, handling what looks like a hundred lines per sail, in winter ice." He waved a hand at their familiar triangular sails, which only required four ropes: a halyard to raise it, a tack to control the weather corner, and a sheet on each side to set it right to the wind.

Inda shook his head. He could still hear Gand's voice from his days as an academy scrub. *Master the details. If you know 'em well enough, you don't have to think about 'em. And you won't be riding blind into a bog.*

While he thought Tau watched him, and sure enough, Inda got that sightless look again. Jeje called it listening to voices no one else heard, but then she'd been raised singing sea songs, and Tau was impatient with the hyperbole of poesy. He'd decided that Inda, though he wasn't yet fourteen, looked back in memory. Bad memory, if his lowered gaze and thinned mouth were any sign—bad memory, yet he was no coward, no liar, no thief, he fought better than most grown men, and he could read not just Sartoran, but the ancient stuff.

"You think I'm a fool." Tau tried to tease out the truth.

"No."

Tau loved poking at this mystery. "So I'm right."

"No." Inda held one hand out. "If I have to spend the rest of my life on ships, it just makes sense to learn everything about them I can."

"Ah, so next cruise you plan to sign onto a Venn ship?"

Inda looked away, then back at Tau, whose teasing was never cruel. "I just know that what you want and what you get can be two vastly different things," Inda said.

Tau thought, *I always get what I want. Except when I lose my temper.*

But that wasn't the sort of thing to say aloud, and so it was just as well that Inda shifted the subject. "Who's the brig? Anyone we know?"

"A Captain Dirbin, out of Mardgar. She's also a captain-owner, so even though she's just a single little two-master brig you're to fly the blue below the white."

Inda had to translate that long washing-line of messages after the green check flag (meaning messages coming), and presently he hailed the deck mate. "News but no mail; pirates seen; Venn two days west; dinner?"

Inda waited while the deck mate relayed the messages down to the captain's cabin, then sent up his counter-invitation.

"Dirbin. Miserly. She'll come here," Kodl predicted. "But she'll know the gossip from home waters, if you can understand her." Kodl stumped toward the hatch. "Better change."

Inda soon reported that yes, Captain Dirbin would bow to Captain Beagar's kind invitation and come over.

A captain's dinner meant that Inda's ease-watch had just been curtailed. He was the lowest ranking of the mids, which meant he couldn't get out of standing behind a chair to serve. But he'd hear any news from home!

He dashed below to clean up and put on his single good shirt. He soon stood with Kodl, Dasta, and Yan, also dressed in their best shore-going shirts, belted with weave, long wide-legged deck trousers, and bare feet clean. Inda's thick hair had been yanked back and neatly braided by Dasta; in turn Inda smoothed Dasta's lank wood-colored hair back and tightly wove the four-strand sailor's tail.

Kodl gave them a quick inspection and just had time to nod in approval as a short, heavy woman with an apple-red, cheerful face heaved herself aboard, her green coat brushed and buttons polished, followed by her equally finely dressed second mate, her first being on watch, a well-scrubbed mid sporting, to Dasta's disgust, striped deck trousers under his beautifully bleached loose white shirt, and then her barge crew, who were taken below by off-watch sailors for their own feast, entertainment, and gossip.

"Hullo, Beagar," Dirbin caroled in a voice made loud and unmusical by years of masthead pitch, as she flung her hand up in the age-old gesture toward her forehead and outward that once had been the doffing of a hat toward the captain.

Beagar saluted her back, equally hatless; no captains wore hats anymore, they hadn't been worn for generations, unless the weather was bad and they had to be on deck. But tradition on the sea was strong.

Captain Beagar led the way down to the cabin. Inda took his place behind Kodl's chair, ready to take the bottle from Dasta, who was stationed behind the captain.

First the wine. Inda poured with care, still not used to these broad-bottomed wooden mugs, sensible as they were.

Having managed to pour without a spill, he silently handed off the bottle to the mid in the striped trousers.

"Fair voyage," Captain Beagar said, hoisting his glass.

"Fair voyage to you," Captain Dirbin responded, and drank. The mates drank, as was proper, in silence.

Dirbin drained hers off, smacked her lips, and said in Iascan, with a strange, gargling accent, "I haff so much news for you out of the west."

Yes, Inda thought. *News behind us, out of the west.*

Beagar nodded, and Dasta gestured to the cook's mates hovering just outside the cabin door. As the platters of grilled chicken and potatoes were brought in, Beagar said, "I heard some at the Nob last month. The Marlovans are taking the coast. Some say they'll push as far as Idayago."

Dirbin thumped her fist on the table. "Damned horse turds. What expect you? Pooh! Pah! They don't innerfere with harbor business, leastwise, and that is a boatload better than the Venn. Strange, these Marlovans! Hear you about their fighting, but! They can't put up no fleet."

"Not with their warships sunk soon's they launch 'em," Beagar said with the indifference of the uninvolved.

"These horseboys attract pirates." Dirbin shook her head. "Not just pirates, but the soul-cursed pirates. Strange. Hah! But your news is month old. You know what's said since about Ramis of the *Knife* in the west?"

Inda waited, not breathing, and started when a hard elbow struck Inda's ribs. "I'll have that bottle any day now," whispered the little mid in the striped trousers.

Inda looked down, saw the bottle sitting there, and passed it as Dirbin finished her wine with a practiced flourish. "There's this new pirate, Ramis."

Beagar sighed. "I've heard the name, but that's got to be just fog. Such rumors always seem to be crossing just ahead, or just behind, never with any fact you tie an anchor to."

"Oh, so Ramis of the *Knife* is just a rumor, is he?" She gargled that "r" in "Ramis" like a hunting cat on the prowl.

Beagar motioned to Dasta to serve the last of the potatoes. Dasta waggled his hand to the cook's mate. Inda saw the mate helping himself to a drink right out of one of the bottles just being brought in. "Pirate independent, or Brotherhood of Blood?"

"Oh, he's an independent, they say. But as tough as the Brotherhood. Tougher, some say. You know how the Brotherhood, they wear a gold hoop in their ear after their first ship kill. But on *Knife*, it means Brotherhood kills. Not mere traders."

Ship kill. It was a Brotherhood of Blood tradition, Inda had learned from other shiprats—some terrified, some impressed. It didn't mean capture, forcing the crews either to take to the longboats or switch allegiance, it meant taking a capital ship, looting it, and setting it afire, killing everyone aboard, just because they could. Subsequent kills were signaled by adding diamonds to the golden hoops.

"He's after the Brotherhood?" Beagar looked surprised.

"So they said, so they said. He fired three Brotherhood ships. Midst of an attack. Took 'em one at a time." Dirbin waved her finger back and forth three times, making a spitting sound. "Three. Makes the independents, with their rules and safe harbors and setting prisoners free inna boat, look like silk-weavers from Colend. As for Ramis' ship, *Knife* is a captured Venn warship, and diddied up to be even faster."

Beagar whistled. "Took it off the *Venn*? Huh. So how does it steer? Did he keep the whipstaff, or put in a wheel?"

The visiting mid smothered a laugh at the looks on the captains' faces. As the two captains embarked on a highly technical discussion of what this Ramis had done to the Venn ship, the new mid whispered behind his hand to Inda, "Pirates! We never get within sniff of them."

"Us either," Inda whispered back.

The boy sighed. "You stay close to shore, like these merch captains always do, and with a lot of other ships, and pirates are just a story." As he spoke he glanced at the captains, who were both leaning forward, illustrating what they meant by moving knives and spoons about on the table. With practiced ease that Inda admired, the mid's fingers nipped the last piece of chicken.

Dirbin finally said, "I had the sved off of half a dozen people, all stone sober. This Ramis is hunting 'em for Norsunder, he is. Taking 'em straight out of the world. Through a tunnel black as night he snaps up with his fingers. I tell you I heard it, with these ears." She flicked both her ears, and then glanced at the apple tarts the mates had just brought in; the heel of the ship sent the tray sliding past her as she hoisted her cup. Unseen by either captain, her mid made good use of the movement to snag three tarts.

"Well, that one I'll believe when I see it," Beagar stated with comfortable ease. Norsunder, in his worldview, was as distant as the time of his grandfather's grandfather's grandfathers, when there were barbaric customs such as leaving condemned criminals out for the Norsundrians to find and harvest, saving the effort of a beheading. "Souleater" was the worst insult possible, but no one saw Norsundrians actually *doing* it any more.

"Suit yourself, suit yourself. You know I never argue, not in the face of this here Alygran wine. Now, this battle. It reminds me of the time . . ."

The visiting mid, seeing that the captains were safely embarked on their battle talk, slid out toward the galley. Dasta poked Inda, holding up two fingers: fetch more bottles.

Inda eased out of the stuffy cabin, glad at least to get a breath. The summer evening was still, warm, and he could hear singing forward; he longed to find someone who could tell him what was going on at home.

No, that wasn't home anymore. His home was here.

He turned away, poked his head into the galley in time to see the mates passing a bottle from hand to hand, each swigging out of it. The new mid took it, glugged down at least six swallows, and then turned without a stagger as the cook expertly topped the bottle with an inferior wine.

Inda silently held his hand out. The two bottles were put into it, and he eased his way back into the cabin.

". . . and so they fired three of 'em right on the water, but they took the biggest, and a fine, sweet vessel it is, fast and clean, danced even with the wind on the for'ard quarter."

He set the bottles down, and saw an efficient brown hand reach from behind and snag one of the last four pastries.

Dasta watched, mouth open; his disgust at the mid's fashionable clothes had changed to respect for so adroit a master thief.

The mid stuffed the pastry into his mouth just a moment before Kodl looked up. "Are you hungry, boy?" he asked with somewhat heavy irony.

Inda said quickly, "You might want to go up and see to it your barge crew has a harness handy for your mate."

The mid bobbed, grateful, his cheeks bulging, and dashed out. Kodl sent an expressive look at Inda, Yan, and Dasta. Dirbin might have a rep as tight-fisted with her crew, but if her mids ate like that one, it was a wonder she could keep her ship in provisions.

The dinner finished up with mutual expressions of good will, and Beagar saw his guest up the ladder. Two big sailors appeared and in practiced silence hoisted the drunken mate—who hadn't spoken once—up after the captains, while Dasta and Inda hastily gobbled down the remaining apple tarts, splitting the last one before the cook's mates could get there.

Captain Dirbin was seen over the side and into her barge as she began singing in her cheery crow's squawk of a voice a ditty enumerating the adventuresome, if unlikely, sexual exploits of a sailor girl's first night on the shore. Inda returned to duty, which was better than trying to make sense out of that patchwork of rumors about home.

Not home.

Chapter Eight

TDOR'S first impression of the royal city was of noise. Carts, voices, horses, dogs, a constant clatter and hubbub magnified by the stone walls all around. Her second was alarm when the fast triplets of war horns sounded from the gates she'd just passed through.

A Runner, a young man in mud-splashed blue, galloped in on a foam-flecked horse. Everyone gave way, even a riding of guards trotting out for a perimeter patrol.

"Has to be news from the front," said her escort. The man was Liet's father, familiar to Tdor since she first came to Tenthen—the older Rider captains often stood as uncles to the girls brought in so young by marriage treaties.

The Runner vanished among the jumble of carts, wagons, armsmen, city idlers talking, flirting, watching. There were sellers hawking fresh rye muffins, in short streets of close-set buildings running perpendicular to the city walls, most with a tree in the center around which people from the surrounding houses seemed to gather to chat, and children to play. Crossing these were the great streets that ringed the royal castle, streets so long she could not see the ends as they curved round the hills. It was a city, a real city, her first, filled with more people than she'd ever seen in her entire life.

Nor was she invisible. People glanced her way, and she watched the

progress of their thoughts in the progression of their glances: first the
owl pennants and livery on her escort, then to her, at the front right of
the bearers; another future Jarlan or Randviar, here for the Queens
Training. No further interest.

They passed beneath the heavy wall built over the main castle gate,
waved on by the watchful sentries—male ones looking outward, female
inward, at least in theory. Just like at home at Tenthen. Tdor was excited
at the prospect of seeing Hadand again after two long years, and Joret,
who had stayed an extra year on an invitation from the queen—an invitation she couldn't refuse. *Maybe I'll even see the king,* Tdor thought.
At the Games, if nothing else.

They rode into a vast stable yard and dismounted. A moment later a
young woman in gray robes appeared before her.

"This way, Tdor-Edli." The woman indicated a door, then said to
Noren, standing at Tdor's right and just a little behind, "Bring her gear
and follow."

Tdor glanced at Liet's father, who gave her an encouraging nod and a
salute, which she returned, and that was the last she saw of her escort.

Tdor and Noren followed the servant, a girl Tdor's own age. Noren
was watching everything intently, her changeable face a tolerable mirror
to her thoughts. When an especially attractive young guard passed by on
his patrol, his yellow horsetail swinging, Noren gave Tdor a covert grin,
her brows raised; the servant leading them never glanced aside.

Immense arched doorways with heavy iron-studded doors led to
shadowy passageways, stairs, and divided courts. From the courts Tdor
and Noren glimpsed such a complexity of towers and higher walls that
they wondered if they'd ever learn. Tenthen Castle seemed tiny by
comparison.

Tdor wondered where the academy was. How it hurt, that chain of
thought: academy, Inda, their last meeting.

Stop that. Watch and learn. They reached an intersection at the same
moment a pair of female guards crossed from the adjacent passages. They
saluted one another, and Tdor heard the taller woman say, "What's new?"

"Nothing in my basket, that's for sure."

Tdor, who'd heard that expression for years without thinking of anything but a nice woven carryall, blushed. She'd recently discovered what
those women really meant.

"Here's the girls' barracks," their guide said, paying no attention to the guards. She indicated the building beyond the last court. "This is where you will stay, Tdor-Edli. Runner—"

"Noren."

"Runner Noren, come with me."

Tdor was left in a plain wood-walled room furnished with nothing but wooden benches. From an open window she heard the echo of girls' voices in drill.

A tall woman in the queen's livery—gray robes edged with crimson—entered. "Tdor-Edli?"

Tdor saluted, hand to heart.

"Please come this way. I will introduce you to your bunkmate, who will show you around and explain. You will not be expected to attend drills until tomorrow."

"Thank you," Tdor said, and followed the woman down clean plank-floored halls, past empty barracks rooms. They reached the last, which was close to a door opening onto a court.

Inside was a single occupant, busy sanding down a bow. She looked up, and then smiled; Tdor studied the girl, who was short, slight, with a square face and curling pale hair escaping her braids.

"Tdor-Edli, Shendan-Edli," the woman said, and then she left without another word.

Shendan Montredavan-An. Fareas-Iofre had said to Tdor, *Your daughter will marry the Montredavan-An heir, and his sister will help raise your firstborn daughter, as their girls cannot marry out. Become her friend, if you can. It will make the loss more bearable one day.*

And on the last day of her last visit with her own mother, she had been given the same advice. Tdor felt peculiar at the idea of having a daughter; the idea seemed weird, even absurd. Mostly she was interested in this new person whose family had such a long, fascinating history. And now were exiles on their own land.

"Hullo," Shendan said in a cheery voice. "Long ride?"

"Somewhat," Tdor said, tentatively.

"Well, you'll be able to hit the pillow early tonight. Take it! Tomorrow it's up before dawn, and whack, whack, whack." Shendan grimaced. "I'll show you what's where. And don't think you have to know it at once. I certainly didn't."

The girl never stopped talking as they moved down the row of barracks and out into the practice courts. It was all quick talk, identifying both people and places, punctuated with laughing comments about mistakes Shendan had made.

Tdor walked slowly, watching the young women who all seemed tall and competent, fighting with wooden knives, with short staffs, with bows, and many, of course, were busy training horses.

Shendan was friendly and funny, but Tdor was wondering if she might also be a little scatterbrained when they stopped in a vast, empty parade court, and she pointed up at the castle.

"The archive is just behind that set of windows, over there," Shendan said, squinting against the high summer sun. "Next to the tower, which is where the king's rooms start." She turned to Tdor, the expression in her wide-set eyes speculative. "Are you going to join the readings on the history of magic, then?"

Tdor drew in a deep breath. "I–I didn't know—" *That we could mention that out loud right in the open*, she meant to say, but she stopped because it sounded so stupid. They were here in the middle of this mighty parade ground, with no one even remotely in earshot.

Shendan laughed silently. "Surely you knew the Montredavan-Ans are part of it?"

Tdor turned to Shendan, saw a sardonic quirk to those watchful dark eyes, and blushed. "I didn't mean that. I only meant—I thought we were not to talk about it, well, so soon."

"I don't, unless it's safe. Which is why we are here on our tour. I don't know what you've been told, but my family is actually the center of this quest, for we began it, and Fareas-Iofre became a part before she was taken away from us and made to marry Jarend-Adaluin. As you might be made to marry Whipstick Noth."

Tdor drew in a sharp breath. "No one has said that."

"No. They won't, until the women negotiate, the men negotiate, and they finally negotiate with one another. Then both you and Whipstick will be told what to do."

Tdor flexed her hands, thinking of Whipstick, the tall, taciturn son of Captain Noth. He was even quieter than Tanrid, but he was even-tempered, and at first had even been a little shy around the girls. They'd all known his reputation at the academy, yet when he arrived he did not thrash anyone, not even Branid, who on the arrival of the Noths had, as usual, made himself unpleasant. Whipstick was the best of the boys in everything, earning their respect.

Out loud she said, "I hope Inda will be back before I reach marriage age, and I won't have to."

"You expect justice? There isn't any justice," Shendan said, such words sounding very odd when spoken in that light voice, with a side-long, merry glance. "We Montredavan-Ans are living proof of that."

Tdor stared at Shendan in silence.

"I hope for your sake Inda returns. I met him once, did you know that? We liked him. My brother Fox liked him, and you cannot imagine how very rare that was." Shendan waved at the archive windows. "You can do what you like during free time, but it's good you'll be joining the reading," she said slowly. "Very good. What happened to us could hap-pen to you, and might even, if the Harskialdna gets his way: you'll lose rank, and holdings, everything but the castle, the daughters can't marry any of the Vayir families, the sons can't fight. And so we girls . . . we study magic. Or try."

Tdor felt as if she'd stumbled into an icy stream.

Shendan gave Tdor a laughing glance. "As for now, we also have fun. This is the only time in my life I get to live among others, and I get as much fun from it as I can. Come! I'll point you to the baths. You can get in a good long soak after that ride, and enjoy it, too. You won't have much time there after today."

She left Tdor at the baths, but before Tdor could shed her clothes and sink into the clean water, a tall girl in Runner blue slipped through the opposite door and beckoned.

Intrigued, and a little afraid, Tdor followed. She really needed a chance to think over what she'd heard and seen so far, but it looked like she wasn't going to get that comfort.

Now came another long walk, then up, and up, and down a carpeted hall with frescoes of hunting beasts and raptors, and above all horses—running, rearing, standing—in shades of light gray along the walls. The hall smelled faintly of beeswax candle smoke, years and years' worth, she realized, and that recalled home, but nothing else did, especially when at last, with a smile, the tall girl opened a door and stood aside for Tdor to enter.

The room was big, with a high ceiling painted with a view of the summer stars. Underfoot lay the broadest carpet Tdor had ever seen, woven gold braiding around the edges, stylized falcons worked in rows through the middle, the royal crimson as background. At the walls sat

large chairs, all of them carved from fine dark woods, edged with real gold
along the swept back wings and legs. Raptor chairs, old ones: at Tenthen
there were only two, one in the prince's own chamber, one in Tanrid's.
Fareas-Iofre had said that the Montredavan-Ans had even older ones.

Completing the room was a great table against the wall opposite the
windows. It, too, had stylized raptor legs. On it rested a huge map, beautifully drawn; even bigger and finer than the one in Jarend-Adaluin's
chamber.

Tdor crossed her arms defensively. It was a masculine room, one filled
with costly things, with a commanding view. She felt unnerved, as if
she'd stumbled into a secret place, a place of power, one into which she
was not entitled to step.

"It's all right," came a familiar voice. Tdor whirled around. There was
Hadand, laughing softly as she entered through an unobtrusive side
door. "This is actually the safest place in the castle right now. The few
who would dare to spy here are all somewhere else."

Tdor knew, then, without being told, that she stood in the king's own
room. She twirled around, staring. The windows looked down over a
very large parade ground—that must be the one she'd stood in with
Shendan, talking of magic—and the windows themselves were high,
framed by heavy curtains, with wall carvings of raptors in flight above
and below.

At last she turned to the short figure in the center of the room.
Hadand smiled as the door latched behind her. "If we see one another
in company, the same sign I taught you is the one we use here for an
unsafe room." She brushed three fingers across her palm in the lily sign.

Tdor whispered, "I remember."

"Two years, it's been," Hadand said, studying her from eyes that
brought Inda right back into Tdor's mind.

"You're in robes," Tdor observed, then flushed at how obvious that
was, how stupid it must sound. Yet it was so strange to see Hadand with
Inda's eyes, but a woman's body. She had gotten short, somehow. Her
fine soft-gray woolen robe with its exquisite edging embroidery of intertwined silver owls, slit up the sides for riding, her voluminous riding
trousers edged with the same silver owls along their hems, did not hide
how wide her hips were, nor how large and shapely her bosom.

Hadand flicked the robe open, revealing a fine high-necked linen
shirt, laced neatly with silken ties, her trim waist sashed, the curved han-

dle of her knife somehow accentuating the inward curve of what Tdor realized was a spectacular figure.

"You're quite a bit taller than I am, now," Hadand said, making her own obvious statement, and Tdor knew it was to set her at ease. She laughed. "I always assumed I'd be a stick like my mother, and not a duck like mother says granny is!" She smacked her hips. "I can barely do a handspring any more, though this fine butt of mine centers me beautifully on a horse. I find I can balance with ease over the most daunting fences." She laughed again, then her smile turned pensive. "I'd like to meet Gran someday. I hear Mother's voice reading her letters."

None of that mattered to Tdor right now. "I'm so glad to see you again," Tdor exclaimed, throwing herself forward.

The two hugged, and when they parted, both were teary.

"Oh, you don't know how very good it will be just to know you are here, even if we seldom get to see one another," Hadand said, her voice low and fervent.

Prickles tingled along Tdor's arms. Hadand just never showed emotion, at least not this kind. She was always practical, or at least merry, calm, kind.

"Don't you have Joret?" she asked.

Hadand drew herself up, and there was the calm, practical, kind face again. "Oh, she's here, but she's so surrounded by spies we almost never exchange more than a word or two, and a few signs, except when we are in the archive, and then it's back to the real work."

"Spies? On Joret? Why?"

Hadand's lip curled. "It's that fool of a Sierlaef. Nobody expected him to raise the staff—to think he's in love with her," she corrected hastily, remembering that Tdor was still in smocks. *Hurry up and grow,* Hadand thought, fighting against the fire of emotion seeing this familiar face from home had sparked. How badly she needed a confident, or at least a friend!

Tdor, meanwhile, translated mentally, and though she understood in a general sense (staffs were men's sex thing, and of course she'd long known where it was supposed to go, but the feelings that were supposed to go with all that were still a complete mystery) it was enough to make her blush. Hadand had grown up. Unsteadiness rocked Tdor for a moment, as if she were on a runaway horse. People changed so fast! She hadn't changed, she felt the same as she always had.

"Alas, we're running out of time. The king will want his room soon, and you will have to take the fastest bath of your life," Hadand said, laughing. "Tesar will take you back down. I'll try to see you when I can. If you like, that is," she amended contritely.

"Of course I want to see you. And the princess commanded me to continue the studies, if that is possible."

"Oh, never fear, I can arrange that. Every girl gets some free time. Most of them waste it one way or another. Joret and I spend ours in the archive, along with Shen—you've met her?—just as Mama wishes. And I will say this: our assiduous reading is so boring to everyone's spies that that's one place they generally leave us alone." When Tdor ducked her head, Hadand grimaced, then said, "Most of the girls are fine, but watch out for Stara Ola-Vayir—some call her Honeytongue. She'll bootlick you something fierce, until she winnows out any secrets you might have, and then you'll wake up one day with everyone knowing, and Mudface—that is, Dannor Tya-Vayir—laughing at you. They both should have been gone by now, but the Ola-Vayirs put pressure for Honeytongue to be a queen's lady, and this is—I hope—Mudface's last year."

Tdor snorted a laugh. "Just as well I don't have any secrets."

"You do," Hadand said soberly. "The magic studies. And Inda being alive."

Tdor winced. Hadand gave her a quick, wordless hug again, and then opened the door to reveal that tall Runner standing outside, her hands in her sleeves. Tdor knew from her stance that those sleeves contained at least one knife, probably two. Even here in the king's castle. Just as Chelis' did, at home in Tenthen, when she guarded Fareas-Iofre. Real life. Adult life.

"We saw a Runner on the way in," she ventured, as they started down the stairs.

Hadand lifted a shoulder. "Runners come in all day, most of them from the Harskialdna." Her voice lowered to a murmur. "He was supposed to take a month, and he's been there half again that long, and from the latest from Cassad's Runners, it might be all summer before they get anywhere. Despite all the news, until Captain Sindan comes back, we don't really know what's going on."

Neither did the Harskialdna.

Riding across the meadows and fields and farmland south of the Trad-heval coast as they pushed east toward Idayago, looking for enemies that were not there, made him wish he could smash something.

A battle in ordered ranks, that he knew he could fight and win. His forces were drilled into instant obedience, their skills unmatched. But where were the ranged forces they had ridden north expecting?

The Idayagans had to be somewhere. It was too easy to envision them slipping along to the north or south, just out of sight, but of course if they were that good, that fast, they would come out and fight. At least if they were Marlovans they would.

There was no *order,* no *sense* to it. It was like reaching for a stone, and finding sand in his hand instead, he thought morosely as he scanned the hazy hills in the north, with their unfamiliar trees that blocked the terrain from view. He longed to set fire to it all.

If he'd been alone, he would have done just that. Or if the northern-ers had not acted exactly as his brother had predicted. But they had. Oh, there had been some skirmishing in the pass, but nothing that really amounted to much. He mostly let the boys get blooded, though it left them all craving more; it was too easy. No one, obviously, wanted to face the entire army of Tlennen-Harvaldar of Iasca Leror.

All they'd found since emerging from the northeast side of the pass and turning east were villages with farmers at the windows watching them with unblinking, angry eyes, a few towns, mostly empty, some deserted castles, and vast stretches of rice plantings in the low grounds and crop fields on the higher. Someone pointed out the Venn might have already been through, but nothing was destroyed, just abandoned. The Harskialdna was certain the missing inhabitants were forming an army . . . somewhere.

His brooding was interrupted when his nephew urged his mount over. The Harskialdna looked up. The king's heir jerked his head at the westering sun. Definitely time to make camp and secure a good perime-ter before they lost the light.

The Sierlaef waited impatiently until his uncle had finished inspec-tion and was waiting for his cook to finish frying up some fresh fish.

Now, he thought, and dropped down on his haunches beside the map. He jabbed the map with his finger, sweeping it eastward into Idayago. "We scout."

"Who?" His uncle scowled.

The king's heir smacked his chest and flicked his fingers at the Sier-Danas, three of whom waited at a respectful distance. Tanrid and Tlen were already seeing to the mounts.

"What? Why?" the Harskialdna asked, frowning, his thoughts scattered between his ongoing worries and this new threat.

For answer the heir swept his two forefingers together on the map, one proceeding east along the northern coast, as they'd been riding for the past month, and one speeding south, then cutting north along the foothills at the base of the Mountains of Ghaeldraeth and back west to meet in the middle.

His uncle sucked in a breath. "But you can't ride alone. Your father would never permit it."

"Not here."

"Aldren, if something happens to you, I might as well fall on my sword. I must keep you safe, it's more important than anything else. You have to see that."

"Take our own men. Each. Flight of gradoo—guh, guh. Dragoons." White-hot anger flashed through the Sierlaef at his stupid tongue.

His uncle saw the anger, and hesitated. Twenty-one, a man for a year, but the royal heir was still a boy to his uncle, and always would be. A boy more intolerant of the Harskialdna's reins each passing day. The Harskialdna thought of the hints, persuasions, coaxings, even downright lies he'd been forced to speak in order to control the damned boy and knew that here, so far away from the king, his control was about as strong as a woolen string on a maddened charger. The heir was still afraid of the king his father, but that fear wasn't enough to keep him under control, not here.

He turned his head, and saw activity on the picket line. Successfully interpreting it—the Sierlaef had already given orders, assuming his uncle's compliance—a surge of anger just as hot as the Sierlaef's scalded him, all the more fierce because he knew that the day he'd dreaded was here, that the boy had chosen now, this moment, to revolt, and there was nothing he could do. The king had given his orders to them both; there was no lying, adding extras on, pretending they were from the king.

So . . . undercut the revolt.

His uncle forced a smile. "You show excellent command sense," he said. "I was just now thinking along the same lines, only I was thinking it might be best if you were to take . . ." Whom could he release? He had to keep the boy safe, but every riding he sent further divided their forces. "Buck Marlo-Vayir's flight, and the coastal riders. Also take your father's Runners." Yes. He'd probably be stuck with Sindan showing up and poking his long nose into royal business before long. At least he could get rid of the other two spies whose reports home he could not control.

And it worked. The Sierlaef's flush of pleasure was easy enough to read. Later on, perhaps, the heir would translate that "excellent command sense" as meaning that his uncle had thought of the plan first. He must keep what control he could.

Chapter Nine

THE first friendly faces in two weeks belonged to young women.

Tanrid Algara-Vayir looked in surprise at the pretty Idayagans standing along a fence, watching the Marlovans ride by. The Sier-Danas had broken formation to ride at the back; the dust still suspended in the hot summer air from the passage of their force made them sneeze, but they could talk freely, and when they arrived, camp would be set up.

It had been a boring ride. Until now. One of the young women leaned against the fence so that the neck of her gown dipped down, half-revealing the promising roundnesses beneath.

Tanrid swallowed. The clothes these girls wore looked to the Marlovans like pleasure house garments, tight at the waist and hips, low at the neck, with gem-colored embroidery and lacy stuff that just called attention to what you weren't supposed to stare at without invite. So unlike the girls at home, who put on the women's robes as soon as they had anything to look at.

Tanrid glanced across at the other Sier-Danas, and saw the Sierlaef's gaze locked onto the one on the end who was lazily twining a curl of hair through her fingers. She too leaned against the fence, her skirt molding the extravagant curve of one hip.

"You boys aren't so bad looking," one of the girls said in strongly accented Iascan.

Another girl giggled. "We heard you were ugly and your horses pretty."

No, these Marlovan boys weren't ugly at all, with those severely-cut long military coats sashed tight at their slim waists, those splendid shoulders, the muscular legs just outlined by the wide-legged riding trousers stuffed into those glossy high-heeled black-weave boots. Attractive, but dangerous, riding so slowly on their beautiful mild-as-milk horses, dagger hilts winking at their sashes, at the tops of their boots, their wicked swords with the curved tip carried slantwise at their saddlepads. On their other side they carried those odd tear-shaped shields, all of them with wings painted on, except the one with the long stylized feathers overlaid in real, beaten gold. Yes, that one had to be the prince, thought one girl, and she gave him her most winning smile, practiced just that day in front of the mirror, while her cousin observed that these Marlovan boys all seemed to look alike, except maybe that rat-faced one in the middle, probably because of the strange way they bound their hair back up on their heads, hanging down like a long tail, and all of it more or less as yellow as old sun-bleached thatch, except the dark-haired one on the end.

"You're all pretty," a third said. She was brown of skin and hair and eyes, her lips curved in a slow, secretive smile.

The first one wore her wavy black hair in a lot of braids tied with ribbon. "We're alone here," she crooned, twirling a ribbon in a way that locked seven rapt gazes to the low neck of her gown. "It's sooooooo booooooring."

"Come in, have a bite?" That was the second one.

The Sier-Danas glanced at the Sierlaef, their faces fairly revealing.

"Ride," the heir said in Marlovan, looking away, and then back again. He made a fist, brought it down: camp first.

"After we see to our camp, we'll be back along this way," Buck Marlo-Vayir said, grinning. "Shall we bring something?"

"Oh, maybe some wine, if you have it," the black-haired one said in a low voice. "Though we have plenty, and no one to share it with."

"We'll be back." Tanrid realized he'd spoken, and bent forward to stroke his nervous mount.

Embarrassment always made him sensitive to sound. He heard soft laughter from one of them, and because he couldn't see her face, because he was listening so intently, the back of his neck prickled.

For a moment there, all he'd been able to think about were those lovely shapes beneath the revealing clothes—that and the peculiar pain of what the boys called saddle-wood, but now he turned his head and looked at the girls.

Still smiling, all of them, lazily raising one hand. Behind them an ordinary house, built here close to the road, which never happened at home except in walled villages. Lots of curtained windows, a truck garden on the northeast side to make the most of the sun. He'd already seen a lot of farmhouses just like this one, here in the north, houses all by themselves, a sign that war seldom came this way, he guessed. An ordinary farmhouse, not a pleasure house.

Tanrid said, "How much you charge for sex?"

The first girl looked confused, the second's lips parted, the third's face tightened in quick, reflexive anger. Then she shook her head, smiling. "Free and friendly. We don't need money. We like pretty fellows, is all, and we're bored."

"Which one is the prince?" the first one asked, tossing her curls and arching her back. She laughed exultantly when she saw the impact in those hot foreign gazes. "I hope it's you," she added to Buck Marlo-Vayir. "You're the handsomest."

"I want the prince. I've never seen a prince. I want a tussle with one," the second one said, jutting a hip and putting both arms up over her head, then running her fingers through her hair. She glanced the Sierlaef's way. It was a quick, assessing look, then she pouted, making kissy lips.

"We like pretty girls, and we're bored, too," Cassad called, laughing. "We'll return."

"We'll be waiting." The first girl cooed in a breathy voice that was now, Tanrid thought uneasily, too breathy.

Cassad made ribald remarks as they rode away, laughing at his own wit. If things were quiet—of course they would be—the outriders were to find a camp beyond the village, where there was grass and water.

"Wine," Buck said presently. "We daren't raid, I suppose. Anyone have any coin? If we sent a fast Runner to the town we rode past this morning, we could have it back by the time we finish camp. What say?"

He spoke to the Sierlaef, but Tanrid said, "No."

The Sierlaef's head jerked round. "What?"

Tanrid looked back. The house was out of sight by now, behind one of the forested hills. Hills that could hide things—like archers, or an ambush. The countryside had been empty for uncounted days, so quiet they had come to assume that nothing ever happened here, outside of the growing of rice along all the river marshland, and cotton in the fields.

But quite suddenly, after days and days of boredom, Tanrid's mind galloped and he was seeing danger everywhere. Real, dream, or cowardice?

While Tanrid wrestled mentally, the Sierlaef was also veering between conflicting emotions. First there was the insistence of desire. It had been so long. Too long. At home, all he could think of was Joret. Now, months away from Joret, he felt desire again, and the prospect of a tumble with one of those tight-waisted, billowy girls made him start to tremble.

And Tanrid had the presumption to say no! "What," he said again, glaring at Tanrid.

Tanrid glanced around at the trees, even at the sky, and then said, low, "Let's talk in camp."

The sun was setting by the time the camp perimeter was laid out, and the Sier-Danas met together at the center, away from the command tents.

Manther Jaya-Vayir said, "Cousin Tanrid. What's wrong? Nothing with the girls, surely. They're just girls."

Everyone knew girls here blanched white as sand at the sight of a knife, unlike the girls at home. Most of the men too, for that matter.

Tanrid drew his sleeve across his sweaty face. The evening was sultry, making everyone feel ill at ease. "They aren't pleasure girls, but they were acting like 'em."

"Flirting," Cassad said with a shrug. "And so were we."

"That's what I thought, but did you watch 'em? They talked and acted like pleasure house girls, yet the one got mad when I asked about money."

Cassad gestured, palm out. "Different customs."

"Except we're enemies," Manther said. "Why so friendly? Not just friendly, but . . ." He frowned. *"Personal."*

"Like they were hiding something. I think it's a ruse," Tanrid said swiftly.

"Ruse?" the Sierlaef said with scorn, miming a stabbing. "Fight *us*?"

"Not a real fight. But, say, they get us drinking, get us into bed, and while we're bare-ass and drunk and humping away, they pull knives on us."

Buck crowed in derision.

Cassad snorted. "Even with our trousers off we could dust 'em, knives or no knives."

Tlen, who'd been silent, looked up, frowning. The Sierlaef punched him in the arm, and Tlen said, "They asked about the prince. They knew who we were."

"That's nothing." It was Cassad's turn to scoff. "They probably spotted his war shield. Even Idayagan girls who've never seen a warrior in their lives are probably smart enough to figure that the only person carrying gold like that has to be royal. I still don't smell a ruse."

The Sierlaef swung his head Hawkeye's way. Hawkeye Yvana-Vayir was the wildest of them all, the first to fight, the one who rode the hardest, yet the half-tamed horses he rode always adored him. "You?"

Hawkeye stroked his sharp-cut chin. "They spotted the shield because they were on the lookout for it. They did seem to know we were not riding at the front."

Tlen turned all the way round, then shrugged. "Someone's been on watch. But we saw no sign of it."

They all considered these words. When they thought about it, it *did* seem like someone had been on the watch.

Hawkeye jerked his thumb at the heir. "I say we send some of our own men in our clothes. If nothing's wrong, they have a good time. If something's wrong, we can be right out there, with a riding, waiting."

"And won't we look stupid, standing around a house listening to them whoop it up, if nothing's wrong," Buck retorted.

Hawkeye shrugged. "Then we go ourselves. So long as we don't see a war party creeping up, we and our own Runners can handle any number of assassins in that house, I should think. So if nothing's wrong we make it out to be a game of our own, and return, ourselves, tomorrow. We're as far east as we can go, we have to turn back and start west again to meet the Harskialdna anyway, so what's an extra day?"

Tanrid had been drumming his fingers in a war tattoo, as he mentally reviewed the map. "Damn," he said.

"Oh, what now?" Buck groaned with annoyance, slewing around to glare at him.

Tanrid dropped onto his knees, smearing the ground with his sleeve. Then he sketched in a rough approximation of the Idayagan coast. "So we're here, hard up against the hills. Two rivers there to the west, which either we or the Harskialdna have to cross, before we meet. Two rivers between us and the rest of our forces. All they'd have to do is bring down their own bridges. If we have to ford rivers on horseback, shooting us is mere target practice."

Buck sneered. "You afraid of shadows now?"

"No," Cassad said before Tanrid could speak, with a characteristic sudden mood swing. "You know, he's right. I mean, if *we* saw so obvious a tactical advantage—forces split by two rivers—"

Tlen stroked his thumb along his knife handle.

Cassad poked him. "And even if they don't have an army, it would be a neat, easy ruse to capture and kill the royal heir and his future Jarls in one night. Catch us in bed, we even look bad. There wouldn't be any songs about that," he added with grim humor. "Not on our side, anyway."

Manther Jaya-Vayir said in his soft voice, "I say we send either liege-men or Runners to the girls. And watch from outside."

Hawkeye turned to Tanrid. "I think you're right." And to the Sierlaef—they all faced the Sierlaef—"Well?"

The Sierlaef wound his finger in the air, and pointed.

The boys each picked out a personal Runner or trusted armsman, and lent them their House tunics and good sashes. Buck couldn't bring himself to tell his armsman anything more than "It's a ruse the Sierlaef wants to run." Cassad, Hawkeye, Jaya-Vayir, and Tanrid all told their men exactly what was going on; Tlen had chosen Kepri-Davan Ain, childhood friend, former academy mate, and now his family's future dragoon captain. They both thought it a prime joke, and Kepa Ain took on his role with enthusiasm.

After some discussion (the armsmen were included) they all decided against the armsmen wearing mail: that would make the girls suspicious, though the thought of the girls believing that Marlovans wore chain mail to bed made them all laugh.

The laughter didn't last long. Tanrid felt strange, watching his own Runner, known to him since childhood, ride off wearing his best green fine-wool tunic, that silver owl stitched by his mother, then he shrugged away the feeling. This ruse affair was too easy, that was what bothered him.

He looked around, sniffing the air. It smelled of dust, of sweat, of summer herbs and grasses. Not a whiff of horse on the wind, but there wouldn't be any. War up here was different, they'd been told that for years.

The others joked back and forth as they slipped into their war gear, for they hadn't even been wearing mail, not since they'd come through the pass and found things so quiet, and the weather so miserably hot. Quilting, mail, and over it their old gray academy war coats. Then they strapped on their wrist and palm guards and loaded up with knives; no bows or arrows, not for scouting a house.

Tanrid finished first and found the captain of his personal guard, who had just sat down to eat.

The man put his food down. Tanrid walked him a little way away, and pointed east, at where the silent, forest-covered hills of Lower Ghael rose, touched with sunset colors. "I want you to take a riding and scout up into those hills soon's you have moonlight. No horses, no noise." He added, uneasy and not sure why, "And I'll see that you get extra liberty soon as we meet the Harskialdna."

The man squinted up at the hills. The subtle quirk of smile narrowing his eyes was not the least derisive; he was used to boys being ill at ease with their first command in real life. He struck his fist against his breast, and that was that.

Soon the Sier-Danas were riding westward again, only this time they circled far around to the rear of the farm, leaving their well trained horses to crop grass next to a stream out of sight of the house and its outbuildings.

It was full dark, the moon just about to rise, as the boys belly-crept through the gardens behind the house, bringing not just their knives but their swords, customarily used only from horseback, though they had also trained to fight on foot. The men's horses waited in an adjacent shed, obviously well cared for, everything peaceful. All the windows in the house were lit, though the curtains were drawn. Inside they heard female laughter and male voices.

"No, I'm the prince!" That was Buck's fellow, an arrogant barracks-raised young dragoon from home named Hemrid. Buck didn't know it, but Tanrid's Runner had warned him, which prompted Hemrid to act the fool. "I command everyone to get drunk!"

The voices rose and fell, punctuated with much laughter, as the moon silently rose and started climbing toward the top of the sky. Then, one by one, the voices softened, and quiet settled over the house.

The Sierlaef peered up between the cabbages again and again, and when an unseen stalk of some sort of weed caused his nose to itch once too often, he became angry and was reaching to smack Buck to signal the retreat when his eyes caught a flicker of movement.

He went still, as he had on so many wargames at home. They had not thought to stain their faces; he knew his pale face might be discerned if he moved.

They were all watching. Silent, black figures moved noiselessly from around the barn beyond the shed toward the back of the farmhouse.

The Sierlaef rose, uttering a strangled yell.

The figures stopped, and then milled about, sharp male voices exclaiming.

"Attack! Attack!" Buck yelled, rising, drawing his knife. "Hemrid! Attack!"

The figures beat them inside, of course, and their leader was smart enough to bar the door and douse the lights. Tanrid and Hawkeye together kicked the door to splinters as Cassad flung a wheelbarrow through a window. At first everything was chaos, fighting in a house—an unfamiliar one at that—but Tanrid, suspecting what had happened as soon as he smelled the mulled wine and heavy herbs lingering in the hot kitchen air, picked up a chair and smashed it into the fireplace, which still contained burning embers. He paused long enough for flames to catch the ragged ends of the chair leg, and then he swept the fire to curtains, pillows, anything that would burn.

Screaming, yelling, sudden lunging figures melded together into a wine-and-herb soaked haze, but one image stayed clear: their liegemen all dead, stabbed just moments before, while slumbering deeply under the effect of sleep herbs in the wine.

The Sierlaef's inarticulate howl intensified the terrifying sound of Cassad's savage yips as he dashed through, knife and sword whirling.

The boys caught and killed everything that moved, a rage-filled murderous attack that had no joy in it, just a lust for vengeance. When all the Idayagans were dead, they ran out; Tlen sobbing with rage and grief combined, Jaya-Vayir hissing in pain, before the fire took hold one of the enemy had lunged out at him from a dish cupboard, scoring him deeply across the back of his neck.

Tanrid himself had a couple of cuts, but he ignored the sting. Beatings back in his academy days had hurt far worse. What drove him now was the growing conviction that this incident was not isolated, that his having been right about the ruse meant he was right about something far larger, far more threatening.

And so he rode hard, bent close over his horse's flying mane as they galloped cross-country toward their camp, the liegemen's riderless horses stringing behind Cassad.

The outer perimeter sentries shouted, Buck waved, and yelled, "Sierlaef!" Tanrid barely registered this breach of ritual, and Manther nearly falling from his horse and being caught by Cassad; his eyes searched the camp, found the camp commander.

Before he could speak a screamer arrow whistled in the distance, and then another, closer: signal arrows, one from the outer perimeter sentries and the other from Tanrid's liegeman.

The Sier-Danas were all waiting, poised with weapons at the ready, when the riding thundered into camp. The captain wheeled his horse, sending dirt hissing into the fires, as he shouted, "Army on the move! Foot warriors coming down out of the hills."

That was what Tanrid had missed: foot warriors. No horses. They wouldn't have speed, but they could use terrain that cavalry couldn't. Like rocky hills.

"How m–many?" The Sierlaef snapped.

"At least a wing, probably more."

All they had was one flight—a third of a wing—plus their personal armsmen.

Tanrid flung himself down, reaching for their map, now much the worse for folding and refolding and coming through rainstorms. He beckoned to the Sierlaef, who had just opened his mouth to command the camp to mount up and ride west at the gallop. "Look," he whispered.

The Sierlaef stared down. They couldn't ride west. Of course the bridge would be ruined. And forcing their horses to swim across would be to provide easy targets for even the worst shots. "South."

The signal to mount up and abandon camp ripped into the soft, still summer air, thrilling rises of notes, followed by the war drums, as the boys grabbed up their shields, bows, and quivers, and cantered southward in the foreign moonlight, riding in perfect formation.

There they saw the lines and lines of waiting warriors advancing from the south.

The Sierlaef's mind veered. They had ridden straight into a well-planned trap. " 'Tack!" That was all he could get out—and no one listened.

Cassad flicked his reins against his horse's neck, sending the animal plunging up next to Tanrid, who scanned back then forward again.

"Fan out?" Manther called from Tanrid's other side in a voice tight with pain. Not to the royal heir, but to Tanrid.

The Sierlaef saw it all as his father's two Runners closed in tightly on either side of him, weapons at the ready: the Sier-Danas, the dragoon captain, turned to Tanrid, not to him. And Tanrid galloped at a slant, catching up one of the heralds' horns and blew three times, the signal for righthand shift. Then the Sierlaef saw Tanrid's plan, and knew it was good. He'd sensed the ruse, he'd foreseen some sort of attack, and now he knew what to do. And the Sierlaef didn't. The real truth was that though he was in command and he would one day be king, he didn't really know what to do.

Except fight.

He clapped his heels to his horse's sides on the trumpet's signal. The well trained riders swept to the west almost as one, then the long horn wailed again, signaling "Shoot!"

Buck gripped his shield close, the shield he'd slung at his horse's side every day for weeks but hadn't really touched since their first ride through the pass. Who would have thought these farmers could put together a whole army? He rode easily, knees gripping his sweet four-year-old mare, who was obedient to his wish. Well, they would go down fighting, then, he thought, exulting in the freedom of righteous rage.

Tlen muttered the Waste Spell three times, but he still felt like he had to pee. For Father, he thought, struggling to find some purpose, some of the elation he saw in Buck's face, but all he could think of was Kepa Ain's laugh before he rode off wearing Tlen's own House coat, his jaunty wave. Tlen's right hand tightened on his sword hilt, his left forearm settling his shield into its long familiar position, aligned along his body so it looked from a distance like the wings of a hawk folded for the stoop.

Hawkeye lifted his head and howled out yips. Battle, finally! Maybe this will please Father at last, he thought, the fox cry burning his throat.

How many times had he been forced to hear, *You're the son of a princess,*
and you haven't yet seen a drop of blood shed in battle. I live for the day
you can show your mettle! This is the day, Father. "Yip! Yip! Yip!" From
behind came answering yips from his men, and he laughed, a laugh
scarcely less wild than his fox yips.

Still galloping, everyone strung bows, fitted arrows, took aim, all as
swift and smooth as in uncounted drills, and shot at the advancing
forms. The lines wavered, serried, and again the horn, and again the
whiffling flight of arrows, but what was that ahead? More of them?

Light? Light! The dragoons, trained to deal with water, bridges, with
fighting once they'd jumped off their horses, now used fire: one carried,
as always, campfire embers in a special silver holder, and now he rode
along just as he had in countless drills, touching fire to oil-soaked strings
that the dragoons bound around their arrows, their fingers nimble even
in the darkness.

On their own signal they fired, sending golden arcs crossing the sky
into that vast, unorganized mob of Idayagans, and summer grasses
caught fire here and there. Again the ranks wavered, but there were too
many of them, the Marlovans could see that now. Far too many, and the
Idayagans were about to close in from the east as well as the south.

We're outnumbered thrice and thrice again, Tanrid thought, slinging
his bow over its saddle clip. He shoved his quiver around to the middle
of his back, then angled his shield up his forearm. He drew steel, in both
hands. Last, because he knew how this horse got distracted and then
turned wild, he put his reins in his teeth. His hands shook, and he recognized desire, but it was a desire different from sex, it had nothing of
tenderness in it, the exquisite husbanding and releasing of force. This
was a different desire, a more powerful one. He rode hard toward the
enemy's steel, knowing that at last he could unleash all his strength, that
there would be no more wargames, not today. Every blow was meant to
destroy.

"Yip! Yip! Yip!" Tlen and Hawkeye shrieked the fox cry, and now
everyone around joined in. "Yip! Yip! Yip!" in a voice that meant "Kill!
Kill!"—a cry that raised the hairs on the backs of the necks of those in
the front ranks of their enemies: maybe they'd caught these terrible
horse warriors by surprise, and they certainly outnumbered them, but
that sure hadn't scared them.

Hearts on both sides hammered faster than horses' hooves, faster than the war drums thrumming at the outer wings of the riders, and the war horns blared their brassy challenge at the sky.

The dragoons slung their bows over their backs and readied their lances and shields, standing up in the saddles, heels locked down in the stirrups. The horses, sensing the imminent charge in the actions of their riders, tossed and pawed and whinnied as they formed up into tight lines.

The Marlovans were outnumbered, but they would go down fighting, and that was all Manther could think. He was already faint from loss of blood, but the pain was gone, and he seemed to float on his horse's back as they homed on the target.

Tanrid grinned when he saw the ruddy light spreading, silhouetting the enemy, to catch the gleam of fire on steel, and then the dragoons galloped straight into the first ranks of the enemy, lances smashing through shields, and the men holding shields, so that rings of shock rippled back through the Idayagans, while horns called and recalled.

The dragoons were halted by the packed mass of enemies, each clearing a space by yanking out their swords and laying into the disorganized, half-panicked masses with ferocious skill and speed, just as the rest of the Marlovans hit in a second wave.

Tanrid wept with joy, with despair, for he did not want to die so far away from home, but—slash, shove, smash! Three, four enemies fell, his cavalry sword too fast, too deadly in its swing for inexpert straight swords to parry, especially upward, or for those big, heavy shields that they couldn't see over, had obviously not been trained to maneuver, to block.

"Tanrid?" That was Cassad.

Tanrid spat out the reins, guiding his horse now only with his knees. But that was familiar, too: one of the first games the ponies played at the academy was riding obstacles with your hands tied behind your back.

"Round the Sierlaef!"

They were completely surrounded now, the front ranks of the Idayagans in total disarray, but unable to retreat as the mass of their forces pressed in from behind. An Idayagan captain shouted, trying to rally his troops, and pointing with his sword at the Sierlaef's golden shield. Tanrid, seeing this action, sent his horse plunging toward Aldren-Sierlaef. The Marlovan strategy had narrowed to that, he thought: their duty was to close around the royal heir, until the very last one fell.

Tanrid obediently wheeled again, tightening in with the others, a circle long drilled. They all fought on, but still the enemy kept pressing forward, untrained, ill-equipped, the real threat their numbers. Tanrid and the Sier-Danas round the Sierlaef struck again and again at faceless enemies until their arms shivered like string puppets', their breath burned their dry throats, the smoke made their vision blur, their horses stumbled with weariness. They circled the heir, just as their own men closed around them. Cassad and Tanrid both saw, too late, four of the enemy force a gap and launch themselves against Manther, who fell, still weakly swinging his sword, his old academy tunic black down the side, before the Jaya-Vayir armsmen closed in and the four vanished under Vayir steel. Riderless horses ran about in rare pockets of empty, trampled field, tails ghostly in the red light, and Tanrid began to weep in bitter rage, for these were not worthy foes—they barely knew how to fight—but they would win from overwhelming numbers.

Rage gave Tanrid enough will to lift his sword again and again, though he knew his last thrust would be soon; his horse had stumbled twice, great-hearted as she was.

It was then that the horns cried in the distance, sounding like an echo, a dream, but coming faster, too fast for a dream. And then the ranks around them faltered, many falling back, faces turning west. The Idayagans knew it before the Marlovans: the Harskialdna, somehow, was there, not way to the northwest riding blind toward the ruined bridges, but right *here*, galloping to the rescue.

And so the Harskialdna had his moment of glory at last, but it was an empty glory, though he would smile and preside over the victory dances afterward while his men proclaimed him *Harskialdna Sigun*, because it was not, after all, his rescue. It was Jened Sindan's.

Chapter Ten

THE Marlovans now ruled an empire larger than Sartor.

Following the news came the repercussions.

For the Pim ships, the first result was the sight of the Pim agent rowing out the day they arrived at the harbor of Bren. "The Venn are putting trade sanctions on Iascan goods," he warned. "Sail fast, or sell up."

Captain Beagar summoned the other two captains, canceled all liberty, and kept the fleet anchored out in the bay, even though it meant paying extra for goods to be brought in and out by the villagers in small boats who made their living doing just that.

The second result occurred when the *Pim Ryala* tacked down the last of the strait, trying to catch the last of the western winds before winter swept up from the southeast.

"Deck hai! Venn sail hull down, west-northwest!"

Venn. They'd seen them before; they'd always passed by. No one paused in their work. The bosun and purser were still arguing about the stowage of the hundred-year glowglobes against the heavy seas of winter; the bosun's mates oversaw a party replacing the foremast topsail lifts and braces; Inda was teaching a new rat how to coil down ropes.

"Venn! Hull up, and closing!" the lookout yelled.

Inda grabbed the rope from the girl and coiled it fast, knowing what would come next:

"Flags!" Beagar yelled from the door to his cabin.

Inda already had the glass from the binnacle. He ran up the shrouds to the mainmast.

The tall ship sailed with such speed the water purled down the sides, leaving a splendid wake. Long, lean as a cutter in line, though quite large, its prow curved up rather than jutting forward in a bowsprit: Inda had seen that singular profile on the horizon a few times. For the first time he saw one close. Towers of square sails augmented by boom-extended studding sails high and low gave the ship the look of a raptor in flight. The spread of the foretopsail stretched in the shape of a highly stylized bird, with symbols above and below.

The Venn ran signal flags up.

Inda checked three times before he called, "Says to come dead. We're to be boarded."

From the look on the captain's face he had expected to be required to report aboard the Venn, not be boarded; the first was humiliating, the second both humiliating and deadly serious. "Sheets up," Beagar said heavily.

The hands ran to their stations, and for a short time the only sound was the flap of loosened sails. The ship swiftly lost way, lolling slackly on the ocean.

Inda watched from the masthead as the Venn ship flashed its tremendous square sails: first the studding sails vanished, then the royals dropped and the lower sails clewed up, all at the same time, with the same sort of deadly grace as a riding of dragoons approaching at a gallop, lances lowered at exactly the same moment. The Venn was now stripped to fighting sail, giving a clear view for archers in the tops.

Everyone on the *Pim Ryala* wondered uneasily why the Venn readied for battle when making contact with a merchant vessel.

The Venn ship closed on the weather side, and then spilled its wind, heaving to beside the *Pim Ryala*. Inda swept his glass aft, and caught sight of the *Ryala*'s consorts, busy shortening sail to maintain a prudent distance. There was nothing else to do. These tall-masted, ocean-crossing Venn vessels weren't just full of highly trained sailors, they were also full of marine warriors and—rumor insisted—mages.

The deck watch lined up on either side of the waist, silent as the Venn lowered a longboat and sent over a large, armed party of those marine warriors, rowed by equally tall, strong-looking sailors in precise rhythm.

Inda watched, then belatedly realized he ought to be down there on deck. He leaned out to catch a stay, but a strong, hairy hand grabbed the scruff of his neck. "Bide," Scalis muttered, spitting downwind. "Don't move."

Sky and sea stayed serene, seabirds arrowing overhead, heads flicking right and left as they watched the perplexing actions of the humans below, crawling about their wooden nests. Scolding, unheard, the birds flapped away. Below, the tall Venn marines climbed nimbly up the side and onto the deck. They ignored the custom of the southern seas and waited for the merchant captain to salute them first. He did, stone-faced, though inside Captain Beagar was sick with anxiety.

His comprehension of the interiors of kingdoms was hazy, but he knew the Venn had taken everything north of the strait except Ymar at the thumb, still held by the Everoneth, apparently with the unlikely help of the Chwahir on the opposite coast.

The Marlovans had now taken the westernmost end of the Sartoran continent, directly opposite the Venn. It was time, apparently, for the Venn to react.

Up in the tops old Scalis knew one thing: the Venn were going to be hunting Marlovan blood. And his boy Inda, his prize scrapper who could even parse his letters, in two languages yet, was some kind of Marlovan, probably a runaway stable boy. Scalis was not about to let these Venn piss-heads get him.

Dun the carpenter's mate paused, setting down his carpenter's tools. *They're coming here because they're searching for us,* he thought. It was not even a question.

Lieutenant Tigga of the *Reed-Skimmer* gave the brig a quick scan. Five years patrolling the strait had given him insight into these southerners. The south was an astonishingly chaotic welter of lands, tongues, customs, and alliances, but even so there were motivations, and reactions, shared by most humans. Universals, you might say.

Fear foremost—to be expected. Trepidation, resentment. Anger, imperfectly hidden in downward gazes, gripped hands, the determined silence when their captain standing up on the aft-castle deck saluted first, aboard his own ship, a salute that Tigga acknowledged with the barest nod.

But no sign of desperation. He knew at once that he would not find Marlovan warriors or spies on this old tub; he was even familiar with the Pim name from a recently acquired list of Iascan merchants. But orders must be followed.

So he said, in Dock Talk, "Return to your duties." Having issued orders on the captain's own deck, he now turned his face up to the captain. "If you will lead the way?"

Captain Beagar descended to the main deck and Tigga followed the furious man to his cabin, ostensibly paying no heed to Captain Vaki of the marines, who motioned his men to their search. Tigga spared a moment of brief sympathy for Beagar, subordinated on his own ship, but it was necessary, not just for the implementing of orders, but to underscore the supremacy of maritime command in these wretched waters. He had no sympathy for Vaki, who longed to get away from sea duty and be promoted to land once again. The command struggles of the land warriors on Drael were almost as alien to him as those of the southerners on their own continent. What interested Tigga—what he understood— were those who lived on the sea.

Beagar indicated, with expressive irony, the door to the cabin, and followed the tall Venn. At least whatever was about to take place would happen in private, and not before the hands. The Venn could, and would at the slightest opportunity, do much more. And no one would stop them.

"Your cargo and destination?" Tigga asked.

His Iascan was clear, fluent, accented with the precise consonants of Venn—or Marlovan. The man himself typical of the Venn: tall, pale-haired, pale eyes, strong features.

In a flat voice Beagar named the cargo and the ports he was scheduled to stop in, as from below came the random thumps and clunks of Vaki's searchers. Tigga's quarry was living and breathing.

"You are now warned. By what you southerners call the New Year, there will be a total embargo against Iascan sea trade. You have three passes of the moon to make other plans. If you have any Marlovans among your mariners, surrender them now."

Beagar did not speak or move.

Tigga dismissed the captain from his attention and paced the companionway of the old brig, scanning the closed, resentful faces of the crew on watch. He dropped down to the lower deck, where the off-watch were obviously hoping to get back into their hammocks and their interrupted sleep. They froze at the sight of him, reacting with bewilderment when he rapped out in Marlovan, "Liegemen of Tlennen-Harvaldar, in uniform or out, will be put to death."

Silence. A few of them realized what language he spoke, but belatedly, without the reaction of the familiar.

He did not see the blond carpenter's mate just behind him in the companionway, who blanched at the sound of Marlovan and retreated soundlessly.

As Tigga moved down to the hold to confront the purser, his two mates, two cook's helpers, and the bosun's third mate, Dun's thoughts raced ahead to the inevitable betrayal on deck, unless he could divert those watchful Venn eyes. Most on the ship were aware of the growing tension between the larboard and starboard mids and their rats, but few cared. Dun had watched, because it was his duty to watch, though he never interfered when Norsh, now a third mate, alternately hounded Taumad and spied on him with frustrated hunger. He never interfered when Norsh was joined in his prowling, glowering enmity by Fassun, smoldering with humiliation over the defeat of Idayago and now hating all southern Iascans, and by Faura, who on passing the threshold from girl to young woman had conceived a longing for the impervious Taumad almost as obsessive as Norsh's. Her own reaction to his indifference was a breach with Jeje, whom Tau had admitted within the guarded citadel of his friendship.

When that voice echoed up from below, "Liegemen to Tlennen-Harvaldar, in uniform or out, will be put to death," Norsh drew a deep breath.

Dun watched the young man grin, his gaze flickering. The easiest way to get at Tau would be through Inda Elgar, the reading mid that some said was secretly a Marlovan—

Dun crossed his arms. His own betrayal didn't matter; the penalty was already death. If that Venn up there heard someone accuse Inda of being Marlovan, the response would be immediate, and final, that much Dun knew. They'd execute the boy right on deck, because Inda would never deny it.

"If you say a word," Dun murmured, staring straight into Norsh's eyes, "you will not live past the night watch." Away, fast, before the mate could recover enough to ask questions that Dun would not answer.

Dun heard steps along the gangway. He paused until Tigga reached the deck, then emerged just as Tigga looked around, then bawled in a topmast voice, for the third time, "Liegemen of Tlennen-Harvaldar, in uniform or out, will be put to death."

Tau had recognized it below, a language he'd sometimes overheard in his mother's pleasure house, and one he hadn't expected to hear out on the water, so very far away from home.

He knew what would come next, and so he had time to think, and to smile, and after the Venn's extraordinary declaration, to laugh, drawing all eyes to him. So that Tigga missed it when Inda, high in the tops, jerked around, his mouth open. Then pain exploded across Inda's face, and a voice snarled, in Dock Talk, "Get it right, ye stupid rat."

Get what right? Inda blinked away the spots in his vision resulting from the clout, and realized he must have missed an order: Scalis wanted those lifts tended. Silently he helped the two men working, but the shock of memory echoed that short speech, and in Marlovan! Wrong word order, odd word endings, but otherwise the accent of home.

Will be put to death.

"Piss-hair is looking for horse turds?" came the hoarse whisper of Niz, who'd swung himself down to the crosstrees. They sat side by side, their skinny bodies blocking Inda from view below, where Tigga was confronting Tau.

"The Marlovan tongue amuses you?" Tigga asked in a soft voice, studying the golden gaze before him, the winning smile, the open hands.

From his earliest days Tau's mother had said, *Smile, sweetie, you have my smile. Use it and you'll get anything you want.* And later, *Smile for Mama, a pretty smile from Mama's pretty boy, and the gold will pour in.*

"I'm sorry," Taumad said, using his mother's open gaze, her tip of the head. The same gestures he'd seen her employ so many times. He'd hated them for their falsity, but they came so naturally now. Inwardly he laughed at himself, the laughter of self-mockery, even though his heart beat fast.

The Venn studied him with a dispassionate coldness.

Tau said, "It's just you won't win any friends here, speaking that tongue, not with Idayagans among the hands."

Tigga sorted Tau's Iascan accent, assessed his looks, the freedom with which he spoke, and decided he had to be the captain's favorite. Vaki appeared from below right then, and Tigga waved Tau aside with a dismissive gesture.

"Anything?" he asked Vaki, in their own tongue.

"Nothing."

Well, he hadn't expected to find any Marlovans hiding on this old tub. In the meantime, these Iascans would carry the story all down the coast, they and their consorts, who still had to be boarded, searched, and intimidated before sundown.

Tigga climbed down into the barge, quite aware of the vast sense of relief, of release, that he left behind him, and Vaki and his men followed. They raised their oars, dipped them on a signal, and after they had rowed round the bow of the *Pim Ryala* in one last gesture of arrogant superiority, they headed back to the *Reed-Skimmer*.

Captain Beagar gave the command to raise sail, put the helm down, and continue on. He did not stay to see his order carried out, but withdrew at once to sit at his table with his head in his hands.

Up in the tops, Inda remained silent during the work of hauling round the foretopsail. When it was taut and drawing again, and the ship had once more come to life, the hands started down, some silent, others talking in low voices, eyes shifting right and left.

Tau was still amazed at his own action. It was the first time he had ever stirred himself to take a risk on anyone's behalf; he who believed in comfort and trusted the predictability of human weakness, was giddy with amazement.

Scalis kept an eye on his Marlovan. Oh yes, young Inda was a real Marlovan, all right, as if anyone had doubted it. Every top hand had seen him jump as if he'd been roped when that piss-hair Venn yapped out that jabber in Marlovan. Scalis had heard it before, when he was small. He didn't understand any of it, but you remembered the sound of it, after those long-haired horsemen in their tight long coats rode through your town, cutting down anyone who stood against them with a single stroke of those curve tipped swords of theirs. But Inda wasn't one of *those*. No. Just a runaway. In Scalis's experience, runaways never talked about their past.

Norsh decided on silence for now. But as soon as they touched land he'd get together some people he could trust and have it out with that carpenter's mate.

Chapter Eleven

TORCH making is an art, an old one. The torches used by the Marlovans had come across the continent from the Chwahir, who had mastered the art of winding oil-soaked, leddas-wax-dipped flax round and round carefully hardened wood, giving off a pungent smell that buzzed in the nose.

Torches (and glowglobes) that burned by magic spell were imported, but the numbers that the distant, mysterious Council of Mages had deemed appropriate to be sold to Iasca Leror were far below what the Marlovans required.

This limit was especially felt at the New Year's Convocation that the Marlovan king hosted every year, and had ever since the days of the plains, when torches were set in a ring on the frosted ground, circling the celebrants who fought, danced, and sang night and day.

New Year's Week was yet a few days off, but Runners arriving with the news of the Harskialdna returning home in triumph had caused the king to order the city lit in welcome.

The glow of the royal city, a dim golden dome against the cold winter sky, could be seen half a day's ride away by the tired conquerors. By nightfall they saw every wall and tower outlined by firelight.

Anderle-Harskialdna and the Sierlaef rode at the front, the Sier-

Danas directly behind them, bannermen surrounding them, and an impressive sight they were.

Only the king noticed how, despite his smiles and his fist raised in acknowledgment of the cheers, drums, and triumph songs raised by the royal city as they rode in, the Harskialdna's brow was tense. And so he sent word for the victory supper to be held half a bell later than planned.

How like our father he is, Tlennen thought. His foremost emotion was pity. He knew his brother conspired against imagined enemies as passionately as he did against the real, that he cherished grudges formed in boyhood. So had their father, as much as he'd craved order—and life was never quite orderly enough in spite of his constant vigilance. First to rise every day, the sounds of bells acting like a rope yanking him from one scheduled task to the next. Last to sleep, thinking of endless lists. Endless preparing, training.

He knew why his brother was tense, but he must give no sign of it. He kept his brother's respect partly because Anderle's loyalties were as long-enduring as his grudges, and partly because of Tlennen's own apparent omniscience that was perceived by his brother as wisdom.

As soon as they were alone the Harskialdna said, before even drawing off his riding gloves, "Here is your treaty, Brother."

"Sit down. Here is some hot cider with bristic." Tlennen indicated the pungent drink sitting on the side table, and while his Shield Arm poured out a drink and sipped gratefully, he took the heavy scroll weighted by seals. He already knew what it said from Jened Sindan's precise reports, conveyed by magic weeks ago, but he took the time to read it through, noting little things like the deliberate angles of the writing here, the angry slants there. Whose name was writ large, whose small. That the king of Idayago wrote only *Idayago* in gold ink and none of his names or other titles at all.

When he looked up some of the tension had already gone out of his brother's face. His cheeks were flushed from the double-distilled bristic.

"This is as good as we could expect," the king said. "Yet you do not seem pleased with your victory."

The Harskialdna prowled around the room, his boots making muddy patches on the fine rug, which would have to be brushed clean. Usually he was aware of such things, as personal fastidiousness was a part of his craving for order, had been clear back in the nursery days, when he and their sister Tdiran would stack all Ndara's and Tlennen's papers and line up their drawing chalk according to size. The muddy prints testified to the depth of his distress. "It was not my victory," he said finally, in short words. His captains would have stiffened at that tone, a little too loud for the room, a little too harsh; his wife had loathed it since they were small children together in the nursery. Too often it had presaged violence in those days. Tlennen knew it to be unhappiness. "It was Sindan's."

Tlennen sat down. "Sindan's? How is that?"

The Harskialdna started to pour another drink, then set down glass and bottle. "I don't want the fumes clouding my head." He paced across the rug and back again. "You know how I chased shadows all summer. You know that your son . . . wished to ride east with his own wing."

"Was his reasoning sound, or was it just boredom?"

The quick look from the Harskialdna's dark eyes was more revealing than the words that followed. "Boredom, and the wish to flush the enemy. Bring them to a fight. He went ahead. I followed more slowly, along the great road. I kept looking for outriders, signs of an army. They knew we were coming. I sent my scouts ahead to find them." He looked out the window, frowning, then turned. "Sindan caught up with me. He heard the reports while studying the map. Waited until he and I were alone, and he said, 'I don't like this situation. The heir is now an easy target.' I said, 'For what? We are here in empty land—they have abandoned their homes, their fields and farms, even their villages.' He asked permission to send Runners out, not ahead as I had done, but out in orthogonals. I said I had already split my force more than I thought right, and so he sent his own Runners not east, as I had done, but northeast, southeast, all along Runner tracks, not the main roads. He kept urging me in private to greater speed, kept studying the map."

He paused, and the king said nothing.

The Harskialdna looked down at his hands, the nails on his thumbs raw and chewed as they had been from time to time when they were young. He picked at the calloused skin on one thumb as he said, "One by one his Runners returned, reporting nothing. Nothing. Nothing, until the one from the southeast came back. He found signs of a mighty gathering in a valley against the mountains. To make sure he waylaid one of their Runners on the way south and got the plan out of him: the Idayagans had formed an army which was hiding in a river valley hard against the Mountains of Ghaeldraeth and were ready to spring a trap from the south and east to capture the heir. They planned to sweep west from there and meet me at the Ghael River with Aldren's head on a pike they did not even know how to use."

Though the king had known about that plan—and how close it came to success—since the day Sindan first discovered it, his gut still tightened against a cold pooling of fear.

"So my son rode unheeding straight into danger, then."

The Harskialdna raised a hand. "Yes, but he figured out their trap before they could close it. It is I who did not suspect any such trap. Sindan also figured it out. No honest or straightforward battle, appointed beforehand. It could hardly be called fighting. But it would have worked if Sindan had not discovered them. So I gave the order to abandon camp and charge. I had—I had death in my heart."

He turned around, a purposeless movement, then said, "And so we were in time. And—your son and his boys, they fought well against those uncountable numbers." The king wondered what he had meant to say. "But the victory was Sindan's. So I listen to the shouts of *Harskialdna Sigun* and preside over the victory sword dances, but it is a sham."

The king said, "No. You gave the right orders when it was the most necessary. That is required of a Harskialdna. It is also required you listen to your scouts when you do not have enough information."

Anderle-Harskialdna stood there, his breathing audible, his chin raised as if he listened to someone outside and far away.

"You are also not done," the king said. "Those people in the north do not think like us, and you have learned they do not fight like us. So they will probably test us, despite the treaty. They will look for weakness. We have to be strong. Sindan acted correctly, and you did too. Now you must appear to know *everything*. You cannot seem uncertain, or they will worry at us forever, distracting us from our real purpose, which is to strengthen their borders against the Venn, who have now cut us off from the rest of the world."

The king studied his brother closely while he spoke, and it was apparent that Anderle had not known about the sea embargo. It was also clear that something else was disturbing him.

The king rose and touched his brother's shoulder. "I fear I have further news." Anderle's head jerked up. "Bad news, yes. The embargo includes every ship that carries any Iascan goods, and they are killing any Marlovans they find in the crews. Your son Barend has been lost at sea."

Anderle's mouth tightened. Then he said, "If he died with honor, if he died fighting the Venn—"

"We know nothing more than their ship was put to flame. Either the Venn, or the pirates who are apparently in the service of the Venn, attacked it, and I am told that the usual practice of pirates is to burn captured ships with everyone on board. Of course, he might have jumped into the sea."

Anderle opened a hand. According to the histories, sometimes humans did that and drowned but other times, apparently, they were taken by those who lived undersea. But they returned again so rarely one might as well say never.

Tlennen saw no real grief in his brother's face, just anger, frustration, another disappointment. "We have the victory supper ahead of us. Or is there anything more?"

The Harskialdna breathed out slowly, twitched his chewed fingers, then faced his brother. "No. There is nothing more. If you consider this battle a success, then I will as well."

"I do. You brought back a treaty. You and I have private reservations, but one thing I have learned from reading the records of our forefathers is that long-sighted kings always have reservations, but they know better than to show them. Part of winning battles is up here." He touched his head. "If they believe us unbeatable, they may or may not try us, but they'll expect to be beaten."

Anderle's face eased. "That makes sense."

"Preside. Take pride. Be seen presiding and taking pride. It is only the beginning. The real war will happen when the Venn come, and everyone will be looking to you. My part, it seems, is to see that we will be equipped for battle, a job for which I am best prepared. You are best prepared to lead, and to win."

Anderle struck his heart with his palm and then left.

Jarls converged on the torch-lit city from all over the kingdom, not just for New Year's Convocation but to hear the news firsthand. Some came to meet sons who had been sent to battle; there were those whose sons had not returned, and there would be drums at First Night held in their honor, the first being for Manther Jaya-Vayir.

Queen Wisthia, loathing the smell of those ever-burning torches, withdrew to her rooms after her obligatory appearance at First Night's supper, windows and doors shut, musicians playing soft music to drown out the never ending thunder of drums, the shouts and clashes of steel and wood ringing day and night during the eight days of New Year's. She did not want to see her sons wielding steel, or dodging it.

She did not want to hear the tight, pain-laden tear-repressed breathing of Ndara-Harandviar. Every day since autumn that brought no further messages from the harbors had increased Ndara's conviction that the Venn had killed Barend. Hadand sat with her, in compassionate silence.

And so Tlennen-Harvaldar sat alone in the stands on Third Night—Debt Day in the rest of the south—which was when a few invited academy boys performed their evolutions.

Tlennen-Harvaldar watched Evred riding as captain. As heralds and chosen guards along the walls drummed, the boys rode in formation, miming a wing at the gallop, splitting into two flights to attack then reforming, wheeling; gallop, split, sword-drill against the opponents, reform, wheel.

Evred, well into his sixteenth year, was gaining height. His dark red hair was modestly pulled back into the club of the younger boys, but it suited the clean bones of his face, emphasizing the strength one could see emerging, his high, intelligent brow. The king watched Evred's smooth handling of his mount, the clean strike and block of his sword work. Nothing brilliant, but strong, assured. Not for Evred the vicious competition ending in blood and broken bones that entertained so many spectators. Evred's style was something new, boring to those who had come from a distance and did not recognize the connection straight back to the summer academy game several years before. The king saw the connection, though, and contemplated how his son had taken Indevan Algara-Vayir's little boy gesture of rebellion in the uniting of the scrubs during the shoeing and had trained these same boys to be loyal to him.

No, not to him. There was something different about that bond, something not exclusive, the way the royal heir closed out everyone but his chosen Sier-Danas, but inclusive. The Sierlaef had made himself the center of his group. Evred seemed to have as center some obscure idea, if not an ideal: the others did not move around him like moons around a sun, but they all moved together, a chain of shared effort.

The king sighed softly. The evolution finished with a loud thunder of drums and a trumpet call, echoing in blended chords up the frozen stone. Then they rode out, breath from human and horse puffing white in the frigid air, and the younger boys ran in for their display—including many of the second class of Tveis, invited here just for this exhibition—most glancing up to see if their families were watching.

The king was aware of the gesture of contempt that the Sierlaef and his friends made to their siblings by not sitting in the stands. It was probably inevitable. They had seen battle. No longer did they care for academy games, and they were too young yet to yearn for those care-free academy days, never again to return.

The king turned to look for his brother.

The Harskialdna had been working hard these past few days, rising before dawn, seeing to reports, speaking to every one of the Jarls and their heirs, to dragoon captains, to Runners. He never seemed to rest; and though he did preside, and smile, and even dance the sword dance to the roaring approval of the Jarls, there was still something wrong.

The Harskialdna did not see his brother's searching eyes. He had chosen a vantage by the stable yard archway, where he could observe both the evolutions and the Sierlaef, who stood with three or four of his followers, making loud comments as the academy boys rode past.

Or rather, Buck Marlo-Vayir led the comments. The Sierlaef wasn't paying the boys any attention. His head was canted upward toward the stands.

The Harskialdna frowned. There was Jarend, old and gray and lined. His son next to him, academy trained and responsive to the Harskialdna, steady and unambitious; and next to him this girl who did not flirt. Did not smile at anyone but her own family. Her straight back, her quiet hands, the deep corners at either side of her smile, all drew the eye, especially his nephew's, but she did not respond.

No, the problem did not lie with Tanrid or his Joret.

The problem lay with the Sierlaef.

The Harskialdna frowned now at his wild colt of a nephew, who had avoided talking to him ever since their triumphant return from the north, and he had to find out why. The boy couldn't possibly know that if it hadn't been for Jened Sindan, he and his friends would all probably be ghosts drifting through fog-wreathed nights on the northern meadows.

It was Sindan himself who had insisted that only the king be told. The next day he was gone, leaving the conquerors to follow more slowly behind him. Yet the boy had not spoken to his uncle once during that long journey, except when he had to.

The Sierlaef had not been brooding about the dramatic rescue that had turned imminent defeat into triumph. He never gave the rescue a thought beyond that first surge of relief; of course his uncle had somehow found out, and came rushing in. That was what a Harskialdna was supposed to do.

What he brooded about was the early part of that battle.

Tanrid Algara-Vayir could have told everyone that it was he who had commanded until the Harskialdna showed up with the main force. But at all the victory dances he sat apart, grieving over the double loss of his Runner and his cousin Manther Jaya-Vayir.

The Sierlaef knew Tanrid by now. He wouldn't strut. He simply didn't care what anyone thought. Tanrid was smart, he was loyal, and he could command. And the future king could not disabuse himself of the truth: he would one day be king, yet he really didn't know how to command an army in the field.

And whose fault was that? The Sierlaef glared at his uncle. He'd been told for years that he'd had the best training in the kingdom, that in the future it would be he who would command with Buck Marlo-Vayir at his side to see to logistics, like the kings of old—and yet when they came at last to real war, he couldn't do it.

The inescapable conclusion was that his uncle thought that someone would command for him after all. He would wear the crown, and wave the sword, but others would really command. Who? Not his little brother. His uncle had seen to that. Buck Marlo-Vayir? At that battle Buck hadn't been any better at command than the Sierlaef himself.

Tanrid Algara-Vayir? No, because he was about—

The royal heir glared up at Tanrid, who sat beside his beautiful soon-to-be wife watching the little boys down in the court. Tanrid was about to ride home. Forever. And by his side would be—

The Sierlaef didn't notice his sixteen-year-old brother passing not six paces away, almost as tall as he was, or Buck's teasing of his own Tvei, who had shot up to Buck's height. He never saw the stricken face of Ivandred, Manther's Tvei, lurking around hoping the Sier-Danas would talk more about Manther. He looked up at Joret because he couldn't bear not to, knowing that she would only be here a few more days, and then would go home. Forever. He would never see her again. Ever. Princesses stayed at home.

No, he couldn't *bear* that. He *had* to find a way to see her. Just once. To be alone with her, once, just once, just the two of them, which was impossible here. Short of riding to Choraed Elgaer, he couldn't—

Riding to Choraed Elgaer. Well, why not?

I'm the next king. I don't have to stand by with my wand waving in the wind. The kingdom is mine. I can do what I want.

He grabbed Buck. "Talk," he commanded, pulling him away.

Chapter Twelve

"U P and dressed, Elgar."

Inda banished dreams of making snow forts with Tdor at Ten-then Castle. All he could see in the thick dark of the mids' cabin was a faint glow on Kodl's pale hair.

The usual pain that came from being woken from dreams of home vanished when Kodl added in a tight voice, "Captain is going ashore. You'll act as coxswain. Get your crew together."

It was not his turn to take the gig to shore, but as a lowly mid, one step above a rat—and there weren't any new rats to do the rat chores, as the embargo meant no new hiring as well—he didn't argue.

Kodl had promoted them anyway, because it was their due, and promised them an increase in wages—when they would be able to land, visit the Pims' guild agent and get their pay—and they were permitted to sit in the cramped little cabin called the mids' wardroom.

First Mate Kodl was doing his best to keep order on a ship full of whispers, threats, ugly sidelong glances between other mids and older hands, between warrant officers and mates. And not just whispers, but sudden scuffles, thumps and cracks, people appearing limping and bruised, while Kodl, who never seemed to sleep, walked the length of the ship every day, in all weathers, back and forth, a knotted rope swinging from his hand.

And the captain stayed in his cabin, as if nothing had happened at all.

Inda pulled his winter shirt on over his sleep shirt, and over that the new long woolen vest he'd bought at the Nob during the spring. He made sure the cuffs hid his wrist sheaths, then put on his thick woolen socks and fleece-lined green-weave deck shoes.

Inda's crew lowered the captain's gig in silence. Being in Khanerenth's main harbor seemed to increase tension, not ease it: as yet they had no guild agents here—the old one had vanished in the change of government—nor were they going to exchange any cargo. Khanerenth was one of the last kingdoms that ignored the embargo—at least if the ship was anchored out in the roads. And no one knew how long that would last.

No one spoke as Captain Beagar took his place on the cushions in the stern sheets—cushions that Inda had helped make—and Inda took charge of rudder and yoke. Zimd acted as bow. Just as she grasped the boat hook came a yell, "Wait!"

The four crew, Inda among them, paused in placing their tholepins. Down swung the second mate, Vorzcin, her short curly hair lifting on the wind as she dropped into the bow beside Zimd.

To the captain's frown she said, "Kodl gave me leave. I'm to get new charts, sir," she said, smiling and holding out the little bag of coins she carried.

She's lying, Inda thought, watching how Vorzcin avoided the captain's gaze. Otherwise she looked exactly like always: strong, breezy, smiling at the great cliffs on the north side of the harbor and at the gulls wheeling overhead. Smiling, though there wasn't any reason to smile.

It was a silent trip, except for the screeching of those gulls, and the swish-splash of water down the sides.

When they drew up to the dock, everyone looked to Inda, coxswain for this trip. He said, "Liberty for a bell, sir?"

"No," the captain snapped. Inda could feel his effort to speak in an even voice when he added, "I am only going to the harbormaster's for news and mail exchange. I will return shortly. We'll want to sail with the tide." He did not look at the second mate, just climbed out and strode away down the dock, gripping the mail bag against him, his green coat flapping in the wind.

Vorzcin gave Inda a rueful shrug as she clambered out after the captain.

At once the four members of the boat crew shipped their oars and leaned on them, Dasta looking back at the Pim consorts anchored farther out, sails bunted, crews busy aboard. Yan frowned toward the harbor, dominated by the huge castle on the far cliffs, in whose storage barns they had spent a winter two years before. Things seemed quieter now, though there were marching warriors all along the docks and riding patrols along the wide concourse at the shore.

Inda watched in all directions though he was fairly certain no one would force him off the ship. No one had said anything more about Marlovans, but the rumors about Iascan trade had gotten worse. If they were true, the entire crew was in trouble, not just him.

Only Zimd seemed in a good mood, but then she was always in a good mood, except if they called "All hands!" during rain or a sleep watch. Zimd lived for two things, food and gossip.

"So," she said, as if carrying on a conversation. "That's one mate we'll never see again, eh? And won't Leugre be mad!"

Dasta snorted; Yan looked up, his round, pale Chwahir face expressionless. "You don't know she's going."

"Yes I do," Zimd chortled. "You were snoring away during snooze watch while I was up in the foretop. Let me tell you, Kodl's voice carries from the forecastle scuttles just fine when he's arguing. She says, 'Get while you can,' and he says 'That sort of talk is mutiny,' and she laughed at him and said he'd have real mutiny soon enough, and then he'd learn the difference between that and good advice."

"She's not the one talkin' mutiny," Dasta muttered.

"We all know who is," Zimd said with her usual cheer, then yawned as she scanned the area. The clouds were thickening, the water graying as the waves chopped and flicked up white foam. But nobody approached. "Anyone want some?" And from her bulky tunic she pulled a sizable flat package wrapped carefully in magic-warded cloth; the frigid air carried just a whiff of baked pastry, causing mouths to water.

Inda, Yan, and Dasta stared as she unwrapped what turned out to be a fresh-baked chicken-and-potato pie, thick with gravy and tender new carrots.

"How did you get that?" Dasta asked. "Not from Cook."

"No. I took it," Zimd said happily. "After all, we really don't think Leugre deserves it, do we?"

All three thought sourly of Norsh's chief crony, who had always liked rough games, the rougher the better. He bullied the smaller rats for sport, but he harbored a special, unrelenting hatred for Inda—and his friends—since Scalis had thrown Leugre out of forecastle drill.

Dasta chuckled, then pulled his hands back as if they'd been burned. "But when we get back to the ship, and Leugre gets off his watch, and the pie—and Vorzcin—are gone, he'll know we got it. And he'll break heads. Starting with him, of course." Nodding at Inda. "Finishing up with us."

"No he won't, because I'll tell him Vorzcin took it," Zimd chortled. "It'll make it far, far worse!"

Dasta snorted again. He didn't mind Zimd, who could be good company, except when she kept on poking her nose into people's lives.

Zimd snorted back, then said, "Norsh wants Taumad, Leugre wants Vorzcin, Faura wants Taumad. What say, when Leugre discovers Vorzcin is gone, he switches to chasin' Faura? If only Taumad would look her way, it'd be as good as a Colendi play! Better!"

Inda said, "You're really sure Vorzcin isn't coming back?" He pointed down the dock where a familiar figure loped toward them, dodging porters, sailors, owners, cargo inspectors, and the squads of fully armed warriors that prowled back and forth along Khanerenth's harbor, walking reminders of the recent protracted civil war.

Zimd rewrapped the pie. The others watched Vorzcin approach, a cloth-wrapped scroll carried in her arms.

She leaped down into the boat, sending shivers through it; handing Dasta her package, she said, "They will call me coward and sved-breaker but no one can call me thief. Those are the charts for Freedom Island, and the chart maker says they did get rid of the pirates. The new holders are indeed open to trade, though it's on free-trader terms. So here's the newest chart to replace the old."

She bent, and caressed Inda's cheek. "Give that to Tau, will you? Though he wouldn't ever give me so much as a kiss." Inda stared, puzzled, as she added, "I'm smart, is what I am. You would be, too, if you run." And, in a husky voice, "Be well. All of you. I will be!" With a smile and a flick of her hand she bounded back up onto the dock and ran toward the harbor without looking back.

"What did I tell you?" Zimd said. "Here. Four equal pieces. And the sweetest part is thinking of Norsh and his mates all eating stale ship-bread and cold cheese."

Inda ate quickly, glad for the warm food; the sun vanished behind clouds, and the wind turned biting, causing all but Dasta to hunch with their backs to it. Cold never seemed to trouble Dasta, who kept watch on the harbor, at last saying the welcome words, "Cap'n coming at last."

They readied their oars. It was unlike the captain to leave them so long without at least sending someone with hot drink, if no word of brief liberty. One glance at his face and no one spoke, not even to ask about mail in the noticeably slim satchel the captain set down by his feet.

Zimd noted that neither Yan nor Inda gave the mailbag a glance; Yan's reason was obvious. He was a runaway Chwahir, but Inda had never shown the least interest in mail, nor had he sent or received any.

She found that so intriguing! Just as she found it intriguing that while Dasta had been seen wearing a heavy coat maybe half a dozen times, Inda wore long sleeves year round. Inda was fascinating because he never told anyone anything. He could be along on liberty and he'd sing the songs, even speculate about the stories behind them, and then the most mild question, like if he had any brothers or sisters, and he'd snap his mouth shut and not speak again, sometimes for a whole watch. But he didn't get angry, or nasty, he just somehow wasn't there.

Zimd chuckled to herself. Mysteries were so much fun. Too bad Jeje was turning even more sour than Faura these days, refusing to talk. And when she was asked her the wrong thing, just teasing, like, she snapped your nose off.

Well, Zimd knew why—and that made life even funnier!

No one spoke during the long pull back to the ship, though wave after wave splashed over the bow and soaked them all. No one spoke when the captain climbed slowly up the side, not with his accustomed briskness but like an old man, blind and infirm. Inda, supervising the gig crew in booming the gig up to its place and lashing it down, heard the captain say in a low voice to Kodl, "No protection from Khanerenth. Their navy is still too busy fighting one another. But we're a day behind a convoy of traders from Venn, all heading down to winter in Sartor if they can. We will join them." He vanished into the cabin—without overseeing the anchor raising, as had been his custom.

Kodl said, "Signal the consorts to get under way."

"Here's the charts." Inda proffered the wrapped scrolls.

Kodl frowned as he took the package. "Charts?"

Inda's face heated. "Vorzcin. Bought them. Said you ordered them."

Kodl's frown deepened as he slipped the wrap-cloth off and unrolled the scroll a little way, then he looked up in fury at the crew members who had appeared in a half-circle all around. "Weigh. Anchor."

"That there is the chart for Freedom," said Black Boots, one of the larboard deck crew under Norsh.

"Doesn't matter if it's a chart to Norsunder," Kodl snapped. "Weigh anchor."

Black Boots looked forward, licking his lips. "We think it's not right. Risking our lives. We think it's time to take the ship ourselves—"

Kodl moved so fast Black Boots never saw the rope coming. Snap, crack, thud, and he fell to the deck. The charts, forgotten, fell away from Kodl; Fassun appeared from the binnacle and gathered them up, sending quick looks around before he bore them back into the binnacle.

"It's true! You know it," roared Gillip, captain of the mizzen. "You keep your rope for yourself, soul-eater!" He brandished a marlin spike, looking from side to side.

Inda realized the two men were trying to start a mutiny. Not in the future, but right here, right now. They looked around for support, and several of the crew stepped forward, everyone looking to the right and left, waiting for someone else to move first, until Kodl struck, the rope whistling, right across Gillip's face.

"My eyes! My eyes! Owww!" the man howled. He covered his face with his fingers, and blood oozed between them, dripping on the deck.

Scalis appeared, his long arms swinging. "Did ye hear the order, then? We're heavin' anchor, and anyone not pullin' will get more of the same from me."

Niz strode up to his side, bandy legs wide, his sharp nose poking forward as he eyed all the crew members who had suddenly appeared climbing down the shrouds or popping up from hatchways. Inda saw Tau and Jeje among them, tousled and heavy-eyed from having been woken from their snooze watch.

"Anchor up," called Dun. He marched up to the capstan, followed by others, shuffling, whispering, and the mutiny, such as it was, ended.

"Brig 'em until the captain decides what to do," Kodl said shortly, pointing to Black Boots and Gillip.

"But I—" Black Boots began, and Inda saw Norsh grip his arm, then with the other hand make a fist, turning the underside of his wrist upward for the briefest moment.

Black Boots muttered under his breath, but followed.

Inda looked up to see if Kodl or anyone else had seen Norsh's gesture, but they were all busy.

Leugre raised his voice, his tone and manner heavy with threat, "I'm second mate now. I'll stay on deck."

A hand knocked against Inda's back. "Let's get the anchor up some-time today, shall we?" Fassun pointed with his chin toward the capstan.

When the anchor had been catted Inda and his gig crew were dismissed. Inda was tired, but he knew he would not sleep, so he retreated to the mids' empty wardroom.

He had been teaching Scalis and his defense team what he knew about staff and sword, gradually absorbing ideas from them as well, most particularly from the carpenter's mate. But that was general of-fense and defense. He had kept his promise to Hadand, and had never shown anyone the Odni. Instead he practiced it alone, with two real blades, two beautiful Sartoran-forged daggers that he'd bought his very first winter away from home.

The drill was so familiar that he didn't need to think about it, he just cast his mind free, whirled and blocked, tumbled and struck, never halt-ing, his breath steady despite the glow of warmth and the prickle of sweat.

It was the sound of footfalls that broke his reverie. He slammed the knives into his wrist sheaths, his loose sleeves hiding them just as Dun entered. Then he picked up the staff propped in a corner.

"Here you are," he said, and looked around the small cabin with its single lamp swinging. "Warming up a little?"

"Warming up" was one of the forecastle's phrases for drill during cold weather. The same sort of humor caused them to call the same drills in summer "cooling off."

Inda made an impatient movement. "You've been sailing longer than I," he said, and Dun smiled and opened a hand, not willing to lie unless he had to. "What does this mean?" Inda demonstrated Norsh's fist, turn-ing his inner wrist up.

"I would call that a private signal," Dun said slowly. "For lack of any other knowledge."

Inda described briefly what he had seen. Dun listened, not surprised. Norsh and his mates had been prowling around whispering; this was the first evidence, if it was evidence, that they might actually be planning an organized mutiny.

But Dun had a more urgent question on his mind. "You were there when Vorzcin jumped ship?"

Inda described that, too.

Dun said, "Of course she's not a thief. In fact, she just lost all her wages since, what, the Nob? We weren't allowed on shore in Bren, were we? That's a sizable sum."

Inda jerked a shoulder up and down.

"She's no thief, and some might call her practical. How much, they are asking, does anyone owe the Pims, since they cannot protect us from the Venn embargo?"

Inda looked surprised. "You going to jump ship too?"

Dun saw in Inda's face that the idea had never occurred to him. "No," he said. "But I hear it around me."

Inda wiped his sleeve over his brow, feeling cold. Once again his life seemed on the verge of disintegrating. He was not sure he owed any duty to the Pims if his life was threatened, but he did feel sure of one thing: if he could sail home in the ship Captain Sindan had placed him on, he would. This vessel was his last link with home.

"I'll stay until the captain, or the first mate, orders me off," he said as carelessly as he could.

Dun's smile flashed briefly. "If they're worried about pirates—or have time for mutinous muttering—maybe we ought to rouse the defenders up for some drill."

Inda grinned back. "Except who listens to us? But they'd listen to Scalis!"

Chapter Thirteen

"CAN you believe it?" Cherry-Stripe Marlo-Vayir muttered on New Year's Lastday, as he checked saddle, halter, and sword in its saddle sheath. "*All* six of 'em going home with us. Including your brother. What are they on about, anyway?"

Sponge glanced over his shoulder. The royal stable was in an uproar as the Sierlaef's and the Marlo-Vayir companies checked saddles, balanced gear on the remounts. Armsmen and heralds jostled for precedence. There was no custom to fall back on. Nobody could remember when a royal heir rode on a tour of all the Jarl-holdings, Ola-Vayir in the north to Jaya-Vayir in the south. Marlo-Vayir was to be the first stop.

Sponge suspected the real intent, but as usual he kept it to himself. "Does it matter?" he asked. "The main thing is, they won't be with you long."

"It'll seem long enough." Cherry-Stripe sighed. "Six of 'em! You just know they'll run me like a scrub. Academy all over again, only I'll be alone, and without any of the fun!"

Sponge laughed in sympathy.

A trumpet outside in the stable yard blared, calling the Marlo-Vayirs to horse. Cherry-Stripe sent one last grimace in Sponge's direction, half-raised a hand, and then leaped into the saddle. Sponge watched him ride out, his ponytail bobbing. Cherry-Stripe had stopped wearing pigtails during winter, though the Tveis had two more years of pigtail level at the academy before they became ponies; so far their Ains had either not noticed, or more likely they'd decided not to deign to notice, now that they were Guards. The current horsetails never gave them any trouble, ostensibly because a prince was their leader, but it helped considerably that the first Tvei group almost always won the authorized games on the fields, as well as the unauthorized scraps behind the barracks.

Men and Guards. *And when I'm nineteen, I will be a first-year horse-tail*, Sponge thought as he dashed up the stairs. He hadn't thought about that when he was twelve, and a new scrub.

And when I'm a man? Sponge thought, passing along hallways glinting with freshly gilt raptor motifs.

A Guard saluted, flat hand to chest. Sponge lifted a hand as he entered the archive, thinking: *And when I'm a man, I still have Buck Marlo-Vayir to face the first Convocation my father is dead, because he expects to become Royal Shield Arm. Nobody says it, but everyone in the academy knows it.* It wasn't right, but there was no use in complaining.

What was it he'd read? *To complain about injustice is to hand power to he who resolves the question.* There was nothing his father could do: the question would arise after he died, and then his brother as new king would order Buck to challenge Sponge to a duel. Inevitable as rain. Sponge had to see to it that he picked the ground, if not the time, or he would be defeated before he lifted a sword.

Silhouetted against the middle window stood the king, hands clasped behind him, gazing out at the slate-gray sky stretching from horizon to horizon, the castle walls with the ceaselessly patroling sentries, and beyond, on the road winding between the gentle, snow-patched hills, the torch-bearing Marlo-Vayir party, riding neatly in column. Those torches looked, if one squinted, like a river of fire.

Sponge was not aware of making any noise, but his father said, "That you, Evred?"

"I stayed to wish Marlo-Vayir Tvei farewell."

His father did not immediately speak. This year's lesson was that the king did not, after all, have unlimited power. That he could be forced to send people to a stupid war, though he hadn't wanted it, and knew it would cost men and money; the original plan of truce with Idayago, bolstered by the seaward protection by the ships, would have been so much better.

Yet my uncle, who is older than I, still doesn't see it, Sponge thought. *He sees only the possibility of glory.* There was no glory in the prospect of a treaty without a battle.

"I was pleased with your brother," the king said at last, as horns blared, echoing from one wall to another. Outside, another family departed. The livery was white and blue: Hali-Vayir. "This is the first time he has acted as heir."

Sponge glanced at his father, saw his profile, so he did not hide his wince of remorse. He did not know that the king could hear his breathing change, could sense his reaction. Profound sadness gripped the king's heart, not just because the Sierlaef's true motivations were suspect, but because Evred felt he had to protect his father.

"What did you learn this week?" the king asked at last.

Sponge glanced up. There was almost no red left in his father's gray hair. "I learned the Jarls all think the embargo is a joke, that we will be fine without outside trade."

"We will be, for a time," the king acknowledged. "We can grow enough food for our people, especially with these new lands. But when the magical aids to life begin to dissolve, one by one?" He spread his hands. "They all talk confidently about living as our ancestors did, but no one will actually do it. It will have the effect of hurrying us into war, perhaps before we are ready. The Venn will be able to name the time. We have already named the place: our own land."

No mistaking that grim tone.

The king turned his head. "Did you learn anything about the Battle of Ghael Hills from listening to the talk?"

Sponge thought back through the wine-soused shouting, the songs and stories from New Year's First Night, told by liegemen and his brother's Sier-Danas. He considered, then dismissed, an observation about how pompous men sounded, with their "History will award Anderle-Harskialdna the accolade of Sigun" and the aggrandizement of individual stories. He'd already had that lesson, years ago. Men bragged. Men wanted to be remembered. Who, and what, "history" actually gave the Sigun did not depend on individual desire, no matter how strong; the truth was that it was future generations who decided what to remember. And why.

He said, "I think the crucial mistake the Idayagans made was in retreating after Uncle Anderle's force appeared."

The king turned away from the window. "Sindan, in his private report, observed that our people were far more savage after the Idayagans broke and ran than during the actual fighting. I've since reread some of the older personal chronicles, and discovered that this is not, in fact, uncommon. Nor is it characteristic of Marlovans. It seems a human trait, to change from fright and desperation to commensurate anger when your enemy gives way."

The king walked to the fireplace. "Do you know what your future wife, the future queen, and some of the other girls are doing in the archive?"

Sponge did not hide his surprise. "Hadand says they are scouting out what they can of our history, since so little of it was written down until just a few generations ago."

"Yes," the king said, "and no. They are scouting out the history of magic, as it relates to us. Think about it. We accept as part of everyday life some very strange anomalies. The lone woman in the cottage is enabled to perform the Birth Spell, and there's a child with the look of his ancestors. We all know, without thinking, the spell to Disappear the Dead, when it must be done—all except those who took the life if it was not self-defense. Why? Who made it that way? Can they take it away again?"

Sponge frowned in perplexity. When he actually thought about it, those things did seem strange.

"Perhaps the project is even larger. I don't know what Fareas-Iofre has in the way of records, as sent by her sister in Sartor or her mother, and it is she as well as the Jarlan of Montredavan-An who are directing the girls."

"Montredavan-An? How? I thought they were sequestered."

"They are. At least the Jarl is. He writes no letters, speaks no messages. That is not true of his wife, who has separate lines of communication. Women delivering cloth and books and luxuries such as Sartoran leaf, women riding through their lands on their way home, women who all know one another. The letters they write are duly read by our border Riders, but who knows what is spoken? I do trust their loyalty to the kingdom, and so I say nothing. But I wonder what success they will have, and what it will mean."

"History of magic?" Sponge repeated. "Why?"

"So that they can find a way to learn it," the king said.

Sponge tried for a moment to imagine Kialen, his fearful, silent future wife, performing spells that made glowglobes light and bound bridges against collapsing. Kialen, who trembled in fear if anyone raised a voice, and fainted if she saw a flogging. The image would not form. And then he realized that Hadand had never told him about these magic studies.

Another secret.

He looked at his father. "What are you saying? That we can't trust the women?" He felt sick as he said it. He had already been over this ground with Hadand once before, and the truth was, he could not imagine honest, steady Hadand conspiring. His champion against his brother's unthinking cruelty, his uncle's well thought out cruelty.

"What, really, is trust?" the king asked. "So slippery a word. I trust those girls to be loyal to Iasca Leror, none more so, in fact. To be loyal to you, and to me. But their vision of what constitutes loyalty is fundamentally different from mine . . . from your uncle's."

Sponge considered his father's words, and realized he would have to think again about trust. It was one of those words you thought you knew, that sparked an instant emotional reaction, but really, what did it mean? For example, his own father's trust. "Sindan says." Yet Sponge knew that Uncle Sindan had not been back in the royal city at all. He was now far north, inspecting, without anyone knowing it, just how well the new Jarls were carrying out their promises made at the treaty. There had to be another secret here, one he'd never before suspected.

"But if the women learn magic, and keep it secret, won't power shift to their hands?"

"Power is another of those words," the king said, smiling. "As long as men are stronger, the power of the sword will lie with them. But if women wielded magic, would that really be so bad a thing? We know that women wielded magic power exclusively in the early days of Old Sartor."

Sponge thought about the northern war, and the future war that it most certainly would bring on them. He thought about the isolation of the kingdom, about his uncle's plans, all in the name of Marlovan glory. He thought about his brother being king one day. And he thought about the glories of Old Sartor, before Norsunder caused its fall.

"No," he said. "It would not."

Chapter Fourteen

TWO weeks later Inda sat in the mizzenmast crosstrees, watching through drifting slants of snow as three pirate craft attacked the slowest Pim ship in the disintegrating convoy, and trying to remember the exact sequence of events during New Year's Week at Tenthen Castle—the songs they sang, who usually drummed, what they ate. He no longer tried to fight memories. They came anyway, if not during the day, then during dreams.

This was the second Pim ship to be taken in a fortnight of murderous sailing against wind, weather, and swarms of pirates in both small, swift sailing ships, and—when they neared one of the countless island clusters—low, fast galleys that skimmed out to overwhelm stragglers.

Down below on the captain's deck, Kodl braced himself tiredly against the binnacle. Already the sun was sinking westward from its low northern arc.

Kodl knew they would never make it to Sartor. Now he wanted to get them to Freedom Island if he could. The island had been the target of vicious pirate battles three times so far during Kodl's years on the sea. The new holders, once Khanerenth's royal navy, supposedly established trade, but on their own terms. Free-trader terms.

That meant Kodl and the crew would have their lives, but lose the ship because they were not affiliated privateers. And, being Iascans, they could not get letters of marque—no government would risk angering the Venn enough to issue one.

The other choice was between becoming victims of pirates or becoming pirates themselves.

Kodl was not the only one whose mood matched the frigid winter air. Captain Beagar had stayed in his cabin since leaving Khanerenth. All his long career a good, careful captain, around the world times beyond count, just a few short years from an honorable retirement. And now his livelihood, his life, was all but gone, and for reasons that had nothing to do with him. The utter injustice had stunned him, leaving him unable to move, to think. The only thing that numbed the pain was the hardest liquor he could find.

The two would-be mutineers still sat down in the hold, awaiting the captain's judgment that everyone knew was not going to come.

And in the mates' wardroom directly below the captain's cabin where Beagar stared sightlessly at his logbook, a half-empty jug at his elbow, Jeje sat at the table, watching the lamp swing, and fighting tears.

"Hey, are you sickening for something?" Dasta plunked down next to her, shedding snow as he stripped off his jacket and knit cap.

"Just a little cold," Jeje lied, annoyed with herself. She'd thought the tears had stayed only a sting, but obviously her eyelids and nose were bright red.

"Is Inda down yet?" That was Tau, sitting opposite them with unconscious grace. His coloring had heightened; Jeje found the sight of his ruddy cheeks and bright eyes so sharp and sweet a pain she had to look away.

Dasta shook his head and wiped his weather-reddened beak of a nose, which had gone numb. "Leugre still snoring. Never took his watch."

"As well," Tau commented, and no one disagreed, even if they had to miss sleep to cover him.

"Inda stayed on for his watch. Snow's thickening up some," Dasta said, crouching down at the iron stove at the forward bulkhead of the mates' wardroom. Ordinarily these lowly middies would be in their airless little cubby of a wardroom, one of the least pleasant spaces in the ship above the hold. But the first mate—now the unofficial captain—almost lived on deck. The second mate, Leugre, was sleeping off a drunken binge, and Norsh, now third mate, was nowhere to be seen.

Dasta pointed a finger at Jeje. "She's sick too."

Jeje peeked furtively. Tau turned his beautiful head, his eyes reflecting with golden radiance the lamplight that swung past, and darkening to shadow as the lamp reached the height of its arc. Jeje saw his quick concern, and not the least hint of the precious, magical fire of ardency that Jeje had so recently, and so secretly, discovered.

"Shall I take the midnight watch? Nothing else to do," Tau offered.

"I hope," Faura said from the door, her dark gaze accusing, "*someone* is going to work tonight."

"On our way." Jeje reached for the coat and hat that Dasta had set aside. They both smelled heavily of wet rope. No one having had liberty for over half a year, those who'd been growing shared their winter clothing around since they hadn't enough stores left to make any. Inda had Jeje's jacket, which was too tight in the armpits for her these days. "In fact, I may's well go bring Inda off, and stay in the tops."

Faura remained silent as Dasta and Jeje passed. Then she stepped up to confront Tau, one hand toying with a ringlet she'd let escape from her knit cap. She glared at Tau. "Everyone leaves when I come. Plotting mutiny?"

Tau said, "Don't."

She said challengingly, "Convince me." Tau saw tears of anger, even of shame, along the rims of her lower lids.

Mutiny. For the past year Tau had been avoiding her hints, touches, gropes, and sulky comments, hoping she'd find someone else to pursue. But Fassun's spoiled cousin seemed to be unshakable until she got what she wanted.

Right now, though, something more than thwarted lust underlay her words, her attitude. He sighed inwardly. *If not me, who?*

"Very well," he said, and took her offered hand, raising it to his lips. He kissed her hand lingeringly, then turned it over and gave her palm a quick bite. Faura gasped.

"Only I might not have time to talk," Tau murmured, and when she smiled in triumph at having at last gotten his attention—and wouldn't that toad Jeje burn!—he smiled back, thinking: *You will.*

Jeje reached the deck and hunched against the slap of icy wind against her face. She saw Testhy's shock of red-tinged pale hair instead of Leugre's wheat-colored sailor's braid, and relaxed. He waved a mittened hand then returned to overseeing the storm sail being set on the foremast. Jeje was glad Leugre was scamping duty; his rotten temper and cruelty were far worse when Scalis, Niz, and Kodl were below on their snooze watch.

She pulled on gloves still warm from Dasta's fingers, then scrambled up the shrouds. Timing her climb against the spectacular roll and pitch of the ship, she hoisted herself up onto the masthead and plopped down next to Inda. "Heyo."

Inda gave her a red-nosed glance, a brief grin, and then smacked the glass back to his eye, aiming it into the wind.

Jeje waited. The night, fast descending, blended sky and sea and ships, except for pinpoints of golden light. She brushed snowflakes from her eyelids and squinted against the wind. Some lights rolled and pitched: sea lights. Other tiny ones arced high: fire arrows.

The confusion of lights close together meant that at least two pirate ships had closed with and boarded the larger ship. Inda had pointed out when the pirates first started shadowing their convoy that they mostly hunted in threes.

Everyone had watched the early attacks, with the same sort of sickening fascination with which people looked at carriage wrecks, or burned houses, then they'd given up, except for Kodl and Inda. Captain Beagar had begun drinking hard after the first Pim ship was taken. The older hands had been wild with anger, all the more because they could do nothing. Now, after seeing most of their convoy disintegrate, no one was there to watch the second Pim ship get snapped up except Inda.

"What do you see?" she asked.

"Watching the defense."

"Doesn't look like there was much of one," she said.

He gestured with the glass. "They all do the same thing. It doesn't work."

"Come down, have a warm bite. You've been here since dawn. Long enough. Testhy seems willing to stay till the next watch, which I'll take."

Inda said, "Did you know New Year's Week is already at least a week past, maybe two? I was trying to count it out."

She snorted. "I didn't know. And I don't care. And won't, until we reach a port, where things like dates might have a meaning—" She stopped, hating herself. Maybe Inda had finally, finally, been ready to talk about his past. And here she was, whining like a scolded brat. "Tell me about New Year's," she said, but she knew it was too late.

And Inda just shrugged. "Oh, I think we'll reach a port. Though I didn't for a while. But I've also been watching that fellow." Inda waved at the lead pirate ship, and then gripped the shroud as the ship gave a sudden lurch, and crew appeared below, handling the gaff to the mizzen course.

Both Inda and Jeje looked up at the sails then into the wind, thinking the same thing: it was time to run under reefed staysails. Testhy, still on deck watch, obviously thought so as well, and called out orders to the watch.

"He watches Niz," Inda continued. "I've seen him on his deck, with a glass to his eye, when Niz is in the tops. They don't want to attack us, not when they can see a Delf."

Jeje felt her numb lips stretch into a grin. "Those noses are easy enough to spot," she said. "Think of that, a Delf nose being our protection."

Delfs all seemed to have bird skulls, pointy at the front, always recognizable in a crowd; what kept the pirates wary was the equally well-known fact that all Delfs seemed to know what ships one another served on, and far too often if you attacked a ship with a Delf on it, Delf traders would appear out of nowhere to its defense. Despite their never ending feuds they all formed instant alliances when they were attacked from outside, and fought ferociously.

Inda and Jeje were still smiling when they reached the deck. They lent a hand to the furling of the mizzen course, and then clambered numbly below, where Inda devoured the lukewarm gruff and stale rocks.

"Did they get the *Pim Olla?*" Tau asked, pouring good Sartoran steeped leaf from the captain's stores.

Inda muttered, "Yup," then chomped another bite.

"Think we're next?" Tau asked, one fine brow aslant. His long fingers ran up and down the edge of a little food knife.

Inda gave his head a shake. "Wary of Delfs is my guess."

Tau held up a hand. Inda frowned, realized that the usually fastidious

Tau was a little disheveled. Tau lifted his voice just slightly, saying, "Yan?"

"Out here."

That meant on guard.

Tau leaned forward and murmured, "So let's talk about us. And Norsh and Leugre."

Chapter Fifteen

TAU told them in three blunt sentences what Faura had revealed, then asked, "Should I take it to Kodl?"

Jeje opened her mouth to blurt *Of course!* but Inda said, "He's going to want proof. And the mood he's in, he might rope it out of Faura. Or Fassun. And then talk turns into action when it might not've."

"From the sound of it, mutiny is imminent anyway."

Imminent, Jeje thought, fighting against another surge of hopeless desire. At least (so she told herself) she could try to enjoy these moments, since she couldn't seem to rid herself of them. *Imminent—the way his mother talks.*

Inda said slowly, "Maybe nothing will happen. Sounds like they don't have a real plan of action."

Jeje said, "What would be a plan of action? All that about killing everyone they hate sounds like a plan to me."

Inda shook his head. "That's just hot talk. If you want to take something, well, like a ship, you'd have to first secure the ship and then those who command. They don't sound like they have thought any of that out. And they both like getting others to run their ruses. Like in Khanerenth."

Tau leaned forward. "You mean, putting Gillip and Black Boots up to it. Though nobody followed their lead."

Inda said, "Right. Leugre is a K—" He shut his mouth on the word "Kepa." Then, seeing puzzlement change to question in the others' faces, he said, "Putting people up to things works only if they wanted to do it anyway. But the whole crew doesn't want a mutiny."

Tau said, "I agree. Sails—Cook—the carpenter and his mates, the bosun and his, why should they mutiny? So we lose the ship. We don't own it, so our only loss is our back wages. We've lost those whatever happens, because we can't get to the Pim guild agents. But if we get to Freedom Island and they take the ship away, those with skills can hire on elsewhere."

"As long as they aren't Iascan," Jeje said.

"You learn an accent and lie," Tau said, shrugging.

A little silence ensued, during which the lamp swung. All of them glanced at the force and height of the arc, gauging the coming weather.

Then Dasta said, "Leugre would love being a pirate. All he needs is this ship to be his."

Inda snorted. "He might be able to take this ship. But he'll never run a battle against another ship and win. Neither he nor Norsh."

The others turned his way, and Jeje said, "Why not? I mean, does he know that?"

Inda shrugged. "Did you watch those pirates take the other Pim ships? From what I could see, they seemed to have some kind of strategy. Imagine Norsh actually planning an attack, instead of talking hot and trying to get others to do the real work."

Strategy. The word caught at the others. Who used words like that? Jeje realized she didn't even know what it meant, except that it had something to do with the military in some sense. Tau's eyes narrowed; he didn't speak, in case Inda offered more. Dasta thought back to the first week Inda was on board, when all of a sudden he, a small boy, decked Fass, who was twice his size and strength. *Strategy.*

But one look at Inda's tightly pressed lips and they knew that, as usual, he was not going to reveal his past.

So Jeje said, "You seem to know what you're talking about. I sure don't. Then you think nothing will happen?"

"No," Inda said. "I think if something happens that Norsh can use, he'll use it. He might even talk someone into doing that something." Inda laid his lands flat on the table. "Then it's going to be one on one, plan or not. If I'm right, we've either got to find proof they're planning mutiny, proof that will convince Kodl and the captain, or get our own defense ready."

Dasta glanced at Tau. "Fass?"

Tau said, "In with Norsh, but reluctantly. I don't think we dare talk to him or any of his mates."

The others agreed. Fassun always followed whoever seemed strongest. That meant if the mutiny could be stopped and Kodl became captain, Fassun would switch sides in a heartbeat.

Inda murmured, "If it happens, it has to be before we get to Freedom Island. Or they lose the ship, too."

Tau played with the little knife, lamplight running and winking on the blade in ribbons of fire. "What would a 'something' be that Norsh or Leugre could use?"

Inda rubbed his nose. "If anything happens to the captain."

Jeje struggled for clear sight, for sense. She hated this feeling that she'd slipped into a dreamworld. No, a nightmare. "So we'd better start listening everywhere we can?"

Inda said, "And put a guard on the captain's cabin."

"All on double watches." Tau yawned. "And just in case we were feeling lazy, the wind smells of a coming storm."

They all watched the widening arc of the lamp, and sniffed the air, which smelled faintly of ice.

"I'll volunteer first," Yan spoke softly from his post at the door.

"It's a toss-up whether they'll do anything to the captain before he drowns himself in wine," Tau observed.

They could all see his regret, which they shared, but since there was nothing to be said, they left for their various jobs in silence.

Four ugly days of fighting rain, sleet, and wind kept everyone busy. It took a full day just to get storm sail on the masts. They lost two foresails, ripped to shreds in moments, before they bent a stiff new storm sail on, Sails and her mates laying aloft themselves to help sheet it home.

The ship ran under nearly bare poles, the half moon just above the horizon casting an icy blue glow over the white-topped breakers, when Jeje finally was sent below to rest.

Zimd had just arrived, stretching and yawning. "Well that was fun," she said, chortling. "I'm ready for spring."

Jeje sighed, too tired to speak.

Zimd jumped onto her hammock, put hands on knees. "Jeje. You aren't heart-achin' for your pretty boy *now*, are you?"

Jeje made a fist, dropped her hand, and walked out, tired as she was. Too tired, obviously. Zimd's teasing was just stupid. So why did it upset her so much? Instinct drove her down below toward the hold, where no one would see her, and she wouldn't see Tau's golden eyes. *I know why I hate it so much, it's because I haven't hidden it, and thought I had.*

". . . dead."

At first the whisper seemed a part of the voice in her head, but that word caught her attention.

Embarrassment snuffed quick as a candle in rain, Jeje tiptoed between barrels and carefully numbered ends of tall rolls of sailcloth stacked outside of the purser's office. "You sure Beagar's dead?"

That was Indutsan's dry voice. Then Leugre's snigger.

"Knife right through his chest," Fassun muttered, his voice shaking. "Face down at the table."

Norsh laughed. "Probably fell on it drunk. He wouldn't have the guts to do it sober."

"Or Black Boots stabbed him in the chest, then shoved him forward. Why else is he hidin' down in the—"

"Doesn't matter," Norsh snapped. "We have to jump. Now. Before Kodl finds out and gets the forecastle shits together."

"So we pick targets?" Leugre asked. "Didn't we say that before? I want Kodl. He's snoring away this moment—"

Jeje backed away, too quickly, she bumped into a thick roll of sailcloth on which a wooden spoon had been balanced, and she saw it too late, her fingers just touching the end of it before it clattered to the deck.

Norsh said sharply, "Who's that?"

Jeje ran. The others slammed out and pounded down the companionway right behind her. She dashed upward yelling "Tau! Inda!" at the same time someone on deck roared, "Capn's dead!"

Norsh shouted, "Get the others! Get the others!"

Inda had been drinking hot cider in the wardroom; he emerged into the waist just as Jeje ran up, Leugre pounding after her, a boarding sword in one hand, a grappling hook in the other.

"Get Kodl," Inda said to Jeje without looking at her.

She vaulted up the ladder to the weather deck.

Leugre stood there, breathing hard, feeling unreal, despite the weapons he kept gripping and regripping in each hand, despite the sharp smell of sweat from his own body, and the faint smell of sweet cider in the air. They were, at last, going to take over the ship. Mutiny! They would be pirates! He always heard about them, but never thought of pirates being actual people like him.

But in his way was Scalis' strutting Marlovan horse turd.

Inda shut out the sounds of feet on wooden boards, the creakings of the ship, the flacking of sails being taken in, and the thumps and yells of Norsh's people running about wildly waving weapons.

He faced Leugre, his eyes flickering from side to side.

Leugre mistook that glance for fear.

"Want it easy or hard?" he asked, licking his lips. "Easy, you have to beg."

The brat shuffled crabwise to the side, a purposeless movement to Leugre, who was trying to decide how long he could take killing him before he had to go find Kodl; then somehow all he could see was shadow, since the deck lamp was now above and behind the Marlovan, the light distracting his eyes.

"Hard," Inda said.

"Leugre?" came the call from somewhere behind him.

Leugre slashed with the grappling hook at the Marlovan, the sword in his left ready for the kill. The grappler clattered on a barrel, and Leugre stumbled against a bulkhead, then pain splintered his throat from a lethal palm-heel strike. He fell, choking to death on his own blood.

Just then Gillip, Black Boots, and one of his mates arrived, saw Leugre fall, and they rushed Inda, who blocked the ladder to the deck, hands empty—

Up on deck Niz and Scalis arrived from fore and aft at a run. They saw the Marlovan boy in the waist make a smooth circular movement with both hands, too quick to follow, but suddenly he stood there holding two knives, not out like swords, but half-hidden against his forearms, and as the sailors rushed him, he flowed into the shadows of the swinging lamp above, whirled around, and within five heartbeats three sailors lay on the deck bleeding their lives out.

Inda leaped over the last one and dashed back to the ladder, looking around in fast assessment—

"Hah!" a hoarse laugh cracked the air.

Inda's head jerked sideways and up. There stood Scalis and Niz, lounging against the binnacle, as if nothing were going on. But nothing *was* going on now, Inda realized, his mind catching up: the fights had all ended.

"That's five you owe me," Scalis said to Niz, his breath clouding in the bright lamplight. "Knives, like I told ya." And significant nods.

Kodl appeared from the cabin. "Where is Norsh? I thought he would come after me."

Sailors assembled from all directions, everyone talking, some frightened, some of them holding violently struggling conspirators, Fassun, Indutsan, and Faura among them.

Niz cocked his head toward the hatchway. "Quiet, sounds it. Who did he get?"

Then they heard noise below. Some grasped weapons as they surrounded the hatchway. To their surprise what appeared was yellow hair, then an unremarkable face: Dun. His expression was mild as always as he gave a vague wave. "I'm afraid Norsh met with an accident belowdecks."

"Accident?" Kodl asked.

"Disagreement with my number one hammer. The hammer won."

Kodl sighed in relief. He looked around then, assessing what they had. Four lower deckhands lay dead in the waist, two on deck, and there would be more below. Sails and her first sail mate had Faura by the arms. Fassun stood distraught, a knife held at his neck by one of Scalis' forecastlemen.

When Kodl saw Fassun his triumph died. "Turn these ones loose into a boat. They can take their gear. Indutsan goes with 'em," he added, catching sight of the purser held by the Delf.

Indutsan searched for allies, his eyes angry, but he'd been caught and knew it.

Scalis ordered a boat to be lowered. The rest of the crew started talking all at once, their voices high and sharp, many of them moving back and forth to no real purpose. All except Inda, Kodl noticed. He leaned on the lee railing, staring at the harbor across the bay; the making tide was steadily bringing them into Freeport Harbor.

Kodl joined the boy at the rail. They stood there as the ship pitched gently on the flowing tide, watching the tiny gleams of golden light strung along the far end of the massive bay, like fireflies in a meadow.

Inda could still feel the impact of Leugre's flesh on his palm. There was no triumph, just a sense of sickness. *He would have killed me*, Inda's inner voice argued. *They all would have killed me*, but the answer was heavy, nauseating silence. His guts heaved, causing cold sweat to break out all over him; he realized his knees and belly had gone watery.

"Good work, Elgar," Kodl said.

Inda made a gesture of negation, realized he was still holding his knives, and that his hands shook. His grip was so tight it took a moment to loosen his fingers. Then he noticed the blood splashed down his shirt. He ripped it off, used it to clean the knives, and pitched it overboard, trembling more from reaction than the cold.

Then he shoved the knives back in the sheaths that everyone could now see.

Jeje appeared and silently held out Tau's coat. It was warm from his body. Inda pulled it on, grateful for the warmth, though he still shivered.

Kodl had been watching the boy, who faced him mutely, his thin ribs, glimpsed through the open front of the coat, expanding and contracting with his labored breathing. Kodl turned his head, saw the entire crew on deck, silent under the creaking timbers.

I am captain now, he thought, but of course there was no joy, only irony. *Captain at last—for the shortest cruise ever known.*

But the work must be done, and done right, in respect to Captain Beagar, who had been murdered. Anger burned through Kodl when he remembered the lifeless body, the knife angled in a way that looked impossible for someone thrust into himself.

But Inda had killed the murderers, which was at least justice, even if it didn't satisfy Kodl's desire for vengeance. All that remained was to honorably finish the captain's work, as much as he could. So he would do it.

"We will sail for Freedom Island," he said, lifting his voice so even those in the tops could hear. "Because we must. There is no longer any convoy that would accept us, and we can't hire protection. We will lose the ship, and probably the cargo as well, because we haven't any money to join the Freedom Island confederation. You pay or you lose your ship, is the word I heard. But I will not consent to piracy. What individuals choose to do after we land is their affair."

"So they won't force us into the galleys?" someone called.

"Not Freedom Island, from what Vorzcin heard and told me, before she jumped ship. Which is why I risked the run here," Kodl said bleakly. "We haven't a hope of keeping our liberty in any pirate port. And nobody in a kingdom port will hire any of us Iascans. Here at least we get a chance, though your choices will be limited to hiring on with privateers or free traders, but I've heard some of them are pretty decent, the free traders being mostly smugglers who run goods buyers think overtaxed. They aren't looking for fights."

Inda flicked his palm up. His head throbbed. Iascan ships were targets now, because of what had happened in the land that was no longer his home. By the Marlovans who had exiled him. But to the rest of the world he was still a Marlovan.

"Is there another choice?" Inda asked, thinking: *Sindan will never find me now.*

Niz muttered something, and Scalis' rusty laugh was just audible over the *slap-slap* of the sea against the hull, and the clatter of blocks as the ship lurched on the making tide.

Kodl raised a hand as if to silence them, and then used that same hand to point southward toward the glittering row of harbor lights, faint and golden at the base of those black mountains. "Let's get ourselves into harbor safely first. There will be time enough to plan after."

Chapter Sixteen

B Y the next watch Inda sensed another conspiracy forming, this one involving him. He saw it in the appraising looks some of the older men sent him, the grins and whispers of Niz and Scalis, who showed no reaction to the sudden deaths of former shipmates. Niz seemed, in fact, to be annoyed that he had been busy on the foremast when all the fun occurred, arriving when it was too late to do anything but witness the end.

Fun. For a time Inda kept flexing and wringing his hand, as if that would get rid of the physical memory of Leugre's neck crushing. He'd killed four people altogether, but somehow that one was the worst.

Tau caught him at it finally, his pale gold gaze flicking from wringing hand to Inda's face and then narrowing. "They would have killed you first," he said. As if Inda had spoken.

Inda leaned against the capstan. "I know."

"You also know you're going to have to teach the rest of us. If you believe, that is, we are worth keeping alive." He walked away without waiting for an answer.

Inda was still brooding about that as he helped with the grim chores of bringing up the dead and performing the Words of Disappearance over them—the crew all lined up in the remains of their best shore-going clothes for the captain's Disappearance—and then the cleaning of the deck of blood, which used just about all the magic on their clean-buckets. Not that anyone cared. The ship was no longer theirs.

And Inda was still thinking during the late watch, when Kodl at last went into the captain's cabin to sort his papers, putting the official ones with Indutsan's books, and setting aside personal ones for the galley fire. He had Inda with him, ostensibly holding an extra lamp, but as a silent threat in case any of the other crew had ideas about another mutiny.

Inda knew there would be no more attempts to take the ship. For each back pat and word of praise, mostly from the forecastlemen, there were ugly looks and obvious retreats out of his way. Mostly from Gillip's and Black Boots' mates.

Inda noticed, but said and did nothing. He had killed four men, there was no escaping the fact. And he knew now why he just felt sick, instead of triumphant. As he stood there holding that lantern and watching Kodl sort the captain's papers, burning his hoarded letters from his family, Inda forced himself to face the truth, that all the training at home, the flags and games and fox yips and the rest, were for this: killing. How could he have been stupid enough to think if he could just go home, the rest of his life would be fun wargames? Iasca Leror had gone to war, and he probably knew some of the men who had fought, who had killed men they didn't even know. Maybe his own brother, who was just old enough now to be included in the Guard.

That's what I am good at, Inda thought, gazing out the captain's open stern windows at the water roiling in a blue wake over the black sea. *I couldn't save Dogpiss, I wasn't fast enough, but now I'm fast and what I'm good at is killing.*

They rode the tide in early the next morning, sailors off watch packing their dunnage below, and speculating on what would happen. On deck there was tense silence as Kodl scanned the shore with a glass. The tension increased when the lookout above shouted, "Cutter beating up direct on the bow!"

Inda glanced back over his shoulder at the point. Of course. Lookouts there, and some sort of signal method. Freeport Harbor would not be taken by surprise.

He rode on the foremast boom, as it was his watch. Niz stood on the topsail yard above him, watching critically as the narrow, single-sailed craft swept around in a beautiful curve and closed with them, loosening the sail. A tall girl expertly hooked them on, and an older woman and a young man climbed aboard, touched their foreheads to Kodl, who stood in Beagar's place on the captain's deck.

A hand clapped on Inda's shoulder. "We'll stay together, eh?" Scalis said, uttering a horse chuckle. "You didn't plan nothin' else, did ya, boy?"

Inda jerked his chin down. "I don't know."

Just then the man accepted a paper from the former first mate. They moved slowly, embarking on a close inspection, as Kodl signaled for the bosun to whistle one last time: *All hands.* They assembled fast, everyone silent.

Kodl spoke a last time to the crew. "We can take our launches in, and leave them tied to the dock. The ship is no longer ours. But the harbormaster will pay, so don't run off before you get your share. Consider it the back pay you were owed."

A quick whisper ran through the crew.

"Cap'n?" called an old hand. "We can't go home, then? If the Pims find out, we be outlaws, no?"

"I signed alone, Reef," Kodl said heavily. "Responsibility is mine."

They understood then that Kodl could, by free trade rules, have kept all the money. Or he could have forced them to sign over the ship, too, but instead he was acting alone but still issuing fair shares. Few understood it was his last gesture to Peadal Beagar, who had been a good captain; they cheered him, then broke into groups, talking and laughing.

"Remember what I said," Scalis muttered, clapping Inda's shoulder.

Inda thought of home, and Captain Sindan. Of Sponge whispering into his fever dreams, *On my honor, on my soul, you will get justice.* Inda winced away from the memory, thinking: *How long before you gave up trying, Sponge?*

Not that he blamed Sponge. He remembered quite well what Sponge's life had been like, despite his being a prince.

Inda's thoughts lingered on Sponge as he worked with the crew on lowering the anchor one last time. He did not hear the subdued songs, barely audible above the hull-shuddering thunder of the anchor chain running free. Despite the singing, for a moment he was back behind the scrub pit before dawn, taking turns with Sponge practicing their blocks and falls. Laughing, naming ancient kings in rhythm as they pitched hay, or making up stupid songs about the masters in Old Sartoran, just for the fun of it.

He was glad that he'd started teaching Sponge the Odni. *Trust your own two hands, Sponge.*

They hoisted their sail bags over their shoulders and climbed down into the launches. Everyone took an oar and pulled for Freeport dock, leaving behind their home of three years with free trader versions of customs inspectors poking into every corner, evaluating and making notes on slates.

Soon enough they all climbed onto the dock below the long, broad boardwalk, built by some king long ago. A huge octagonal spired building dominated the north end, obviously the harbormaster's headquarters, a white flag flying from its spire. Along the boardwalk ranged a row of huge buildings, once grand, probably housing aristocrats with huge retinues, now used as warehouses and shops.

Inda and his companions glanced upward at the weatherworn buildings with their old scrollwork, graceful iron railings in a lyre motif, the old-fashioned artistry contrasting with the more conventional harbor pleasure dens and shops they now housed. Then they trudged up one of the two curved stairways to the boardwalk, their dunnage burdening their shoulders. A harassed flunky waved them toward the first warehouse. There they stood around in a rough circle near the disconsolate crews of two other ships that had limped in on the previous tide—one of them a high-sided caravel from Sartor, half dismasted by weather and pirates, the other too far down the harbor to see in the hazy sunshine, but a round-hulled brig from the north.

Inda glared at the placid sea. No one to turn to, no authority to guarantee fairness. No one cared why they were there, what had happened. They had brought a ship to a port that existed outside of any government's law.

He sank down onto his bag between Jeje and Dasta, Yan still standing nearby. Tau had vanished, which was usual for liberty landings. Inda wondered if he would return this time, realized he expected Tau to come back, and contemplated for a brief, weary time why he expected it: Tau was a friend, not just a fellow mid. A comrade, just as were Jeje and Yan and Dasta. Or at least he had been, but maybe Tau did not see it that way. If he did scout off, nobody could blame him.

By the end of a long, thirsty afternoon they all braced themselves to end up with nothing after all, especially after witnessing a prolonged, vehement argument over the tea traders between customs people and what had to be privateer captains, standing just outside the warehouse. So they were surprised when a young man approached Kodl at last, a young fellow with an air of authority, dressed in stylish striped trousers, wide at the bottom and tight at the top, and a frilled shirt under a tight, quilted vest. He read out in fluid Sartoran a long list that they soon realized was a scrupulously rendered percentage of value of ship and cargo.

Inda saw a boy his own age busily writing down everything that was said on both sides. He wrote with pen on paper, indicating that records were kept.

Kodl agreed to everything the young man said—there really wasn't any alternative—and then the speaker finished in a loud, clear voice, "So you'll sign on receipt of the agreed-on payment?"

"Yes," Kodl said heavily.

The free trader misread his reluctance, and said, with an impatience that didn't quite mask a residual fear, "Look you. These slow round-bottom tubs, that's a fair price. No one gives full price for 'em. And glowglobes, so close to Sartor? Why carry those here? They won't bring much more than was paid for them before cargo prices."

Kodl said in a heavy voice, "Picked them up on the Nob, out west. From a ship needing extensive repair. Supposed to sell them on the other side of the strait. But we couldn't land, on account of the embargo."

The young man nodded. "Dumped cargos are too common these days." He hesitated. Though Kodl did not yet know it, this was the harbormaster's assistant, a quick-witted, observant young man; he realized Kodl was not reluctant about the price, but about matters he could not control. And so he motioned to a woman who, dressed in money-changer brown, with silken counting strings dangling at her belt, pushed forward stacked coins in three different issues, all purported to equal the same amount.

So there was some authority behind them! Kodl sighed, inwardly hearing his opening words of defense to Ma Pim. Both Niz and Scalis made what they thought were discreet nods and pokes toward the smallest pile, the six-sided Sartoran coins. Not that Kodl needed reminding that Sartoran coinage was generally accepted all over the southern hemisphere at full value.

The coins having changed hands, the free traders all looked relieved. The boy blew the ink dry on his record and they vanished toward the dock and the next ship, leaving Kodl and his crew standing there with the coins and their dunnage.

"We may as well divide up and pay off right here," he said, since no one was chasing them away.

Inda, Dasta, Yan, and Jeje waited as the older hands were paid off. Inda breathed in the familiar smells of a harbor: fish, brine, rope, wood, overlaid by a trace of exotic spices. The voices around spoke in the usual mishmash of tongues expected in a harbor. Dock Talk was the most prevalent, but Khanerenth and Sartoran were also often heard.

Dasta's thoughts seemed to come from far away, squeaking like mice in a wall. Until recently his life had lain before him: rat, mid, mate, maybe one day captain, around and around the globe, events marked by fierce storms or escapes from pirates, always safe in convoy, never far from a coast. All of it gone, leaving him in a world with no rules.

Yan hunched up, willing himself to be invisible. He had escaped the home that was not a home, he had escaped the galleys, he had escaped death. He refused to think about the future. It was enough to stand, breathe, and think, *I'm alive.*

Jeje was the only one besides Inda aware that Taumad had slipped away. She watched as old, familiar crew members parted, vanishing into the crowd: cook, steward, bosun, carpenter, sailmaker all knew they could find work fairly swiftly, even if not on a legitimate kingdom trade ship. Testhy lingered, watching as well.

Sails was the last, a tall, skinny, strong older woman, frowning Jeje's way the while. At last she separated from Cook and the other four women who had chosen to band together, and said in Dock Talk, "Come with us to Sartor, Jeje. I can get ye work as first sail-mate anywhere but the most finicky yacht or royal ship."

Jeje looked toward Inda, then shook her head mutely.

Sails hesitated, then murmured, "Those pretty ones like young Taumad, it's never any good even if y'do get their bowsprit aboard ye. They never has to learn to please."

Jeje's face burned, but she didn't speak.

Cook said, as Sails joined her, "Don't tell her sex is mostly in your own head."

Sails laughed. The two moved out of Jeje's life.

"Ramis," Inda said suddenly, and the others turned his way. "I keep hearing the name Ramis the One-Eyed."

Jeje opened her mouth, then shut it. She was unwilling to be the one to speak Tau's name, but Yan said it for her, "Tau will have gotten the sved, soon's he finds us a place."

Quick steps brought all their heads up. There was Dun, the carpenter's mate. They were mildly surprised he hadn't gone with the carpenter, but no one really knew the pleasant, soft-spoken Dun, and were too busy with their own thoughts to ask questions. "Kodl says we'll find you later." He smiled. "I take it you'll be in your usual haunts?"

Inda said, "I think Tau went to scout us a place."

Dun gave a casual wave. "We'll find you. Then plan." He moved away, Testhy, after a last pause, following him.

Tau dashed up shortly after, golden hair flying, drawing the usual stares from both men and women. For Taumad the world was little different than before. When he'd left home he had at first scorned his mother's advice on always finding a pleasure house to stay in, but his first liberty night in an overpriced, nasty backwater inn, stinking of fish, listening to the shrill battles between cats and rats through a night on a hard bed with mildewed blankets, changed his mind.

Now his ship life was stitched between houses of comfort, cleanliness, and always the best local news. Using the secret words his mother had taught him he always got the best lodging for the cheapest price. Free, if he took a turn upstairs.

Inda grinned, relieved to see Tau. "I got your share of the final take," he said.

Tau smiled back, one fine brow quirked, as if he was reading Inda's mind. As he led his friends up a narrow brick switchback, he said in Iascan, "While we were rounding Khanerenth Lands End, Ramis the One-Eyed of the *Knife* smashed a local alliance of pirates. Bad ones. Killers."

"Brotherhood?" Yan murmured.

"No. Someone building a fleet to join them. They said Ramis must be going for dominion over these island seas. He stayed here a day, said he'd be back if he heard that the free traders weren't trading free. That means keeping the peace."

Inda jerked his chin down. That might explain the almost unnatural order he saw about him. Oh, there were still the bawling, raucous sounds of drunken sailors from open windows in the dock dives, and loud, shrill voices haggling filled the air, but people seemed to be more careful, somehow. Though there weren't any guards here, far from the reach of any government, and so everyone went armed like brigands.

"I found a place," Tau said, and the others followed wordlessly.

As usual, the places on the hill that commanded a view and fresh air were the most expensive. These houses were set right into the hills, many with streams tumbling down between them, some paved with marble in ancient times. Huge windows bowing out testified to gentler weather patterns.

"Here we are," Tau said, pointing.

The Lark Ascendant was built on a hillside, commanding a truly spectacular view of not just the harbor, but the rest of the island lying northward. Inda stared out at the tangle of silvery branches, the rocky hillside, and wished with violent suddenness he could run off and go exploring, despite the crunch of frost underfoot, and the cold searing his throat.

But he followed Tau inside, where they were soon settled in a first floor room at the back that looked out onto a pretty little tiled court. The four of them had to share a room, of course: all of them except Tau were still passing as underage.

Inda watched Jeje stowing her stuff and pondered, for the first time in months, the mysteries of sex. He knew Tau had at least a year ago, if not longer, crossed over that strange bridge. He, Dasta, and Jeje hadn't—though sometimes he wondered about Jeje, despite her preference for dressing like a rat in shapeless long smocks and old trousers. There'd been something different about her since late summer.

"Inda! Come on!" A meal was waiting, they were starved.

After that, they all fell into bed. When morning came they had just decided to explore the main causeway—called the King's Saunter—when Kodl arrived.

"Time to talk," he said.

Tau cast Inda an inquiring look. Inda remembered that sense of conspiracy—Niz and Scalis talking with Kodl, all while glancing his way—but he said nothing as Kodl led them downhill to a low, rambling, but clean inn at the very end of one of the quieter streets that catered mostly to mates and captains of the smaller craft, where he, Niz, Scalis, Dun, and some of the forecastle and topmen had taken rooms.

Chapter Seventeen

THE room Kodl led them to contained an old, battered plank table. The single window looked out over a narrow alley down which carts creaked and sailors on short liberty were already weaving along, drunk and singing merrily.

Around the table sat all Scalis' favored forecastlemen except one, Dun, Niz, three of Niz's topmen, and the mids Zimd, Testhy, Yan, Jeje, Tau, Dasta, and Inda.

"Now, here's what us think," Niz said.

Scalis took over. "Way I see things is, no smart ship wants us merch hands when we aren't trained for speed sail, and most of us are Iascan. So we offer something else, see, something they need so much they don't ask where we're from."

Another general nod, and Niz said, "Defense."

Everyone looked at Inda. He slouched on his bench, staring down at his hands. *I'm a killer,* he thought, wincing. *They all think of me as a killer. Because I am one.*

Of those watching him, only Dun, Tau, and Jeje recognized the pain in Inda's lowered gaze, the white line of his lips.

"We'll become marines?" Tau asked, arms crossed. Drawing attention his way. *"Us?"*

One of the forecastlemen cackled, to be thumped on the arm by his mate. "Shaddup. It's Scalis' idea."

"Oh. Right." The forecastleman hastily sobered his face.

Tau went on as if no one had spoken, "Who will hire us? The only ships I see that carry marines are kingdom warships carrying their own people. Merches sometimes, when they are carrying very expensive cargos, but will they take on Iascans instead of their customary armed companies-for-hire?" He shook his head.

"We offer ourselves to the independents," Kodl said. "The ones that can't afford the price of those companies of marines-for-hire. Begin with privateers in the Freedom alliance, the ones that sell cargos taken off their enemies, or smuggle past customs cruisers. No one looking deliberately for trouble, in other words."

Scalis rubbed his hands. "But if trouble comes, we got to be ready for it."

Kodl gave a nod of agreement. "In these waters, there's a need. Piracy's got worse ever since Khanerenth turned to civil war. We spent the night talking to people." He indicated Scalis, Niz, Dun, and himself. "We all heard pretty much the same thing."

Scalis leaned forward. "Fact is, there's no protection on these eastern seas. Sartor mostly trades west. Sarendan same. Some of them trade up the coast, but not enough to rate notice by their kings. Geranda is Venn held, so they ignore the islands and face north. Colend is land bound and never thinks of the sea at all, and the Chwahir fight everyone else, so what other big kingdom is there to patrol here in the east?"

"Khanerenth used to," Kodl said. "Until they got so busy fighting themselves. Half their old fleet is right here, as privateers—three people told us the harbormaster used to be the Admiral of the Royal Fleet. So everyone else out there, if they see something slower, weaker, they turn pirate. And who's to fight 'em?"

Scalis smacked his scrawny chest, snuffling a breathy laugh. "Us!"

"How do we turn into marines, then?" Tau asked.

Niz spoke. "There's two things, ship chase, and then the fight. Us learns the fighting skills." Then he turned Inda's way. "Yes?"

Skills. Inda looked up, feeling for the very first time the urge to tell them where he got those skills, that he was supposed to be a Randael, protecting his home, and not just a killer.

But Leugre would have killed him . . . and become a pirate.

Memory brought Tanrid's voice, the single time they were in Daggers Drawn. *I just hope if you defend Tenthen without me you won't show pirates any mercy.*

He would have fought pirates at home, if they had come again. They wanted him to fight pirates here. Niz called it skill. That wasn't being a killer, was it? He was supposed to do it at home, so why not here?

He pressed his palms over his eyes briefly. *I lost my home. My name. The ship Captain Sindan put me on. All I have left of home is the promise I made . . .*

So he would hold onto the promise. And maybe, just maybe, if he held onto honor—whatever that was—he would somehow be able to go home again.

But first, it seemed, he had to fight pirates.

He dropped his hands and looked up at the waiting faces. "I only saw my first pirates, same as you, when the Pim ships got taken."

"But you watched," Kodl said in an encouraging voice. "What did you observe?"

Inda shrugged again, feeling awkward. "Couldn't see so much, as it was always dark when they attacked. But they seem to go in threes. Come up on either side, grapple to, board."

Niz poked his nose forward in his Delf manner of agreement. "What I heard, it's all that way. So you need speed. It's like this. Merch sailors, us trains while doin'. Practice bending sail on land, no one does it. Fighting, it's nothing you can practice for. See you? They come up fast, tie on, everyone attacks everyone, so how you drill that, except for sittin' in the crosstrees and sendin' fire arrows into their sail? Merches don't know fighting. Our convoy, watched you them? Us has someone trains us better, hire as hands on a big, independent merch. With something to lose. If pirates comin' hull-up, us fights. You trains us, Inda Elgar."

"In staff and archery and sword, maybe." Inda thought ahead, trying to find weaknesses. "But ship maneuvers? I don't know any more than you do about ship warfare."

Niz snorted. "What us needs to know is speed. Get away. If no getaway, they comes, we fight."

Just like what happened to the Pim ships.

"We've been training all along," Tau murmured.

"Yes, but not for—" Inda shook his head. They weren't going to attack anyone. Marines were there for defense.

He'd already figured out that defense of the Pim ship was akin to land warfare on an island. You couldn't get off. Just the same as being driven against a lake or river or ocean at home.

Land warfare to Inda had meant dragoons. Master Gand had told them that they'd learn dragoon skills first, the dragoons being the ones who charged, dismounted, then fought close in, on foot. Cavalry was war on horseback, dragoon was the toughest fighting, because it was both horse and foot.

So he'd begun the training with dragoon skills, though they hadn't known what it was called. He would continue with what he knew, and though it wasn't what the older boys had gotten, maybe they could get fast enough and strong enough to make it work. That meant it needed to be all day. Like the academy.

"I think . . ." he began, again feeling that urge to tell them about dragoons. But that would lead to questions, and more questions, and then he'd break his word.

Dun held his breath, gaze switching from the waiting sailors to Inda, whose young face was so expressive of his inward struggle. He wondered bleakly if Inda would still keep his secrets after all this time, and what it would mean for them both if he talked.

But then Inda looked up, as brisk as when he conducted drill. "What about pirates? I mean, do they all fight alike? Do they have a different style?"

Kodl said, "Most pirates, we were told last night, fight much like the privateers who go after warships. That is, they abide by certain rules once they take a ship. They board, but if you surrender, they stop killing. Set the crew adrift, take the cargo. Some take cargo and ships."

"Privateers attack only the enemy of a kingdom, and pirates attack anything weaker, is that it?" Inda asked.

"Yes," Kodl said, and Niz bobbed his head several times, his Delf nose poking forward. "Then there is the Brotherhood of Blood. They are the worst of all pirates," Kodl added.

Scalis made a spitting motion over his shoulder. "Brotherhood is Norsunder on water, what we called 'em at home. Some think that life a free one. No rules."

"But it's a bad life." Niz made a curious warding gesture, hand up, fingers fluttering. "Bad."

"The Brotherhood," Kodl said, "kill innocent people and take not just their goods but their ships, or burn them just to watch the fire and listen to the screams."

Scalis put in, "Some do it just to swagger about with gold earrings, see everyone scuttle out o' the way."

Kodl continued. "As for fighting ability, what I was told last night by an old captain is that they haven't any order, they're just more savage than anyone. Fighting any of 'em is a skill that seems to be in demand."

Scalis gave a crack of laughter. "We saw ya, boy, when that filthy soul-eater Leugre came after ya with a sword and a grappling hook. And Black Boots and his mates right after."

Tau sat back, again drawing attention from Inda, who had flushed and looked down again at his hands. "What about this Ramis everyone talks of?"

Kodl shook his head. "All I know for certain is everyone is afraid of him. He sails the *Knife*, a fast Venn three-mast warship he took. Venn haven't been able to take it back."

"The Venn?" Tau asked. "Is he a pirate?"

"Some sez yez, some sez no," Niz put in, pointing his thumbs in opposite directions.

"The clearest sved we could get is that he seems to attack Brotherhood," Kodl said. "He was here not long ago, and everyone said we'd have to talk to some fellow named Scubal, but in the next breath they claimed he's a liar and a coward. He was the sole survivor of Captain Ramis' last attack on the leader of the eastern arm of the Brotherhood of Blood."

Scalis snorted. "Why repeat all that shit? Sounded like drunk talk. Or rabbit talk."

"Excuses or stories, apparently this Scubal talked some strange stuff about this Ramis ripping a hole right in the air, and sending the pirates through into blackness. We heard he rode his ship *out* of blackness to attack," Kodl retorted.

"What?" Jeje asked. "Norsunder is a *sea*?"

"I never heard that," Dasta muttered.

Inda said slowly, still looking at his hands, "That first thing, well, you can read it in old records. Norsunder isn't in the world, but we know it still exists. If they rip a hole from beyond the world and pour in, no one can stand against them."

Uneasy glances all around.

"But no one has actually seen this night-rip? Other than the drunk, what's his name?" Zimd asked.

"No," Kodl said. "From what we heard, anyway."

"So let's just forget all that," Scalis muttered, waving his gnarled hands like he was shooing insects. "Moving on to this here Ramis, either he's got mages that do things like that, or he don't, but he's gone, and so's this Scubal, and there's no straight sved, just sailor talk, so let's get on with our plans."

They all looked Inda's way.

Inda flexed his fingers, resisting the urge to touch those blades up his forearms. Sharp and ready. *At home it would have been the Venn, if not pirates. Here it's going to be pirates. Yes, I can do that.*

He looked up and saw Tau watching him, arms crossed, brows raised, and he heard Tau's voice again, *If you think we are worth keeping alive.*

Inda sat up, knowing he'd already decided. It was time to act on it, then. "If I agree, you have to do it my way, or else go your own. Sailors don't know how to shoot. Not really. Longbows in the tops only make sense when you have a huge ship with lots of room. And while most sailors are strong enough to pull the bows, they have no idea how to aim. You can't learn to hit a target, shooting maybe twice a year, or even twice a month. So we have to make cavalry bows, and we all have to learn not only to shoot but to make arrows, and I mean good ones—my kind, fletched in a spiral. And then there's staff and sword work. Knives are a last resort, because that means the enemy is already too close."

Scalis chuckled. "There'll be nothin' like us on east or west waters. Nothin'."

Dun murmured, "It will take time."

Kodl frowned. "Then I say we pool our shares of the take, to last us all the longer. If any leave, they get a portion back and fare-thee-well, but the rest of us ought to train as long as the money lasts."

Again everyone turned Inda's way. He had no idea how long money would last. "All right," he said, because they all seemed to expect it.

Kodl sat back. "Good. That's decided. Make no mistake. We'll be laughed at, first off. If we get hired, it'll be with something small and poor. We have to prove ourselves. Niz knows fast sail, which is different altogether from what we're used to, so he can advise our hiring captains on evasion or attack. And young Elgar here will drill us in defense until we're good."

He looked around. No one spoke.

Kodl said, "Whoever is with me, stay: otherwise, go and I hope your life will be long and profitable."

No one left. Even Testhy stayed, chewing his lip.

Inda, watching him covertly and wondered if he was in contact with Fassun, Faura, and Indutsan. Then he shook his head. He had enough to worry about, with the hands believing him to be some kind of dragoon captain though a dragoon of the sea, not the plains.

Thinking of how long it took to really train people (Gand had been quite fluent about that, back in Inda's scrub days), and about how ignorant he knew he was compared to the horsetails at the academy, much less the masters, he said, "Then we better begin right now."

Inda faced his scrubs: Kodl; Scalis and a cluster of big, brawny forecastlemen; Niz and his two topmen, both Olarans from the Nob; Dun, once a carpenter's mate and now the carpenter for the marines; the mids.

"It will," Inda said, "take at least half a year before you can use a weapon and expect to do anything but lose against an experienced warrior."

Surprise, astonishment, dismay met his words. Disbelief, too. And a few shifty side glances and shuffles.

"So let's get started. Now, here's your stance . . ."

It actually didn't take as long as Inda had feared.

As winter closed in, Inda drilled them all in a little cup meadow up behind Lark Ascendant that no one knew about. They spent mornings in weapons training until their muscles felt like unraveled yarn and their clothing was drenched with sweat despite the snow on the ground.

"Break for midday," Inda called three or four times a week if they'd done well. "But be back at first-bell."

Groans and curses initially met his announcement, until they established a rhythm. Within a month they expected to spend afternoons clambering over a beached schooner in a dried creek bed in the next inlet over the hill from the pleasure house, or running uphill and down.

Inda worked twice as hard. He still thought of himself as just a scrub, and how much could a scrub really know?

Dun could have answered that. He had seen Inda working at daily drill for well over two years, gaining steadily in strength and speed as he grew; Inda saw his own advancement as having stopped when he left Iasca Leror. Mindful of his promise to Sindan, during those years of forecastle drill Dun had taken care to introduce his own Runner training as suggestions, added so gradually that not just Inda but Niz and Scalis had been unaware of how much they had learned.

After practice invariably Inda came to him, no matter how tired he was. "Dun?" he'd say. "Got plans for the evening?"

"No," Dun would always reply.

And so at sunset, while the others retreated to well-earned rest and recreation, Inda and Dun moved to the outer court of the pleasure house, and by the light of the lamps along the rooftop, as music and the noise of revelry spilled out, the frosty air smelling of beeswax candles, perfume, and spiced foods, they sparred for bell after bell.

Dun no longer pretended to make suggestions. During those private sessions they worked with sword, staff, and knife, the close-in knife work that the Runners learned that was not quite like the Odni, but related, being shaped around defense of one's Dal or Edli, and thus adaptable to the confined space of a deck. In turn Inda trained Dun with the Odni, though he never said where he had learned it, and was relieved the man never asked. Dun criticized with fluent precision, and Inda, who wanted to go home as badly as he did, worked all the harder.

He never questioned where Dun's skills came from, never questioned how Dun was able to make—perfectly—the composite bows and the staffs that snap apart and were used exclusively by Marlovan dragoons.

Neither spoke of anything but the work at hand. The two could have been one another's greatest support, for they both longed for what they could not have—Dun for his beloved Hibern, Inda for his home. It would have been so comforting to talk about home.

The only tie they had to the possibility of return was their shared conspiracy of silence.

With the other mids, Inda was somewhat more forthcoming.

"I want to find out more about this Ramis," he said one night when they were all gathered in the mids' back room at Lark Ascendant while a sleeting thunderstorm roared outside. It was a warm room, and they had expensive hot chocolate in hand—all of which was somehow arranged by Tau in ways they couldn't guess, though Zimd was always trying to find out. They lived quite well, even though they were trying to be careful with their money. But then Tau sometimes vanished at night, Zimd insisted upstairs, and would appear at practice looking tired but determined to work.

"Why?" Dasta asked. "Most of it sounds like ale talk."

"And if Ramis is fighting pirates, he's no threat to us."

"Anything to do with Norsunder is a threat," Inda stated. "Norsunder wants power. That means war. He might be taking pirates because they fight hard. What if he wants us for the same reason? We need to find out what we can about him."

No one argued with that.

Zimd chortled, "If there's any real news, I'll find it!"

"So what if there's snow falling outside?" Kodl roared. "If pirates attack under cover of snow—and I would—are we going to ask them to wait until the weather is better? I said, get outside! It's nearly sunrise!"

Kodl, Scalis, and Niz, strong and tough and experienced on the sea, took to the training with the ferocious enthusiasm of those who meant never again to face the fears of their recent journey. Kodl was worried at first that they had too large a force. Aware of the costs of hiring, he knew that a large force could only be considered by captains of capital ships, and those mostly had their own protection. *We will have to be not just good, but the best*, he thought, and every day, no matter when he'd retired the night before, he was the first one awake.

Before the snows came and covered the ground Niz and Kodl were even willing to spend time each day scouring the island for the right feathers, the ones that fletched arrows, and to spend evenings learning how to string a bow, aim and release, arm snapping back in a line from fingertip to fingertip, all in one smooth motion, over and over, though their arms already protested from the morning's weapons' practice.

Scalis and Niz were determined, and Kodl passionate with the peculiar focus of the man with a vision. When the hard snows came at last, and they could not search for fallen feathers, Inda's drill began to mean all day, sometimes wargaming all day and night for two or three days.

Kodl was surprised to see the mids all stick with it, even Testhy, who had hoped to replace the purser's mate in preference to the strenuous outside work. He became the purser of the marines, scrupulously keeping books, and scouting bargains whenever possible when Dun needed more wood and good steel for their weapons; as for his training, he toiled away grimly, never standing out but not falling behind either. Jeje brought to archery the same precision of eye she brought to sailmaking, and she rapidly became the best in the group and stayed that way until one came along who was better. Zimd (who spent most of her free time roaming the King's Saunter and even less savory dens and listening with unending interest to every bit of gossip anyone would tell her) turned out to have an unexpected flair for staff work, being short and strong and very light on her feet. Yan and Dasta showed steady improvement in all areas. Tau excelled. In part because he was naturally strong and quick, but also because he was a close observer—after each lesson, he withdrew somewhere alone, drilling himself until he had mastery of the new lesson.

"We lost another one last night, sir," Testhy said after the second snowfall.

"Who?" Kodl asked, with less interest each time; by the end of First-month seven of Scalis' forecastlemen and one of Niz's topmen had taken their share of their pay and vanished aboard one or other of the ships coming and going.

Kodl reported each loss to his mates, and though Niz snorted with derision and Scalis cursed each fluently for cowards and traitors, Kodl laughed inwardly at his worries about his marine troop being too large a number.

But no more left during Secondmonth, and by Thirdmonth's first day the troop had gained four new recruits.

First came a pair of big, smiling, round-faced young men from Sartor, who'd arrived at Lark Ascendant with pockets full of coin from their first journey. Raised to be bakers, they had run away to sea in search of adventure. After a wild weekend at the Lark Ascendant they were down to their last couple of coins, and wondering what to do. They saw the marines leave early in the morning, weapons in hand, to troop over the hill to the meadow and begin practice.

"Hi! Hey! We join ya?" came the pure Sartoran accent, startling them all.

Everyone looked at Inda, who turned to Kodl. "You can try," Kodl said, and waved back at Inda to take over.

Half a day later both volunteered with enthusiasm. "We do anything," Rig said. Then frowned. "As long it's not hire on as cooks."

Rig, the youngest, was the smart one. Hav, his big, even-tempered older brother, seldom spoke, but he adapted to the training rapidly, exhibiting enormous strength.

Wumma appeared next, brought by Niz. Wumma and the Delf had engaged in a drinking contest the night before, and though few could beat Delfs in that regard, Wumma was one of those few. He was welcomed by Dun as he'd had training in woodworking. He was even faster than Dun at making smooth, straight arrows for their stash. Dun had more than enough work for a mate. Wumma was tall, lean, strong, tough, dark of face and hair with startling pale blue eyes. He hated pirates with the passion of someone with personal experience.

"I heard you be training to fight pirates."

The soft voice was almost inaudible, carried away by the cold winter wind, but Tau's hearing was acute. He lowered his weapon when he saw the tiny, platter-faced Chwahir girl by a scraggly tree, her lank black hair half-hiding her face.

She looked about twelve.

The others also stopped, and Kodl looked pained, calling out, "We don't hire children."

A thin hand pointed at Jeje, who wore her old winter smock to fight in, and then opened toward Inda.

Zimd muttered behind her hand, "I know who that is. Got stranded here by *Windskimmer*. Picked up from a pirate wreck."

And Yan said, almost a whisper, "Her family was destroyed and she was forced on a pirate ship."

Zimd snickered. "So you're the one who's been slipping her extra coins to keep her out of the workhouse. I heard about that. You tell her about us?"

"Everyone knows about us," Tau said in Dock Talk, sparing Yan, who studied the ground. "They all think us crazy."

Kodl snapped his fingers and they fell silent. He faced the girl. "Look, you're just too small, too young."

"You want to die?" Scalis shouted, hoarse, derisive.

She lifted her voice. "I want to fight pirates." That voice, so cold, so quiet, gave them all pause.

Kodl waved to Inda to resume the session. Inda sent a sympathetic glance at the girl, who just stood there, watching, no expression on her round face, and he snapped his staff out and tapped Dasta's.

The girl stood there all day. Next day she was back, and the next. The fourth, Inda said, "At least let her show us what she can do."

Kodl rolled his eyes upward.

The girl did not smile, or frown. She just ran down, held out her hand for Jeje's composite bow and a handful of arrows. Then, with a speed and exquisite precision of form that silenced them all, she sent all six shots squarely into the center of the clout.

"What's your name?" Inda asked, glancing Kodl's way.

Her chin lifted. "Thog. Daughter of Pirog."

Kodl said, "Welcome, Thog, daughter of Pirog."

Jeje said kindly, "You can stay with us, if you don't have a better place."

Flower Day.

In Iasca Leror, the first day of spring was celebrated with the last of the winter's hot spiced wine, with cakes and dancing and song. To the Marlovans spring had meant the year's first war games. In Sartor and Colend, the first day of spring brought out flower boxes and flowered silks; on that day, all distinctions of rank ended, and anyone could flirt with anyone else. And where Sartor and Colend led, the rest of the eastern end of the continent followed.

"Why would anyone here care?" Inda asked, as they met just after dawn on the hillside above their meadow. He looked in some bemusement at Freeport Harbor down below; rails and balconies draped, flower boxes put out overnight, people strolling about dressed in formal fashions of different lands. "Why celebrate? There isn't any rank here. Or any one custom. People do what they want anyway."

Tau laughed. "Why does anyone celebrate anything? It's an excuse to have fun." His brows twitched upward on "fun."

Dasta hunched his bony shoulders and began swinging his sword. "No consequences." His voice had of late taken to growling more than squeaking. Tau had noticed, with private amusement, that Jeje no longer had the lowest voice among their particular group.

Inda hadn't seen any evidence of consequences either, but then he didn't really understand what Tau meant. He was fourteen, busy running drills by day and roaming the docks by night, studying the ships that came in, from round-hulled merchant vessels to narrow-built, rake-masted pirate ships with overlong jib booms with sharpened steel affixed to the end, as were the other boom-ends, to cut up the rigging of their prey. Sometimes, for a coin or two to the mate of the watch, Inda was even able to get on board and climbed the masts, so he could look down, envisioning where one might strike—and where one might repel strikes—and then he'd apply what he'd seen to the drills on their hulk. He was too busy to think, to dream.

Kodl appeared at the top of the rise, and exchanged looks with Scalis and Dun. "There are a couple of contests," Kodl said, "we ought to enter."

"Like?" Tau crossed his arms, the brisk morning air bringing magnificent color out along his cheekbones, his fine-cut lips curled sardonically. Jeje glanced away, down into the harbor, ignoring Zimd's knowing snicker.

"The weapons competitions?" Inda said, looking doubtful. "But the prize is so small, and if any of us get hurt—I've heard how they cheat—then we have to wait for recovery."

"Time," Kodl said, "to measure ourselves against others."

Niz growled. "Cheat fightin' is part o' war on the seas."

Kodl lifted his hands outward, fingers spread. "Let's enter a band for the gold bag run."

They had all heard about this one of the popular entertainments of Freeport Harbor. The biggest ship at anchor was always chosen, or as near the biggest as was willing to trade the trouble of a messy deck for the best anchorage Freeport offered, directly out from the boardwalk. A bag of gold was suspended from the tallest mast; bands of sailors launched in boats from the dock, and the first one to get to the ship, board it, and reach the bag of gold got to keep it. People lined the King's Saunter, the nearest docks, and the windows of the shops on the other side of the Saunter, laying sizable bets, laughing and hooting and cheering as the boat bands attacked each other on the water, and then as they tried to board, and finally when they reached the decks—those who even made it that far. Real weapons were allowed, though there were supposed to be no fights to the death; about the only rule was you couldn't use fire. Damage to the contestants was expected, but no one wanted damage to a ship.

Inda said, "But from what I've heard they don't fight so much as cheat. Throwing pepper. Soaping ropes. Twice I've heard about people killed, just for a stupid bag of gold."

Dun hoped the others didn't hear the aristocrat in Inda's "stupid bag of gold" remark, the boy who'd come from royal rank who never had to think about money.

"It's also a hiring test," Niz said, looking from Kodl to Inda and back again.

Scalis was rubbing his lined cheeks. He added, "We'd be up against some of the toughest privateers. Maybe even that big privateer brigantine down at the south end, if they put up a team."

Everyone paused to consider that. They'd discovered that some privateers were little more than pirates with a scrap of paper claiming legitimacy—a scrap of paper they couldn't always prove was genuine. But these were always escorted in by the harbormaster's ever-watchful fleet, and their captains had to undergo a sweatbox of questions, so gossip along the Saunter said. If permitted to land they were enjoined to obey the rules of Freeport. They had to know that not just Freedom Island's defense—which used to be a royal navy—but everyone in the harbor would go after them if they didn't.

Kodl said, "We'd be watched. And also we need that gold. Testhy says we've about a week left in our pool. Five days, if we drink anything tonight."

Several of the men gasped, two or three looking guilty as everyone looked Testhy's way, and on his nod, back again.

Dun spoke up. "Think of it as a kind of war game."

Kodl said, "And if we win, we might just be able to use it to get us our first hire."

Inda said, "But we're not ready! Not for real warriors."

"No one's ready for war except those makin' it. What we need is experience," Scalis said, making a spitting motion.

Dun watched Inda, sensing the inner debate: the scrambling drills on the hillside and aboard the hulk would take years to match what Inda remembered of Marlovan standards. Meanwhile Inda was still a boy. Did he not understand the real issue here?

Niz said to Inda, "Us can't win against 'em, you mean?"

Inda's expression hardened, eyes narrow, jaw jutting out, a look Anderle-Harskialdna would have recognized from the morning he tried to persuade Inda to submit to public dishonor for something he had not done and that Fassun saw on the first Restday when he threw the stupid scrub out of his bunk just for laughs and ended up flat on his back, a finger's breadth from death. Dun had never seen that look before, and once more he wondered what exactly had happened three years ago, on the far side of the world.

"That's a different question," Inda said. "We can win against anyone here. Whether we be good enough yet to win against pirates out on the sea is . . ." He opened his hands. "Moreso as we don't really know exactly how pirates fight."

Niz just cackled. "Maybe time for practice, yez? No learning like practice, is what us Delfs sez."

Jeje looked troubled, Tau laughed.

Kodl glanced about with a peculiar air, a familiar air, that brought to Inda's mind his first glimpse of Captain Beagar walking his ship on Restday. "Let's make up our band."

And Inda remembered that he was not in command.

Chapter Eighteen

KODL stood on the boardwalk, looking over the competition ship once more, a long, narrow, flush-decked trysail, the bag of gold tied to the top of the mainmast. The ship had been stripped clean fore and aft, and had been anchored at both ends, sails stashed below. It lay alone, stern on toward the boardwalk, which had been built out over the water between two rocky fingers of land, forming a small inner bay.

The competing teams waited along the wall, fingering weapons, some talking and laughing, others exchanging insults, some, like Kodl, studying the ship.

About the only rule the harbormaster's people insisted on was that the launch boats of each team be the same size, or as close as could be managed, oars only, no stepping of masts. Teams could be as large or as small as competitors wished.

Someone blew a horn, and a man on the balcony outside of the harbormaster's office roared, "To the dock!"

The teams scrambled toward the pair of stairs leading to the floating dock directly below, where all the launches had been tied up. As the teams ran, the spectators crowded in behind them, lining the boardwalk, elbowing and shoving as enthusiastically for a good view as the competitors did for position on the stairs. As Kodl fought his way down the dock to their launch the noise rose behind him, spectators howling, cheering, jeering, shouting advice and insults.

Kodl shut them out and flung himself into their launch. The positions had been assigned by drawn lot; they were slightly downwind of the best launch spot, the current against them, but a mild current, near the height of flood tide.

The next boat up had only six people, but all six were huge, brawny, tough-looking privateers bristling with weapons, including suspicious looking bags and ropes, probably pepper to fling in faces, or soap, or honey.

Well, Kodl thought, turning his gaze away, his band had their own pepper, Scalis had one or two suspicious bags of his own, and they had Kodl's bag of weapons at the bottom of the launch, which he was now uncovering and laying at the ready: one long staff, assorted knives, grappling hooks, and rope.

The launch on the other side was crowded with an equally rough-looking gang of over a dozen, its rail just barely clearing the water. Their strategy was obvious, to overwhelm the competition by numbers.

Kodl looked at his band as they set their oars and lifted them, Scalis, Niz, Wumma, and Hav leaning forward to get that heartbeat's extra time. "Remember," he murmured in Iascan, meeting each pair of eyes. In the other launches, others were also talking, except for the crowded one, where half the crew seemed to be drunk, shouting insults and laughing at their own wit. "Stay with your team, don't get separated. You older hands be shields for the mids. Watch me for navigation."

"And you take good care o' my gear, you," Scalis growled, pointing at the grappling hooks and coiled rope at Kodl's feet.

They all agreed, including Inda, who had taken his usual place at bow oar. He had accepted Kodl's commands without a word of opposition, despite half a year's command, despite Kodl following his orders for that half year. Inda had never shown any ambition whatsoever aboard the *Pim Ryala*. He had accepted promotion with the same blank-faced sobriety he had accepted everything aboard the ship, never talking about the future or the past. The night after the foiled mutiny Kodl had lain in the captain's cabin staring at the swinging lamp and thinking back through memory for anything Inda had ever said about his past. Hitherto it had been a subject of no interest; Kodl had noted but not pursued the fact that of all the crew, Inda alone never spoke about his home or previous experiences. Even Yan had let things slip—it was clear he'd been a runaway from the Chwahirsland coast—but as far as Kodl could remember the single inadvertent revelation Inda had made was their very first winter, when they stepped ashore in Sartor, and Inda had gazed at the signs, exclaiming, *Oh! It's the modern script!* He'd then shut up and wouldn't say anything more.

How many knew that Sartor had had another alphabet, utterly different, more than three thousand years ago? Kodl hadn't. Yet apparently Inda not only knew about it, he could *read* it. What kind of background trained for that? Niz said mage, when they discussed it after the mutiny attempt, but they all shook their heads. Inda had never made the smallest spell outside of the everyday magic they all used.

Kodl looked at Inda sitting at the bow oar, bending slightly to listen to Tau. No ambition—but then he was only fourteen.

Har-eeeeeee!

The horn signaled the start, and Kodl yelled, "Pull!"

He was echoed by voices from the other boats and from the spectators along the boardwalk, whose roar sent the few seabirds perched along the roof poles of the harbormaster's buildings flapping skyward, scoldings unheard.

The big launch promptly tried to ram them.

Scalis howled "*Pull* hard! *Ho,* yah! *Ho,* yah!"

Their arms and backs straining, Kodl's marines matched rhythm. The launch shot well past not just the big one (followed by drunken insults and invitations for the cowards to return) but past the three launches on their north side.

They matched speed with two others, one of them a narrow, low riding skiff, captained by a tough looking gray-haired woman who kept up a running stream of comments in a language Kodl did not know; as the launches converged on the stern of the ship, he heard her change her tone, and her crew whirled their oars in a well-drilled move. She yanked hard on the tiller, and Kodl saw that they were using their speed to ram them.

Kodl tried to think of a command—he had not planned for attacks before they reached the ship. But then he saw Inda prod Tau, who rose, grabbing up Scalis' staff from the bottom of the launch. He balanced perfectly, left foot on the rail, right arm cocked back with the staff held like a throwing spear. It *was* a throwing spear, Kodl realized, seeing the long, wicked blade affixed to it.

Tau's pose, the wind fingering his long golden hair in its four-strand sailor's queue, the tight pull of his plain sailor's clothing against what had always been a slim, graceful body and now, after six months of drilling day and night, was as muscular as one of the figures on one of those tapestries you find in really rich nobles' palaces.

"Get 'em Goldenlocks!" The shout, in high, shrill female voices, rose above the clamor on the Saunter.

"Commere, Sweetlips!" crooned the gray-haired captain from the threatening launch. "Come 'n wave your stick at me. Tickle my ribs, and I'll tickle *yours*."

"Ooh, I'm so scared!" a man cried in a high voice.

"Come closer, let's see if your prick is as pretty as the one yer holding—" Another man yelled, amid raucous laughter.

Tau made no move for two, three breaths, and then with a single, powerful thrust he drove the spear not into any of the taunting crew, but straight into their launch, just below the water line. Grinning, he jerked it one way, then the other, and yanked it free. The crew on that side instinctively lunged forward, and the laden boat dipped, water surging over the side as the captain screamed, "Backwater!"

Wallowing dangerously, they fell behind. Two tried to stop the hole first with weapons and then their shirts, the others either paddling or bailing as their captain screamed abuse at them, at Tau, and again at her crew. On the Saunter, above the roar of laughter, a woman shrilled, "Go at 'em, Goldenlocks!"

Bump! They reached the stern of the competition ship just as the other launches did, one on either side. Somewhere behind they heard a roar, a mighty splash, and another shout of laughter echoing off the buildings from the boardwalk watchers as a boat capsized.

Scalis whirled grappling hooks and tossed them up, one, two, three; Kodl sent one fast glance at the other launch to see them doing the same as Inda and the others swarmed up the rope. Kodl was last. Two more boats smashed into their hired launch. Competitors scrambled over it, fighting to get to Scalis' ropes just as Kodl gripped one.

"Climb, climb!" Niz shouted.

Fingers gripped at Kodl's ankles. He kicked free, and a surge of strength sent him fast, hand over hand, up the rope. Then Scalis and Niz pulled sharp boarding blades from their waists and cut the ropes, sending the team swarming behind them howling down to smash into the boats or splash into the sea.

Kodl straightened up. *Have to see, have to see, where is everyone, must see*—and pain sent lightning across his vision. Pain, then blood. He half fell, heard an indrawn breath behind him. Someone was raising a weapon again, and this time his well-drilled muscles took over and he whirled, slamming upward with his short staff, not even remembering when he'd pulled it from its sling at his side. The staff broke the descending stroke and angled right the weapon past to clip his attacker on the side of the jaw, the move automatic, the stroke powerful after all that drill.

The boy—he was hardly older than Tau—stumbled back, clutching at his head with both hands, and fouling the approach of two cursing adversaries, both of them waving swords. Kodl whirled then staggered, his head pounding. He couldn't see. Red, sting. Blood in his eyes. He smelled the sharp stink of sweat, stale wine, brine, the sickening tang of fresh blood, heard thumping on the deck, howling, grunting, cracks and groans and curses and clangs.

I'm in command, I have to— He scrubbed his sleeve across his eyes, and again he was accosted, this time by a pair of women who obviously worked as a team. They rushed him, and he swung the staff until it whistled, catching and tangling their whirling rope ends. He yanked, pulling both of the women off balance; a kick to the side of one's knee sent her into her companion, and both fell, the one screaming, the other rolling up to come at him with a knife.

Niz loomed up behind her, one gnarled hand grabbing her scruff, and with a grunt and a heave he tossed her overboard. She screeched invective all the way down.

Kodl straightened up, scanning the deck, but all he saw was a roiling mass of surging, swinging, screaming, kicking, and punching bodies, some on the shrouds, others trying to bypass those by hurling grappling hooks into the rigging and climbing up. He'd lost them, lost—

There was Inda, poised on one of the shrouds, facing his way, Tau and Dasta below him fending off attackers with enthusiastic swings of staff and rope end.

I can't do it, Kodl realized. His body hurt too much for him to feel any emotional reaction, and he shook his head slightly. Inda flashed three fingers in their hillside drill signal.

Tight threes. Of course! Kodl's original plan was already worthless. But their old war game drill of roving threes, yes!

Niz and Scalis joined him at either side, weapons up, Scalis chuckling hoarsely.

They moved as a unit, smashing their way up to Inda's shrouds as backup; Kodl knew he'd lost command, but this was his first battle. He'd learn it. Now they just had to look good.

Tau and Inda climbed side by side up the starboard shrouds, unhampered for the moment by rivals; Kodl and the two older topmen held the shrouds at deck level against all comers. Inda scanned the deck with speed honed by the war games of childhood, and he spotted those moving with purpose as opposed to those who fought wildly with no direction or plan.

First priority: the two teams of adversaries now taking to the larboard shrouds.

Wumma, Rig, and Zimd caught a boom with the last two of the grappling hooks, and Wumma swarmed up the rope, the other two behind him. Rig brought up his hand and blew a cloud of pepper into the open mouths and eyes of the climbers; Wumma grunted, sent the rope swinging so Zimd could smack down attackers with impartial zeal.

Below, Dun, Hav, and Jeje formed a triad, fighting shoulder to shoulder to keep more competitors from jumping onto the larboard shrouds.

Inda and Tau reached the crosstrees same time as two of the peppered privateers, eyes streaming, through that was not slowing them down. A third appeared, and tossed a glop of something glistening and slimy looking onto the starboard shrouds leading to the topmast, just over Inda's head, where it glistened with a slow moving, oily sheen.

The privateers dashed across the platform, knives upraised. Tau whirled in, a staff in each hand. Inda put his foot on the boom; he'd use the stay line if he couldn't get up the mast the usual way, but then he heard the rhythmic shout from the boardwalk, "Goldenlocks! Goldenlocks!"

Inda paused, and for a moment he did not see Tau, his old companion, he saw what they saw, the tall, slim figure moving with dashing grace, laughing as he fought back two, no, three enemies, holding them all for the moment, though they pressed forward a hand span at a time.

"Goldenlocks!"

Instinct thrust Inda in front of Tau, his own staffs whirling as he grunted over his shoulder, "You go!"

And when he heard the frenzied howls from the spectators as Tau took in the situation, then leaped out and sped, hand over hand, up the stay line to the topmast cross trees and the bag of gold, he knew he'd been right.

Inda was the better fighter—he wounded all three, sending them back into the shrouds—but no one was watching him except from below; another scream rose skyward, a wailing scream of triumph from countless voices as Tau made a spectacular slide down the backstay to the deck, his sleeve ripping to tatters and his arm wealing, the bag of gold clutched in his other upraised hand.

"Are you all right?" Jeje asked Inda later that evening, as the triumphant marines drank, laughed, and sang riotous songs in Lark Ascendant's biggest hired room. "You've got some prime bruises. Want me to get some salve, or steeped willow?"

Inda sat alone at a corner table, an untouched cup of ale between his empty hands.

"I'm all right," he said. The bruises were no worse than he'd gotten during overnight war games when he was a scrub; what hurt most was one shoulder, which he'd wrenched trying to favor his bad wrist.

He turned the ale cup around and around with his fingers. What he had to think out was what he'd learned that day. Not about fighting. He had vastly overestimated the fighting skills of privateers, if that competition was anything to judge by. Of course some of the more raffish, gem-bedecked, swaggering ones had stayed on the boardwalk, drinking, betting, and shouting. But then expensive strut clothes and swagger didn't necessarily equate with fighting skills. All he could be sure of was that they were successful enough that they hadn't needed to exert themselves to win that bag of gold.

But there was something more to think out—and it came back to looks—swagger. Displays of wealth and swagger seemed to be taken as signs of success.

Inda knew his instinct at the very end had been right. It was Tau's dashing looks as much as the band's skill that had resulted in the hire offers they'd received all afternoon since the gold bag run. Tau had been the focus of all eyes on both sides: it was he some of those competitors had aimed for, and it was he the crowd had cheered for. He drew them all, enemies and admirers, and just how close were fighting and, well, the mysteries of desire? To Inda, they both looked the same, though he knew the flame of satisfaction when a war game goes right, and the other one was still just puzzling.

But to talk this matter over with Jeje would bring the hurt look into her eyes that appeared whenever Tau was the subject of discussion, and so he finally said, "If we're really shipping out tomorrow, I need sleep. I hope I can get Kodl to go over the new hire before we leave. If we're attacked as soon as we leave harbor, we're gonna look pretty stupid."

"But we'll be dead, so we won't have to worry about looking bad." Jeje snorted a laugh. "All right. Long's you don't need a healer."

"Naw. Just a scrape on the ribs, looks worse than it feels, and a wrenched shoulder." He flexed his wrist that he had broken so long ago; it had never healed right. Maybe a wrist guard, he decided. Though he wasn't horsetail age . . . oh, yes. Of course. No more academy rules. *Time to get one.*

Zimd appeared at his table, her broad face even broader with a triumphant grin. "Look who I found! I told you," she added, pulling forward an old, scrawny man with a lined face and red-rimmed eyes, and a single earring in one ear. "I promised him you'd buy him some wine," she added meaningfully.

Inda said, "Testhy has my share of the money. Grab a coin from him and order the wine."

"Only if I can hear the good stuff, too."

Inda agreed, Zimd dashed away, and Scubal sank down at the table. He smelled of old clothes, salt, and stale drink. "She said you won't scorf," he muttered.

"Huh?" Inda leaned forward.

Scubal sent an apprehensive glance at the rest of the revelers, his Dock Talk an older version of what Inda had learned, jumbled with Sartoran slang and words from half a dozen other languages. "When I first come, they all scorf. Every 'un. I stop tellin' me story, and ship out, topman, on the *Royal Oak*. I'm never goin' out again, no, not if I have to spend me whole life in the workhouse, makin' rope and blocks and sail."

Inda understood this blatant plea for a donation. He knew the workhouse wasn't a bad setup—it was clean and the food plain but plentiful—but most sailors hated rules and compulsory sobriety, and both were in force there. Residents worked for food and board, but didn't get paid so if they wanted to drink they had to find a way to it elsewhere. "I'll give you what I can. Tell us what happened with Ramis."

A shadow drifted at the edge of his vision, and Tau sat opposite, next to Jeje, looking elegant despite various bruises and cuts, despite his bandaged arm; he'd burned it sliding down the rope.

"I was takin' pris'ner by the *Damnation*, Captain Lum. Head o' the Brotherhood in east waters, and bad, bad, bad. Kill everyone right on deck, if you say no to join, and even then, just for fun, like, if he mislikes your voice, or your face. Or forget to hop quick, when he gives an order. But I'm quick and quiet, see. Those two years is bad. I do my duty in the tops, and try not to see what they's doin' below. Ah, I need me a drink." He shook his head, his earring swinging against his lean cheek. Odd, how gold metal looped through a hole in one's ear added a savage kind of strut to one's appearance; most people, seeing man or woman with such a hoop moved circumspectly out of the way. Even Scubal retained a faint trace of a sinister air, Inda thought, looking at the wizened old man, his strong forearms, his bony back under his thin old shirt ropy with muscle, and wondered what he had done, even if he hadn't wanted to do it, to get that hoop.

Zimd appeared, set down a tray with a wine bottle and four glasses. Scubal grabbed the bottle and took a long pull out of it. When he set it down and wiped his hand across his mouth, no one touched it or the glasses.

"Go on," Inda said, wincing as he pawed awkwardly with his good hand at his aching shoulder.

Tau's eyes narrowed, then he rose and stepped behind Inda. "Straighten your arm out," he murmured, and Inda glanced up, distracted. "That shoulder. Let me try some of my mother's trickery. Why waste years of enforced training?"

Inda smiled, obediently stretched out his arm along the table, but turned back to Scubal. "Go on," he said, and then he grunted in pain as Tau's long fingers dug into his shoulder just beside the wing bone.

"So one night, end o' last winter. Two days' sail out of Freeport. Lum's formin' a fleet, see. Four sail. Comin' to take Freeport. But I looks up into the direction of the wind, blowin' out of the northeast, and see the sky black from there to there." He pointed up, then down. "It's night, but this is blacker, no stars, and they all see it too, not just me. And suddenly we see this Venn warship come sailin' out, square sails, studding sails, jibs'ls, all black, with lamps high and low, all alight. Single ship, see, but he comes out right in the middle, out of nowhere, because then when I look the stars is back."

"Clear night? No fog?" Tau asked, over Inda's head.

Inda had begun breathing somewhat harshly, his eyes half-closed. Jeje tried not to look at his face, tried not to imagine what those long hands would feel like on her flesh.

"Clear as glass. No fog. I tell you there's a rip in the world." Scubal's voice rose to a whine, and Inda motioned with his free hand for Tau to be quiet. Scubal gave them all shifty glances, drank again, and when no one had said anything more he went on. "So they tack about, fastest I ever see, and swing out cut booms more vicious than ours, and take the shrouding down on the weather side o' the *Soultaker*, our consort. They lose all three masts, one after t'other, and they lose way, no steering, see, so they ram up tight against *Glory*, and I see nothin' o' what happened. The bosun swearin' he sees that Ramis wearin' an eyepatch. One side of his face all burned. Standin' at the prow o' the *Knife*. Stretch out his hand, and comes this green light, and then the sails on *Abrin*, our fourth, breaks out in flame."

Tau whistled softly. Jeje felt the sound go through her like someone had drawn a string of fire through all her veins.

Scubal drank again, drew an uneasy breath, then said, "So then he comes after us. Lum roarin' orders. No good. *Knife* closes with us, keepin' the weather-side, and then boards, fighting real silent. Real good, all together-like, not like pirates where they just go in roarin' and do what they want."

When he paused for a drink, Inda let out a long sigh of relief; all of a sudden the massaging had ceased to hurt, and felt good. His shoulder no longer ached, and Tau lifted his hands and moved back to his chair. He sat, giving Inda a meaningful glance in Scubal's direction: their first real word on pirate fighting tactics, if the man was to be believed.

"Ramis' crew kill half the *Damnation*'s crew before Lum's surrender. I'm in the tops, hidin'. Lum's on deck, first threats then pleading, when this Ramis come on the captain's deck, and he just shakes his head, holds out his sword, a real old style. Black steel. Three strokes it takes,

and Lum, long a fighter, he took the *Damnation* by fightin' its old captain, and they say he killed fifty men in duels and the like before he
turned twenty. Three strokes, and Lum's dead. You can't see that sword
move, I tell you. Then they drive all the pirates down into the hold, and
I think, what I do now, he looks up. The fire on *Abrin* spread to *Glory*,
make all this light, see, and I see him clear as glass, patch, purple all
down here." He touched his temple down to his jaw. "He says, 'Come
down, Scubal'."

Zimd gasped. Jeje frowned, more aware of Tau's breathing than she
was of the story. She was stiff and achy too, yet Tau did not offer her any
massage.

Tau said, "So this Ramis knew your name." The tilt of his head was
one of polite inquiry.

"He do, he do! It be true sved!"

"Someone told him," Zimd said, shrugging.

"I know nothin'. Just says me name. Then he says to me—in me home
language, I haven't heard in years—'You were never here by choice, and
if you foreswear piracy, you may live.' I comes down, and swear it's true,
I'm cryin' like a baby, I admit it, and then he takes me arm, and I feel
like he's gutting me, only I blink and I be standin' on Freeport shore, just
like that."

"Transport magic? He's a mage, then?" Inda asked.

"All I know is what I seen. Then that rip come again, and the other
ships, *Glory* and *Abrin* still on fire, sail in the blackness, and be gone.
Like that." He snapped dry, wrinkled fingers. "So then I tell people what
happen, no one believes me. I ship out on the *Royal Oak*, free trader,
but when she, Captain Gannis, I mean, is takin' this big prince sort of
yacht, probably full of goods, I'm sweatin' and beggin'. Tell her what
that Ramis say. She says they always use privateer rules even if everyone else be turning pirate now't there be no law. But after half a year,
every night I'm afeard to see that rip in the sky again, and so when she
docks here yesterday I jumps ship, though it means only half-pay, and
little enough o' that."

He drank the last of the bottle, swayed in his seat. It was clear enough
why he'd had little pay left on the *Royal Oak*'s books.

Inda said, "Thank you. I'll go find some coins, like I promised." He got
up and walked away.

Scubal squinted after him then got up too, afraid he would be abandoned. Zimd went with him, asking questions in a low voice.

Leaving Tau and Jeje alone at the little table. Tau said, "Quite a story,
eh? Do you believe it?"

Jeje's throat was dry. She wished she had the courage to ask for a
massage, but that wasn't what she really wanted, and she was afraid he
knew it, and would scorn her. No, he would never do that. But he would
stiffen and withdraw, just like he had to Norsh and Faura and all the
others who had wanted him. "Um," she said witlessly.

Tau smiled at her. "I'll go see if Inda needs a hand."

She watched him go, then rose herself. Tears blurred her vision, and
so she eased along the perimeter of the room, hoping not to be noticed.
She did not see Tau slip to the front room and hold a quick exchange
with the proprietor, she just was glad when she finally made it to the
door, and started down the hall toward their chamber in the back.

Where she stopped, looking up in surprise at the bountiful figure of
the proprietor, Mistress Lind, standing there right in the hallway.

"Come along, my dear," the woman said, and Jeje followed her exquisitely draped silken skirts. Upstairs, past the hired halls, to the quieter landing above, where she had never been, though she knew (and
had tried not to know) that Tau had begun obliging the mistress—or
himself. She tried not to know because she was jealous of the unknown
people who chose his custom, who thus could touch him, hold him, and
be held in turn and if she thought she could buy his custom she would,
but she knew he would refuse; that if she offered to buy what he did
not want to share for free, she would forever lose his friendship.

The woman said, "You people are good for business, and I suspect are
going to be better. Turnabout is fair trade."

Jeje just stared at her as she opened a door.

"This is Tivonais," the mistress said, indicating a young man who
waited in a pleasantly furnished room: table, chairs, a couch. A bed. "His
art is with first timers."

Tivonais. A house name, Jeje realized, secretly relieved. A house
name, putting them on anonymous footing, the fantasy image being that
famous Sartoran Prince Tivonais of historical times whose reputation
had supposedly sent half the females in Sartor running and half seeking
him.

Jeje darted a single look at the young man, who was of medium height, pleasing enough of person, dressed only in trousers and a loose shirt. He smelled clean, as if he rinsed his hair in herbs; she realized she'd left her share of today's winnings downstairs, tied into a corner of her extra shirt. "I–I—"

Tivonais shook his head, grinning. "Mistress Lind says your crew has brought us enough custom. And young Goldenlocks will bring 'em again when you return."

He took her hand, and drew her in, and shut the door. Fear and anticipation fluttered inside her, like moths frantic to find the flame inside the lantern. He led her to a chair, and she plumped down onto it. "Mistress Lind wants your mates happy, too. Starting with you."

"I–um, er—" she began, as he deftly began undoing her short braid, massaging her tight scalp, her rigid neck.

A soft kiss pressed just behind her ear. "If Goldenlocks ever does notice you, why not give him something to remember you by?" was the laughing question, in a warm, breathy whisper that made her arms tingle with gooseflesh.

The questions winked out, just like those inward moths, burned in the flames of pleasure.

Chapter Nineteen

THE next morning Kodl took Inda to meet their new captain and tour the ship while the marines assembled their gear and Testhy paid off their lodgings. They pulled up anchor the following day, and began their first cruise, which turned out to be uneventful except for fierce weather; they spent two months as badly needed extra hands, beating against both wind and current until they finally reached Sartor. That journey gave them the chance to drill on board a real ship.

Their second journey was even more eventful, though for weather alone. A series of bad storms dismasted the ship not once but twice, and again they served as hands, limping back after nearly half a year to Freeport a few days before New Year's Week, not having fought a single battle, but having had plenty of time to drill and to work on Niz's ideas on evasive tactics in managing sail. Inda sat in the tops with him, whatever the weather, absorbing the wily Delf's knowledge.

The morning they landed, they settled in at their usual lodgings. Kodl threw his bag into the small upstairs chamber he'd come to think of as his and ran downstairs, telling Scalis (who was putting on his best shirt before heading up to the pleasure house) that he was going to stroll the boardwalk to catch up on news and scout for possible hires.

At the Lark Ascendant, Inda chucked his gear into the back room he still shared with Dasta and Jeje, then said abruptly to the others, "I'm going to see what the weather did to our meadow. Map out some new drills."

Inda had already made up new tactical ideas, adapting drills to support them, on the voyage in. Now he just wanted to be alone, for the first time in months. It was almost New Year's, his Name Day had again passed without him noticing it, but again there was no family to celebrate it with. The urge to get up, keep busy, practice his Odni routine at full strength now that he was not confined to the heaving deck of someone else's ship pulled at him, and he knew it for what it was: the only way he could escape the memories that still hurt when they came in dreams.

So he sat on a rock gazing westward and let them come. First Tdor. Then Sponge. And Tanrid, Joret, his parents, the other Tveis—he could still remember exactly which bunk everyone slept in . . .

And in Iasca Leror it was still night.

Camped on the border of Choraed Elgaer, the Sierlaef sat brooding in his tent.

On the cold night air the sudden and discordant clangor of bells echoed over the distant hills, followed by the screech of whistler arrows. Trouble! On the border of Choraed Elgaer! The Sierlaef's first reaction was fierce joy.

His camp was already rising, some of them groggy from the long day's ride and half a bell's sleep, but he strode among them, kicking those who didn't move fast enough, and snapping his fingers as he pointed to the southwest.

Three more signal arrows whistled, one on fire, a glowing red pinpoint against the sky.

"Attack!" he shouted. "Rescue!"

Buck took over, issuing a stream of orders that really didn't need to be spoken, but his curses and buffets prompted haste. The camp divided, armsmen left to bring the tired horses of the day before, perforce now remounts. The royal heir, the remaining Sier-Danas, and the rest of the armsmen took the fresh animals, stringing bows as they rode.

The half moon rode low over the distant hills, the sky brilliant with stars, all shining enough light to canter by.

Orange light glowed ahead. Fire! Though there was no road he gave the sign for a gallop, already feeling the sweet fire of Joret's reaction when he rode into Tenthen as the rescuer, just as his father's own men had been thirty years ago.

That inner vision spread its warmth through him as the fire spread in the distance, becoming doused, as the fire was doused, when they topped the hills. His signalers winded their horns as they clattered into the riverside village and saw the burning boat and half-burned houses, the dead men in the village square, and heard, rising on the cold air, the triumphant yips—academy yips—that meant Tanrid Algara-Vayir had no need of rescue.

The villagers who were not involved in bucket brigades stared at the Marlovans who rode into the village in strict formation, but the Sierlaef ignored them. His attention was all for Tanrid, who'd won; he'd been too late.

"What happened?" Cassad called. "Looks like we're after the fun, but I assure you, we ripped out of camp fast enough."

He laughed, and Tanrid, surveying them in the torchlight, at first just saw tired faces. Buck yawned, and Hawkeye Yvana-Vayir looked disgruntled, but the Sierlaef's white-lipped rage acted on Tanrid like a dunking in a winter stream.

He turned away, fighting against his own fatigue; it had only been the day before that the heir had finally released him to go home and prepare for the royal visit. They hadn't even been to bed yet when the villagers rang the alarm bells.

"It's nothing much," he said. "Just some pirates, who the people tell me have been getting a lot worse since the Venn cut us off." He indicated the dead or captured pirates, some of whom reeked of drink on the cold, still air. "I think they were raiding upriver, decided to stop here for a bit of diversion, just after we arrived. We thought there were more of them, which is why we used the signal arrows, but if there were, t'others slunk off and missed the entertainment."

Tlen gave a crack of laughter.

Tanrid turned to the Sierlaef. "Shall I ride on home?"

The Sierlaef was still furious. "Camp," he said, looking at the drooping animals. "Horses."

His horses were tired, but the Algara-Vayir mounts hadn't even been used. No one gainsaid him, of course. They set about making camp and

Tanrid kept his distance from the tense heir, knowing quite well what the problem was: Joret.

As he stretched out in his bedroll, Tanrid thought of Joret. Yes, she was now full grown, and yes, it had been a year, and yes, she was beautiful, probably the most beautiful of all the girls he'd ever seen. Beautiful, loyal, smart, and cold as that moon up there.

Your visit, he thought grimly, watching the Sierlaef's yellow head across the campfire, *is not going to bring what you think.*

The Sierlaef brooded all the way to Tenthen, refusing to let Tanrid ride ahead. It had been difficult enough the first time. He couldn't bear the thought of Tanrid being there with Joret first, maybe being permitted into her bed as celebration for thumping a few pirates. It didn't matter that that was her right, and his, according to law and custom—his uncle always got around law and custom both when he wanted. The Sierlaef believed it was the future king's right to find a way to do the same.

They all rode together until they reached the company of green-and-silver Riders on their unending patrol of the outskirts of Choraed Elgaer.

And so he had to see their excitement, their joy, their pride, when the armsmen retold the stupid little raid and rescue. And at the celebration on the night of their arrival at the castle he was forced to listen to the Algara-Vayir heralds sing hastily composed songs about Tanrid's prowess.

A celebration endurable only because *she* was there. An entire year he had waited, touring the entire kingdom, thinking about her, dreaming about her. And now she was here. In the same room. At first he could scarcely bring himself to look at her, yet all he could think about was her end of the table, listening for the rare words she spoke, and once he was certain he heard her breathing.

She was breathing hard because she saw Aunt Joret's ghost again, walking down the middle of the hall during a song, her blue eyes gazing above the royal heir's head as Tanrid offered the Sierlaef the toast of honor.

Stranger still was Jarend-Adaluin's stark, unblinking gaze tracking the floating progress of Aunt Joret's form until she drifted to the hearth, outlined for a single heartbeat in fire, then vanished. No one else saw it—they all smiled, lifting their glasses together in salute to the king's heir.

When the meal was half over the Sierlaef began to sneak peeks at Joret. Any more than just a brief glimpse and his face heated up, his body kindled into flame, and his hands trembled so he could scarcely hold his eating knife. But several gulps of wine, and the fact that he never once caught her gaze, enabled him to lengthen the glimpses into longer looks, sweet and dangerous as they were: it was all very well to think about flouting custom while in the saddle far from anyone, but he knew what his father would say if he broke custom while a guest in the Adaluin's castle. Because custom was quite clear: it was for the host or hostess to favor or refuse your company if you wanted to dally.

And he didn't want just to dally. He wanted . . . he wanted . . .

Drinking off his wine, he stared hungrily at her. She sat very still. She did not gaze at Tanrid, or whisper to him, or take his hand, for both hers remained above the table. She did not act, in other words, like someone who has been longing for the company of a lover for over a year.

By the end of the meal the Sierlaef had regained his equilibrium, and had even begun to hope that the chase was done, and he just had to find her alone. And so he retired in a far better mood.

He had no idea how many people had observed those hungry glances Joret's way.

In the royal castle Sponge finished another session with Hadand and then raced upstairs to check over his gear for New Year's Convocation. Some of the other Tveis—still pigtails though, like him, some had reached seventeen—were coming to demonstrate riding exercises during the Fourthday Games. He checked his own gear because he still did not have a personal Runner—nor did he want one. There were enough spies in the castle reporting to his uncle without his accepting one attached to him personally. The thought was sickening.

The sight of his academy gear cast his troubled mind ahead to spring. On the surface it seemed he'd return to another good year at the academy, an even better year, surrounded by friends, granted more freedom, and more interesting training: this year, for instance, they would be given battle problems for the first time, the solutions to be drawn out on paper. But it was that freedom, and those friends, that also troubled him. He could not endure the possibility of losing either of them.

If you do nothing that the others do not do, then there is nothing to worry about, is there?

At the north end of the castle, down in the queen's barracks, Tdor did not spare New Year's a thought.

She was entirely preoccupied with Shen Montredavan-An, on whose Name Day last year—this very week—had proved that she was not as frivolous as she led the world to believe.

Last year Tdor had gone to their bunks, having seen a Runner in Montredavan-An black and gold passing through the stable where she was working. She expected to find a happy Shen surrounded with little gifts and what was always more welcome, letters.

Instead she found Shen face up on her bunk. Not weeping, no. That would have been easier, somehow. But that rigid body and compressed breathing, the blanched face, the tearless eyes staring upward, eyelids tight with just barely controlled anguish, had sent Tdor tiptoeing right out again.

It was through Hadand that she discovered that the news that Shen's beloved brother Savarend, who had been making sporadic cruises at sea from a young age, had been aboard the *Cassad*, and her Name Day, by cruel coincidence, was the anniversary of the day she'd found out about its destruction six months after the attack. Tdor had realized, with silent compassion, that Shen, who professed not to believe in hope or justice, had silently passed the intervening years waiting for news that Savarend had survived, just as Ndara-Harandviar silently hoped that Barend might yet turn up alive.

Apparently this anniversary she had decided it had been too long to wait.

Now, a year later, Shen's Name Day was again here. Tdor—again having been assigned early morning stable duty—was braced to see that same unhappiness. She approached their bunk bed, her tread soft in case she must vanish again.

Instead she found Shen sitting on her bunk, smiling a very strange smile, a characteristic one, wide, with the corners quirked tight. In anyone else it would be a sarcastic smile, but in her somehow it was merry, an inward sort of laughter that reminded Tdor again how little Shen actually revealed of herself. Remarkable in one who talked so much.

She was fixing a bulky pouch to her belt, looked up, and dropped her hands to her knees. "Oh, there you are."

Tdor hesitated, not sure what to say.

Shen gave a soft laugh. "No, our Runner isn't here yet, and yes, we'll make merry later. I only had one brother to lose, and I've finally accepted that he's dead. So there is nothing to fear." And before Tdor could fumble out something sympathetic, Shen tipped her head. "Your Name Day is in a month or two. Do you want a coming-of-age fete?"

Shen's asking now meant she must have somehow known that Tdor had had to use the Waste Spell three times now for monthly courses. Tdor wondered what about her had changed, since she was still as flat in front as she'd been at ten, and the rest of her seemed more or less the same as she'd always been.

Her face burned. "I think I want to wait until I return to Tenthen." She knew that many girls did that, celebrated their coming of age at home.

Shendan opened a hand, and the subject dropped. Obviously Tdor wasn't in any hurry to sample the delights of the pleasure houses; Shen, like some, went every chance she could get.

Shen turned thumb toward the door. "Then let's get to mess and eat fast. We'll want to get right to our break-in."

Tdor sighed, relieved to have the personal questions over with. "I was just grumping to myself about it. You'd think at least the snowstorm could have waited a day. But no, we get all that mess to slog through—leaving huge tracks—and a clear sky, to assure we'll be spotted even by girls half asleep. We'll be caught before midday."

Shen's smile deepened at the corners. "Oh, we'll get in."

"We will?"

Shen laughed without making a sound. "This place is rife with hidey-holes. The Venn will never be the ones to find 'em."

Tdor asked, "Is that why you volunteered to lead? I mean, you never have before."

Shen gave another of those smiles. "Do you think it would be universally welcome, a Montredavan-An wanting to lead?" She left without waiting for an answer.

Tdor opened her mouth, and then shut it. Once Tdor had seen a brief look exchanged between Shen and Marend Jaya-Vayir—who had been Savarend's intended—when the fox banner was seen streaming past at the head of a riding of horsetails, and Tdor remembered that that had once been the Montredavan-An banner, carried by the heirs.

She flushed, though Shen's words had in no way been directed at her as accusation. *I keep thinking I'm the only observant one,* Tdor thought as the two raced through the halls to the mess hall for a hasty breakfast. *Maybe I'm like the girl in the old song, counting acorns on the ground and not seeing the crows in the air flying from the coming storm.*

The defending ridings were already at the archery court. The rules were that the riding assigned to break in had half a bell to get out and in place before the defenders were released to start guarding.

Shen and Tdor gathered their riding and Shen led them past the older stables, past the outer wall, over the old road that was slushy from countless feet and hooves even at dawn, to the fields just south of the half-frozen river.

"All right, girls," she said with breezy cheer, her breath clouding as she handed out strips of cloth from her belt pouch. "This exercise is going to benefit us as well as the other girls. I am going to tie these on personally, and I will lead by voice. You, in turn, are to use all your other senses but sight, and after our win, we will compare notes on how much you observed of our route."

"After our win." No one had won a break-in since last year, and that had been by a superb ruse, led by Hadand herself. She'd set the older girls in an uproar, for apparently quite a number of bets had been laid. It had also been her last training exercise with the girls before she moved to training with the Queen's Guard.

It was thus in an atmosphere of intense anticipation that the girls stood in a row, holding hands as Shendan tied on the strips of cloth, checking each one to make certain that no sliver of light penetrated. Each girl felt the visible world shut out, her head bound tightly, the sensation intensifying the helpless feeling. Hearing sharpened, smell, and touch, though in that they were limited by having to hold hands. Strange! Shen's plan was so strange, but it did sound fun, especially if they managed to win.

Tdor stood last in line, waiting for hers, but Shen shook her head, and indicated for Tdor to pocket the cloth and take the last girl's hand. Then they began to walk, in a slow, snaking line. Tdor, closing her eyes briefly, realized she would have thought they were going straight when they actually veered from the road over to the rocky outcrop in the river where the falls would be in spring.

Then they stood, and Shen said, "Hands down. Now, listen hard. Here's the first exercise, just for us. It's midnight, and foggy, and the enemy is coming, but we can't see them. How will we sense them? Count up how many things you detect, and remember them for tomorrow."

Then Shen pulled a broom from behind some rocks, where it had obviously been placed to await them, and handed it to Tdor. Shen motioned to the snow up to the road, and Tdor at once moved away, smoothing out their tracks.

When she caught up with the group, it was to find a hole gaping in the rocks behind where the fall would be. How had Shen found *that*? Inside was a tunnel lit by glowglobes!

"Form hands," Shen said. "Now we're the enemy in the fog, finding our way. Again, listen, smell." As she spoke she took the broom, then motioned for Tdor to gather snow in a shallow bucket that was also waiting.

The girls were led into the tunnel, and from time to time Shen fanned the girls with a Colendi court fan that she pulled from her pouch—a strange, rare sight indeed—and then she dripped snow on them, just as snow might drift down from a roof in a light wind. Three or four times Shen brought from her pockets various pods and spices, and dusted the air with them.

Tdor realized at last what Shen was doing: she had no intention of the girls discovering they had been inside a tunnel. That meant the tunnel was secret—a secret of the royal castle known by a girl who had not grown up there.

Tdor set aside her conflicted feelings for later consideration and watched the girls register the smells, the snow, and several times the sound of water dripping, and once rushing by in an underground stream—all commented on by Shen in a misleading way, to make them believe they were aboveground.

No one spoke except for Shen as they made their way steadily but gradually down, twice making sharp turns, and finally up, up, up.

The tunnel appeared to be very old. Moss covered walls, and there were a number of branches. It gave Tdor a strange feeling to know that it lay under the city, yet she had never heard of it, not even from Hadand. She wondered if Hadand knew about it, and how old it was.

Shen's thoughts ran in a stream: the girls, Tdor's blank surprise and then speculation, the timelessness of tunnels, and what, really, is time, anyway? *Is it truly imposed on us, or do we impose on it?*

Up, up, and again a stop, near water, then forward, through a wooden door that turned out to enter one of the old storerooms behind the kitchens. Shen led the girls through, and Tdor watched triumphant smiles crease the girls' faces as they each registered the familiar cabbage and braised chicken and bread smells of the castle kitchens. "Bindings off."

The girls obeyed.

"We're in the kitchens," said Ondran Stalgoreth, looking around in wonder. "How did we *do* that?"

Shen grinned as, for a short time all the girls talked at once, each convinced she knew the route through the castle grounds that they had taken naming the two canals, and several buildings that had distinctive smells, not realizing those smells had been evoked by dust.

Finally Shen said, "We'll talk over your observations tomorrow. Now we have to capture as many as we can before they discover we breached the defenses. I suggest we capture riding leaders, for it shows far more finesse. Tdor and I," she added, "are going for Mudface."

The girls all smiled. Tdor was certain no one actually liked arrogant, mean Dannor Tya-Vayir, sister of Horsebutt, who had gotten her nickname after she'd done something exceptionally vicious when small, vicious enough to cause the austere Jarlan of Yvana-Vayir, once a princess, to take her by the scruff of the neck down to the kitchen garden and scrub her face in the mud. Friends she did not have—and she made it clear how much she despised any girls below her rank—but she did have followers who obviously wanted her influence, for she came from one extremely powerful family and was marrying into another.

It was either influence or something else that had gotten her leave to stay an extra year or two here in the royal city, when by rights she should have gone home for good long ago. But she was bored at Yvana-Vayir and liked the excitement of the city, so she was here, ostensibly as an auxiliary tutor. Hadand had said to Tdor, *I suspect the Yvana-Vayirs are hoping she'll learn a little civility while they're rid of her.*

Shen nodded. "Now, in the interests of making ourselves look as good as possible, let's divide up. We'll be that much faster." She assigned girls to the city and the outer buildings of the castle, reserving the residence portion for herself and Tdor. Everyone agreed—they all knew quite well that Mudface would consider it beneath her to patrol any area outside of the royal living area—and dispersed.

Shen said, "Let's get rid of Mudface first."

Tdor realized then that Shen's brisk hurry all was to a purpose, one that lay outside of the game.

"Shen?"

The curly blond head turned, though Shen did not slow her pace as they bustled through the old storage hallways. "Maybe it's a cheat to use a tunnel, though I don't care. I will never have to defend this castle, so it's no matter to me." She laughed softly. "And yes, I knew about the tunnel. And now so do you."

Yes, and if I ever break confidence and tell someone, you'd find out, Tdor thought, feeling unsettled. Shen had obviously thought of everything. She'd also waited, with amazing patience, for the right time to use that tunnel.

Their capture was absurdly easy to make. The two sneaked up the servants' passageways and surprised Mudface, who was indeed dawdling outside the queen's suite. They bound and gagged her, and left her, furiously glaring, sitting just inside the despised servants' entrance, where she'd be sure to be overlooked, most scrupulously and correctly— servants never interfered in the games, unless, of course, bribed—until Shen's triumphant band sent someone for her.

"Now," Shen said, laughing as she shut the door, her chin high, her eyes wide with more real emotion than Tdor had ever seen in her. "Now we meet the future."

Shen was not aware of sounding portentous. She was aware only of her heartbeat, faster than the drums for a charge. *Time,* she thought. *It is mutable. When you love something enough time races ahead like the wind chasing autumn leaves, sending them skipping and dancing out of reach, no matter how fast you run. But when you want something and must wait to get it, time stops.*

Now the time had come for both love and want. She couldn't walk fast enough, though she tried, despite the trembling in her knees and hands. Her mind reached ahead to the archive room where she knew

Hadand waited, her body working as hard as it could to close the distance.

Still, training was training: she noted Ndara-Harandviar's own guardswomen at key intersections, and no one else about, for the king was busy in council below.

Tdor, meanwhile, trotted alongside Shen, thinking: *Meet the future? What does that mean?*

For a horrible moment she felt a little like she had the day she'd swum in the river in late spring, when the water was moving fast, and she'd stepped out confidently, remembering the shelf from the summer before, just to find herself underwater, struggling against the cold, fast current as she fought for grip or ground.

Shen paused outside the archive door. Tdor waited for her to open it. Instead Shendan leaned her forehead against the door, her braids falling forward, half-hiding her face, her hand still on the latch.

Tdor pressed her knuckles against her lips.

Shen whispered, so softly her voice was scarcely audible, "If Foxy is truly dead, then it is *my* son your daughter will marry. And their daughter might go to Sartor to study magic."

Shen fought to still the trembling in her wrists as she thought of the future while Tdor stood there thinking not about magic, but about Shen. *She calls her brother Foxy.*

And Tdor thought once again of those Montredavan-An runners in black and gold and the fox banner that the academy carried, belonging once to the Montredavan-An heirs.

Chapter Twenty

THE door opened, and Hadand looked relieved. Tdor realized that Hadand had arranged this interview, whatever it was, to occur while the game was going on.

In fact, Ndara-Harandviar's own women were on guard. That meant neither king, queen, nor Shield Arm knew about it.

Hadand said in Sartoran, "This is Mistress Resvaes of Sartor's Mage Guild."

Tdor's mouth opened when she saw the old woman in the strange gown sitting there in the best chair. Both girls bobbed awkwardly; Queen Wisthia had taught them all curtseys when they served in her rooms, so they knew it for an outland sign of respect, though it felt peculiar.

"Come. Sit down," Mistress Resvaes said, indicating the chairs around her. Tdor obeyed, distracted by the green-edged linen robe the woman wore, how soft the fabric looked, how well it was made. "I come in response to a letter of invitation brought to me by an influential member of the Sartoran Royal Court, on behalf of the Duchess—what do you say—the *Jarlan* of Cassad, and on behalf of her sister, who is, I understand, a princess of . . ."

"Choraed Elgaer," Tdor whispered.

"Ah! Yes, thank you. And you are . . .?"

Shendan's smile was practiced, her eyes appraising. Tdor's smile was the quick, inadvertent smile of one caught by delight: that Sartoran accent was the real thing, and how beautiful it seemed! Not at all like the labored enunciation of their tutor at Tenthen, and yet Tdor could hear at last what the poor woman had tried so hard to teach them.

Tdor spoke, glumly conscious of her inharmonious Iascan accent: "I am Tdor Marth-Davan."

"I am Shendan Montredavan-An," Shen said, in a fair copy of Resvaes' own accent.

"The Mage Council has been told that you have been trying to collect rare and ancient scrolls, mainly historical. You want ones that concern magic. We wish to know to what use you intend to put these scrolls, should we release copies."

Shen worked to hide the elation caused by this woman's presence; her mother had warned her it might be generations before they would get a hearing with so august a visitor.

Mistress Resvaes watched their reactions: Tdor's interest, Hadand's sobriety, Shen's triumph.

She had been sent against her will to visit this rapidly expanding empire, a return of a favor owed to a well-respected Sartoran noblewoman who was sister to this Princess of Choraed Elgaer. What the noblewoman, and the sister, would not find out was that she came to observe and question with an eye to warding this empire of warriors, if necessary.

"The study of magic use in history," Shendan said.

Hadand looked at Shen's wide, unblinking gaze, the tips of her teeth showing in her smile, and instinctively tried to draw the visitor's attention from the passion so plain to see there. "We study history. Our interest is in the far, far past. We know that women used to control magic, largely. That's why there are spells for waste, and why there is the Birth Spell, and the spell that makes our wombs unable to conceive a child unless we take the herb gerda, though we know that women alone didn't make that magic. There are, or were, some sort of beings that gave them the magic in the first place, who also made that magic."

"Because we couldn't," Mistress Resvaes said, her pleasant manner giving no hint to how closely she watched Hadand's anxious care in choosing words, Shen's hunger that she could not mask, and Tdor—obviously a girl with a good heart—who seemed not to question the Marlovan view of the world.

She said slowly, "Not even with the skills vouchsafed to us then. And as you probably know, those were far superior to what we know now. We lost so much in the Fall, knowledge and skills we might never recover. But you know that, too."

"All the old ballads attest to it," Shen said, chuckling.

"They do. Go on."

Hadand winced inside, sensing that this woman knew very well what they really wanted: access to magic. But she said, "We've learned that women were the first to get magic in coming here from some other world. And besides the other changes I mentioned, women were able to effect changes like eradicating terrible sicknesses."

They also killed, Mistress Resvaes thought. *They killed sexual predators until that instinct was eliminated from humankind, because they knew if they didn't, these "beings" you so blithely referred to were going to destroy us all, down to the oldest grandmother and newest born child. They tried to kill off the instinct for war, and maybe would have succeeded, but for one foremother's taste for yet more power, inviting in what became Norsunder's Host of Lords. But you are not going to find out any of that until I know a lot more about you.*

"We just want to understand how we are what we are. We don't even know if those beings hinted at in the old records were wiped out by magic too, if they even still live."

We don't know that either. Or what that means.

Shendan said, "It is very difficult for us to get older works that we can trust, and that we can comprehend."

Hadand said, "We know we have only pieces of what has shaped our lives. Fareas-Iofre, my mother, is a descendant of Lineas Cassad, as well as the Princess of Choraed Elgaer." Hadand waited until she saw an encouraging nod. "Well, she told us we have only a leg of the table, and though we study its carving, and even its grain, we still are only speculating about the rest of the table, and the other legs."

"True. So let's discuss what you do know. Tell me," Mistress Resvaes said, "what exactly does 'Marlovan' mean?"

They exchanged glances of surprise. Tdor looked down at her hands. Shen hesitated, still searching for the right words to tell this woman whatever it was she wanted to hear.

Hadand said, "Marlovans have no written history. The oldest songs and stories tell us 'Marlovan' means 'accursed of the Venn.' By studying

Iascan history, we've found out that the word really is a blend of three words, meaning 'outcasts of the Venn.' "

"I see. So you have corrected the songs, then?"

"Corrected the songs?" Hadand repeated, taken aback. "The songs are songs. Separate from, well, anything else."

"Who sings these songs? Everyone in Iasca Leror?"

Hadand said. "We do, the descendants of the Marlovans."

"Who speaks Marlovan? Not everyone, I apprehend."

"No," Shen said. "Just us. In fact it wasn't even spoken for several generations. Or only at home, on festival days."

"Why is that?" Mistress Resvaes asked, leaning forward.

"There are different ideas," Hadand said slowly; at first she'd been surprised at the woman's ignorance, for mage teachers were supposed to be quite learned. But now she suspected the woman knew the answer, and waited only to hear how the girls framed it. "My mother says it's because nothing was written down, that we had only stories to go on. Iascan, being written, was more useful for government and trade. Others claim that Marlovan must only be spoken by descendants of the plains, a custom denoting pride. Yet the Cassads tell us that most of the Marlovans of the second generation after the kingdoms joined were ashamed of their language, because it wasn't written, it hadn't—" Hadand frowned, seeking words.

"The sophisticated vocabulary," Shendan said, watching the mage for the tiniest reaction. "And yet it does, but for life on the plains. For weather, for seasons, for matters of the open air, my mother says, Marlovan is far more subtle than Iascan. There are nineteen verbs just for rain."

"For weather, for seasons, for matters of the open air such as war?" Mistress Resvaes asked. "So I have heard. I have also heard that Marlovan is called 'the language of war.' "

No mistaking the girls' reactions: surprise, followed swiftly by wariness in Shendan, resignation in Hadand, and the puckered brow of inward questioning in Tdor.

Shen's lips parted, and Mistress Resvaes said in a gentle voice, "Do not attempt to tell me it's just the men who say it thus. It was Ndara Cassad, the one you term Harandviar, who told me just last night, when we had our private interview. Our secret interview, unknown to any of the men here, at which she told me pretty much everything you have told me—except what you would do with knowledge of historical magic."

Silence.

Mistress Resvaes breathed slowly, searching for the words that would bring these girls to a wider understanding. "And I must observe, if men and women are so divided here, you will never really have peace."

Shen said, eyes wide, "So because we are Marlovans you'll withhold knowledge from us? Ignorant we might be, but we're trying to fight against that, and meanwhile, we're informed enough about other kingdoms to know they aren't perfect. Yet they have trained mages, and not just healers, living among them. Why should we be condemned to ignorance? Is it because we won't permit the Venn to conquer us?"

"There are so many wrong assumptions lying behind your words I hardly know how to begin," Mistress Resvaes said. "But I will try. First, no one is withholding knowledge as knowledge. Magic, yes, for a time, but I shall see to it that you get better records, for I think you must begin to understand what happened to us before the Fall, the chain of bad choices humankind made, often for the best of reasons, and the results. It is we humans, not anyone else, who nearly destroyed ourselves. And we used magic to do it."

"But we don't want magic for war," Hadand said, her hands gripped together. "No one ever thought that. We all want it to make life better."

Tdor spoke for the first time. "Fareas-Iofre taught us magic can't be used for war. Only for improvement of life."

"It can be used for anything," Mistress Resvaes said to her, and though her voice was kind, her gaze was serious. "And we have made some very terrible mistakes. Not just in our ancient history, but more recently. Far more recently."

She went on to ask some more questions about their history, and heard the eager answers. She had been trained well, and so the girls saw no sign of just how alarming Mistress Resvaes found them, with their passionate desire to master magic for "peace" when they so clearly accepted war as an expected way of life. Yet she felt an unexpected sympathy: she knew that these girls did not lie, they really believed just what they said.

That made them even more frightening. Their intentions were the best, but they had accepted the mandate of their kings that Marlovans conquer their neighbors for their own good, and then rearrange their lives so that they would live the Marlovan idea of peace and plenty. And prepare for war against their ancient ancestors, a cycle that promised never to end.

They would get their ancient records, but ones that detailed politics and lives and laws, nothing about magic except as result. Not method.

Shen fought tears. She had let herself hope, and she *hated* hope, for the only thing about it you could trust is that it would always, without fail, be denied.

And so she and Tdor withdrew with silent steps, watched ahead by Ndara-Harandviar's women, until they reached the Royal Armsmistress, just as all the girls were returning from the game. The Royal Armsmistress declared their break-in a win.

And so there was a celebration that night, their triumphant riding given leave, and in their midst Shen talked, and laughed, and drank, but at night Tdor lay in compassionate silence below her, listening to the harsh breathing of grief that lasted until dawn.

Chapter Twenty-one

JORET looked down at the intertwined gilded lilies circling her beautiful porcelain cup, and knew that this interview with Fareas-Iofre was not going to be an easy one.

Late summer light streamed in the west windows, painting tall columns of glowing gold up the bare peach stone of the opposite wall and reflected back into the room, glinting on the rims of the cups.

Fareas-Iofre poured out summery scented steeped leaf, all the more precious since the embargo. They talked of training games, of who would be sent to the capital to bring Tdor and Whipstick Noth back now that his last year as a horsetail was done and Tdor was finished with the queen's training. He would take over as the Algara-Vayir Shield Arm, and his father would ride back north, to honorable retirement, unless the king required him again.

"My dear," Fareas-Iofre said, after they had finished a cup. "You must speak to the heir, or his visit, I suspect, will stretch on for another half a year."

Joret looked as if someone had taken a dagger to her heart. Fareas thought, *Is it possible she returns, in some wise, the Sierlaef's passion?* She studied the girl's unhappy face and considered the tall, good-looking royal heir who sat a horse so well, whose silences held him aloof and perhaps made him seem a mystery to the young.

But Joret was not thinking of the Sierlaef, she was thinking of ghosts. She looked into the pale green liquid in her cup and breathed the fresh scent as she considered how she'd seen Aunt Joret's ghost three more times, all three when the heir was present. And no one else had seen it, for on all three occasions Jarend-Adaluin had been absent.

Once again she wished she could confide in Fareas-Iofre—except she knew the princess could have no insight to offer. Joret had been through all the Iofre's books and scrolls, and so she knew whatever the princess knew about ghosts. Probably more.

What she really craved was comfort, but at what cost? Hadand had made her promise not to tell her mother when they were girls of ten and eleven. *She sometimes forgets I'm here when my home visits first begin, and I overheard her talking last year, saying how difficult it is to live with a ghost. But she doesn't see ghosts. I asked her later. I figured it out, she means how everyone always talks about the old Iofre, your Aunt Joret. I don't want Mama knowing she has her real ghost here as well.*

And though Joret now knew she was not alone in seeing this ghost, that the Adaluin also saw it, it never would have occurred to her to talk to him. He had always been courteous but remote—she once thought he probably spoke a hundred words to her in as many days. Maybe in a year.

"My dear?" the Iofre said, and Joret wrenched her mind back to the wretched question.

"I don't want to talk to the Sierlaef," she said, turning her cup purposelessly in her fingers.

Fareas-Iofre said, "The royal heir does not appear to perceive your preference not to dally. After all, many would consider it an honor to be so noticed. Perhaps you need to make it clear." And offered more steeped leaf.

Joret accepted a third cup, but she did not see the liquid, or taste it. Instead she looked back most unwillingly over the past half a year, and how she always knew when the king's son was there in a room, how he watched her. In truth, she did feel attraction, but she likened it to the attraction of fire, which was bright and strong and powerful, and had its own kind of grace. But get too close, and it would burn.

"I fear," she said, low, "it will be difficult for me to send him away. I fear he will take it as hurt."

"It is possible," Fareas-Iofre said. "That family is known for its long-lived passions. But it has to be you, it cannot be any of us, because of who he is."

Joret said, "I've never spoken to him, beyond polite necessity. That should be enough!"

Fareas said, "Not enough for obsession, it appears."

Obsession. A spasm of disgust caused Joret to grimace slightly. The attraction she'd felt for the Sierlaef from time to time, and for one or two others, only flickered—and it was a pale flicker, not nearly what others called a spark—when watching them afar. With the Sierlaef, when he rode or performed the sword dances. But when he looked at her in that way of his she felt crowded and stuffy, like a room too long shut up in summer, with too many people in it. She did not want intimacy with him, or with anyone, really, though she'd settled it within herself that intimacy with Tanrid would be her duty one day. Life, she thought (perceiving herself as very wise at the advanced age of eighteen), would be far more tranquil without sex.

But wishing life was different did not solve the problem of the king's heir—who was supposed to marry Hadand—and his obsession. Hadand! That gave her an idea. "Will it seem less of an affront if I say that honor and love cause me to regard Hadand as sister, and thus him as brother?"

"Nothing you say will be pleasant, but that does not offer insult to a hot-blooded young man. Honor is always a good reason," Fareas-Iofre said, and shook her head, thinking, *it's a good excuse, especially for the young.* "We endeavor to rely on the halter of custom, though no set of rules truly tames the human heart."

Joret used those words later to the Sierlaef, when she finally agreed to meet him on the west wall. The sentries saw they wanted privacy and obliged with silently shortened patrols.

When Fareas-Iofre had said that, it sounded so wise, so right, but as soon as the words were out of her mouth she wished she could reach and catch them and clap them into nothingness, for she could see how wrong he heard them.

Nothing can tame the human heart. His breathing changed, and his chin came up, so that moonlight shone in his eyes, startlingly green, and then he smiled, his hands trembling as they reached for hers.

She put her hands behind her back and stood, poised to run if he should touch her, but instead he fought his tongue, rehearsing his words over and over, for he would not bleat, not before the love of his life. "Find a way," he managed, his voice low, and rough, his body trembling.

"No, no," she cried. She realized that any explanation was useless, for he would hear only what he wanted to hear. "Please. Go back to Hadand, who is my dearest sister."

He opened his hands. Of course she would be loyal. It was part of her perfection. "Find. A way," he said again, with more emphasis, and then he left, his self-control almost at an end. His entire body was on fire. Another moment—if she brought out her hands again, if her glorious blue gaze touched his—he would kiss her, and he sensed from the sound of her breathing that she would take fire too, but it would be the fire of anger as well as passion. Honor. She wanted everything honorable. It just made her more perfect.

He strode off to the tower door, his long pale hair swinging between his shoulder blades, leaving her there alone, sick with despair, thinking, *What have I done?*

And so he ran downstairs, summoned his liveried men with a snap of the fingers, and made the flat-handed sweep they had all been waiting for: pack up. In scarcely repressed relief his Runners set about preparing for a morning ride. They'd been waiting every single day for the command to leave, while enduring the firmly closed world of Tenthen. Nothing ever impolite, not to those who served the future king, but bearable when people get on with their lives if it's only for a few days. When the time lengthens to six months, and people still do not know your name, or move around you as if you were fragile furniture, you begin to wish you were as invisible as they pretended you were.

The Sierlaef was, of course, utterly unaware of this silent struggle going on belowstairs. All he could think about was bracing himself for his last glimpse of Joret.

Before dawn Tanrid was thumped awake by Cassad's impatient hand. In the weak blue light Cassad's sharp face altered from impatient to thoughtful as he glanced at the empty space on the bed beside Tanrid, and he plumped down unasked, mail faintly jingling. "We're gone," he said.

"What?" Tanrid realized Cassad was dressed for riding, his hair pulled up in its gold clasp, his House colors on.

"Your Joret finally turfed him out last night." *And she's not in here. Interesting.* Cassad thought of that beautiful face, the polite, honest, but stone-cold manner, and his guts warmed at the prospect of being reunited with Carleas Ndarga, who might be plain to look at, but they made one another laugh—while they shared the fun things they had learned at the royal city pleasure houses.

Tanrid didn't waste time asking if it was truth or just rumor. Cassad always knew the gossip almost as soon as it happened. "Huh." He flung out of bed, thinking: first day worth getting up for in almost two years.

He scrambled into his own colors, but without the mail, since he was home, and would be able to stay home.

The entire household turned out to see off the Sierlaef and his entourage, all of them saluting with hand over heart. The royal heir kept his gaze on the beautiful figure there between the Iofre and Captain Noth, her fine, glossy black hair ruffled in the cool breeze, her color bright, but not as bright as her eyes. She met his gaze unsmiling, her hand at her heart like the rest, the other hand straight at her side.

He raised his fist. His outriders gave vent to their feelings by galloping through the gates, banners held high. The Sierlaef's mare, excited by the sudden departure, danced impatiently and so he loosened the reins and he too was gone at a gallop, his guard thundering after.

As they rode north the Sierlaef began to brood about his promise. For the first time he sent his thoughts ranging ahead of the present. Perhaps it was the prospect of being home again and all those duties closing in.

Honor. He had no honorable reason to visit again, and even if he did, he knew a brief dalliance would never be enough. Tanrid would have her by his side his entire life.

Tanrid. *I wish he was dead,* the Sierlaef thought, feeling a jab of frustration-spiked jealousy. Because he'd never agree to give her up, he or his stiff-assed father. Even though it was clear as day Joret didn't want Tanrid. But she would marry him and share his bed just the same, because she was honor-bound to do so. *If Tanrid was dead, she wouldn't care.*

He considered that, and yes, it seemed true. Then the sun rose inside his mind, full of the light of possibility—

If Tanrid was dead I could marry Joret.

Marry her. For a time he did not see the bright summer sky, or feel the heat reflecting off the road as the sun climbed higher in the sky. Insects chirruped and dust hung suspended on the road and a warm breeze rustled through the broad green five-fingered oak leaves along the ridge above the river. He was oblivious to it all, dazzled by the sunlight of this new vision, Joret standing on the dais in the throne room, the Jarls crying out *Joret-Gunvaer,* her beautiful blue, straightforward, fearless gaze, her straight, strong body beside him, wearing his own crimson and gold, and later they would go together into the king's rooms . . . her warm flesh under his hands, her lips raised to his. The sun inside flashed to intense heat, and his body tightened, causing his horse to sidle, which made the other horses prick their ears and swerve their heads, their riders as well.

He reined both mind and horse with an impatient jerk. *Think like a king!*

But his mind promptly answered, *She deserves to be a queen.*

The thought was fine while it lasted, but as soon as he began to explore it, he came hard up against Hadand, and everything faltered. He liked Hadand. Everyone liked Hadand, but still she never strutted, unlike some of those females. He frowned at a memory: Hadand helping him with his reading, quietly, so no one ever knew. No one. She never told anyone, except maybe that little rabbit Kialen Cassad, who didn't count for anything.

If Tanrid were gone, would she agree to let him marry Joret? Of course she would. She'd always done what he asked. But *her* honor required she be given a marriage just as good. She deserved one just as good. So, well, he could send Hadand off to marry some prince somewhere, just like his own mother had come to this kingdom. That was it! A peace treaty, honor all around. Might even be good policy! If Tanrid were dead—

But Tanrid wouldn't die. Nobody as brave, as smart, as loyal, as good at command would trip over a rock and break his head, like that stupid Noth boy long ago when they were still horsetails.

The Sierlaef's hands tightened on the reins. The mare tossed her head, snorting. His mind veered away from actively plotting treachery. *I always get what I want,* he thought. *Somehow. I do what I want, and my uncle makes it right. He's of no other use. He certainly can't command.*

Chapter Twenty-two

THAT night, far to the north, Sponge flipped his hand up. "Go!"
And with shrill yips of triumph an entire riding of scrubs burst
from their hiding place in the hedgerow, charging toward the enemy.
The two ponies spun around, torchlight revealing their dismay. A double trap!

They fought, of course, but the well-drilled scrubs divided into two
groups and each took down one big boy. By the time Sponge crested the
slight ridge and surveyed the field of battle, the two ponies were
crushed flat in the tall summer grass, pinned by four small bodies each.

Was I ever that little? Sponge thought.

"We won!" The fifth boy danced around, holding the red banner aloft.
"We won, we won, we won!" And he yipped the fox yip, high, shrill, triumphant, joined instantly by the rest of the boys under Sponge's
command.

Sponge jerked his chin as a signal to the two boys behind him, they
dipped their torches with conscientious care, and from a distance came
the triumphant bugle calls signaling a captured flag.

Now that the banner game was decided both armies disintegrated
into chattering groups, with bet payoffs, hoots of derision, scarcely-
heeded words of critique and would-be plans exchanged: everyone
wanted to be talking.

Or almost everyone. Sponge did not listen. What he contemplated was the relief in the two older boys' faces when they saw him approach. Nothing said—nothing was ever said—but it was clear that they had both, without speaking to one another, mentally surrendered to the king's son and not to a litter of scrubs.

They reformed into one big group for a campfire dance, hoarded drums coming out of saddle packs, real swords brought out for the sword dances. Sponge sat on a rock near Noddy, who had been the opposing army commander. Noddy watched the boys with his usual impassive expression.

"Not bad," Noddy said. Lower, "Second spring."

Sponge opened a hand in acknowledgment. Only their own group recognized variations on Inda's old plans.

Noddy grunted, not a grunt of agreement. Sponge studied Noddy, whose dark eyes reflected fire, shadowed and lit again as silhouettes capered round and round between them and the blaze. "What is it?" he asked.

Noddy's eyes narrowed. "Heard my lot blathering about the summer with no banner."

Sudden reminders still kicked like an untrained colt. Sponge looked down at his hands. So much for justice. Ten heartbeats ago, he'd felt a mild triumph at having commanded a successful banner game; now he found himself face to face with his own powerlessness.

Justice. He'd promised Inda justice, but if he came back there was no way to give it to him. Sponge had the desire to achieve justice, but not the power. He could not even prove that injustice had been done; to his father he would have had to bring proof, not just accusation.

"Nobody knows the truth. Except us. Still," Noddy went on. His voice had altered slowly to a mild tenor over the past couple of years. When he was angry his expression still didn't alter much, but his voice lowered to a soft growl in his chest, the same timber as Cama's voice, which had still been a kitten squeak when they broke for winter last year, but when he returned it had dramatically dropped to a rough, husky burr.

Thwack! A heavy hand thumped them each on the shoulder, and they looked up at Cherry-Stripe Marlo-Vayir, arrived just behind them. He turned away, stooped, then came up again gripping a wine bottle in each hand. Strictly forbidden on banner games, but nobody made trouble for the king's son and his particular friends. Especially with all the talk of changing the once steel-forged rules. With all the trouble up north and spreading down the coast, the first Tvei class might be put into horsetails early, accelerating their training so they could finish and get home to guard their castles. The horsetails were not commanding this game, despite tradition, because they'd all been sent to the Guard early as replacement for the Guards sent north to reinforce the Harskialdna's army. All, that is, except their leader, Whipstick Noth, who had been just recently sent down to Choraed Elgaer as escort to Tdor Marth-Davan, in order to take up his new life as Randael to the prince.

They all missed Whipstick. He'd given them excellent challenges on the game field.

"Good job," Cherry-Stripe said, though he'd been Noddy's second in command. He jerked his chin at some small boys nearby. They scrambled out of the way to sit elsewhere, one of them glaring and muttering about frost. Ignoring them, Cherry-Stripe dropped down where they'd been and passed one bottle to Noddy, who took a swig. "Inda, game upriver, second spring."

Sponge tipped his head in agreement.

Cherry-Stripe uttered a laugh, motioned for Noddy to keep the bottle, and he took the other one to Cama, who was overseeing the packing and the horses. Noddy reflected on the past as the sweet wine sent fire through his veins. Their third year, the first one with Inda and Dogpiss gone, no one had talked about Inda. Not until their first overnight game. There under the stars somehow they couldn't talk about anything else. Except that last banner game, once they realized no one knew anything. Instead they reminisced over Dogpiss' stings, and discussed endlessly the details of Inda's wins, what he'd said, how he thought.

Noddy had come to realize that Inda had somehow found the weakness in their training strategy, which was to force the boys to a standard on games, but to favor the sons of the Royal Shield Arm's privileged Jarls during training. Inda had known by instinct that practice would be more successful if the person was driven to match the standard, but on an action the goal was matched to the person who can best achieve it.

It sounded so simple when put into words, but it first required being able to stand back and ignore rank and politics and see everyone clearly, their strengths and weaknesses.

Politics. Noddy glanced Kepa's way; he was clashing swords with Master Kavad to begin the dancing. Smartlip Lassad wavered, as always, between whoever was most friendly to him, but Kepa—now heir to a Jarlate in conquered Idayago, and so full of frost some of them privately had taken to calling him Snowballs—was bluntly loyal to the Harskialdna. Such words as he'd just been thinking, spoken aloud and reported to the Harskialdna, would be perceived as dancing mighty near the edge of treason. And there wasn't any way to change it.

A fist struck his arm, and Noddy passed the bottle into Tuft's waiting hand. Tuft drank, then carried the bottle to Cama, who tipped his head back and chugged a few fast swallows, unaware of the cluster of younger pigtails who watched his every move with intense fascination.

Cama and Flash, along with Mouse Marth-Davan, were the fastest and most reckless riders in the entire academy. Cama and Flash were the best with archery in the first Tvei class, and they were also the handsomest, though Cama's curling black hair and above all his eye patch—for the embargo against Iasca Leror had prevented him from any more trips to finish the work on his eye—made him, in the eyes of all the younger boys, the most dashing senior in the academy.

It was a matter of utter indifference to Cama. His interests, outside of rec time forays to Heat Street, were confined solely to competition in the field—and to winning them. He, Noddy, and Sponge, sometimes with Cherry-Stripe and Rattooth, often sat on the barracks roof (since Sponge never had been introduced to Daggers Drawn, the others had mostly forgotten about it) and talked strategy and tactics, shaping new plans from Inda's old ideas. And they won, time after time. So far, no one outside the academy really noticed the wins, or Sponge's popularity. The Sierlaef had been gone almost two years, and the Harskialdna spent spring and summer riding the north and trying to put out Idayagan fires of resistance, sparked by increasingly bold pirate attacks along the northern coast. The king was reported to be struggling with the strains of trade agreements broken, of the need for more money, of the need for allies.

Not that these distant, dreary doings mattered to the herd of little boys riding for glory here at home in the academy, which comprised all their world.

Cama, Noddy, and most of all Sponge were not sure if they wanted them to wake up or not.

The next day the academy rode back, group year banners streaming before the winners, and at the head of the cavalcade two banners, the Montrei-Vayir stooping eagle and the academy fox.

Just about the time they spotted the welcome sight of the castellated royal city on the horizon, far to the south the Sierlaef—after a full day of brooding—had his plan. The Idayagans were constant trouble, so who better to send north to put down uprisings than the hero of the Ghael Hills battle?

The Sierlaef smiled for the first time in weeks, and the ride home looked a lot easier to his much exasperated Sier-Danas, who had been forced to behave circumspectly far too long, and who could think of nothing but the week (at least) they would spend at the pleasure houses, as soon as they got through the city gates.

The pleasure houses were also on the minds of the older Tveis, who knew that coming back from a successful banner game meant liberty, and while liberty for the little boys meant Daggers and bragging, for the older ones, it meant time to get laid.

When they dismounted, there was Headmaster Brath himself, granting liberty to not just the winners but to all of Sponge's Tveis for their excellent conduct, on the recommendation of Master Kavad, who had accompanied them.

As soon as Master Kavad was gone Cherry-Stripe leaned against the door of their pit, eyes closed in an ecstasy of anticipation. "Oh, Morgand! Here I come!"

"And come, and come, and come," Rattooth added.

"I'm first with Mdan," Kepa declared, eyes flicking from one to the next as he named one of the most popular dollies at the pleasure house the boys liked best.

"First and worst, first and worst," Smartlip taunted as he, too, sidled looks to see who was laughing.

"Lances at ready: Charge!" Flash howled, leading the race to the baths, Smartlip yipping loudly right behind him.

Sponge ran with them because it was expected. In the baths he avoided looking at strong, hard young bodies of the others who were now young men, envying them their careless, unconscious freedom. He was the first dressed, the second out, but the last through the academy gates. The others, as usual, never noticed that he did not run into the city streets.

He ducked up the back way into the castle, hesitating outside the archive when he heard several female voices, then moved on to his room without noticing the ubiquitous, unobtrusive women on guard at key landings. Nor did he notice one of the Guards make a signal to a young Runner sitting in an ancient recessed window, studying her Old Sartoran letters. She crushed the scroll into her tunic and flitted back to the archive.

So Sponge was surprised not long after he reached his quiet bedchamber when his door opened and in walked Hadand. He turned, unaware of how sharp was his movement until he saw her draw back against the door. "Should I have knocked?" she asked.

He flushed. "Why? We never have before. What have I to shut out? Or shut in?"

Hadand considered him, her brown eyes narrowed in the way that always called Inda to mind. "There was a problem on the banner game?" she asked tentatively.

Sponge looked out his windows at the dust hanging suspended in the air over the practice fields: young horses in training. His emotions swooped, and he resolutely turned his back on the window.

"No," he said, when he saw her expression had altered to worry. She, too, still missed Inda, and still felt the shadow of that terrible summer. And he could see it. "We won."

Her brows went up. "You don't look like you won."

He lifted a hand, palm out.

It could have meant anything. She asked, in the same tentative tone as before, "Where are Cherry-Stripe and Rattooth and Noddy and the rest of your friends?"

"Heat Street." He saw the trap too late.

It was a trap formed by kindness, its bait the best intentions. Hadand whispered, her eyes wide. "Sponge. Don't tell me no one's taken you to a pleasure house yet?"

"I won't, if you like." He managed to sound wry.

Hadand pursed her lips in a soundless whistle. "Your uncle wouldn't, of course. And I don't think your father has ever been in one in his life."

"I doubt it." They both knew that he and Jened Sindan had formed their bond as senior horsetails, a bond never broken by either of them since.

"Your brother?"

"Oh, he offered. Before he left on his journey." Sponge made an inadvertent gesture of warding. "But I wasn't interested at the time."

"I see." Hadand studied him.

"It's nothing I want, particularly. Or I think I could find my way there on my own," he said. "I just want to sit and relax. Banner games are not days of comfort and rest."

That was weak—he knew it was weak as soon as he spoke—and Hadand quite properly ignored it. She was still studying him with that narrow, penetrating gaze that had characterized her ever since she was small. Inda had had it too. Sponge turned away, looking out the window at the long late afternoon shadows, wishing he was dead. No, he wished he was away, far away, maybe lost at the sea . . .

"It's men, isn't it?" she asked finally, not tentative but practical, as if she'd solved a puzzle at last. "Or are you not sure?"

Sponge had to laugh, though the sound was as forced as his smile had been. "Oh, I'm sure." His mind flung its way back through last year's painful memories: waking up with what the older boys called saddlewood, furtive experimentations with the older Tveis in the dark, in the baths, in the stable, hiding from discovery by the younger boys (who would inevitably hoot and crow with laughter or disgust, just as he and his fellow-scrubs had when they stumbled over evidence of the existence of sex); laughing and lingering fun during their rare moments of real free time and privacy, most of those in meeting places passed on by cooperative silence from the older boys to the younger who had just crossed the threshold as yet invisible to the rest.

Shared laughter at the discovery of the real meaning of terms the older boys had used for years, the brief, violent passions for one another. His first real craze had been Cama, who had come back this spring handsome beyond belief, with that rough, compelling voice. Cama had, mercifully, remained unaware of Sponge's crush, which seemed to last an eternity but was in reality no more than a month, followed by an even briefer, more violent infatuation with Flash, after a drunken encounter in the baths that Flash apparently forgot within a day.

Sponge winced, remembering the exhilarating dreams he'd had last winter of a band of friends who were also lovers, as had happened now and then in history, burned into cinders when just this year Cherry-Stripe (of course it would be he) discovered the Real Thing: women.

One by one the others had joined him, when they could, and there had been no turning back—except for Flash, who found boys and girls equally attractive, the more the better, but rarely the same one twice in a row. They were still pigtails, and Heat Street ought to have been two years ahead, as well as the privileges of command, but Sponge was not only a prince, he was also not the only one who had had to get the healer to do the Beard Spell within this last year. So the masters looked the other way. The Tveis were young men, with the brains of young men as well as the desire—and nobody said no to a prince.

"Are we disgusting?"

Sponge looked up, to meet Hadand's considering gaze. She'd stepped closer, and he hadn't noticed. "Huh?"

"Are we—girls, I mean. Are we disgusting to you?"

"No!"

Hadand tipped her head. "It's seldom that definite, from what I understand. But it can be. Both ways. Our arms mistress loathes the smell of men even more than the sight."

Sponge, thinking of that grim, spear-backed figure, smiled. "I'm not surprised."

Hadand's hands fumbled at her robe, and before Sponge could say anything, she had shed it, and brought her hands up under the generous swell of her breasts beneath the fine linen of her shirt. "I had to stop drilling in a shirt during summer," she said matter-of-factly. "When I discovered most of the sentries watching as if they'd been struck by lightning. So I nearly die of the heat, wearing a winter tunic if I have to drill outside, but a future queen can't be waving these things around and causing the lookouts to miss the occasional invading army."

Sponge laughed.

"Are you the least bit stirred?" she asked.

He looked at the extravagant curves in her hands, he looked at her trim waist neatly sashed with its knife handle curving upward, and watched as she thrust a hip out. He saw what the men saw, the spectacular figure of a young woman who is also in superb condition. But there was no inward flare of heat.

"No."

"What do you feel?"

Sponge shook his head. "It looks . . . motherly."

Hadand pulled her robe back on. "I know what to do." She started toward the door.

Sponge snapped, "Don't do anything."

"Why?" She looked back, hand on the latch.

"I don't want a willow wand any more than I want a dolly." He used the slang terms for professional lovers—male and female—in a sharp voice, and turned away, pacing back to the window to glare out at the sunlit court.

"Why not?" she asked, sensible as always. "I mean, why not a man if you don't want a woman?"

Because none of my friends do, he wanted to say, but he hesitated.

He'd already been through the difficult decision-making process, and was not going to thrash through it all again. There was nothing she could say that was new. They'd grown up aware that the taste for one's own gender ran through the Montrei-Vayirs, men and women, that no one would be surprised that Sponge was the one in whom it emerged in this generation, though they'd all expected it would be the Sierlaef. He knew that eventually he'd act on it, and everyone would shrug.

But that would be after his friends had gone home forever to their castles to take up their lives as Randaels.

Because far, far more important than sex was that friendship. He would not have his passions separate him from his friends. If it had been any of them who'd turned to men, it wouldn't have mattered, but this accursed rank as second son of the king—if he formed a craze for one of them, for anyone they knew, there suddenly would be the intrusion of rank. And imagined obligation.

He struck a fist lightly against the window sill. *Nothing*, not even sex, was as important as the free, easy companionship with Noddy and Cama and Cherry-Stripe and the others, an unthinking bond of cama- raderie that meant more to him than anything else in his life: unthink- ing on their parts, both guarded and cherished on his. And sometimes, sometimes, like on the banner game, he didn't have to think, it just *was*.

The urge to speak, to tell Hadand—talk to her as he always had— subsided. Women had their secrets, and he wouldn't make his personal life one of them.

The sound of the door closing brought his head around with a wary jerk. She'd gone out while he was brooding; now Hadand slipped back inside, and said, "I sent my Runner for some wine. I could use some too."

It came, swiftly, and she poured out two glasses, talking the while of her first visit to a pleasure house, with the other girls during New Year's Week. "After all who could take me? Queen Wisthia summons her favorites to her. Ndara has nothing to do with sex, we all know that. Joret was gone, and anyway she loathed the very notion. My mother would have, but I can't see her again. So Shen Montredavan-An made up a party. I thought I'd be the first clumsy one, the first silly one, and everyone would know, but I discovered that they have people who are trained just to be the first. They are everyone's first. Did you know that?"

Sponge gulped wine. "Yes. No."

She poured out more, and Sponge drank it, though he knew he must not return drunk, and he hadn't eaten all day, so the fire of the wine burned through him with frightening rapidity. But to escape the uncomfortable subject, he drank anyway.

Hadand talked on, making the story funny: her fumbling dialogue, her panic, her discovery just how much fun sex could be, and the inevitable violent crush, thankfully as short as it was violent. After a time she said, "Would you like to try with a girl? If you could have one who knew what to do?"

He glowered, thinking, *And what if I see this girl and can't raise the staff?* But he couldn't bear to speak the words. His wine cup crashed down. "What have you done?"

She gave him an exasperated look. "Sponge. You *know*, because the healer *told* us when we got that long lecture about sex, that if you let the heat build you burn up here." She smacked her head. "If you were able to shed the heat with a trained dolly, and it would make your life simpler, why not at least try?" She waved toward the academy on the word "simpler" and he realized that once again she had parsed at least some of his inner thoughts.

"Look, Sponge, if it doesn't work nobody will know. The pleasure house people have to guard their business, and big mouths can ruin it. They talk when someone wants to be talked about, and they also talk when someone is hated. You won't be either."

His lips buzzed. "But castle people would find out. They always find out everything."

"That's why I sent for a girl," she said in that practical voice as she used her robe to daub the table clean of the drops of wine he'd spilled, and then poured out some more. "If your friends do find out, nobody pays the least attention. They won't always be watching you in case you want one of them, and worrying about princes and privilege and favorites and the like. I can just imagine Smartlip trying to seduce you, just to get preference over the others."

Sponge flung up a warding hand, grimacing with distaste.

"I can see you already thought that out, too. Listen, if this experiment doesn't work, you can tell everyone I cried after that first time," she said, smiling crookedly. "Oh, my, was I dreary to Tdor, boring on forever about how much I was so in love. Or thought I was."

Sponge snickered. He sounded to his own ears like someone else, a second-year scrub who couldn't hold his wine. "How long did that last, anyway?"

"Two weeks." She chuckled. "Two very intense weeks."

A knock at the door.

"Enter," Hadand called, before Sponge could get his numbing lips to say, "Go away."

In came a boy dressed in riding clothes, about their age. No, not a boy, though at first she seemed to be one. The strong chin, the adze-sculpted cheekbones, the swinging stride and short curls, all signaled male, but the smoothness of her cheeks, the neck, the hands, were female.

"Meet Dyalen," Hadand said, and then she was gone—the traitor!—leaving Sponge to blink owlishly at this boy-girl, and wipe at his sweaty forehead with shaky hands.

"Where did you come from?" Sponge knew he sounded rude, but he was terrified.

"You mean, just now? From Heat Street. House of Roses. It's a short enough trip, if you go up the back way through the old sentry walk." Dyalen flashed a quick grin, then she sobered just as quickly. "Hadand-Hlinlaef has been good to my family." Her voice was low, a husky contralto. "If I can repay her I will."

The women again, with their hidden webs of loyalty, but he lost the thought, because Dyalen had stepped up, and stroked his hair back from his forehead. With the other hand she took away the wine cup. She bent slightly. Her shirt was open at the neck, showing a brief glimpse of collar-bone, and flat breastbone between two small breasts. Boy and not boy.

"Humans actually cleave to both," she said. "To degrees. Pretty youths, strong women. You probably have friends who like both males and females, don't you?"

Sponge thought of Flash Arveas. "Yes," he said. "One, anyway." *If the others had been like me you wouldn't be here.*

She laughed again, that free laugh, sounding like the Tveis in the bath house. "Come on, get to your feet."

"What? Don't we have to—" He motioned toward his inner room, which was his bedchamber.

"Nah." She grinned, a wide grin with teeth. "We're going to wrestle. Bet you can't pin me, either," she taunted. "I'm a lot stronger than I look." And she reached up, casually, and slapped him.

He stepped back in surprise. It wasn't a hard slap, just a sting. A tingling sting, and she laughed again, swatting the air just before his face. "Try to get me back. I dare you."

He lunged. She caught his wrist and twisted it up behind him, sliding the other hand into his tunic, a fast grope that left a feeling of burning on his skin, kindling in his guts. Wrestling, like boys wrestle.

She smelled of the outdoors—sage and wind, a little of snap-vine oil, and horse. Academy smells.

He lunged, only half trying, but she evaded his grip and danced away, taunting, taunting, until he used some of his fighting knowledge and caught her, just to be flung off again. And so they played at battle, no blows made in anger, and she teased him with voice, with tongue, with teeth, with tutored hands, until the wine, and the warmth, and her easy strength, brought him spiraling down into the sweet urgency of desire, and even then she made him fight for it until he couldn't hold himself back, and those expert hands brought them together, breath mingling, hearts thumping, until white, searing fire obliterated memories of the past, worries of the future, consuming him in the now.

Chapter Twenty-three

KODL'S marines' third hire forced them through more sudden squalls full of lightning, choppy cross seas, and sinister drifts of fog that hid shoals and rock-bound islands, but this time they saw their enemies. Twice fast, small galleys swarmed out of the islands toward them, but both times they hauled their wind, as the mate of the deck followed Niz's orders for setting fighting sail. The galleys' glasses revealed the tops full of sailors armed with composite bows, and more sailors armed with steel lining the rail, obviously waiting.

Both times the galleys veered off and sped back into the fog, oars lifting and splashing in strict rhythm.

The marines were as disappointed as the captain was happy to have avoided battle; the benefit was that he paid off at journey's end with loud-spoken enthusiasm.

Their fourth hire was found that day. The captain of the *Loohan*, having heard about the marines who scared off pirate galleys, came directly to their lodgings in Khanerenth's main harbor, begging Kodl to take ship with him at once.

Kodl had been alone, studying the new charts he'd bought first thing off the ship. When the *Loohan*'s captain left, Kodl ran downstairs to the common room, where he found half of his marines eating, and he figured the other half had to be at the pleasure house across the square, spending their earnings a lot faster than they'd made them.

"I'll fix it, I'll fix it," Inda mumbled, awkward and red-faced.

Kodl stopped where he was, observing the gawky teen picking at a ripped seam in the side of his weatherworn, stained, threadbare shirt as Tau and Jeje laughed at him. Who could look at him and guess he was the real force behind the marines' skill? *When will Inda realize it—and what will he do about it?*

"Why don't you just *buy* one, Inda?" Jeje asked in exasperation. "Your sewing isn't any better than it was when we were rats! You had plenty of money after the gold bag run!"

Tau crossed his arms and leaned back, staring up at the ceiling as though he'd just discovered a fabulous painting there.

Inda hunched over his food, his ears now scarlet. He mumbled something.

Jeje leaned forward. "What do you mean, you ran out of money? Inda, you didn't buy any new weapons, and you have never gone upstairs at the Lark. What did you do with it?"

Inda's shoulders hitched up, and Kodl thought, *Good question.* But a pang of self-loathing forced him to dismiss his suspicions, as Jeje said in haste, "Well, never mind, I know it's none of my affair. It's just, we want to look successful, so good liberty clothes make us look successful."

She instinctively reached for Tau's arm, covered in very fine linen, then snapped her hand back, and brushed it down the front of her sturdy green-dyed tunic. Tau picked up his mulled wine and looked intently at it, as though counting the cloves floating on top.

Jeje said, "You got paid today, so how about I take you to the clothes makers street tomorrow? They can make you up whatever you like. Sometimes they even have ready made things. You just pull them on and see if they fit."

"There won't be time," Kodl interrupted, and all three looked up at him, Tau self-possessed, Inda miserable, Jeje startled.

Kodl paused, framing the words, but a loud voice from the next table caught his attention.

". . . yes, we heard that too," a tall, swarthy man spoke in a masthead voice to another table of sailors, his Dock Talk Brennish in accent. "The Delfs is sailing west, on account o' the Venn sailing west. Badrik of the

Fleet Deer says it's on account of the Venn needing to protect the northern waters from them damned Marlovans on their flying horses—"

Inda choked on a swallow of ale. Dun, at the table directly behind Inda, looked blank; Tau whacked Inda with unnecessary vigor on his back.

"Nobody can beat soul-eaters ridin' flyin' horses. That's everyday sense! But whatever's goin' on the land, the western waters been closed off. And the strait, they say, is so full o' Brotherhood you can't sail a bowline without hitting five of 'em in a single watch. We be stuck here in the east. And so we will go to try northern waters, up Everon way."

"Good plan," Kodl said, and eyes turned to him. He opened his hand to his people. "As for us, we stand south for Sartor."

"Already?" Yan asked, putting down his fork.

"On the tide," Kodl said, laughing. And, lower, "We're getting a rep, we're getting a rep at last."

Three weeks later dawn brought three fast pirates bearing down, all sails set and taut.

"Pirates ho!" called Yan from the masthead. The Chwahir was normally soft-spoken, when he did speak, which was seldom. His shout roused the deck, and the sudden running feet woke those belowdecks.

Inda whirled out of his hammock, yanked from a vivid dream: he was still eleven, the air smelled of summer fields, and Dogpiss had joined Sponge and Inda in the secret practice out behind the stable. The dream vanished, abandoning Inda for moments somewhere between *there* and *here*.

He strapped his knives on, and was thrashing his way into his newly-mended shirt as he raced up to the deck, where he found all the marines assembled before Kodl, faces grim, eyes alert, hands fidgeting and restless.

The captain, a cautious older man whose stiff demeanor and well-brushed green coat called poor Beagar to mind, said, unnecessarily, "They have the wind."

Inda had known that with the first warm blast on his face and the sight of three blue-painted shapes, hull up, bearing down squarely on the beam, which meant that the *Loohan* couldn't escape.

Kodl held two glasses. One he handed to Inda and they both snicked the glasses out to the longest reach. For a time there were no sounds except the slapping of water against the hull, the creak of wood and rigging, and the low thrum of wind in the sails. No one noticed the cold, eye-stinging drops of dew falling from the rigging above.

Inda and Kodl observed the pirates on their slow, inexorable approach. Kodl watched for changes of sail and direction; Inda watched those pirates visible on the deck.

"What're those booms?" he asked.

Niz nipped the glass from his hand, peered, grunted, said, "Them's cut-booms."

Inda took the glass back and peered. Now that the primary pirate was closer, he could see the huge extended boom, an open angle secured to the foremast and to the hull for support, its end glittering in the sun, some kind of massive blade fitted to its end. The three booms, one to each mast, seemed to be maneuverable—there were teams on each side of a boom with double-blocked lines.

Cut booms. Their effect would be like enormous swords or spears. Inda saw from the angle of approach, the way the booms jutted, that the pirate meant to come up at that angle and then throw the helm hard over, using the wind and the pirate's own speed and mass to sweep that beam along the shrouds of the *Loohan*.

With a flash of blue the sails on the first ship changed, some flapping down, others bowsed tight. The ship leaned, the wake changing, and Inda saw the plan—yes, this had to be the exact same plan used against the Pim ships. "Fire their sails," he muttered, glass still raised. "Two will sweep our sides, and that third will run right up over our stern so they can board."

"Arrows aloft!" Kodl snapped, and feet drummed on the deck, racing to the weapons locker.

Inda smacked the glass closed and turned to the bow team. "Arrows first, one to sail, one to a man on the cut-boom crews, sails, man, until they close. Make each one count so they think twice about us." He hesitated, facing Kodl, who just nodded, hiding his own trembling hands behind his back. *I only see what they're doing. Inda sees what they will do.*

Inda said, "Dun, your band starboard, Scalis, yours larboard. Get rid of those cut boom crews first! Niz, see to it your band is ready with staffs and steel to hand on the captain's deck in case they make it over the stern."

Scalis' low, breathy chuckle of anticipation was the only answer as they all ran to fetch their gear, the arrow bands swiftly dipping threads in the oil that Thog had left open for them, in preparation for setting the shafts alight.

The mariners' swift deployment was watched keenly by the *Loohan*'s regular crew, who knew they could not beat off one ship, much less three.

Inda never noticed them. He kept the glass pressed to his eye . . . not yet . . . not yet . . .

"Now!"

Spang! Tcheng! Simultaneously, in two disciplined waves, the bow teams sent arrows aloft, keening through the air, their flames leaving faint smoke trails. Fire arrows . . . Inda's mind flew back to lingering images from the dream.

He was a scrub again. The dream was so vivid, not just the scents, but the quality of the light, a blue glow with faint gold undertones highlighting strands of Dogpiss' untidy hair, warm and bright on the rough reddish scarred skin of his knuckles.

"Yulululu!" That was Niz's Delf triumph cry.

Stinging dew dropped into Inda's face, blurring the pirate ship. Just as he wiped his eyes the pirates hauled wind, weaving around to try another angle of attack, head on to diminish the target area of the fire arrows.

"Them's comin' at a sharper angle," Niz declared.

Everyone muttered and grunted in agreement. This angle would make it tougher for the pirates to make the maneuver successfully, Inda saw.

Loohan's captain, seeing their sails change, shouted orders for his own crew to tack, orders carried out faster than Kodl had thought possible with this merchant crew.

"Halt," Kodl yelled to the bow teams. "Wait till they come round." Jeje, far above, motioned to her band to change position. "Ready?"

The wind favored the pirates, as did the shape of their craft—long and narrow.

The first pirate came in fast, aimed now at the weather-side of the stern; the second one maneuvered in more slowly on the lee side, sails constantly altering to compensate for *Loohan*'s tacking.

With a flash of courses the first pirate threw his helm over—

"Now!" And to *Loohan*'s helmsmen, "Hard over!"

The second pirate, still too far back, permitted them to yaw leeward, the deck slanting, blocks clattering, a spoon someone had laid on a barrel clattering down the deck.

Fire arrows sizzled across the intervening sea in deadly, hissing sheets, so fast and well-aimed that the pirates again hauled wind, to repair and replan. Then Jeje, captain of the band aloft, shrieked, "Sail ho! Forward on the weather quarter!"

Inda, Kodl, and the *Loohan's* captain swung glasses toward the windswept bow to observe a small, fast schooner bearing up rapidly, white water feathering down both sides.

"Delfs!" Niz cried.

Three more behind—a fleet of four. As soon as it was within range the first Delf loosed a hissing canopy of arrows at the untouched third pirate, who had been hanging back as either reinforcement or to close with the *Loohan's* stern.

The pirates abruptly hauled off, this time sailing away in search of easier prey. Kodl grinned up at Inda.

"Heave to!" the Delf captain roared.

Soon a small party of poke-nosed, bandy-legged Delfs scrambled aboard, their weather-wrinkled eyes searching out the scrawny form of Niz, busy helping stow away their still vast store of arrows while everyone laughed and chattered.

"Hya, there," said the leader, in the Delf version of Dock Talk. "Heard us there was a Fussef in these waters."

"No Gams among ye," Niz replied, nodding in approval.

The Delfs invited Niz and the *Loohan's* captain over for drinks and the latest news, which Niz brought back aboard and shared, once he'd sobered up.

While they waited, Kodl, almost giddy with triumph, said, "What amazes me is that on the sea they set aside their feuds. But they've been known to make dates a year ahead for duels on shore when they meet clan enemies. All quite cheerful."

Their ability to know all the current news on the seas extended homeward. That news was grim and getting grimmer. Niz ended his report by saying, "Venn—" He spat over the side. "Soul-sucking Venn, wardin' off all else. Let red sails attack on shore. Hit Delfin Islands twice, hard. Venn wants 'em a land base in mid-ocean, and so they agreed to let Ghost Islands stay in pirate grip if red sails shits attack Iascan coast.

So red sails fired the Nob. Delfs headin' home after winter. Defend, if Venn come back in spring, try to take us while pirates busy 'gainst them horse-boys."

"Prick Harbor? Gone?" Scalis asked, astounded.

"So them sez."

Kodl murmured, "If the Brotherhood of Blood attacked it in force, you know they'd leave nothing standing."

No one spoke as they all imagined what it must have been like to see the Brotherhood's red-sailed ships on the horizon, landing launches full of pirates . . .

The *Loohan* set sail again in a sober mood. Later Scalis muttered when Niz was safely aloft, "Them Delfs is known to put a touch of color into their tales. It just don't make sense to torch the Prick, when them Venn shits trade there too."

Inda glanced down at their hoard of feathers as they all worked on carving and fletching fresh replacements. It made sense in terms of army movement: the Venn were obviously making certain the Marlovans couldn't launch armies from the harbors. He said nothing, though, even when Kodl joined him at the rail—they weren't going home.

Kodl sighed. "If the Delfs sail west, so go our allies."

Next hire: a wealthy Silk Guild schooner. Pirates, recognizing a fortune in ransom in the beautifully appointed craft, attacked under cover of fog-wreathed uncertain winds.

This pirate ship was single, with only one cut-boom, but they were so skilled they did enormous damage along the weather side of the schooner, making escape impossible.

Four times they tried to board, and each time they were repelled, after very hard fighting. Inda commanded the first two, and Kodl the next, once he saw the pattern of attack and Inda's response; Inda learned that his much drilled signals worked, and that most pirates apparently had no training at moving in disciplined units, instead relying on noise, terror, and brute strength.

But it's not always going to be this way, he thought, prowling around the ship and trying to think of new defenses. If the next enemy were trained, what then?

Kodl, standing in the middle of the sprawl of fallen rope, jumble of blocks and tackle, and splintered wood as the ship's crew launched desperately into hasty repair, watched Inda with the same intensity the *Loohan*'s crew had watched the mariners one hire ago and when Inda looked up at last, and said, "We need our own cut booms, something we can carry and rig when needed. We need new defenses. Beginning with spiked shields along the rails, to be snapped over just before they board."

Kodl whirled. "Dun! Wumma!"

One was helping with sails, the other at the helm. They both ran forward, and Kodl described the shields in a few words, then said, "Can you make us something to try out?"

They looked at one another, Wumma muttered something about extra steel, then Dun said, in his even voice, "We will do our best."

They dropped down the hatch.

Inda said, "Now for some drills to use 'em," and he started walking back and forth, back and forth, unaware of this pattern he'd begun while thinking furiously.

Kodl, seeing it, was reassured: when he stopped walking, Inda would have a plan.

Summer lengthened into a very busy, successful autumn. Their cruises were all short, sometimes a matter of a single week when convoys broke up and single ships wanted extra protection. They had a few more brushes with pirates, but each time beat them off. The others crowed, but Kodl saw Inda sitting on the taffrail staring out, or prowling the deck moodily. Kodl watched, his feelings conflicted. He knew the boy had no ambition. He showed no interest in hiring out and stayed by himself or with his particular friends. The perfect first mate, Kodl thought of him, but for how long?

"What's wrong?" he asked abruptly one hot summer night, as the sound of singing rose from below.

Inda's profile was bleak, looking much older than his years in the swinging lamplight. "We haven't seen the worst of what's out there," he said. "We have yet to face the red sails. But it is going to happen."

Kodl had no time to answer. Scalis, flushed with success, came up, motioning for them to listen. "We all did thumbs, and we don't want to hire out over winter. No pullin' watches in freezing storms."

Behind, his remaining forecastlemen gestured agreement.

"All right," Kodl said, doing a quick mental calculation. "I'll set a goal. If we earn it, we buy winter free. But we'll drill," he added, remembering Inda's words.

The others agreed—winter training was nothing new—and Kodl drove their hiring price up. The only captain who'd meet it owned a weatherly independent trader called the *Dancy*, fast for a merch, and heavily laden with some sort of expensive cargo kept locked up tight.

And just two days outside of Freeport Harbor dawn brought two narrow craft bearing down with all sails filled.

Jeje and her band pounded up on deck, arrows ready, Thog with her lantern. Inda motioned them into the tops, then watched Kodl, who studied the oncoming pirates through the cold mist drifting across the blue-green waters. Those sails, a sweet, sharp-cut curve that was so expensive to cut and sew to precision they had to have been taken off a royal yacht, bellied in a way that worried him. Both ships' foresails wore crossed swords painted on, licks of flame above and below. Fire Islands pirates.

No cut booms on these. Inda had learned by watching that they required skillful handling—too close in to a much heavier ship and the booms just tangled, could even cut into the mast, immobilizing the pirate.

These two relied on speed, then, so they'd be boarding, which meant—

Kodl faced Inda, flashed his hand open: over to you.

Inda turned his head up. "Jeje!"

"I see it," she cried down. "Cut-arrows ready!"

"What's the matter? What's the matter?" asked the cargo master, a nervous landsman dressed in Guild Livery, his fashionably short blond hair lifting in the wind.

"Sails are wet," Inda replied briefly.

"That's bad? That's good?"

"Go below and guard your cargo," Kodl snapped.

A sound like a whimper escaped the man, who wrung his hands. "You're supposed to be the best! You were paid double—"

"Get!" snarled Scalis, waving a freshly honed cutlass.

"Dun," Inda said, forgetting about Kodl being in command. He was too intent on watching the perfect tacking of those low, fast craft, narrow built, clean lines. Men, mostly young, crowded in the bows, armed and ready to leap over.

"Wet sails," Dun observed at Inda's left, standing in his accustomed shield arm spot.

Kodl frowned. "They planned for *us*."

That's what getting a rep means, Inda thought.

Up on the yard above, Tau leaned toward Jeje, who stared down, her face unhappy. "Worried?" he murmured.

Jeje flicked him a glance. "About Inda. Why does Kodl watch him like that?"

Tau laughed inwardly at himself. So much for thinking he was the only observant one. "Kodl doesn't understand Inda. He doesn't see that the problem, when it comes, will be Scalis."

Jeje glanced down at the forecastlemen, who laughed and joked, stroking their weapons. "You think he wants to turn pirate?"

"Not yet, but—" No time to finish his answer. The first ship came in, as usual on the weather side, the other sailing for the lee. Inda signaled to Jeje and steel-tipped arrows whined across the intervening sea, all aimed at the weather-leech of the mainsails, the ones tightest and drawing the most against the wind.

The arrows cut through again and again, making tiny holes. Inda forced his eyes away; though it was a desperate measure, it had worked twice against pirates who had attacked under the cover of rain squalls, but in sails that were worn, or badly made, causing them to rip and flag out, catching in shrouds and lines, and spilling way off the ship.

Then he forced his attention away. It would either work or it wouldn't.

He signaled to Scalis and Dun. Both bands crept along the rail under the hastily put together spiked shields, bows and steel thrust in clothing, even clenched in teeth.

Arrows whizzed overhead, some aimed at Jeje and her band, others shot high, with little licks of flame to catch in their own sails. Yan would already have the regulars organized into a pump team, so Inda did not even look; he gauged the oncoming ship, felt the wind, shook his head, and signaled to the helmsman to put the helm hard over.

The heavily-laden trader moved too slowly, and the lee pirate's bowsprit caught in the foremast shrouds. The wood creaked and groaned, the ship's own bulk worked against it, and with a rending crack the foremast came down, flinging the upper-yard sailors into the sea.

The first pirate boarding party screamed in triumph, brandishing weapons as they stood on their rail or held onto the mainchains, ready to climb onto *Dancy*'s higher deck the moment the two ships came together. With a roar Dun's band lunged up—Wumma, the Sartoran brothers, and Tau—shooting arrows with practiced, lethal accuracy directly into the pirates. Few were wearing mail, which was not liked at sea—no one could swim long with mail weighing them down—and they started falling. The spiked shields slowed the boarders. Scalis' band hacked into the few pirates who actually made it over the rail and flung the bodies right back onto the pirates' deck.

Inda motioned to Hav and a forecastleman. Dun came, pushing Hav aside, who shrugged and rejoined his band.

"Oil," Inda said.

Niz and his fighters flung lighted empty barrels and bits of flotsam down at the pirates, who were hanging back, many looking to their own captain for a change in orders.

Dun led in bowsing up the mizzen course tight, then fashioning a net sling at the end of the boom. Arrows flew all around them, one hitting Testhy in the side. He staggered, but did not let go of his rope. Dun and a big forecastleman wrestled a barrel of oil into the net sling, set it afire. They waited to see the blue flame curling up from the surface and then Inda cut the rope holding back the boom, which snapped out, causing the entire ship to lurch. The barrel launched across the short distance to the deck of the pirate ship, where it broke, spreading flaming oil in all directions.

Another barrel. They readied the third and the big forecastleman holding it recoiled, shot through the neck. As he fell, Dun caught the barrel, slapped it into the net. They released it upward at the long, beautiful curving mainsail of the second ship, setting it alight.

A launch full of pirates shot around from the far side of the second ship, oars like beating wings. Scalis shifted his attack of fiery debris toward it, but it hit *Dancy* with a crash, sending a judder through the hull. The pirates climbed up in a tight mass, some wearing shields on their bent backs; hammers and carpentry tools took care of the spiked shields along the rail as arrows clinked and plinked unmusically on the shields the pirates wore, falling harmlessly into the sea. They swarmed up.

Inda whistled sharply. Kodl's own feet and hands obeyed, falling into position, cutlasses, knives, and the wickedly efficient dragoon staves that Inda had drilled them with at the ready. The *Dancy*'s sailors watched in amazement as their defenders charged the boarders, stabbed those in front, and the reaction rippled back through the pirates, who recovered in a few moments, stampeding over their fallen crewmates, roaring and shrieking, weapons high. In a single movement the defenders twisted their staffs apart and waded in swinging two humming cudgels with deadly effect.

Inda led the wedge into the mass of attackers, Dun fighting shield-arm position behind and to his left; Kodl took a hard-held position at the right.

They ripped into the enemy like a knife cutting rotten rope. A spike of sharp triumph flared through Inda, igniting bones and muscle with high-singing joy. The attackers began to fall back, some of them slipping in the blood of their fellows who fell with crushed throats and cracked skulls, hacked limbs, smashed ribs. Inda felt none of the blows and jars inevitable in hard fighting—his mind had disengaged, he had fallen into that cascade of events, only he was the power driving it, driving it—

Up above, Thog, daughter of Pirog had been peering intently at the pirate ships between shots. Jeje, puzzled by the strange behavior of the Chwahir girl, was busy scanning for Inda and Kodl's next signal, and so she almost missed it when Thog suddenly smiled—a horrible smile with her teeth bared—and raised her bow. She said something in her native language and then shot one pirate captain square in the chest. A heartbeat later she whirled round on the masthead they shared, aimed at the second pirate captain she'd obviously marked before, and shot. And as he fell, an arrow through his throat, Thog laughed, her voice high and shrill as the cry of a gull.

Chapter Twenty-four

THE next day they listed into Freeport Harbor, foremast fished with timber and rope, red flag at the mizzen and white at the main, sailors either cleaning or nursing the sails at the jury-rigged mast with tender care.

Damage was always interesting. The docks and boardwalk lined with idlers and workers pausing in their labors as the *Dancy* was signaled for a place close in; they'd get a dock as soon as one of the refits warped out.

"Ho *Dancy*," came a bull's roar of a voice from the dock as the oars on the first launch began to dip. "What news?"

"Pirates," cried *Dancy*'s first mate, in an equally topmast-in-a-squall voice.

That was obvious from the damage.

"Brotherhood-allied?"

"No. Fire Islands."

"Brisk fight, eh?"

"Brisk enough," came the justly proud answer. "Burned one, drove t'other off, listin' bad."

"This is going to kick our price up," Kodl muttered to Inda and Scalis as they clambered into the second launch.

Scalis chuckled at the thought of more gold to fling about, and Niz muttered, "Winter's on us. You keep that gaff bowsed up tight, mate. Us'll need t'make our pay last—Inda wants us havin' all kinds o' new weapons."

Scalis spat over the side, his glee undiminished.

Niz said to Testhy, their official purser, "Don't let him chousel you outa no extree, now."

"I won't," Testhy said cheerily. "I know his tricks."

Scalis uttered an explosive snort.

Inda, sitting at the bow oar, thought: *You are not going to have time for tricks. And you're going to be too tired for sex.*

Kodl thought, *They say Inda, not Kodl. But he's the one with the ideas.* He'd already wrestled with his inward conflict: there was a way of military thinking he just hadn't grasped yet. Inda saw a weapon, he thought of the easiest way to resist it. Spiked shields that flip up to resist cut booms . . . the cut arrows . . . This idea of force against force was simple when Inda explained it, but as for actually carrying it through . . . Kodl knew he just did not have the experience applying it in real terms.

So where does a small boy get that kind of experience?

To dismiss his uncertainty, he leaned forward. "Inda, what first?"

By the time they reached the main dock, Inda and Kodl had begun revising the drill schedule.

Inda, sore from the fight and desperately hungry, loathed the prospect of the long walk up to Lark Ascendant. At least this time it was Dun's and Scalis' turn to make sure the wounded got over the side and to their beds; though their injury count was about half the band, they'd only lost one of Scalis' forecastlemen in that fight.

The dock master was waiting as they tied up. Within moments he was in conference with the *Dancy*'s captain about harbor fees. Inda climbed up the slimy ladder, glancing at the dock support poles to check the height of the tide, an automatic glance. It would be months before they launched again.

He hoisted his gear bag into a better position on his back as he passed the captain and dock master. Behind them lounged the assistant who kept records for the harbormaster, a tall, thin, young man dressed in plain sailor wear—long vest over shirt and loose trousers—but who always managed somehow to look elegant. Tau, who was always equally elegant, could have told Inda that that was what you got when you had your clothing tailored, but it had never occurred to Inda to ask. He had no interest whatsoever in clothing. Despite the others' teasing he still made his own shirts the way Sails had taught him when he was eleven and a new rat on the *Pim Ryala*. It was something to do with his hands when he had watch on rainy nights, when he could revisit old memories, and try to imagine where his friends were now: did Sponge ever get to Daggers? Did Tanrid stop going now that he was a Guard? And Tdor . . . she had to be . . . he mentally counted. He had turned sixteen sometime before they took the *Dancy* hire. So, if that was true . . . he was stunned to realize that if he was sixteen, she'd be eighteen come spring! Tdor seventeen? Not in memory. In memory, she was forever twelve.

The real world intruded itself once again when the harbor master's assistant spoke. "Ho, Inda."

"Heyo, Woof."

"Squalls ahead," Woof said in Sartoran, motioning behind by rolling his eyes and flicking his head.

"What news?" Inda flexed his aching wrist.

"Came in with Ramis," was the surprising answer.

"What? Ramis One-Eyed? Is he here?" Inda turned around and surveyed the harbor in the fast-fading light, but saw no sign of a tall-masted, square-sailed Venn warship with its raised, curved prow.

"Was. Left on the morning tide, stayed just till the ebb. Off to some secret base to refit, some say." Woof jabbed toward the sea with his quill. "You think *Dancy* looks dusted up, you should've seen *Knife*. Norfa—on morning duty—she heard they took on three Brotherhood, two big cut-boom brigantines, and a schooner. Sank two, took the third. And when I say took, I don't mean took a new ship, I mean sent 'em right into night, though it was the middle of the day."

Norsunder again. "Three! What does he look like?"

"Ugly." Woof smacked the side of his face. "Half burned off. All over purple, eye patch. They say that the dead eye looks straight into Norsunder. I don't want to know." Woof grimaced. "The good one is terrible enough. But he brought—"

"Elgar!" Kodl yelled from across the cobblestone causeway, Testhy close behind him.

Woof stepped back, made a gesture both courtly and ironic, and Inda, remembering the beginning of the conversation, wondered what awaited them. Surely not a disgruntled captain!

Testhy looked glum as he fingered his bandaged side. His light eyes flickered to either side. "I hate it when anyone asks for me by name. Just means trouble. I hope it's just Scalis' unpaid shot in some den. He has the money to pay it now."

"Why us, then?" Inda countered. "Wouldn't the person he owed ask for him? And if some captain wants us to hire, shouldn't it be Kodl?"

Of course Testhy couldn't answer these questions. He just hitched his shoulders closer to his ears.

The trader clerks waved them through canyons of silk bales stacked neatly and well away from the big rooms with their damp air, past other sorts of cargo, some of it hidden in boxes painted with cryptic markings, to a small office with a battered door.

Kodl opened it. A tall, thin, black-browed young woman looked up from the table she sat at, and Kodl stopped short so that Testhy and Inda nearly ran into him. Testhy's breath whuffed out as if someone had smacked him on those wounded ribs.

"Ryala! Ah, Mistress Pim," Kodl croaked, wiping his grimy eyes as if he were dreaming.

Inda stared, and three gear bags thumped to the dusty floor.

The owner's daughter stood, and they recognized worn Iascan travel clothes. She held up some wrinkled papers and pronounced in a loud, forceful voice, the sort of voice one uses when one has mentally rehearsed an encounter for months and months, "If you do not have the price of my family's ships and their cargo, then I accuse you of theft. And murder. And I'll see that I get justice."

Testhy sat down abruptly on a barrel, his hand pressed to his side. Inda stared from one to another, completely bewildered.

Kodl said, "Testhy told me that Fassun wrote to you."

"Two letters," Ryala Pim stated, her eyes wide, her face taut. "He sent two letters, in case one should go astray. And he paid for magic transfer."

Testhy forced himself to speak, though his throat had gone dry. "Look, Mistress Pim. Fass was angry when he wrote those. He told me just before he left the island he wished he hadn't. He was going to earn some more money and tell you what really happened."

She faced him, her shoulders tight. Until Testhy spoke everything had gone as she had envisioned during her long, weary months of travel, but now the interview was completely different from what she'd expected.

Everything was unexpected. No one, at first, had been willing to take

her from the mainland to Freedom Island until a messenger from that
ugly pirate captain had come with his invitation. Her mind fled back,
briefly, to the utter quiet of that inn in Khanerenth, an absence of sound
probably unfelt in there for decades, so all that could be heard was the
rain dripping on the cobblestones outside, the fire, and a lot of people
breathing, after the innkeeper whispered, "Ramis." Only desperation
had given her the courage to accept.

"What do you mean?" She shook her head to banish the memory and
glared at Testhy, one hand clutched tight around the magic talisman
she'd been given so unexpectedly by that scarfaced pirate.

Testhy glanced Kodl's way, watched by Ryala. She did not know
Testhy, or his habits, so his normal shifty-eyed gauging of others' reactions appeared as collusion.

He said, "Fassun stayed in Freeport over that first winter, then he
went to the mainland. Him being Idayagan, he meant to find a capital
ship to hire on, since what comes through here are privateers and allies
of the free traders—"

"You mean pirates," Ryala broke in.

"We don't have anything to do with pirates," Kodl said.

"You don't?" Now she was back to familiar mental terrain. "Oh, then
you still have our ships? Even one of them? The cargo, perhaps?"

"No. They were taken when we entered harbor here."

"You sold them," she accused. "Fass said you sold them."

Kodl shook his head. "We would have lost them anyway. Possibly our
lives as well, had we not run for this harbor. The sved is that Norsh and
Leugre led some crew in a mutiny; they wanted to keep the ship and
turn pirate, and they lost. Norsh, Leugre, and some others were killed.
Fassun was with them, but I don't believe by true choice. We let him
and Indutsan and Faura go. As for the money, we paid off the arrears of
everyone's wages."

"You didn't pay Fass," Ryala retorted, glaring at them all in turn: three
brown faces with pale hair, for all she could see of Inda was the top of
his sun-bleached head as he stared at the dusty boards of the floor.
Three heads gone pale in the sun from sailing around, attacking people.
Like pirates. Maybe even in her mother's ship, for who was to say they
didn't just keep it and sell the cargo?

Kodl said, "No. As I said, we let Fassun and his cousin and the others
go. In the launch before we sailed into Freeport."

"So you say." Ryala Pim flushed with rage. "Convenient, that mutiny. And the fact that all the other crew are gone, except your *pirates*."

"That's not true," Inda protested.

Ryala Pim glared at him. "So you didn't know about the mutiny beforehand? Fass said that you did, and that you—*you*, a *Marlovan*—used that as an excuse to kill off your enemies."

"No! Oh, yes, we knew, that is, we suspected they were planning a mutiny, and it's true I killed Leugre and Black Boots, but that was because they were coming after me."

"If they were suddenly so evil, why didn't Captain Beagar place them in the brig for justice?" Ryala demanded, her voice shaking.

"He was . . . sick," Testhy said, his eyes shifting, when he realized the other two would not answer.

"Fass said he was *drunk*! Or you never would have gotten away with your mu—"

Kodl cut in, angry now. "He was drunk, yes. The embargo, the blockaded harbors—he'd lost everything that mattered to him most. And now he is dead, and beyond blame."

"Fassun said that you killed him. You, the expert with the knife." Ryala pointed at Inda, and stated in her slurry north-coast Iascan, "I know who you are, *Lord* Indovun Algraveer."

"Indevan-Dal Algara-Vayir," he corrected automatically, in the accent of a Marlovan aristocrat. "Of Choraed Elgaer." Her derision in saying the name he had not used, or even heard, for four long years made him flush with painful prickly heat all over.

The other two gaped at him.

Ryala sneered. "And I also know why you went to sea, *Lord Indovun*. Because you cheated in your stupid war games, and killed the boy who tried to stop you. And you expect me to believe you!"

White-hot rage seared through Inda. "That's a lie!" Inda shouted, for the first time in all the years the others had known him.

"Oh, so Lord Kethadrend Keperi-doo–Kepur-dow—now one of your nasty, bloody Jarls, who rules the entire Andahi Pass all the way up to the Nob. He's a liar? It's his daughter who told my mother who you were and what you did. His son was there when it happened."

Inda's rage turned cold, bringing back all the pain and humiliation of his eleven-year-old self. "It is a lie, a damned lie, and Kepa is a liar," he declared, realizing he'd spoken in Marlovan only when he saw the reaction in all their faces. In Iascan, "Kepa lied to the masters. It was a frame up. Though I don't know why."

Ryala turned away from him, her movement expressive of disbelief and contempt. "There is no sved for pirates." She waved her papers. "You're *all* a lot of liars. I believe Fassun. Knew him all my life. He was my friend, his words were sved." Her voice quavered with both grief and anger.

Testhy said in a low voice, "He told me before he left for the mainland he felt bad about lying, especially about Inda, because, well, because."

"Because what?" Ryala and Kodl exclaimed at once.

Inda gave a shaky sigh. "Zimd told me Testhy was meeting him in secret. Fassun didn't have any money. I told Testhy to give him my share of the gold bag run. Tau shared his with me until we got our first pay, and kept the secret."

"I don't believe it," Ryala stated. "Why would you do that? He hated you!"

Inda flushed with guilt, dropping his head again to glare at his hands. He was determined not to speak. Ryala felt sour triumph at having caught him lying at last. Of course she could not know—because Inda would never say it out loud to anyone—that his reaction was a mixture of guilt over Marlovan conquering of Fassun's homeland, and guilt because Scalis had thrown Fassun out of the forecastle drills after Inda decked him, and Inda hadn't found out until it was far too late to make amends. Neither was his fault but he felt guilty just the same, for reasons he still couldn't parse.

"Why else would you give him money?" she demanded, waiting obviously for his next lie.

"Doesn't matter why." Inda dug his palm heels into his eyes. "I wasn't there when Testhy gave him the money. Never saw him. But Testhy said Fass told him to tell you what really happened if he ever saw you again."

Testhy said, "He's telling the truth. Fass told me about the letters, Mistress Pim. Then he used Inda's money to buy passage to Khanerenth. We left on our first hire, and we never saw him again."

Kodl opened his hands. "I myself heard nothing about Fass until the last time we touched here between hires. Adun-Cook had just returned from Khanerenth and had gone again, but she left me a letter, saying he'd died in a fight in Lands End while stealing some sailor's purse. Said he'd been drinking heavy. He couldn't get hires because people insisted he sounded Iascan, and then because of the drink."

Ryala stared sightlessly down at the papers crushed in her trembling hand. The other hand still clutched that transfer token as memory erupted into her thoughts again, bringing before her mind's eye the terrifying pirate Ramis, who had ignored her until a couple of days ago, in the middle of the sea, he joined her beside the rail. She said to him, *Are you certain I will find Kodl and that Lord Indevan there in Freeport Harbor?*

He shut his one eye, lifting his face as if hearing voices beyond human hearing, or seeing a vision that others could not see, then said, *They are in a battle right now. If they live through it, you will find them.*

How could he *know* that? Maybe they were all secretly united together. So why did he give her the magic talisman before he set her on land?

Ryala shook her head slowly, smashing the letters unheeding against her chest. "It's true that Fass died while stealing. I found out that much when I was in Lands End, before I crossed to here," she said in a low voice. She blinked rapidly. Her jaw hardened. "If he was that desperate, then blame falls to you."

"It was a mutiny, Mistress Pim," Kodl stated.

"So you say. But who am I to believe? I crossed the entire continent just to find out the truth. The only evidence I have is Fassun's letters, and the fact that you are all still here, still fighting like Marlovans and killing people." She slapped at Testhy with her papers. "Here's the sved: my ships are gone. Gone! *Everything* is gone. Those ships—the talk of war in the north—-we had pledged the very last of our credit on that glowglobe cargo, at Captain Beagar's request. Gone. Sold by *you*. But we still owe the original owners. How am I going to repay it? There is no shipping, no work, no money. Just before I left, pirates attacked and burned down Lindeth. And then the Nob. My mother is left with no roof over her head, same with my cousins at the Nob. We are forced to take charity from the Guild. I will have justice, Handar Kodl."

He spread his hands. "It was either take refuge here, or be taken by pirates. The ship was lost either way."

She smacked the papers against the back of her chair, her mouth quivering. "Back to that again? All right. I can see that my journey was for nothing." Tears wet her cheeks. "But I promise you this," she said in a low, trembling voice. "You set foot in any kingdom that has justice, and I will see to it you get it. Thieves. *Pirates.*"

She closed her eyes, her one hand clenched on something and her lips moving. As the other three watched in stunned disbelief she vanished in an eye-tearing crackle of light, leaving only a faint breeze caused by displaced air to stir the heavy air in the room.

"How'd she do that?" Testhy squeaked.

Kodl turned to Inda in amazement. "You're the son of a lord? No," he corrected, calling up what little he knew of Iasca Leror's government. Choraed Elgaer. "A prince."

Inda looked back with that blank face they'd all known since he was a rat. They stared at his bruised jaw, red knuckles, the filthy tangle of yellow-streaked hair escaping from his braid, and his old, weatherworn shirt and deck trousers, thinking: prince? Aren't they supposed to be different?

He's different when he fights, Kodl thought.

Inda, reading accusation in those stares of bemusement, said, "I did not betray Dogpiss Noth." His gaze slipped past them, straight into the past, old pain renewed. "It was a plot, and I still don't know why, but the king's own Shield Arm was part of it."

Kodl whistled softly. He could well believe that. Marlovans were notoriously bloody-handed, so why wouldn't they plot against each other as well as their neighbors? He stared at Inda, reflecting on years of travel, round the world twice, and how you thought you knew people, then surprise. Like Beagar, so calm and wise and steady during bad weather and nasty customs officials, turning to drink and despair.

Now it made sense, the boy who could fight two-handed against grown men. The boy who would forget and use proper Sartoran verbs in Dock Talk, even though he'd never actually been to Sartor. That all added up to a prince's education. A cowardly, treacherous prince?

No. Kodl was sure of that much. Inda Elgar might be a prince, and might have left scandal behind him, but he was no coward. Nor was he treacherous, or he would have been leading that mutiny on the Pim trader, and further, he would have succeeded. He was a natural commander—who didn't want to take command.

At least, not yet.

Would the rest of his band of mariners follow the son of a prince if he decided he wanted to be the leader? Kodl said, "Look. Scalis' family was killed in a Marlovan raid, long ago. He's talked himself, and the others, into thinking you were one of their horse tenders, a stable boy, exiled for refusing to murder people. Let's keep what we heard between the three of us. Some of the others have similar attitudes. We don't want to run the risk of dissention in the band when we've been so successful, do we?"

Testhy shrugged. Princes were rare, but they were also only of real interest in their own sphere, that is, surrounded by wealth and power and thus dispensers of largesse. Inda Elgar, or whatever his name really was, obviously possessed not the smallest vestige of largesse.

Inda nodded. It was clear he still wanted to keep his secrets if he could. Kodl would exert himself to keep it that way.

Kodl murmured, "That knife fighting. The staffs. Is that what they teach the horse boys?"

"Dragoons," Inda corrected numbly. His mind droned over and over again, *Never go home again. Never go home again.* "We haven't horses on ships, so you're getting a combination of dragoon work—-those are the ones that ride ahead and fight on the dismount—and . . . another kind of defense." He stumbled at revealing the Odni. That promise had been to his sister, and through her, to his mother. *Never go home again.* But he would keep that promise.

He struggled to get a grip on his emotions. All right, so now two knew who he was, what had happened to put him here. But they would keep his secret.

A short breath, then, "Pirates don't do sveds? Or did she mean they always lie?"

"You won't often see sveds in pirate-held ports," Kodl said. "Very few mages will work for 'em, and also, merchants who try to cheat end up dead. On the mainland so-called respectable traders cheat each other all the time unless their Guilds are on the hop. It's against the law to kill someone for cheating you. Pirates don't *need* sveds."

Testhy straightened up, shrugging away pirate trade custom. "Ryala said it too, about Lindeth and the Nob. That must mean it really happened. What do we tell the others?"

"It no longer matters whether the Nob is there or not." Kodl rubbed his aching forehead. "She'll lay information against us at all the kingdom harbors. We daren't land in any kingdom port unless we want to be jailed. Maybe hanged outright. Until, at least, we somehow pay her back for the cost of ships and cargo. Which I had intended to do anyway, but did not get the chance to tell her." *That was my oath to my old friend Captain Beagar, not to the Pims.* Kodl gave the skin between his brows one last pinch then dropped his hands. "Just as well we're successful here, then, isn't it? Woof told me there are at least ten or twelve likely people who've been asking how to hire us on, and I guess I'd better talk to some of them. Freeport Harbor is our new home. We're independent mariners."

Inda looked up then, his eyes bleak, his mouth tight. In a flat voice he said, "We need more people for boom crews once we build our own. We have to learn how to mount them and use them right. That means drilling with sail teams who can be in the tops, directing the crews of our hires. We'll start the people you hire on our regular training. But until they catch up, they run the cut booms and sail so we don't have to run both. We also need more staff drill—we need moves for that downward angle, when they're boarding. Last, we also have to find ourselves a cutter to scout the p—" He pressed his lips together, then said, "What we used to call the outer perimeter. We need to scout the sea around us, not just wait until they are on us. We'll need crew for that. Maybe some old weatherworn craft with good lines. We can rebuild them. But from now on we must always have scouts—we pick the fighting ground instead of allowing the enemy to do it, if we can."

The other two agreed, neither giving voice to the uneasiness they felt at the unhidden misery in Inda's face.

Chapter Twenty-five

THE Harskialdna looked out the king's window at the men marching out to the great parade ground to set up for the long postponed summer games. "You waited on my return."

Tlennen-Harvaldar opened one hand. "Too many of their fathers, cousins, brothers were with you up north. It was not . . . seemly to hold the games with stands so empty of banners."

The Harskialdna fretted at that pause. If only Tlennen would say what he meant. Just once. That, and stop looking so old. There wasn't any red left in his hair at all. The Harskialdna, tired from the long ride, felt unsteady, as if he'd been gone ten years. It underscored his worry that, despite careful orders last spring before he left, things had changed without him here to oversee to see them.

"You could have filled the stands with civs," he finally said, an attempt to provoke his brother into being more revealing.

"The city people always enjoy what they see, but they cannot evaluate the youth as you must do," the king said. "Then we had to wait on the weather. After a dry summer, all the rain came at once, a hailstorm that smashed most of the crops. It took half a month to dry out the grounds."

"Of course, of course." Crops didn't matter. They'd grow more next year. What did matter was sudden change.

A steward appeared to offer food. Tlennen deferred to his brother, who flung his riding gloves to the man and then dismissed him, all in the same motion. "That can wait."

Tlennen murmured, "What of recent developments?"

"Little beyond what I sent by my last Runner. What I did not trust to written word was the totality of the destruction of both Lindeth Harbor and the Nob. The pirates with the red sails brought down every building, and burned every single ship in both harbors."

"We must rebuild," said the king.

"Yes." The Harskialdna began pacing back and forth. After so long a ride he needed to move. "And so I told our new Jarls." He stopped, smiling with grim pleasure. "I told them to gather up those Idayagan and Olaran rabble who seem to have nothing to do but attack us from behind hedgerows and trees and force them to labor. If they will not work, put 'em to the sword. And the townsmen can pay for the supplies."

The king's face did not change. "You misunderstand, brother," he said. "We must rebuild. *We.*"

"We?" The Harskialdna stopped, and swung around.

"It is in the treaty."

The Harskialdna frowned, remembering the silent figure standing behind him during the negotiations: Jened Sindan.

They both considered those negotiations, the king through Sindan's report, and the Harskialdna looking back in sour pleasure on the defeated, and stricken, Idayagans.

Sindan had noted, and the Harskialdna had gloried, in Idayago's shock at the Marlovans' savage mastery of the vast Idayagan hordes during that battle below the Ghael Hills, a shock so deep and severe they would sign anything. Almost.

The fat, wily old king of Idayago had only spoken once: *You declare you are here to protect the integrity of the continental borders. Does that mean that you defend them, and rebuild if someone attacks?* The Harskialdna, reveling in the privilege of speaking with the King's Voice, had stated with an air of impatience, *Yes, yes.* And so the king had signed.

"We should have acted." The Harskialdna rapped a table. "By staying our hand afterward, by not rooting out the leaders of that trap and executing them publicly, we showed ourselves as weak. They think they can ignore a treaty they now say was forced on them. You've seen my reports: never an honorable battle. Constant cowardly reprisals. Sneaking around behind bushes and barrels at night, ambushing any of our people they catch alone."

"Nevertheless, it was a treaty. We must abide by it," the king returned. He said in the King's Voice, using the verbal mode of future-must-be, "In spring those harbors shall be rebuilt. We shall pay those who do the labor."

The Harskialdna saluted his assent. So precious gold would go north next campaign season. The Harskialdna must obey, but he could also see to it that he would not return a third time—not to oversee what by rights was a harbormaster's job. "Shall we give the boys the signal, then?" He forced a smile. "They must be impatient enough."

"I will send it," the king said, sensing how little his brother liked his decree. But the treaty must be kept.

"Then I will ready myself." The Harskialdna indicated his mud-splashed riding clothes and left.

He expected to find the heir sulking somewhere about, and so was not surprised to find him waiting in his own rooms. The Harskialdna already knew from his ears among the heir's Runners that the boy had had no success with that black-haired icicle Joret Dei.

"Come with me to the baths. How find you things here?"

"Same." The Sierlaef was already in his House tunic.

"Your brother's progress?" The Harskialdna flung off his dirty clothes.

The Sierlaef shrugged, making it clear he was no longer concerned with the academy and little boys. He was ready to take his place in the men's world. "Headm–muh–mum. *Brath* says he's good." Another shrug. Of course Headmaster Brath would say the second son of the king was good. Of more interest was the report from his uncle's castle Runner Retrend Waldan, chief among the spies.

"Drink." A waving hand. "Favorite. Liberty nights."

The Harskialdna ducked his head under the water, and emerged laughing at the image of Evred Varlaef in a teenage drunken wallow with a dolly from the pleasure house.

He rubbed the soap through his scalp, and flung back his long dark hair that, he noted with a spurt of pride, showed not the least hint of gray. "Never expected it." He dismissed Sponge with a wave of his hand. "What is the talk of our progress in the north?"

"Most want—" The Sierlaef smashed a fist into his palm. "Others—" He flicked his fingers. "Not much news. Hearsay."

His uncle surged out of the bath, and the royal heir broached the subject he'd been mulling for weeks. "Spring. Send Tanrid north."

His uncle paused in the act of toweling his hair, his eyes narrowing. "Haven't you finished with that absurd pining for his wife-to-be? You'll make a joke of yourself."

The Sierlaef waved a hand, hiding the angry jab of victory: his uncle had said just what he'd thought he'd say. "Draining marshland. Planting. Storms bad here, nothing in the south. Crop hoards." It took some time to get those words out, but his reward was the lift to his uncle's brows, and the considering expression.

Iasca Leror was far from starving, not from one bad harvest. But they both knew that northern resources would be diminished greatly, between the embargo, harvests neglected by Idayagans unwilling to grow crops for the conquerors and whose farmers were slinking off to join the ambush parties, and the king's insistence on rebuilding those harbors against his unrelinquished plan of launching an attack northward against the Venn. In the south—in Choraed Elgaer—the lack of war meant abundant crops, and people to plant and harvest. And that meant war tax increases, plus demands for men, horses, equipment, and foodstuffs for the next season.

The Harskialdna flicked his splendid House tunic straight, the gold embroidery gleaming in the leaping firelight, then pointed a finger at the Sierlaef. "You're beginning to think, my boy. I mean to see to it that my brother's loyal prince in Choraed Elgaer meets the realistic needs of our kingdom. Perhaps having his son in the north will increase his . . . enthusiasm for meeting the realistic needs of war. And to the people, his hero of a son is being honored with a command in the troublesome north, eh?"

The Sierlaef smiled, irritated though he was at being called "my boy" when he had been a man for nearly two years now and had seen war before that. But he'd gotten what he wanted, so he smiled. And as he'd been ready ever since the tired outriders arrived at dawn heralding the return of the Harskialdna, they descended together through the castle and out to the stands, talking of horses, new Jarlans, who had died in Idayagan reprisals (no one of import), and who replaced them.

The Harskialdna was in a good mood as he signaled the start of the games. He listened to the crowd cheering and watched the eager scrubs running out to compete in the shoeing, as if anyone but their fathers really cared.

He relaxed into a complacency he had not dared permit himself, not so long away, with success in pacifying an angry populace eluding him for months and months. He had come back to little change. His wife still moped, secluded in her rooms, running the girls' training from there. Good riddance. The king dealt patiently and endlessly with those soft-voiced fools from the east about trade. Evred-Varlaef had apparently fumbled his way from frowsting about in the archives to frittering over a pleasure house dolly, which kept him busy and out of trouble. And the Sierlaef was still his to command.

His complacency lasted through Thirdday, which was when the ponies ran their competitions. They were usually sparsely attended.

The Harskialdna came down after a night of listening to his House ears' private reports and reading copies of letters to see the stands crammed, which ought to have warned him that something was amiss, but he was tired. He noted only that the royal heir was gone, probably to Heat Street.

The first sign of trouble was the tall, slim young man whose resemblance to a young Tlennen hammered him like a fist to his heart. He rode at the head of the ponies, with two full-grown, powerful young men, one pale-haired and one dark, riding at his left and right shoulders respectively—Marlo-Vayir Tvei and Noddy Toraca, who would be Randael to the influential Khani-Vayir family. Behind them the one-eyed Tya-Vayir boy, now looking impossibly dashing, and from the way the girls abruptly started screaming from the stands, extremely popular. Next to him was the second Cassad son, as rat-faced as the rest of that family. Every one of those boys from powerful houses—and obviously at least as tight as the Sier-Danas ever were. Tighter, in fact, judging from the exchanged grins, the joking back and forth, always with Evred-Varlaef in the middle. Aldren-Sierlaef had never led his followers like that.

The Harskialdna snapped his gaze back and stared down in open mouthed dismay at Sponge, who somehow, unnoticed, had grown into a handsome young man: high, intelligent brow, bringing Wisthia's subtle, dangerous father to mind (only met once, but never forgotten), clean jaw, mouth shaped like Tlennen's, even to the controlled lack of expression. Waving dark red hair worn properly in a club, but not the least childish. Severe, that was the word.

The war games commenced, and any hope the Harskialdna had had that the boy—could one call him that anymore, really?—that *he* was still the ink-stained, awkward puppy of yesteryear vanished with the first charge.

Now he watched with a sickening sense of just how vast his error had been to keep Evred-Varlaef upstairs an extra two years in order to send him down to be the oldest, the most awkward of the scrubs, to be laughed at with contempt by his brother and the heirs, while the Harskialdna firmly bound all those future Randaels to his own command against need in the coming war. The heirs had gone on, leaving the academy to the boy who had somehow learned not just competence but a fast, deadly sort of grace.

Oh, but even that wasn't the worst miscalculation.

No, that came in the afternoon, during the mock war on horseback. Sponge had learned how to command.

The Harskialdna, who had been gnawed all his life by the worry that without rank he would never have earned command, that he couldn't command, recognized the flair when he saw it. He'd seen the natural flair in that Algara-Vayir brat and had gotten rid of him, though exactly how still troubled him from time to time. But as long as he was gone, so was the problem. Except that now he was seeing a far more potent version, for this was the king's own son, who could hardly be made to mysteriously vanish, dead or alive.

The Harskialdna leaned forward. The game did not matter. He concentrated on that slim figure in the center, watching in all directions, guiding his horse with trained expertise. Evred did not snap and point in the manner of his brother, the Sier-Danas obeying with the scarcely hidden resentment and then resignation that came from a realistic view of rank and its privileges. No.

Tlennen, with hidden pride, and Hadand, with hidden pleasure, watched the evolutions through the rising dust as the ponies all turned to Sponge, and Sponge signaled with glances, with minute relaxations of his mouth, and finally just by attitude, what he wanted.

The Harskialdna watched, watched so closely he scarcely breathed, but he still could not characterize what he saw. That oblique communication of his will, it was so different from what they taught, so subtle, almost too subtle to discern, built as it was on . . .

Trust? The word "trust" had lost any meaning for Anderle-Varlaef his very first day as an academy scrub. In those days, the only younger brother permitted in the academy was the royal second son. It ceased to be a privilege when four dragoon captains' boys jumped him to see just how tough the future Sirandael was and Tlennen-Sierlaef—seventeen, strong, admired by all, who had promised to watch out for him—wasn't there to help, and didn't come, because he was watching Jarend Algara-Vayir in the archery court.

He ached, three fingers and one rib throbbed with the pain of breaks, all his front teeth felt loose, his nose dripped blood down his gray tunic, but he made it on watery legs to the fence just to see his brother staring at this older boy named Jarend with hot-eyed longing. Next to him, totally unnoticed, ten-year-old Hasta Marlo-Vayir stood, still trying to get his attention to come to Anderle's aid.

A shout! The memory was gone.

Evred-Varlaef's band won, amid echoing cheers, drumming of hands, and yells. And they were all—just as the wretched Algara-Vayir boy had been years ago, and why hadn't he seen the danger then?—they were all loyal to *him*.

"I'll kill Brath."

"What's that?"

Tlennen's voice jolted the Harskialdna. He'd spoken out loud! "What? Nothing. I'm astounded."

Tlennen's austere mouth relaxed, that mouth exactly like his son's below.

Anger boiled in the Harskialdna's guts. He clenched his hands, refusing to raise them, though he knew he would have to. Why had Brath not told him? Because he'd consider Evred's improvement and the boy's grasp of command testament to the success of the academy teachings; it was more effective displayed. No one could fault Brath for doing his job.

He wouldn't see that the true future king rode down there. One day the Sierlaef would be Aldren-Harvaldar, who would ride around seeking little instances of glory, while his brother gripped the true reins of power—not his uncle, with age and experience, who should be by his side, as guide.

He *had* to be there as guide. He'd spent his whole life preparing to be there. But the Sierlaef was getting harder to control; perhaps another long inspection tour. To the south.

More important: for the good of the kingdom, if he did not guide one brother, he must find a way to guide the other.

He shifted his gaze to those boys below.

Now all of the remaining first group of Tveis were there, ranged on either side of Evred-Varlaef: Marlo-Vayir, Cassad, Arveas, Basna, Fijirad, and Fera-Vayir . . . one-eyed Camarend Tya-Vayir . . . Toraca . . . and the Tvei of the most powerful of all the eastern families, Kethadrend "Tuft" Sindan-An! All loyal to *him*.

It didn't matter any longer how it had happened, it was done, and must be mended.

The crowd still shouted for the accolade, and he looked up to see not just Tlennen looking at him in question but Hadand as well. He raised his fist, thinking: *Strut now, boys. This is your last game. When winter is over, it's time for real life.*

Chapter Twenty-six

HALF a year later, on the first day of spring, Sponge was checking his gear for yet another academy year when he was surprised by a summons to his father.

Inside the interview chamber his father and uncle both waited. He turned his gaze to his father, who said, with his faint smile, "Your uncle feels that it is time for you to taste command. You will go north this season, and protect the shorelands, and see to the rebuilding of the harbors from which we will eventually have to launch our defense."

Sponge was stunned. On the walk he'd been considering what window might be best to bunk under in the horsetail barracks. He shifted his gaze to his uncle, just to see the usual white grin, false as a summer wind midwinter. His uncle said, "You'll have not just a wing or two, but an entire army, and your captain will be Tanrid Algara-Vayir, who has distinguished himself up north. Runners will be sent ahead to our holding forces that they are to report to you, and you will personally visit all the Jarls to oversee civilian matters."

Sponge swallowed. He wanted to protest, but he couldn't. They'd decided. A protest would sound merely cowardly, not sensible, since it wouldn't make any difference.

The king, seeing the doubt furrowing his son's brow, felt a pang of remorse. If the Harskialdna judged Evred ready, he was ready, yet he well remembered the uneasiness that came with the weight of command before one thought oneself ready.

"We are stretched somewhat thin this year," he said. "I need your uncle here in case there is trouble with the east."

"The Adranis march to war?" Sponge asked, eyes widening.

Tlennen shook his head. "I don't think it's them. The king will stick to his treaty, but some of his ambitious nobles appear to see the Venn embargo as an excuse to try us."

The Harskialdna said, "Your brother remains in the south, reporting that we must send more detachments west to protect our own harbors against attack. Your brother was your age when he rode to Ghael Hills and victory."

The king, watching his son, knew that it had been a mistake to surprise him. *Don't tell him*, the Harskialdna had said weeks ago, when the plan was first broached. *We'll wait until the first day of spring, and instead of playing at command with the horsetail boys he will have his own real command! Who would not love such a surprise?*

He said, "You will have Captain Sindan's eyes and ears at your command." And because he was watching his son (and saw the relief there, which eased his mind) he did not see the spasm of irritation that tightened his brother's features.

But Sponge saw. His uncle added, "You will also have Tanrid Algara-Vayir, and your dragoon captains, to give you wise advice." And, on Sponge's nod, he said in a voice of dismissal, "You depart tomorrow, while the weather holds."

Tanrid already here? Of course. On orders given long ago. Everything was done without consulting him: he was a boy being given a man's command. If he actually held any authority. That was not a question he could put to his father; what was said could mean less than what was not said.

"Your mother wishes to see you before you leave," the king murmured.

Sponge saluted and left, feeling as if someone had put his head inside a bell and struck the metal.

The first sound to break that strange ringing was his mother's convulsive grip on his arms, her soft kiss, her whispered, "Remember, my child, every man is someone's son."

Then he crossed back to his own rooms, acknowledging the salute of the duty captain. Strange. Though he himself had just been given the surprising orders, it seemed that everyone knew. The salute was not a flat hand to the heart, but a fist: the salute to a commander under royal orders.

He ran up the back way, through an archway mossy on its south side, old Iascan carvings worn to random bumps. Color caught his eye and he stopped, head lifting as he watched young linnets braiding upward into the sky in a mating dance, their song faint on the spring-scented wind.

He stood in his outer room, his gaze wandering from chair to table to the door to the bedchamber as if to find some meaning hidden there while his brain labored to disengage from the predicted path of his future. There would be no academy for him today. This spring, this year. Maybe never again.

No Noddy, no Cama, no Cherry-Stripe or Tuft or Flash—

Pain burned through him. Then he heard a noise, and Hadand and Kialen emerged from his inner room, Kialen pale, thin as a reed, her large eyes dark with the fear that seemed to shadow her through all the seasons. She didn't speak; she almost never spoke anymore.

Hadand turned her head to give a last quiet command, and when the servants were gone she paused, her hands hidden in her robe, aghast at the unhappiness she saw in Sponge's eyes.

He said, "I'm to go north."

Color highlighted Hadand's cheeks and then leached away again. Her brown eyes—the warm, intelligent, sometimes relentless eyes he'd known all his life—lowered, hiding their expression. How often she brought Inda unexpectedly to mind! But this expression, a new one, had never been Inda's. Inda had been absent from time to time, when his mind was racing the winds of possibility, Sponge had learned, but never secretive. "I know," she said to the floor. "My brother told me this morning."

"You've seen Tanrid, then? What does he say?"

"The Harskialdna has been keeping him busy since his arrival yesterday, and of course wants to oversee all the details himself. I breakfasted with him before dawn, and he showed me his map and outlined his orders." A brief smile, more wistful than warm. "Your father invited him once before—a gesture of kindness that was a disaster. Did I tell you about that?"

"I don't think you ever have."

"It was when you were, oh, three or so. I was about six, I forget now, but it was when Tanrid first came as a scrub to the academy. The king invited him to a Restday meal in the nursery. It was horrible—your brother wouldn't speak at all. In those days, I found out later, he never spoke at the academy because he didn't want anybody to hear the stutter. Tanrid didn't say a word, either. Just sat there shoveling the food into his mouth. He never talked much then, still doesn't now, but he was far too intimidated to try. So we endured an entire meal in silence, and the king took pity on us all and it never happened again."

"Did he sit in silence today?"

Hadand smiled, but again the smile was poignant, not happy. She was picturing her brother on the other side of the table, so unfamiliar, despite their being in the same family. He'd grown quite tall, and broad through the chest, and though he obviously was out riding in all weather, his hair had gone dark. "He spoke mostly about his preparations. He thinks the command a great honor."

"So it was explained to me," Sponge said, but Hadand's smile was gone, and though her hands were still hidden inside the sleeves of her robe, he could see that her shoulders were tight.

She turned to Kialen, whose face was pale and stricken, the same expression she'd worn in the old days when Sponge or Barend had been beaten. They'd all comforted Kialen, who was so terrified it was as if someone had taken a stick to her instead.

Hadand said in same the light, tender voice she'd used ever since they were all little, "Will you tell the queen we will be there in a few moments?"

Kialen, one day to stand by Sponge as his wife, glided noiselessly away. He watched, feeling helpless as he always did around her, then he forced his mind back to his new command. "I should have seen it, or something like it, when my uncle so suddenly required me to drill all winter in the Guard, where I was all but forbidden before." He did not talk about the strange conversations with his uncle, always one sided, full of empty laughter and meaningless jokes at others' expense. He had known his uncle was testing him, but for what? He'd thought loyalty. Now, all his old speculations were blown. "You think it a plot to disgrace me? Or something worse?"

"You are capable," she retorted. "You know that."

Sponge shook his head. "I don't trust what I know any more. Not after this morning. But this, it's no secret my uncle has wanted to bind the Marlo-Vayirs more tightly to him, and one of his longest plans was to replace me with Buck Marlo-Vayir." She inclined her head, and he went on, "I think he expected me to dishonor myself in action or by accident by now. It hasn't happened. My first thought on receiving these orders was he sends me ill-prepared for command, meaning for me never to return."

Hadand made a tense gesture. "But you've trained for years for command. You're only a year or so off the time when your brother left. And you will have not just Tanrid, but Uncle Sindan. He will not let anything happen to you."

"True."

"I do know this. You must be vigilant, Sponge. No." She shook her head. "I think—I really think I ought to call you Evred, now. They have decided you are to take a man's place. It might help if you—if we all—begin to think of you with a man's name." Hadand's face was tense as she turned away.

Inwardly he thought: *It is time to be Evred*. It seemed right.

"I gave the orders for all your things to be readied, including a mail coat, so the rest of your day is free," she went on, walking with quick steps to the old ornament casket that sat unused in a wall niche. Evred had had it all his life but in her hands, now, it looked unfamiliar, a box so old the corners were worn, the color dull, the carving of overlaid raptor wings crude, as if carved in the field with a belt knife, which it was. As he watched, wondering what she was about, she opened the casket and pulled out the engraved gold hair clasp that had lain there for all these years, the one worn by his grandfather's Harskialdna. She laid the clasp into his hand, replaced the casket, and walked to the doorway. "Be sure to put up your hair. And send for the armorer, to fit you with proper wrist guards." Then she was gone.

He fingered the heavy gold clasp, the motions empty of intent; what needed to be done was being done by more experienced hands. The day's liberty stretched out long and long before him, and so he tossed the clasp onto his table, gave in to impulse, and sent for Dyalen.

Dyalen. He had always understood that it was better to observe than to ask. As summer had faded into the chill of autumn he came to understand that if he expected her to come when he summoned, then he must not just pay for the time but to contribute to her support; he discovered that somehow everyone knew about her, that he was envied by the other boys for having a favorite. Envied, and admired. Not resented. They accepted it as the prerogative of a prince.

And because she was a female from outside the exclusively male confines of the academy, there was no speculation, no competition to become a favorite, which he knew would have happened if Dyalen had been a male.

In his room, they were always alone, and so the servants did not know what happened there. Sometimes they only talked, for he'd discovered that sex was impossible without the distance that wine created between his thoughts and his body's own desires, and sometimes he could not afford the luxury of waking up with an aching head. They talked about men and women, and her observations, within her view of the world, were acute. They did not talk about war, they did not talk about the future, and though he sometimes wished to ask if she cared about him at all, he didn't, and after a time he realized that she came only when he summoned her, that on her free time she did not; and so he accepted that theirs was a relationship of need, one for sex and companionship, the other for a living. At his request—in case Kialen would, on their marriage, invite him to her bed, though he could not imagine that happening—she taught him how to give pleasure to women. There would be no other woman, he knew by now, unless it be his wife, in his own bed.

Dyalen arrived, wearing her boy's riding clothes, her hair short and free on her neck, like a city boy. When she sat she dropped down like a boy, knees apart, hands on her knees, head to one side. She always smelled of sage, of wind, and a pleasant hint of hay and horse. Smells he loved.

"I am being sent to the north," he said.

"Ah," she said.

He gave her a bag of gold. "Here's for you."

She tipped her head the other way. "I was told that after a long association, it's not so easy, at the end."

He shook his head. "The rules. They govern the physical intimacy. But not that of . . ." He couldn't say "love." The word, misused, could be so sickening.

"Of spirit, of heart," she finished, her eyes steady. "We've shared a kind of binding, the kind that comes of pleasure shared, and I think yours is also a bond that comes of gratitude. I know mine is, for you've been generous and kind. I hope you find what you seek."

"Thank you."

Desire was impossible. She saw, as she always did, and departed. Time returned to its heavy tread. He endured it alone.

Two weeks later Evred was jarred from reverie—he was still thinking over that last interview with Dyalen—by a sudden squawk. A flight of ducks launched from a nearby pond, their fat bodies stretching into the unexpectedly elegant arrowlike shape they took in flight. The beat of their wings diminished in the breeze, and Evred looked around. The plains were unchanged, showing the green tufts of early spring, pools of melted snow below dripping trees sending out slow rings that intersected and vanished.

He rode at the front, two banners flapping just ahead of him. The horses were restless, he realized; his own sidled, her head plunging up and down. One of the horses behind him farted, causing a muffled snicker, and farther back down the line Tanrid Algara-Vayir spoke in a low, soothing voice to a young scout dog who obviously thought it was time to run and investigate whatever it was he smelled on the wind.

Evred lifted his head, peering into the haze under a pewter sky, the silvery gray reflected in the ponds, and in the old sun-bleached stubble left over from the winter. Today silver, at sunset yesterday the sedge had glowed very briefly an astonishing ruddy gold, the sun dropping beneath the layer of clouds just long enough to send out horizontal shafts of radiance, backlighting the hawks drifting over the tips of new grass blades, before sinking beyond the western sea.

Insects, birds, voles, busily went about their lives, noticed and then forgotten: humans looked about for danger, and that meant they watched for one another.

Horse hooves approached from behind, mail jingling, and there was Tanrid, narrowed brown eyes that unexpectedly brought Inda to mind. "Outriders?" he asked.

The asking was pure formality. They both knew it, but still they both scrupulously stuck to the forms. "Take what you need," Evred said, and he watched Tanrid cut out a riding of his own armsmen, snap fingers to the delighted scout hounds, and gallop off to investigate.

The columns stayed steady, everyone watching the scouts dash ahead, mud flying, some sighing in envy. Evred gentled his mare with an absent hand, thinking about Tanrid. He'd expected to despise him. His memory of Tanrid from scrub days had been of a huge, unsmiling tough whose expertise with his fists had been evident on Inda's skin at the beginning of both springs. He'd been one of the Sierlaef's Sier-Danas, too, after that first year. No recommendation in Evred's eyes.

Tanrid had proved to be not just competent but easy to ride with. He seldom talked, and it was never just chatter. He did what needed to be done without strut or indecision. The second night, when two of the older Guards got drunk while on watch, he hadn't bothered with parade or saddlebag searches, as Evred felt sure his uncle would have required, for it was regulation. He'd offered each of them the first hit—traditional but not regulation—after which he'd dealt out the punishment himself with no words wasted, an efficient thrashing with his own hands, not a stick, that left the two men able to ride. Just. Nothing was said, but Evred observed the silent comprehension of all, veteran and new rider. They respected him, young as he was, and all the dogs adored him.

After that there was no breaking of regulations.

The scouts returned almost immediately, their number considerably augmented. Evred recognized that leading figure, his pale yellow horse-tail flying in the wind.

"Cherry-Stripe!" he shouted, and then wished he'd been silent, but Marlo-Vayir Tvei crowed, "Hey, Sponge! We got word you'd crossed into our land day before yesterday, and my dad sent me as a welcome party!" He added, sick with envy and not caring who heard, "And none of us get to go north with you? That reeks worse 'n shit!"

There was a brief whisper that echoed down the columns, obviously repeating his words; two or three laughs, and when Evred did not respond, the entire command erupted into laughter.

Evred grinned wryly. So much for worrying about protocol.

The two parties joined, Cherry-Stripe riding beside Evred. He never stopped talking. Despite his frequently expressed envy, and his plentiful insults not quite naming whoever'd seen fit to deny Sponge's own trained Sier-Danas this prime opportunity for adventure and maybe even glory, he exhibited pride in his land.

Evred listened, noted, smiled when it seemed he ought to, and watched ceaselessly. He had not wanted to stay with the family who conspired to replace him, but those words could not be spoken out loud.

The Jarl, Hastred-Dal Marlo-Vayir, was at his castle gates as befitted one greeting a member of the royal family; his brother Camrid-Dal, behind and to the left in Shield Arm position. The Jarl limped at Evred's halter, leading them inside the court, his face seamed by two sword slashes: one from a border skirmish, one from a duel.

As they exchanged words of greeting Evred listened to his tone. This man did not appear to be subtle. He was loud and jovial in his welcome, his light blue gaze keen but not threatening. Buck Marlo-Vayir was also there, at least long enough to speak the words of welcome. Evred expected to see, and did see, annoyance at the disturbing of their routine, which he found oddly steadying. Somehow it restored some sense to the changing world to see plain emotion in Buck's face, instead of smiling friendliness that might conceal more subtle, and deadly, plans. In any case Buck's mood changed for the better when he spotted Tanrid riding up the column from behind, and that, too, was easily seen.

Buck beckoned to Tanrid and they vanished inside.

Evred was conducted into the castle by both the Jarl and his wife, but the one who caught his eye was the tiny, long-toothed Cassad sister who would be Cherry-Stripe's Randviar. Twice she gave him intense looks from unwavering hazel eyes, but she didn't speak except to add her own version of polite welcome.

"Your men will have our own Riders' campground as the weather's good. My brother is seeing to that," the Jarl said. "Here is your guest chamber, if you'd like to rid yourself of the road dust."

Up old-fashioned stairs through the middle of what was once a main hall, to a second floor built, like most others in these old square castles, within the last two hundred years. Evred slowly entered a huge room clean-swept, newly made raptor chairs at either side of a clear fire, and a bed turned down, with fresh herbs strewn on the sheets.

While he stood absently unstrapping the wrist guards he'd forced himself to wear every day to make them familiar, he contemplated the strangeness of life that would bring him here as guest, when he'd assumed for the past seven years that the next time he saw Buck Marlo-Vayir would be over swords in the grand parade court, only one of them able to walk away.

In the courtyard, Buck jerked a thumb upward. "So?"

Tanrid gave his characteristic one-shouldered shrug. "He's a Varlaef," he said. "They seem to have figured it out at last, and now he's riding off to try out the duties of a future Harskialdna."

Buck brooded on that for a time, as they paced across the long courtyard between the great stable and the outer wall. A scout dog loped up, snuffing at Tanrid; Buck would have swatted the animal out of the way but Tanrid knelt, running experienced fingers over the dog's back, chest, under the chin, while its eyes narrowed and its body stiffened in ecstasy. When Tanrid rose again Buck said, "Sponge's good? Despite what the Sierlaef kept telling us when we were horsetails?"

Tanrid shrugged one shoulder as the dog trotted on to resume its patrol route, waving tail high. "They're calling him Evred now. But yes, he's good."

Buck gave an explosive sigh. "I thought Cherry-Stripe was like a colt full of bran gas about their wins and flags."

Tanrid flashed a brief grin.

Neither spoke as they vaulted up the worn stone steps to the wall. Sentries saw them, the last rays of the sinking sun catching in the silvery stitchery around the great owl in flight embroidered on Tanrid's House tunic, and gave way, leaving them to stand in the cold western wind, staring down at the two great campfires below, ringed with Marlo-Vayir men and those of Evred's new command.

Buck's profile was dark against the campfire below. "Evred. Did you know my given name is Aldren, same's the Sierlaef's?" Tanrid shrugged. "For nearly ten years, I thought—" He tipped his head east toward the royal city. It was as close as he could come to saying the words that never were supposed to be said, and now couldn't be: that the Harskialdna had promised he'd be the Sierlaef's Shield Arm.

Tanrid grunted.

"You think all that talk in the past was just some kind o' test for *him*?" He tipped his head back toward the guest chamber.

Tanrid opened a hand. "Doesn't matter. What they want comes true."

Buck then remembered that Tanrid's own brother had somehow—no one knew how—crossed the Harskialdna's attention and had vanished. Completely vanished. Buck stared down at the men below who were bringing out drums and drawing swords in order to begin the old campaign dances, overseen by his uncle, but he didn't really see them. He tried to remember, and couldn't, what exactly had happened on that banner game so long ago when they were horsetails. The details were gone, except for the sight of Whipstick Noth's little brother lying there beside the stream, dead. The first dead person he'd ever seen, and not an enemy: one of their own. After that, he did remember Tanrid here swearing he'd find out the truth, but then one morning his brother was gone. Missing, no one knew where he was, and Smartlip Lassad and Kepa Tvei—now an heir himself, after his brother's death at the Ghael Hills battle—swearing that the brat had been cheating.

What they want comes true.

Yes, so it seemed. Well, he loved Marlo-Vayir land, and as they'd gotten older, he'd wondered just how much he'd enjoy being Shield Arm to the Sierlaef, with his moods and his wild jaunts after some female.

He sighed, a sound barely discernable over the thunder of drums rising on the dying breeze. He realized he did not resent that solemn red-haired boy upstairs; if anything he felt sorry for him.

Pointing below he said, "They'll expect us to join the dances."

Tanrid shrugged, a short, sharp movement that hinted at memory for him, too. "Let's go."

Buck indicated the stairs, then said with grim humor, "The only good recollection of that summer is what Kepa Tvei—do you know they call him Snowballs now, he's so full of frost—what he looked like after you caught him out."

"Huh," was all Tanrid said. But he grinned.

Behind them, in the castle, Cherry-Stripe and his wife-to-be, fourteen-year-old Mran Cassad, came to fetch Evred.

"Are you ready?" Cherry-Stripe asked, pride and delight shining in his big, handsome face. "Wanta show you over the castle before we get down to the camp. You know they'll expect you in on the sword dances."

Evred had recollected himself, changing hastily into his good tunic. Cherry-Stripe and Mran both stared at the crimson and gold, splendid in the firelight. Cherry-Stripe had never seen Sponge in anything but academy gray, with his hair clubbed modestly. Now he wore his House tunic, and his hair was pulled up, clasped in gold, a long tail hanging down his back. Cherry-Stripe paused, the fond, familiar Sponge sticking in his throat. Somehow he'd become Evred-Varlaef, the future Harskialdna. And he looked like the king.

Evred saw the bemusement in Cherry-Stripe's face, and muttered, "So, Cherry-Stripe, where's this famous room where you and Flash scared your Ains into thinking you were ghosts?"

Cherry-Stripe's crack-voiced laugh echoed down into the great stone hall below, and they clattered back downstairs, the Jarl relieved to hear the sounds of the boys' laughter. This Evred-Varlaef looked far too much like Tlennen-Harvaldar, who had been incomprehensible ever since their boyhood days, when he'd appeared so suddenly after his little scrub of a brother had gotten thrashed by the dragoons' boys for either frost or snitching, and had sat with him all night long, watching over his sleep, then vanishing with the dawn back to stable duty.

"You forgot your sword," Mran pointed out.

"What? Oh!" Cherry-Stripe looked down at his side, and snorted. "Don't ride off." He ran down the hall.

Mran, who had hidden the sword to guarantee a few moments of privacy with the overnight guest, put out a hand to keep Evred from following. She was very small, the prince tall and imposing, but he courteously stood still, and she said, looking up at his unreadable face, "I just want you to know I know who made Landred—ah, you call him Cherry-Stripe—made him bearable."

Evred gazed down at that heart-shaped face, so determined, so serious, and he did not know what to say.

"Landred learned from you," she murmured, and still there was no comprehension in his face, no acknowledgment, so she rather desperately finished what she'd been planning to say all these weeks they'd prepared for this visit. "And Buck learned a little from him. If I can help you in any way, send me word."

He smiled then, a kind smile, though inwardly he was bemused, but it was enough.

She flitted away, and was gone when Cherry-Stripe came clattering back, waving his sword. "Let's get the dancing over with. Then it's back for supper, and just wait till you see what we have planned by way of eats . . ."

Chapter Twenty-seven

EVRED looked down at the woven carpet, its pattern of spring green vines obscenely splattered with a thick brownish stain. From there he scanned child-sized furnishings, scattered toys, small clothing, all picked out in clear gold-touched morning sunlight.

The body had been Disappeared, but the disorder remained, violence caught out of time.

He looked up at the waiting faces and found that of the older woman accused of the child's murder. Her hands rubbed together, fingers stiff, as they had since Tanrid's men had brought her in.

Evred forced himself to concentrate. They all stood there in the small circular room high up in the tower of Sala Varadhe castle at the north end of Andahi Pass, Idayagans and Marlovans alike, waiting. He knew what must come next, had sat listening in judgments conducted by his father.

"Was it an act of war, or of personal conflict?" he asked, in Idayagan.

The woman stared at him as if he had spoken in Venn.

Evred repressed impatience. He had, on the two months' journey, mastered enough Idayagan vocabulary to understand and to be understood, and he knew his pronunciation was clear enough.

He enunciated slowly, "You killed Nadran Kepri-Davan. Was your motivation one of war or of personal conflict?"

The woman's heavy face flushed with rage, with hatred. Her chins trembled. He could see in that flat, angry gaze that she'd already chosen judgment for herself, though the trembling in her hands, the sharp smell of fear, betrayed the body's unswerving wish to live.

When he spoke, it was for the others listening. He said, in that same careful voice, "Your king signed the treaty, and so you come under our laws. An act of war means you are subject to the laws of war. A personal conflict among us is a civil complaint, and there are choices, depending on reasons and actions. For example, you murdered a two-year-old child, so we can assume that he had not threatened you, stolen from you, or dishonored your family."

Two-year-old child. How evil, how cold, when stated so flatly! Someone gasped, and farther back in the crowd, a sob. The woman's face blanched. She said, her voice thick with loathing, "War. It was war."

"Then your action falls under the rules of war. There was no flag of battle, and the slain carried no weapon, so your action is termed covert, and for that you will die—"

Her voice sharpened in desperation. "I demand a public execution! Let all witness you butchering more civilians—"

Evred cut through. "A public execution is for commanders captured in battle. You murdered a child who was asleep in bed. You will die by the same method, in the same length of time, as far as can be discovered under questioning, as the slain. It will not be public."

The woman gasped, and she began to scream, "But you are invaders! Norsunder-damned, blood-handed—"

"Next," Evred said, pitching his voice to be heard.

Tanrid jerked his head, and one of his armsmen shoved the woman out, still screaming invective.

Evred followed Tanrid, stopping at the line of rooms comprising the castle's residence chambers.

"Next is the murder of Garid Kepri-Davan, heir to the Jarl. These four are responsible." Tanrid indicated four men, two young and two old, waiting in the hallway under guard. All four were wounded, two badly.

By Kepa, fighting for his life. Evred felt sick. He had never liked Kepa in their scrub days, even less when Kepa had become the strutting Snowballs, heir to a new Jarldom. It had been a relief when his father, the new Olaran Jarl, had pulled him out of the academy after their last banner game.

Personal reaction aside, the discovery that the Kepri-Davans had been murdered the night before his arrival was a direct jab at Marlovan honor. Motivated, it was clear, not just by a general wish for revenge, but by bad governing.

He walked on to see the room where Kepa had died; the chamber, rich with new furnishings, was hacked up, the floors strewn with blood-smeared belongings.

Evred moved on, forcing himself to listen one by one to the voices of accusers and defenders. He passed judgments, one by one, and at the end of the long morning, when at last they departed the blood-stained, dishonored house, he and Tanrid left behind heavy reinforcements to hold the place.

Neither spoke for a long time. Evred breathed in the clean, frosty wind flowing down from the western peaks. There was still snow gleaming on those peaks. Around them green grassland sloped downward toward the river winding along below the ancient road. Behind them the castle overlooked the north end of the pass. Evred felt its violated presence still.

He watched shadows move over the grassy slopes, cast by clouds overhead: blue-green, then light green again. Finally he said, "As bad as the Kepri-Davans were, these people seem to think we'll be worse."

Tanrid glanced back. "They used your name as a whip."

"The Kepri-Davans? How so?"

"More than one of them said that the Jarl used the same threat: *You think I'm cruel, wait until the King's Voice returns in the spring.*"

"What was the spark?"

"The woman who killed Kepa's little brother. Her own son, flogged to death by Snowballs Kepri-Davan himself last summer. The Harskialdna was here to witness."

"What was his offense?"

"Conspiracy. According to her—under kinthus—they'd talked but hadn't actually done anything. The execution was a supposedly a warning. One of many."

Evred made a gesture, ending the subject: he didn't need to hear more. He could imagine the figures bound to a post in a military court, their backs raw and bloody, Kepa leaning forward watching greedily, perhaps licking his lips like he did in the old days whenever anyone was beaten, or even talked about floggings. He could feel the anger, the desperation, the woman dashing into that quiet room with the green rugs, steel in hand, and once she'd forced herself to act, there could be no return. *You got your welters and weepers, Kepa.*

"You'll have to put someone in," Tanrid said. "Soon."

"I know." He'd read it often enough: the most dangerous of times was not during an attack, but after, when people had become accustomed to violence, when they felt they had less to lose, when change, by anyone, had become the norm and not the abberation. Custom and habit were two of the strongest legs of order, besides law and plenty. Take any of them away, and what was left was imbalance.

They each fell silent, then, Tanrid wondering how many more chases like that lay in the future. Running down a bunch of scared servants! He'd rather face battle, even the trickery of Ghael Hills. "I feel dirty," he said suddenly.

"Yes."

After a grim pause, Evred spoke again. "The best defender, the most reasonable judge, would be Dewlap Arveas." They both had grown up hearing about Cavalry Captain Dewlap Arveas, Flash's father, who with Dragoon Captain Horsepiss Noth had commanded the king's forces in the days before the war. Evred frowned. "But the next command was promised to one of the Sindan-An or Tlen families."

Tanrid lifted one shoulder. "That's your worry, not mine." He looked sardonic.

"Not much of one. No appointment of mine is a true promotion. Just a holding command," Evred said. They both knew that, but he said it out loud, trying the words, listening to what they meant.

He had command, yet he didn't have command. Things had changed, yet things hadn't changed. He saw the evidence of it, but knew he still did not yet fully comprehend the sense of it.

"Tell Captain Sindan first," Tanrid finally said, and with that, Evred knew that though Tanrid disliked politics, he was aware of its machinations. He was also aware of the importance of Sindan's getting Arveas' appointment to the king before the Harskialdna's Runner reported to him.

Runners—

For a moment his mind wrestled with two important questions, leaving him in a jumble of images without a point. He frowned in frustration, then lifted his head, trying to find the end of the mountains through which they'd ridden so recently. Behind them lay the northlands proper. At the south end of the pass he knew that he'd find Uncle Sindan waiting, with his gathered report on the rest of the northern shores. *You will have Captain Sindan's eyes and ears at your command.*

And his eyes and ears would, in turn, send all Evred's doings back to the royal city. Evred did not resent that. It was as it should be. He would also be surrounded by men chosen by his uncle and his father—again, all good captains, good warriors, as it should be. They were there to lend their experience to his command.

Experience, and possibly authority. He did not know what might happen if he disagreed with their orders, or if he simply wanted to talk out his ideas without his words being repeated. He felt a strong, desperate wish for his own friends: Noddy, Cama, Rattooth, Tuft, Cherry-Stripe, and Flash Arveas. What a luxury that had been, and they hadn't even known it: to be able to talk over their plans, and have no one else hear their words.

He thought about each of them, sensing that he was on the verge of some insight, some very important insight, but it hovered just out of reach, like the sun behind the sailing gray clouds.

Captain Sindan was indeed waiting at the south end of the pass with the captains of the occupation forces. He agreed with Evred's decision about Dewlap Arveas' appointment to hold Sala Varadhe. Not only agreed, but approved: unsaid was the fact that what was needed was not just someone tough—that sort of Jarl was easy to find—but someone fair. Dewlap had a reputation for fairness.

They regrouped, some to ride back north again through the pass and then east on patrol, the rest up to the Nob to inspect. Evred had expected Tanrid to take the eastern patrol, as he'd learned the territory during the invasion with the Harskialdna and Sierlaef, but he declared his wish to accompany Evred.

"I want a glance at the defenses myself," he said to Evred's overt surprise, and Sindan's mute question.

Evred accepted that with no questions. So far their cooperation had been amicable. Evred worked to keep it that way. It was easy enough to guess that Tanrid did not trust the Olarans, who were known for their independence, in spite of their former alliance with Idayago.

And so they rode together up the old roads above the rocky, wave-smashed cliffs toward the distant harbor city. At their left, the sea, green, blue, gray, silver, by slow-changing degrees, the wind fresh and stringent, the horizon almost without limit. At their right the mountainous line that formed the spine of the Olaran peninsula, hiding old valleys, and—it was said—ancient geliaths in which the mysterious white-haired morvende hid. Evred surveyed all hollows, cave mouths, and other mysterious nooks that they rode past but they never saw a morvende or heard eerie singing on the night winds.

Evred did sense, and rightly so, that they were being watched.

But they rode with two armed columns at their backs, scout dogs sniffing the wind, tear-shaped shields within easy reach, hooked on their saddles upside down so from a distance they looked like raised wings, bows slung and tested from time to time, dragoons with lances couched.

As the old month blended into the new, the warm winds carrying hints of summer, they rode downhill into the Nob. Lindeth Harbor had been a grim enough sight. Evred was prepared for more fire-blackened desolation. What they found was that the Olarans, in typical and arrogant independence, had thrown up a shanty town on the edges of the ruins, bastioned against the crashing winter storms, while they waited for the great orders of wood and stone they had put out the autumn before, expecting that someone—whatever government claimed them—would pay when the orders arrived this year.

With spring long wagon trains had begun to arrive, disgorging stacks and heaps and rows of building materials from the eastern harbors where the forming Guild Fleet was struggling to maintain trade despite the embargo. The makeshift houses swarmed with people, music poured from the tumbledown doors and cubbies. Everywhere, the sounds of pounding, rapping, sawing, some of it pausing as the newcomers were surveyed, riding down the hill in their long columns, steel glinting in the bright sunlight.

Tanrid, at Evred's side, turned constantly in his saddle, looking everywhere at once. Evred puzzled over this behavior until he turned his questioning gaze from Tanrid's grim face to what he surveyed.

Tanrid Algara-Vayir was not gauging walls and fortress layout, he was searching faces.

He was looking for Inda.

Evred felt a cold certainty in his guts, but then his own attention was snared by a long, lean body lounging near a ramshackle house, the languid posture a contrast to the wary, staring people to either side. Evred stared across the muddy expanse of the street straight into the smiling, speculative gaze from a pair of light eyes. The eyes belonged in a narrow, bony face, surrounded by curly hair lifting on the wind. Evred turned as he rode past, and watched the young man shift his lounging stance just slightly; arms crossed, one long, muscular leg propped on an upturned wheelbarrow, scruffy riding boots.

That gaze, unwavering, with just a hint of a smile—a sardonic smile midway between defiant and beckoning—sent fire straight through Evred, more potent than the most powerful distilled bristic.

He forced himself around again, and made himself busy surveying the burned docks on the other side, the broken walls and rubble piles, as his ears burned.

How many songs had he yawned through about the mysterious snap of magic when eyes met eyes! During his brief, mostly fun wrestling matches that had burned so swiftly into desire back in his academy days, it had always been laughter that caused the spark, or a grab, and from someone he'd known for years. This was the first time ever that a mere glance from a stranger smote him with a message so clear and strong.

His mind stubbornly presented that light gaze to him again and again as he busied himself with the orderly fuss of setting up camp, establishing perimeters, and then negotiating the priority of those who had waited all winter to present their complaints and demands.

Tanrid was equally busy, carrying out the logistics of survey and patrol, and then tramping all around the remains of the ancient harbor with the harbormaster, the head shipwright, and guild representatives.

Thus there was no time to talk until nightfall, when the tired Marlovans, glad to be finished with their long ride in full war gear, were given campfire liberty. Evred watched as the drums came out, the war songs sounded over snapping fire and reached skyward. Tonight they expected limits, but those makeshift hostelries were going to be a temptation. He had to decide what was wiser, to make them off limits now and try a few liberty parties, or set no limit and wait for the trouble that was probably inevitable.

A note arrived, carried by a small girl in a ragged gown. She was waved from person to person by the Guards: no one questioned the intentions of someone no older than six.

The girl came directly to Evred, frowned a little as she studied the crimson and gold splendor of the device on the breast of his war coat, and his crimson and gold sash, and then thrust out a crumpled piece of paper.

He took it, but before he could speak she whirled, dirty hair and ragged skirts flying, and scampered away.

Evred looked down, knowing whom it was from, and knowing made his fingers burn. He crushed it into his fist as Tanrid came striding around the rocks set up as an inner barricade and sat down next to him.

"I'll ride out tomorrow," he said.

They were alone, more or less; everyone else was busy. Messages— Runners—plans—that pale, intriguing gaze.

Evred shook his head. "You're leaving," he repeated. One thing at a time. Then he looked at Tanrid's dark eyes, bleak in the leaping firelight, and everything else spun away like burned cinders as he said, "You *were* looking for Inda."

He hadn't meant to speak, but when Tanrid looked up, he was glad he had. "You know, too? Of course. Hadand would tell you. He's alive, that's all my mother told me, and she probably wouldn't have said that much, had I never been sent north. But she did tell me, between my re- ceiving my orders and my departure." Tanrid looked grim. "According to her, Inda is alive and put to sea. My first reaction was to turn down the Harskialdna's offer of a command unless he provided an explanation for that whole stinking situation that damned summer. Yes, I know what that means." He waved an impatient hand at Evred's startled reaction. "Same as flinging down a war banner before the throne. I figured why not now instead of later, when I inherit? But my mother insisted I take the command, that I could better find him if I were here myself. She's right." He looked up, waiting. Watching.

Evred said, "Sindan put him to sea, that's all I know."

They both looked across the fire at the tall Runner dressed in blue who stood talking to three other runners. "I figured as much. No use in saying anything to him. If he hasn't spoken, it means he won't. But it does tell us the king acted, and on my brother's behalf. It makes a dif- ference."

He didn't say in what. Evred knew. They both knew that their talk now skirted the dangerous edges of treason, though the subject was a scrub and the incident some years old. Evred then saw what was needed, what Tanrid couldn't honorably ask, and he said, "I will continue the search. And if I find out anything, I will send you word."

Tanrid's face eased. They said nothing more; Tanrid had his ride to prepare for, and Evred had the paper in his hand. Tanrid saluted and left for his chores. Evred looked around, saw focus turning toward the cooks, and unrolled the paper, now damp from his tight grip.

If you want a proper Olaran welcome, I'll be waiting.

No titles, no name, only a little drawing of three clover leaves. He flicked the paper into the fire, fighting to control the burn of anticipation, more potent than any liquor.

In the morning Tanrid departed, halving their force, but Evred's arrival with gold—and promise of more from the distant Marlovan king—had changed the locals' attitude enough for the harbormaster, and then two guild leaders, to say after a morning's discussion, "The Venn will be watching."

To which Evred replied, "Let them watch."

From then on he was plunged into a flood of activity that made for impossibly long days. Everyone, it seemed, wanted a better place to rebuild on what was essentially a long, narrow promontory. Evred had to learn about defense from sea attack, which was the exact opposite from building for land attack: the former, you are looking for attack from the water, and the latter uses the water as a last defense, the constructs formed for attack from inland. He listened, he learned, and from time to time Sindan appeared at his side, offering in his quiet voice the king's own view.

Evred never questioned how Sindan knew. He'd grown up with the man at his father's side; Sindan's knowing with almost instant certainty what the king would want done in this or that matter was, to him, no mystery at all. They thought with one mind, those two.

Three nights passed, with liberty granted first to captains, and then, when dawn brought no trouble, more of the men. Sounds of merriment rose up the hill to the encampment—good smells, the tang of liquor. On the fourth night, under a downpour, Evred faced the prospect of yet another long, watchful night, and gave in.

He knew where to go. Down the only street with buildings, and there was one, a low, raw-brick affair, with a freshly painted sign with three clover leaves.

There *he* waited, with mulled wine, and that smile.

After a drink or two, and no talk, the man said in accented Iascan, "You realize we are enemies, you and I."

Evred said, "I'm not here to make war."

A laugh. "What shall I call you, then, enemy prince?"

"Sponge." It came out, just like that. He really thought he was anonymous, but he was too bedazzled to consider how public his movements were.

At the time his reward was a slight lift to those mobile brows. "Sponge. Short, uncomplicated. Call me Dallo."

Evred was unable to repeat the name, lest his voice squeak. Sweat beaded on his brow, his legs and arms had gone watery, his heart drummed in his ears.

Dallo laughed suddenly, and pointed downstairs, to where the old cellars still existed, relatively undamaged, and quite clean. A door clicked, and they were alone in one fitted up as a private chamber, with only a burning candle.

The flame went out, and soon—far too soon—Evred was consumed by the sun. The second time took longer. The third, Dallo piqued and provoked instead of leading, spinning out anticipation just short of agony, and when at last the lightning struck and then shimmered into cool quiet, Evred fell briefly asleep. He woke up when someone commenced hammering somewhere outside. He found himself alone, so he dressed and walked out into the fresh, cold air of morning, with everyone busy starting the day. The family at the inn all smiled at him as he left, and he was happy enough to smile back.

On his return to the camp, he found Sindan waiting. Wariness, worry, a little resentful anger for that observant watchfulness, all boiled in his empty stomach until Sindan nodded to the harbormaster, whose weather-seamed face showed no expression at all.

"Fishing smacks had to come back in," the man said without preamble. "Spotted a Venn scout craft on the horizon."

Sindan said, "They'll see the building going on. How long can we expect before they send someone against us?"

The harbormaster shrugged. "Don't know. If they're ahead of a fleet, tomorrow. If they aren't—and word is, they're massing against the new Guild Fleet building in the strait to try to defend it—they might send pirates, and we don't know where they lie up."

The strait was north of Andahi Pass, that was all Evred knew. "Who can tell me more about this Guild Fleet?"

The harbormaster's gaze shifted down, then up, and the Marlovans successfully followed his thought: *Ought I to have spoken? Why not? The Guild Fleet lies outside the borders.* "All the big guilds, or most, are forming this fleet. To defend trade along the strait because the Venn don't defend against pirates, all they do is cruise, take toll, look for anyone from our coast. There's someone just arrived with news about the Guild Fleet from over the mountains. Staying for a time, we being cousins and we got our Guild refuge up first before returning down to Lindeth."

"I'd like to talk to your source," Evred said, and the man bowed in the manner of local people. And, because it seemed he ought to say something about the problem, he added, "We'll begin drilling for defense." As soon as he spoke he realized they had already decided the same thing, if they hadn't already issued orders.

Jened Sindan saw in Evred's narrowed eyes the recognition that his order had been anticipated.

The harbormaster bowed again, and walked away to where his own people waited. As they closed into a circle, everyone talking at once, Sindan said to Evred, "We have discussed nothing else since the sun came up."

As a hint it was fairly oblique, but Evred had been subtle ever since he was small. Color burned in his face, but he only said, "Of course you'd know what to do."

Because they were isolated, and because Jened Sindan alone knew what lay in the king's heart, he said, "Your father wants you to be ready for whatever happens. Think of this particular command as a long drill."

Evred's gaze shifted to him, unexpectedly green, very like his brother's in the clear morning light. "I know," he said. He grimaced slightly. "I also have read the same records as my father has. I have seen that old Sartoran admonition that princes who feel ready to rule have ways of finding their way to power. I'm in no hurry."

"There's enough to do here and now." Sindan uttered the platitude as reassurance, and saw that it worked.

Evred returned to Dallo twice more, each time after three days. He went there, Dallo did not come to him. The family greeted him with smiles and casual waves as they went about rebuilding their inn, but he spoke to no one, and they did not speak to him.

The fourth time he broke his pattern and returned at sundown the next day, his excuse a driving rainstorm, which he thought provided cover. Instinct prompted him to seek a door at the back rather than face the entire family no doubt shut up inside the half-finished common room.

He heard voices coming up through the unfinished wall from the room below: Dallo and another man. They were laughing.

He's got someone else, and they're laughing about me! Fierce, jealous anger blazed through Evred, then the inward chatter of self-mockery smothered that laughter. What absurdity, to assume that laughter had anything to do with him—or that he had claim enough for jealousy!

Still, he could not resist crouching down to listen to the low voices, despite rain dripping off the half-built roof onto his neck. He had to be certain.

They spoke in the local language that Evred had studied so hard on the ride up the peninsula, their conversation not even remotely one of passion—and all the names and places were unfamiliar. Another jab of self-mockery caused him to turn away, but the clink of glassware froze him.

Then the unfamiliar voice said, "I should run. This is usually the time your fierce little prince shows up."

"Not until day after tomorrow. I think he thinks he's being unobtrusive." And Dallo's familiar laugh, musical and just a little sardonic.

"Have you put Mardric's questions to him yet?"

"No," and again, the careless laugh, once dangerously attractive, but now, in the cold, with no sight of that teasing mouth, just sounding smug. "It can wait. I want him devoted to me first, body and soul. Give me two weeks."

This time Evred did get away, backing up straight from the wall so no one inside would glimpse him, though the windows were shuttered against the rain.

He backed up until he was between two other buildings, and nearly tripped over a pile of bricks awaiting the next day's work. He swerved, orders to secure and kill the spy—to arrest everyone in the family—shooting like arrows through his mind. No. The family probably knew nothing. Mardric, Evred had learned, was the name a local resistance leader went by.

Evred drew in a deep breath. Yes, he had been a fool. He would do nothing foolish now. Dallo was a spy, but had learned nothing, so far, beyond that the Marlovan commander was a fool. He had even admitted they were enemies, the very first time they met and Evred had returned that stupid answer that at the time he had thought so very sophisticated. Whether or not Dallo's words were fair warning was immaterial. Dallying with the enemy had gotten people executed before.

Evred wandered at random along the new street being built for the harbor officials. Humiliation made him long for isolation. His position in command, which he had come so very close to jeopardizing for the sake of a dangerous smile, required him to think through what he'd learned, and what he ought to do, before he faced anyone he knew.

But he'd scarcely passed ten buildings when a tall, thin young woman caught sight of him in the generous golden light pouring from the windows of the harbor guild house and her brows rose. Despite the pouring, shockingly cold rain (a cold he did not yet feel) her lips parted and she changed direction, pulling her green cloak tighter against the wind.

Evred had just time to recognize the harbormaster's chief scribe when she said, "You wanted to meet someone. She said she will meet you." Her Iascan was heavily accented.

Evred thought about spies, assassination, but his mood was so vile that right now he did not care. He lifted a hand, palm out: show the way.

"In here." The scribe gestured to the harbor guild house, which was now a warren of makeshift little rooms occupied by officials and displaced families.

She opened doors and shut them again three times. Very soon he sat down, shedding pools of water, in a tiny parlor that smelled of baking bread, furnished with a small rough-planed table and four chairs. A young woman sat in one. The room was made smaller by a curtain drawn across half of it. From beyond the curtain the little clinks and scrapes and rustles indicated someone preparing a meal in a tiny space.

The scribe motioned for Evred to sit, and so he took his place across from the tall young woman. For a moment they stared into one another's faces, Evred seeing heavy dark brows, a mutinously angry mouth, thick black hair braided back, travel-worn clothing.

And she saw, instead of the expected arrogance or contempt or cruelty, a young man with dark red hair, clear hazel eyes, and a courteous air.

From the doorway came the voice of the harbormaster's scribe. "Ryala Pim just arrived from the east. She saw the Fleet forming, but said she'd talk to you only if you answer some questions."

Ryala flicked a look beyond Evred at the scribe, then returned her dark, unfriendly gaze to Evred. "Are you really the Marlovan Prince, or are you some underling dressed up?" She poked a finger toward his travel-stained riding coat with its crown stitched on the breast.

"I am Evred-Varlaef Montrei-Vayir of Iasca Leror," he said, adding wryly, "I don't know how to prove it unless you come to my camp. You can ask anyone there who I am."

"I don't want to go to your camp. I want restitution for my ships," she said. And then stunned Evred with the words, "Your Prince Indovun Algraveer stole them."

"Indevan. And he's not a prince." Who said that? Evred realized he'd spoken as shock gave way to a flood of delight and then apprehension. The whipsawing emotions, after what he'd just experienced, made him feel slightly dizzy.

Ryala slammed her hand on the table. "But he *is* a pirate." And at his expression of disbelief, "If you don't want to listen—"

"Speak." Evred rapped out the order quite sharply. It was unconscious, and he'd meant to be polite, but the tone reassured Ryala that he really was who he said he was.

"They *said* the ships would have been taken anyway. That the embargo made them targets. But they sold our ships. At least one, probably all three. Sold our cargo, and my mother and I, we have nothing left. Nothing. I have to go back to Lindeth and tell her we have to hire out as cooks, or scrubbers, because all we know are ships, and you Marlovans made it impossible for us to do any trade."

"How much?" Evred asked.

"How much what?" Ryala was so ready for disbelief she struggled to make sense of this unexpected response.

"How much are you owed?"

She drew in an unsteady breath. "Three ships—the cargo—"

Evred gestured, and the two women saw it as kingly command. "Find out how much you are owed. Bring it to me. I will pay whatever it is."

That simple! It couldn't be true. It had to be some Marlovan trap. Ryala glared across the table, her limping thoughts trying to fight their way to clarity, but then the young man leaned forward, his eyes wide, the pupils large, so large she saw the lamplight reflected in them, pin-points of golden flame. "When did you see him? What did he say?"

"Who?" she squeaked.

"Inda. The Dal—you would call him Lord Indevan."

"I saw him in Freeport Harbor. Just before winter. It–it's a pirate is-land somewhere east of Khanerenth. He was all battered up. Some bat-tle, supposedly against pirates, I was told, though I don't believe . . . well. He was there, with Handar Kodl, who was once first mate to Captain Beagar—"

She stopped when she saw the young man rub one hand along his jaw. His fingers shook. Her voice stuttered to a stop.

The hand came down, and his face was calm. "Is that all you can tell me about him? That he's, what, become a pirate?"

"Yes. Well, they are calling themselves something else, but—" Again she stopped, remembering that she had no evidence, really, except her own angry assumptions. "Whatever they are or aren't, they won't get hired anywhere honest, being Iascan. Everyone knows about the em-bargo, thanks to you Marlovans, and the Venn take Iascans off ships. No one sees them again."

The prince said, "Bring your total to—" His eyes went hazy, and then he looked up. "To the harbormaster. I'll see to it that your sum is made good." He looked in question at the scribe, who gestured agreement, not hiding her surprise.

Ryala stared in even greater surprise, but before either could speak the young man rose, his soggy clothing smelling of wet wool, and stepped out, closing the door quietly behind him, and Ryala said, "He didn't even ask about the Fleet."

The scribe dropped onto one of the chairs, letting out her breath in a slow whistle. "I suppose we can send word of what we know through the harbormaster. It's not like we know much, but I guess we owe him that."

Ryala did not respond. It was so much easier to hate these Marlovans, to regard them as so many mindless killers, all alike in their evil. To be dealt with fairly by one was almost as upsetting as the clues—covert, but there—that they cared for one another.

Chapter Twenty-eight

E VRED realized he had no one to send to Tanrid.

That was it, the thing that had been bothering him all along—ever since Mran Cassad exhorted him to send word if he needed her help. How could he send word? Everyone had their own Runners, trusted Runners, Runners who kept their own business quiet and reported everything of everyone else's. Everyone except him; he'd never wanted a personal Runner because he knew they were all spies for his uncle.

Runners . . . and sex.

There was nothing, Evred thought grimly as he toiled straight into the rising wind, like humiliation to force clear sight. Now he could see what had probably been obvious to everyone not only along the main street but in his camp: that Dallo had been on the watch for a likely connection with the Marlovans, and instead of having to exert himself to seduce one of the warriors, it was the prince himself who'd come to heel at the first hot glance.

Well, he wasn't the first and wouldn't be the last to be blinded by lust, and suddenly those songs, too, made a lot of sense. He grimaced, but there wasn't any pain, at least not yet; not in the face of the news about Inda.

Inda, alive. And . . . a pirate.

Evred had promised Tanrid, but there was no one to send—a general message would be opened. They had not set up a code.

I need my own Runners, he thought, as the first perimeter guard called out the challenge, and Evred responded with the day's password. Chuckles behind him made his ears burn, and accelerated him toward his tent, before which he paused. How simple! How easy. He was in command, so no one could stop him from taking the news about Inda to Tanrid himself. Meanwhile it would get him out of Dallo's territory.

Evred ducked inside, and as he shivered out of his wet clothing into dry, he mentally reviewed the situation here at the Nob. There was nothing that couldn't be done by Sindan.

By morning he had his gear packed and his story ready. The captains were surprised, and Sindan concerned, when he announced that he was riding east to perform a surprise inspection himself along the north coast, which he still had yet to see. Sindan insisted he take two Guards and two Runners and then suggested Evred wear Runner blue, at least along the peninsula, so he wouldn't be a target. And so three Runners and two Guards rode splashing through the mud that dawn, steam rising from the puddles, the air brisk and clean.

They had a week old report on Tanrid's movements at Ala Larkadhe below the south end of the Andahi Pass. At Sala Varadhe Castle at the north end of the pass, which would soon be held by the Arveas family, as Evred had desired, the Runners were able to give him a report three days old, and at Trad Varadhe castle in the western region of Idayago called Tradheval, a report half a day old, sending them south on Tanrid's trail ("Here, take a pair of scout dogs and let them sniff Tanrid Laef's bed upstairs; they'll find him faster than a hawk stoops") as Tanrid rode out just that morning to investigate a report of marauders in the river towns on the other side of a great forest.

They set out after him—a ride almost not made, because they were weary, and the weather was cold. But Trad Varadhe had fresh horses and Tanrid was so close, so very close.

It was near midnight, midway along the forest road, when they spotted, between tall stands of trees on another ridge, the pinpoint of ruddy light that was probably a campfire, and then they heard echoes, faint shouts and the ringing of steel.

Bavas, one of the king's Runners under Captain Sindan's command, jerked in his saddle, his face a pale blotch in the weak moonlight. "It sounds like fighting, Evred-Varlaef."

An attack? Just then someone blew the academy ride-to-shoot signal. Once. And again—until the sound was cut off.

One of the dragoons drew a hissing breath. "That's not locals."

"Ride!" Evred shouted.

The horn had brought more attackers. The noise intensified as Evred's party splashed across a stream, galloped up the ridge and into the camp. The fight was desperate; the attackers looked up, saw the Runner blue, and redoubled their efforts in maddened desperation.

Most of them clustered around Tanrid Algara-Vayir, who was alone except for three ferocious scout dogs trying to defend him. Hot with fury, Evred closed the last distance at a gallop, dismounting in a perfect drop and roll, coming up with sword in hand as the two standing attackers retreated into the trees, leaving Tanrid lying alongside two dead dogs and a wounded one, and surrounded by dead enemies.

Tanrid tried to rise, and sank back. The dragoons chased the two fleeing attackers, the Runners searched for more. Evred cast his sword onto the mossy ground and knelt by Tanrid, who lay facing away from the fire, half in shadow. Evred did not see any arrows or knife hilts. Relief washed through him. "Tanrid."

"Evred. Not yours?" Tanrid coughed, a ghastly, liquid sound. He turned his head. His mouth opened, and horror froze Evred's nerves when blood bubbled out. Tanrid gasped for breath, and now Evred saw the terrible wound in his side, under the gripping hands. His eyes were stark, desperate, as he fought to understand. "Evred." Each word took a breath. "Evred. Not. Your ambush?"

"Ambush?" There were many words for ambush in Marlovan. Tanrid used the word that implied treachery.

Evred looked at the bodies littering the area, saw tattered northern clothing. Idayagan brigands wouldn't see an attack as treachery, but defense. And Tanrid would know that.

He forced himself to focus, his own purpose coming first to mind. "I came to find you. Tell you myself. I found out where Inda is—" But the words about piracy would not come.

"Inda." Tanrid's eyes eased, though his teeth were clenched against pain. Then he forced in a deep breath, an effort that Evred felt in his own guts. "Bring him back." Tanrid's bloody hand left his side, and clutched at Evred, his long dark hair, loosened by a blow to the head, falling down over his arms. "Promise. Bring. Him. Back."

Evred hesitated, bitter memory forcing him to hear his own voice promising Inda justice, a justice he couldn't possibly give.

Tanrid wheezed. "Bring . . ."

"I will." Evred's eyes stung, blurred, as Tanrid's grip loosened, and he fell back, his red-stained lips moving. Did he whisper "the Sierlaef"? Evred bent nearer, but all he could hear was the labored breathing.

Tanrid's eyes remained open, looking up into Evred's face, even after his breathing went shallow, then stopped. Evred knelt there for a long time, staring down, scarcely hearing the long, nerve-prickling mourning howl of the wounded scout dog, until Bavas came back and said, "Evred-Varlaef. We have the two who ran. The others are all dead."

Two prisoners. Trial, execution, retribution. Except there was no real retribution. The Idayagans would only become more righteous, the Marlovans more cruel. But it must be done. It would be done.

Evred picked up the fine silver hair clasp that lay gleaming a stride or two away, and pocketed it. Then he forced himself to rise, to act. He had to witness, they all had to witness, had to Disappear the bodies of the attackers, and so he walked around, counting them all where they lay, and reconstructed what must have occurred. One of them men tended gently to the wounded dog, who lay patiently under the bandaging, but once it was done, once again lifted muzzle to the sky, and howled long and low and hoarse.

Evred found what he expected to find: five dragoons with Tanrid. Against them had been twelve, all wearing shabby local garb. It was so easily construed that he almost missed the horn, lying not by Tanrid, or even by one of the dragoons, but by an attacker.

Evred pulled it up, and stood there, turning it over in his hands, and then he looked around again. Two dragoons lay near the brigand who'd had the horn, and all three were across the camp from Tanrid.

Think! He knew the horn was important. He looked down again, hearing that academy signal. Dragoons, none of them academy trained. Only their officers came from the academy and learned its signals; among themselves they used whistler arrows, not horns.

Neither Tanrid nor his dragoons had blown that horn.

Ambush. Tanrid had heard that horn signal, which could have summoned targets to attackers who were combing the woods just as easily as it could summon rescuers.

And Tanrid would know the fighting style whatever clothes the enemy wore.

Ambush.

Evred whirled around to face the two prisoners, held in the grip of the Runners, both badly wounded, hands bound behind them. In the firelight he could see their rough north country garb: long shapeless tunics, woolen trousers, moccasins. They were dressed as Idayagans.

He said in Marlovan, "Did you really believe you would escape?"

One stood stolidly, the other's eyes flickered toward the fire and back. They all heard it then, the rescue, riding far too late to the sound of a distant horn. Evred saw the plan: brave Tanrid, set about by brigands, blowing for aid, which came at the gallop, but too late. It would have worked, too, except for Evred being there to catch the "brigands" and to hear the horn signal and identify it.

The question was who had set this ambush?

No one moved, until Evred faced the two prisoners, and said in Marlovan, "Whatever you were told about safety or reward was a lie. You're going to die, and it's going to be slow."

Neither spoke, but the one's eyes flickered again.

The sound of horse hooves approached, at least a riding. Evred flung back his head, wondering for a moment if this, too, would be part of the attack. No, it didn't make sense. These would be genuine rescue, and sure enough, he recognized the commander from Trad Varadhe, who halted near him, saluted fist to chest, and said, "A Runner came to us on road patrol. Said he heard a horn signal."

Evred opened his hand. The man looked about, horror and disbelief lengthening his face when he saw Tanrid.

Evred said, with a glance at the prisoners, "Take these back for questioning. I will supervise it myself."

The ride back was silent. When they reached the castle the wounded dog was carried to the kennel to recover, and the prisoners were jerked off their horses and shoved toward the prison, their treatment testament to Tanrid's reputation and esteem, short as his stay here had been.

Evred had risen before dawn and now it was past midnight; he asked the hovering commander for something to drink while they sent for kinthus from a Healer. Evred needed sleep, but even more badly he required answers to his questions.

But even so short a wait, so late at night, was a mistake. When the Runner arrived, it was not to announce that they had their kinthus. "The prisoners are dead!"

Evred and the captain both ran down to the prison cells, and saw the two men lying in the farthest cell, still bound, their throats cut.

Evred turned on the commander. "Find out who did that. Now. Or my father's men will."

The commander blanched.

Evred trod back upstairs. His head ached, his eyes burned, but he knew he would never sleep until he found out what had happened. Before long the commander came himself. "Evred-Varlaef. It appears someone gave conflicting orders, one by one, to my guards. Sent them on various errands, in my name. All that's known is that the orders were carried by Runner. But we don't know who."

The remainder of the night was spent in interrogation, tension escalating steadily as tired men tried to reconstruct what had happened, the guards insisting they had followed orders brought them by a Runner, the Runners insisting they had not carried any such orders.

The prison guards had all been handed written orders, which was common enough if you did not want prisoners hearing spoken orders; everyone remembered the stories going round about Tanrid's death, people running back and forth, and Runner blue, yes, but not who it was who handed them the little strips of paper.

When asked for the order papers, each man said that the directions had been to put them in the fire. This, too, was accepted practice.

Evred listed all the Runners' places and times, beginning with Farnid, the Harskialdna's Runner, who had heard the horn signal just after he left the castle to head south with a report, and returned to alert the commander. But Farnid had spent the time between their arrival back and the news of the dead prisoners with the older dragoons, drinking and talking, seen by everyone. He could not have carried those orders.

And so Evred kept listening, posing questions first to Runners and then to stable hands and kennel keepers and orderlies, until one of the stable hands mentioned another Runner's name: Vedrid, personal Runner to the Sierlaef, who arrived that day with a message for the commander about supplies. The other Runners all thought he left again that afternoon, except this one man.

"Midnight is when I saw him," he reported. He smelled of fear sweat, and kept looking past Evred to his commander as if for clues, for safety, but the commander just sat, angry and grim, and the man went on somewhat hopelessly, "Took one of the Runner horses from the meadow, rather than from the stable. I–I thought Vedrid just wanted a very fresh mount. Thought no more about him. Hadn't seen him near the castle."

"So you never saw him hand out any order," Evred said, forcing his voice not to show the corroding sickness he felt inside: all he could see, over and over, was Tanrid's dying face, the blood pouring out of his mouth.

"No." And the man saluted, his fist thumping his chest. The sound somehow underscored the truth of his conviction.

And so Evred dismissed him and continued with the questions, despite thirst, hunger, a growing headache driven by that memory that would not go away: but all for nothing.

As Vedrid's name spread through Sala Varadhe Castle by whispered conversations, Evred came to realize the Runner's name was like a magic spell that turned men to stone. No one would say anything, anything at all, now, because of who Vedrid was. There was no positive proof to convict him, and far too much danger in speculation—at least in open speculation.

Evred stopped the questions.

There was therefore no trial of malefactors to slake the thirst for justice, no public execution to expiate the sense of shame—it was worse, far worse, than the Idayagans. Tanrid's betrayal and death had been ordered by one of their own.

And so there was only the torchlit gathering in the great court at dawn and the singing of the "Hymn to the Fallen" before Tanrid, one of his two personal Runners, his Dragoons, and the animals who died defending them were Disappeared.

And during the ceremony, Evred stood by the bier on which lay the still figure, his tunic smoothed, weapons at his sides, watched by shocked, dazed, angry, weary, shamed men, grubby and sweating and looking ill in the weak blue light. Evred held the flaming torch, thinking: *Once again justice is impossible. But if I confront my brother about what orders he gave his Runner, he will probably lie just like he did about Dogpiss the summer with no banner.*

The truth is, my brother had Tanrid killed, with my uncle's permission, but I cannot prove it; therefore I can say nothing.

Chapter Twenty-nine

"IS that all you need, Elgar?"

Inda tried witlessly to make sense of the question while not staring at the rounded neck of the clerk's cotton blouse. He looked up at the rough-hewn ceiling, at the smoke-stained fireplace, at the west windows, as though the answer lay out there in the harbor.

She chuckled, a soft, attractive sound.

Heat flooded his face, rushing down to what was already painful enough. He winced, leaning against the counter. "Seizings." His voice squeaked, compounding his wretchedness.

The clerk took pity on him and turned away. "Seizings it is. You'll want enough for the gaff o' the cutter, then, and an extra set or two? Looks like it got mighty chewed up in that storm that brought you in."

He scarcely heard the well-meant chatter. From the back she was just as round, her worn skirt molded to the shape of her hips, and when she reached, that blouse pulled tight against the swell of her breasts—

"Glarg." His tongue caught somewhere in his throat.

She glanced back over her shoulder, her eyes dark, merry, and knowing. "I'll send the cordage over to the slip, shall I? Thog isn't on board now, is she?"

"Thog." That almost sounded human. "Send. Thanks."

She turned away again, deliberately, for she was past twenty, and had brothers besides. Though she was amused, she had the kindness to hide it. Inda managed to get himself out of the cordage shop and into the open air of Freeport Harbor. It was a cool summer day, everyone busy, for after a miserable month of pounding storms the first clear weather had brought in fleets of sail. He walked with a kind of painful care, but at least no one paid any attention to him—

"Inda! Caught your bowsprit in the shrouds?"

Tau's cheery voice caused Inda to sit down abruptly on a convenient pile of canvas rolls outside a sail shop, forearms over his lap. He looked up, his face a peculiar blend of misery and sheepish grin that caused Tau to hoot in delight. He looked back at the cordage shop, and comprehended immediately. "That Lorenda, gets you tight against the seam even if you're blind. I heard she's walking out with no fewer than three, besides Kodl—"

Inda groaned. "She knew. I—"

Tau's smile turned pensive. "Inda, how long have you been getting torch without fire?"

Every morning for months, Inda thought gloomily, about the time the others suddenly twitted him for face fuzz, making him hunt up a Healer for the Beard Spell. And he'd finally gone and bought a made shirt, because his old one had ripped seams during practice within the space of four weeks, after he'd reseamed it twice.

He grimaced, recalling that morning's dream, a jumble of images involving one of the women at Lark Ascendant, an older and much differently shaped Thog, and for some weird reason a grown version of Liet from back home. Only they'd been speaking in Marlovan, which made him feel homesick. "Dunno," he mumbled, since Tau seemed to be waiting for an answer.

Tau's sympathy turned to impatience. "If today isn't the first time, why haven't you gone upstairs in the Lark?"

Inda hunched and looked away at the forest of masts, glimpsed through the narrow opening between two weather-beaten buildings. He wished he were out there, preferably under water. "We're low on money," he mumbled. "Kodl just saying it a week ago. And Scalis keeps going up anyway."

"For an old geezer he's sure hot at hand," Tau agreed. "But he's doing all their wood repair, so he's square."

"Mrfle."

Over the past day or two Tau had been exchanging speculative glances with a hip-rolling young first mate who'd recently landed from Sartor. She was tall, handsome, red-haired, and from a successful privateer crew. And here she was, damn, having just spotted him.

He forced his attention back to Inda; the red-haired first mate, in the mood for dalliance with the prettiest man on the island, saw his attention stray to the knot-limbed clodpole hunched there on the sails, and so she passed by, thinking, *Oh, what a waste!*

"Inda. I can see you being circumspect on board ship—I am myself— but why on shore? Girls here not—?" He hesitated on *not good enough*, frowning down at Inda's averted face.

When did a joke become a jibe? When there might be truth in it. Tau sorted through memory with the swiftness of habit. Though Kodl and Testhy had scrupulously kept their secret, Tau had very soon—once winter began and they were all holed up together—perceived subtle differences in their attitude toward Inda, and once he'd noticed, he tracked unerringly back through memory to the day it had changed.

Tau had been taught well. He watched, listened, and during New Year's Week, while Kodl and Inda took some of their new recruits out for a two-day training run on their rebuilt cutter, he got Testhy drunk, listening in growing amazement to the mumbled account of that confrontation with Ryala Pim.

Now Tau rubbed his chin, staring down at Inda, who looked out at sea, his face closed and grim. Son of a prince! There certainly had been no royalty turning up at his mother's harbor house, horns blowing and outriders clattering. Tau knew little of Marlovan royal custom. Maybe a brother or father or uncle was expected to haul him off and show him how to set his sails the first time. Or maybe an expert in first timers was brought in. Testhy hadn't known any details about Inda's family, being an outlander, and Tau knew better than to try Kodl.

Inda's mood soured as his thoughts winged back to Tdor. He'd always expected his first experiments would be with her. But she was still a child in his thoughts. He cherished that tender memory of the summer afternoon they had napped, limbs entangled, on his bed and despite their well-meaning intentions, no closer to solving the mystery of sex than to reaching to touch a summer sky. Where was she now? They might have sent her back to Marth-Davan . . . or there could be a new Shield Arm being trained. Maybe even Branid! The idea of Tdor being forced to marry that whining bully turned his mood to rage.

Tau's voice pierced through the fug: "You know, if it's a tumble with the boys you want, we can walk over to Cock-Robin's den, or you could go with—" Again he hesitated, not wanting to mention Yan's name if no one else knew. The Chwahir was a friend, and Tau had worked hard to keep his friendship by pretending not to be aware of Yan's long, hot gazes, the sound of his breathing. As he'd done with Jeje, until he'd asked Mistress Lind to show her upstairs.

The idea of sex with friends was disgusting to Tau, he who had been raised knowing about the wide varieties of sexual tastes. He'd experimented with many of those, over the past couple of years, but never with friends, who he permitted within his own personal citadel of friendship because they did not grab him, touch him, strive to bind him with the febrile, maudlin emotions of possession.

Inda looked up, recalling the sounds, the stale, sweaty smells afterward, of Norsh and his friends, mostly Leugre, who'd liked an east and west wind—males and females—down in the dark hold, when they should have been on night duty. Grimaced. "No Cock-Robin," he said shortly. "All it reminds me of is Norsh and his mates."

Tau laughed softly. "My mother always said that sexual preferences are like boiled persimmon. If you've a liking, it's superb, if not, it's poison. And then of course there are those of us who say it depends upon the pie."

He looked down at the wide brown eyes before him, saw Inda's confusion. His mother had also said: *A secret without the why of it is as useless as speculation.*

"Come along. Kodl is down scouting hires now, and you won't be any use to anyone hobbling around like a sea turtle caught on shore."

Inda blushed as deeply as Tau had ever seen him, but he managed to get to his feet and then shambled, shamefaced, at Tau's shoulder back up the hill where Tau made sure to get Mistress Lind alone. Then he looked back in exasperation and a kind of hilarious wonder at their tough, even frightening marine tactical trainer who stood in the doorway as if fire burned his toes, his face now blanched. But then Tau thought, studying that compact, powerful body, the awkward elbows and feet of someone who has grown fast within just half a year: *I keep forgetting—he must be somewhere around sixteen.*

"Oh," Mistress Lind said, after a glance. "I wondered when that one would wake up. Inda, is it? Come along. You've arrived just at the right moment. Three of our first timers are free as business is slow, it being such a fine day. Everyone is down on the King's Saunter if not on deck."

"Er," said Inda.

"Now, do you have any preferences? Lissan is dark and quite fiery, then there's Ziri, who is fair and as cool as a spring stream. And also we have Nanog, who comes from Chwahirsland, and she's probably our very best first timer—"

"Um," Inda said.

"Ah. Like that, is it?"

Nanog was tall, taller than Inda, with the kind of rounded curves he liked at once, her round face merry with dimples in her broad cheeks. She took Inda's hand, and welcomed him into a bright room with a lot of rose-colored furnishings, and she didn't seem to notice that his clothes were already drenched with sweat.

Nor did she react after a very short time—far too short—when he gave a cry of dismay.

"Never mind that, it happens *all* the time," she said with that merry, dimpled grin, her black eyes sparkling with light from her windows. She ran an idle hand along his smooth, strongly-muscled young flesh, and leaned in to whisper, "Now it's *my* turn."

A couple weeks later Inda was perched high in the foremast of their new hire, thinking about sex.

It was a mild morning, the haze just burning off, their convoy all in stations behind them. Their new scout craft wasn't in view, but that wasn't unusual, especially with the morning mist still lying heavy over the water, and a darkness in the east, diffused by the mist, that might be a series of squalls boiling up.

So Inda wrapped an arm more comfortably around a shroud and thought pleasurably back. Sex was fun. Or at least, it was fun once you got over that first desperate time. He winced, thinking that the pleasure house people who dealt mainly with first timers probably had to train for years first in learning how not to howl with laughter.

But fun as it was, it also lit a lamp on a lot of previous mysteries.

Some ships had strict rules about affairs on board. Some didn't mix genders at all and Inda could see why, now. But a rule like that wouldn't have done any good for Norsh, who unlike Leugre and Tau, only sparked to his own gender. Or would it be worse for the ones who liked both? No, not for Tau, who didn't dally with friends. As for Norsh, Inda found himself, after all this time, feeling a kind of sympathy for him; life on board ship, whatever the rules, would be terrible if you happened to find yourself yearning for someone who paid you no heed.

Some sympathy, anyway. What he couldn't understand was how he could want to destroy someone he felt passionate about but couldn't have.

Inda grimaced as he thought back over how stupid he'd probably looked, giving all those excuses to return to the cordage shop, and for nothing. Lorenda had been nice to him while making it quite clear she had no interest in dalliance. Yet he never wanted to destroy her, the way Norsh had wanted to hurt Tau. And Faura had wanted to hurt Tau as well, in a much sneakier way, at least as much as she'd wanted to bed him.

Inda groaned with impatience. Thinking about Lorenda did nothing except bring on that burn belowdecks, as did thinking about that curly-haired cook's mate on the other ship who Inda really found attractive. The rules of their contract were strict: no pillow jigs at sea.

Unlike Inda at this particular moment, Thog, daughter of Pirog, had her mind on business. This is not to say that Inda did not think about business frequently, and did not in fact do more than his share. But Thog was passionate about business—which she defined not as defense but as fighting pirates—and because she was passionate she rarely ever thought about anything else. It was far better than the horror of memory.

When Thog was on lookout duty, she stared outward in full expectation—almost anticipation—of seeing the red sails of the Brotherhood of Blood appear, hull down, on the horizon. Ugly raids in her hometown, time and again over a generation, had burned bloodred sails into her worst dreams even before the night all the adults in her family were killed, her home village burned by drunken, laughing pirates, and she was dragged aboard their ship to scrub and serve, to learn piracy or die, until she had escaped by diving overboard during a storm. She had intended to die, but then she saw she was not far from shore, and so had clung to wrack until she drifted to safety, leaving her alive and with a passion for vengeance.

The ocean, she felt right now, was far too empty.

She'd been up on the mizzenmast since the dawn bells. Tack and tack again; the four ships moved together slowly but smoothly on the calm ocean, just as they had each day of the week they'd been sailing. The wind had held steadily against them so they continued to tack night and day, all four on signal.

Everything as it should be. So why did she feel this sense of impending threat?

Because something was wrong. She just had yet to see it.

She scanned for the scout, which ought to have appeared by now, though maybe it was up there in the east, caught in the crazy winds of those oncoming squalls. That wasn't it.

She glanced at the sun, then back at the *Toola*, last of the four. They were now on the starboard tack, so she ought to be seeing Yan at his fishing at any moment. Was that it?

She trained her glass on the *Toola*, almost a silhouette in the glaring light reflecting through the dissipating haze. No sign of anyone at the sides at all.

She scanned the deck at the base of the mizzenmast. Uslar, the young Chwahir runaway she herself had rescued from begging on the docks was at the side, fishing for breakfast, Chwahir-style. Others not on watch stood about, some with work to hand, others sipping a drink and chatting idly.

She felt wind on her cheek. Below her the great triangular sail bellied slowly and the ship came alive, beginning to pitch slowly forward as the wind rippled the smooth water up into playful cats' paws.

She peered under her hand down the row of ships, trying to block the strengthening glare. Heads moved about on two of them, but the fourth, still mostly silhouette, seemed oddly calm.

Yes, there were lookouts' silhouettes at the masthead. Then she glanced down at her own deck, saw tousle-haired Mutt, the next youngest new boy, moving forward to get out of the way of the expected command to take in sail.

"Mutt," Thog called, without moving.

The boy squinted up through his tangle of brown hair.

"Stroll over and tell Elgar I want to talk to him. Don't hop, don't make it look like alarm."

The boy's face changed, and he sauntered forward with rather obvious care. Thog remained where she was, watching the *Toola*, listening to the rhythmic creak of mast, the hum of rope, which had changed slightly in timber as the wind began to freshen.

A very short time later Thog heard Inda's voice from below; he stood directly forward of the mizzenmast, where no one aft could see him.

"Yan isn't fishing," she said, without changing her posture. Yes, that foremast glass was trained straight on her, she could feel it. "No one is moving on *Toola*'s deck. Just at watch at their stations."

"Can you make out individuals?"

"No."

Splash, creak. Inda said, "Seen the scout?"

"Not aft."

"Not forward either."

Creak, splash. Thog realized that the entire ship had gone quiet. People still moved about their stations, but there was now an air of expectation.

Inda dropped down into the waist, which would be invisible to the ships behind them. Thog saw his head near Dun's and Kodl's sun-bleached ones, both just woken from their snooze watch, and she turned her attention back to the sea and those ships.

In the waist, as others drifted up, Kodl said, "We'll send a scout band down under cover of that squall." He pointed to the greenish-gray line growing in the east.

"I'll go," Tau said, reckless as always.

Overhead the bosun's whistle tweeted and stamping feet thundered all around them, as hands swarmed aloft to reef up the sails and bowse them tight.

"Wind's swinging round," Niz said, nodding in approval. "We'll have to use the big launch to scout. Rig, Wumma, and the Fisher boys can go with Taumad."

Kodl opened a hand, said, "Dun, you take Rig's watch, then, and check our gear in case."

Dun lifted a hand, signifying agreement.

"Do we take weapons?" Wumma asked. He stroked his knife hilt. He wanted to fight pirates. Kill pirates.

"Just your—"

A wiry, shirtless body landed lightly among them and they looked over at Dasta. He pointed south. "Got a clear peek. Better send a boarding party. Not ours on lookout."

Grim reactions. Yan and Zimd, in charge of the marines on the *Toola*, were original shipmates. If Zimd was not at her post and Yan was not fishing, then it was very probable that they were dead. Neither would desert their posts for anything else.

"I'll go," Inda said, thinking: *If something's wrong, I should have seen it.* He dashed below to fetch his gear.

Dun caught Kodl's arm. "I'll be one of that party," he said, pleasant as always, but with the steady, unsmiling intensity that characterized him at times.

Kodl opened his mouth to point out that he already had his orders, then hesitated. Dun only got that way if his action station was shifted away from Inda's. They fought well together; during the battle aboard the *Dancy* Kodl had thought that Dun fought just like a bodyguard, an observation he'd forgotten when confronted by Ryala Pim. Over the winter he'd asked Dun a few questions, but, he remembered, somehow they'd always either been interrupted by something else, or some more pressing questions were raised that set aside the subject.

Kodl, remembering the stunning revelation about Inda, wondered for the first time if Dun had a similar secret. Kodl now had enough military training to recognize that Dun had *always* been good—he'd just matched his ability to the skill level of the others. The way an adult with a secret might hide the extent of his skill, unlike a boy like Inda who revealed it in the first fit of anger.

Maybe it was time to get Dun the Carpenter alone, no interruptions, and find out the truth.

But that was for later. Kodl jerked his thumb, and Dun vanished below to fetch weapons.

And so, as the first squall sent slants of rain to curtain them they boomed the launch over the side and dropped in. The rain was warm, the wind unsteady, flinging gouts of water at them from east and south, so most of them had stripped off their shirts and wore vests only, stitched with sheaths for extra knives. Dun took a signal bow, though in this weather it would be next to impossible to shoot.

They didn't risk stepping the mast, not with the current moving so quickly. Each took up oars, and it seemed only a few sweeps later they slipped along the lee side past the second and third ships, all full of hands fighting snapping, whip-cracking sails, and *Toola* loomed, a silhouette, curtained by rain.

Inda divided them into two bands with a wave and a gesture.

One band climbed silently up the forecastle. In three surges the launch slipped aft, Dun hooked the launch onto the mainchains, and up they swarmed. Inda shook rain from his face, then peered over the taffrail at the sailor at the helm. He had made it a rule to learn the watch bills on their hires, and he expected to see a big, square older woman, cousin to the fleet captain. Instead there was a tall, brawny fellow with at least two knives evident. Bloodstains were all over the deck.

The *Toola* had been taken by pirates.

They had the advantage of surprise, but they were only ten. Dun landed lightly next to Inda as rain pattered all around them, washing rose-colored water down toward the scuppers.

"None of ours aloft," Dun said directly into his ear.

No legitimate crew in evidence. Then it was easy: everyone was an enemy. Wumma appeared on the other side, and Inda motioned the teams to steal along the rail fore and aft.

This, too, they had drilled. Rig, who was nearly as fast as Niz aloft, sneaked up the mizzen, knife at the ready, and Wumma vanished fore to direct the attack there. One by one they took the pirates, while Dun and Tau secured the hatches.

Inda stood looking down at the hatches as rain poured off the sail overhead onto the back of his neck.

"Set fire to 'em?" Rig asked, white around the mouth. Hav, his brother, had been part of Yan's crew.

Disgust twisted Inda's insides. The pirates' plan was lethally simple, and had nearly worked: take the ships from behind, one by one, under cover of darkness and fog, keeping station and signals. The crew had to be dead, including Yan and Zimd, but they'd had a chance to fight, however ephemeral. Trapped in a wooden box, there was no chance at all.

"Pirates burn prisoners all the time," Wumma muttered, his blue eyes shifting sideways.

They were all waiting for his order, Tau lounging against the aft hatchway rail, arms crossed, face turned away. He would never say—for some reason he hated to be caught making any kind of moral judgment—but Inda could sense his repugnance at the idea of firing the ship with the pirates below.

"We can save the ship if we fight," Dun said mildly from the helm, which he had taken over. "Captain will be better pleased than losing a ship."

Inda said, "We don't know how many there are. Dun, send an arrow forward for reinforcements. We can at least let them fight for their lives as they come up."

" 's fair," muttered one of the boys everyone called the Fisher Brothers, their fishing smack from Geranda having foundered, and their family name being Venn. No one really liked anything Venn these days, but Kodl had found the boys to be tough, resourceful, willing to work hard.

The wind was veering again as the squall moved on. Wumma took the helm. Dun had brought oil-thread, and under the binnacle got it flaming well before he went forward, planted his feet and took his time to aim. For a moment all was still, except for the high plunging of the ship on the green-gray cross seas as the tall, blond man slowly drew the arrow back in a straight line from elbow to fingertip in long practiced, perfect form. He sent the arrow whizzing through the air to arc over the second ship, where Thog would see it.

Reinforcements arrived in the rest of the boats.

It went as Inda ordered. Those who wished to fight pirates as they emerged did so. There were a lot of them. But they killed them all, until the deck ran again with blood, mixing with the rain, washing crimson out the scuppers. When they were done, and they stood about looking at one another, at the bloody deck, at their mates' gear bags—mostly rifled through—quietly piled aft. There was no joy or even triumph, not in a fight like that, just a bleak satisfaction in some, and weariness in the rest.

When the captain of the fleet arrived with a launch full of sailors, and gazed about appalled, Inda said shortly, "The pirates will be back."

Inda was in a bleak mood as he returned to the first ship. Guilt mixed with grief. He should have seen something was wrong. Thog's happening to think about Yan's habit of fishing was too accidental. Now Yan was dead; Zimd too.

He brooded below as the others, minus the five who stayed to hold the ship, laughed, drank, talked the wild talk that always seemed inevitable after a fight, as on deck above, the captain conferred with his own mates in order to replace the dead hands for the rest of their journey.

No one believed the danger was over: the pirates who had taken *Toola* were dead, but no one had seen their ship. Or ships.

Inda brooded even after the scout craft showed up, blown far north by the squalls, and Jeje came aboard safe. She did not hide her tears when she found out about Yan. She and Tau and Dasta retreated up to the masthead with a bottle of distilled mead, and no one bothered them as they drank and Jeje and Tau sang wake songs, ballads, and old sea tales, her unspectacular voice harmonized with Tau's beautifully trained tenor weaving the melodies with heartrending intensity through the soft night air into the sailors' dreams.

Inda did not go aloft. In their cabin, alone with Kodl, Niz, and Scalis he said, "They knew about us. It'll be that way from now on."

Niz rubbed his chin. "Rep, we got."

"Rep means others hear o' us, like ye said once," Scalis agreed, chuckling. "I just wish ye'd let me come along for the fun."

"Next one," Kodl said

Inda grimaced and left, mumbling about his snooze watch.

Kodl took a pull of his ale and wondered if he should confront Dun now. Only what would he say? Dun never singled Inda out, had told everyone he was raised on the shore just below Lindeth as a carpenter. He'd never spoken about the Marlovans, not once.

Marlovans. A Marlovan prince, and no one knew. Kodl had started the marines thinking of Inda as a resource, but over the winter he'd begun to regard the boy as a weapon, one perhaps to be used for more ambitious plans—as long as the boy stayed loyal.

He leaned forward. Time to sound out part of his idea, leaving Inda out. See what the others said. "I want to get us a ship. Build a fleet, even, protecting convoys. No more serving on someone else's vessel, having to put up with their rules. Join Freedom as independents."

"Them raffee-sails we laugh about," Niz said, as Scalis bobbed. "Them bein' tricksy sails, lookin' prissy. But the fact is, in these here tricksome airs, and with all them isles, speed is your first need. And a raffee becomes a good ship. Pirates like 'em. We could use 'em to chase pirates."

"So we take us a pirate ship. Set crew afloat." Scalis chuckled. "See how they like it!"

Scalis already thought like a pirate. Kodl thought, *He might have gone his whole life as a forecastleman. Take away the rules, and see who begins to make new rules.*

But he only nodded. Unspoken was the obvious: here in the east, with the nearest land being Khanerenth, which was in a constant state of warfare, it seemed as if every local trader turned pirate when something slower or weaker hove up on the horizon. So they take a ship. First he would keep his promise to Beagar and repay the Pims. And then they could make themselves rich as convoy guards, using Inda's brains and training.

As for that Dun—

Kodl sat back. Maybe it had best wait until they landed. There'd be plenty of time afterward to get the carpenter drunk enough to talk, and then figure out how to use what he knew.

Chapter Thirty

"THEY'RE out there," Inda said early one morning a few days later, hitching up onto the taffrail beside Kodl, a knife in one hand, an arrow in the other. They sat amidships on the weather side, their acknowledged spot by the ship's regular crew when they weren't drilling or on watch. As always they had something in hand, making, repairing, sharpening. "I wish the Delfs hadn't all sailed west!"

Kodl rubbed his hair, bleached nearly white by the sun, back off his brow before returning to knife sharpening. It was ferociously hot, the sky as clear as a burnished bowl, the sea placid and deep, deep blue. Sails thrummed with pleasant tautness. To starboard the scout craft skimmed through the water, graceful as a dolphin with the new, sweet-curved mainsail Jeje and her mates had made. The little craft, so battered and ugly when they first acquired it, so sleek and beautiful now, had been named *Vixen* by Inda. A few thought it odd, had wanted to name it after a fast-moving fish or bird, but it had been Inda's idea to get it, he'd supervised most of the work on it, and no one was in the mood to argue since the killing of their mates on the *Toola*.

Dun sat a neat coil of rope, sanding down new arrows and guiding Mutt in shaping them. He glanced across at Inda, perched there barefoot, wearing patched deck trousers, hair escaping from his sailor's queue blowing back, rough shirt rolled to his elbows as he fletched arrows in the Marlovan spiral. He had left boyhood behind, and perhaps that mysterious boyhood scandal that had caught the royal eye. Dun had resolved, after that pirate attack, to tell Inda the truth about his oath to Jened Sindan, captain of the King's Runners, once they reached land, and could not be overheard. Perhaps Inda would respond with his own truth, and perhaps not. Dun realized he no longer cared what that story was. And he had accepted that Hibern, so sweet in memory, had mostly likely by now found another man. That was the way of nature.

It was Inda himself who had his loyalty now: for the king's sake, yes, but more truly for Inda's, Dun would guard him until they both could go home.

The time has come, he thought as he polished the wood on his sleeve. The decision released a tension inside he hadn't previously been aware of: soon as they landed, it would be good to release the truth at last. To know, and be able to hear, one another's true names, to be themselves, at least while they were alone.

Mutt said with a grimace of both fear and excitement, "So who's out there, you think? Fire Island galleys? Or those ones from down south that Scalis was telling us about?"

"Brotherhood."

The word snapped away the easy atmosphere as quick as a sail rips from bolt-holes in a high wind. Scalis' raspy chuckle was the only answer, so familiar no one paid any heed.

"How d'you know?" Kodl asked, stroking his chin with the edge of the newly sharpened knife.

"It's . . ." Inda's face went blank, his eyes unfocused, and he shook his head. "It's the way no one's out there. Nothing happened after we took back *Toola.*"

Wumma spat over the side. "You think them soulsuckers is massing against us?"

Inda sighed. "Either them or someone as bad. It's just too quiet. Independent pirates—the kind we've been facing till now—would have come against us right away."

Kodl and Dun both gestured agreement.

"Cap'n says if the wind just stays steady we got two-three days till we hit Lands End," Testhy offered, more as a statement of hope than as news. They all knew that depended not just on what ships appeared on the horizon, but if the wind shifted and began to blow offshore to the east, which was common this time of year, it could take up to two weeks of wearying, exacting sailing to beat that short distance directly into the wind's eye.

Thog didn't speak—she seldom did unless she had to—but her expressive dark gaze lingered in Inda's mind as he dropped his finished arrow into the bucket and climbed aloft. She'd been silent since Yan's and Zimd's deaths. He considered that. He had tended to avoid Zimd outside of duty because she had been so indefatigably nosy, but he'd seen her laughing and making merry with the others. Had she managed to make friends with the quiet Thog? And as for Yan, he and Thog hadn't been twoing (Inda was pretty sure Yan preferred men to women in that way) but the Chwahir stuck together. Odd people, they were, hard working, whispering in their own language as if it were forbidden. He knew little about life in Chwahirsland except that they suffered under the double ax of Venn and pirates attacking from shore, and the harshness of their own government inland. Their rope was some of the best in the world, and they built fine trade ships. Their land supposedly wasn't good for much, catching more storms than any corner of the continent; a good summer, Yan had said once, making one of his rare jokes, had seven full days of sun in it, never together.

Thog's grief was the angry kind, the thirst-for-vengeance kind. Uslar, too, young as he was.

Inda looked down at the Chwahir boy, so similar to the other Chwahir: pale skin, round face, black hair. He was scrub age, but his back was scarred from flogging. Not just one, either. There was a lot of cursing about the Chwahir, here in the east; apparently they fought so hard and so consistently to take Colend, famed for its beauty and wealth, that mages had thrown up an entire mountain range to block them hundreds of years ago. They seemed to be as cruel to one another, in their bleak land, as they were to their neighbors.

Inda, watching Uslar's fingers plait his blue-black hair into a sailor's queue, considered how coastal Iascans casually cursed Marlovans out in the west the way these easterners cursed the Chwahir.

"Signal!" Rig called from the foremast. "Three sail, maybe more, comin' downwind out o' the northeast!"

Inda scrambled out onto the staysail boom, squinting out at the *Vixen*, now slicing through the water in the path of the liquid light created by the newly risen sun. Up arched another arrow, following which the blue flag aft dipped four times.

Four sail as vanguard between them and their safe harbor.

"Anything on fores'l or tops'l?" the captain's voice snapped. And, what they all dreaded, "Sail color?"

No one spoke. The lookouts would be straining to peer directly into the morning glare, of course, but the marines all watched the *Vixen*. Skimming ahead, the scout craft would see first, and signal if there was real danger. The captain stubbornly maintained that ordinary pirates did not dare try flying the colors of Jara or Khanerenth as a ruse because the penalty in mainland courts was death. But first you had to catch them, and pirate life was a violent one by definition; Jeje would not just accept colors as genuine, she would watch for signs of preparation for battle.

Rig drew in a breath. "Jeje's raising something—"

They all saw it: the red signal flag that meant pirates, and to make certain, Jeje dipped it three times in the age old signal to *flee*! At least the black flag did not come after, the signal for the Brotherhood of Blood.

They were hull down now, only the masts nicking the horizon. They'd appeared on the starboard bow—they had the wind for fire and chase. By the time Inda reached the deck, the ship's crew was already hauling the sails around and forcing the ship to come about; the other three were almost as fast.

Now they were running downwind, southward and away from Khanerenth and safety, the sails bowsed up as tight as they dared. The marine leaders lined the taffrail and smacked their glasses to their eyes. The vanguard appeared, sharp and clear, hull up now—they were terrifyingly fast—and behind them a fleet of smaller, equally fast sail.

Tension sparked in the summer air, and except for Scalis' low mutter of rough oaths, no one spoke. The only sounds were the creak of wood, cord, and sail, the percussive splash of water against the hull aas they strained every sail to escape to the south. All they had now was the wind, and in these seas, it was notorious for its treachery.

Midway through the night the wind betrayed them, first dying, and then shifting around to the southeast to drive them toward their enemy, who had sailed easily down along the western and land side of their convoy. Though the captain called for all hands, and everyone, including marines, laid aloft to bring the ships about as fast as possible, the pirates had the advantage and they attacked before sunrise.

The pirate fleet at first seemed to be a mass of lights, a deceptively beautiful sight. Those resolved under the hazy, cloudy darkness into a great many smaller craft, all narrow, knife-sharp, built for the chase and the kill and not for trade. In command were three rake-masted raffees, their foresails blank, and one older trysail. These were magnificent ships, built for speed.

All of them equipped with cut-booms swung out and secured.

Niz appeared at Inda's side, eyes nearly closed. "You know what blank tops'l means."

Inda nodded once. "Woof told me, hire before last, just before we left Freeport. They want to join the Brotherhood."

Niz spat over his shoulder, down into the sea. "Means them has to do something bad enough to catch redsails' eye."

They watched in grim silence as smaller two-masted pirates swarmed up in pairs, one sailing windward and one to the lee, aiming to sheathe the row of traders.

The four ships, on signal, veered in two directions, attempting to evade, but they were just too slow. The pirate craft closed in.

Inda's fire teams were the first to respond from the tops of all four ships. The raffees and the big trysail hung back until Inda's convoy was beset by bands of small craft, many of which were set ablaze by Inda's bow crews. But as soon as they veered away to repair their damage they were replaced by more pairs.

A crack from behind was followed by another—the mainmast of the second ship lurched and fell, taking the top of the foremast with it; the *Toola* lost its foremast, pirates swarming over its rail.

"Take command," Kodl shouted.

Inda stood on the taffrail, ignoring the arrows flying, as he observed the battle, the impossible battle. Even though the pirates had not yet gotten close enough to sweep those cut-booms down their side, two of the convoy were partially dismasted, and pirates were now closing on the third.

They wouldn't win this one.

But they would fight as if they could.

He signaled to his marines. Rage and despair twisted his guts into knots of fire at the sight of the four great silhouettes drifted along, watching the smaller ships do the work.

He shifted his gaze aft. The hammocks had long ago been brought up, the fire netting, and both sets of shields: ones to use if needed, and the others the small round spiked shields tipped outward from the railing to ward incoming arrows and to slow boarders.

Kodl met Inda's eyes, saw the grim, distant battle look that tightened his features. Inda pointed toward the *Vixen*, and Kodl said, "Dun, Mutt. Signal Jeje to run north for aid."

The fire arrow arced up into the sky. Inda knew the pirates were watching, but the *Vixen* was too fast for them to chase, at least with this wind. Mutt stood on the gaff boom, despite the arrows whizzing around, and held up a lamp, counting five and covering it twice. Then he jumped down.

Jeje hauled wind in so tight an arc the little craft slanted at a steep, sharp angle, the rail nearly submerged, then it scudded northward, gathering speed like a bird in flight. Signals flashed from the command ship and two small, fast pirate schooners separated out to chase. Everyone on both sides watched the pale blobs of sail as long as they could. The distance between the *Vixen* and its pursuit increased just before they all faded into the thick darkness. The pirates, perhaps judging that the fleeing scout might actually find aid, decided to launch all their small craft to the attack.

On Inda's signal Thog and Uslar took all the young marines aloft to shoot boarders. They carried all their reserve arrows.

Three times they repelled boarders through the remainder of the long night—doing enough damage to the enemy that the first of the big ships finally sailed in at an angle, aiming for the weather rail of Inda's ship, cut booms out and steady, fire reflecting like heated blood along the steel blades. Using their oil barrels and Thog's fire team's superb shooting, they nearly destroyed the trysail by fire. There was no triumph in that, not with two raffees still drifting along, the railings lined with pirates watching the entertainment by torchlight as the eastern horizon slowly brightened, revealing the spikes of pirate arrows everywhere— masts, rails, deck, binnacle, helm—like some kind of creature at bay, and splashed along the sides shocking amounts of bright red blood from where they'd repelled the early boarding forays from launches.

Daylight revealed further horror: *Toola* and its consorts had completely fallen into enemy hands, launches going to and from the third big pirate ship.

On some hidden signal the last two raffees flashed their sails and bore down, fast, sleek, and expertly handled, one lee and one starboard. Their sails had been wet; close-woven nets, also wet, were raised as well. Though Inda's bow crews shot as fast as they could, the arrows may as well have been grass stalks for all their effect.

Aching with exhaustion, Inda saw at close quarters the effect of a massive ship driving expertly handled cut booms. The crew made one last tremendous effort to evade, but the faster ships adjusted course, the one on the lee only slightly slowed by the wind catching in the trader's sails.

The sound of the cut-booms was unforgettable, a shrieking, grinding extended crash, and the trader's mizzen- and mainmast shrouds ripped free, the mainmast falling with excruciating slowness.

A flicker of white and gold brought Inda's gaze around as Tau rode a boom out in a wildly desperate act, snagging Thog round the waist just before she would have fallen overboard, tangled in ropes. She cried "Let me die!" and Inda heard Tau's "I can't."

The mast slammed across the stern of the lee pirate. Its boarders had retreated safely forward, lining the forecastle rail; on a signal they shouted and ran aft, kicking aside the trader's topsail hands who had been smashed with the mast to the pirates' deck. The boarders leaped up onto the mast, using it as a bridge, and swarmed onto the trader's deck.

Inda and his fighters took up their stations. No one spoke, but they gripped their weapons, breathing hard, limbs trembling. Inda's heart thundered in his ears, throwing him back in memory to the drums on the plains beyond the academy, and the horsetails preparing for attack. He heard Tau's laughter rising, and Inda felt the urge to cry the fox yip, an urge so strong he gave in for the first time since he'd left home, shrieking on a high, harsh note that raised the hairs on listeners' necks.

And the pirates were on them, gold hoops in their ears, smelling of blood and sweat, and swinging steel.

Inda snapped apart his staff and stamped forward, wood humming.

His body fought as it had been trained to fight, his mind, cut loose from worry and memory ran free, and there was even a brief echo of the ferocious joy that drove him in other fights as he smashed flesh and bone, sending sprays of pirate blood back into the faces of their fellows.

They were human, they could die.

In fact, his disengaged mind noted certain things: these pirates had been drilled, were under command; that some were far better than others at fighting.

That some of them were scanning.

Searching.

He shrieked the fox yip again, and this time there was an echo from Dun at his left, almost immediately taken up by Kodl and then Wumma and the rest. Inda did not dare to glance behind him; he only saw, when he jerked his head to fling sweat out of his eyes, that the captain of the trader lay dead, his first mate beside him, on the companionway. Then the fighting increased in fury, and the impressions were no more than flickers: Scalis shouting curses—abruptly cut off. Niz toppling overboard, a dozen arrows stuck in him, his hands outflung loose and empty as he fell.

Tau lying on the deck, one hand groping for his knife, and then relaxing. Next to him Rig falling, clubbed from behind.

At Inda's right Kodl went down on one knee. Inda lunged to cover him, then a hot spray of blood nearly blinded him and Kodl fell back, weapons dropping, hacked apart by three pirates.

Dun pressed up to Inda's left, a dark-smeared sword in one hand and a broken staff in the other, blond hair spattered with red, his face distorted into a rictus of effort and hate. *He's never fought so well*, Inda thought, ducking a humming sword. Dun's sword was a blur of light, whirling in strokes and shield defenses that brought back images of Captain Gand.

They did not speak. Could not speak, as they retreated step by step to the mainmast, Thog's arrows zinging down in a lethal rain all around them, but the pirates still pressed forward, trampling the fallen from both sides.

And so Inda fought until his breath burned his throat and lungs and his arms felt like logs. He fought on, blinded by tears when with a groan Dun stumbled to his knees, a sword thrust through him from the back. The dying man tried even then to shield Inda from a blow aimed at his head, he said something, reaching with one blood-sticky hand, the other pawing uselessly at the steel standing so obscenely out from between his ribs, but Inda could not hear over the roars and clashes, and then Dun collapsed onto the deck.

Just a glance, a painful glance, but Inda paid for it; the staff was smashed out of his weaker hand and he backed up, his breath keening in his parched throat.

Pirates leaped over Dun. Two, three, four—but at an incomprehensible shout two of them retreated back, and the first pair closed on Inda.

Inda hurled the other short staff straight into the face of the closest pirate, who ducked—and laughed.

Inda whipped out his knives and fought hand to hand.

Tried to fight hand to hand.

The tall, slim black-clad pirate who came at him was far better at fighting. He seemed to know every throw, every feint, before Inda made it, he even held his knives up his forearm like Hadand's arms mistress in the royal city at home: fast, deadly, but all blocks, he didn't use the knives on Inda. Instead he sheathed them at the last moment and used his hands once, twice, and Inda was down, gasping for breath.

Sunlight glared into his eyes, half-blinding him. He blinked to rid his eyes of stinging sweat as the pirate with the black bandana dropped down beside him, red hair drifting from under the kerchief, his face silhouetted by the sun directly above his head. But the morning light shone on the face just behind the redhead, a triangular face. A familiar face . . . A Cassad? *Here?*

Someone flung Inda over then wrenched his hands behind his back and bound them. He was yanked up and slammed back to the deck, face up.

And then the redhead bent close, the Cassad blocked the sun, so light reached the redhead's face as he whispered urgently in Marlovan: "Act stupid, and I can keep you alive."

Memory threw Inda back to when he was ten years old, the days just before he first arrived at the academy. He knew that voice. He knew that sharp-boned, sardonic face.

It was Savarend Montredavan-An.

Epilogue

THE day following the Disappearance ritual, Evred-Varlaef worked long on his tribute to Tanrid-Laef Algara-Vayir. The official version would state that he was killed on the king's service by a band of brigands. What he took great care with was the private letter to Fareas-Iofre.

Evred, hating the necessity of a lie, wrote both letters by his own hand instead of dictating them to a scribe. He told the truth in describing how bravely Tanrid had fought before he died. That much he could do to honor Tanrid, and his family. The real message—about Inda—had taken careful thought, and many burned pieces of the imported heavy linen paper only used for important communications, expensive and limited as it was.

What he finally settled on was a tribute in the form of verses of an Old Sartoran ballad about the long sought beloved son who had sailed west to unknown lands. To that he added a line in the same rhyme and meter that described in typically convoluted Sartoran symbolism how watchful eyes sought him still.

Evred trusted that Inda's mother, never met but whose three children he had come to know well, would be able to tease out his real intention. And find a measure of comfort.

But his mood was bleak as he folded Tanrid's hair clasp into his own letter, sealed it, then handed it to the grim-faced young man in blue with the owl over his heart, and a black sash round his waist.

The sight of Tanrid's personal Runner in his black sash dashing tiredly into the courtyard of Tenthan Castle two months later, seen from her upper window, was a shock of ice to Fareas-Iofre's spirit. At first she did not even notice the herald at his side as the dogs in the kennel began to howl, first one, then all of them, hoarse with misery. The hairs on her arms and the back of her neck prickled, then grief struck hard, a knife straight through flesh and ribs to the heart: Tanrid was dead.

How could the dogs possibly know? she wondered, walking to the window, her eyes burning with pain. The same way they had known the day before Tanrid returned from the academy each year, and afterward, from his long rides either for the Shield Arm or at his father's command. *What world exists side by side with ours, yet unperceived by us, for the animals with whom we share our homes, our lands, our lives?*

She had time to prepare herself, to hide shaky hands in her sleeves, as Evred's royal herald and Tanrid's Runner were both brought upstairs to her formal room. The herald handed her the official letter, which she laid aside, then he stepped back with a courteous salute, leaving the Runner to give her the bulky personal letter.

She unsealed it and the heavy silver hair clasp fell into her lap: Tanrid's grandfather's clasp, and no son to hand it to. Grief struck again, harder, and her fingers closed convulsively around the cold metal. She drew in a painful breath, forced herself to read the words written there, and then handed the letter to Joret.

"Please go downstairs, refresh yourselves," she said to the two men. "This is to be delivered at the funeral fire?" She touched the official scroll, and when the herald saluted again, she gave it back to him unread.

To Tanrid's Runner she said, "Were you there?"

A shake of the head, and a spasm of pain, and helpless anger. "He left me with orders to see to the horses. We'd just arrived, you see. He took fresh ones—" He stopped, swallowing.

"We shall speak later," she murmured. "Rest now. You have had a hard ride."

They left without further speech.

When the door had shut behind them Joret looked up, her face blanched, her body still as death for two, three long breaths. "The verses?" she said finally, and handed the letter to Tdor, who stood behind her chair. "He means Inda, doesn't he?"

The Iofre pressed the palms of her hands against her eyes. "I believe it means he intends to continue the search." Fareas dropped her hands. "Evred-Varlaef honors us by writing to us himself. That is no scribal hand. Yet there is that in his wording that makes me wonder what it is he does not say. Brigands."

"With no more identification or explanation." Grief made Joret feel cold all over. Tdor looked on in silent compassion. Tanrid had been a part of Joret's life, as much a part as the castle, as the seasons. The prospect of life with him, while not exciting, had given her purpose.

Joret, still in the icy grip of shock, couldn't believe she would never see him again, until she looked into Fareas' face and saw the anguish there.

Jared-Adaluin arrived home a day later, and knew as soon as he saw his black-sashed Riders on the castle wall what must have happened.

He felt his age as he trod up the stairs. He was alone now, so he could let the tears fall, but they did not come. Pain, braced against ever since he married the second time, was just as steely a knife as the first time. He had kept his sons by his second marriage at a distance so he would never again suffer like that and all it meant was that the pain was worsened by regret. He had just begun in recent years to know Tanrid, to speak freely to him, and listen to his words. Just a year or two of knowing one another, after all that enforced distance, and now he was gone. *Dead.*

Fareas-Iofre found him on the first landing, leaning against the wall with one trembling hand, rocking slightly back and forth, his breath coming in quick rasps.

"Come," she murmured, touching his gaunt cheek. "Come. They are laying the bonfire. We must decide what we will say."

He saw the red rims to her eyes, the bruised skin beneath. Together they entered their son's rooms, so still, and stood amid the splendid old furnishings that Jarend-Adaluin's father, the Tanrid for whom Jarend had named his son, had inherited from his own grandfather.

"I have something to show you," Fareas-Iofre said, relieved that at last, after all this time, she had a reason to bring up Inda's name without betraying Ndara-Harandviar.

He held out shaking fingers, and she laid Evred's letter into his hands. He looked at it without comprehension, and she pointed out the verses at the end. "There, in Sartoran, he repeats an old song, but what it means is that he knows where Inda is. He's at sea. He's *alive*."

Jarend-Adaluin stared at the meaningless letters in confusion, then he looked up, frowning. He was about to ask why the prince wrote in so strange a fashion, but then he remembered the conference in the king's room, and Jened Sindan promising to take Inda away somewhere.

Jarend crushed the paper against him and recalled that day, which seemed so remote in memory but so immediate in emotion. He still did not know why Inda had been singled out for disgrace, only that, somehow, the Sierandael had been behind it. But he could not make that kind of treasonous accusation without proof, unless he wanted civil war as a direct result. Jarend therefore had not spoken, contenting himself with Sindan's assurance that Inda, though surely going to some kind of exile, at least would be safe.

That decision he had regarded as an act of prudence as well as of loyalty, but now, with his heir dead, he wondered if he had been a coward not to force the issue, even at the cost of his long friendship with the king. *Except that Anderle-Sierandael surely wanted just that . . .*

He rubbed his stinging eyes with the back of his free hand. Then turned to his wife, who waited, patient and quiet, her hands hidden in her sleeves. "What think you?" he asked.

"That we declare Inda the heir, and we await his return. It is enough to avow he lives." She gestured toward the stairway. "We can tell the Noth boy the truth."

"He's a quiet one," the Adaluin said, nodding once. "I find him as trustworthy as his father has always been. Yet my aunt's side of the family will be expecting Branid to be named."

Fareas hesitated. Branid, as descendant of Jarend's uncle, had a claim though a distant one, as custom seldom acknowledged entitlement older than a generation. But the Randviar previous to Jarend's first wife was still alive, a hateful woman still angry at being forced out of her position by the deaths of her husband and the old prince and her replacement by Jarend nearly forty years ago. She was correspondingly jealous of every prerogative for her direct descendants.

For a moment both of them pictured Branid as prince, Jarend trying to envision him commanding the Riders, and Fareas seeing Joret forced to marry him, to endure his interference in home defense and regulation—his manner of rule the terrible combination of threat, wheedling and spying he had always used on the other boys in his struggle for precedence, and that he now used on the Riders. Branid as prince would destroy the Algara-Vayirs, they both knew it.

"We shall say," Jarend murmured as he studied the owl rug, still bright, lying there on the floor, "that Indevan is alive, and travels to learn. I have never disowned him, so unless the king requires that of me—and he would have to give a reason—I can therefore make him my heir."

Fareas felt a spurt of joy, so intense that fear immediately followed it. Inda. Home again. Somehow, she must get word to him. To her husband she said only, "It is good."

And so they walked down to the great court a little later, as the sun sank in the west. The bonfire was already lit. They joined the waiting circle, and the "Hymn to the Fallen" rose skyward with the smoke.

After that Evred's herald read out in a slow, formal voice the letter that the future Shield Arm had written attesting to Tanrid-Laef's loyalty and courage, and all the while Joret felt Branid's hungry gaze on her, and Tdor watched, feeling sick and apprehensive by turns.

Joret looked away so that she would not have to see Branid's unhidden desire. She was a Marlovan, adopted into the Algara-Vayir family, and unless she was sent elsewhere her duty was to marry the heir, a duty she had accepted, but which now closed in like a threat of death, as they all waited for Jarend-Adaluin to come forward and name his new heir. Joret stared into the fire, not thinking about Tanrid, who was now beyond pain or care, but about the bleakness ahead for those remaining; she was jolted, but not surprised, when once again a black-haired, blue-eyed face emerged from the flames, and her Aunt Joret stepped out, flames shimmering through the blue of her gown.

Joret turned her head, and yes, there was Jarend-Adaluin, staring, so silent his people stopped their murmuring and watched, no sound rising but the crackling of the flames.

Many saw the ghost that time. The old kennel master, for he sobbed aloud, and once again the dogs began howling in the distance. The Adaluin. Joret herself. The cook, the old arms mistress, several of the grizzled Riders with whom she'd dallied thirty years ago, though afterward many claimed to have seen her ghost, Branid loudest of all.

The ghost drifted toward the house, her ethereal blue gown blowing in a wind distant in time from this warm, still summer night. Heads turned, watching, and others watched the watchers, until she blended with the golden-lit stone walls of the castle, and vanished.

It was at that moment conviction gripped Joret by the heart, a grip cold and icy as death, and she knew why her aunt haunted this castle: she had died as the result of treachery, and was bound to Tenthen until such treachery was expiated. Her message now, or warning, or the mysterious power that gave her the strength to appear was the fact that Tanrid had also died as a result of treachery.

So the question was, should she speak, and risk touching off a civil war? Because there was only one person who could have arranged that death.

The Adaluin's voice was strained. "We shall await the homecoming of Indevan-Dal, who shall be named henceforth Indevan-Laef, my heir." He walked inside next to his wife.

Joret turned to Tdor, both keeping their faces still, but seeing their relief in each other's breathing and stance: no Branid. That much, at least, they were spared. They would talk as soon as they were in a safe room.

Joret followed the prince and princess inside, still second in rank, now betrothed to someone she had not seen since he was a little boy.

Branid Algara-Vayir, on the other side of the fire, glared, looking for a victim, and everyone except his grandmother avoided his gaze as they dispersed. She walked beside him to their wing, whispering in a low, venomous voice.

Whipstick Noth waited for Tdor, who stared at the fire, her hands pressed together. They'd gotten to know one another on the ride home from the royal city; each had found the other quiet but direct, concerned with duty. But he had a sense of humor that reminded Tdor so much of Inda he in turn sparked her own sense of the ridiculous, far too long suppressed. They swiftly developed an easy friendship, and they had talked about every aspect of life in Tenthen. Right down to Joret's ghost.

Finally Tdor looked up, her hands still locked together. "Did you see anything? Something happened. Too many of them looked shocked. Including the Adaluin. Did you watch their eyes?"

Whipstick said, "Has to be that ghost of Joret's. Look, here's what I'm thinking. If we see the Sierlaef here before long, I'll know who was really behind Tanrid's death."

Tdor breathed slowly. "So you think Sponge was hinting at something? Was it not brigands, then?"

"They were dressed as brigands, that's as far as I'll go," Whipstick said. "Sponge's wording was close. Careful. He never wasted words, or said the wrong thing." He frowned at the worn flagstones in the court and then added, "I got to know him pretty well these last couple of years in the academy, when I was a horsetail and they treated him like one. We were almost always enemy commanders. He'd gained influence, y'see. Despite, well, despite them all."

No need to define "all" further—they both knew.

Whipstick squinted up at the Riders now taking up their places on the walls—everything as it should be—then said, "He can't promise to find Inda. Or restore him. He hasn't got the power. But he's gaining influence outside the academy, just the same."

Tdor looked at the fire, at the women on the walls facing inward, some of them talking quietly. At the windows above as lamps were lit behind them, a soft golden glow shining down from each one by one. She looked at anything and anyone to avoid the possibility of seeing pain or even betrayal in Whipstick's face. They'd talked on that long ride back to Tenthen about castle life, both of them knowing they would never leave again. But one subject she'd avoided, and he'd never mentioned: the academy, and everything concerned with it. Especially the summer Inda vanished, after the death of Whipstick's little brother.

It was only the extremity of worry—necessity—that forced her now to murmur, "Would you . . . I mean, if Inda comes back—"

Whipstick comprehended immediately. "Listen, Tdor. Week or two after Dogpiss died, Tanrid finally came to me, after he was permitted inside the Guard keep. Said what Inda told him: he tried to stop him from going down to the stream. That Inda followed him, and after Hawkeye smacked Dogpiss—and I'm not saying he didn't have the right, rules being what they are on banner games—Inda tried to catch him. I remember how tired those scrubs were, the Sierlaef's gang riding them hard all week. They were stumbling over their own feet by that last night." Whipstick's voice dropped, and for the first time his even-tempered, toneless voice was rough and bitter. "I know who is to blame. And it wasn't Inda. But he paid the price just the same." Whipstick lifted his head so that torchlight reflected in his eyes, and then added, with quiet conviction, "If Inda comes back, I'd be honored to serve as Randael to him. For the rest of my life."

Tdor's neck muscles eased. Life had gone twisted out of its regular stream, she had sometimes thought, the day that Inda was summoned to the academy. Nothing happened the way she expected—or wanted. The prince and princess were locked in grief. Tanrid dead, Inda gone to sea somewhere in the world. Joret now betrothed to Inda, and she herself probably expected to marry Whipstick, walking here beside her, a thought too strange to examine right now.

But there was one thing she knew, in heart, mind, spirit. The world would be right again once Inda came home.

Marlovan Terms

Adaluin—prince of a territory, as opposed to a son of the royal family

Convocation—the New Year's week gathering at the royal city, for the Jarls to renew their oaths to the king and kingdom. Derived from an old ceremony of clan kinship, and undergoing constant friction between definitions of ownership, kingdom, and king, ever since Marlovans first conquered the land of Iasca Leror and settled.

Dal—honored male, the nearest equivalent is "lord."

Edli—honored female, the nearest equivalent is "lady."

Gunvaer—queen.

Harandviar—Royal Shield Arm's betrothed or wife.

Harskalt—King's Voice.

Harskialdna—Royal Shield Arm at War. (See Sierandael.)

Harvaldar—War King. (See Sieraec.)

Hlin—betrothed or wife of second royal son.

Hlinlaef—betrothed or wife of crown prince.

Iasca Leror—the name of the kingdom the Marlovans conquered. It meant "land of the Iascans (Yaskans, originally)," and their language is one of many branches of the Sartoran tree.

Iofre—princess of a territory, as opposed to a daughter of the royal family.

Jarl and **Jarlan**-territorial titles, similar to "earl."

Laef—second son. Royal second son is Varlaef, and he only takes the title Sierandael when his brother becomes king, under ordinary circumstances, though older Sierandaels (uncles, usually) have been known to keep the title, especially in wartime, when their experience is particularly needed. (Others were reluctant to retire when their brothers died, and as they have control of the royal Guard and of the training of the Jarls, they can be difficult to oust, especially by very young kings and would-be Royal Shield arms.)

Marlovan—from Maralo-Venn, or "outcasts from the Venn." Their language derives from Venn, which in turn derives, centuries ago, from a Viking exploratory fleet that was propelled through a world gate to this world. They sailed north, looking for home, and eventually settled on the northern continent that during Inda's period was called Goerael. Marlovan was not a written language until its people conquered the Iascans. They then adopted the Iascan alphabet, as well as a good deal of the Iascan language, eventually altering it to fit Marlovan verb endings and word order—during Inda's time, Marlovans were raised speaking both languages, ostensibly confining their use of Marlovan to matters of war and defense, though that custom blurred as the languages blended.

Montre-Hauc—("King of the Mountain Dwellers." Hauc meaning "mountain," Montrei from "mund" or "mond," the Venn term for hand, or leader.) Earliest of the three ruling families of the Marlovans. Subsumed into the Montredavan-An family.

Montredavan-An—(from Montrei-Davan-An, "King of the Forest Dwellers." "An" being forest, and the alteration of "mond" into "Montrei" being, it is said, subsequent to marriage with the mysterious Dei family.) The Montredavan-Ans led the Marlovans from a nomadic existence on the plains to rulership of nearly the entire Halian subcontinent; it was they who discovered the superior Iascan steel of the Aurum Hills forges, and subsequently conquered Iasca Leror.

Montre-Vayir—("King of the plains." "Montrei" being, it is said, subsequent to marriage with the mysterious Dei family, and "vayir" meaning plains.) During Inda's time, the ruling family of the Marlovans. What exactly happened during the generation the Marlovans conquered the Iascans and settled into their castles is unclear to the Marlovans of Inda's generation as their ancestors did not at that time keep written records; the result was that the Montredavan-An family was reduced by treaty to exile on their own and in the province of Darchelde, which was half forestland, for ten generations. All the songs point firmly to betrayal on the part of the Montredavan-An family, though they did, and still do, regard the Montrei-Vayirs as the betrayers, but of course the winners write, or rewrite, history. The immediate result was the old king was assassinated in his own bed on a visit to his home castle, following which most of the family was killed, as well as their most loyal servants. Pleading on the part of the former queen's family for the life of the heir ended in the final compromise: home exile for ten generations. Their renown as leaders and fighters keeps the Montrei-Vayirs nervously assiduous in guarding the borders of Darchelde during Inda's time. It was after the Montrei-Vayirs took the throne that greater autonomy was granted the new jarls (this may have been the price of betrayal of the former kings) and they were permitted—some say encouraged at sword-point—to add "Vayir" to their family names, as a gesture of solidarity with the Montrei-Vayirs, who hitherto were the only ones with *vayir* appended.

Randael—Shield Arm, usually brother or cousin to a jarl.

Randviar—Shield Arm's wife or betrothed

Sierandael/Harskialdna—the king's brother or cousin or appointed Royal Shield Arm, if there is no brother or cousin, in peacetime. If he goes to war, he becomes Harskialdna, and, of course, if he is victorious, he also gets Sigun added to his title.

Sierlaef—heir to a king, almost always first son.

Sieraec/Harvaldar—terms for kingship. A Marlovan king during peace-time appends Sieraec after his name. When he raises his war banner, he becomes Harvaldar—even if he doesn't actually lead the battle (this distinction evolved after the Marlovans established themselves as land owners). If he is victorious in war, the term Sigun is added to his title.

Sigradir—-King's Counselor (not used in Inda's time.) Different from Harskalt, which is used only for specific tasks, and almost always by Runners.

Sigun—a title appended to that of a victorious king or Shield Arm.

Vayir—old meaning derived from "plains," now appended to the names of jarls' families, denoting ownership of a territory. Ownership depends upon oaths renewed each year at Convocation.